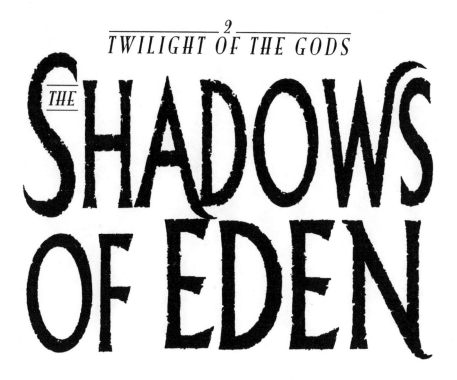

2

TWILIGHT OF THE GODS

THE

SHADOWS OF EDEN

MICHAEL R. JOENS

D0096980

MOODY PRESS
CHICAGO

ISBN: 0-8024-1697-7

1 3 5 7 9 10 8 6 4 2

Printed in the United States of America

To my son, Brandon.
"A wise son makes a glad father."
You overflow my cup with gladness.

CONTENTS

PRONUNCIATIONS

Allyndaar	Allen-dar
Aeryck	Air-ick
Boadix	Bode-ix
Bolstroem	Bole-strem
Brynwald	Brin-wald
Caelryck	Kale-rick
Dagmere	Dag-meer
Hauwka	How-ka
Joens	Jens
Killwyn Eden	Kill-win Eden
Terryll	Tare-el

THE MAP
OF
BRITAIN
CIRCA A.D. 450

GRAMPIANS

River Tweed

River Nith

River Cree

River Annon

Loch na Huric

CAER LUHL

IRELAND

BOWNESS

WHITLEY CASTLE

River Eden

Solway Firth

KILLWYNEDEN

BRIGANTES

PARISI

NORTH SEA

IRISH SEA

River Ouse

PENNINE CHAIN

GLENRYTH

River Trent

CAMBRIANS

CORITANI

BADONSWARD

River Severn

River Avon

COTSWOLDS

TRINOVANTES

LONDINIUM

River Thames

AQUAESULIS

STONEHENGE

DUMNONI

SARUM

CANTII

THE CHANNEL

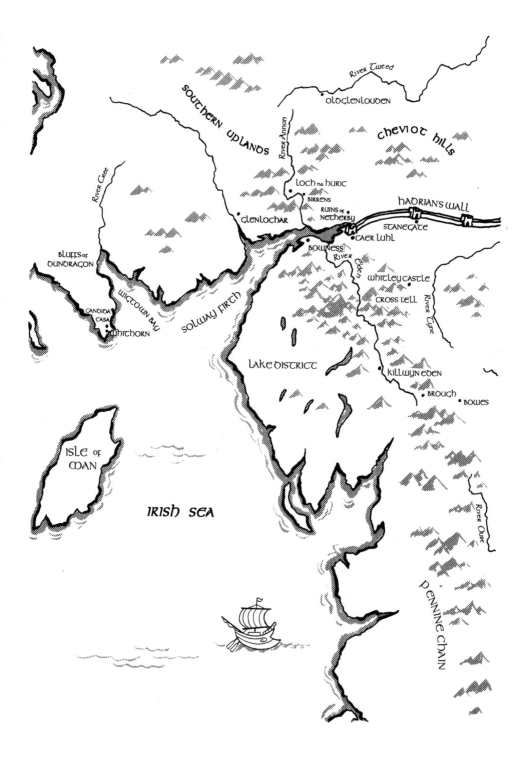

PART ONE
THE DEAD OF WINTER

1
TERROR IN
THE WHITE

The killers were onto their scent and moving quickly now, gliding silently through the trees, then coming out and over the lee of a treeless ridge. They dropped into a shallow bowl and paused, crouching warily, listening, eyeing the broad-valleyed terrain with a cunning appraisal. Everything was quiet. Nothing stirred that could be seen with the naked eye. Then the cold hush of the wind blew over their savage snouts, fanning their eyes ablaze, and they took off in a dead run.

Yes, they were onto the scent.

Sullie was restive, sensing something dangerous in the air, not knowing what it was but knowing that it was drawing nearer. Her ears flicked nervously as she whinnied and snorted her warnings into the cold December morning air. Warnings that fell on deaf ears.

It was just dawn in this stalwart land, this wind-blasted sod of Scots and Picts, and the winter came hard against it, storming its ancient bastions of whitened cliff and marshaling its icy forces down lonely, plateaued highlands, along infertile dells, and over the bleak and desolate reaches of the moors.

It came calling the stouthearted out from behind comfortable and secluded walls, where warmth crackled in stone hearths and cheer flowed from lifted flagons; it came taunting the brave, and only the brave, to forsake Reason's counsel and to do battle in the frigid elements.

There was at least one soul who picked up the gauntlet this breaking winter dawn: a Briton, a boy—the once beggar boy who had in earlier days answered to the name of Worm.

Riding astride Sullie's broad back, Aeryck had just left the village of Glenlochar, heading west to the coast through a fresh fall of snow, and, finding a narrow thread of trail (nothing more than a shallow impression in the snow), he reined the big, gray draft horse off the main road.

Sullie whinnied again, swinging her huge, blunt head up and down, and shook her mane as if to protest the change of direction. But the boy paid her no mind; he reckoned her complaints to the cold.

But Sullie knew different. She was attentive to the imperceptible shifts in the air that warned those who would listen and sneered at those who would not.

The sky was an implacable steel gray. In the grayed light of dawn Aeryck was reading from the *Iliad and the Odyssey,* the little leather-bound volume given to him by Tillie two months earlier, and was struggling with it. Grunting, he dragged a sleeve across his nose and looked up from the page.

There was a pristine clarity to the colorless landscape, now rolling away from him in a series of low hills. His path—a lazy snaking trail following along the curls of a frozen creek bed—unfurled before him through the knolls and marked his course.

For just a moment the snow's brilliance blushed with a tint of magenta as the breaking sun spilled through an opening in the sky and pushed long blue shadows before him, hard-edged, cold shadows that were miserly and friendless. There was a sparkling demonstration upon the surface of the snow, like diamonds, and the wind polished over them.

Ahead lay a tract of woods, mostly broad-leafed trees stripped clean of foliage and newly dusted with snow, that fell below and between two long and blunted folds in the terrain, and the trail wriggled through the middle of it.

Aeryck took a deep breath and coughed it out as his lungs burned from the bitter cold. Then gazing about him, the boy pondered the day before him and his spirits rose.

He was traveling to the coast to meet a contingent of men from Ireland, mostly monks, sent by Patrick to nurture the new church in Loch na Huric. They were also coming to attend the feast of Christ's Mass, which would celebrate a new alliance between the Pictish chieftain Brynwald and the British chieftain Allyndaar—men who were once sworn enemies but now brothers knit together by a common faith.

Aeryck was told that his uncle, Finn MacLlewald, a kinsman on his mother's side, whom he had never met, would be coming from Ireland as well, and so he had answered winter's challenge bravely—or foolishly.

Possessing neither the gift of prescience nor Terryll's hunter's instincts, there was no way he could have known that his life was in peril, for the horizons on either side of him were sparse of trees and offered no sign of life, good or ill.

But Sullie knew, and her ears were suddenly back, and her easy gait stiffened with alarm.

"What is it, girl?" Aeryck said, patting her thick neck. Warily the boy scanned the scattered trees, now cloaked with a heavy burden of snow. "I don't see anything."

Sullie whinnied, then blew out several more uneasy snorts into the biting winter air. Blasts of little clouds marked her hot breath.

"I know, I know," the boy said. The cold bit his cheeks and dripping nose. "It's cold. But it'll warm up soon, I promise." He waited a moment as his mind collected another thought, then added, "Besides, you're all woolied over with your winter coat now, so I don't see why you're complaining about the cold."

Sullie gave vent to a final disgruntled snort and watched the trees.

The snow quickly muffled all noise to a tomblike quietness, covering death and decay beneath a shroud of cold white. Aeryck turned in his saddle and viewed their back trail. Sullie's large feet had left deep impressions in the snow and showed their track disappearing around a crook in the hills, then showing it again at the other end of the crook where the trail reappeared farther away.

There was nothing the boy could see betraying life, except a few tendrils of blue-gray smoke curling up here and there from the distant village of Glenlochar, now obscured by a low ridge of white trees, and a large brown owl that swept low across the sky carrying something small and furry in its talons. Then it was gone from sight. And again the stillness, the treacherous cold and stillness, the pause before the hammer blow.

Peering intently through a blind of spruce and fir, the large black wolf narrowed its eyes to yellow slits as the boy came into view over the rise. He was still a dark gray speck against the snowy white, but the wolf's keen eyes could see him clearly. The wolf raised its snout to the wind. Yes, it was he, the single boy on horseback. They had found him at last.

The hunt was over. The upper lip curled along the wolf's snout, unsheathing the long canine teeth, and a low growl rattled in its throat, alerting the others in the pack.

The dark heads turned in unison and became motionless along the bright and bleak ridge. The glistening yellow eyes fixed on the gray speck, blinking occasionally against the wind. The wind was up, lifting the fine spray of powder over the shimmering surfaces and carrying the electric scent into their wet nostrils, exciting the feral instincts. A charge of blood lust crackled along the line of wolves, and the heads moved excitedly to the ancient soundings.

The black wolf took off below the rim of the ridge toward a wooded tract ahead of the boy's position. The others followed soundlessly.

And the wind moaned and whistled through the trees and lay a fine sheet of snow over the trampled area where they had been.

And then there was quiet.

Aeryck looked up at the leaden sky. It was a cold sky, low and heavy. The clouds fell quickly and swallowed the horizon and the breaking sun, leaving a dull, gray cast upon the terrain. *It'll snow again before the day is out*, he thought.

Sullie snorted again, once, long and loud, and then it was quiet. And for the longest time it was quiet.

The quiet was lonely, aching, pervading the countryside with a foreboding melancholy, touching the boy's heart with an awful soundlessness, suddenly moving him to fear, then strangely to panic, and his hand was on his father's sword.

Looking about him—startled as though he had been caught in some unlawful act—he searched the blank slopes of grays and whites for anything, his eyes quick and darting and the hair on the back of his neck standing on end. His breathing became shallow over a racing pulse.

But there was nothing—only the quickened fear that was all about him, clinging to his mind, stripping his inner fortitude until he was all-consumed by a choking, hollowness of sudden, unexplainable terror, a terror that whispered into his mind, *You are a fool. You are a fool, Worm, and you are mine!*

Collecting himself with a shudder, Aeryck shook his head and blew out a cleansing sigh, shrugging it off, censuring the thoughts and emotion with contempt. Then, returning to his book, he sifted idly through the worn pages, easing his mind and soul with pleasant thoughts. He gave up struggling with the words and was now musing over the pictures and letting them carry him to faraway places.

He looked up once more, turning a page, and scanned the ridgeline. Nothing. He shook his head, then let his eyes fall upon the new page.

His mind was soon drifting along the shores of the Peloponnesus on the Ionian Sea, where he imagined himself leading great sea battles during the ancient Trojan War. It was a familiar dream and easy to get into, being refined, as it had been, by time and exercise to its purest essence. During one of his many glorious conquests, he managed— through many death-defying feats of heroism—to rescue the beautiful Helen from the city of Troy and spirit her away on his golden vessel to the land of Eire (his own addition to the Homeric epic), where they lived forever in blissful marriage. The boy envisioned Helen's features to be those of Dagmere—always Dagmere's beautiful face with her bright blue eyes shining through the murky mists of his memory like a beacon.

He replayed the dream in his mind several times, each time savoring the moment when she would kiss him appreciatively, and then with enthusiasm, for having saved her. Each time the dream condensed in scope until, at last, there was nothing left of it but the kiss—the lingering kiss and the light of her eyes burning into his soul.

In the quiet, in the aching stillness of the dream's aftermath, the image of Dagmere haunted him. She wouldn't let him be. Finally he let out a sigh, wondering in his heart if she would be accompanying her father to the feast of Christ's Mass in two weeks. He doubted it. After their last encounter, now two months past, she had probably forgotten him and was in love with someone else.

A blast of icy wind whirled about him, and he shivered back to the thread of trail and Sullie's large head bobbing in front of him. Pulling the heavy woolen cloak around his shoulders—Brynwald's cloak—the young Briton returned the little book to its place, then hunkered down lower into the fleece-covered saddle for warmth.

Brynwald had given him the cloak and a bronze brooch to fasten it, both symbols of the chieftain. The boy was on official business, acting as the chieftain's surrogate. He remembered the glint of pride in the large Pict's eyes as he had watched him fasten the brooch in place. His wife, Tillie, had cocked her round face to one side and flashed him her broad, infectious smile, revealing the little gap between her two front teeth as she always did. And then she had kissed him. She kissed him often, it seemed, as if he were her own son, and it never ceased to embarrass him, though inwardly he cherished the warmth it made him feel.

He had made the three-day trip to the coast twice before with Brynwald, stopping off each time in Glenlochar to meet with the chieftain there, a thin, balding Scotsman named Oswald, who had an easygoing manner and a thirst for knowledge. He and Brynwald had long been friends, and he hoped to hear of this new religion of Brynwald during the upcoming feast.

Sullie whickered. She cast a white eye back at the boy, then looked ahead. Aeryck shifted his eyes from one point on the horizon to another, trying to pick out a familiar landmark. He grunted. Although he knew the trail, he hadn't counted on the snow. Things looked different under white. But no mind. Sullie knew the way, and he gave the big gray her head.

By nightfall he would arrive at the Fords of Wig and stay the night there at the tavern of Pea Gants, eating his fill of broiled whitefish and cabbage. Then the following morning he would begin the final leg of his journey across the Macher's Peninsula to the village of Whithorn, where he would await the arrival of the boats from Ireland.

19

It would be a cold, two day's journey from his present location, colder than he had planned for, but it would be worth it. He was going to the sea, and there at the mouth of the Solway Firth he would meet his Uncle Finn for the first time.

Black boles were soon cutting through drifts of snow all around them, obscuring Aeryck's view as he and Sullie made their way into the midst of the wooded tract. Below a sharp embankment to their left, the creek lay frozen and hushed and directed the course of their trail. On either side of the track were gentle slopes of snow, guiding the tract of woods like an earthen sluice to a broad expanse of clearing a mile ahead.

A headwind picked up and swept through the boughs overhead, sending sprays of snow from the sapless limbs upon the horse and boy, a cold, wetting dust. Sullie shook her mane free of it, then snorted anxiously as she settled into her rocking gait. Her head bobbed as she plodded through the deep drifts of powder, ears switching first one way, then the other.

A branch whipped Aeryck in the face and showered him with icy clumps of snow, most of which found the back of his neck. The boy mumbled something under his breath as he scooped a handful of the stuff from his collar and tossed it aside. Then he stuck his numbed fingers in his mouth to thaw them out.

Suddenly the big gray startled and froze in her tracks. A red fox bounded out from behind a screen of hawthorne bushes into their path, paused as it eyed the large draft horse and curious-looking rider through small, obsidian eyes, then darted across the frozen creek below and disappeared into a thicket. Aeryck's hand was again on the handle of his father's sword, his heart pounding.

"You see?" Aeryck said, again patting Sullie's thick neck. "It was just a little old fox. Nothing to be afraid of, girl. Nothing to—"

Aeryck wasn't expecting Sullie to bolt, and he nearly came out of the saddle when she lurched forward suddenly into a dead run.

Wolves came at them from all directions, shattering the awful quiet with a violent rush, howling, snarling, snapping, their teeth flashing in the winter light.

The big gray, her eyes peeled white with terror, made straight for the treeline and the clearing beyond. Her instincts commanded her to flee into the open. However, the terrain provided only a press of trees and thickets, with a thread of trail between them—choked now with wolves forward, rearward, and along either flank. Her hooves were a muffled thundering of iron slamming against the snow.

The boy, near blinded by the biting spray of snow and the numbing cold as the wind rushed against his face, grabbed somewhere for his lost reins, somewhere for his lost stirrups, settling desperately on a handful of Sullie's mane and the grip of his legs as he clung tenaciously to life.

Almost immediately he felt something big slam hard against his leg. Looking down, he saw a large wolf, a black one, fall away from him snarling, with a snatch of his trousers in its mouth and its yellow, hateful eyes riveted on his.

The wolf lunged again, snapped and missed, again and nipped his leg, this time drawing blood.

Aeryck swung at it with his sword, slicing a broad silvery arc through the air, but the blade struck against an overhanging limb that raced past his face, and he nearly lost the thing. In the whirring sweep of branches, the sword was useless, a threat to him and to his mount. Aurelius had not yet taught him the sword's use astride a battle horse, and the boy suddenly felt quite naked.

Another wolf leaped onto Sullie's hindquarters, clawing her rump, and was at the boy's neck, its fangs snapping inches from his nape, its hot breath sending icy shivers down his spine.

Aeryck swung around in the saddle and jabbed the animal hard with the butt of his sword, and the wolf slid off Sullie's rump into her hind legs. The horse whinnied and crow-hopped at the same time, pitching him forward onto her neck, then kicked wildly at the beasts that lunged and bit at her hocks. She caught one of them on the snout with a dull crack of her iron hoof that sent it reeling into the snow.

But there was no letup from the attack. The wolves, driven by a savage bloodlust or some other hellish inspiration, came in a maddened frenzy of flashing teeth and claws that was terrifying.

A fallen tree lay across their path, and in an almost dreamlike rift of time—as the whites and grays and blacks rushed past him in a blur—Aeryck recalled this snag with supernal clarity, without the cover of snow. He recalled how he and Brynwald had to skirt around to negotiate the obstacle, both going and coming on their last two trips. And then the big gray was over it, her hooves cracking hard against another wolf with the up-kick thrust of her rear legs as she leaped.

The jolt of her landing again pitched the boy onto her neck. Unclenching his eyes, Aeryck saw to his horror that Sullie was off the trail and into the trees, now into the thicket heading uphill.

The big gray crashed into the tangle without breaking stride, startling the boy and probably the wolves as well. She whinnied and squealed as branches and bramble tore against her flanks and clawed at Aeryck's face and limbs like long black talons, ripping his clothes and tearing at his flesh.

Sullie made headway as best she could, thrusting and lurching, but the deep snow and the tangle of stripped branches pulled against her massive bulk and slowed her down to laborious plowing. The wolves, however, fared none the better, now stripped from her flanks by the thicket and having to bunch up in the deep snow behind the kicking iron hooves they had grown to respect.

And then the big mare spilled out of the bushes into a broken clearing near the brow of the hill, dotted sparsely with trees and large boulders, and was soon out of them altogether and into the open. At the summit the snow was less deep, blown free by the fierce winter winds sweeping the ridgelines, and Sullie was able to gain some ground.

Gripping his sword and the reins, Aeryck swung around in his saddle. The wolf pack was not far behind, into the open now, howling and yapping again with renewed ferocity. The brutes surely sensed it was only a matter of time before they drove the big gray into the ground and it would be over. So did Aeryck.

As he crested the hill, a movement caught the boy's eyes on the slope off to his left across the frozen creek, and his heart sank with despair. Forty or more wolves were angling down the slope, attacking it, kicking clumps of snow into the air, and would intersect his path in seconds. He reined Sullie over the ridge away from them, but she was ahead of him with the same notion, and immediately they were flying with abandon down the leeward slope into deeper snow, heading toward another forested tract below.

As they dropped down the incline, falling through the deep powder in a series of bounding leaps, the declivity choked off the baying of the wolves behind, and all sound muted to a muffled hiss of wind high overhead. Wave after wave of snowy powder sprayed skyward from Sullie's massive, thrusting bulk—cresting high and hanging suspended in midair, only to smack the boy's face with a biting freeze as he fell through each of them.

The sensation was surreal. Encompassing him was the dazzling omnipresent white, blinding his eyes, and the bitter cold that numbed his senses, and all the while the fear, the out-of-control fear that consumed his rational thoughts with a bolt of white-hot terror.

Strangely, it was exhilarating. And as the boy fell down the white slope astride the lunging gray, brandishing the sword of Caelryck wildly, through the crashing breakers of snow waves, consumed by the cold and the numbing fear, all he could do was let out an ecstatic howl of laughter.

Then there was a jarring jolt, and to his surprise he was sailing through the air without the horse. Reaching the tract of woods, Sullie had apparently caught a foot on a buried stone and the two of them pitched into the trees. The boy landed abut an outcropping of huge boulders, and Sullie rolled into a thicket off to his right.

For a moment Aeryck lay in the snow, spread-eagle and dazed. The black boughs overhead formed a curious pattern against the pewter sky as they swirled into focus, and for just a moment he had no idea where he was. Then his thoughts cleared, and he scrambled to his feet, and there they were.

Filtering into the trees from every direction the wolves came, slowly, deliberately, heads lowered and every eye trained on him. The boy shot a look over at the thicket, but the big gray was nowhere in sight. He was glad that at least Sullie would make good her escape.

Suddenly he remembered his sword, and panic shot through his mind. But glancing down at his sword hand, the boy was surprised to see the gleaming blade extending outward from his frozen grasp.

Then looking up at the wolves, his features cast in a grim mask, the boy flexed his frigid grip on his sword hilt and backed up against the wall of boulders that prohibited his escape.

"All right! All right!" he snarled, as he eyed the line of wolves before him. "C'mon, then. I'm going to take at least one of you with me."

2
OF MEN'S THINGS AND WOMENFOLK

Do Pictish girls wear linen dresses as we do, Mother? Or should I make myself a new outfit?" Dagmere asked, as she laid out her wardrobe on her mother's bed. On the floor nearby were two large traveling trunks, opened and filled to overflowing with women's apparel. "Something . . . I don't know . . . something with more cowhide or furs in it." She giggled impishly.

"Now how would I know what Pictish girls wear, Dagmere?" Helena responded, not catching the humor. She was frowning at herself in the full-length bedroom mirror that stood in the corner. "You have several lovely dresses. I'm sure that you would look just fine in any one of them." Then angling her figure to catch each of her contours, both fore and aft, she grumbled to herself, "This dress fit me fine last Christ's Mass. How could it have shrunk so in just one year?"

"Ah! This is the one!" Dagmere held up a beautiful linen dress, the one Helena had made for her on her fifteenth birthday. The material had been imported all the way from Constantinople and was of the palest blush of pink.

Presently the red one caught her eye. "Hmm. Now this one might really—" she broke off "—but he's never seen me in this one be—" Again she broke off. Glancing back at the pink dress, she was suddenly caught in a quandary.

"I suppose I'll have to let it out," Helena mumbled at her reflection. She took hold of the gathering at her waist and stretched it from side to side, determined to coax it a size larger.

"You look beautiful, Mama," Dagmere said, charging in front of the mirror with both dresses held against her bosom. Favoring the pink one first, she angled her head to one side and fluttered her eyelashes. "This one really brings out the color in my eyes. Don't you think, Mama?"

"Hmm?" Helena was distracted.

Then favoring the red one, Dagmere's eyes lit up. "But this one—yes, now this one—what do you think, Mama?"

"You don't think it looks a little tight?" Helena asked, fiddling with the bodice of her dress. "Maybe up here a bit?"

Dagmere glanced back at her own reflection in the burnished mirror, gazing at her features pensively, studying them as though she were looking at them for the first time. The first rays of the morning sun, the cold winter sun, were just spilling into the bedroom through the small, Roman-arched window and catching the myriad hues of brown and red and yellow highlights in her long auburn tresses. The sun's reflection bathed her face with a golden bronze luminance, bringing to light a thin, faded line of freckles across the bridge of her nose. Noting them, she scrunched up her nose with a scowl.

"Are Pictish girls pretty, Mama?" She traced the soft lines of her features with her eyes.

"I suppose," Helena replied. She was tugging at a pleat.

"Do you think there might be many of them in Loch na Huric?"

"I don't know. Perhaps." Helena arched her brows resignedly and compressed her lips. "Maybe if I loosened it just a stitch or two. Yes, that's what I'll do. Now, what was it you were saying, Dag—" She glanced at her daughter's two selections. Then immediately picking up the question in her mind, she answered, "Oh, definitely the pink one. It makes you look so much like a fine, well-bred young lady—a British lady. So demure."

Dagmere raised the pale pink dress a bit with a contorted expression. Then turning away she mumbled, "Demure?"

Suddenly Allyndaar blew into the bedroom and stopped. His eyes took in the room with a masculine sweep.

Dagmere crossed behind him as she made her way to the bed. "Hello, Papa."

"Hello, Dag," he replied, distracted. "Has anybody seen my emerald cloak?"

Helena's eyes shot open, and she caught Dagmere's eyes reflecting a startled look at her in the mirror. "Your emerald cloak, did you say?" A flush of pink colored her cheeks.

"Yes, my emerald cloak. Have you seen it anywhere?" Then spotting something green, he continued across the room.

"What would you want with your emerald cloak?"

"What would I want with my emerald cloak?" Allyndaar repeated. He was rummaging through a pile of his clothes at the foot of the bed and pulled out a green pair of woolen trousers. He frowned. "To wear at the banquet, of course."

"But you haven't worn your emerald cloak in . . . in . . . ."

"Months!" Dagmere said quickly, trying to help.

Helena shot her a look. *You're not helping.*

"Weeks?" Dagmere squeaked, trying again.

"Well, I want to wear it now," Allyndaar said, now foraging through to the bottom of the pile.

"Uh-oh," Dagmere mumbled under her breath. She started to leave the room, but another look from her mother caught her and drew her back.

"Why not wear your scarlet cloak?" Helena asked innocently. "You look so much more . . . more dignified in it."

"I don't want to look more dignified," Allyndaar grunted. "I want to find my emerald cloak." He stood up from the pile and, tossing a shirt back onto the heap, threw his hands onto his hips. A measure of frustration was building in his voice. "Now where did it get off to? Have you seen it or not, Helena?"

"You can't wear your emerald cloak," she answered flatly.

"What?"

"I said, you can't wear your emerald cloak," she repeated, abruptly crossing the room to a corner, where she began rearranging an assortment of flowers and other knickknacks on a small table.

"What do you mean, I can't wear my emerald—"

"Tyrrell has it," Helena said, moving a little vase a half inch to one side, as if it mattered.

"*Terryll* has it!?" Color flushed into the chieftain's face. "What is Terryll doing with my emerald cloak?"

"No doubt impressing Gwyneth with it right now," Dagmere offered under her breath.

"I didn't give him permission to wear my emerald cloak," Allyndaar objected, his voice rising to his "angry pitch."

"No, but I did," Helena said.

"*You* did? Wha—"

"Yes, I did," she said again. Helena, her attention now back on the floral arrangement, picked out a couple of flowers, healthy-looking flowers, and carried them to the window. "I thought you were going to wear your scarlet cloak. You told me that you were, just last week," she hastened to add. Then she tossed the flowers out onto the courtyard below.

"I did, did I? Well, that was *last* week," Allyndaar roared. "This is *this* week. This week I want to wear my emerald cloak. I ought to be allowed to change my mind once in a week!"

Dagmere raised her eyebrows and pretended to be interested in one of her dresses.

Helena crossed back to the corner and shot him a scowl. A strand of hair blew out of place, but she let it fly. "Well, Terryll asked me before

26

he left yesterday, and you were—well, who knows where you were when our son left?—so I gave him permission. I didn't think you'd throw a fit about it."

"Are you blaming *me* now? Isn't that marvelous? I want to wear my emerald cloak, so now I'm throwing a fit, and it's all my fault. Just marvelous."

Helena was back at the floral arrangement choosing more victims. "I don't know what you're so all fired up about your emerald cloak for anyway. You always told me you liked your scarlet one best."

Dagmere brightened. "How about your blue one, Papa? That's the one I like the best."

Both parents shot her a look. *Stay out of this!* And the girl slunk back to her dresses. She was mumbling under her breath.

"Now, what am I supposed to tell Baldwyn?" Allyndaar bellowed.

"The ale monger?" Helena asked, stuffing the petaled victims back into the vase. "What's Baldwyn got to do with anything?"

"Yes, what's Baldwyn got to do with anything, Papa?" Dagmere echoed, suddenly back into it again.

Allyndaar was looking at Helena. "Because it just so happens that he asked me if I was going to wear my scarlet cloak to the banquet."

"So?" Helena pulled the strand of vagrant hair out of her eyes, but it fell again, coaxing a few more insurrectionists with it.

"Yes, so what, Papa?"

"So I told him no. I told him that I was going to wear my emerald cloak to the banquet—thinking foolishly to myself that it belonged to me and that it would be where I had left it. So Baldwyn asked me if he could borrow my scarlet cloak to wear at the banquet and, seeing as how I wouldn't be needing it, I told him that I would be pleased to let him borrow my scarlet cloak."

"Since when is Baldwyn coming to the banquet, Papa?" Dagmere asked, her eyes widening with concern.

"What?"

"Well, you'll just have to retrieve your cloak from Terryll when we meet him in Bowness then," Helena interrupted.

"I wouldn't have to 'retrieve' it if people around here asked me before taking my things," Allyndaar countered, starting for the door. However before reaching it he pulled up sharply. "And I'll have you know that yesterday I was busy making arrangements for the trip. Terryll and I said our farewells the night before."

Having said that, the chieftain stormed out of the room, grumbling to himself about the way things ought to be around his household.

Helena stood in front of the little table watching the empty doorway clearing of its thunderheads. "Oh, bother," she said, composing her-

27

self. "I've really messed that one up, haven't I?" She took a breath and blew the brown strands of hair out of her face, then looked over at her daughter.

But Dagmere seemed to be caught in a trance, staring at nothing out the window.

"Dagmere?"

"Mother, is Baldwyn's family coming along with him?" Dagmere asked, breaking free of the trance. "I was just wondering."

"I believe so, Dagmere. Why?"

"And I suppose . . . er . . . Fiona too?"

Helena raised an eyebrow. "She's part of the family. I'd expect she'd come along too. Yes. Now, what is this all about?"

Immediately Dagmere's countenance fell.

Helena caught the collapse and understood at once. Aeryck. It was no news in the village that the beautiful sixteen-year-old girl with the flashing green eyes and raven hair was Dagmere's eminent rival. There were other rivals, to be sure—Aeryck was handsome; he was also the son of Caelryck—but there was none so beautiful as Fiona and certainly none that had kissed him. Helena let her be.

Walking across the room, she stopped and looked appraisingly at the image of herself in the mirror, an image that had blessed her over the past thirty-seven years, one that was devoid of the toiled furrows etched by grief, hardship, and the sculpting of time that lined the faces of other women her age.

Helena's was a face of Latin verse, composed of splendid lines and soft contours. Her figure, at once shapely, aristocratic, and chaste, bore her through life with graceful womanly cadences, finding their counterpoint in the mannish rhythms that beat thunderously in the breast of Allyndaar.

A tiny squall of lines gathered around the corners of her rich, chocolate-hued eyes as she considered the twin bronze image standing before her. The twin gazed at her with haunting feminine scrutiny, warning her that time, though it had passed her by in the full flower of her beauty, pausing only to touch her temples with silver, would one day return to collect its rightful due. The turbulence moved from her eyes across the smooth olive plain of her cheeks and settled at the corners of her mouth. Shaking her head, she set the strands of hair that had gotten loose back in place with an ivory comb.

"There!" she said triumphantly, the coup attempt overthrown. Then she started to undress from her gown, a fine silk garment imported from India and of the deepest azure blue.

Dagmere stood by the bed—a brooding scowl furrowing deep lines across her brow—gazing down at her selection of dresses lying out before her. She picked up both the red and pink gowns and eyed each thoughtfully. A few moments passed, after which her brow suddenly cleared to a look of fierce determination.

"Definitely the red one," she said, and she let the pale pink dress fall to the bed.

And immediately she did, a cheer rose from the village.

She glanced out the window and brightened. "They're here, Mama! The people from Brough and Bowes have just arrived!"

Her mother joined her at the window and gazed at the throng gathering at the south gates of the village. Coming up the road from the south was a caravan of horses and wagons and about twenty people besides—mostly men, but there were a few women and children as well.

Just then Allyndaar swept back into the room. He was wearing his blue cloak. "The men from Bowes and Brough are here. Is everything packed?"

"We will be ready in one minute," Helena said, hurrying over to her trunk. Folding her gown, she placed it neatly on top, then closed the lid, and fastened the straps. "There. You may take this out to the wagon, Allyn, while I finish getting dressed."

"You'd best dress for the weather and not for appearances. There's a front blowing in from the north, and it's mighty cold outside," Allyndaar said, crossing the room to the trunk.

"Since when does one have to exclude the other?" Helena returned with a smile.

Hefting the chest, the chieftain immediately dropped it. "Forsooth, woman! What have you got in here anyway—stones?"

Helena pretended not to hear him.

"Mine is ready too, Papa," Dagmere said, carrying the red dress over to her trunk.

Allyndaar grunted as he dragged Helena's trunk to the doorway. "And you've probably got bricks in yours. Right?"

"Not too many bricks, Papa." She smiled.

3
THE WHITE ONE

The wolves came through the black trees and into the snowy vault like so many ghosts. Their lank spectral shapes hunched in wild postures, their heads lowered with intense gazes, their feet moved soundlessly through the white and cold. Drawing to within twenty feet of the boy, they peeled off into two lines—one angling to the right and the other to the left—and surrounded him in a large semicircle, sealing off any avenue of escape.

Then the wolves sat down on their haunches and stared at him. Others filled in behind the two lines, and soon they were three wolves deep. And the sky was hanging an iron ceiling overhead, dreadful and oppressive and void of sympathy.

Aeryck's eyes darted along the semicircle, searching the wolves' faces, anticipating which would be the first to lunge. His gaze swept about him furtively, from the intertwining of boughs and branches overhead—their twisted and gnarled fingers stretched in sapless reach, entombing him—to the outcropping of stone jutting behind him like some ostentatious marker for his head, prohibiting escape. He was alone. A thought eased through his mind, a placid thought and without a hint of fear: it seemed as good a place as any to die.

Aeryck brandished his sword, determined to stand this frozen plot to the death. For Death itself seemed its keeper and was all about him, measuring his lines for its cold embrace. He was set in battle stance, tense, shivering from the cold, and wondering what they were waiting for.

"What's the matter?" he taunted. "Lose the stomach for a fight?"

But the wolves remained motionless, fixed in their wild hunched-shouldered vigil, like gargoyles raised from stone, keeping watch over the dead. Only the vapors of steam marking their breath betrayed any sign of life. Presently the circle opened to allow room for a smaller contingent of wolves, about twenty, now padding into the wooded tract, swelling their numbers to sixty or better.

"Didn't want anyone to miss out on the fun," Aeryck said under his breath. Then his eyes opened with a start.

Last to join the pack was a large wolf that loped into their midst and took its place in the clearing between Aeryck and the semicircle of wolves. Pacing in front of the others, the beast studied the boy for several moments, its feral eyes narrowed on him with a wild intensity.

Immediately a cold breeze rustled through the wooded tract, lowering the temperature, and in the gray morning light the wolf's thick coat of winter fur glistened a bright luminescent white. Aeryck recognized the animal at once; it was the white wolf that had been shadowing him for the past several months.

"You again?" He shifted in his stance. "Well, whatever else happens today, Whitey, I'll take you with me to the dust."

But the white wolf didn't make a move toward him. It continued to pace slowly in front of the others, staring at the boy through yellow eyes that neither blinked nor averted their hold on him.

With each passing moment, Aeryck grew more perplexed, more tense, certainly colder. *Why don't they attack?* he wondered. *Why are they just staring at me?* He was anxious to get the fight over with. It was freezing. His toes were numb, feeling too big now for his boots. At least a fight would warm him up, and afterward—well, afterward the cold would no longer be of concern. It was then that he noticed the patch of blood that had dried into the white wolf's fur around its mouth, as though it had recently killed.

Suddenly the white wolf turned its head and barked at the others.

Aeryck readied himself. But to his astonishment, the white wolf turned then and loped out of the wooded area, followed quickly by the others. The boy's head took a little jolt, and he blinked hard. Then he settled into a sort of dumbfounded trance as he watched the pack charge up the snowy hill without a sound and disappear over the crest.

A moment later the white one reappeared on the ridge and looked down at the boy, its familiar lupine shape cutting a fearsome silhouette against the dull gray sky. The wolf let out three quick barks, then, throwing its head back into a terrible arch, it howled loud and long with a kind of mournful quality to its voice that seemed to be revealing some ancient mystery. It was hauntingly beautiful.

Then the beast disappeared behind the ridge, leaving Aeryck alone with the wind soughing through the boughs overhead, alone with the white and the cold and an assortment of thoughts that didn't make any sense. And the boy looked on where the wolf had been, and he wondered.

Sullie's neigh pulled him from his bewilderment. He looked over to the thicket on his right and saw the big gray pawing at the snow, snorting her contempt at the foul winter cold.

31

"There you are!" he said disgustedly. He walked over to her, stamping the numbness from his feet as he went. "Where were you when I needed you?"

Sullie looked up from the lifeless dirt, not finding anything edible, and whickered softly. Aeryck smiled at her big brown eye as he patted the side of her neck, then took hold of the reins dragging in the snow. He looked up at the hillcrest and shook his head. "I don't understand it either, Sullie. No, I surely don't."

Mounting, the boy spurred the big, gray draft horse up the hill, and, reaching the top, he turned in his saddle and looked away at the wooded tract in the distance where he had been ambushed. Immediately a horrible thought filled his mind, a thought that had an unfamiliar distinction from his own thoughts. *I have found you, Worm,* the thought taunted. *I have found you.*

The boy shuddered, and a light snow began to fall.

4
THE TAVERN
OF PEA GANTS

The blizzard struck the Fords of Wig sometime around mid-afternoon, punishing the port and the countryside around with an unyielding downpour of icy, wet snow. The temperature was driven to well below zero by fierce, offshore devil winds that howled and screamed with unrelenting fury. A few cargo ships and some smaller fishing boats, straining against their moorings along the leeward quay, pitched and yawed, and their furled masts kept time with the rolling swells like large metronomes. And the dark and surging gray water—laced with creamy foam—pounded the rocks and sent geysers of spray and wash into the frozen air.

The usually busy port was spread out along a crescent stretch of bouldered quay and held a clutch of stone shops and mercantiles, a few taverns, warehouses, and livery stables, each enjoying a thriving maritime business, each clinging tenaciously to the rocky coastline like lichen, now battened and braced against the fierce winter storm. At present, however, one wouldn't know to look at it that anything existed there at all, for the little seaport town was obscured to vague shapes of gray by the blinding gauze of driven snow. Although most of the traffic had already headed south to trade in warmer climes, a large, single-masted Byzantine-styled ship laden with trade goods and bound from Constantinople by way of Carthage, Iberia, and Ireland, had put into port earlier that day just ahead of the storm front. The sailors, a swarthy lot out of Crete, had quickly unloaded their cargo into nearby warehouses, then scurried into their favorite haunts for warmth, ale, and wenches, their pockets full of gold and silver.

Inside the tavern of Pea Gants were handfuls of sailors and fishermen grouped about the room in little fraternities, attending to their peculiar creeds. They were hard, driven men, with tough faces that were leathered and lined and beaten brown by the bitter, unforgiving elements and time, faces quick to smile and quicker to scowl.

There was a collective loneliness in their faces, a collective knowledge of the sea's seduction and her briny kiss upon their lips that left their souls each a ravaged wasteland. And now they were cast ashore by the ocean's caprice and her heartless disfavor, left stranded now with a common knowledge of themselves. And so the mariners pitched and yawed over foamy swells of ale, and they plunged headlong into the glowing amber philosophies of the room with abandon, hiding the loneliness, drinking away the briny kiss with a mariner's abandon that was hearty and full of reckless cheer.

Off to one side, near the great stone fireplace, Aeryck sat by himself at a small round table, taking in the scene with boyish awe. His firelit silhouette was hunched over a wooden plate of broiled whitefish, boiled potatoes and cabbage, and a mug of cider—steaming apple cider—and the hot, therapeutic vapors wafted up and enveloped his face with sensorial comfort. He had arrived a half hour earlier in the thick of the storm. It was fortunate for the boy that when the blizzard struck, he had just reached the River Cree and was able to follow its course south to the Fords of Wig without too much difficulty. Had he been anywhere else when the snowstorm hit, he would have immediately lost the trail and quickly perished.

Sullie had kept faithfully to the track, plodding along in her easy, rocking gait, seemingly oblivious to their earlier encounter with the wolves or further peril from the elements. She was an anchor in the storm.

He found the livery as his first order of business and paid handsomely for Sullie's needs to be tended properly: a box stall bedded thick with straw, plenty of hay and oats, and a good brushing down.

He left her in good company, eating her fill in comfort, then quickly found the tavern of Pea Gants, an inn on the quay known for its good food, lively atmosphere, and the latest world and local news. Brynwald knew the taverner well and had taken Aeryck there on their last two visits to the coast, so the boy at least had a point of familiarity in this faraway port on the way to Whithorn.

Basking now in the warmth of the fire—the warmth, acting as a balm, eased his thoughts and tensions—the boy massaged his eyes to coax life back into them. For they were heavy—like leaden, salted balls—bloodshot and burning within their sockets from having strained at the white ridgelines all morning and afternoon for further signs of the wolves.

Once during the morning he thought he spotted the white wolf peering at him through some distant trees, but as it turned out it was only a clump of snow-covered bushes that had played tricks on his eyes. Still, it had looked like the wolf, and it was enough to work on his nerves for the rest of the day.

He started at every sound, imagining bloodthirsty wolves lurking behind every tree and shrub, watching him with their yellow eyes, waiting for the moment when he would get drowsy and least expect ambush. And he had been driven to near madness by the all-encompassing white and the cold and the sensory distortions of vertigo upon his mind. But there were no more signs of the wolves. They had vanished for the time being. The blizzard had seen to that. Now he was bone tired and ready for the comfort of a warm, goosedown bed awaiting him upstairs, a comfort he had grown fond of in the home of Brynwald and Tillie. Aeryck smiled at the thought and breathed a prayer of thanksgiving.

The door opened then, and someone entered the tavern, and the howl of the wind and the cold and snow outside rushed into the room, and everyone stopped in the midst of their conversations and turned and scowled at the intruder until he closed the door. Aeryck looked up in time only to see a hooded shape retreating into the shadows on the far side of the inn.

He was quickly finishing his plate when Pea Gants ambled over to his table. The taverner was a portly man and was possessed of a blithe temperament. His sea-gray eyes, always sparkling, were quick and shrewd like a weasel's, never lighting on anything for more than a blink or two. He maintained a white stubble on his round cheeks, and a fringe of unkempt white hair floated recklessly about his ears as it caught the vagaries of currents that whistled about the place. Aeryck enjoyed watching him.

Wiping his chubby hands on a dirty apron, Pea laughed gregariously and loud as he slapped the boy on a shoulder. "Well, mannie!" he bellowed. "It does a soul good to see a lad who enjoys a fine eat. Most of the sea buzzards that roost in here come only to fill their heads with ale."

He shot the sailors at the nearest table an affable scowl. "Aye! They wouldnay ken a good leg o' lamb iffen it walked up and bit 'em. But that's all right, laddie!" he added, appraising a week's crop of whiskers with his palm. "They mostly get too drunk to waste good food on 'em anyways, so when they've had their fill, I just sends 'em up to the wenches. Either count, I get their gold, and they get a warm thought that'll keep 'em on the chillin' lonely seas."

Aeryck looked up at the man, not sure what he meant.

Pea Gants took no time to read the boy's vacant expression. He chortled, then bent over close to the boy. His chubby fingers lay gently on the back of Aeryck's chair and drummed a little tune. "So what brings a lad here in such a blow as this then? What, with all the murderers and cutpurses lurkin' about the port for a throat to slit and a little gold to pinch? Why, I wouldnay doubt there's one or two of the dreg-lickers in here right now, sizin' up the take."

35

Wiping his hands on his apron again, Pea Gants shifted his gaze across several of the tables. Most were filled with sailors and fishermen from different ships and boats that had put into port—a group of Italians at one, some Gauls at another just behind the boy, and of course the Cretans. But there were also tables along the periphery of the tavern, set back into shadowy nooks and hollows, where other men huddled in conversation—men who were neither sailors nor fishermen but were men who had the look of time and violence in their eyes.

Aeryck took a draft of cider and scanned the room over the lip of his mug, acting nonchalant. "I can take care of myself."

"Aye. That I'm sure, mannie. That I'm sure," Pea said, testing the boy's shoulder for strength. "Brynwald told me how you relieved old Sarteham of his sword hand." The portly man thrust back suddenly and let out a hearty guffaw, startling the boy. *"Och!* That I would've like to seen!"

He bent over the chair again like a confidant, and his fingers tapped a furtive cadence. "Laddie, he's a mean one, all right, that rascal is. And he's got a wheen friends in these parts, you can be sure of it. I'd take a mindful concern, I would."

Aeryck took another draft of cider. "Like I said, I can take care of myself."

"Whisht! That you did. But I wouldnay be a braggin' on it, none the same. Not in these hereabouts, leastwise."

Pea Gants wiped his hands on his apron, paying particular interest to the fleshy spaces between his fingers, as though he were working off some absolution, then picked up the boy's empty plate.

Aeryck was intrigued by this peculiarity in the man and watched him with some amusement. He couldn't imagine how anyone could be so concerned with keeping his hands clean, since it was plain to see that they were the cleanest pair in the establishment.

"Tell me then, mannie," Pea Gants continued, "what brings you out here to this scrape of the earth? And by the look of your leg," he added, "not without a bit of trouble."

Aeryck had forgotten his leg wound, and he glanced down at it. The torn opening in his trouser leg revealed an ugly, dried smear of dark rust red on his calf, radiating from a three-inch scab. But he managed to hide his reaction to it. "It's nothing," he said, looking back at the man. Then, changing the subject, he answered the taverner's question. "I'm on my way to Whithorn on the morrow to meet my uncle—"

"Whithorn, say you?" Pea Gants interrupted. "Whatever for, lad? To catch your death perhaps in this weather?"

"To meet some men who'll be putting into port from Ireland," Aeryck said.

The round man arched an eyebrow and cocked his head. "There'll be nay ships landin' there for some time, laddie. Not with winter settin' in as it done, of a sudden. If your mates was plannin' to put into port on the morrow, as you say, they'll be in for a time of it. Aye, that I'll warrant you."

Aeryck looked into his mug of cider and considered the taverner's words. Slowly panic began to rumble across his mind, and his brow furrowed with dark lines.

The thought of there being weather trouble for the men during the crossing had not occurred to him. But hearing it now from Pea, it made perfect sense. Since the boy had never been to sea, he wouldn't know of such things. He had only dreamed dreams of the ocean and the faraway places it could take him, the romantic idealism of it all. However the notion of sea gales and blizzards and ships lost at sea had never been factored into them.

Pea Gants seemed to read his face at a glance and be about to say something, when one of the Cretan sailors jumped up from his table, brandishing a saber. He began to shout untranslatable expletives in his frenetic tongue.

Every eye in the room turned at once to the scene, and a hush fell over the place. Laughing, the other Cretans immediately waved the man back to their table. But the one with the saber would have none of it. He was drunk and stood reeling before the strong currents in his mind. He began to hurl threats at the man who had been sitting next to him, jabbing at the space between them with his blade. The seated sailor flashed him a toothy smile and said something in a conciliatory tone, waving the man back to his seat. "Come, come," he said. "Come, have more wine!"

The drunken Cretan's eyes began to wander in their sockets as he tried to maintain a focus on the other's flashing white teeth. But he gave it up as a lost cause and a faraway glassy stare edged into his eyes. Then his body seemed to settle in on itself, listing to one side. His mouth parted as though he were going to speak, but he belched instead, and his saber fell out of his fingers and clanged against the floor. He gaped stupidly at the thing, chuckled, then pitched headlong to the floor under the table.

The Cretans, joined by the others in the tavern, roared with laughter, and everyone was soon carrying on as before.

"Don't worry, mannie. Iffen those Cretans get too lively for you, I ken how to knock 'em about a bit," Pea Gants said, patting a stout cutlass at his waist that was hidden partially beneath his apron. "We get the ragabashers in here from time to time, but this lot looks the peaceable kind. Theirs build up to a fast squall, but it blows over just as fast. It's the quiet ones you got to keep the grapes peeled on," he added, shifting his eyes suspiciously about the inn at some of the other tables. "They'll

37

glide up on you like sharks, roll about with the blink of death in their wee black eyes, and take you to the ghosts. To the ghosts, mind you!"

Looking at the man's cutlass, Aeryck had no doubts that Pea Gants knew how to use it and indeed had used it. Brynwald had told him so. Aeryck knew that under the man's corpulent rolls of flesh were muscles strong enough to break a man's neck.

"Now, don't you be troublin' yourself nane about your mates, laddie," Pea Gants said, returning to his earlier thought. "If there be a salt dog among 'em, you can be sure he'll have some sense of the blow and not get hisself and the others kilt."

The boy smiled woodenly, and the squall on his brow cleared some.

"And I'll wager you could go for another plate of whitefish and cabbage, eh?" Pea Gants asked.

Aeryck nodded his head. "That would be fine. And some more potatoes as well."

"Right you are, laddie! And we'll get a poultice on that wound o' yours, lest it fester."

"It's fine. Really."

But Pea Gants had turned away, chuckling to himself, wiping his free hand against his apron, and seemed not to hear his protest. "Aye. It does a soul good to see one who enjoys a fine eat—" his Scottish burr trailed off into the kitchen "—aye, it does."

Aeryck glanced down at his leg and wrinkled his nose at it. Then, taking another draft of cider, he looked around the room with boyish interest. It was a warm place with the smell of men and the sea about it.

Everywhere he looked were paraphernalia of the seaman's life, hanging from the rough-hewn timbers that framed the low paneled ceiling or from the stout walls: harpoons of various kinds displayed proudly, fishing nets piled against one corner awaiting another haul, block and tackle draped here and about, and from every vantage point in the room, it seemed, sharks' jaws were hanging, bleached white and ringed with rows of wicked-looking teeth, their maws gaping menacingly at the men below.

Having never seen a shark, Aeryck pondered them for a long time. His mind was stirred to envision the most horrible atrocities, and he shuddered over each delicious invention.

Just above him, hanging over the fireplace, was a crude wooden sculpture, faded to a sea gray by the sun and salt air, depicting the Celtic sea god Manannan mac Lir in his sea chariot, a local deity that was indigenous to the nearby Isle of Man in the Irish Sea.

During their last stay in the tavern, Brynwald told him that the figurehead was found adrift off its very shores, broken apart from the prow of an Irish cargo ship as the vessel was dashed into pieces against the murderous rocks in some storm two hundred years before. As the boy studied it, he was reminded of the picture in his book of Odysseus, standing on the prow of his ship as he braved his epic journey.

The sights and smells of the tavern fired Aeryck's imagination and reminded him of his purpose. It put some wind back into his sails, and he took heart. His Uncle Finn could take care of himself, he thought. He was an Irishman. Irishmen knew everything there was to know about weather and the sea. They were seafaring men who had spent much of their lives before the mast or servicing those who did. So he had been told. Yes, his Uncle Finn would know such things. The boy took a deep breath and blew it out, his spirits much improved. The room was bustling with activity: mariners with time on their hands in lively conversation, tavern maids—the wenches, Pea called them—fending off the men as they brought trayfuls of food and drink, mostly drink, from the kitchen. The noise, ascending steadily to an obstreperous din, was trapped by the low ceiling and deadened the senses.

Aeryck turned his attention to the Italian sailors at the table in front of him and studied them for a time, trying desperately to pick up some Latin words or phrases that he had learned from Aurelius. But the men were talking too quickly, too loud, and their antics were too wild and animated to make any earthly sense. They were easily a match for the volcanic thunderings and the occasional eruption belching from the Cretan table.

Behind him, the Gaulish traders, a lively bunch in their own right, were discussing the bloody events surrounding one Attila, king of the Huns, who at that very moment was marching across the continent toward Gaul with an army of Huns, Ostrogoths, Burgundians, and Franks, leaving a bloody wake of destruction in his path.

As Aeryck listened in, he remembered Aurelius referring to the little Hun as the "scourge of God." Aurelius told him that the Roman general Aetius, under whom he had served as a centurion years before, was at that time marshaling his legions, as well as the Visigoths under Theodoric, near Châlons to withstand an imminent invasion of Gaul. It was clear that on every front the fate of western Europe hung in the balance. The battle at Châlons would determine which way the scales tipped.

Across the room, a table set back into the shadows had caught the boy's attention while he was talking to Pea Gants. A handful of men huddled there, bent and twisted over flagons of ale, jerking their hunched heads back and forth in clandestine asides to one another, seemingly oblivious to their surroundings. Occasionally, though, one of the men with his back to the room would jerk a squinting look over his shoulder to inspect the goings on in the tavern, then quickly return to his covert business.

39

They were certainly a curious bunch, "quiet ones," Aeryck thought, surely the kind Pea Gants must have had in mind earlier. So he studied them for a while, careful not to let them catch him doing so, his mind freely imagining them for the worst. No doubt cutthroats and thieves.

Without thinking, he reached inside his cloak and patted the small purse of coins tied at his waist.

Maybe even pirates—Irish pirates. But none of them had the look of the mariner about him, so he dismissed the matter with a shrug and pulled out his little book. Being in a roomful of mariners, men who had traveled far and abroad, men who could tell him stories of the sea, stories of seafaring men given to plunder and violence, he was inspired to read *The Iliad*.

Aeryck had been reading for a few minutes, struggling to concentrate in the noise, when he looked up suddenly and his eyes met those of a solitary figure—a boy perhaps seventeen or eighteen, wearing a dark brown cloak—sitting in a recessed area near the back of the tavern.

The torch above the youth's table spilled a dim pool of light over his hands, revealing that he was holding a sheaf of papers. He was undoubtedly, like Aeryck, trying unsuccessfully to read in the din. The stranger smiled at him with the look of one recognizing a kindred spirit, a fellow traveler, then returned to his reading. His eyes glimmered in the shadows.

Aeryck was intrigued by the youth. He studied him for several moments, wondering where such a one might be traveling to or from. Was he journeying on his own, like himself? Or was he waiting for someone? Had he come from one of the ships? He didn't look like a seaman, so he dismissed that at once. A thought dropped into his head to go over and meet him, but at once several reasons shot into his mind that convinced him otherwise.

A tavern maid crossed in front of the boy, obscuring him momentarily from Aeryck's view. When she had passed by, Aeryck was startled to find the boy looking across the inn at him again. Aeryck flushed, embarrassed at having been caught staring, and jerked his attention down to the worn pages of his book. There would be no meeting him now.

"There's a fine-looking shoot," a voice soon interrupted his privacy. "Not the usual barnacle scrapings I see around here."

Aeryck looked up, startled.

Standing next to his table was a rather large woman looking down at him. Bands of faded blue tattoos ringed both her arms, and two large brass rings dangled from her earlobes. *My, she's a big woman,* he marveled. And those tattoos . . .

She wiped up a spill on the table with a rag, then lowered a steaming plate of food before him. "Here you are then, lad," she said, offering him a broad, toothless smile. "Old Pea said you had an appetite on and to fix you right up before you withered away."

Aeryck nodded awkwardly. "Thank you . . . er . . ."

"Gilda. Call me Gilda," she said, settling a squall of hair into place. She stood back with her hands on her hips to take a good look at the boy, eyeing him as one would inspect a yearling colt. "You're a right handsome frame of a lad. I seen it, right off, the last time you come in here with old Bryn. With a ruddy boon face to boot!" she added, pinching his cheek.

Aeryck flushed, adding red to her pinch mark.

Chortling to herself, Gilda took a step backward, angling her gaze at the bloody tear in his trouser leg. "Now, dinna worry none aboot your leg. I'll be back in a switch to lay a poultice on it." She turned to leave.

"No! That's all right!" Aeryck called after her.

But she was gone, and the boy was left alone with his second helping of whitefish and boiled cabbage, which he attacked heartily.

Ten minutes later Gilda was back with a bowl of hot water, some clean strips of linen, and a poultice made of herbs, crushed roots, nettles, and a mixture of salts. Before Aeryck could object, she had his trouser leg pulled up and was cleansing the wound.

"Old Gilda'll have you fixed up in nay time," she said, dabbing the gash along his right calf with a wet cloth. "Had to wrestle the bowl out of Silvie's hands though, 'cause she wanted to take care of you herself. Hoot! Ooie! She begged me, she did. But I told her nay. She dinna ken the first thing aboot doctoring—though she was flint set on learnin' of a sudden." Gilda chortled and shook her head. "I swear. The poor girl."

"Silvie?" Aeryck had a hard time keeping up with her.

"Aye, my friend Silvie." She jerked a thumb at a girl leaning against the entrance to the kitchen. "That's her over yon, a-gaping at you."

Obediently Aeryck looked at the girl. It was a lass with a bonny figure he was looking at, with mousey-blonde hair pulled back into two long braids, and leaning easy with her back against the doorjamb. She was playing with one of the braids, brushing the roses of her cheeks with the ends, and staring at him with a wistful, pouty look.

"She's a strange one, she is. Pretty enough, but a bit daft in the bean, I'd say. Cannay help it, though—was dropped as a child, says she in her defense. Got a permanent lump on the back of her skull where the floor fetched hard again' it. Troth, I felt it! Aye. Like a turnip, poor thing."

Gilda shook her head as she pressed the poultice into the wound. She angled her head toward the boy with a squint in one eye. "She's got it powerful hard for you, lad. She told me so."

Aeryck flushed again, bright red.

The girl at the doorway smiled demurely at him, then disappeared suddenly into the kitchen. Pea Gants was shouting something at her from inside.

A howl erupted from the Latin table.

Gilda shot them a scowl. "Animals," she growled. "Knock their heads together, and only a single thought would escape."

Turning back to Aeryck, she wrapped a strip of linen around his leg, tore the end of it, then tied it off snugly. "There, that ought to do it." Climbing to her feet, she asked, "So, what'll I tell Silvie?"

"Tell Silvie?" The boy looked up from his newly bandaged leg, completely bewildered.

"Silvie," the woman said. "What d'you think I been scratchin' at?"

Suddenly Aeryck felt very light-headed. For a moment he wasn't sure that any of this was actually happening. It had all come on so suddenly. He suspected that maybe he had somehow fallen off into a bad dream, bone tired as he was, and that at any moment he would wake up and the large woman would be gone. Gone so that he could eat his meal in peace, or at least gone out of his dreams so that he could sleep better. But as he looked up at her, with the mariners in the tavern providing the ambience of revelry, there she was, big as life, peering down at him with her broad, toothless smile and faded tattoos ringing her arms, waiting for his answer. He gaped at her with a vacant, stupid expression, and all he could muster was, "Uh . . . I don't . . ."

"Suit yourself, handsome," she said. "It's nay skin off my teeth. Not that I got many left to skin, mind you." She threw her head back and laughed. "But I cannay say aboot Silvie. She'll be heartsore about it, I ken." Giggling, the woman gathered up the bowl and the strips of excess linen, then turned and left, shaking her head. "Poor girl's daft in the bean, I tell you, daft in the bean. Ah, well."

Aeryck breathed a sigh of relief as he watched the woman crossing the room. As she passed by the Italians, one of them, a skinny one, said something to her, then hooted drunkenly.

Gilda let out a howl. Immediately she grabbed a flagon of ale from their table and broadsided him with it, sending the man sprawling. Then she tossed the remaining contents of the flagon into his lap as she walked past him toward the kitchen, singing a tune.

The others in the room broke out laughing, thoroughly entertained by the show. The skinny Italian sat on the floor rubbing his skull, presumably wondering what had just hit him.

Aeryck laughed in concert with the other men and exchanged a few clever nods and winks with those around him. He was even amused

42

by the vulgar remarks hurled at the skinny Italian as he staggered to his feet. He knew the meanings of the words at once, not by recognition of sound and syllable, but by the universal interpreters of gesture and tone, and they addressed an earthy place in his soul. It was all in good fun.

Even the skinny Italian was soon roaring with laughter and swinging a flagon in the air. It was a demonstration of international solidarity and bonhomie. The sea had returned its broadcast orphans from the four corners of the globe to huddle and congregate together beneath a common roof and atop a single deck of scrubbed planks.

And there was an aura of comradery among the mariners that transcended race and creed and tongue. For just a moment in time the single lurid exchange had stitched the little separate fraternities into a single common fraternity, a brotherhood of the mast as it were, and the boy felt at one with them. He was no longer an outsider watching from some isolated perch along the gunwhales. No. Through his laughter he became an initiate into the order, and he reveled in it.

It was then, as Aeryck sat chuckling at the scene and shaking his head, all aglow in the amber wake, that he glanced across at the youth sitting alone in the darkened recess of the tavern, as though to strike a pledge with him, to entreat him too to "enter in" and take his ease among brothers.

Aeryck was surprised to find the youth staring at him now, his face placid and luminous in the aureole of torchlight, his eyes glittering dimly in their quiet orbits. However he beheld not a look of amusement upon the stranger's face but a little tract of pity. It startled Aeryck like a slap on the cheek. He blinked hard to clear his focus. Perhaps he had misread the look, he thought, looking again, but his eyes had not deceived him.

The terrible look of pity glinting in the boy's eyes from across the shadowy room reminded Aeryck at once of the waking dream he had had two months earlier, wherein his father, standing amid a throng of radiant saints before the resplendent city of gold, had looked upon him from across the fiery chasm with that same look of pity.

It unnerved him, and a ripple of shivers swept along his spine. Moreover he was touched by a chilling sensation of nakedness, reaching down to his marrow, it seemed. And unable to hold the boy's gaze, he retreated to the fireplace and drew his cloak about him for warmth.

But the chill clung to him, clinging not to his body, however, but to his soul. The prick of conscience—the little despot enthroned upon his brow, who railed and pronounced implacable judgments—moved him to shame, and he writhed beneath it like a nocturnal snake caught in the sudden white eye of a light. His expression unfurled a hidden knowledge of himself. Gazing heavily into the fire, a little astonished and disheveled of spirit, the boy shook his head as the gentle wooing of an inner Witness caught him unaware.

Aeryck looked away from the fire to the youth's table, determined in his heart to go over and join him, but to his surprise he was gone. He wheeled his head around and just caught a dark-hooded shape disappearing behind a door that led to one of the rooms upstairs. Aeryck looked on for a moment as the disappointment seated itself securely in his mind.

Curiously, he was struck with a sense of loss. Immediately a melancholy shroud settled over his spirit.

Then, as he gazed about the room at the lively mariners, each one with his sheets to the wind and sweeping along to some obscure horizon, he was struck with a vision of stark clarity. These were men who had trodden decks of teak upon the open, tossing seas; fearless men of lark and laughter; men who were in love with the infinite line between earth and sky and were driven there by a burning wanderlust in their souls; men whom he had admired and, indeed, still admired for their vision and courage; men in whose company he still desired to be.

But he wondered if any of them had any salient notion of the Creator who had breathed the wind of life into their earthen vessels; indeed, who would captain their mutable and trackless charts if they would but let Him.

It troubled him.

For the first time.

Letting out a heavy sigh, Aeryck turned back to his plate of food and his book, and, in such solitude, next to the warming fireplace, he was soon sailing across the seas of his imagination, braving the worst of storms and rescuing the beloved image of Dagmere from the clutches of savage Irish pirates.

Looking up from the book (he had made a connection to an earlier thought), it suddenly dawned on him that he had no idea whatsoever what Irish pirates looked like. For all he knew they might look just like one of the quiet men across the room in the shadows.

He glanced at their table, and one of the men who had had his back to him the entire evening turned in his seat and began to stare at him. And as the torchlight pulled his rugged, almost simian, features from the darkness, Aeryck found that it was the face of a man he knew quite well, one who had at one time delighted in inflicting much torture upon the boy.

He was looking into the face of Spang.

5
OLD DEBTS

Well, if it ain't the British shoat—what—and up here all by hisself," Spang said through a wicked grill of teeth.

The Pictish warrior, a churlish brute of a man, got up and made his way through the crowd toward Aeryck's table, causing no small stir as he pushed and bullied mariners out of his path. Four other tough-looking men followed in his wake, casting hard looks at the mariners. All about the tavern, heads turned and followed their progress, with expletives abounding on a gaggle of quick tongues.

"What're you doin' here, sonny?" Spang asked, still coming through the crowd. "Seems you've stepped a touch out of your reach, iffen I'm not mistaking."

"I didn't come here looking for trouble," Aeryck said, rising to his feet.

"And who says you've found any?" Spang said behind a throaty chuckle. "I just come over to see an old friend is all. Thought perhaps we might tidy up a wee bit of unfinished business."

Aeryck recognized the sadistic tone in his voice from his earlier encounter with the man.

Spang and the others pulled up to within a few paces of Aeryck's table and spread out a little, keeping to just outside the large oval of fire-glow cast onto the wooden floor. The light kept them at bay long enough for the boy to step away from his table and secure the advantage of the hearth at his back. Judging by the squinting sneers and the deadly manner in which each fingered the haft or hilt of his weapon, it was clear that trouble had indeed found the boy. He swept back his cloak to free his arm and lay his palm gently on the silver pommel of his sword.

"I wish to do you no harm," he said.

Spang eyed the sword greedily, then let out a throaty laugh. "Did ye hear that, lads?" he chortled. "The shoat here dinna wish to do us nay harm. Ain't that nice?"

The men chuckled.

"Whisht! But ye see, lads, this here's nay laughin' matter," Spang said to his men, with a melodramatic aside. He was clearly enjoying himself. "Why, there's good reason for us to be trembling in our skins—meltin' in the quakes, I tell ye. *Och!* Did I not mention to ye that this here's the shoat what cut oft Sarteham's right arm?"

The men gasped and shook their heads, gaping wide-eyed at one another as they played along with him. "Imagine that!" one of them exclaimed.

"We're in for it, sure," another added.

"Surely not this young sprig," a third put in. "He has a face as pretty as any I ever kissed."

"As I live and breathe, he's the very same," Spang said in earnest. "I was there and seen it with my own—" He broke off and addressed the man nearest him. "Why, you was there, Coswold, weren't you now? You seen how he done it too, I'll wager—with his shiny sword and all."

Coswold, a tall slope-shouldered man and powerfully built, stepped out of the shadows and gaped stupidly at Spang, nodding his head vigorously. Aeryck recognized him at once as the one who had helped Spang stretch Terryll and him between the menhirs in Loch na Huric.

"Sure ye did," Spang added, finishing his thought. His brow suddenly cleared of any humor, and something malignant quickly drew his features into a savage scowl. Turning to the boy with a kind of gloat clicking through his teeth, he fixed his gaze on him. "But you ken—now as I recollect it—I seen it as a lucky blow of yours, what took his arm."

"Aye, them's my recollections as well," Coswold agreed.

"Maybe so," Aeryck countered, growing tired of the sport. "Just the same, the worms have picked his bones clean by now, don't you think?"

Spang grunted contemptuously. "You got a smart mouth, laddie buck. But it dinna count for spit. Nay more, anyhow."

Aeryck edged a pace to one side and fixed himself into an easy stance. However, his muscles were taut, like coiled springs, ready to leap into action. His weight shifted forward onto the balls of his feet, and his mind was a recitation of sword drills. "No one has to get hurt here, Spang," he said calmly. "Like I said, I don't wish to do you any harm."

"It ain't the harm you was to do to me that was on my mind, shoat," Spang rasped, stepping into the light away from the others. The firelight flickered luridly on his face, and his hand was reaching for the hilt of his sword. "What if I was to tell you that I was going to prick your guts open wide, and spill 'em all over the floor?"

"Then I'd suggest you cut the lather and get on with it," Aeryck said, drawing his sword.

As both blades cleared scabbard, the familiar ring of steel rent the air, then, trailing off, drew a terrible silence over the tavern. Every eye was now riveted on the business at hand, and every eye was agleam with a sudden thirst for blood. The silence hung still, and there was a collective intake of breath.

Spang lunged at the boy like a crazed bull, and with a broad arc his blade fell hard against him, and the boy staggered before the blow. This seemed to loose some pent devils in the room, and the air was immediately rife with an ejaculation of hoots and hollers and impish shrieks. There was a sudden furious clambering for better vantage points.

Spang howled exultantly.

Ringing his blade off the boy's, the Pict hammered and thrust time and again, slicing great yellow arcs through the air as he swung his blade down with astonishing power. Each time, however, his punishing blows were fairly met and countered by Aeryck's honed steel and skill.

The room was a roiling gallery of faces that jumped here and there out of the shadows into the saffron halos of torches, and here and there white teeth flashed, and eyes winked, and encompassing the spectacle was an unabated roaring clamor.

But the lad's focus fell away from these and narrowed to the two glowering slits hovering before him and the slanting point of metal. His ears were acutely attuned to the grunts and snarls jerking in Spang's throat. His feet moved with the frenetic speed and agility of a mongoose in a terrible dance, his eyes seeking the moment of weakness, the uncertain glint in his enemy's eyes, waiting for the opening to strike; his mind, hammering out the inner cadence of Aurelius's rhythmic commands. *Sidestep, parry, thrust . . . step forward, parry . . . weight forward, parry, thrust . . . sidestep . . .*

The moment came quickly when, parrying Spang's blade to one side, the boy thrust forward with a feint. Spang fell for it and jerked back awkwardly to catch the blade, leaving himself open. Then with a quick flip of his weapon, Aeryck thrust his swordtip at an exposed part of the man's left shoulder and pricked it gingerly, drawing a thin rivulet of blood onto Spang's leather jerkin. It had been as easy and natural as drawing a breath.

Spang jumped back and looked down at his bleeding shoulder incredulously.

An astonished quiet fell over the room. Those who were with Spang let out a succession of gasps, this time without any sport in it. Others in the room gaped at the boy in wonder; they had obviously assumed it would go the other way. Immediately odds were given and bets taken, and the crowd soared on a tumultuous updraft.

47

"I could've killed you if I wanted to," Aeryck warned Spang. "If you come at me again, I will." He looked intently at the man, measuring his angry eyes for a response.

The firelight betrayed a hint of fear in them, playing at the corners. He hoped it would be enough for Spang to back away and leave him alone in peace. But he knew better. As he stood watching the Pict, waiting, lithe in his battle stance, the boy beheld a stubborn rage smoldering on his brow, and in that moment he knew that it could only go one way.

Encompassed now by a welter of gluttonous onlookers, shouting for the contest to resume, for the spillage of blood, the brute stood in the center of the lighted ring, cornered by his pride. His barrel chest and heavy shoulders heaved like a lanced bull before the matador, his nostrils flaring, snorting, and his eyes burning red as blood rage consumed the last of his reason.

Aeryck read the pathetic transformation and wagged his head slowly. He rolled his weight forward onto the balls of his feet as Spang let out a loud curse and lunged. The spectators roared. Aeryck leaped to the right of the man's clumsy charge, again adroitly parrying his blade, and Spang's weight carried him just past the boy. Then as Aeryck was about to twirl and thrust his blade into the man's now exposed flank, he caught a glint of light out of the corner of his eye. Immediately he ducked and rolled, and a massive wedge of blade cleft the air where his head had just been. Rolling up onto his feet, Aeryck was faced with another man reaching for a second battle-ax. It was Coswold.

He sidestepped warily to his right, crouching in his battle stance, keeping Spang in his left field of vision and Coswold in front of him, his eyes darting back and forth from man to man as they advanced.

"So that's how you cowards are going to play it," Aeryck spat contemptuously.

"Aye, sonny," Spang snarled. "Aye, that 'tis."

Coswold stepped to the boy's right to outflank him, a wicked chortle rattling in his throat. But as he raised his ax to make another strike, a flash of metal twirling across the tavern caught him square in the chest. Coswold's arm slumped to his side like a felled limb, and his weapon clattered to the floor. A bewildered expression screwed over his face as he gaped at the small hilt jutting from his chest. Then, staggering backward, he tripped over a chair and crashed heavily onto the table where the Cretans were sitting, scattering them like crabs.

Aeryck reeled to see Pea Gants advancing toward him from the kitchen, wiping his hands on his apron, and the wreath of hair floating about his ears seemed charged with electricity. Gilda was just behind him, wielding a broadsword with her tattooed arm.

48

Looking back at Spang, Aeryck said, "Come on then, coward. Let's get on with it."

The crowd took up with the boy and hurled insults at Spang and his men, seeing now that Pea Gants had thrown in with the young Briton.

Spang had different ideas of a sudden and angled back into the shadows.

Pea Gants and Gilda drew up alongside the boy, and, drawing his cutlass, the taverner stepped ahead of him and shook it at Spang and his men. "G'wan. Clear out, you lot! I'll not have the likes o' you dreg-lickers soiling up my establishment."

Spang and his cohorts made for the door through a gauntlet of jeers like whipped dogs, but not without exchanging words.

"I ken where you are, shoat," Spang snarled at the boy. He chortled a wicked, throaty laugh. "That's certain. I'll be watchin' the place for when you take your leave, you can count on it. Aye. There'll be nay hidin' from old Spang—nay—not from this time on. I'll be laying for you." He spat on the floorboards.

Pea Gants moved toward him and threatened him with his blade. But Spang and his men were out into the blizzard, and the door slammed shut behind them.

A kind of awe settled over the tavern. It took a breath, then an effervescent murmuring commenced.

Pea Gants returned his cutlass to his waistband and ambled gregariously toward the boy. "'Twere a fine bit of swordplay, laddie," he said, clapping his chubby hand on Aeryck's shoulder. "'Tis true, I see, what Brynwald spake about you! Aye. A fine play of the sword, that was. Now—tell me, mannie. Who was that scurvy pack of dogs then?"

"I only recognized the one that I fought with," Aeryck said. "His name is Spang. Oh—" he remembered, "and that fellow lying over there with your knife sticking out of his chest—him too. He and Spang are both Sarteham's men."

Pea Gants strode over to the Cretans' table, where the dead man lay draped over the edge.

Aeryck followed the taverner through the crowd, which was now gathered around the corpse like monkeys and buzzing with erudite commentary. Some were eyeing Aeryck as he passed by, doubtless taking a new measure of the boy, who, until the fracas began, had been just another bent shape against the wall. Others were just eyeing his sword covetously.

"Sarteham's men, you say?" Pea Gants asked.

"Yes," Aeryck replied. "Though what they are doing away out here, I haven't a clue."

"Aye. Unless they be laying for mischief."

Gilda drew up next to them, her eyes shooting a scowl at the door. "There's a bunch I'd not be taking lightly," she said. "I heard 'em talking at the table as I was tendin' to my duties nearby. Not that I was eavesdropping, mind you!"

"You heard what they were saying?" Pea asked.

"Oh, they was keeping low and secret like with their ratty business—hissin' like snakes, they were," she replied, "but old Gilda's got ears. I was pretending not to be interested, but I gathered enough to ken that they was plotting murder—troth! Murder, it was!"

Aeryck stared at the woman until she turned his way and grinned, revealing her too-few teeth hanging tenuously from her gums.

"Plotting murder, you say?" Pea asked her.

"Aye. And they was squinting with the sheer pleasure of it, they were."

"Is that so?" Pea Gants grabbed the knife handle sticking out of the dead man's chest, pulled it free, then wiped it clean on the man's trouser leg. "Well, this'un," he said, indicating Coswold, "his plotting days is over. Leastwise this side of the hereafter!" He laughed at his humor.

Then pointing to a few of the men who were following the proceedings with rapt enthusiasm, he said, "Here, you lot. Take this rubbish and toss him into the bay. Reckon the fish'll have more use for him than any of us in here—hold it!" Pea Gants interrupted himself, as the men grabbed hold of the corpse.

He cut free the little coin purse that dangled from the man's waistband. "Wouldnay want him leavin' without payin' for what he enjoyed, now would we? A fellow would go broke. Besides, he ain't got need of it nay more." He laughed again, hefting the purse in a chubby hand.

"I ken one of them too," a quiet voice spoke from just behind Aeryck.

However the quiet voice startled the boy, perhaps because it was quiet. Turning, he was startled further, for standing no more than a foot off his left shoulder was Silvie. And she was looking at him with a longing brown-eyes-fluttering look.

"What's that?" Pea Gants demanded.

The girl shrank from the man's gaze. "I said, I ken one of the men," she replied. "The wee fellow with the weasel eyes. I don't think much of him though. He owes me."

Pea Gants crossed over to the girl and drew her toward the kitchen away from the mariners, many of whom were now arguing over who had won the fight in order to settle the bets. Gilda and Aeryck followed close behind.

50

"Well, go on then, lass," Pea Gants said curtly. "Tell us the sum of it."

Silvie edged toward Aeryck, drawing alongside him a pace.

It worried the boy some, and he shifted uneasily. Presently a powerful inclination came over him to reach over and feel the back of her head, to see for himself how large the knot really was. He almost did too, so powerful was the urge, but he restrained himself and allowed only his eyes to peruse the area surreptitiously. He couldn't see any lumpy spots, none out of the ordinary at any rate, and he reckoned Gilda to be a teller of tales.

Silvie cleared her throat and, casting a sidelong glance at the boy, said, "I was . . . er . . . entertaining him, ye might say, just the other night."

She was now looking at Aeryck wistfully and brushing her lips with the ends of her braid.

Aeryck fidgeted anxiously and averted his eyes from her to Pea Gants, suddenly feeling quite warm. The scowl brewing on Pea Gants's brow told him that he was getting impatient.

"And . . ." the taverner snapped.

"And he told me some things," Silvie snapped back, shooting the man a sour look. She straightened a bit and raised her head. She was in the possession of some information that was suddenly important.

"He told me he was meeting some fellows from up north—away up north near the River Tweed somewheres," she began. "Said he were meetin' with these fellows to plan something big—'real big,' says he. But he couldnay tell me what. Said it was too big and too secret. Well, he was acting cocksure of hisself, like he owned the place, and himself thinkin' that I were impressed and all—well, I weren't, and I told him so. That got it out of him real quick, you can be sure. Him and his weasel eyes squintin' at me." She grunted. "It weren't hard a'tall."

"Get to it, girl!" Pea groaned. "You're wearing me out."

Silvie grunted again and turned her attention to Aeryck. "Well. Like I said, I was actin' unimpressed, and the little man—his tongue was flapping crazy, sayin' things like, 'This fellow what got his arm cut off'— I dinna recollect his name—'is finally comin' to get his revenge on this other fellow.' Some important man, I gathered—dinna get his name either. 'Raising an army,' he said, 'going to plunder his village and slit his throat.' By my troth, he said it!"

Pea Gants and the boy exchanged looks.

Silvie straightened a bit more, arching her eyebrows. She continued, making an appraisal of her nails. "He went on, saying that these fellows up north was offering him a tidy sum iffen he could interest enough men to lend their blades, as 'twere, to do this other fellow harm.

51

Though he dinna let on how tidy a sum they was talking, of course. Said he knew plenty of blades for hire though, no problem. 'I'll be fixed soon,' says he.

"And now I'm thinkin' he dinna got a token for my trouble. So I spake to the wee fellow—Fek, I think was his name—to pay up. Well, he just looks at me with his little black weasel eyes and smiles. The rat. And now I ken I'm out what's coming to me, so I tell him to leave. He got riled, expecting I owed him for the tale, and threatened to do me harm. That's when I called out to Gilda. Ain't that so, Gildie?" she said, turning to the large woman.

"Aye," Gilda said. She made a gesture with her broadsword. "Had I kenned the mischief he were up to, I'd have snatched him by the nape and slit him up to his brisket."

Pea Gants had grown reflective and had taken to scrubbing his fingers like a penitent. "They're meaning to do old Bryn some harm, laddie," he said at last.

Aeryck drew his lips together and nodded.

"I tell you what—there are yet a wheen blades in these parts that'd never cross with Brynwald's. The man's got friends around here—he can count on it."

"Aye," Gilda put in, indicating her well-worn sword.

Silvie was staring at the boy.

"But that's the morrow's game," Pea said. "In the meantime, you'd best be watching your back. That Spang fellow's got it in for you. Aye, mannie. Iffen the storm blows over tonight and you're leaving on the morrow, I'll send some men to keep you safe on your journey."

"I can take care of myself," Aeryck said.

"*Och!* That I've seen with my own eyes, son!" the taverner boomed heartily. "Still, I'd rest easier kennin' that you were free of the fords before you got your throat cut. I ken old Bryn'd be expecting as much— you being like his own bairn and all."

Aeryck shot the man a curious look. He wondered if Brynwald had told him that or if the man had surmised it on his own. He was about to ask, when one of the Cretan traders came up to him and asked to look at his sword.

"What for?" Aeryck asked, annoyed at the intrusion. He was suddenly bone tired, sullen-minded, and spent of any social graces.

The Cretan smiled broadly, flashing an even row of white teeth below his thick black mustache. "Perhaps I might purchase it," he said, eyeing the workmanship on the hilt.

"The sword isn't for sale."

"Never have I seen such a beautiful blade. I would offer you a generous sum in gold," the man said, undaunted. He produced a fair-sized bag of coins from his cloak.

Pea's eyes lit up, and he massaged a chinful of whiskers. Gilda blew out a long whistle. Silvie continued to stare at the boy.

"I'm sure you would," Aeryck returned. "But like I said—the sword isn't for sale."

"May I at least have a look at this sword that isn't for sale?" the Cretan persisted.

"I don't see the point in it." And with that Aeryck walked over to his table, gathered up his belongings, then bade Pea and the others good night.

The Cretan stood gaping, stunned. It was a large sum of money.

Silvie saw her chance and made a move for the boy. But Pea Gants caught her by the arm and withheld her.

"Leave him be, lass. Leave him be."

6

THE WOLVES OF BADONSWARD

Miles away to the east the moonlight spilled through an aperture in the thick ceiling of clouds, bathing the blue-white hillside with a shimmering cold luminance and revealing a dozen dark shapes that lay still against the icy slope where they had fallen, each one mostly obscured now by blankets of newfallen snow.

Other shapes were on the hillside, shapes that moved black against the brilliance of the moon wash, shapes with their shadows going out long from them, dozens of them, gliding down from a ridge and converging upon the place where a recent battle had been fought. Once there they paused, then separated and covered the field of snow, searching the quiet forms.

The large red wolf plodded silently among the dead, looking down at each lifeless form as he passed by, pausing momentarily by each to register the face, to sniff the wounds, before moving on to the next. A series of staccatolike barks aroused his attention, and, turning, Gray Eye wended his way heavily through the snow.

Finally he stopped at the place where a large black wolf lay half buried and frozen stiff in a bloody swath of snow behind some boulders. The young wolf that had discovered the body shied from his terrible cold stare. Gazing down at the body, the red wolf's mind fell into a kind of malefic transfixion, his eyes narrowing to two glazed and yellow crescents.

A cold, shrilling wind blew down from the ridge as if on cue and raked through his thick fur, ruffling the hair on his nape so that it stood on end like a collar. His body shivered as he tilted slightly against it, though his mind was far from the cold. A growl heaved in his breast and took black flight. Trailing it came a low succession of growls that rattled about in his throat with his breath. Evanescent tendrils of steam escaped the ports of his snout in rhythmic intervals, like spirits ascending woefully from a tomb. It was a malevolent skein that winged against the ghostly pallor of the night.

Then another draft of wind rushed upon him and swirled about his shape, lifting handfuls of white powder into the air. A violent shudder rippled along his flanks, so chilling was the blast, and with a startled intake of breath his head jerked to one side, and his eyes blinked open. For a voice was in the draft, the command of his master, it seemed, to hunt down and kill.

The other wolves formed a dark circle around the large red wolf and waited patiently, shivering in the bitter cold of night, and the bright moon cast their long, sharp shadows over the glimmering snow. And they waited.

Suddenly Gray Eye threw his head back into a violent arch and vented his threats to the moon, baying long and baleful, and heralding the presence of his pack. The other wolves did likewise, each in his turn, each according to his place in the order, and soon the night air was filled with an unending succession of their malicious cries. Their voices reached, like black tentacles of fear, unto the furthermost wind-blasted moor, fore and hinder, there touching, gripping, the trembling hearts of all creatures that had paused in their businesses, their nocturnal scurrying and foraging, paused in their lowly and tiered places in the created order to hear this chilling message.

The wolves fell in line behind their leader as he led them down the slope into a dell cut out by a narrow stream, heading east toward the village of Glenlochar.

What they could not know was that they were being watched, listened to, for hidden downwind in some trees along the ridgeline was a shape of monstrous size, a black, starless hole against the night sky that sat studying the strength and movement of the wolves with rapt attention, its wet, coal-like eyes mirroring the pale orb of light in the sky.

The creature sat motionless, like an inanimate fixture of granite jutting from the landscape, long after the wolves had been spirited away into the night. Finally it moved. It blinked twice to moisten its eyes against the drying wind, then, raising its massive bulk onto its hind legs, it stood a full fourteen feet above the earth and smelled the air. The wolves were gone.

The great beast blew out a snort of contempt as it lowered onto all fours, trailing clouds of vapor from its snout as it settled with a shake of its mane. Then slowly it lumbered along the ridge with a regal majesty— like a prince—with a noticeable limp betraying its gait. And the creatures of the night looked on in wonder.

The snow-laden clouds closed over the hole in the sky, swallowing the moonlight with blackness and drawing a curtain of gloom over the terrain and the dead that lay scattered over the hillside. A cold and sinister wind moaned through the pines.

And the snow fell.

___7___
GHOSTS

Opening his eyes, Terryll slowly blinked in the awareness that the world had changed dramatically during the night. He was thrilled with the change, and the morning greeted him with a rush of promise. Winter had come at last with a grand flourish. All about him was a fresh lay of snow, blanketing the third quarter of the year with a clean slate.

The young hunter took in a draft of the new season and blew it out heartily, showing his breath in a dissipating cloud. He was again on the road, away from the confines of the village, away from the scrutiny of adults and suffocating goose-down beds, and he reveled in the liberty and the chilling, livening whiteness all around him. Rolling out from under a blanket of heavy furs, Terryll crawled out of his lean-to of yew boughs, got to his feet, then arched and twisted into a wakening stretch, coaxing the kinks along his spine to move elsewhere. Then he shook his head and blew out a shudder.

And then he let out a hoot.

A movement overhead caught his eye. Through the canopy of yews he spotted a golden eagle carving lazy circles against the pewter sky, searching the unyielding landscape for food. It would be a desperate hunt. For though beautiful in her whitened folds and pleats, winter can be a treacherous mistress to those who fall out of her favor; to the unprepared, a merciless executioner.

A red squirrel poked its head out of its cozy tree hole and chattered noisily. Moments later it was answered by a chorus of squirrel chatter. One scampered across a network of limbs overhead, kicking loose fresh snow that fell, broadcasting a fine white powder onto the camp.

Terryll smiled. The day was off to a superb start, and he about burst with a good feeling. He hooted every now and then to vent the pressure.

Clearing the ground of snow, he built a small cooking fire with a handful of dried tinder and his flint and soon had a healthy blaze warming his little camp.

The boy prided himself in his culinary skills and made full use of them when he was out in the wild. Retrieving a small tin from his saddlebags to cook in, he fixed himself a tasty meal of pork sausage, chunks of potatoes, some boiled eggs, and a mug of hot tea, adding various herbs and spices to bring out the savory flavors of his meal. He wasn't in a hurry—he knew he'd be there in plenty of time, so he sat on a smooth stone near the fire and laid his back against a broad girth of yew. Then, taking in a leisurely survey of the sights and sounds and smells of the early winter morning, he enjoyed his breakfast. On the other hand, Tempest, his spirited stallion, had to make do with whatever he could uncover around the trees and complained—stamping impatiently—with snorts and whinnies as he snatched mouthfuls of cold grass from the frozen earth.

"What's the matter, boy?" Terryll chuckled. "Miss your warm stall and hay? Or is it the mares you miss?" He laughed. Laying his plate aside, he reached into a gunnysack and pulled out a handful of oats and offered them to the horse. "Here's something that will take your mind off your woes."

Tempest shoveled the oats out of his hand greedily with his thick lips. Then, finishing, he sniffed the gunnysack Terryll was holding and nuzzled it for more.

"No, no." Terryll smiled, pulling the string taut around the sack's mouth. "That's enough for now. Don't want you getting too excited on the trail."

The stallion pawed his hoof and shook his mane, then snorted in protest.

Terryll chuckled again and broke camp. Stringing his longbow, he shouldered it and was soon astride the black charger, his stomach full and his heart swollen with a youthful contemplation. He was finally heading northwest to Bowness, to his love, tracing the familiar path through the forested Pennines, with the mission on behalf of his father now completed.

Having left Whitley Castle the day before, the last stop in his itinerary, the boy had climbed steadily into the mountains, finally reaching the summit known as Cross Fell, the highest point in the Pennines, where he had made camp for the night. It was his favorite place in all the earth, for it commanded great vistas on each point of the compass— "the top of the world," he called it, "a place where the heavens touch the earth and one could dance with the stars."

Looking back on his trail to the south and east, he could see the South River Tyne, like a silver necklace glistening in the distance, coiling through the swelling rolls of the hills, its headwaters rising from the mountains north of Killwyn Eden. To the west lay his beloved Eden Valley, a fertile skirt of land stretching from the Solway Firth southward for sixty-five miles to include his village. To the north was the fiery-haired Gwyneth, and after a month's absence he was anxious to see her.

For the past two days he had traversed the countryside acting as his father's surrogate, informing various chieftains in the area that Allyndaar and his party from Killwyn Eden, Brough, and Bowes would be arriving at Whitley Castle sometime later that day. There the chieftains and their traveling parties would rendezvous and spend the night before heading on to Bowness on the morrow.

But of course, Terryll would not be with them. His thoughts were upon Gwyneth, and he planned to be holding her in his arms and kissing her before the noon. Unable to contain his joy he burst into a lively song:

"When Love is fair, and fares thee well,
   The lonely soul takes wing;
   The turtle doves, though twain of breast,
   With single heart shall sing.

"But woe the heart when Love is cruel,
   Think not that soul shall fly,
   When maidens turn on fickle heel;
   Wither 'way, light heart and die."

The song carried on with such warbling sentiment for another five stanzas, seven being the sum and number of perfection, which of course was only a fitting tribute to such a subject as prenuptial love. There was further mention of lotus petals, and whitened breast, and blush of cheek, and limpid pools of azure blue, and so on. But to the heart "smitten with Cupid's airy dart," as was Terryll's, such words bore witness to divine inspiration. He sang it again and again, then trailed off after a time with a whistling refrain.

Wending his way through the snow along the ridge, Terryll presented a striking contrast to his surroundings. His jet black hair, full of the morning sheen, hung neatly about his shoulders and framed a generous smile. The heavy woolen cloak that he drew around him for warmth cut through the myriad grays and blacks and whites a bright emerald green, a flag heralding both his presence and his father's clan and authority.

Terryll's chest swelled just noticeably, and the blue in his eyes sparkled with anticipation, for he knew that Gwyneth would think him handsome in it. She had told him so before.

Joyfully he retrieved the great ruby he had taken from the cave of the Tuatha Baalg and held it before him, dangling upon a little chain of gold that Bolstroem, the blacksmith, had fashioned for him. Peering at its brilliant luster, he blew out a shrill whistle through his teeth, then clucked his tongue in concert.

The grayed spectrum of hills to the north seemed to bid him now, "Come, my love—my turtle dove! The dewy roses of my lips await your sweet kisses!" Within his breast there sounded an echo of Eden's first trembling stir. The boy took a deep breath and let out a wistful sigh, then returned the precious jewel to the pocket in his cloak. He was feeling powerfully good about the day.

He hadn't gone but a mile or so when he smelled smoke. *Odd*, he thought, as he pulled up on the reins. Standing in his stirrups, he scanned the horizon for its source. Nothing. Being downwind, he could tell that it was coming from somewhere to the northeast, perhaps a mile or so away. However the wind was fair and steady, so it might even be farther. Tempest whickered and stamped his foot at the delay.

"I know, boy," Terryll said, sitting down into the saddle. "Probably just a woodcutter or hunter."

Again the stallion whinnied and threw his head back, unfurling his mane and tossing his tail.

Terryll chuckled, then spurred the horse ahead on his course. As they dipped into a shallow glen, he cast another glance back to the hills beyond Whitley Castle, and then the horse and boy soon disappeared behind a screen of spruce trees, heading on to Bowness.

"The turtle doves, though twain of breast, with single heart shall sing . . ."

Moments later the two of them reappeared plodding back up the trail, heading in the direction of the smoke. And Tempest clearly didn't like it one bit.

The first image that caught Terryll's eyes were their shields, and immediately the hairs on the back of his neck bristled with alarm. Upon each was emblazoned a crimson wolf's head arched against a field of black—the coat of arms of the Saxon underlord, Norduk.

"What are they doing up here?" He scowled.

The Saxons were fifteen in number, heavily armed, and from what Terryll could see, peering through the blind of conifers, there were two boarhounds as well, maybe three. A scouting party, he figured. It was a good thing they were upwind of him. Otherwise the hounds would have caught his scent long before he had smelled their smoke.

Their camp was situated along a tributary of the River Tyne, perhaps five hundred feet away in a dingle of stripped maples, elms, and alders, some ash as well, and the men were making little effort to conceal their presence. They were clanging swords and shields, calling out to one another, and cursing the inclement weather as if they had a right to. A few were hunched over a cooking fire, eating a hearty fare and laughing, while others thrashed noisily about in the trees gathering firewood.

"Fools," Terryll said. He squinted into the glaring snow, trying to make out their features, straining his ears to pick up any words or clues as to the why of their presence. But with the distance, and through the cover of trees, it was difficult to make out anything but their black shapes and the blood color of the wolves against their black shields. And the thick insulation of snow muted all sounds.

The boy was torn between curiosity and the intense desire to continue on to Bowness to see his Gwyneth. The scales were tipping slowly back to the fiery-haired beauty, but the boy in him constrained him, and he stayed a while longer just to see what they were up to—mischief, no doubt.

Then one of the men, one who had been stooped over the blazing campfire with his back to the boy, stood up and turned, facing him. Terryll's eyes jerked open. At first sight he thought he was looking at a ghost. Rubbing his eyes to clear them of sleep and glare, he shielded his brow and looked again, squinting into the dazzling white.

It was not a ghost. It was a man now rising from the earth like a fiery shade from the Underworld to remind him of a past horror. The boy let out a gasp. For there was no mistaking the winged helmet and thick, blond mane of the Viking Olaf—the large man cut an all-too-familiar and terrible silhouette against the snowy field.

"So you've escaped the Pictish blade," Terryll growled under his breath. And there was no more question as to what he would do. He studied the man for several minutes, squinting, searching for answers. None were forthcoming. Then stroking Tempest's muzzle, he whispered, "You stay here, boy. I've got to get a closer look."

The black horse whickered softly.

Removing the bright green cloak, Terryll unshouldered his longbow and, using the cover of trees and boulders to conceal his advance, was gone. His years of hunting in these hills gave him the advantage of the terrain, and as he made his way down the blind side of the hill, across and along the river and into the periphery of the Saxon camp, he moved with the stealth of a cat and the silence of an adder. The young hunter was in his element, and the wind held in his favor.

He was soon peering through a tangle of yew bushes not thirty feet from their campfire, his eyes sweeping the clearing with the cunning of a predator, taking in essential information, pausing to consider each new piece taken.

The boarhounds (there were three of them) were tied near their horses across the campsite sixty feet away and seemed interested only in whatever scraps of meat were tossed to them.

The men resembled so many bears, clothed, as they were, in thick furs to warm them against the cold—bears with battle-axes, armor, and broadswords, each assaulting the air with his harsh, too-many-consonants, German language.

Terryll searched his mind for translation, having learned much of their tongue from Gaulish traders, but the words came slow and stubbornly. What he did gather consisted mostly of grumbling about the cold and snow, pedestrian business of the camp, and crude humor laced with insults, and nothing whatsoever to reveal their purpose—though he heard the mention of Whitley Castle more than once.

The boy's gaze swept over to the large Viking standing next to the fire, his eyes falling upon his old enemy with an admixture of keen fascination, boyish admiration, and hatred.

Olaf carried himself with a confident, proud bearing. His gestures were broad and condescending as he stood a full head above his men, his lessers. The latter were separated from him not only in rank and station, a distinction that needed no interpreter, but in stature as well. There were none among them his equal. He was a big man, of Scandinavian height and brawn, his limbs thickly muscled, and his hands quick to snatch some miscreant by the nape and set him on a rightful course. The men's eyes seemed continually darting over to him, watching him like spaniels, their ears attuned to the timbre of his voice as though waiting for him to define their existence with a command. The Viking turned his blond-maned head in profile to the boy, revealing the long jagged scar that fell, a cruel mockery, across his face, the cold having changed its hue from a fleshy rose to a wicked reddish-purple. He traced the length of it with his thick finger, stabbing at it occasionally as though he were brooding over matters far removed from his present society.

The boy watched intently, recalling the details of his harrowing experience with the man months earlier, when, as his prisoner, he was inflicted with the cruelest of entertainment by the men under his command. Had they not been surprised and overrun by a Pictish war party that night, and had it not been for the timely appearance of the great bear, he would have undoubtedly been killed after a considerable torturing. Until this morning Terryll believed himself to be the only one who had escaped the battle.

You must be a wily one, he thought, studying the man. *What are you doing up here again?* His mind was a riot of speculations. Glancing to his right, Terryll noticed a quiver of arrows next to one of their bedrolls, about ten feet from his position. Then he returned his attention to the Viking, but his eyes immediately fell back on the quiver as an idea began to take shape in his mind.

Looking back and forth from the quiver to the Saxons, he decided he would steal it. It seemed a good idea at the time. However there was no cover of rocks or bushes between the bedroll and him, so in order to steal the quiver he would have to be exposed for about ten feet, with nothing to shield him but the depth of the snow and his cunning. He should have left immediately to warn his father. But such reasoning was far from the young hunter's mind.

If I can just get to within six feet of it, I can hook it with the end of my longbow and pull it over the snow.

It was a foolhardy scheme. It was dangerous. It was thrilling.

Immediately he set to work. From his cover of evergreens he began to burrow a trough through the snow, being careful as he inched along at a snail's pace to build up a protective berm of snow facing the campsite. Then if one of the men happened to glance in his direction, he would see only a slightly raised mound of snow between the trees. Hopefully it would be perceived as a pile of rocks or a fallen branch covered with snow, and the man wouldn't give it a second thought. Hopefully.

Again, it was a dangerous game and a foolish one, and Terryll knew it. But he received an immense satisfaction from pitting his wits and skills against his prey, be it man or beast, knowing that whatever he had come up against he had bested. He could hardly help himself. The boy was, after all, a boy—and a hunter.

Burrowing an inch at a time, Terryll managed two feet without detection. It had taken him ten minutes. So far so good. But no sooner were the words framed in his mind when he heard the scrunching snow-sounds of footsteps heading his way. He blanched, then without hesitation scuttled backward, crablike, and ducked into the bushes. A moment later a warrior lumbered past him into the trees. Terryll recognized the man at once—another ghost—a mean one named Druell.

Terryll's eyes narrowed. The man had felt the bite of Terryll's broadhead in his shoulder months ago and had inflicted much torture on him because of it. He would surely enjoy finishing the job if the boy were discovered.

Druell finished his business and returned to the campfire.

Terryll waited a few moments, debating whether or not to continue with his foolhardy scheme. A half hour later the young hunter was now five feet out in the open, with only a foot-and-a-half rise of snow berm shielding him from view.

Every few minutes he raised an eye above the barricade furtively to scan the campsite. The men seemed in no hurry to go anywhere. Some even stretched out on their bedrolls to rest after their meal—a fact that concerned him. What were they waiting for? Why were they here? The answers were withheld from him.

Terryll determined that he needed another foot of berm before making his move. He peeked over to inspect the men's positions. He was safe. Most of them were huddled in conversation around the fire. His eyes fixed for a moment on the fire—the warm, thawing fire, throwing sparks and shimmering heat waves carelessly into the air. A small shiver rippled through his body, just watching them wriggling warmly upward.

It was then that he noticed his feet going numb with a burning cold, both of them feeling heavy as though molten lead had somehow gotten into his bloodstream. He hoped that if he needed to call upon them quickly they would respond. And then he felt the cold numbing away through his limbs, and the chills working their way up his torso. A large shiver shuddered down through his length, over the backs of his legs, then trembled back up along his spine to his head, his teeth clenching to put a halt to it. Suddenly it felt as if everything inside him was breaking apart.

Terryll returned to his work, hoping to shut the cold from his mind. He scooped handful after handful of snow from his path, surreptitiously pressing each against the berm to build his shield. It was tedious work, and the cold hindered him. His fingers burned now, refusing the cradling warmth of his mouth, and he began to have serious doubts as to his intentions.

The cold. Shaking, he wished now that he were straddled atop the warming back of Tempest heading north to Gwyneth away from this place. The cold. He wished now that he had not smelled the smoke. The cold. He would be on his way, enjoying the ride and the out-of-doors, descending now into his beloved Eden Valley with Bowness just on the horizon.

But he had smelled the smoke, and he had come to investigate. Such was his fate. But why had he not raced back to tell his father when he had discovered the Saxons? Why was he here instead, crawling on his belly in the freezing snow, mere feet from those who would kill him with cruel pleasure if he were discovered? Such was his nature.

The quiver—only a foot of burrowing to go.

The boy shifted his eye from the men huddled around the fire to the three boarhounds, and to his horror they were now looking directly at him. He froze. Immediately the blood rushed into his head, thickened at his temples, pounded heavily down along the thick cords of his neck. He felt as though something the size of his fist had lodged in his throat.

Then the hounds were on their feet, pulling at their tethers, howling and yapping, and creating an awful chaos with their throaty barks.

Terrified, the boy melted into the snow, burying his profile as much as he could. Adrenaline raced through his veins. His breath came in shallow scoops, if at all. A warm wash went over him.

He could hear the men rising to their feet, muttering puzzled queries, their attention now on the dogs. And the hounds were tearing at their tethers, snarling and snapping, and now the warriors were all looking in his direction.

One of them called out, pointing. *"Achtung! Ein Hirsch!"*

Another warrior drew back on his bow.

Terryll almost bolted, but the whistling scream over his head held him in place. A moment later the arrow struck a tree with a hollow thunk. At once the warriors let out a collective groan.

Suddenly a warrior crashed into the trees not fifteen feet in front of the boy, nocking another arrow to his string as he plowed into the deep snow. An instant later Terryll heard the distinctive, twanging bow shudder and the whistling shaft as it was loosed at its mark, and then the cursing—the gushing of profanities that needed no translation.

The Saxons shook their heads and grumbled, returning to the fire. Even the boarhounds settled down and returned to their previous dog concerns. Why? The boy was too stunned, too confused to move, and he lay there in the freezing trough behind the berm trying to figure it out.

Ein Hirsch? Ein Hirsch? What was it? Terryll searched his mind for the—and then his face cleared. Deer! That was it! They had spotted a deer behind him, somewhere in the trees.

As the man returned to the fire, the others began hurling insults at him, many throwing their arms at him in disgust and cursing his foul marksmanship. The bowman returned their insults; then, cursing his bow, he flung it into the snow.

Wasting no time, Terryll seized the opportunity of distraction and hooked the end of his longbow through the loop of the Saxon quiver, quickly pulled it into the trough he'd dug out, then crabbed back into the shelter of the bushes. No sooner did he make cover than he heard a muffled thunder of horses pounding along the riverbank in his direction, and immediately the relative tranquillity of the camp was interrupted by the arrival of eight more Saxon warriors. The crimson wolf's heads arched proud against their black shields.

"Guten Morgen, Olaf!" the lead rider shouted as he raised his spear. *"Wie geht es Ihnen?"*

"Gut, Erhard—danke!" the Viking returned. And his breath hung in the air like smoke.

Erhard slapped some circulation back into his arms. *"Es ist kalt! Ja?"* he groused.

But Olaf had more important things on his mind than the weather. *"Ja, ja! Was fur schones Wetter!"* he said without humor. "Now, what news do you bring?"

"We have scoured the countryside to the south of Whitley Castle. The land is peaceful—the Britons do not suspect a thing. There will be much glory when we have conquered them."

Olaf pulled on his mustache, seemingly indifferent to the man's enthusiasm. Erhard continued. "Yesterday afternoon we spotted a group of Britons on horseback, fifty or more in number, along the road leading to Whitley Castle. Many wagons too. By now they are probably about six hours away."

Olaf raised his head. *"Wie bitte?"*

"I said, we spotted a group of—"

"Were they armed?"

"Heavily," Erhard replied. "But there were some women and children in the group as well. I do not think that they are a war party."

The horsemen with him concurred with an assortment of grunts and nods.

"Hmm," the Viking mused. "Still, it will not serve our purposes if we are discovered. We must leave!"

Terryll caught most of the conversation, though he still had no idea what the Saxons were doing here, or what they were scheming. What he did know, however, was that the party of Britons consisted of his family and the men and women from Killwyn Eden, Brough, and Bowes. His thoughts of Bowness and his beautiful Gwyneth suddenly vanished as he gave his mind to a more immediate concern.

The young hunter filtered back into the trees as silently as he had come and quickly retraced his steps into safety along the riverbank. It felt good to feel his legs moving beneath him again, surging with warm blood. Behind him he could hear Olaf barking out commands and the clangor of men scrambling to break camp. He thought he heard one man growling about a missing quiver of arrows, though he couldn't be certain. It was a difficult language to grasp, and he wasn't of a mind to translate.

8
THE BLUFFS
O'DUNDRAGON

Aeryck had slept poorly. Even in the soft, warm comfort of his goose-down bed he barely got a wink of sleep. His dreams almost ruined him. Throughout most of the night he was chased by wenches with faces twisted into greedy, lurid looks; wenches with tattoos all over their bodies and scraggy teeth, chasing after him with flagons of ale and then with drawn swords.

However these latter wenches with the swords took on faces that looked like Spang's, conjuring in his tortured mind the most hideous of apparitions. Several times during the night he had jolted upright in his bed, his face clammy with sweat and his pulse racing. Pea stuck his head into his room once after he had let out a yell, then let him be.

Aeryck was happy to finally be away from the tavern. The boy took a deep breath of the morning air—the sea air—as he scanned the trees and ridgelines for mischief. Nothing. Nothing that he could see, at any rate. But something horrible was in the air; he could sense it. Like the smell of death. It gnawed at his ear in furtive whispers. Finally. Finally the instincts of the hunted were being honed.

There was nothing in the offshore breeze that betrayed it, nor was there treachery in the strident cries of gulls and ospreys on wing overhead, nor in the muffled and irregular cadence of horse hooves shogging through the snow all about him. But it was there. It tolled at his ear like a single, monotonous, repetitious note, and Sullie's own ears twitched nervously back and forth in counterpoint.

The blizzard had passed sometime during the night, leaving a thick blanket of snow covering the land of Scots and Picts. Gusts of wind whipped along its broken surfaces, lifting sprays of fine white powder into the air and smiting his face with hundreds of icy needles. The sky was cast in iron gray, with peepholes of blue struggling here and there. And occasionally the sun would spill through the holes and warm the small company of men heading south along the bay road toward Whithorn.

Some crows and a few gulls gathered in clumps along the low stone wall that traced the seaward length of the track, their obnoxious cawing punctuating the quiet of the morning with irritating exclamations. Annoyed at the intrusion of the horsemen, each bird lifted off the wall with a heavy flapping of wings as they drew near, and rejoined his compadres farther down the wall. They repeated the cycle as the riders once again approached, and repeated it again, leapfrogging along the length of the wall until they grew tired of the sport and winged southward.

Pea Gants had been told that Spang and his men had left the fords before dawn, heading north along the River Cree. Aeryck had tried to dissuade Pea from sending his men along with him since he was heading due south. But Pea would have none of it, remarking that Spang wasn't the kind of man to take such a beating as he did lightly.

"Such a man is cruel of heart and mean of spirit," said Pea. "He'll be scheming villainy till he's laying cold for the sod! Aye. That I'll lay the money on!"

"Aye," said MacTibber.

"Aye," said Doone.

"Aye," said the others.

And so Pea's men would accompany the boy as far as the bluffs o'Dundragon, a journey that would take them a little more than two hours. If all was clear by that point they would return to the fords, bidding the lad a bonnie farewell. Aeryck knew in his heart that Pea was right, and he had agreed, reluctantly. He was proud. The beggar in him still lived.

The men were a gladsome bunch, full of mirth, seamen every one, Scottish seamen, not long from Eire, their faces leathery and tanned and bitten hard by the ravages of the sea. If they sensed any trouble in the air they didn't show it, for at once leaving the Fords of Wig they broke out into several rousing chanteys, the likes of which moved the impressionable soul to wanderlust.

Aeryck liked the men at once and was grateful that Pea Gants had persuaded him.

The leader, a lanky fellow named MacTibber, rode out in front and kept his eyes fixed on the treeline and the occasional outcropping of rocks for villainy. He had long black hair and wore it in the fashion of seamen—pulled back and tied in a tail to keep it out of the way while they were doing their chores. Aeryck liked the look. It had a certain fraternal appeal to it—a symbol of the initiated—though he wasn't bold enough to wear his own hair in such a way. He hadn't been to sea.

Not yet.

He pressed the lanky man for any seafaring adventures he might relate. At first MacTibber looked at the boy and dismissed him with a roguish chuckle, then led off with another chantey. But Aeryck was persistent, and after a few miles MacTibber fixed his eye on him with a scowl.

"The sea's a harlot and a thief, laddie," he said. "You'd best be givin' any thoughts o' her a wide berth."

Aeryck was taken aback by the remark. "But you've made your living by the sea," he protested. "Sailing to faraway ports with strange people and customs and who knows what else—trading and making good profit too, I'd be bold enough to say."

"Aye, lad, that I have," MacTibber said. "And more besides!" Then he jerked his thumb at himself and with squinted eye added, "And what do I got to show for it? Answer me that. You cannay. All I got to my name is my tote and a wee room behind the tavern where I stow with these other lost beggars. Aye. 'Tis a lonely calling, to be sure. Profit?" The man threw his head back and laughed. "We've had a muckle show of it, eh, lads?"

The other men threw in their laughter as well.

But the boy took it as they intended, in good stride. Waiting for quiet to settle, Aeryck asked, "Have you no family?"

MacTibber flashed a fierce look at him. "*Och!* And what do you mean askin' me aboot such a thing, mannie?"

Aeryck was again taken aback. "I'm sorry—I didn't mean—"

"That you didnay!" the man interrupted. "And leave it be!" Then he grunted and turned away, and silence fell on the little company for a time.

Aeryck wore a hangdog look as his mind whipped him the while.

MacTibber suddenly animated to life. "I had a bonnie wife and two wee'uns," he said out of the blue. There was a wistful, faraway gaze in his eyes, and his voice was low and rueful. "But the sea—the sea bewitched me. Took my senses, she did. Took me away from my bairns year after year, castin' me adrift on the brine with all the other lost beggars of the mast.

"Every time I'd put into port for the winter, so glad was I to see their gleamin', laughin' faces, crying with tears of joy, I'd swear upon their wee brows 'twas my last time at sea. By my troth, I did.

"But come a-spring and she'd be callin'—the Temptress—a-blowin' her kisses 'cross the bay. I'd turn my face away like a stone, though my heart would be trembling with the wicked spell. For it kenned she had me—a matter of time, is all. A day—maybe two—would pass, and I'd be holdin' strong again' her. But lang aboot the third day, when the first square of sail'd cut against the sky, I'd be gatherin' up my tote, and there'd be my bonnie wife looking sweet and lost and sad, a tear swellin' in her eyes, not kennin' what I seen in the Temptress over her. My bairns 'ud be clinging to my legs a-beggin' me not to go. But I'd refuse 'em. Aye. 'My duty,' said I, and every spring the door'd be behind me, and me a-running like a fool into her cruel embrace."

Aeryck looked at the man, suddenly feeling terrible, though he was aching now to hear the rest of the story. "You said you had a wife and children . . . er . . . bairns . . ." he said tenuously, then broke off, leaving the query hanging.

"Five years past, I come home from a journey what took me half way round the world," MacTibber continued. *"Och!* The places I seen! The treasures I had in my tote for m'wife and bairns. Swinging open the door to my bonnie home, when I find to my surprise a fam'ly I dinna ken. There they were, a-gapin' at me, nay doubt, for the rogue I was. Four wee towheads, laddering aboot a cheery-faced woman and her husband—a merchant, I gathered by his girth, and him smiling too."

Aeryck was stunned. "What happened to them?"

"'Gone,' says they. 'Your wife and bairns cleared out in the spring.' 'A-where to?' 'She dinna let us ken, 'ceptin' this note she left behind.' Aye, lad," MacTibber continued. "Not a trace, 'ceptin' that note saying she had left me, is all. Saying she couldnay take another tide comin' in without her man. There were tearstains on the note to be sure. I brake her heart—and such a dear one." The man paused as a tear welled in his eye, and then, "Ah! Bless her!"

"But couldn't you look for them?" Aeryck wondered. "Surely they're—"

"Nay, lad. 'Twas for the best. They're a-happier for it, I'm sure." MacTibber looked over the bluffs at the sea below and paused in thought for several moments. Finally he said, "I'd give my eye teeth to spit at the harlot and ne'er give her 'nother thought. But she'd only laugh. She always does. I'm cursed, I tell you—cursed for ever layin' eyes on her. I cannay help m'self now—not till she lays the murky fathoms o'er me—" The man broke off, and his posture prohibited further inquiry.

Aeryck was quiet. His breast swelled with sorrow, and he was nearly moved to tears, thinking of those two children without a father.

He took his eyes off the lanky mariner and followed his gaze over the low stone wall to the sea. The coastline framing the horn-shaped Bay of Wigtown was a jagged wall of glacier-carved bluffs, sometimes sheer in its presentation, rising out of the sea upward into the hundreds of feet. Like some gargantuan paternal sentinel, whose broad, masculine shoulders and arms were formed of granite muscles and sinews and bones, the bluffs reached outward from the port into the tempestuous sea for miles, beckoning sailors—the rebellious prodigals of its earthy embrace—to come home at last and find refuge in the rugged cradle of its arms.

The road they were traveling shagged the crest along the brink, affording travelers spectacular views of the bay, and Aeryck was near overwhelmed by the sights and smells and sounds that rushed him from all sides.

He looked below at the rocks just as a gray-green breaker crashed against them, smashing against the boulders with a murderous thunder and fury, shooting white spray and spume skyward and breaking the light into a spectrum of watery colors, only to fall back a million tiny droplets against the glistening rocks. Moments later another breaker followed, and another wave, and another, attacking the rocks incessantly, tenaciously, whittling them down a grain of sand at a time with eternal patience.

The sea knew that in time the rocks, the cliffs, the land, and the very souls of men who trod there would be hers. A wash of salt air splashed upon his face with a bracing burn—a seductive saline fragrance —lifting the boy's gaze and luring his eyes to the horizon. What he beheld filled him with inspiration.

The rolling plain of the sea rose to meet the endless wall of the sky, like two gray halves of an infinite book. Each met and was bound at the horizon, a perfectly curved line that stretched from one end of the earth to the other, and dreams were written upon that line. He thought about some for a while. And while he did, brown pelicans skimmed gracefully over the white-capped surface of the deep, searching for schools of mullet, diving into the waves, shoveling mouthfuls of the ruddy colored fish out of the watery fields.

The distant screeches of gulls called Aeryck's eyes heavenward. He laughed in his spirit as he watched the reckless birds piloting the capricious winds along the sheer bluff walls, racing the updrafts, soaring atop thermals that took them, like prayers, into the clouds. Such glorious freedom, he thought, such defiance of the earth, such love of the Creator. How he wished for wings that he might join them. Aeryck took a deep breath and settled instead for a wistful sigh, a long, wistful sigh. The sea.

The sea and all of its miraculous ambience worked a curious and impetuous magic on the boy's senses, and strangely—and regardless of the mariner's desperate warnings—he wanted her. He too hungered for the spring.

They had been traveling the bay road for about two hours, without the slightest hint of villainy afoot. Only a single set of horse tracks leading out of the fords and heading south suggested any human activity.

MacTibber had taken note of them right off and said, smiling, "Probably just a poor lost soul seeking a friendlier port." But just the same, he warned the men to keep their eyes peeled. He agreed with Pea Gants that Spang was none to be trusted, none to lower the guard against.

The bluffs o'Dundragon lay just ahead around a broad, forested crescent, and it seemed that Pea Gant's concerns, though profitable for the companionship, had proved erroneous. The bluffs were a sheer wall jutting out into the horn-shaped bay near its mouth, made of broken granite, chalk, and sandstone, and with fingery veins of lava rock striping the face horizontally, indicating tremendous volcanic activity at one point in the land's formation. When the rising sun hit the cliff face, it touched off a burnished dun color in the rocks, giving the impression that the bluffs were on fire—hence the name Dundragon. The effect was momentary, but altogether stunning.

"Like the face of a god!" MacTibber exclaimed upon their approach, to which the other men responded with a resounding, "Aye!"

Atop the bluffs were great outcroppings of rock, pushing upward in violent posture, dominating the skyline for several hundreds yards. The road cut through a break in the formation, submitting travelers to the possible treachery of ambush from above, for there were many boulders behind which to hide and as many vantage points from which to strike the unwary traveler. Beyond Dundragon the land opened into flat, tabletop expanses, with a sparsity of trees and a greater density of population. And though the terrain remained rugged and rock strewn, to lay an ambush would take a considerable doing, especially in the broad of daylight.

Aeryck was musing over the whereabouts of MacTibber's family when Sullie's ears shot back and she stiffened with alarm. The boy jerked his head away from the sea and peered into the hills for any sign of trouble. But there was nothing, just the sound of the wind and two crows flying south overhead, squawking obnoxiously.

"A horse coming through the trees yonder," a man called out. He pointed ahead on the road.

The boy followed his point and beheld a horse running toward them. His pulse quickened.

"Aye," said MacTibber, cupping his hand over his brow. "And by the looks of it, there's no one settin' aboard. Still, you'd best be looking lively, lads. There's maybe treachery here."

The men drew their swords, cutlasses mostly. Aeryck's broadsword was the exception, but it had cleared the scabbard first.

The riderless horse charged along the tracks with clumps of snow flying along its flanks, its reins flagging wildly. It came at a full gallop, wide-eyed with terror, and only as it drew to within a few feet of the men did it pull up abruptly. The horse blew out several snorts as it trotted nervously back and forth. The other horses immediately smelled the fear in the air and became restive, whickering and tossing their manes as it fell upon them. One reared and nearly threw its rider. Even Sullie, who had been taking the journey in her usual easy gait, broke her stride and was throwing her head up and down with her ears still pinned back.

MacTibber immediately took the lead, putting his horse into a trot. His eyes searched the trees ahead for any hint of movement. His cutlass was drawn and at the ready. The others followed, likewise poised for a fight.

The riderless horse, a chestnut gelding, held back at first, frozen in its fear. But its instincts for the herd compelled it to stay with the others, and it was quickly alongside Aeryck's stallion, its reins dragging in the snow.

Upon entering the wooded area the men slowed their mounts to a walk, and every eye was keen and busy among the stark tree boles and overhanging limbs. But everything was quiet, eerily so, with nothing stirring. Only a light breeze whispered through the boughs. A raven winged overhead and lighted somewhere in the trees out of sight. Another one followed. There was bird chatter somewhere in the distance, muffled by the snow.

The men rode warily forward. It was a narrow tract of trees they had entered, and, passing through them quickly, they came upon a broad, shrub-dotted clearing that spanned from the bluffs to a line of trees some distance to the west. Ahead lay the formation of rocks—the dragon—sprawled across their path like a monstrous carcass from another era. Its jagged spine, broken by some great and primordial upheaval, was arched defiantly against the elements and time.

Aeryck was awed by it. It seemed a living thing.

Then immediately clearing the trees the horses became restive again, needing sharp coaxing to move forward. Something dreadful was in the air. Aeryck sensed it more clearly now. A continual buzzing in his ears like some buried instinct had suddenly come alive.

The chestnut gelding separated from the other horses and angled over to a depression in the snow, lowered its head and whickered softly. Aeryck followed with his eyes and spotted the red-and-yellow fletching of an arrow protruding over the snow and guessed the mischief.

"MacTibber," he called out.

"I see it, lad." He signaled to one of the men, and the man dismounted to examine the body. As he made his approach, his eyes, though fixed on the red and black feathers, seemed mindful of the trees and rocks about him.

"Careful now, Doone," MacTibber cautioned.

"Aye."

MacTibber's eyes swept across the rock formation. But nothing was to be seen except the small black silhouettes of some crows and ravens that had gathered there and were hopping about.

72

"The rest of you lot—spread out and look for signs," McTibber said. "Be watchful of them rocks yonder, mind ye. Whoever done this is sure to be lurking 'round some'eres—might be drawing a line on one of your gullets even now."

"Aye," the men retorted, and they hunkered down into their saddles as they fanned out across the clearing, each looking this way and that for anything out of the ordinary.

"Who is it?" Aeryck asked, angling the big gray toward Doone. The hair on the back of his neck was bristling, for the "something horrible" that had whispered in his ear earlier was shouting at him now.

"Just a lad, it appears," Doone said.

"What?" Aeryck flew off his horse and hurried to the man's side. Gazing down at the body lying in the snow, he let out a gasp and staggered back a step. It was the boy he had seen across the tavern the night before, only now with a thin, feathered shaft of spruce protruding from his chest.

"*Och!* Poor soul. And such a pretty face," Doone remarked.

The dead boy's eyes were staring up into Aeryck's face with a quiet peaceful look; his mouth parted slightly in a kind of smile. So warm and full of life was his gaze, with only the hint of death beginning to edge his lips with its pale blue touch, that Aeryck had the queerest sensation the boy was just lying in the snow and that at any moment he would sit up and speak. But then there was the arrow sticking out of his chest—a conspicuous reminder that the peaceful-looking form would quickly decay into a ghastly corpse.

A small shudder wracked Aeryck's frame.

"What is it, lad?" Doone asked, gauging the look on his face. "Did you ken him, then?"

"Huh?" Aeryck was interrupted from his thoughts. "Er . . . no. Not exactly. I've just seen him before."

Then, with a curious expression working into his features, the man looked back and forth between Aeryck and the dead boy. "*Och!* But he could almost be one of your kin by his looks. Dinna you think?"

Aeryck didn't respond. He just stared numbly at the boy's face—that serene and kind and altogether dead face—not more than a couple years older than himself, he calculated. A face that seemed to gaze up at him with a frozen look of pity, that same look he had recoiled from the night before.

"Looks like he were one of them holy men we see around from time to time," Doone observed.

"What?" Doone's words had pushed their way into the boy's mind, pushing through dark, cerebral mists and finding him lost and adrift on a faraway thought. "What did you say?"

"A holy man," Doone repeated. "One of them . . . now what is it they call themselves?"

"What are you talking ab—" Then Aeryck's mind made a jolting landfall.

He had not noticed before, because his attention had been focused on the boy's face, on his eyes, on the feathered shaft of spruce. But now that he observed the other details of the body, the image that assaulted his eyes filled him with an even greater sorrow.

The dead boy was wearing a brown woolen birrus, the hooded robe worn by the peasantry of the Roman Empire, and his head was shaved tonsure-style. Both were symbols adopted by Christian holy men: the birrus, a sign of their identification with the poor; the tonsure, worn to resemble the plait of thorns around Christ's head, reminding them daily of His sufferings and humility.

"A . . . monk," Aeryck said at last, quietly.

"Aye, that's it—a monk. Queer name."

"Here's another one!" a man called out. "But this'un here weren't kilt by no man, by troth."

"Another monk?" Aeryck cried out as he started toward him, leading Sullie.

MacTibber pulled up his horse next to the man and looked down at the horrible gashes across the dead man's body and face. "*Och!* Upon my naked word! What kilt him?"

The man on the ground scratched his head. "I cannay tell. Some kind of wild beast perhaps."

"Wild beast?"

"Wolves." It was Aeryck who had answered. He approached the body on foot and stared blankly at it, staring now with a measure of relief. The dead man was not a monk.

"Nay, lad. I've never heard tell of any wolves in these parts," the man on the ground said. He was examining the deep lacerations along the dead man's throat. "Could be a bear though. A big 'un."

"Bears hibernate in the winter," the boy said flatly. "It was a wolf. Look at the tracks in the snow."

"And what would I ken about tracks?" the man retorted, shaking his head. "'Tis nay business for a sailor, this. Sharks, I ken well enough. Wolves?" He shuddered. "I prefer the sharks, by troth!"

MacTibber looked at the boy curiously. "Wolves, you say?"

"Aye."

Suddenly one of the men who had fanned out across the clearing called out from behind a low screen of shrubbery midfield. "Over here! There's several more of the poor beggars! *Och!* What a sight!"

74

As the other riders converged on this man, their horses reeled in horror and refused to advance further. For before them lay an area about twenty-five yards square where the dazzling white of snow had become an appalling crimson. MacTibber and the boy drew up on their mounts and scanned the grisly scene. Strewn across the bloody patch were the bodies of five men who were lying disheveled, with limbs all crooked and tangled like mannequins on display, arranged as though for some ghoulish effect.

Wolf sign was everywhere apparent.

The scent of a large pack clung to the air with dreadful talons, clinging to the minds of men and beasts alike. Sullie stamped her hooves and whinnied her primal fears, as did MacTibber's mount, as did the other mounts.

The men bunched together in a single anxious clump, like a circle of wildebeests facing hyenas; each man facing outward from the hub, looking anxiously at the rocks and treeline with his sword or ax clenched tightly; each man casting curious, squinting looks at the dead below them on the ground and satiating his mind with the gruesome exhibit.

"Here's one what's still among us," the man who had discovered the bodies called out. "Barely."

Aeryck dismounted and joined the others. Looking down at the torn man lying in the snow—his tunic a mass of bloody shreds—the boy recognized him at once from the night before.

It was Fek. His neck was opened by a jagged slash. The little man gazed up at the Scottish mariners, and his little, black weasel eyes searched the shapes above him with both relief and panic. "The wolves— they was everywhere," he said with difficulty. "Dozens of 'em. Hitting us afore we knew what happened. Dinna ye see 'em?" His chest heaved. A paroxysm shook his body, and he started to cough violently.

"He's not lang for it," one of the men observed.

"Aye."

"So it was wolves what laid ye low, was it?" MacTibber asked, as he joined the group. "Well, 'twarn't the work of nay wolf what kilt the lad laying cold over yon."

Fek's eyes rolled heavily across the men's faces looking down at him and found MacTibber's. A thin, wicked smile curled over his lips. "Aye. You guessed it, did you?"

"You killed that boy?" Aeryck demanded.

"'Twarn't me what did the killin', but it dinnay matter," Fek replied, shifting his gaze. But immediately he laid eyes on Aeryck, they jerked open with a start. "You! How could—" His eyes narrowed on the boy with a puzzled look, and then his lips began to tremble. It was as

75

though he were beholding a ghost. "You've come back to haunt me, have you, laddie?"

"What are you talking about?"

"By the oaks!" Fek stared at the boy curiously for a moment and raised his hand as though to touch him. Then his brow cleared with a thought. "Are you not dead, then, laddie?" he chortled, and the wicked smile returned to his lips. "Old Spang'll be surprised, I'll warrant you. I daresay now, in the light of your face, it were an honest mistake."

"Mistake?"

"Where's Spang?" MacTibber interrupted. "Are there others of ye?"

"Aye. Fifteen in all. If they're not lying cold on the ground, they cut out then, leaving the rest of us here to die. Aye, and we're kilt, sure enough." He coughed.

Aeryck stooped next to the man. "You said something about a mistake. What mistake? And why did you think I was dead?"

"You see, we was layin' for you, boy," Fek continued. "In them rocks over yon, waiting for you to come down the road. We kenned you'd come this way—hearin' of your plans south'ard and all. And Spang—" He broke off, coughing again. "He's a mean one, that Spang is. Nane too bright, neither, and he had it hard for you. You'd best not be letting him ken you ain't kilt."

"What—"

The little man chuckled. "Like I was sayin', laddie, when we seen you clear them trees on your horse, old Spang he took a line on you with his bow and sent an arrow straightway to your brisket. Knocked you clean out the saddle. Oooie! A sight it were. Spang, he let out a glory holler. We was going to cut oft your head to show Sarteham when they come."

"But I wasn't—"

"Aye, laddie! Your mother-wit's got the sum of it now!" Then Fek rolled his eyes toward the dead boy. "S'pose I'll be joinin' that young fellow over yon in a trice. Trust he won't be too upset we kilt him." He began to chuckle again, until a coughing spasm shook his body. Finally settling to a calm, his little, black weasel eyes rolled open and searched lazily for the boy's face, and finding it he gave him a wink.

Aeryck gaped at the man dumfounded. He struggled hard to receive the incredible thought, but the words kept crashing into each other in his mind, scrambling the message into a single line of utter nonsense.

Fek's thick tongue slowly dabbed the rim of his lips with moisture. "'Twarn't . . . like I had it in for you, lad," the dying man continued with labored breath. His speech was slurred, and the agues raked his limbs at regular intervals now. "You never done . . . me nay harm.

76

Troth . . . it was the gold, you see. Just the gold and the thrill of it." His eyes widened just perceptibly with a little gleam in them, like a candle flaring in a draft. "Aye, and the thrill of it. Could've been a hoot—" And with that his eyes rolled back into their sockets, and he was a dead man.

Aeryck grabbed hold of his cloak and shook him. "What are you talking about? Tell me! Why'd you kill that boy?"

"*Och,* laddie! Leave him be now," MacTibber said. "There's no reasoning with a corpse."

For several moments Aeryck stared at the dead man in a little trance. Then he looked over to where the boy lay still in the snow with Spang's arrow marking his chest.

His mind buzzed with a welter of thoughts and images: thoughts screaming at him, accusing him, and images of the boy's face—that kind, smiling face—staring up at him with that frozen look of pity. He could feel his palms collecting the moisture that had deserted his mouth, leaving it parched and tasting of bile. Feeling himself in a swoon, Aeryck stretched out his hand involuntarily to steady himself against Fek's chest.

"Aweel, laddie," MacTibber said quietly. "There's nay mair we can be doin' here. Best leave the dead to their business."

The heavy voice jolted him back to his senses. Aeryck's eyes slowly focused on his hand, still pressed against the dead man's chest, and he snatched it away. Then a confluence of rage and horror swelled in his breast as he stood up from the corpse. He stumbled to catch his balance on uncertain legs, then steadied himself.

MacTibber clapped the boy on his shoulder. "We'd best be clearing out, lad, if we're going to make Whithorn by sundown."

"I'm going on alone from here," Aeryck said, starting over to his horse.

"Nay, laddie. 'Twere Pea's charge to see you safe to your destination. And it isnay safe with that Spang fellow and his jackals laying for you."

Aeryck wheeled in his tracks. "I said, I'm going on alone! You can tell Pea Gants to mind his own business!"

"Whist! Well, I'll be boiled in oil," MacTibber said, stroking his chin. He peered at the boy for a moment, studying him through a squint, then grunted. "Suit yourself, laddie. 'Tis no matter to me if you want to end up starin' at the sky like that mannie yon."

"I can take care of myself."

"'I can take care of myself,' says he. *Och!* And what are we doin' here then, men?" MacTibber said. "The lad says he can take care of hisself again' a crew of boy killers and a pack of wolves. Aweel, I ken where there's mugs of hot mead a-waiting to take the chill off. What of it, lads?"

"Aye," they replied as one man.

The lanky mariner strode to his horse, grabbed the reins, and mounted. "You're a fool to be sure, mannie," he said. "But you got sand. Aye. That I'll whistle for you. I'd've made a sailor out've you had you lived into the spring." Then with a wink and a hoot he reined his horse, and the Scot was heading north toward the narrow tract of woods, followed by Doone and the others of Pea Gants's men.

Aeryck stood watching until they entered the trees. Falling behind the others, MacTibber looked back at the boy and nodded sharply, solemnlike, as though acknowledging the revelation of some terrible oracle. Then with a final salute he too was gone.

Aeryck attempted a wave but caught himself mid-salute, and his arm fell to his side and hung limp. He had no heart for it.

Turning, he glanced over his shoulder at Fek and the other bodies strewn about the snow. Drifts of snow were already mounding against their lifeless forms as the shrill, low wind planed over them. Aeryck wagged his head grimly. And then a funereal hush eased into the void left by the mariners, like a ghostly presence sidling up to him. For the first time in many months he felt very much alone. Suddenly he felt what seemed like an icy hand clutch his shoulder, and a shiver went through him. He whirled about, thinking someone had come up from behind, one of MacTibber's men perhaps. But there was no one.

And then a breath of wind blew coldly through the trees, curled over and down the broken back of the dragon, and spirited up behind his ears in a whisper, telling him that he was out of place amid these quiet denizens of the bluffs . . . telling him that it was time to leave . . . that this was no place for the living.

He glanced up at the sky, wincing at the brightness of the overcast, and saw a lazy spiral of black shapes high overhead, gathering over the place of the dead.

And the crows and ravens already present were quick to swoop down from the arched back of the dragon and set to their tasks, hopping and flapping here and there among the dead, cawing and squawking greedily as they inspected their boon. They eyed the boy with malignant little eyes, awaiting his exit.

Aeryck hated the birds. It was a hate born out of his beggar days in Glenryth, and he thought to shoo them away. But he let out another sigh instead. This was their place now, a place to tidy up. And then he didn't care anymore.

Let them have their fill.

9
THE CALL

Grabbing hold of Sullie's reins, Aeryck walked over to the boy monk and looked down at his face. Immediately he clutched his mouth over a gasp. Death had been here, attending the monk's features with its grisly handiwork during his short absence. The boy was looking up at him now through black, soulless eyes, no longer with a pitying gaze but with one of horror. And the once ruddy and lifelike coloring of his skin was now cast with an ashen pallor, like that of old porcelain, and the thick blue rim of his lips seemed to twist over an unuttered moan. Any notions that he would ever sit up and speak to anyone again were dispelled at once.

The chestnut gelding, still standing vigil over his fallen master, whickered softly, mercifully pulling Aeryck's attention away from the corpse. Then he noticed a pair of canvas bags tied behind the saddle. He went over to the horse and began to rummage through their contents dazedly, hoping to find some clues to the boy's identity.

A blanket was rolled up inside the one, some foodstuffs and a small skin of wine. Provisions for a day's travel, he thought. Nothing of importance. Inside the other bag, however, was a complete copy of Jerome's Latin Vulgate, the "people's translation" of the Bible, a sheaf of papers written in a language Aeryck couldn't read, and a folded piece of paper that was fastened shut with a wax seal and imprinted with the chi-rho—the Greek symbol for the risen Christ. He broke the seal, and his eyes fell upon a letter of introduction. It read:

To Brother Thomas of the monastery of Candida Casa:

Greetings in the name of our Lord and Savior Jesus Christ, and may His grace and peace abide with you always!

The brothers here are pleased to send to you Stephen, a novice in the Order of Hermits of St. Augustine, whose zeal for the Lord, whose purity of mind and humility of soul, and whose love for the sheep of the holy Shepherd are unequaled among men. He carries upon his shoulders the burden of the cross for the

Lord's work at Candida Casa. Day and night he prays for you with many tears. He is filled with great joy at the prospects of being of service there and reaping a harvest of souls among the Picts and Scots of the highlands.

Though the work there is, without doubt, fraught with many hardships and dangers, we, bearing witness in our spirits, felt it right in the Lord to send young Stephen to you for a season, until the time of his confirmation into the Order. We are confident that he will bear much fruit in your fertile soil and that his holy pilgrimage will season his life and yours in the Holy Spirit. Receive him as you would receive the brothers here.

In the fellowship of His sufferings and shed blood—

Brother Lupus, Bishop of Troyes, Gaul

Aeryck read the letter time and again until his eyes blurred from the strain, each time sinking deeper and deeper into a disconsolate mood. Every one of the words in the letter was like a dart loosed from the pen of the faraway Bishop of Troyes, and every one of the darts found his heart and pierced him through to the marrow of his soul. He was stricken with the anguish of an irretrievable loss, with bitter remorse, with shame and a host of other emotions that were suddenly yanked from their moorings. The incredible waste of such a life was more than his sensibilities could bear.

Why?

Why, God? Why?

Why him and not me?

Why would You take this young monk's life—a holy man dedicated to Your service—and leave mine? I am but a recent convert to the faith—nothing more than a beggar and a thief who once hated You, who once mocked Your Son.

Why?

Why, God?

But the voice of God, the inner Witness in his soul, was mute. There was only the steady rush of wind blowing off the ruddy bluffs, and the muffled crashing of the breakers below, and the occasional insufferable cawing of crows that seemed to be jeering at him from the broken rocks of the dragon and from the sprawling carnage in the snow. Something black flapped overhead, trailing a vague shadow over the dead face, laughing—or so it seemed—and the mocking echoes of the voice sounded a terrible thought in the boy.

Aeryck's head jerked up with a start, his brow darkening with a scowl. A strange glimmer smoldered in his eyes, lighting over a dark contemplation, like a prophet's. And the prophet eyes were fixed unyieldingly on some distant point that existed in another dimension, gazing wildly and recklessly into some forbidden knowledge. And the birds looked on suddenly from their inanimate perches.

He had heard the call.

It sounded with pristine clarity, somewhere from the shadowy netherworld of his heart. The call, with resonant timbre to its voice and with seeming divine fiat, had made a pronouncement, a judgment, and a verdict in one blazing bolt of illumination: Spang had murdered the boy monk Brother Stephen; Fek had borne witness to the crime; the verdict was chillingly lucid—there were no reasonable doubts, no grays. The brutish man was guilty.

He must die.

Aeryck's mission was unequivocal, the mandate clear. He would simply find Spang and, with the detached emotions of the executioner, administer the judgment. This time there would be no mercy. This time there would be no pricking of the man's shoulder to warn him. No. This time he would find Spang, draw his father's gleaming, beautifully crafted sword, the one with his family's crest engraved upon the hilt and the tongues of fire along the length of the blade, and execute him. Yes, that was what he would do.

Immediately there was a vague stirring in his soul. The little despot held a hasty court upon his brow and began to voice objections. But Aeryck turned a deaf ear.

A half hour later, with the body of young Brother Stephen secured over the chestnut gelding, Aeryck mounted Sullie, and the sprawling formation of rocks was soon receding into the jagged bluffline behind him, the broken face o'Dundragon falling away to the north in full retreat.

Tiny black shapes swirled and swooped against the hinder gray sky, indicating the presence of many birds. Their screeches and cries punctuated the windless calm like a clarion of the macabre, heralding to others of their kind that the feast had begun.

Aeryck's new course had not changed from his original, even with the dead boy in tow, for the monastery of Candida Casa lay just on the outskirts of the little village of Whithorn. The boy had visited there on each of his trips to Whithorn with Brynwald and on both journeys had met with the kindly abbot, Brother Thomas. The only change in his plans now was that, whether by divine providence or by the mockery of coincidence, he would deliver to the abbot Stephen, "a novice in the Order of Augustine, whose zeal for the Lord, whose purity of mind and humility of soul, and whose love for the sheep of the holy Shepherd, are . . . were . . . unequaled among men."

He looked back at the dead boy draped over the chestnut gelding, swaying in tempo to the horse's gait, his lifeless arms slapping out a slow, mournful cadence along its flanks, as though to a dirge.

The wind moaned through the trees, and it had a heavy, somber kind of sound to it. Sadly the boy let out a sigh. And as the little cortege made its way along the bay road, the overcast darkened, and a light snow began to fall, dropping large fluffy flakes the size of birch leaves over the frigid winterscape. The snowflakes swept past Aeryck's face, and some lit on his nose and cheeks and stung, and some got tangled in Sullie's mane.

Hunkering into his woolen cloak, the boy scanned the low, blunt hills and sparse trees for any sign of mischief, for any hint of Spang. But there was nothing. Not now. There was only the unshakable feeling that he was being followed.

Not long after he had set off from Dundragon, he had seen the tracks of several horses heading north, presumably those of Spang and his bunch of assassins. He could tell by the length of the strides, and by the way the snow had been kicked behind the tracks, that the horses had been running—fleeing, more likely. However he hadn't seen any more wolf sign. He was pleased with himself that he had made such observations, though he doubted that Terryll would have been impressed.

The thought of his friend rushed him and brought a much needed respite to his troubled mind. A smile began to soften his grim face. He missed him. It seemed like a year ago now that he watched Terryll riding away from the village of Loch na Huric after the fiery-haired girl from Bowness, all rolling-eyed and lathery and smitten with love. Aeryck shook his head of snow and laughed loudly at the thought, startling the horses. Sullie glanced back at him with a big brown eye.

"It's all right, girl." Aeryck smiled as he patted her wooly neck. "I haven't lost my senses."

And then an ache sounded from his stomach, reminding him that it had been several hours since his parting meal at Pea Gants's. It had probably been aching for some time, but with the harrowing events of the morning he had ignored it—the instinct for survival having superseded any pangs of hunger.

Then he remembered the leg of mutton in his saddlebag that Silvie had put there as he departed, her eyes in a desperate flutter. But as he reached behind him for the flap a movement along the treeline caught his eye.

Sullie's ears shot back. The gelding whickered.

At first the boy reckoned it to the falling snow, a trick of perception. Then peering into the distance, his eyes widened with alarm, and thoughts of the leg of mutton suddenly vanished. Survival was again his only concern.

Wolves!

There were at least fifty of them, gray ghostly shapes, hunched heads lowered in wolfish attitudes. Yellow, feral eyes peered at him from just inside the trees.

Both horses snorted nervously, each keenly attentive to the carnivorous predators that were shagging their vulnerable course.

And Aeryck's hand was on the pommel of his father's sword.

10
RECONNAISSANCE

The sun was presumably high in the sky. However one wouldn't know it for the low cloud ceiling that obscured everything but an even cast of dull, gray light upon the landscape.

It had taken the Saxons two hours to reach the low forest-ringed bluffs overlooking the village of Whitley Castle. They hid themselves in a stand of conifers, like so many roosting birds of prey, watching the goings-on in the village below, scrutinizing the quiet grounds for any signs of life. There wasn't much activity in the village: a man carrying a load of firewood into his cottage, a woman exiting a barn hefting two pails of milk, the inevitable dog or two making their rounds, a few birds. A rooster crowed in the distance. But guessing by the number of cottages, stables, and sundry outbuildings, the Saxons were able to approximate the man strength of the village.

They also took note of the surrounding terrain. The Pennines rose sharply in the west to their high point at Cross Fell, catching the morning sun when it shone. To the east were several ranks of lower hills arrayed in a monotone spectrum of grays that fell away into a distant bank of fog, their ancient rounded backs stretching north and south and sparser of trees than their taller western siblings. Running through them was a long river valley through which the South River Tyne coursed northward until it doglegged to the east at Hadrian's Wall to spill its contents into the violent turbulence of the North Sea.

It was a hard land, this north of Britain, wild and masculine, and cut out of a coarse fabric—a land bereft of the graceful, feminine lines that rolled for miles like folds of emerald silk spread sensually across the southern plains of the island.

But Olaf liked it. He liked it because it was hard and masculine. It reminded him of his home on the tiny, sea-pummeled island of Föhr—a larger sibling of the Frisian archipelago west of Denmark—where his Ingrid stood waiting, waiting as she had done for the better part of her life, looking to windward, hoping for the telling square of canvas upon the horizon.

When this campaign is over, he thought, *I will bring her back here with me. We will build a cottage on a choice plot of land and raise cattle or sheep—herds of them. We will have children—a tribe of them. They will be mighty warriors, as hard as iron, beaten in the forge of this tempering land that favors only the strong and stouthearted, a land that is merciless to the weak and cowardly.*

Yes, Olaf liked this land. It moved him to inspiration. He let out a sigh. It was a good dream. However this was not the time to give one's mind to dreams. It was the time to give one's mind to war. He turned his attention to the man-made fortifications and studied them dispassionately, as would a professional warrior, and began to strategize battle tactics with his men.

Encircling the village was an earthen berm packed with stones, and an eight-foot wooden palisade surmounting its circumference. But there were several gaps along the palisade, blinking lazily at the peaceful quiet of the wintry landscape, seemingly unconcerned with the world beyond their quiet precincts and certainly oblivious to the several pairs of squinting eyes that were hidden upon the brow, canvassing their measure in full.

Inside the compound were a dozen or so Roman catapults and onagers and, here and there, their larger cousins the ballistae, sitting behind the walls like petrified monsters from another era. These awesome machines of war, like gigantean reptiles, had once roamed over the land on great wooden wheels, hurling huge boulders and javelins hundreds of yards, smashing flimsy bulwarks of wood and spewing balls of fire at puny men, devouring them with voracious appetite, pummeling them into Roman subservience.

However, after the Romans left the island forty years earlier, these once terrible monstrosities were left to decay, standing now in various stages of disrepair along the walls as fitting symbols of a crumbling imperial age, some having been dismantled and picked clean by scavenging villagers for use as firewood, others having yielded to the games of inventive children.

For the Britons cared little for the Roman methods of heavy mechanized and ordered warfare. A fast horse and a good spear or bow, where the warrior could hit his enemy fast and be gone before he could retaliate, were the preferred weapons and tactics of the British Celt.

"What do you think, Olaf?" Druell asked.

The Viking leaned against the thick wet trunk of a rowan and brooded. His eyes were fixed upon the village like a cat's upon a mouse, taking in every whisker of detail, and his expression evinced a growing weariness. After a time he let out a sigh.

"Is there to be no challenge in this campaign—no glory?" he groaned, voicing his mind. "Are there no warriors left in this land that I might pitch battle against them and win Odin's favor?" He shook his head reflectively, almost ruefully, and grunted at the thought. "It is the same everywhere we have patroled. The Britons lie sleeping like thought-less *kinder* beneath the blanket of some past splendor, lulled into some delusion that their villages are still impregnable, made secure by legions of Roman ghosts. What glory will there be in crushing these fools, Druell? What glory? The Britons of the north, whom our leaders once feared, it seems have women to rule them now."

"It escapes me, Olaf, why we have we waited so many years to attack them," Druell replied.

Roth, a smallish Angle with nervous, icy blue eyes that never blinked, began to chuckle. "Perhaps we too have women for leaders," he offered.

Olaf shot a cold scowl at the man. It was not the thing to say to one who placed a high premium on loyalty and station.

Roth's eyes jumped open and began to dance a little jig. Quickly he shrank from the Viking's gaze. "I didn't mean you, Olaf." He chuckled nervously. "Why, I was referring to Hengist and Horsa, of course, and—it was only a jest—a jest, is all!" Looking at Druell and the others, he shrugged his shoulders. "That's all it was—a jest!"

"You'd best mind your tongue, dimwit, lest it get cut out," Druell sneered. "Now go and see to the horses. Perhaps they will find you amusing."

Roth melted into the trees. "It was only a jest," he grumbled under his breath. "Nothing more. Meant no harm by it." He took a good ribbing from the other men along the way.

"We've seen enough." Olaf grunted contemptuously. "They are ours! Let us ride now to Killwyn Eden and see what Odin has given us there. Perhaps we will yet find some warriors worth fighting. Warriors worth killing!"

The men nodded their heads at one another with churlish grunts, each of them contemplating the acquisition of land, the plunder of goods, and the ravaging of women. The swagger of conquerors was in their tread, and as a whole they were feeling mighty good about their business, glory or no. The easier the better.

As they turned to leave their sheltered perches, one of the boar-hounds let out a surprised yelp and flew into the air, twisting its powerful back into a grotesque, wild-eyed attitude of pain. It fell hard to the ground dead—or soon to be—with an arrow sticking out of its throat. A thin tendril of steam rose tenuously from the wound.

The men nearest the hound froze in their tracks, stunned. Others were still chortling over the thought of British women as they filtered carelessly out of the trees into the clearing. But immediately seeing the feathered shaft jutting from the animal's throat, they became like stones. The terrible silence that ensued was intruded upon by the distant hammering of a woodpecker. The rooster crowed a second time, sounding this time like a laugh.

The Saxons quickly scanned the trees along the clearing for the bowman. An astonished buzz fingered through their midst. Then with their hands clenched over haft and hilt, the men crouched low and began to angle cautiously back into cover. Their eyes warily traced figure-eights against the enemy trees that stood against them with a silent conspiracy. But there was no sign of anything moving, and not a sound. There were only the black boles cutting vertically against the omnipresent white—and then the whistling sound of iron, spruce, and feathers rifling through the air toward its second mark.

The dull *thwump* that followed was answered at once by the startled howl of a second boarhound, the deadly missile hitting it high on its back and just behind the rib cage. The animal writhed in the snow, and its shrilling cries pierced the otherwise calm of the noon, shattering the brittle tension.

Olaf's eyes were white with rage, and immediately his battle-ax fell upon the animal's neck to quiet the air. Two or three dogs from the village below barked protestations.

"What's going on!?" the dog handler queried. He jerked his head from side to side with an astonished rhythm, looking for the unseen attackers as he tried to quiet the remaining boarhound. But the hound would not be quieted and strained at its chain leash, snapping angrily at the air with deep, throaty barks that added to the confusion.

"British pigs! Cowards, I'll wager!" a man answered. His eyes were taut and betrayed a fear of his own. "They must've sneaked up from the village and somehow gotten behind us. That's a trick!"

"Why don't they rush us?" Roth asked, as his blinkless eyes began to blink out a frenetic semaphore. "Why, do you think? Gunther—why, do you think?"

"Who? I don't see anything!" Gunther countered as he squinted at the trees. "Do you see anything, Erhard?"

"No," Erhard grunted.

"Me neither."

"What was that? Was that something?"

"I'll give them a taste of something!"

"Why don't they rush us? Huh? That's what I'd like to know! Why don't they rush us, Gunther?"

"It doesn't make sense."

"Not a bit!"

It didn't make sense. However the large Viking did not engage in their speculations. Instead his piercing gray eyes were trained on the trees across the clearing behind them. They were steely eyes, cold and void of emotion, eyes belonging to the consummate warrior, challenging the trees to reveal one of their enemies' unseen positions with the slightest of movements, commanding them by the force of his will to betray one of their countrymen.

But there was nothing, only the wind mocking him through the overhead boughs. Why? Where was the enemy? The Britons had had the element of surprise, and yet they hadn't taken advantage of it. They could have killed many of their number quickly, perhaps all of them, but only the two hounds lay dead in the snow. No. It made no sense at all.

The snarling boarhound drew the man from his thoughts.

"Shut that dog up, or I'll take its head off!" he snapped.

The dog handler, a stout, powerfully built man wearing beneath his furs a brass-studded leather shirt and trousers for protection, immediately straddled the massive boarhound from behind and thrust his leathered arm around the dog's throat, pulling its head back into the cradle of his thick arms. The hound jerked its angry head in the man's grip, trying to break free of the viselike choke hold. But the handler knew his business and quickly slipped a leather muzzle over the dog's snout and pulled it taut. Around the hound's muscled girth was a wide leather girdle that was belted on top, with two iron rings fastened to it, one on either flank. The ringed girdle served to protect the hound's flanks and underbelly in battle, and—by attaching a second leash to either of the rings—the dog handler was able to control the dog's hindquarters by pulling against it. The handler quickly attached his second leash to a flank ring, and the boarhound was secured.

The men waited several minutes crouched behind various offerings of cover, each man searching the trees for man shapes, a glint of light off armor, anything that moved, anything that might provide a mark. But the brow overlooking the village of Whitley Castle was as still as a morning lake with not even a breath of wind over it. It was eerie. Unnerving. The air was rife with a sinister uneasiness. The rooster crowed a third time.

"I don't like it, Olaf," Druell said, drawing up next to the big Viking.

Olaf grunted a retort. His eyes probed the trees for betrayal of life, something that he could face, could attack, something that could die.

"Let me take four men and search the woods," Druell offered. "I cannot abide this waiting. It works against my soul."

Olaf nodded consent.

Druell and his men took off along the periphery of the clearing, keeping just inside the cover of trees. The others waited, watching as the tree trunks took their savage forms, expecting at any moment for the cry of battle to shatter the quiet. Ten minutes later the five men returned, shaking their heads and shrugging stupidly.

"There is no one, Olaf," Druell said. "Not a sign anywhere."

"Impossible."

"It is true," Druell retorted. "We searched the entire area around the woods, and there was not so much as a single footprint in the snow. Nothing! Not a trace! Whoever—or whatever—killed the dogs walks without touching the ground."

The Viking grunted in disbelief. His gaze quickly swept the trees again and then eyed the hog-backed ridgeline beyond the forest to challenge Druell's report. There had to be tracks, his logic screamed at him. Men leave tracks in snow.

The Saxons along either flank looked at one another with various expressions of bewilderment and suspicion.

"I tell you, there are spirits in these blasted hills!" Roth muttered as he shot a shuddering glance back to the trees. "Likely as not we're being watched right now."

This fell on fertile soil. Fearless though these warriors were in battle against men, they feared that which could not be killed with ax blade or sword, and a terrible inspiration descended upon the group. Heads wagged anxiously back and forth as each man looked into the trees for anything that might resemble one of his nightmares, a horror born of ancient mythology handed down orally from father to son and now given flesh.

They had heard tales in Saxony that the hills of Britain were haunted by strange peoples, ancient peoples, inhuman; haunted by spirits that rose out of clefts in the earth and caves, and even from the many, long barrows that pimpled the landscape; haunted by demonic creatures that took captives from among humans in order to make slaves of them in the Underworld. Each man knew that there were powerful malignant forces at work in this hard, enigmatic land against which no mortal could stand. And from the quiet cloisters of each pagan soul, the incense of prayer wafted heavenward to a pantheon of Teutonic gods—austere, warrior gods that reveled in the glorious deaths of their children—each warrior hoping in secret blasphemous thought that his gods were more powerful than the Celtic gods of Albion.

Olaf had no such fears. In his mind there was no god as fierce or powerful as Odin, chief of the Norse pantheon. Odin was the protector of heroes, the god of war who rode into the storm of battle mounted on his eight-footed steed, Sleipnir, with the Valkyries going before him to collect and bear the souls of fallen heroes back to Valhalla.

The Norseman's fear—his only fear—was that he might not die a glorious death in battle. Anything less would dishonor Odin. He considered the tales of British mythology inconsequential, fireside entertainment at best, designed to frighten old women and children and to fatten the purses of the traveling bards who created them.

However the arrow shaft protruding from the boarhound next to him was no product of a fertile imagination, no act of any Underworld creature, no British god. It was real, and it suddenly commanded his entire focus.

With all the confusion of the last several minutes, he had not taken note of it before. He bent over and pulled the arrow from the hound's side, then twirled it slowly between his thick fingers, carefully studying the markings along the shaft: a crimson crest, ringed against a black shaft, with two black vanes and a crimson cock feather. He looked up from the arrow and again searched the ridgeline beyond the trees.

"If there are spirits in these hills," he said, "then they kill our dogs with Saxon arrows!"

"What?" Druell gaped incredulously at the arrow. "How can this be?"

Olaf reviewed his men as if to find the answer in one of their faces, any look of treachery, of infidelity, the look of a stranger that was not there moments before, anything out of place lurking in the umbral contours of a man's face that might betray him, might turn on the traitor with a kiss. Olaf searched for it, but it was not there.

"I do not know," he replied. Suddenly his brow darkened with a thought. He looked away at the hills.

Druell caught the shift in his eyes. "You suspect treachery?"

The Norseman did not answer. His mind was fixed on the ridge beyond the woods, seen only through a few narrow corridors allowed by the trees. He made a mental calculation of the distance.

"It is Ruddbane," Druell said.

Olaf looked at Druell. The man was a brute, a merciless fellow of ruddy complexion and a slightly protruding simian brow, bull neck, and heavy shoulders that sloped clumsily into a pair of thickly muscled arms too long for his frame—a configuration of body parts that many might recognize as the dwelling of a dullard.

Yet Olaf knew that beneath the man's bovine exterior and slow wit lay the cunning of a deadly and somewhat cruel viper who grew restless in times of peace, whose singular ambition seemed confined to the killing fields of land and sea, where he took sadistic pleasure in meting out pain upon his enemies. Though Druell was a Jute from Schleswig and Olaf a Dane, they were kinsmen. They had sailed together, taken plunder together, left the bones of fellow Vikings bleaching on faraway shores. Olaf trusted him like no other man.

"No, it is not Ruddbane," he said.

"Who else could it be but Ruddbane?" Druell countered forcefully. "The man is dangerous—he'll stop at nothing to undermine your power and take it himself. Not three weeks ago I overheard him telling some of your warriors that you were weak and incompetent—said it was your fault the Picts killed so many of our warriors on our last patrol. I called him on it, but he denied it, of course—the others too. The snakes."

"A man is in less danger for knowing who his enemies are," Olaf returned. "Besides, you said yourself that there were no tracks, and unless I'm mistaken, Ruddbane hasn't sprouted any wings of late."

Druell grunted. That one small point had escaped his reasoning. But no matter; he nursed a private hatred toward Ruddbane and enjoyed discussing his demise, a violent demise preferably, one brought about by his own ax. It was a well-nurtured fantasy. "Well, you wouldn't have so many enemies if you'd let me split a few skulls."

Olaf chortled. "What? And wipe out half our army? Perhaps you would do better to join the Britons!"

Druell failed to see the humor in this and stuck to his argument. Hefting his ax, he said, "I'd kill just Ruddbane and a few of his lapdogs, is all. They'd know some treachery."

"This isn't the work of Ruddbane . . . or spirits," Olaf mused, his mind working through a raft of possibilities. "He would've killed us all and not left any witnesses. No, there is some other mischief at work here. I'm sure of it." He looked hard at Druell. "Take three men on horseback and search for tracks along the ridge. You'll find your treachery."

"Why, that must be at least two hundred yards away," the brutish warrior protested. "What archer could possibly hit a mark from so great a distance? And through trees!"

"Arrows travel farther through the British air," Olaf replied, picking up his earlier thought. "Even Saxon arrows. You of all people must remember that."

Olaf's words stung the Jute with a remembrance of pain. He began to rub his shoulder as a vague image of a late spring night and the pursuit of a young Briton filled his mind—a boy who had killed most of their hounds with his arrows—a boy who had loosed an arrow from a distance of more than a hundred fifty yards and knocked him out of his saddle. It had been a magnificent shot, he was told, one that immediately gained the respect of the other men, though Druell had been in no position to admire it. He shook his head, erasing the imagery. "But he's dead. I saw him fall in battle."

"So did I. But certainly there must be other archers in Britain who are skilled with the longbow," Olaf argued. "A hunter, perhaps, who has a taste for dog meat. Now go and search the hills. If you do not find any tracks there, then I will be forced to believe that these hills are indeed haunted by spirits. Catch up to us ahead. We will be in the hills east of the road."

"It's Ruddbane, I tell you," Druell mumbled as he turned away. He was still rubbing the phantom pain in his shoulder.

Olaf glanced at the Saxon arrow in his hands, then swept the hills with his eyes. The barren ridgeline mocked him. He grunted at the puzzle, then, starting toward the horses, he snapped the arrow in two and threw it into the snow.

"The rest of you men, mount up!" he rasped. "We leave at once! We have already wasted too much time!"

Within minutes the Saxon horse soldiers were heading south toward the village of Killwyn Eden, each warrior casting furtive looks behind him to the forest-encircled brow, each man entertaining his own version of what had just happened there. Most of them agreed in a kind of silent pact that the hills were haunted with all manner of evil.

11
OF HERESIES
AND RIVALS

B y stating that 'as we are procreated without virtue, so also without vice,'" Helena said, quoting, "Pelagius has denied the existence and power of original sin."

"This is true," Aurelius admitted. "Then you must see that if 'man is able to be without sin, and that he is able to keep the commandments of God,'" he said, also quoting the man, "then Pelagius denies the need for the grace of God, and hurls man into the bondage of legalism and the pride of self-will."

"What need is there, then, for the cross of Christ?" Helena observed.

"You have struck at the heart of the matter, daughter." The Roman monk smiled. He never ceased to be amazed at Helena's scope of education and intuitive grasp of theology. "Would that your fellow Britons could see the danger of such teaching if it is allowed to spread without reproof."

"Why do they not?" she asked.

"They are dullards," Aurelius replied, with an edge of anger. "Rebellious hellions who mock the good council of God."

They were discussing Pelagianism, a heresy named after its progenitor, one that was sweeping rampant across the island and causing schisms in many of the British churches with its ascetic emphases.

The monk clucked his tongue and snapped the reins, more to check his anger than the gait of the horses. Then he looked off into the distant white hills that fell stark against a cold shale sky, his brow fighting a foreboding thought. It was a dark maleficent thought that had lighted upon him months before, like some black bird of prey perched atop his mind that he could not shake, its invisible black talons piercing his soul, mocking his smallness, swatting his feeble prayers back into his face.

"It is a damnable thing that Pelagius has brought upon us," Aurelius said ruefully. "Daughter, I fear for the church of Britain. I fear that her divided light will be swallowed up in this black heresy. Shall be unable—nay, unwilling—to stand against the principalities and powers of darkness that threaten to overwhelm the land like a flood."

Helena nodded gravely as she pondered his words, her eyes looking inwardly at some foreboding storm front that troubled her soul. She said a quick prayer against it in hopes that it would blow away. It did not. Letting go a sigh, she then allowed her eyes to wander thoughtfully to their team of horses that was shoveling obediently through a fresh lay of snow.

She and Brother Lucius Aurelius were riding tandem on the family's carpentum, a two-wheeled Roman carriage that was covered with a decorative canvas awning and woolen curtains fore and aft, designed to shelter driver and cargo from inclement weather.

Now she lifted her eyes from the team to include her husband, riding in front of the long caravan of carts and wagons with a group of chieftains and fighting men from Brough and Bowes. Their colorful cloaks of blue and red and green and purple and yellow snapped proudly in the sunless December air like so many banners unfurled against a field of white. It was a breathtaking sight, those handsome men in their finest woolen cloaks—like watching a triumphal parade of Roman soldiers—and Helena swelled with excitement just taking it in. For a moment she was distracted from her concerns and enjoyed the beautiful winterscape.

And then her brow darkened with a thought.

"Are you all right, Mama?'

She looked up at her daughter riding alongside and smiled. It was a maternal smile mixed with blessing and fear. *What kind of world will you inherit, my daughter?* she wondered. *Will you know peace, or war? The growth of faith, or persecution?* "I'm fine, Dagmere," she replied unconvincingly, then quickly changed the subject. "Aren't you cold riding out there? Perhaps you'd prefer to join Brother Lucius and me in the carpentum?"

Dagmere shrugged her hooded woolen cloak around her and replied, "Oh, no, Mama, I like the cold." She took a deep breath of it and blew it out hard. "It makes me feel so—so alive!"

"Well, there's a warm seat right here, if you'd rather feel comfortable," Helena offered. But she knew better. She shook her head and smiled.

Dagmere had been riding alongside the carpentum on a sorrel mare, sidesaddle, intermittently listening in on their conversation, though most of the time she was distracted by her own little world of thoughts.

94

Observing the men riding along proud and handsome in their glorious attire made her think of Aeryck—as most things did—and how wonderful it was going to be to finally see him after two months. Had it only been that long? It seemed longer. It was longer. It had been an eternity.

She let out a long, wistful sigh. She wondered if Aeryck had missed her as much as she had missed him, or if he had missed her at all for that matter. That thought had concerned her over the past few days. After all, they hadn't exactly parted on the best of terms. What if Aeryck had forgotten her by now? Or worse, what if he had found another girl and fallen in love with her—even married her? She wondered again if Pictish girls were pretty, and she let out another sigh.

It was still several miles to the north. Dagmere glanced over at her mother, who had resumed her discussion with Aurelius. She tried to listen in, but her heart wasn't in it. Then she adjusted her seating, and a frown crossed her brow. She cared little for sidesaddles but had conceded to her mother's request to present a ladylike appearance on the trip.

She preferred to ride astraddle a horse like a man, "the only reasonable way," as she put it. After all, God gave a woman two legs just as He gave to a man, and two sides of a horse over which to put them. It seemed silly to her to throw both legs over one side of the horse and risk falling backward over the other. The girl wondered how many women had fallen over into a ditch and broken their pretty little necks, or ditched into a puddle of mud, presenting to all the world the most unflattering postures, all for the sake of a ladylike appearance. Life could be a sufferance at times.

She contented herself with another dream, one of the many dreams in which Aeryck held her warmly in his big strong arms, while looking down at her lovingly with those beautiful blue eyes a moment before kissing her. Her insides began to flutter. She giggled. She held onto the dream as long as she could, but the image was fleeting, not having any substantive history to it. So she let it go with another wistful sigh, wondering what it would be like to really kiss him. Wonderful, she knew. Yes, it was going to be wonderful seeing him. Just wonderful.

There was a sudden shift in the wind, and an icy chill ferreted out a fold in her cloak and shivered down her spine. Then she heard a horse drawing up alongside her. She looked. It was Fiona. She might have known.

Fiona was riding sidesaddle on a speckled gray, and she was making a great show of it. The thought would never have occured to Fiona to ride any other way than proper and ladylike, and if it did she would have chased it out of her mind with a switch. The girl with the raven hair and flashing green eyes looked over at Dagmere and nodded her pretty little head, showing her gleaming straight teeth as she smiled. She was a year older than Dagmere, and it clearly showed. She made a great show of that as well.

"Isn't this wonderful, Dagmere?" she gushed. "I've been looking forward to this trip—forever, it seems!"

Dagmere gave her a curt smile. However only the corners of her mouth were in it. She eyed her suspiciously from around the lip of her woolen hood and replied, "How nice."

"Isn't it a lovely day?"

"Just grand," Dagmere said flatly, still eyeing her skeptically. "Getting a bit chilly though."

"Nonsense! I love the bracing air. It makes me feel so—so—"

"Frosty?" Dagmere offered sweetly.

"Er . . . yes. That's it, I suppose. Frosty." Fiona looked at her uncertainly, then let it drop. "My father just told me that we'll arrive in Whitley Castle in just two hours!" she went on. "And then on the morrow we'll be in Bowness! Just think of it! I'm so excited, I could just burst!"

Dagmere didn't comment, though she was tempted. If the truth were known, she couldn't stand the girl. It was a point in her daily catechism that she struggled with. The fact that Fiona was the prettiest girl within a hundred square miles didn't bother her so much—the raven-haired beauty could easily have any boy in the north of Britain eating olives off her toes. It was the fact that she knew she was the prettiest girl that rankled Dagmere.

Today was no different. Dagmere felt a terrible squall rising in her chest, as she did whenever the girl with the flashing green eyes, and a figure that belonged more to a woman than to a girl, was around, and she knew she was in for another catechismal struggle.

A losing struggle.

"Did you notice the boys from Brough and Bowes?" Fiona asked, shooting a flirting glance behind them. "One of them is kind of good-looking, don't you think?"

Dagmere followed her glance, more out of reflex than any interest. Six boys were riding in a clump, twenty yards back, most of whom were on the dangerous precipice overlooking manhood. Each of them was trying to look as fierce as possible with sword and longbow in full display, hoping desperately that one of the girls might take notice. But when Dagmere caught the boys staring apishly at them, two of their mouths fell open at once, one began to snicker uncontrollably, two others exchanged sophisticated winks, and the one who was passably good-looking nearly fell off his horse for no discernible reason.

"No, I didn't notice them," Dagmere replied.

"Neither did I," Fiona returned. "They're probably nothing more than childish bores.'"

"You would know," Dagmere muttered under her breath, wishing that the girl would just leave her alone.

"You wish it would snow?" Fiona looked around at the white fields and hills and shrugged. "Why, you silly." She giggled. Then she cast an appraising look at Dagmere, her only real competition where beauty was concerned.

There were other girls in Killwyn Eden of eligible age. Some were pretty, others would make wonderful child bearers if given the opportunity, but Dagmere was clearly in another league. She was of a beauty that came natural and unaffected, like her mother's, with full, graceful lines— Latin lines—that were well-turned from head to toe. She had a beautiful face that was clear and of a milky complexion—save for a thin line of fading freckles that spilled daintily over the bridge of her nose—with eyes so deeply blue they were almost violet.

Many boys in the village had vied for her hand, no doubt each of them pining away every night on his pillow, dreaming of the chieftain's beautiful, if headstrong, daughter, dreaming of creative ways to win her lasting affection. But each offer of love had been summarily rejected. That was fine with Fiona. It kept the field open, it simplified things, but it did occupy considerable time in her musings.

"Has anyone ever told you that you're a pretty girl, Dagmere?"

"What? Er . . . thank you," Dagmere replied, taken aback by the remark. Flattery was a new twist.

"It's true. Why, with a change of hair—perhaps a different dress —you might even be considered beautiful. It just doesn't make sense to me."

Dagmere braced herself. *Here it comes,* she thought.

"It just doesn't make sense why on earth you would carry that thing around with you wherever you go."

"What thing?"

"That weapon you're always carrying." Fiona pointed at the long-bow slung across Dagmere's back. "Boys don't like girls who can shoot better than them, you know. Especially pretty ones!"

Dagmere glanced down at the bow. "I don't care," she countered. *That wasn't so bad.*

It was no secret that she was probably the finest archer in Killwyn Eden next to Terryll and her father—a note of celebrity that deeply vexed Helena, but she had long ago abandoned it to her failure as a Roman mother. And there had been no winning her husband over to her side on the matter either. For apart from being the chieftain of Killwyn Eden,

Allyndaar was a bowyer by trade, a maker of the finest longbows in all of Britain, and a devotee of their children's skills with the bow.

"You don't care about boys?" Fiona giggled. Her giggle was more like an airless twittering that could instantly sour a treeful of songbirds. "With all the boys in the village I've seen looking your way? Why, that's the silliest thing I've ever heard you say. I'm sure that there must be one boy that you care about," she said, edging the conversation forward to the next level.

Dagmere cast her another suspicious look. *So that's it!* The squall in her chest immediately took on a considerable turbulence. Fiona wasn't there to amiably chat away the time. She was there to establish the ground rules for the game—her game—a game that Dagmere had no intention of entering. Only winning. Fiona eyed her appraisingly. Smiling, she continued, "There's only one boy that I'm particularly fond of, you know. Oh, there have been lots of suitors, mind you, but they're of no interest to me."

"As I recall, weren't you interested in my brother for a while?" Dagmere wondered innocently.

"Terryll? Hah!" Fiona roared, and her horse spooked a bit. "He's such a child! I called the whole thing off at once!"

"After he told you to go fall in a well," Dagmere muttered the other way.

None the wiser, Fiona took a deep breath. "Ah!" she sighed dreamily. "But love between two mature adults is quite another thing, isn't it? It's such a wonderful feeling to be in love. Don't you think, Dagmere?" She paused affectedly. "But then again, you're much too young to have ever been in love, aren't you?"

Dagmere rolled her eyes plaintively to the heavens.

"But don't worry—" Fiona smiled, again showing her teeth "—there's plenty of time for you yet. Perhaps in another year or so, when you're tired of your little arrows and things. With me, love came like a wondrous visitation from heaven—just recently, you know. Pure, majestic, a fiery wind that was simply glorious!" She sighed dreamily again. "He's a veritable god."

"A *god?*" Dagmere had had enough. Enough with the civilities. Out with the foils. "What in the world are you babbling about?"

"Babbling?" Fiona appeared wounded. "Why, Dagmere, is that what you think I'm doing? Honestly, I just thought you would be interested to hear about the boy who's in love with me—the one I hope to marry soon. But I can see—"

"Marry?" Dagmere was stunned. "Who is this poor fool?"

"'Poor fool?'" Fiona twittered sharply. "Why, the 'poor fool' is Aeryck, silly. I thought you knew. Everyone else in the village does."

The raven-haired girl threw her hand to her mouth. "Oh, dear me—you *didn't* know, did you? And here you were so fond of him, weren't you? How unforgivably clumsy of me. Do forgive me, won't you?"

The temperature around the girls had risen markedly during this last exchange, enough to melt winter.

"And does Aeryck know that he's in love with you?" Dagmere parried.

"I would imagine so." Fiona giggled, with a feint. "It would seem silly otherwise. Don't you think?"

Dagmere was fuming now, so much so she couldn't find an apt retort.

"One usually kisses the girl he is in love with—" Fiona lunged for the kill "—and Aeryck kisses wonderfully. Well, you saw how he kissed me, didn't you? Since that morning when his lips last touched mine, I'm sure he's thought of nothing else. I know I haven't." She giggled again, chopping the air with her airless twittering, and somewhere nearby a bird must have choked. "When we get to Loch na Huric, I'm sure he'll ask me right off to marry him. Of course I'll accept. He's so handsome, and strong, and wonderful, and—" She broke off and smiled sweetly at Dagmere. "Listen to me going on. Honestly. You'd think I was a lovesick fool."

"No, just a fool!"

Dagmere blew a shrill whistle and spurred her horse with a sharp kick—a difficult task considering that she was sitting sidesaddle—and the sorrel mare lurched forward suddenly, spooking Fiona's horse.

What followed made clear that Fiona had spent more time contemplating boys than riding horses, for as her mount shuddered wide-eyed and bucked, the raven-haired beauty quickly took off in a graceless swan dive one way while the speckled gray and ladylike sidesaddle crow-hopped the other.

Dagmere didn't look back, but she heard the scream and the muffled *ka-flumph* of a body landing spread-eagle in the snow. *Do forgive me,* she mouthed, scrunching up her nose. Every one of the commandments began to roar stentoriously, and she knew that she would be having a difficult time in prayer that night.

For the moment, however, she just smiled.

12
OLD FRIENDS

The Saxons were keeping to the low hills east of the South River Tyne, swinging wide of the road and using tracts of forests, dingles, and river valleys wherever offered to shield their movement, circumventing villages inconsequential to military purposes and lonely farmhouses, which dotted the landscape in abundance. Here and there the horsemen were challenged by the distant protests of dogs, who had picked up their scent, and were forced to mind a more circuitous, always more untoward, route. The dogs were a constant irritation to the Norseman, who, though it was beginning to look doubtful, hoped to reach Killwyn Eden before nightfall.

The temperature had plummeted, and if there were a more skulking, clandestine, miserable-looking troop of specters slithering about in the contrary bleakness of winter, they had apparently found more amiable haunts and had yielded the right of way to this rum lot of interlopers. Curses ejaculated with mounting frequency along the grumbling line of horsemen, these whose gray silhouettes were pitched forward in sullen attitudes against the inclement metal sky, each of their minds contributing to a corporate fantasy of blazing hearths, flagons of hot mead, and the warmth of women.

Olaf had sent Erhard and Krueger on ahead to scout the whereabouts of the British column traveling north along the Whitley Castle road. It would serve no good purpose to engage with the enemy before the proper time, and it was deemed that spring was the proper time.

Spring was always the proper time for a good battle. With the rebirth of the land—the swelling of rivers, the bursting of spectral colors over hill and dale, the happy choruses of birds on wing, the lazy droning of bees collecting nature's alms—came the renewal of passion, hot, sensual, masculine passion that was the necessary prelude for the procreation of the earth, necessary to fight a good fight, necessary to conquer. Yes, spring was always the proper time for a good bloodletting.

The Viking knew that if the campaign in the north were to be successful they would have to take Killwyn Eden. It was the key to success. It was the seat of power, if not commercially like Caer Luel (Carlisle) or Eboracum (York), certainly militarily. A hint of a smile prowled beneath Olaf's thick blond mustache. He had heard that there were men in Killwyn Eden, men who were led not by women but by warriors, notably Allyndaar, their chieftain, a man whose skill with the longbow was legendary.

He held onto this thought for a moment. It would be a glorious battle, he added to it. *Odin will smile upon me that day.* Breathing deeply, he exhaled an exultant blast of steam. The wild challenge of this land had taken him in completely.

Presently the Norseman led his men into a broad tract of yews and raised his hand, and the file of horsemen came to a halt. The yews were so thick they arched into a great pavilion of evergreen boughs overhead, with their stolid trunks forming long, dark aisles that stretched away like those in a Roman basilica. So intertwined were the branches of the bowery that many places on the needled floor were untouched by snow. An icy current soughed overhead but was quiet at the ground level. Flecks of snow drifted occasionally from the ceiling.

The place would provide a good windbreak, Olaf thought, a shelter from unwanted observation, and would filter out most of the smoke from a campfire.

"We will rest here until we hear from our forward scouts," he said. "Gunther, you and Hörst secure the horses and tend to their needs. Medwin, you tend to our stomachs."

The Viking looked behind them for signs of Druell and the others on their back trail. He frowned. His eyes were dark and brooding, the lines of his countenance interpreting nothing of his thoughts.

Through an aperture in some fir trees Erhard and Krueger observed the long line of horses, wagons, and colorful cloaks filing below them around a bend in the broad Roman road.

"They've made good time," Erhard said.

"Yes," the other agreed. "And they've added to their number, by my count. Sixty or better now, and half of them well-fitted for battle. It is good that Olaf is being cautious. We would do well to avoid a confrontation with this lot."

Erhard grunted savagely. "We came here to kill Britons, not hide from them."

"You will get your fill of Britons in due time, my friend." Erhard shivered and countered with a curse. Then, "If this isn't the coldest plot on earth, I don't know what is. What do we want with it anyway?"

Krueger chortled. "I thought you wanted to kill Britons."

"Kill Britons—yes. Live here? Let the dead keep it, I say."

Then the two scouts reined their mounts and headed back the way they came.

Olaf and the others were stooped around a large fire eating a hastily prepared meal when Druell and his men rode into camp.

"Doesn't the sun ever shine in this infernal land?" Druell groused as he dismounted.

Gunther and Hörst immediately gathered their reins and led the horses to where the others were tethered some distance from the fire.

Olaf waved the riders over to the him.

"Smells horrible," Druell remarked as he strode across the campsite. "You cooking up one of them dead hounds, Medwin?"

Medwin shot him a surly look.

The remaining boarhound looked up sleepily at their approach, then returned to his nap.

"Must be," one of Druell's men added in the shelter of his comment. "Even the dog don't want any part of it."

Some of the men chortled; others eyed Medwin out of the corners of their eyes, knowing that he didn't take kindly to being the brunt of ridicule.

Medwin grunted a string of curses, then wagged a wicked-looking cooking knife. "I'll cut the livers out of you lot and boil 'em, if you'd prefer." He scowled. "Makes no nevermind to me."

Medwin was a portly man with cheeks purpled by surface capillaries, who served as cook. He had been chosen for the thankless task not for any manifest culinary skills but for his voluminous girth. Anyone who was as substantial as he had to know something about the subject of food, it was reasoned. He was more proficient in battle though, so it wasn't often that the men complained about his cooking.

As the man who made the crack sauntered past, Medwin kicked his feet out from under him, and he fell hard to the earth. "That'll teach you to bridle your words, see!"

The man jumped to his feet and squared off for a fight with the stout cook.

But Olaf constrained him. "Enough of this!" he growled. "Save your killing for some other time. The both of you!"

Medwin and the other fellow glowered at one another for a few moments. Then, after exchanging a few broadsides of threats, they went about their business, muttering to themselves.

"Now, what news do you bring, Druell?" Olaf asked.

"We found the spirit," Druell said, pushing himself next to the fire. "He was riding on horseback, just on the other side of that hog-backed ridge. Probably just a hunter as you suspected."

"He was alone?"

"There was only one set of tracks."

Olaf grunted his satisfaction. "You killed him, then," he assumed, as he bit into something that resembled a sausage.

Druell exchanged a glance with one of his men. "We followed his tracks to a small river where they disappeared."

Olaf looked up. "And . . ."

"There was no sign of him. We split into two groups and searched along the banks for two miles in either direction. Nothing. His tracks never come up."

"You lost him?"

Druell looked at him for a moment. "He's a clever one, this hunter."

Olaf's brow darkened with a curse. This time he was not so pleased with himself. "To your horses, men!" he snarled. "We cannot dally here!"

"We just got here, Olaf," Druell protested. "Surely there's time to at least fill our bellies."

"Not with the little bird you've let loose to fly about the country-side—no doubt singing a fine tune by now!" Olaf growled. "Every British idiot north of here that can shoot a bow may soon be onto our trail. You can eat as we ride!"

Druell snatched a piece of meat from the man next to him and bit into it before he could protest. And when the man began to object, Druell cut him off with a sneer.

Roth was busy enlightening a little aggregation of scholars off to one side of the fire and making a grand show of it. "I tell you, its tracks vanished just like that," he said, snapping his fingers. "There are strange goings-on in these hills. Spirits, I tell you—skulking about everywhere! And they're onto us!"

"I'll stand no more of that talk!" Olaf snarled as he brushed past the smallish man. "Now, get to your mounts and look lively!"

Suddenly there was a yell from across camp, immediately followed by a sound of muffled thunder and branches cracking, and the ground beneath their feet began to shake and rumble as though it were about to give way. Everyone started to his feet wide-eyed as their horses stampeded into the camp, squealing and whickering and careering as if their tails were on fire.

For the next few minutes there was a terrible uproar. Men scrambled desperately out of the horses' paths, with everyone yelling and

103

swearing and shouting confused orders at one another. Some waved their hands to deflect the course of the stampede, some were getting bowled over, some getting trampled, some grabbing frantically at loose reins.

Olaf stormed about the camp in a rage, barking commands while snatching the reins of frantic horses and controlling them with brutish strength. Here and there he snatched the nape of a man, slapped some sense into his panicked skull, then flung him back into the boil to help wrangle the horses. And in time, by the sheer force of his size and will, he commanded reason into the tumult.

Finally a kind of snow-falling quiet spread through the bower as order was restored. Horses stood splay-legged and wide-eyed about the clearing, heaving and huffing in frozen wonder, too panicked to move, each snorting out the residue of its terror through flared nostrils and shuddering hides. Men began picking themselves off the ground and filtering back into camp from the safety of trees, astonished and beat up and disheveled and grousing angrily at the sudden turn of events. Heads wagged here and about, searching warily for the cause of riot, looking gape-mouthed at their surroundings.

When they took stock of their losses, it was discovered that three pack horses had bolted south for the winter with most of the camp's provisions, the remainder of which were scattered over the clearing and into the trees and would take at least an hour to salvage. One man had suffered a broken arm, and another (who had been severely trampled) lay on the ground next to the fire, bleeding to death internally.

Then Gunther and Hörst—who had been tending the horses— staggered into the clearing rubbing the backs of their heads.

"What happened?" Olaf demanded furiously.

"Ugh . . . don't know." Gunther groaned. "I was hit from behind—a rock, I think. Out of the blue."

Hörst nodded sickly but was too nauseous to add anything more to the account. He was listing a good fifteen degrees to port. The side of his head was a bloody mass that he was supporting gingerly with his hand, and his complexion was sallowing quickly.

The Viking glowered at them, and it seemed for a moment that he might strike them down with his ax.

Then Hörst's eyes quit their focus of a sudden and rolled inward, and he crumpled to the ground and was sick.

"Somebody take care of these idiots!" Olaf scowled and turned away in disgust.

Suddenly the boarhound began to howl and tear at its leash as though possessed by a legion of devils.

"Now what?"

"He's onto a scent, Olaf!" the dog handler shouted over the furor.

"Then loose him, fool!"

A moment later the hound was bounding out of the trees and into the snow. He was onto a scent all right. Then immediately a yelp jerked from his throat as an arrow rifled into his heart.

"By Odin's beard!" Olaf roared, as he ran to the edge of the trees where the dog lay stone dead. "What madness is this?"

"Olaf, look!" one of the men cried. "It was killed by another of our arrows!"

"By the gods!" Olaf shouted. His eyes flashed murderously as he stared at the wicked black shaft with the crimson and black fletching. "By all the gods, I'll have a head," he exploded, looking up from the dead animal. "I swear it!"

"There!" another man shouted, pointing. "By those rocks! A horseman! Alone, I think."

The Norseman followed his point to an outcropping of large rocks situated on a blunt knoll more than three hundred feet away. Adjacent to the formation stood the gray silhouette of a single rider on a black horse, a swatch of emerald green waving smartly behind him providing the only hint of color.

Olaf shielded his eyes and squinted at the ghostly shape. There was a vague familiarity about it that was strangely haunting.

The lone rider began to prance about the knoll on his black charger against the hinder gray cast, his emerald cloak flashing brightly as gusts of wind caught it and hurled it recklessly about him. It seemed his eyes were fixed unyieldingly upon the Saxon camp below, taunting them, daring them to join him in combat.

The lively charger stamped its hooves and arched its neck proudly, thrusting its mane and tail and snorting contemptuously at the earth, and the terrible blasts fell upon the Saxon ears a muffled challenge. For just a moment the leaden sky opened a port in its great vault and let spill a trove of sun upon the little knoll, and the single horseman and his steed paraded gleaming in a great coin of silver. They were a splendid apparition.

A contagion of awe trembled through the warriors' midst, and there was anxious murmuring. Speculations bred like rodents and scurried about the camp. Oohs and aahs radiated worshipfully. It seemed to many that the solitary figure was a manifestation of some god—perhaps a British deity come to mock their presence. Perhaps even Odin himself astride the spirited Sleipnir. To others it was a phantasm; to others still, a demon. Who else but an immortal would dare challenge so large a troop of warriors singlehandedly?

But to Olaf, to the Norseman, the intruder was nothing more than an enemy to be killed. A low growl rattled in his throat.

"The Saxon army must be running low on dogs by now!" the horseman hallooed at last. "'Tis a pity . . . I prefer dogs over Saxon curs."

"He speaks our tongue, Olaf," one of the men remarked.

Druell squinted at the shape, convinced now that Ruddbane was indeed behind the treachery.

"Who are you?" Olaf bellowed.

"What is that to you who trespass on British soil?" came the defiant reply.

"Your tongue has an edge that cuts against a friendly company," Olaf said. "We have come in peace."

"You're a black liar, Saxon!" the rider replied. "Britain has already given many of her sons to the sword edge of your peace."

"You're an insolent knave who could stand a lesson in manners!"

"And you are the spawn of your father the devil!" the rider countered. "And my arrows strike well the hearts of devils!"

Olaf was suddenly intrigued by the horseman's audacity. A braver fool he had not seen in some time. "Who are you to address us with such insults?" he inquired. "A chieftain, perhaps? A prince of the land? Or perhaps you are nothing more than a loon who's escaped his chain!"

"Nay, but I am an old friend, Norseman."

"Come closer then, friend, that I might know the pleasure of our acquaintance."

"And have one of your archers send an arrow into my brisket? Not likely! Besides, you know me well enough, Olaf!"

Olaf started at the mention of his name.

Druell drew alongside the Viking and grunted. "Who is this crazy fellow that he knows your name?"

The other men turned to one another, gaping with astonishment, many of whom were now convinced that this was some deity of the land. Some argued that he was a water deity since he had disappeared into the river, and no small debate arose between them.

However, Olaf's mouth compressed into a grim smile as the vague familiarity of the horseman took form in his mind. He began to chortle. "Still killing dogs, I see," he boomed, taking a step forward. "I thought you were dead, Briton."

"My next arrow will convince you that I'm not, Saxon," Terryll replied. "And it is a British arrow, which has a better cast as you will see."

He loosed his arrow, and it straightway struck one of the eagle wings on Olaf's helmet, knocking it off his head. The boy laughed. "There's a buzzard for your cooking pot! You see—I can kill preening birds as well!"

"I see that you are still full of arrogance," Olaf said, his choler rising. He plucked the arrow from the wing and returned the helm to his head. Then he searched the hills beyond the boy for more Britons. "Do you expect to escape so many of us?"

"Hah! One Briton is worth any twenty Saxon dogs. And I can change those odds as I please."

Druell leaned over. "Let me work up behind him, Olaf, and I'll clip the tail feathers off this strutting cock."

"No. The fool has just admitted that he's alone," Olaf mused aloud. "No, we'll let him strut a while longer."

Terryll raised his bow and took aim at Druell. "Perhaps the half-wit next to you has acquired a taste for my arrows," he called out, guessing their conversation. "Tell him that I'll give him his fill of arrows if he so much as blinks!"

Druell glared up at the boy, his hand flexing savagely on the haft of his battle-ax.

Terryll regarded the men below him with contempt. They were trespassers. They had stolen his land, killed his countrymen, raped his countrywomen, threatened now to do more of the same. His eyes burned with vengeance.

But now the question arose in his mind as to what to do with them. He couldn't press an attack, and he couldn't sit out in the cold all day either. It was a stalemate. He grinned as he watched the men casting surreptitious asides to one another and shuffling about like squirrels. From his elevated position he could keep them pinned down indefinitely with the greater range of his longbow, at least until he ran out of arrows.

Suddenly a black shaft buzzed inches past his face like a furious hornet. He reeled to see the savage shapes of two horsemen bearing down on him at a full gallop.

"Ah! Erhard and Krueger!" Olaf laughed exultantly. "We've got the rooster now! After him, men!"

The Saxons were mounted in a trice and thundering out of the trees.

Terryll whirled about and spurred Tempest toward the two scouts. Immediately he loosed an arrow at the lead horseman and took him square in the chest.

The rider let out a startled gasp and jerked backward out of his saddle. The other Saxon appeared stunned by the unexpected charge. He swung his ax wildly at the boy as Tempest sped past, but he cleft only the wind.

The Briton let out a whoop and reined the spirited black on a southerly course with a score of Saxon warriors hot on his tail. Terryll flew over hill and dale as he made his way toward the road, now about two miles ahead. The image of the place burned in his mind as he fled across the winterscape. The Saxons were about a hundred yards behind, struggling to maintain the distance. But there was no matching the speed of Tempest, whose winged gait seemed a mockery of the earth.

The wind rushed past his ears, roaring like a beast, biting him with its cold teeth and drawing water from his eyes. And Tempest's hooves drummed softly against the snow, and it was a comforting rhythm. Behind him were the muffled cries and curses of men and a thunder of hooves, and feathered shafts of crimson and black screamed about his head like angry falcons loosed on the fleeting prey. But they were wildly cast and fell spent about him in the snow. Then one homing shaft caromed off his stirrup, and the boy laughed scornfully at the Saxon's poor marksmanship. He dug his heels into Tempest's flanks, and the black jumped ahead with a snort.

The land favored her native son as he led the Saxons through the treachery of woods and over frozen streams, around great outcroppings of boulders, and across the untoward, rock-infested terrain of Britain, terrain as familiar to the young hunter as his own village. But Terryll knew well that such favor could turn like a capricious wind—like a woman's fancy—and strike at him from beneath the placid lay of snow with a hidden rock, or ditch, or fallen limb that would spell his certain doom. So his eyes were kept busy about his stallion's hooves, alert, as he guided them with the lightly held reins.

Twice Tempest stumbled, twice the boy's heart leaped into his throat as the fingers of death clutched at his snapping emerald cloak. But each time the stallion, scrambling, kept his gait and snorted angrily at his feet, and great blasts of steam marked their course.

The boy and horse charged a wooded slope, and the black boles of trees fell past him on either flank in a flickering blur, black and black and black against the white of the incline, and the gnarled limbs of trees snatched at him, arching before and over him to frame a kind of corridor of white and black through which he must flee to survive. Then, spilling into the clear, he crested the hill and immediately let out a laugh.

"'Tis a grand sight, isn't it, boy?" Then, casting an impish look over his shoulder at the Saxons advancing through the trees, he whooped and hollered and raced down the other side of the hill with glorious abandon.

The muted howls and tiny patch of emerald green sparking about a half mile away caught Dagmere's attention. "Papa! Papa, look!" she cried out. "Someone's coming! It looks like—"

"Terryll!" Allyndaar exclaimed, as he reined Daktahr to a halt. He beheld with rapt attention his son's shape, enshrouded in his chieftain's cloak, flying down the hill like a bird, whooping and waving. The chieftain's eyes were wide and busy and taking in the scene as would a father.

Helena and Aurelius drew alongside him in the carpentum. "Are you sure, Allyn?" Helena inquired, like a mother. "Why would Terryll be here?"

"Up there, Allyn!" one of the Britons interrupted. "It seems he has the devil on his tail!"

Allyndaar jerked his gaze to the brow of the hill, as did the other British warriors. There was a collective grunting of men's voices, and then a rattling of blades.

At the summit Olaf drew back on his horse, and his men shuddered to a halt around him. The Viking scowled, swearing bitterly as he beheld a group of British horsemen, like little dark animals, breaking off from the caravan and galloping toward the hill, their battle cries deadened by the wind and distance.

"Shall we fight?" Druell asked, brandishing his battle-ax.

"No," the Norseman snarled, and he reined his horse to the southeast. "We shall ride!"

"To Killwyn Eden?" another man called after him.

"To Badonsward!" came the reply, and the hill was soon quit of them.

13
CANDIDA CASA

Aeryck and the two horses persevered against a bitter barrage of snow. It seemed for a time the regiments of the lowering sky strove to bury them beneath the sum of its infinite arsenal. The winds, like artillery spotters, howled martial commands at the dark gray batteries overhead, directing their unyielding volleys against the little flecks of life that dared challenge the frigid Scottish winter. The landscape surrendered quietly to the furious pummeling of the cannonade, but the harrowed little troop merely hunkered lower and pressed onward.

The wolves had worked their way to within fifty feet of the horses during the recent deluge. Sullie's ears twitched nervously as she eyed their lank shapes shadowing them off her right flank. She and the chestnut gelding traded anxious snorts.

"It's all right, girl—it's all right," Aeryck said, patting her thick neck. "If they were going to attack us, they would have done it by now." He caught himself. "I think."

Then he stared through the lace of snow at the lead wolf. The white one's eyes were busy, wary, and, meeting the boy's gaze, paused only briefly to appraise him, then continued to intently work the hills on either side of the road.

Aeryck looked on with amazement as he regarded the wolves. They were beautiful creatures really, he mused, moving through their gaits so fluidly that it seemed they were floating over the earth. Still that did little to ease his fear of them, for after all they were wolves—man-killing wolves.

And then a thought struck him. The white one had been trailing him for several months now, ever since the night he stood vigil over the slain body of the shepherd. Why? And why had the wolf obviously saved his life yesterday morning when he had been attacked by the other wolves? Wolves were territorial, he had heard, but killing Spang's band of assassins had nothing to do with territory. It had everything to do with saving his life again. Why? Why would a pack of wolves do such a thing? And then it dawned on him that he knew very little about wolves.

Letting out a sigh, he shifted in his saddle and gazed at the body of Brother Stephen draped rigidly over the chestnut gelding. The wolves had distracted him from more weighty concerns. Looking upon the outstretched arms of the dead monk, arms that seemed to be imploring the sweeping-by earth for its covering, he ruefully shook his head.

"Why did they not save *your* life?" he wondered. "What could be so important about the miserable hide of a beggar, that a holy one such as you would be taken instead?"

He turned back in his saddle, and his features were again grimly set with a dark purpose. He remembered the call.

The angry regiments, brooding darkly over the puny creatures below, took pause to replenish their armaments of snow, and, during the interval, visibility of the winterscape was of a beautiful pristine clarity. The sun shone dark red behind the western rim of hill.

Immediately the wolves fell away.

The horses' gaits clipped livelier. A small covey of grouse skittered across the road into a barley field during the lull. A skein of geese winged southward, honking, late in their rendezvous with warmer climes. Aeryck envied their wings, and he gave air to a familiar fantasy.

Suddenly he looked over his shoulder, sensing queerly that someone's eyes were upon him. But as he scanned the long line of wolves, each seemed intent on the business of wolves. Over his other shoulder there was nothing but snow. He shrugged off his feelings to the cold and jitters and turned back to the breathtaking panorama before him.

Everywhere the land betrayed the presence of man. Farms and villages began to crowd the little coastal road, and airy tongues of blue smoke lapped at the clouds from hidden chimneys. Low stone walls and hedgerows crisscrossed the countryside tartanlike and separated harvested fields and retained great snowdrifts. Brown stalks of cut grain poked through the snow, and orchard after orchard stood bare in perfect little rows, their winter limbs rattling in the wind.

Presently Aeryck crossed a stone bridge as he approached the rise of Whithorn. The tiny village of wattle-and-daub shops and cottages was swept away from the coast a mile or so and lay nestled in some low hills west of the road, now obscured by a coastal fog.

The wolves made a circuitous detour into the hills but not without first drawing attention from a contingent of dogs on guard near the village gates. At once there was a heroic uproar. The wolves ignored them, and the dogs, who lunged and twisted and barked rabidly at the air, weren't sure whether they should press some sort of attack or hold to their ground. They held.

Off to the boy's left the muted sound of gulls, mingled with the dim roar of breakers in the distance, betrayed the presence of the bay, as the wind allowed. Aeryck's mind took a brief respite from his sinking gloom and entertained thoughts of his Uncle Finn's arrival.

As he entered the cheerless streets of Whithorn village he pondered the mental scene that had impelled him gaily forth from Loch na Huric three days before: merchant ships happily arriving and disgorging their cargoes from great bellies of teak onto the spray-washed quays, and the frenetic hustling and bustling of merchants and sailors, who, like compulsive ants, were singularly consumed with their business, and children running and squealing happily because of the breach of tedium, composing airy little chants, and the glad faces of passengers disembarking and embracing. The image was well-rehearsed. But now the village, in grim contrast, was draped with a dreary soundlessness, and a melancholy gloom overshadowed its once gleaming facades. It was as though the dream had fallen off into a deep hibernation and was not to be stirred until spring. A desperate prayer escaped the boy's lips as a sigh.

Thick fog clung to the coast and obscured everything but a field of twenty feet or so around him. Beyond was an oppression that stymied inquiry. Sounds filtered through the sullenness as though from great distances.

Quietly Aeryck passed before a gauntlet of curious eyes peering at him through various dark apertures. Rosy-cheeked children gathered in mute clumps behind door slits, looking on impishly at the strange little parade that shuffled along. Occasionally mothers would appear suddenly and, shooting Aeryck skeptical looks, would yank them away, scolding. Cries of protest would ensue but were quickly silenced by the muffled slamming of doors.

There was a single man outdoors, one with a scarf wrapped about his head, and he looked up from his pigs and eyed Aeryck passing, eyed the snow-covered body of Stephen behind him, eyed Aeryck again, snorted, then resumed his feeding chores as if a stranger leading a corpse through town were a common sight.

Aeryck nodded to him, but the man had turned an apathetic shoulder.

Suddenly a dark shape loomed out of the obfuscation like a giant and startled the boy, and he immediately corrected Sullie's path to avoid stepping into the tavern of MacMaw.

Voices of merriment hailed him from inside. The skirl of pipes sang out with a haunting wail. Listening, it seemed to Aeryck that the pipes alone understood his thoughts, bade him to come in out of the cold, to be at ease from his woes. The boy had stayed in this tavern with Brynwald, and he imagined the happy scene around the hearth. He imagined hot plates of food and cider warming his belly, and leathery-faced men amidst the ale casks, mostly mariners, telling fantastic stories of their adventures, mostly lies. He knew there was a warm comradery glowing inside and a soft, warm bed to comfort him.

"Come on, Sullie, let's go." He sighed ruefully. "No oats for you just yet." And clucking his tongue, he spurred her along the road. He plowed ahead into the fog, benumbed with thoughts of the cheery scene he had witnessed in his mind. His shoulders were weighted with a profound loneliness. His spirits grew more and more despondent as the sirens of the pipes faded on the wind. Sullie exchanged a repertoire of complaints with the chestnut gelding. Immediately leaving the village precincts, Aeryck took the little road that climbed swiftly to the monastery of Candida Casa. Built in A.D. 397 by the British monk Ninian as a base from which to evangelize the Picts and Scots, Candida Casa ("white house") was set atop a noble promontory and commanded a panoramic view of Whithorn and the Bay of Wigtown beyond. The little white church, clinging tenuously to its lofty height, was like a beacon guiding the weary traveler away from the treacherous rocks of Celtic paganism. And from this elevated prow the good bishop was the first man to take the word of Christ to the southern Picts. His ministry eventually reached even as far north as the Grampian Mountains—a place of great spiritual desolation.

It was a half-mile journey into the hills to the monastery, though in the dense fog, and now with the light of dusk beginning to fade and the advent of night quickly gathering the vigor of outlines, it was slow going. And cold going. A wet chilling cold, going through the skin to the bones.

Aeryck's mind was singularly fixed upon pleasant warm thoughts, slowly making a transition from the warm tavern behind to the warm monastery ahead. When he had reached the halfway point up the hill he started when he became aware that the wolves were alongside him again, unannounced. However their dark wraithlike shapes were now no more than fifteen feet away, moving silently across the bluing hues of snow. He had no idea how long they had been there.

Sullie whickered and sidestepped, nearly stumbling at the sight of them.

"Easy, girl. Easy," Aeryck whispered quietly. "That's it."

The boy looked fore and hinder, and in either direction the fog concealed the beginning and end of the wolf column. There might have been fifty or five hundred of them for all he could tell. They paced beside the horses with a purpose, it seemed, their yellow eyes scouring the clouded terrain greedily, as though hunting. They appeared unaware of the boy's presence as they glided forward toward some objective, the snow scrunching softly beneath their pads as they moved stealthily along.

Now the density of the fog began to play tricks on the boy's eyes. Dark shapes emerged from the blue mists before him like multi-limbed monsters, chimeras likely. Then, floating quietly past, they were perceived as trees and shrubs. Large boulders appeared as ogres, crouched and huddled in stolid groups. A hedgerow was a rank of warriors poised to attack.

Chuckling nervously, Aeryck glanced over at the wolves and discovered that one of them was staring at him, a black wolf with gray-and-white splotches. There was such a malefic quality in the look that he cringed, and, blinking, he looked again, thinking his eyes were at play. But at once the wolf's yellow eyes narrowed into a glower.

The boy's eyes had not been playing tricks, and very quickly a prickling sensation came trundling along his spine with a terror. It was as though some black thing reached out of the fog and clutched at him with an icy hand—like the one he had felt on the bluffs. He had a sudden sensation of violent wings rushing about his head, and his hand quickly fetched the hilt of his sword.

The black wolf fell back in the line gradually, subtly, its narrowed eyes fixed on Aeryck the while, and as the pack entered a tract of conifers it did not reemerge with them.

Presently a sleepy clutch of edifices with white-plastered walls rose out of the formidable gloom with a ghostly luminance. Groves of huge oaks and yews, their thickly gnarled trunks cloaked with years of moss, stood in lamenting postures on either side of the curling path. Their great limbs were thrown up in astonishment at his approach. And then a soft, shivering wind moaned through the boughs, rustling the stalwart leaves and sweeping sprays of fine snow into the air. Aureoles of amber light blinked mournfully at the boy through the purpling twilight mists, as if the little church were prescient of the arrival of the slain novice.

The somber ambience of the night worked upon the boy's mind, and he felt his stomach tightening at his immediate prospects. A kind of dread reached up from the twisting knots in his belly and pulsed heavily in his throat. It seemed he was about to give an account of himself. His mind began to rehearse an apologetic concerning the dead boy, adroitly winnowing the chaff of the account from the meritable, each line of exposition designed to turn away a terrible guilt that had been continually nagging him.

Just along the murky periphery of his mind, however, anger crouched like a panther, waiting its turn, waiting for this thing of guilt, this nuisance to its schemes, to be gone that it might prowl about undeterred.

He produced a bronze medallion from his cloak and fondled it thoughtfully, caressing the worn edges as he was wont to do when troubled by a matter. He well knew the image of the bear's head and laurel wreath engraved upon it—the bear wreath, as he called it; the crest of Caelryck—and the tips of his fingers translated to him fond memories of his father and of the giant bear, Hauwka. Looking off to his flank, he noticed that the wolves were gone. They had disappeared sometime during the retrospective interlude into some dark lair, spirited away. The wind whistled about his ears.

And then the fog put forth the robed figure of a man, who, stepping into the deserted skirts of the monastery, raised his arm and hallooed. "Welcome to God's house, friend. Come—come now—be quit of your burdens! Vincent! Andrew! Come quickly, brothers! We have a guest!"

The boy took a deep breath. "It is only me, Brother Thomas," he hailed upon his approach. "Aeryck, from Loch na Huric."

"Why, so it is!" Brother Thomas cried. "So it is!" He was elated and began to wave his arms excitedly. "Brothers, come quickly! 'Tis young Aeryck! Bryn's boy!"

A handful of monks filed out of the various outbuildings that supported the church proper, and the yard was suddenly bustling with an air of unexpected welcome.

Brother Thomas, a short, barrel-shaped Scotsman with alert, little black eyes and a short-cropped tonsure of wiry gray hair, strode over to the boy with a gregarious smile. "*Och!* And what brings you out here in this deffil's brew, little brother?" he inquired. "And what of my friend Brynwald—is he not with you then?"

"No. I've come alone to meet a ship from Eire," the boy replied. Then hoping to forestall the inevitable examination, he asked, "I don't suppose any have arrived?"

"Whist! Nay, little brother! And not likely till this weather blows over, neither! Come in! Come in, before you catch your death," Thomas boomed heartily. Then casting a skyward look, he added, "It has the look of the Apocalypse aboot it, dinnay you ken? Brother Milius, take the lad's horses to the stable and give them a shovel of oats—apiece now, mind you. Give them a good rubbing too, if you like! You will, I ken, and treat them like the poor creatures of God they are!"

Brother Milius, a tall, loose-jointed man, nodded and smiled. The two horses whinnied their approval and blew snorts into the foggy air, and as Brother Thomas passed by, Sullie took hold of his sleeve and began to nibble on it.

"Aweel!" Thomas laughed as he grabbed hold of the gray's blunt nose and stroked it. "There's a girl! We'll take good care of you, dinnay you fret now."

Then the monk noticed the strange-looking cargo upon the second horse. "And what have you got there then, little brother?" he inquired. "Come alone, did you say? Then who—" He suddenly stiffened and put his hand softly to his cheek. "Mercy!"

There was an immediate murmuring of men's voices.

Aeryck swung his leg heavily out of the saddle and groaned dismally to himself.

Brother Thomas approached the dead boy haltingly, as one would a coiled snake. Then stooping, he angled his head to look up at the ashen face. "God have mercy!" he exclaimed, and he immediately turned away from the corpse, aghast. "Have mercy!" he repeated, as he stared incredulously at the ground. Then looking up at Aeryck, he asked, "A monk is he? But—but who? How?"

Aeryck's defense immediately fled before the man's torn eyes, and he began to stammer like a drunkard. His eyes shifted furtively beneath his hood, avoiding the other's gaze. He was sure that his eyes would betray some terrible guilt in the matter. It was then that he remembered the letter of introduction. He retrieved it from his cloak perfunctorily and handed it to the monk. Then, taking a step backward, he slumped into a kind of melancholy stupor.

Thomas gazed momentarily upon the broken seal in a trance. Then his eyes knit a path from the letter to Aeryck, then to the astonished faces of the monks gathered around him, then back to Aeryck. "A letter?" he asked, bewildered. "How can a letter explain . . ." Averting his glance from the dead boy, he opened it and began to read. Pausing, he looked up at the somber huddle of monks.

"It's from Brother Lupus," he said quietly, then continued to read aloud until the last of it. He stared at the letter for a few moments, rereading it to himself, folded it carefully, then looked up at the boy. "How is it that you have cume by this one, Aeryck?"

Aeryck glanced at him quickly. Then, compressing his lips together, he began to review certain of the pertinent details of the events of the evening and morning. It was strange, but he found in his voice a kind of absolution. The tale did not accuse him in its telling as he had supposed it would.

His brow cleared during the course of the briefing, then arched judicially. "Spang, it was, who murdered him," he concluded, with a renewed indignation. "He's the guilty one."

Thomas looked at the other monks. "We must pray for the men who did this," he said with a heavy voice.

The others nodded solemnly.

Aeryck was incredulous. *"Pray* for them? I'm going to kill them!"

116

he exclaimed vehemently. Then he drew his sword from its scabbard and brandished it at the trees.

Brother Thomas searched the boy's face intently. His little black eyes glistened in the wan light of the torch spill from the church. For a moment it seemed he was in pain.

Aeryck was haunted by the look, for he had seen it on the face of Stephen the night before in the tavern of Pea Gants. It was more than he could bear, and he lowered his eyes to the ground, where they continued to burn agitated circles in the snow.

Thomas turned sadly to the other monks. "Come, brothers," he said, "let us take young Stephen inside."

And so they did.

A tongue of fire leaped into Aeryck's breast. "But they killed him!" he protested angrily. Then he started after them. "Did you hear me? I said they killed him! They deserve to die, don't they? Well, don't they?"

Brother Thomas wheeled about and faced the boy with a piercing gaze. "Aye, little brother—that they do. By troth, they deserve a swift and fiery judgment, like as we all. But if it's a judgment you're demanding, son, look upon the cross—there's the sum of it!"

Aeryck fought a little shudder. "But—"

"*Och*, but there's murder in your heart, son," Thomas interrupted with a travailing voice. "It rises like a serpent out of the blackness of your soul to consume you. Who are you then, to exact the Laird's vengeance and so deny His sweet mercy? I ask you, son, are you any less guilty than the men who did this terrible, hateful thing?"

Aeryck stared at the man dumbfounded.

"I will pray for your soul as well, little brother. That I will," Thomas continued sadly. "Perhaps the Laird will show you a kindness to repent." Then he turned and walked away.

The boy blinked stupidly at the abbot's retreating form, his mind reeling from an emotional assault.

Sullie and the chestnut gelding were led away to the stable area and, swinging her gentle head toward the boy, the big gray whickered softly. But Aeryck was unaware of it. He stood alone in a glimmering pool of light, gaping at the Scottish monk as he stepped into the little white church after the others. Then he looked down at his sword. The amber cast of light flickered over the blade, giving the engraved tongues of fire along its length a curious vitality.

Suddenly the boy felt a breath of hot air on the back of his neck. A rush of shivers crawled over his head and spine as he whirled about, sure that he would see some ghoul standing just behind him, grinning.

But there was nothing—only the lingering shivers loosed over him and a subtle stirring of wind that crept chillingly through the umbral shadows of his brow and seemed to whisper, *The man is a fool, Worm. He is nothing but a kind and gentle old fool. You know what you must do.*

Aeryck glanced again at his sword, then returned it to its place and started toward the church with a heavy tread. As he reached the stoop, the muted cry of a wolf pierced the murky veil surrounding the monastery and arrested the boy in his tracks. Turning, he stared into the blackness beyond the light with a strange look.

14

HATE IS A DEFFIL OF A THING

The sky was a brilliant sapphire with fluffy white clouds scudding upon it like a gay regatta. And the sun beamed warmly over the gleaming white countryside, calling to mind the healthy, masculine sinews of the land. Icicles hung from the eaves of the monastery like a rake of glistening diamond teeth. The storm had passed during the night watches, rumbling away to the north, and Candida Casa presided now over quiet vistas. And the sun shone a great square of golden light upon the floor and wall of Aeryck's little room, warming where it touched.

The boy looked out his small window that faced south upon the moors. The barren bleakness of the terrain seemed to reflect his mood, which had grown even more sullen during the night's passing. He let out a disgruntled sigh. Then, looking through the trees to the east, he could see a narrow crescent of the ocean, iridescent and shimmering. His eyes strained to conjure an image of sail upon the dark rim. He took a deep breath and blew it out hard.

He watched for a while as a little bird—a swift—harried the flight of a hawk, swooping and diving, driving it doggedly away from some sanctuary, slicing at the flight feathers of the great bird with each knife-like pass. The hawk, though five times its size and weight, and though it could easily tear the swift apart should it get the thing in its talons, could do nothing but yield.

Abandoning this diversion, Aeryck shifted his attention to a small oak-studded knoll. There several monks were gathered in a somber wheel around the linen-wrapped body of young Stephen as it was being lowered into a frozen hollow of earth. The boy sighed as the words of Brother Thomas floated down to his window upon a gentle stirring of wind and breathed over his sullenness like a bellows.

"And 'except a corn of wheat fall into the ground and die, it abideth alone: but if it die, it bringeth forth much fruit. . . . He that loveth his life shall lose it; and he that hateth his life in this world shall keep it unto

119

life eternal . . . I am the resurrection, and the life: he that believeth in me, though he were dead, yet shall he live.'"

And so the young novice from Troyes was buried.

Aeryck blinked hard upon hearing the "Amen," and with eyes burning red through a mist of tears, he continued to gaze upon the place, attending it with a multitude of mournful sighs long after the monks had retired to some other place.

Then a look of determination swept over his face like a dark overcast. He quickly gathered his things and was about to leave when there came a light rapping on his door. He eyed the door warily. "Come in."

Brother Thomas entered the room and saw that the boy had made ready to depart. He smiled warmly. "A good morning to you, little brother."

"Good morning," Aeryck returned, without much heart.

"Such a fine day the Laird has given us," the monk said, glancing out the window. "I would not've thought such a storm could pass so quickly." He took a deep breath. "Such a fine scent, dinnay you think? Makes a body rejoice to take it in!" Then turning to the boy, he added cheerfully, "We are all gathered at board and await your company. Do you care for some porridge, son? It'll warm your insides against the cold."

"No thanks. I'm not hungry."

"Not hungry? *Och!* And when is a lad of your size not hungry then? And doubly so since you hardly touched your supper last night."

Aeryck averted his eyes to the window, fearful of falling under the man's scrutiny. "I'll eat once I reach the village."

There was a long pause during which the monk eyed him thoughtfully. "You're welcome to stay here with us, Aeryck," he offered. "We have food a-plenty. Plain of taste, I'll warrant. Not like you'd fare in the village. But it'll nourish you just the same."

Aeryck looked at the man and smiled. "Thank you, Brother Thomas. You've been very generous, but I'll be taking lodging at MacMaw's tavern until my uncle arrives. It's closer to the bay, and I might hear news of some kind or other concerning the movement of ships. It shan't be long now, I shouldn't wonder—assuming the weather holds."

"Aye, that's sound, that's sound," Thomas admitted, pulling on his chin. "Then might I have a word with you before you go?"

Aeryck shrugged, and his eyes darted about the man's face uneasily.

The room—nothing more a large cubicle—was large enough only to accommodate a cot, a nightstand with a wash basin set upon it, and a small desk and chair that were suitable for reading or writing. There seemed little enough room for one person, let alone two. There were ten such rooms in the dormitory, one man to a room, this one being used for guests.

Thomas took the chair, scratched the side of his nose, then looked up at the boy. His little black eyes, wet with age, glistened like marbles in the light. "You're carrying a burden upon your shoulders that was not meant for you, little brother," he said.

Aeryck glanced quickly at the man, then his eyes stole away to the desk and looked steadily at its surface. "I don't know what you mean."

"'Twere God's will and purpose to take the boy, through nay fault of your own," Thomas continued. "His loss is a grievous thing to the living, and we shall mourn him as one of our own. But he's in the Laird's hands now, son, with the angels attending. 'Tis a better place, I'm sure."

Aeryck searched the dark pools that were the monk's eyes. They seemed to draw him out of himself into a kindlier place.

"That's right, by troth," the monk continued, "you are not to blame for what happened to young Stephen, though you be floggin' yourself with the deffil's cords. I ken 'tis hard to understand such truth—God's ways being infinitely higher than ours—but you must come to terms with it, lad. You must put it behind you now and move on in the grace of God, lest this thing be your undoing."

The boy looked out the window. "I wish I could." He sighed remorsefully. "But I can't seem to shake it loose. They meant to kill *me*, Brother Thomas, but instead a boy completely innocent is lying cold in a grave with my wound in his breast." The grim determination quickly edged back into Aeryck's features as he considered the matter. "All I can think about is finding the men who did this, and—and I will—" He broke off and stared at the pommel of his sword, fingering it with his thumb.

The monk grunted thoughtfully. "Hate is a deffil of a thing—a terrible master, if you 'low it. It'll take from a man his youth—eat it through like a canker till there's nothing left of his soul but the black hate itself. 'Tis an insatiable appetite that works within you, Aeryck. I ken 'twill be a struggle, but the Laird through His grace will work His sweet mercy in you, if you dinnay withhold Him."

Aeryck turned sharply to the monk. "You don't understand," he protested. "How could you? You're a monk—a holy man. What could you know about such things, living up here in this place?"

"Whist! 'A holy man,' you say!" Brother Thomas retorted, with his little black eyes flashing. "And what is a holy man but a wretched sinner clinging to the gapin' wounds of the Savior? I ask you, little brother, think you that I have earned but a single drop of His precious blood? Nay, by troth! Nay! The deeds of ten thousands of His saints couldnay purchase such a wee amount.

"And what things might you be referrin' to then, that I cannay understand? Lust? Greed? Hate, perhaps? Aye! I see by your look, I've fixed upon it. Do you think that because I have taken a holy vow and have shaven me pate, or because my robes bespeak a humble estate, that I dinnay covet or have the same passions as another? Hoot, lad! You thought, perhaps, the Laird fashioned me from a piece of wood instead of clay?"

"I don't know," Aeryck replied, a little taken aback. "You just seem so . . . so . . . good. I guess I just thought—"

"It is not what you can see with your eyes that marks the sum of a man, Aeryck. Nay, but 'tis what you cannay see," the monk interrupted. "'Tis the heart, lad, the heart of a man that must bear a fiery scrutiny to fix his measure. Aye! For therein is laid up the inheritance of Adam, the full trove of it. And could you look upon my heart then—*och!* There's a sight for you now. You'd see a heart all right. And you'd ken then that the heart is wicked and deceitful, as the prophet says, so full of evil thoughts and adulteries and murders and the like that, gazin' upon its horrors, a man must either flee into some pit of despair to dwell therein a wretched worm or flee into the loving arms of the Father for His mercy. For troth, lad, there is nay reinin' the heart's hellish bent but by His grace. A 'holy man,' you say! Nay, but this holy man is the least of the redeemed, little brother, the very least."

Aeryck looked upon the man astounded. Never had he imagined such words coming from the mouth of a Christian, let alone from a man of God. He began to speak, but his words stood in revolt against his mind, and so he stammered like a fool until he sat down upon the bed, his mouth agape and quit of its riot.

Thomas strode over to the window. "I ken well this thing of hate that's got a hold of you, little brother," he said, gazing across the moors. "I've seen it taking the lives of my family one by one through the blood feuds up north, till nane but my wee sister and I were left to tell it. I was but a young lad like yourself, full of hate and fire and vengeance, spewing out cursings and blasphemies. I wanted to kill the world, I did. Aye— imagine that.

"Then one day, when the heather was a-bloom on the slopes of the Grampians and the air was sweet with a gentle birdsong, the saintly Ninian come into the mountains and there fetched me—fetched me there a-stewin' in some dark contemplation beneath the shade of a rowan. And he at once shone the light of Christ into my black heart. Set me free, he did, from the living hell in my soul. Taught me a better way, aye—the way of the cross and peace. Troth! I was filled with such joy as I cannay express, such—Oh, merciful Savior! Merciful Savior!"

The man broke off full of tears, and, overwhelmed with emotion, he began to utter, "Thank you, merciful God, for lifting me out of the pit. Oh, thank You." And a little hymn sprang from his lips as from a pent wellspring.

> "Holy! Holy! Holy!
> Omnipotent King of Kings;
> The heavens declare Thy glory,
> And angels rush to sing.

> "For love of Eden's ruined race,
> Thou left Thy great estate;
> Thy hands outstretched to sin's embrace,
> Thou bore Thy Father's hate.

> "Come now, Immaculate fount of God,
> O wretched man, draw near;
> Take hold the Lamb on Calvary's sod,
> Be cleansed and no more fear."

Aeryck beheld the man with rapt attention as he sang quietly. A sweet spirit filled the little room, such as he had not known, and he scarce knew how to respond. He did not know the words to the hymn, but he found himself humming along, his body gently swaying to the tempo, and his eyes brimming over from the wonder of it. Indeed it near overwhelmed him.

"Ah, yes, such sweet joy He filled me with." The monk sighed as he wiped his eyes with his sleeve. Then turning to Aeryck, he said earnestly, "Give it over to the Laird, little brother. Give it over to the Laird, and He will surely heal your soul. For if you've a mind to cling to it, 'twill doubtless scuttle your faith and bring you to shipwreck."

Aeryck considered his words for several moments, and a desperate struggle tore at his brow, tore savagely at the mystic ecstasy lingering there from the hymn. "But—but how?" he asked. "What do I do? I don't understand. It's like there's a war going on inside me, and I'm growing weary of fighting it."

"*Och*, but you're just gettin' knocked about a wee bit." Brother Thomas smiled. "Your 'old man,' as the apostle Paul says, wouldnay be givin' ground wi'out a good fight. But you must fix your eyes upon the Savior, Aeryck. There is nay greater picture of His love and mercy than that as He hung torn and bleeding upon the Roman cross—there, with the great weight of sin bowing His noble brow in shame before the world of His making—with His arms opened wide to forgive us.

"Can you fathom it, little brother? Can you fathom that God would pour out His wrath upon His only Son that He might be just to embrace us with His infinite mercy and kindnesses? If you can, it will move you to a greater love for God and, wicked though they be, His pitiful creatures. Fix your eyes upon the Savior, Aeryck, and I'll warrant you that notions of hate and revenge will wither in the light of His glory."

There was a hush in the room like that to be found in a dense summer forest. It weighed heavily on the boy, and his head sank slowly to his breast.

"Will you be quit of your wrath, little brother?" the monk asked, breaking the quiet. "Will you lay down your sword and take up the cross?"

There was a lengthy pause.

"I'm told that my father was a righteous man—that he gave his life protecting helpless people from evil men," Aeryck said. "Am I to do less? Should I not raise my sword in defense of my country? And what of its women and children? Should I let them be raped and killed without coming to their aid?" The boy let out a great sigh. "With all my strength I want to serve Christ, and I will. I swear it. But this teaching of yours is hard to understand."

"Aye, 'tis a difficult problem, I'll grant you. There are those of the faith—righteous men, nay doubt—who would say, 'Aye, take up the Laird's holy sword against your enemies like sons of thunder, and let the deffil take 'em all.' But 'tis not our way here at Candida Casa. We choose to learn of Christ's love, His gentleness and easy yoke, wielding only the weapons of the Spirit against those who would do violence to His little ones."

Aeryck shook his head sadly. "Why is the world in such a mess? Everywhere I go, it seems, no matter how I try to avoid it or outrun it, death is always close behind me, stalking me like a lion. If I lay down my sword I feel it will surely overtake me and tear me to pieces."

The monk smiled. "The way of the cross is ofttimes a lonely and desperate journey, fraught with struggle and hardships, miseries and diverse temptations of spirit and flesh. And throughout the pilgrimage you can expect nay comfort from man but rather his scorn and ridicule and—aye—perhaps even the edge of his sword. But in the epistle to the Romans, Paul said, 'In all these things we are more than conquerors through him that loved us.' Look upon the Savior, little brother. 'Tis a fierce love He has for His own. Nane can separate us from it. Take comfort in it."

For several moments Aeryck stared at the palms of his hands as though they were two mirrors, reflecting an image of himself. He slowly closed the fingers of his right hand into a fist. "But what of justice?" he asked the monk. "What of justice? Am I to just sit back and do nothing? Am I to allow the men who committed this terrible crime to fly freely about the land doing the devil's bidding? To murder again perhaps? Don't you understand, Brother Thomas? If I had killed the man when it was in my power to do so, Stephen would be here now, alive—alive to further the work of Christ!"

The monk gazed sadly at him for several moments. "Have you heard nothing I've said, little brother?" He rose to his feet and walked over to the door. Before exiting, he paused and looked back. "I will pray for your soul, Aeryck. I will pray that God may open your eyes of understanding and give you wisdom—that He may preserve you from the evil one who roams about like a ravenous wolf, seeking to devour the straying sheep." He smiled affectionately, then left the room.

Aeryck looked down at the crest on his sword while he pondered the monk's words. His brow was knit with lines of intense bewilderment. "I don't understand, God," he prayed earnestly. "I just don't understand."

Then glancing out the window he beheld that the sky was clear, save for the little swift that came swooping happily back alone upon the gentle currents. It seemed a fine day for sailing.

15

AN INVASION
OF BRITONS

A steady westerly breeze off the Solway Firth swept the tart smell of the sea over the Bowness promontory and the surrounding winterscape, raising the temperature a few coveted degrees of warmth, and the skies over Bowness were bright and brittle clear, as bright and clear as ever shone in the eyes of a woman in love.

Dagmere leaped out of bed and rushed to the window and gazed out upon the dawning world. It was a glorious dawn. Like no dawn she had ever witnessed.

The circle of the earth could be seen a deep cobalt blue beyond the tiny clutch of fishing boats anchored off the lee point of old Bowness harbor. Their prows bobbed up and down on the swells, their masts pitching to and fro as the little vessels kept time with the ancient rhythms of the sea and the mariners gathered in huddles along the quay, working the nets and the baits with their gnarled and wise seamen's fingers.

The air was rife with the high-pitched screeches of seagulls and the keening of ospreys as the birds sliced back and forth through the currents, their keen eyes ferreting the dazzling blue waters for fish and, finding them, folding their wings and plummeting like daggers.

And there was a continual drumming of the surf, the *boom . . . boom . . . boom . . . boom . . .* that was the heartbeat of the earth. And the terns skittered after the fiddlers in a never-ending dance. The birds and the fish and the boats and the mariners composed a timeless song of the sea.

Dagmere could scarce contain the melody that surged in her breast. She giggled with excitement, then, thrusting herself away from the window with a squeal, hurriedly threw on her clothes and proceeded to awaken everyone in the house.

Later that early morning a crowd of people was gathered outside the village gates to bid farewell to the company of Britons, who, having visited there now for a few days, were mounted and ready to make the

126

final leg of their journey to Loch na Huric. It was grand the way the men sat their horses, with their cloaks of various hues of blue and yellow, crimson and orange, emerald green and purple, and the people in the crowd looked admiringly at them. It was the chieftain of Killwyn Eden who wore the emerald green now, and he sat on the Arabian stallion Daktahr, off to one side of the others, addressing Belfourt, the chieftain of Bowness. "You sure you won't change your mind about coming with us, Bellie?" Allyndaar asked his good friend.

"No, Allyn. There is still much bitterness in my heart. I doubt whether I'll ever be able to fathom the thought of sitting down to sup with a Pict staring at me across the boards. No, Allyn, the river of bitterness flows deep in my soul. Too deep."

"Yes, but the river has taken a new course," Allyndaar retorted. "They are Christian now."

"That is your religion, my friend, not mine." Belfourt placed his thick hands on his ample girth and patted it sagely. "I told you before that it would make you soft in the head, Allyn. I see now that I was right."

Allyndaar chuckled. "We will debate the faith when we return. But for now, suffice it to say that Brynwald has come to believe in the Christ, a miracle which I must see for myself. If it is true, as it is reported to me from many quarters that it is, then we would be fools not to form an alliance with them. A pledge of friendship with Brynwald will only help to preserve our borders—perhaps even deter any northward movement of the Saxons."

"Aye, if it's true. Perhaps," Belfourt agreed. Then he lifted a prophetic finger. "But there's still a passel of beggars up there that'd cut your head off in a blink. I know them, Allyn. You don't."

"So I cannot persuade you to come?"

"No, I doubt that I would be fair company for you, my soft-headed friend," the portly chieftain said, his eyes twinkling. "You'd best get along."

"Then I bid you farewell," Allyndaar said, clasping his arm. "Look for us in about a month. We'll send word to you from time to time to let you know how we fare."

"Aye. You do that."

And with that Allyndaar reined Daktahr to the head of the column, where Dagmere had been prancing anxiously about on her sorrel mare, and he motioned for everyone to get under way. Dagmere let out a little whoop.

Then the long column jerked forward with whistles shrilling and whips cracking over the teams, and the carpentums and wagons and horsemen were soon clattering and spaced from head to terminus over a distance of a quarter mile. They were a majestic sight against the brilliant

127

white: the men in their polished armor and battle accoutrements glinting brightly in the sun, and their multicolored cloaks, like so many banners, curling on the breezes. The crowd waved and cheered happily. The children ran and threw snowballs at the horses.

Smiling, Belfourt turned to Terryll and Gwyneth, whom he knew were champing to get going. "You take good care of my lass, you hear, Terry? She's all I've got in the world now that Sophie's gone." Suddenly his eyes suffused with tears, and he quickly wiped them.

"Don't you worry, Bellie," Terryll said. "I will take care of her like the apple of my eye."

Belfourt pulled himself together and chuckled. "Of course you will, Terry, though I don't know whatever you see in the lass," he said, winking at him. "She's plain of face, as you can see, but she's got a good heart. 'Tis good that you show her kindness."

"Father!"

Terryll looked at Gwyneth and smiled. She was radiant in the morning sun, with the light igniting the myriad red hues in her hair to a glorious blaze, and her big green eyes sparkling at him. "I'll have to differ with you there, Bellie. Your daughter is the most beautiful girl I've ever seen."

Gwyneth blushed and looked away.

"Ah, love is blind, they say," Belfourt boomed, laying hold of his swelling girth. "It's just as well then, for you're all she talks about. Every minute of the day it's 'Terryll this' and 'Terryll that,' or 'when is he coming? and will he be here soon?' I tell you, son, there's no end of it."

Gwyneth flushed and cast him a reproachful eye. "Really, Father!"

"Would you have me say you never spake of him at all then, lass?"

Gwyneth cast a demure glance at Terryll, who was grinning stupidly at her.

"I think not!" Belfourt grunted. "Now be off with ye two love doves, before I change my mind. Off with ye now!"

"Farewell, Father!"

"Farewell, Bellie!"

"Off with ye, I say!" the big red-bearded chieftain bellowed, his eyes suffusing with tears again.

But as they started to rein their horses toward the others, a mousy-looking girl of sixteen or seventeen, with quick nervous eyes, stepped forward from the crowd.

"Terryll?" she squeaked.

"Yes?"

And turning he saw that it was Corrie, one of the girls whom Aeryck and he had rescued from the Sarteham's black altar. It was the girl who had fallen and twisted her ankle.

128

She drew up next to Belfourt and handed a little package to Terryll. "Will you give this to Aeryck when you see him?" she asked meekly. "It is a little carving that I made that he might remember me."

Terryll glanced at the package, then looked down into her eyes.

They were searching eyes, imploring him. Although she was decidedly more at ease with herself since her trauma two months earlier, he could still see the ghosts of her pain flitting around the edges with their little torments.

He smiled warmly at her. "I doubt very seriously whether he will ever forget you, Corrie, but I would be happy to give this to him as soon as I lay eyes on him."

Corrie smiled embarrassedly, and as she turned to leave she caught herself and said, "And tell him that I pray for him every night." Then she hurried back into the crowd.

"I will."

Pawing the ground, Tempest whickered contemptuously. He seemed not at all pleased with the delay or the fact that all the other horses were ahead of him already. He blew a great snort.

"Take it easy, Tempest. We're going now." Then the boy saluted Belfourt and the crowd, and he and Gwyneth galloped away.

Belfourt watched the long column snake its way down the broad escarpment toward the trees and the wall beyond. Ten people had joined their company from his village, and a dozen or so more from Whitley Castle and Caer Luel, swelling their numbers to around eighty-five, the majority of whom were fighting men, skilled with both sword and longbow. Were it not so, he would never have allowed his daughter to go with them.

Still, his face darkened with apprehension. His mind returned to the battle fought two months before, where these same people from the north had come and ravaged their village, killed many of their warriors, killed many of their women and children, including Sophie, his wife of twenty years. How was it possible that such a brutal people could be tempered so by this religion of the Romans? He shook his head doubtfully. Fearfully.

And as the column began to enter into the trees, he could just make out his daughter's shock of fiery hair near the front of the column. She was looking back at him and waving. He smiled weakly, pondering deep matters in his mind. And by the time he had raised his hand to return her salute, the trees had swallowed her.

Everyone in the column felt it the minute they reached the mile castle in the Wall and the doors were shut behind them. They had closed with such resolute finality that everyone looked back at them out of reflex. Even Allyndaar at the head, even the giant blacksmith, Bolstroem, who feared no man, looked back with a start.

What the company felt began as a vague uncertainty, like a warm mist settling quietly over the gathering and clouding hearts. Mother Britain was behind them now, hearth and home, kith and kin, the security of the tried and familiar. And now the untried, the unfamiliar, and with these the danger of the unknown, the unknown save for the knowledge that they had entered the land inhabited by their sworn enemies.

Who knew what lay ahead? Imaginations flickered to life, quick to provide a spate of suggestions, even cruel inventions. Then the deeper they penetrated the seemingly fierce, brutal land of Picts and Scots, the quiet uncertainty became a gnawing apprehension, and then it grew into a garrulous fear.

Eyes flickered anxiously along the long line, each British mind recalling tales of horrible atrocities committed on their kinsmen by these savage, uncultured barbarians. Winds whistled over the broken terrain, around and through scraggy winter-stripped trees and rock formations that jutted violently over the earth, adding a suitable ambience to their mindscapes. A kind of dreadful shudder tremored along the column at regular intervals.

The men wore grim expressions as they scanned the hills and trees for mischief, their eyes busy, their ears quick, their fingers darting out of the warm folds of their cloaks and fidgeting nervously along their sword hilts or the grips of their longbows, ever mindful that death could leap out of the blinds and take them unaware.

Occasionally they would pass a farmhouse or a small village, with thin wisps of bluish smoke curling from chimneys hidden by clumps of trees or low hills, and immediately the thought was telegraphed along the column: Picts lived there—the headhunters—the painted devil worshipers —the sacrificers of children! The darkest of heathen!

And indeed Picts did live there. And sometimes they would come out of their homes and stare warily at the long column of Britons clattering by, neither extending a greeting nor brandishing weapons. Just staring. The man, the woman, the children staring, especially the children, with their dark, curious eyes boring intensely from beneath wild brows, as curious of the spectacle passing before them as the spectacle was curious of them. It seemed that a dark chasm, invisible and unbridgeable, separated the gauntlet of glaring eyes.

And dogs would rush out, Pictish dogs, the devil dogs barking ferociously, and then they too would stop at the invisible brink and stare.

And as the Britons passed, a shudder of gloom would again tremble through the column.

Some fleecy clouds scudded quickly by, some birds winged beneath them and disappeared to who knew where, but the wind was always there, whistling or moaning, adding to the pervading atmosphere. And the eyes of the men were busy over the hills, and the eyes of the women were mindful of their children and their men and every so often turned inward on themselves with furtive peeks, recalling the refuge of their homes.

And so it was as they traveled east along the narrow road that threaded treacherously through the land of Picts and Scots, with Mother Briton to the south beyond the Wall, falling ever away into an indefinite gray haze.

But as soon as they came to the road heading northwest from the old Roman fort at Netherby, the gloomy mood of the column suddenly lifted. Dagmere was first to sense it and indeed may have been the one to trigger it, for at last seeing the road that would take them straightway to their destination, she burst out, "Isn't this wonderful, Mama! We're almost there! Only two more days to go, and then—why, we'll be there!"

Helena looked up at her from the carpentum and smiled. She knew what she meant, and her own apprehensions quickly scurried away before her infectious effervescence. Indeed the good cheer bubbled like a contagion through the column, calming every troubled heart, and at some point a song burst forth from its midst:

> "Thou crimson stain of ruined estates,
> Plunged 'neath the blackest flood;
> The purest white made solely by,
> One drop of Ransom's Blood.
>
> "Away! Away! Let the soul sing away!
>
> "Break forth Thou Light in darkened breast,
> Command the gloom away;
> Rejoice ye lights on sullen wicks,
> For holy breaks the Day.
>
> "Away! Away! Let the soul sing away!
> Away! Away! Let the soul sing away!"

And upon completion of the song, happy chatter splashed along the column. Men talked of hunts and recited the secret catechisms of their trades, their eyes now appraising the hills with broader sweeps. The women returned to the ministrations of the nest, chatting the warm relational businesses of women, and the children rejoiced in the loosened reins and hurled happy squeals at the infinite vault of sky.

131

The road was easy to travel, ranging from forty to sixty feet in width, and gave the impression that civilization had indeed penetrated this wild land. The spaces were wide on either side, with moors and low ranks of hills sparsely dotted with trees that stretched from horizon to horizon.

Allyndaar sent out scouts to patrol along their flanks, forward and hinder, and the reports they brought back throughout the day were favorable: the people of the land seemed peaceful, most of them tucked away in their cottages before blazing hearths and mugs of hot mead. And everyone was heartened.

Allyndaar looked up at the sky. The sun was past its zenith and descending quickly to the west on this the shortest day of the year.

Bolstroem drew alongside the chieftain on a big, white draft horse. "Best be finding a place to camp for the night, Allyn—today being the solstice and all."

"You stole my thoughts, Bol," Allyndaar said, then he looked over at his son who was riding close by, talking with Gwyneth. "Terryll?"

"Yes, Papa?"

"You say you know of a place to camp along the road?"

"Yes. There's a big stand of yews with a little stream about two hours ahead. We can't miss it."

"Two hours, you say?"

"No more."

Allyndaar looked up at the sun again. "We ought to just make it before sundown." He looked at Terryll. "Son, I want you to ride on ahead and scout it out for us."

"I'll go with him, Allyn, to keep him company," the big black-smith offered.

"Good."

"Where are you sending Terryll that he needs company, Allyn?" It was Helena's voice calling out.

Allyndaar looked back at his wife. "He's just going up a piece to scout a camp for the night."

Helena's brow wrinkled. "Do you think it wise?" Her eyes darted anxiously over the terrain. "I mean—"

"We need a place to camp," Allyndaar said, sealing the matter. "Besides, it's a peaceful land, and Terryll knows it better than any."

Helena's eyes fixed apprehensively on her husband's. He looked away, smiling.

On a small rock-strewn knoll, about two hundred yards west of the column, six Pictish warriors watched curiously as two riders broke away from the long British cavalcade, one wearing a blue cloak and riding a

132

black horse and the other—a giant by the size of him—riding a big white one. Their eyes followed the two riders for a moment, then returned to the column. A succession of churlish grunts followed.

"What do you make of it, Taelbork?" asked a smallish man with a scraggy brown beard.

Taelbork's eyes flared with a reddish light. He was a larger man with a flat misshapen nose and thick leathery features. "Look at 'em, Clynne," he snarled, his eyes narrowing on the length of the column. "Bold as brass they come. Bold as brass."

"Dinna think it's a war party—there's women and bairns with 'em."

"I've got eyes too, mannie."

"We've got to tell Sarteham aboot this."

"Aye." Taelbork looked at him. "You and Ruppie hightail it and tell him what you've seen—eighty Britons headin' north, by rough count. Sixty of them well-fit fighting men."

"What are you going to do then?"

"We'll tend to these! Now, off with ye!"

Clynne and Ruppie dug their heels into their horses' flanks and galloped away to the north.

Taelbork and the others observed the Britons until they disappeared around a bend in the road. Then they reined their mounts off the knoll and, keeping out of sight, shadowed them for a while over several low hills and valleys, eyeing them with savage looks.

When the Britons at last turned into the stand of yews, the sun was dipping below the trees, and there was already a big fire going and fresh haunches of venison turning over it. Terryll and Bolstroem waved them in, and, with the sun throwing an exhibition of reds and yellows back over the bright turquoise gloaming, the Britons made camp, lighting several more fires, pitching tents and lean-tos with oiled tarps, and nestling cozily under a canopy of yew boughs.

Allyndaar posted sentries, and the horses were tended to. Then as the night herded shadows in from the fields and the stars winked on in their fashion, the men and women gathered around their bonfires, eating hearty meals, swapping stories, singing songs, and discussing their soon arrival in Loch na Huric. There was an air of jubilant expectancy in the camp.

Dagmere gazed up at the stars and listened to their stories. She sighed between each one.

After supper some of the men gathered in little knots to discuss the goings-on in the world or to listen to Aurelius's heated discussion on Pelagianism with a recent convert from Bowes. Others were laughing, others still were cleaning their swords and tending to their accoutrements, their lively faces flashing as they turned to the fires. And the women busied themselves with supper cleanup and sleeping arrangements, chattering noisily and herding children.

Helena and Dagmere rolled out their beds inside the carpentum. The girl, however, was moving with a listless indifference, as though distracted by a matter.

"Mama," she said, fluffing a pillow for the third time, "when did you first know that Papa was in love with you?"

Helena looked at her thoughtfully. "I don't know. I suppose it was when we first met." The woman smiled, looking back at that moment in her mind. "Yes, it was. I could see it in his eyes."

"His eyes?"

"Yes, the way your father looked at me like there was no one else in the world." Helena giggled. "Someone has said that the eyes are the windows of the soul. It's true! Your father was as proud and full of the thunder of his youth as they come—tough as iron on the outside. But I could see at once, the way he looked at me—looked into me with those piercing blue eyes of his—that there was a tenderness behind them, a tenderness that wanted only me and no one else."

Helena blushed as she came back over the years. She collected herself and said, "The eyes, Dagmere, you can always see love in the eyes."

Dagmere thought about that for a while, thought about the times she would glance up from her plate at supper and find Aeryck gazing at her—how it made her flush and look away. Was that love she saw in his eyes? she wondered. Or the times she caught him staring at her from the stables while she was working the horses. Or the surreptitious glances, the "eye tags" as they passed in the halls of the villa or in the fields. Was that love? Or was that something else—perhaps the shyness of youth? She wasn't sure.

"Don't worry, Dagmere," Helena said, taking her hand. "When the time comes, you'll know. I can't explain how you'll know, but you'll know. Trust me."

Dagmere let out a sigh. "Thank you, Mama."

She climbed out of the carpentum and breathed in the clean winter air, then, glancing across the camp, she found a pair of emerald green eyes glaring at her. Fiona. There was no love in those eyes, she thought, as the girl continued to stare. There was trouble in them.

Later in the evening, when the moon was up and filtering through the interlacing boughs, Terryll and Gwyneth huddled next to the dying-down fire, with their legs drawn up so that their chins rested on their knees and their eyes gazed into the other's. Then Terryll put his arm around her and drew her close, and she nuzzled affectionately in the warmth of his cloak.

Every so often she would pull out the ruby and dangle it against the fire and look dreamily into it, watching the rubescent lights dancing in its lustrous center. "It is beautiful," she kept saying. "Just beautiful."

And when they were sure that no one was watching they would steal kisses.

But someone was watching. Someone was always watching.

For not a stone's throw from the bonfires, a black man shape was crouched in the shadows and listening in on every word that was said. Only the flicker of firelight glinted now and again on his narrowed eye slits, marking his position and giving them a smoldering glaze. The man fingered the haft of his ax as he observed the goings-on in the camp, taking note of the number of warriors and gathering bits of information— information that could be used against them.

Then a sound to his right caught his attention, and just his eyes shifted to it. *Nothing of concern,* he thought. *Just two sentries meeting and passing away their watch with conversation.*

"Fools," he snarled under his breath. "I could kill you easily." Then just as silently as he had come, he stole away into the night.

Taelbork ran a big finger along his flat nose as he considered the news. Then he grunted. "Loch na Huric, is it?"

"Aye, that's what they were saying," the spies reported. "Something to do with a religious festival of some kind in four days—Christ's Mass, I think it was."

"A religious festival?" A thin smile curled along Taelbork's leathery mouth as he thought about it. And then he chortled wickedly. "Troth! Sarteham will be pleased to hear aboot this, now won't he? Come, there's no further need of us here!"

And the four Pictish warriors mounted and rode north under a bright, gibbous moon, their silhouettes black against the silvery hills.

135

16

THE WINTER SOLSTICE

Miles away in the southlands of Britain, inside the hill fort of Badons-ward, the northernmost stronghold of the Saxon army, black smoke curled from a single torch and disappeared into the nigritude of the ceiling, then drifted back in languid rolls and drew thin smoky layers, like diaphanous palls, over the gloomy inner chamber of the Wolf. An insufferable sullenness choked the air, a bitterly cold and wet charnel oppression beading up on the stone walls. For there was neither fire in the hearth to warm the room, nor had there been all winter, and indeed it seemed doubtful that a fire could be kindled in such a dank and smothering chill.

Olaf stood in the amber spill of light, a picture of proud devotion to duty, his bright warrior eyes twinkling, his body drawing what little warmth it could from the torch, if nothing more than to warm his mind by it. He had just finished briefing the underlord on his northern reconnaissance. He cleared his throat anxiously, and his breath hung before him in little clouds.

"That will be all, Commander," the voice rasped.

The big Viking jolted at the curt dismissal. The torch cast a frantic reel of shadows over his face, contorting his grim features into a mask of grotesque incredulity. He peered intently into the darkness at the darker wolfish shape that was sitting, perhaps crouching, in a large oaken chair just beyond the periphery of the torchlight, searching for the eyes that he might measure the intent behind the voice. But they were hidden now beneath the protruding snout of the wolfskin shroud, sheathed in darkness. The eyes were hidden—yes, but they were studying his every move, he knew.

Recovering, flexing his body with masculine deliberateness, he said, "I will take another patrol to scout the area around Killwyn Eden."

"It is not necessary," the voice said with a guttural ferocity. And from the shadows a gnarled hand penetrated the flickering aureole. The light flashed luridly on the skin and waved him off. "I have told you before that I have eyes that you know nothing of."

What eyes? Olaf wondered. Instinctively he continued to search the shadows for some telling feature, some definition of form or expression that might unveil an insight, but he found there only a vague and sinister outline of something altogether malevolent.

"But Horsa specifically commanded me to scout Killwyn Eden," the Viking said, resorting to the martial certainties of his mind. "It is the key to our campaign."

"And you've failed him, haven't you?" the Wolf said evenly.

The Norseman flinched, and his face colored with anger. Glowering, he lay his palm on his battle-ax, rubbing his thumb menacingly along the haft. Then he saw them—the eyes, floating it seemed in the shadows—two ocher orbs glinting dully beneath the wolfskin shroud, taking everything in, giving nothing away.

Norduk chortled throatily, then, edging pantherlike into the umbrage of the torchlight, he asked, "You would like to strike me, perhaps?"

There was a bestial timbre in the voice that sent a little shiver up the big Norseman's spine. For just a moment he wasn't sure if he were talking to a man or to some demon incarnate. He was repulsed by the thought and said nothing. The Viking eased his hand from the blade to his side, and the little clouds streamed from his nostrils at quicker intervals. The light played floridly over the folds of his skin and revealed dark lines of uncertainty.

Apparently gratified, the Saxon underlord moved stealthily back into the shadows, and only the faintest outline of the wolf's pointed ears and snout could be seen, and the grayed impression of the crimson wolf's head arched against his black jerkin. "We are old friends, are we not, Olaf?" he said, with sudden warmth in his voice.

"Yes, Wolf," the Norseman said warily. "We have fought many battles together."

"Indeed. You were always the right arm of my strength."

"Then you must know that I do not suffer failure—nor insults—well."

"Have I insulted you then?" the Wolf commiserated.

"You said that I have failed."

"You have not failed me, Commander. You have never failed me, and that is all that matters, isn't it?"

"Still—"

"You are under my command," Norduk said, cutting him off, "or have you forgotten?"

"No, my liege, I have not forgotten."

"Good. Then that will be all."

Olaf struck his chest sharply. "As you wish."

"Oh, and by the way, Commander . . ."

"Yes?"

"On the morrow we will talk again."

Olaf looked at him strangely, for there was a queerness in his voice. "As you wish, my liege," he said again, then stared into the darkness, waiting.

But there was no dismissal, nothing. There was only the faint guttural hissing that rattled forth from the wolfish silhouette at regular intervals. An unsettling pause followed, during which the atmosphere seemed to close in and around the Norseman's mind like a malignant growth, suffocating his thoughts, taking control of them with spidery tentacles. He felt himself sinking into some vague darkness that was taking shape around him.

And then he saw the yellow eyes that were moving toward him from the shadows, the dark wolfish features approaching animallike, taking on sudden light and contour. And Olaf could not move from the eyes. And more, he could not think, for he felt his mind sinking, the vague darkness becoming a black tunnel that was cold, bitterly cold, numbing his senses, his will.

The Wolf was before him now, inches from his face, chortling throatily, shifting stealthily around to his side, around to the broad, muscled back, his sinewy fingers now folding and unfolding in the locks of the Viking's golden mane, now tracing a nail along the purple scar that jagged down his taut cheek. And drawing around to his front, the Wolf, gazing steadily into the eyes of the big Norseman, said, "Tell me, Olaf, do you miss her—your Ingrid?"

Olaf's eyes started at the question, just a little flicker of light entering them, but the eyes of the Wolf would not release him. They held him captive, the feral yellow eyes floating before him, though the Norseman's thumb was again stroking the haft of his ax with some lingering force of his will.

What was the question? Do you miss her? *Yes, yes, I miss her,* he heard his mind respond. Then his eyes drifted over the underlord's dark visage, over the pale, ocher eyes gazing at him, the eyes setting him free now to drift over and beyond to the bright little cottage on the rocky coast of Föhr, where he last saw her waving to him, his beautiful Ingrid.

At once the image of her young face filled his mind, the beautiful Scandinavian features, her sparkling blue eyes gazing at him longingly, with the long blonde hair. Yes, the hair, full of the sweet sea smells and the tiny wildflowers of spring, cascading down and splashing over his face, and she was smiling at him, and laughing, kissing him as a young bride in love kisses her man. Beautiful Ingrid.

"Yes. Yes," he said, caught in the trance. There was an ache in his voice that came forth from a deep, aching place in his soul. "At night she visits my dreams. She is always there, waving at me, calling me to come to her."

"Ah, yes. I can see her now," the Wolf said, a satisfied smile curling on his lips. "Perhaps you could send for her. There is room here in the hill fort."

"Yes, I will send for her," Olaf repeated, the torchlight flickering over his glazed eyes.

"Good . . . good . . ."

Then Olaf looked at him suddenly, the vision bursting in a million lights. "No," he said, shuddering back to the yellow eyes still gazing at him. The Wolf stood now over by the window.

Olaf was stunned. How did he get over there? he wondered. His eyes darted to the empty chair in the shadows. *I'm tired, weary. Must have blacked out.* Suddenly he felt a shudder of horror go through him, a shudder of revulsion, as though his soul had somehow been laid bare to the world, then trampled upon and sullied.

"No," he repeated and, collecting himself, added, "Ingrid would be a distraction to me. I will send for her once I have crushed the last glimmer of hope in these Britons. Once I have taken Killwyn Eden. Any time before then, and she would think me weak."

"Is that why you hold your ax? To show that you are not weak?"

"My ax?" Olaf looked down at his right hand and was astonished to see it indeed clasping his battle-ax. Another shudder wracked his big frame as he slipped it back in the frog, and he wondered for a moment if he were going mad.

"No, you are not weak, Olaf. You are tired. You need rest." And as the Wolf peered at him, the feral light curled subtly off his eyes. "You are a good warrior," he said. "Odin is pleased with you, I'm sure." He paused, eyeing the Norseman now with an almost paternal affection, the thin smile lingering, becoming something else. "You will celebrate the solstice now with your men?"

Olaf was surprised with the underlord's familiarity. "Yes," he said, his mind still reeling from the recent sequence of events. Then chuckling, he added, "Though I'm sure their ale has taken them far beyond knowledge of the occasion."

The underlord smiled. "That is good. That is good. They are good men. Give them my regards, won't you?"

"I—I will, my liege."

"Good, good." Then, turning, he looked out the window and took

139

a deep breath, blowing it out hard. "It will be good when this is all over, will it not?"

"Yes, it will," Olaf said, just wanting to get out of the room.

"To the spring, then!" Norduk said, with a kind of triumphant flourish in his voice.

"To victory!"

"Yes, of course. To glorious victory," Norduk said, moving back to his chair in the shadows. "And one more thing, Commander."

"Yes?"

"We will also discuss the business of Killwyn Eden on the morrow. I will fill you in on any details lacking from your own reconnaissance, so that Horsa need not be any the wiser."

Olaf eyed the bestial silhouette curiously, not sure what he meant by the last phrase. "As you wish," he said, then he turned smartly on his heels and strode out of the chamber, sorting through the madness that had suddenly come over him.

The Wolf sat alone in the dark chamber for a moment, brooding. And then, "I hear you rattling over there, little man," he snarled. "You may come out now and treat me to your hideous form."

"I feast upon the flatteries of your most delicious tongue, my liege!" a voice answered from across the chamber. From a dark niche a little bulbous-headed man, nestled in a cocoon of woolen scarves, toddled out of the shadows. Boadix the druid. "An interesting little exercise that," he said, slapping warmth into his arms. "Brrrr . . . it's freezing in here!"

Ignoring him, Norduk said sullenly, "The Norseman has a strong will. I could not hold him long."

"No, but you will soon. Come the spring, when everything is made right, you will."

"And Horsa?"

"Him too."

Boadix halted in the aureole of light and began to hop back and forth on the balls of his feet. He resembled a large toad with bulging eyes, bright red varicose cheeks, and a russet nose that beetled out over the scarves like a lump of mud and blew cloud streamers. A rebellion of long white hair floated like gossamer down about his ears and brows. "A spring that won't be too soon in coming, if you ask me," he groused.

"I didn't."

"Why don't you light a fire in here? A yule fire, perhaps, to celebrate the solstice?" Boadix continued, blowing into his cupped hands. "I could catch my death."

The Wolf narrowed his eyes on the squat little druid. "You might at that."

As Boadix chuckled, the torchlight, catching the glass orb that was his left eye, flickered over its gleaming surface. "It was a figure of speech, of course."

"Of course." The underlord slumped over onto his left elbow, his thumb and forefinger supporting his chin. He peered intently at the druid from Gaul, scrutinizing his dwarfish features with contempt. "Now what of your trip to Londinium? It was profitable, I trust?"

The light twinkled in the druid's glass eye, as the other peered into the shadows at the wolfish silhouette. "Profitable? No, no, no, my liege!" he exclaimed. "I should say that 'profitable' is a poor choice of words. But to say that my trip was enlightening—then, oh, yes! Most assuredly!"

"Out with it!" Norduk snapped.

Boadix, bowing obsequiously, grinned impishly at the floor under the lip of his scarves. "The Britons believe, as we hoped they would, that Hengist's suit for peace is genuine. They have withdrawn their forces from the battle lines and are even now preparing to celebrate the *natalis solis invicti.*"

"The what?"

"Oh, how imprudent of me!" Boadix chuckled. "The 'birth of the unconquered sun,' of course—the Roman Saturnalia." Turning from the underlord, he began to make little leaps at the torch to warm his hands. "Though it . . . has decidedly . . . been conquered . . . in this . . . infernal land."

"You could always go back to Gaul."

The druid grunted as he collected his breath. "What—and have my other eye gouged out? No, I will celebrate the winter solstice here and pretend that the sun has not been conquered."

Suddenly the lone howl of a wolf sounded over the wintry skies, a malevolent voice, and the wind carried it into the chamber and troubled the torch.

Norduk looked out the window and listened intently. The moon shone big in the east now over the luminous folds of terrain and cast a pale arch over the flagstones in the chamber. There were two more howls, followed by a succession of staccatolike yelps and a single sustained cry. Then as the last echoes of the cry sank beneath the shrill winter winds, a malignant light crept beneath the wolfskin shroud.

"Good. That is good, my brothers," the Wolf said, stirring in his seat. And then there was only the wind, and the shadows flickering violently against the wall and floor.

Boadix adjusted the scarves around his pudgy neck, for the temperature had quickly dropped several precious degrees. "G-g-good news, my liege?" He shivered.

"The boy."

"Ah," the druid said, bouncing now. "And w-what of the white wolf?"

"Lukar too will die."

Boadix frowned, the white wisps of hair knitting on his brow. "He is c-c-unning, this Lukar," he said, now hopping and slapping his arms. "We m-m-must not underestimate his resourcefulness."

"You accuse me of underestimating him?"

The druid's single eye shot open. "No, no, no, no, no!" he squealed. "It's just that so far he has managed to elude the most venerable Gray Eye at every turn. Heh, heh, heh!"

A low growl rattled in the throat of the Wolf. "You play dangerously close to the line, little man," he said, rising menacingly from his chair and stepping from the shadows. "It would be a pleasure to see you cross it."

Boadix took a step backward and gulped. "W-without me, you will never inherit your k-k-kingdom," he stuttered. His single working eye blinked nervously. The other, its membranous lid stretched taut over the glass, merely twitched.

"It might be worth a kingdom to see your pathetic little heart beating in my hand."

"What is one p-p-pathetic heart, my liege, when the wise son of Cernunnos might hold t-ten thousands!" A violent shiver rippled over the little druid's body. Then he threw his hands over his face and waited to be torn to shreds.

Norduk grunted contemptuously as he angled over to the window. He looked to the north and fell deep into thought. After several minutes, he said, "We have easily four times his numbers. When the son of Caelryck leaves Whithorn, which he surely must sooner or later, we will simply rip out his throat and have done with him." He grunted again. "And any of Lukar's wolves that are foolish enough to protect him."

Boadix blinked warily through his stumpy fingers and, seemingly surmising that Norduk's anger was abated, breathed a sigh of relief. "Good, good!" He chuckled. "Who can stand against the armies of my lord, the most favored of the gods?"

Then he began to hop back and forth again. It seemed he was turning blue.

Norduk did not respond. He continued to gaze north in silence for several minutes, the wind rustling through the fur of the wolfskin shroud. Then, swinging his head to the south, he gazed steadily out upon the soft, feminine contours of the land. The moon shimmered lightly over them, the winter stars twinkled softly down, and his eyes turned inward.

"Tell me, druid, how is she?" he spoke at last. "Well, I trust?"

Boadix eyed Norduk's back questioningly, then brightened. "Rowena is well. Yes, she is very well," he said enthusiastically. "And more beautiful than ever I've seen her! But she—" he broke off and considered his words carefully "—she wonders why you have not come down to see her. She thinks that perhaps you—" He hesitated.

Norduk glanced sharply over his shoulder.

The druid started at the glare in the Wolf's eyes. "Well, it's nothing, really," he said, chuckling nervously. Then he quickly averted his eyes to the cut of his nails, which were decidedly purple. "You know how vain women can be. She thinks that you are avoiding her, because—imagine this!—because she is expecting Vortigern's child. Heh, heh, heh. 'Such silliness,' I told her. She actually feels you will not want her after the child is born." He chuckled again.

"It disgusts me," Norduk snarled, as he strode back into the shadows. Turning, he slumped heavily into the oak chair and groaned.

Boadix's eye flared open with alarm. "My liege! You haven't reconsidered your oath to her, have you? No, no, no, you cannot! If she thinks that you will betray her, then she will not give us the child!"

"It disgusts me to look upon her, knowing that the weakling Vortigern's child grows in her womb—that—" He broke off and looked away into the dark recesses of the chamber and brooded for several minutes. "Do not worry, little man!" he said, rousing from some dark reverie. "You will have your sacrifice at Stonehenge."

"You must see her then! You—" He quickly corrected himself. "Let me say it would be strongly advisable then, my liege. Rowena is not one to be trifled with. She holds her father in the palm of her hand, and the success of your plans in her womb. Without the sacrifice, Cernunnos will not—"

"Did I say that I would not see her?"

"No, no, you didn't," Boadix admitted.

"Then do not trouble me again over the matter."

"Perish the notion."

Norduk grunted. "On the morrow you will travel again to Londinium and meet with her. You will—"

"So soon, my liege? My ponies have scarce rested from their last journey."

"Whip them!" Norduk snarled.

"Consider them whipped."

"You will come to me before you leave, and I will present you with a gift for her. You will allay any fears she may have over the child. Instead, tell her with the utmost diplomacy that my concerns here have painfully detained me from coming to her. She will understand. Tell her that I will come to her in a week's time. Is that understood?"

"I shall be your willing surrogate, my liege." Boadix giggled. "Your devoted suitor. My tongue will be your most capable and wise ambassador, your ready scribe, dipped in the most delicious nectar of all the cherry blossoms in Saxony, to write the choicest love words over her heart . . . words that will flow from my lips like the reddest wine of Gaul, to bring the heady luster to her eyes, the rosy blush to her bosom and cheeks. Ah, yes! The beautiful Rowena will be powerless before the potency of my impassioned elocution. She will verily melt—"

There was a faint, low rattling hiss.

"As you wish, my liege." And the druid bowed with a little flourish.

"Leave me now, little man," the underlord growled, "unless you wish to climb the hill of Badonsward and celebrate the solstice with me. I am in good appetite."

The druid's eye flared just perceptibly as a raft of gruesome images flashed through his mind.

A wicked smile curled along the Wolf's lips. "I thought not," he chortled. "Go then and tend to your little animals and birds—peer around in their guts. Look closely now—you may find some tasty gizzard or bowel to celebrate the solstice."

Boadix shuddered, then he bowed curtly and toddled disgruntledly across the chamber, adjusting his scarves and muttering to himself.

As Norduk watched him leave, his smile twisted into a wretched scar. Then as he lowered his head into some dark and restless contemplation, his mind began to dredge through the bleak desolation of his soul. Minutes passed. The chamber grew darker, colder. It was as though the darkness were a living thing, a maleficent thing, and it came stealthily out of the black reaches of the night against the light of the torch, encircling it like a big cat, gathering itself for the leap, then pouncing.

Suddenly Norduk's head jerked up, and there was a faraway gleam in his eyes, the ocher-colored eyes looking out of the umbral womb into the bright tunnel of his mind.

And then she came to him.

The vision of Rowena came to him, gliding through the cerebral mists like the goddess Freya, her gown a luminescent sheerness floating behind her on the heady air. His jaw slackened, for she was more beautiful than all of the women in Britain, more than all of Saxony. And as she stretched forth her hand, beseeching him, her haunting gaze was fixed upon him, devil-eyes looking through him, exploring his wretched soul uninhibitedly, finding the secret nooks, the cryptic desires, luring him.

His soul writhed in the agony of her electric touch. His eyes rolled back in his head, the eyelids fluttering over the dark torture of his mind.

The moon, casting its pallid light over the British winterscape, found the little carpentum shoveling along the road beyond the hill fort, the team of hairy ponies chugging through the snow toward a secret place in the hills.

Boadix, wrapped in a mound of blankets, so that only his single living eye could be seen peering through an aperture in the folds, was mumbling to himself. "'Go here . . . go there . . . do this . . . do that,' he says. Hmmph! 'Go play with your bird entrails,' he says. Go ahead and mock the druid ways, my liege . . . you'll see . . . you'll see," he grumbled, then clucked his tongue. "Get on now, girls!" He whistled shrilly then snapped the reins.

The ponies startled and lurched forward, trotting a few yards. Then, snorting angrily, they settled quickly into their former sullen gaits, the clumps of snow kicking out from their small hooves.

"Gizzards, indeed! Hmph!" the druid grunted. Then he thought of a proverb. "The way of the ant may seem insignificant to the rook, whose belly aches for want of meat. But while the one works and eats his fill, the other eats his belly." He chuckled at the humor, imagining himself to be the dutiful ant, the faithful servant who, as he selflessly, tirelessly served the will of the gods, never complained, never questioned their caprices, always maintained a stiff upper lip in humble devotion.

His face was aglow with a happy reverie. He was the chosen one, the one through whom the gods would reinstate the ancient ways, the priesthood, and he would rule over it as the high priest. He would be honored for his great wisdom, men would travel from all around, even Gaul, and bow to him. Imagine that: big oafish men bowing down to him. He giggled at the thought.

Then his eye glanced heavenward, and he noted the stars, bright against the jet of winter, nodded with affirmation at their correct positions, then grouped them into their constellations. He marveled at their constancy, their immutable courses, then he took a deep breath and blew a great cloud through the woolen scarves.

"Ah!" he sighed. "Life will be good again."

Then his face screwed back into a miserable sourness. *Mock the ways of the druids, will you?* he thought. "I'll show *you* a bowel . . . the idea!"

He nearly jumped out of his seat when he heard a howl, a deep, agonizing wail keening over the hills, sounding like a wounded animal. His skin crawled with a legion of chills. Then listening, his single eye darting among the trees, he heard only the wind soughing through the branches, moaning lugubriously at times.

He was mindful to goad his ponies into a trot, and they seemed only too eager to comply.

_____17_____
AT LAST!

S o cold was the room that the plaster on the walls was wet with conden-
sation. Watching his breath hang in little puffs of cloud above him,
Aeryck wondered whether or not it was actually colder inside his room
above the tavern than outside. He decided that it was. Then, as he lay
beneath the warmth of his down comforter, he pondered the frigid sequence of events that he needed to negotiate before he could be seated
beside the blazing hearth downstairs eating a hot bowl of porridge. He let
out a moan, then rolled over for just another minute of delicious sleep.

An hour later and he was bent over the edge of his bed in some
dismal contemplation, shivering, and groaning the sleep out of his mind.
His head hung limp and heavy between his shoulders, and his long,
sandy hair was a tangled insubordination that he raked from time to time
into greater lawlessness. With his elbows firmly planted into his knees,
and his hands dangling where they willed between his legs, the boy
stared, blinking heavily at his two feet that presided over the floor like (as
Terryll had once called them) "two sides of beef." But with the illumination of morning light upon them, it was clear that Terryll had grossly
understated his simile.

Aeryck chuckled. Then, putting his toes through their morning
calisthenics like some drill sergeant, he wiggled them, stretched them,
bent and splayed them, noting the affluent community of dirt and grime
that had gathered in the fleshy parts between their ranks. They could
stand a good scrubbing, he thought, still drilling them, but he immediately shrugged it off. He'd take care of that maybe once he got home.

His stomach rumbled and barked. Then he shivered up from his
bed and stretched into a great yawn, punching at the ceiling with his fists
as he emitted a variety of bestial noises. Then, raking his nails along his
flanks, and belly, and shoulders, and back, and head, and points south,
as though he were currying a sackful of spiders that had been loosed over
his person, he trudged over to the wash stand accompanied by the *ka-*

slap . . . ka-slap . . . ka-slap sounds that his sides of beef made against the smooth planks of the floor.

Reaching the stand, he broke the thin crust of ice that had formed overnight in the basin, then dipped just his fingertips into the water and sprinkled a dewy ablution over his face. He shuddered and shook and blubbered, wiped himself vigorously with a towel, then proceeded to climb into his clothes that were every bit as cold as the water. Shivering and savoring a sour disposition, he went downstairs to break fast.

Still shivering (the hearth had been but a smoldering ruin) and in a degenerating mood, he returned to his room from a leftover meal of cold pork, some bread, and a bit of goat's cheese (the hot porridge having been cleaned out by the early risers).

He looked around and found a square of sunlight in the northwest corner that gave a suggestion of warmth. A cat was already curled in the middle of it, a skinny orange thing with splotches of haphazard colors spattered over it, that seemed oblivious or contemptuous of all the world save for the elusive square of warmth.

The boy crossed to the window and gazed out upon the Bay of Wigtown. The weather had been holding now for several days, though there had been a steady decline in the temperature. But this morning an ominous dark smear of clouds loomed over the southern horizon.

Aeryck shook his head and groaned—a storm front. Only four days were left until the eve of Christ's Mass, and if another storm were to hit now, there would be no way for Uncle Finn and the monks to cross the tempestuous Irish Sea and arrive in time. And waiting for the weather to clear, he would miss the celebration, he would miss Terryll and his family, he would miss Dagmere. Dagmere. Again he shook his head and groaned.

Huddling in Brynwald's woolen cloak, Aeryck sank into the light next to the cat and attempted to read the bit of Scripture that Brother Thomas had given him upon his departure. Perhaps it would lift his spirits.

He followed the cat and the patch of sun around the room for the better part of the morning, struggling with the words, with their meaning, until the golden oblong of light finally was spirited up the northeast wall and was gone. Somewhere along the way the cat had left too, and the boy was alone now with a mind full of questions. He fell asleep on the floor, wondering.

"Ho, a sail!" a man cried outside. "Ho, a sail on the horizon!"

Aeryck's head jerked up with a start, and immediately he was on his feet. Springing to the window, he scoured the horizon and at last caught a tiny, square silhouette climbing over the gray rim of the bay. He let out a howl and danced a little jig in the middle of his room.

147

Ten minutes later he was standing on the stone quay, panting and squinting beneath the cup of his hand into the distance. His heart pounded in his throat with anticipation, and his mind was a riot of thoughts. Happy thoughts. Warm and wonderful thoughts. Thoughts he had treasured and guarded and kept locked within his heart. Thoughts that were now storming the prison walls and inciting giggles in his throat.

His Uncle Finn was coming.

And then, inexplicably and without warning, he was overwhelmed with a rush of fear. His breath became labored, his mouth parched, and moisture collected in the palms of his hands, collected between the grimy ranks in his boots, and little rivulets of sweat trickled here and there along his flanks. He had a sudden and absurd urge to run and hide, and he even looked around for a bush. He was terrorized. Stagestruck.

His Uncle Finn was coming! His mother's brother, his own flesh and blood, his kin. *His* kin! And presently he was going to meet him! Since the day when he had watched his father walk away from him to die in battle against the Saxons, he had lived as an orphan without any hope of kinship. But now his Uncle Finn was coming. *His* Uncle Finn!

Hope called unto hope as Aeryck steadily watched the sea, steadily gazed upon the dark green horizon as the tiny black canvas square, in its slanting course and in the course of time, took the form of a ship, took the shapes of tiny men working its decks, took light from the sun and glinted off beam and spar, took hues from its spectrum and dabbed clothes and banners and sails with color, took the muted sounds of men's voices singing mariner's chanteys, took now the larger shapes of men working its decks, shining bright and colorful, took the luff of sail as the ship's bow turned two points off the quay to windward, took the splash of wave against the pitch and roll of its creaking hull, took the exultant cries of gulls on pointed wing as they swooped and hovered overhead and followed the ship to its safe harbor.

Hope called unto hope, and tears began to well in Aeryck's eyes from the overflow in his heart. His Uncle Finn was coming. He hoped.

"Can you see him yet, lad?" A voice spoke, as a big hand clasped the boy on his shoulder.

Aeryck spun around, startled. "Oh, hello, Brother Thomas," he said, recovering with an anxious giggle. "You scared me."

"I didnay mean to startle you, little brother," the monk returned, with a gregarious smile. "We come to meet the brothers from Eire and to see you off on your way."

Brother Milius, the tall loose-jointed man, and two other monks stood smiling behind Thomas and greeted the boy.

Aeryck smiled, then looked seaward.

"Ho! We beat the starm. 'Tis a blow comin' from the so'west!" a lanky sailor cried out to a gray-haired, portly man on the quay (a merchant of some kind), then tossed him a line. The sailor corkscrewed off a sheet line and arced over the gunwale onto the dock, then quickly tied off the bow to a cleat. The ship heaved and flexed and creaked upon the green swells, groaning as if it were some great beast of burden that was finally quit of the plow. And now, as it lay secure before its crib, the trapped waters along the quay lapped gently against its great sinewy flanks.

"Give 'er breathin' room now, lad," a stout, bearded man on board called out to the sailor. The storm'll give her a rum shimmy!"

"Aye, Captain."

"Did ye have a fair crossing?" the portly man on shore called out to the captain.

"We gave an Irish pirater a go of its sails off the Isle of Man! 'Twere a race I'll not soon forget!" the captain cried with a hearty laugh. "But we're here with our skins, and the sharks go a-wanting!"

"Pirates?"

"Aye, pirates. The black devils are everywhere up and doon the coasts it seems—like wolves they are, rapin' and killin' and plunderin' where they may!"

"There's one benefit the Romans took with them," the merchant on the quay said. "At least they kept the sea lanes safe for commerce."

"I'll take pirates any day!" the captain boomed, flavoring it with a dash of contempt. And then he barked at several sailors on board. "Batten down the hatches, lads—stow the sheets—secure that gear over there! Come! Come! The blow'll be upon us in a whirl! Look lively, lads! Look lively! Tie it off—there! Aye! *Och!* not there, you lunkerhead—over there! There! That's a lad."

Aeryck studied the bustling activities like a scholar, studied the bronzed and weathered faces of the sailors as they manhandled rope and canvas and teak, listened as they sang songs and shouted oaths to the love and hate of their work. It all seemed to him a kind of organized chaos. A thrilling chaos.

It was a merchant ship of Byzantine design with a full load of cargo, and the air was rife with the clamor of merchants anxiously awaiting their goods on shore. For a moment—just a moment—the boy was caught up in the business of the sea and shore and forgot why he was there.

Then the gangplank was lowered, and soon after a group of about twenty men began to descend to the dock, some waving, some calling out to men who were waiting on the quay, some to women and children who hurried through the crowd to greet them.

Aeryck studied each of the men as they disembarked, examining each face, looking for something (he knew not what), a certain look, a nod, perhaps a smile in his direction, anything that would single out his Uncle Finn from the others. Again his pulse began to race.

"Make way for the passengers!" the captain bellowed. "Out the way, you lot! Hear now! Stow that over there. There's a lad!"

"Toss me that line!" a man shouted.

"Lend me a hand over here," another replied.

"Gang a-way! Gang a-way!"

"And you must be Rebecca's boy!" a voice boomed over the crowd.

Startled, Aeryck turned and found himself staring at an older man, maybe a few inches taller than he.

"Er . . . yes. Yes, I am. Are you . . ."

"Gildas! Brother Gildas! And this is Brother Rupert," the man said, indicating a smaller man to his left. "We were told to look for you. Aeryck, isn't it?"

"Er . . . yes."

Gildas, a Briton, appraised the boy's features thoughtfully. "You favor your mother, Aeryck. Right off I picked your face out of the crowd. What do you think, Rupert? Does he not have the touch of the MacLlewalds about his eyes?"

Rupert nodded and smiled. "Aye, that he does. Though a sight handsomer, I'd say!"

"Where is my Uncle Finn?" Aeryck asked anxiously, as he looked beyond the two men.

Gildas took the boy by his shoulders and looked him square in the eyes. "Your Uncle Finn couldn't come, son, through no fault of his own."

"C-couldn't come?" the boy stammered.

"Aye, son. There's been a number of pirate raids of late. Bold as the sun they've been, coming inland to wreak havoc among the villages— put many to the torch."

"Been seen in the hills north of Armagh," Rupert put in. "Your Uncle Finn didn't think it wise to leave his kith and kin behind right now with the threat of violence hanging over the isle," Gildas added. The monk produced a thin leather pouch from his cloak and handed it to the boy. "Here, son," he said, obviously noting the sad look that had swept over Aeryck's face. "He sent this to you—a letter. I'm sure his words will tell it to you plainly. I'm sorry, Aeryck. I truly am."

Aeryck looked down at the pouch and stared blankly at it for several moments, then turned and stared at the sea for several more, his shoulders weighted beneath the crushing blow. And then all at once, his back straightened, and he brightened with a thought.

"Then he needs me," he said, addressing the horizon.

At that moment the captain of the ship strode by, and Aeryck took hold of his sleeve.

"Here, what?"

"When are you leaving for Eire?" the boy inquired earnestly. "I wish to book passage on the return voyage at once."

"*Och*, kipper, you may book passage whenever you like. But it'll be a tiresome wait till you collect," the captain said, fixing his eyes on the boy. "We'll not be setting sail again till the spring."

"The spring?"

"Aye, kipper, we're puttin' her up here for the winter," the captain said, at which point something caught his attention on board the ship.

"You—men—ho, there!" he cried, starting for the gangway. "Watch what you're doin' wi' that. *Och*, you'll drop it. Over there, you two, give 'em a hand now!"

Aeryck glanced at the sea, then ran after the captain and took hold of his sleeve again. "Are there any other ships that'll be putting into port—one, say, heading back to Eire?" he asked desperately.

"Troth, lad! What're you in such a hurry to meet the fishes for?" the captain replied, distracted. "There'll be nay ships comin' or goin' from this port . . . leastways not till the thaw! Only a fool or a lander'd try it this time of year." Then leaning over, he squinted at the boy and asked, "And which of the two might you be then?"

"Huh?"

"A fool, I see," the captain grunted, "and a deef one at that. Now, stand aside, kipper. I've got a cargo to unload. *Och!* Mind your step there!" he yelled as he ran up the gangplank. "You'll be spillin' the load into the drink!"

Aeryck followed him a few steps, then stopped. He looked down at the leather pouch in his hands, his features torn and wrought with despair. He turned and walked a little way from the monks, at which point his shoulders sank and he began to cry.

Brother Thomas came up to the boy and put his arm around his shoulder. "'Tis a shame to hear aboot your uncle, little brother," he said. "I ken how you were—"

But Aeryck wrenched himself away. He glared at the monk with a pained expression, hiked his shoulders, then ran up the hill toward the tavern of MacMaw.

Brother Thomas, Brother Gildas, and the other monks looked on, shaking their heads, until Aeryck disappeared into the building.

Then, as the monks made their way along the quay, Gildas turned to Thomas. "Patrick sends his greetings and blessings to you, as do the brothers in Armagh! Your work at Candida Casa is ever in their prayers."

"We thank you," Thomas returned. "Will you lodge with us at the monastery tonight?"

"Thank you, no," Gildas replied. "We'll stay with the boy in the tavern, if that's where he's lodging, then leave at first light. We can't delay a moment if we're to arrive in Loch na Huric for Christ's Mass."

"Then we will sup with you in the tavern," Thomas said. "There is much we would hear concerning Patrick. Is he well?"

"Yes, though he is advancing in age. He's not as spry as he once was."

"Better not let Paddy hear you say that." Rupert grinned. "He says he can still fight an army of demons on his knees—and better them."

The men laughed.

"He may have to," Thomas added without humor. "He may have to."

●

18
CAT AND MOUSE

Indeed, upon the first hint of light, Aeryck and the two monks took their leave of Whithorn and struck north along the coast road to the Fords of Wig, where they hoped to find lodging in the tavern of Pea Gants. The monks had purchased two horses and a donkey for their travel, and upon the latter—who was none the wiser for it—was secured the sum of their worldly possessions.

The day was cold; however it was bright and clear with only a few fleecy clouds floating overhead toward some distant gathering of the same. The storm front that had come charging the coast the day before like an unleashed mongrel, thundering and threatening violence, had curiously pulled up before reaching shore, barked a few times, then moved up the western seaboard to continue its rounds.

Throughout the day Aeryck kept his eyes peeled for the wolf pack that had given him escort several days earlier, but he saw no sign of them. However, he was never without the feeling that they were being watched. Sullie must have sensed it too, for her ears switched back and forth constantly, and the horses conversed regularly with nervous whinnies and snorts.

The monks, on the other hand, were quiet for the most part, conversing between themselves in low tones about the weather, or the Scottish countryside (how it varied from Eire), or matters concerning their mission in Loch na Huric.

They had tried to engage the affections of the boy and lighten his heart with stories of his Uncle Finn and of other members of the MacLlewald clan. But these only served to heighten a growing despondency in his heart, and in the course of time his disposition toward them became more and more reserved, if not cold. It wasn't long before he distanced himself from them altogether and rode about fifty feet or so ahead, "to act as scout," he said, "for there are many dangers afoot."

However his scouting proved fruitless, as the day was without incident. And so they arrived at Pea Gants's a little before sundown and were there refreshed with a succulent joint of lamb, boiled potatoes, and cabbage.

The place was lively, and the mariners were anxious to hear the news from Ireland. Many had heard of the recent spate of pirate raids there and were concerned how it might affect their trade. The monks obliged them with a detailed account, as well as a rehearsal of their own escape from a pirater the day before. And upon the completion of their tale a tumultuous row arose from the tavern.

The lanky MacTibber was in fine spirit and voice, and he led the Scottish mariners in a heroic assault against the Irish pirates, if only from the ale-washed decks of the tavern. The men cheered and howled before the winds of inebriation. Some wanted to set sail at once in pursuit of the sea scourges, others pounded flagons for more wind. And it wasn't long, as the bravado soared to billowing heights, that the pirates were forgotten and the men merely howled.

But Aeryck was sullen. He sat alone in the shadows off to one side of the hearth with his mind adrift on a dark sea, not the least interested in the goings-on in the tavern. He had pulled out the leather pouch and was rereading the letter from his Uncle Finn for the dozenth time.

The notable points were: the MacLlewald clan was full of joy that he was alive . . . God be praised for His wonderful mercy . . . they could hardly believe such news and looked forward to seeing him . . . Finn was terribly sorry that he could not make the voyage now . . . villainy afoot in their land . . . it was necessary for him to stay behind . . . perhaps he could come in the spring, or perhaps Aeryck could visit them in Eire. Whichever, Finn knew that he would understand.

The boy didn't. He folded the letter with a sigh.

Silvie made several amorous advances while he was reading the letter, ranging from a subtle sashaying by his table, with eyes fluttering, to a blatant whisper in his ear. But her feminine arsenal had no effect upon the boy whatsoever, and after the latter salvo was fired he told her to leave him alone. The glare in his eyes told her that he meant it. The girl threw her head back haughtily and flounced away from his table to work the other side of the tavern.

He gazed down at the letter.

Presently Pea approached him, wiping his hands penitently with his waist towel. "Well, mannie," he said with a gleam in his eyes. "Might I have a word in private with you?"

"Uh . . . sure." Aeryck grunted, glancing sourly at him. He put away the letter in the pouch.

Pea Gants took a seat opposite the boy and advanced conspiratorily across the table.

Aeryck recoiled an equal distance, now regretting his consent. "I have news which concerns a friend of yours, lad," the taverner whispered.

"A friend of mine?"

"By the oaks. I've news pertaining to a certain dreg-licker who's had a taste of your blade."

Aeryck's eyes started. "Spang?" And he leaned forward to reclaim his ground. "Tell me."

"Aye—" Pea smiled "—that I will." His eyes quickly ferreted out the shadowy recesses in the room, then settled on the boy. "Seems this Spang fellow has been seen in the vicinity of Glenlochar."

"Glenlochar? When?"

"Two days past."

"But Oswald—"

"Would've run him off?" Pea interrupted. "Aye, and that he did. Chased him north into the hills—to the moors likely. He's a good man, that Oswald, a truer friend Brynwald never had. Troth but there's more, laddie. I'm told this mongrel's gathered quite a few more curs in his pack of hellions—been scraping up every murdering cutpurse north of the Wall, it seems. They're scheming something for old Bryn, there's nay doubt of it."

"I should have killed him," Aeryck said flatly. "I should have killed him when I had the chance."

"Aye, but you didnay, and now you've let the deffil on the loose." Pea Gants stood up and took hold of his towel. "Best be mindful as you make your way through them parts, mannie," he said, giving his hands a good scrubbing. "Like as not there's trouble layin' for you."

"But Spang thinks I'm dead."

"Aye, perhaps," Pea admitted. "Just the same, I'd keep me eyes peeled off the quarter, you can believe it. I wouldnay trust your thinking on the matter, laddie, not when it concerns the likes of that scum."

Aeryck looked hard at the man. The information had drawn him from his bilious disposition. However, by the murderous scowl that set over his brow, it was clear that it was none for the better.

Pea stood up and made his way to the kitchen.

The boy thought about the information for a minute, staring darkly at the place in the room where he and Spang had fought. He compressed his lips with a grunt. Then, looking up with a thought, he glanced across the room and caught the eyes of a man who had apparently been staring at him. Meeting Aeryck's eyes, the man quickly looked away.

Aeryck considered him for a moment. Was he one of Spang's men? Had he seen him in here the other night? Or was his imagination just getting loose? He couldn't be sure. Then another fellow approached the man, said something to him, and the two of them laughed.

They seemed harmless enough, Aeryck thought. Then he peered skeptically about the room and noticed a few heads turn at the approach of his eyes. His head took a little jolt. Then as he looked further, several pairs of eyes dipped out of his line of sight the moment his gaze swept past, as though they'd been caught in a stare.

Aeryck tensed warily. Instinctively his fingers edged near the hilt of his sword. Suddenly he felt as though everyone in the tavern was watching him. His eyes darted here and there, digging about in the dark recesses for a telling glint of eyes, a clandestine aside, a murderous sneer or chuckle. Everywhere he beheld narrowed eyes winking in and out of dark huddles as they plotted his death. The skin curled along his neck, seeing it now coming to light—the dark conspiracy—taking the serpent's form and bearing its fangs. There was a continual hissing in his ears.

Then he felt the stealthy approach of someone behind him. Screwing out of his chair, the boy drew his sword and faced the assassin with a violent scowl. His eyes were wild.

"Easy, lad, easy," the man said, waving the boy down with his hands. "It is only I, Brother Gildas."

"What?" Aeryck didn't hear him at first. His mind struggled to comprehend.

"Has the journey been unsettling to you, lad?" Gildas said, somewhat at a loss for words. "Perhaps the news of your uncle . . ."

Then Aeryck saw that it was the two monks. "Er . . . no, that's not it," he said, his brow clearing of its violence. "I just thought you were somebody else is all."

The monks looked at one another. "We'd best turn in early if we plan to get an early start, don't you think?" Brother Gildas asked.

Aeryck glanced quickly around the tavern, for it seemed a hush had fallen over the place. And now he saw that it was no longer his imagination—everyone was indeed looking at him.

"Yes, yes," the boy said, sheathing his sword, "I think we'd better turn in."

The next day Aeryck and the two monks left early, heading due east now for Glenlochar, where they would end the second leg of their journey in the home of Oswald, the chieftain there. The sky had clouded some, complementing Aeryck's dark mood. Icy winds shrilled over the wolds. The temperature had dropped to a bitter cold.

Again the monks tried to engage Aeryck in conversation, but the boy remained quiet and aloof, answering their queries with curt monosyllables. There was much on his mind: Uncle Finn, the advent of Christ's Mass, Terryll and his family, Dagmere. And of course Spang.

His eyes skirred the hills and stands of trees and rock formations and any other point of terrain that might conceal an ambush, that might screen the treachery of an assassin's arrow. If Spang and his men were out there somewhere, waiting for him in hiding, he would be ready. *Let them come*, he thought, daring the countryside. *Let them come*. And then he looked quickly over his shoulder.

Like the day before, he had the unshakable feeling that they were being watched. They were.

The wolves came gliding out of a blind of woods like specters, materializing it seemed out of thin air, their dark, lupine shapes hunched in feral posture, with scores of yellow eyes glinting dully and fixed upon the three humans and their animals.

Gasps—or prayers—winged from the mouths of the two monks, and their horses whickered loudly and tossed their manes. The donkey brayed and froze in his tracks, his eyes white with terror.

But when Aeryck caught sight of the white wolf taking the lead, he loosened his grasp on his hilt and took an easy breath. Sullie sensed also that these wolves meant them no harm. She reproved those behind her with snorts and cocked her head proudly.

"What should we do?" Gildas wanted to know. "Should we run?"

"No," Aeryck replied. Then he quickly explained to the monks a brief history of these wolves, how strangely they had followed him on his journey south and protected him from the attack of another wolf pack.

"Why would they do that?" Rupert asked incredulously.

But Aeryck merely shrugged his shoulders. "Some wolves are just friendlier than others."

However his explanation appeared to do little to assuage the monks' anxiety. After all, there were seventy or more wolves in the pack they saw, eyeing them curiously. The monks stared at one another doubtfully.

The wolves kept a distance of about a hundred feet, maintaining an easy trot as they had before, but it wasn't long before Aeryck noticed a sudden change in their demeanor. Abruptly they became distracted, agitated, as though some dreadful thing had suddenly burst upon them, rifling through their midst with a hidden knowledge.

Four wolves immediately broke away from the pack, two heading northeast, the other two heading northwest. *Scouts*, Aeryck guessed. But why? What was out there? His eyes swept the hard reaches of the terrain, dug about in the shadowy folds where treachery might lurk. Nothing. Nothing he could see. Still, he was learning not to trust his eyes.

The pack traveled along the coast for a few miles, each pair of eyes keen and wary, driven by instinct or by an intelligence unknown to men.

157

Presently the scouts returned with some news that caused a sensation among the other wolves. They were definitely agitated now.

The white wolf—Lukar—began to pace up and down the line, a growl rattling in his throat, the hair along his nape standing on end. The wolves moved immediately to within fifty feet of the humans and maintained the distance.

Sullie's ears began to work furiously. A strange scent was on the wind, an evil scent hissing through the trees. Her head began to bob and wag, and, whickering, she cast a wild eye back at Aeryck.

"Easy, girl, easy," he said, patting her neck. But he sensed it too. Death was near.

Then a howl cut through the broken slate of sky from a distance. Immediately the wolves perked their heads and scanned the low hills from whence it came. There was an evil quality to the voice that sent a legion of shivers along the boy's spine and his hand to the hilt of his sword. As if on cue the wolf pack now moved to within twenty feet of the humans and quickened their stride. The horses kept pace, no longer afraid of the wolves. They were afraid of what was over the hills beyond their sight, the thing that smelled of death. Nervous snorts blasted the air.

There was another howl, closer now it seemed. And then another —yes, closer. Suddenly the air was charged with some electrical current that galvanized the line. Eyes burned intensely, ears twitched, hair bristled, senses honed to pristine acuity. The humans prayed silently.

Two more wolves were dispatched in the direction of the howls. Another howl pierced the air just ahead, and moments later another answered from a place not far behind.

"Over there, look!" Gildas said, pointing.

On a low ridge to the north a group of twenty or so wolves stared down at them menacingly.

The white wolf growled just audibly. He looked behind him, then, halting, threw his head back into a violent arch and let out a terrible cry, one that carried far into the hills and came back on the wind a muted echo.

Aeryck knew nothing of the language of wolves, but he knew at once that there was nothing conciliatory in the cry. Indeed, it seemed a challenge. It seemed to him a majestic voice.

The wolves on the ridge continued to look on silently like stones, like treacherous black stones stabbing out from the earth, and for several moments there was only the hiss of wind over the snow as it whipped icy needles into the air. And then the silence was broken.

"There's more of them!" Rupert called out. "My God, have mercy!"

Looking swiftly back on their trail, Aeryck caught sight of what appeared to be fifty wolves, cutting against the clouding sky. Immediately a prayer escaped his lips. Sullie let out a terrified whinny, as did the other horses. "Are those friendly wolves?" Gildas asked.

"I don't think so," Aeryck replied. "No, I don't think so. I think they mean to do us harm."

The monks shuddered. Prayers winged off in harried flights.

The wolves alongside picked up the pace, and the horses broke into an easy lope. The wolves on the ridge mirrored their movements. Those that followed hinder maintained their distance.

Ahead, about a mile or so, a dark sawtooth blade ripped a jagged tear across the earth and sky. Aeryck knew the place well, for it was the very tract of woods where he had been ambushed by wolves on his southward journey, a seeming lifetime ago. Before the margin of the trees was a line of tiny, black shapes that stretched from the road to the ridge, a distance of about a quarter mile. The shapes were moving slowly toward them like a large net drawing closed around the white wolf and his companions.

Aeryck's eyes glared open, and he reined Sullie to a halt. The monks did likewise, and the three gathered in a little terrified clot.

"There must be a hundred of them—or better!" Rupert gasped.

"Closer to two hundred," Aeryck said. Then he noticed more coming up from behind.

"I take it that they're not friendly either," Gildas said.

Aeryck did not reply. His mind was working furiously.

They were surrounded on three sides by a rough count of two hundred or more wolves, putting the odds against them at better than three-to-one. And with the sheer cliffs on their right flank, falling an easy hundred feet to the jagged rocks and coast below, escape was not possible in that direction.

Lukar's wolves stopped and formed a semicircle around the humans and faced outward to the hills. The white one paced out in front of the others, eyeing the long, dark line of wolves before them, waiting, it seemed, for some sinister revelation. An eerie silence pervaded the air. A deathly stillness descended like a smothering tarpaulin over the snowy tract of ground, such stillness and quiet the ilk of which weighs the courage of men before great battles of spirit and flesh.

A biting wind came keening over the ridge, and the long, black line of wolves began to close on Lukar's position, advancing slowly, predatorlike, until they closed to within a few hundred feet and stopped. Those wolves on the flanks also closed to a similar distance. The line of wolves lowered onto their haunches and stared intently at the boy.

Aeryck felt their eyes burning into his brain, felt some vague wickedness fingering around his ears.

Presently a large red wolf, flanked by two others, stepped ahead of the line and made their way to the midpoint between the two forces, then lowered to their haunches and waited.

Lukar and a monstrous brute named Three Wolves padded out to engage them on the gleaming slopes. Drawing near, Lukar's eyes moved to the wolf on Gray Eye's left. It was Kill Bear, a hothead, he knew; a fierce warrior in battle, he knew also, but predictable. Hotheads always are.

Then glancing to Gray Eye's right, his eyes started just noticeably. Sneering at him from the shadow of his superior was a dark wolf with gray-and-white splotches—a wolf that was once a loyal member of his pack, was once a good hunter, was now a traitor. It was Wumok.

The white wolf snarled at him fiercely.

Wumok shied, drawing a narrow look from Gray Eye.

Then Gray Eye stepped forward, and Lukar rose to meet him. The two wolves began to circle one another warily, each eyeing the other with animal contempt, each baring his fangs threateningly, each with hackles up and head lowered. Each canine mind drew upon the ancient dictates of the wolf pack, heard the drummings of a primordial voice that sounded the arcane instincts of his kind, moving through him to either fight or flight. Neither wolf seemed disposed to the latter.

An interlude of tension passed during which each tested the other's dominance—the alpha of the pack. Gray Eye, the larger of the two, effused with the confidence of his size and experience and the greater strength of his pack, growled tauntingly, stabbing the space between them with short jabs of his forepaws, daring Lukar to leap.

But Lukar was too cunning to fall for that. Though he was slighter of stature and weight than Gray Eye, he was more compact of build and quick like no other. His muscles and sinews were taut and coiled, waiting for the right moment, gathering to release a lightning-quick strike. The circling continued, the two wolves looking for the glint of weakness in the other's eyes.

"What are they doing?" Gildas asked, as he observed the strange goings-on fifty yards away.

"Are they going to attack?" Rupert added anxiously.

"Ever see a cat play with a mouse before it kills it?" Aeryck asked.

"A cat? I see," Rupert remarked, suddenly comprehending. "And we are the mice then?"

"No," Aeryck said, his eyes burning with a sudden vision. "I am." He turned to the monks with a fierce glare. "You must flee from here as fast as your horses will carry you," he commanded them. "Glenlochar is only another ten miles or so. Hasten now with Godspeed! Fly and do not look back!"

Bewildered, Gildas asked, "What about you, son? Are you not coming?"

"Just fly!" Aeryck growled. "If you stay here, you will die, and I'll not suffer another dead monk on my account!"

Then he slapped the rumps of their horses with his reins, and the monks took off down the road in a dead run.

Aeryck wheeled about on Sullie, "This is the only way, girl!" he cried. Then digging his heels into her flanks, he broke out of the semi-circle of wolves and charged up the hill at the others, brandishing his sword. "High! High!" he yelled wildly. "We'll give them a day of it!"

19
THE TERRIBLE FLIGHT

The wolves of both packs reeled in wonder. Neither had expected such a move, and those along the slope even jumped aside out of reflex to allow the thrusting bulk of the big, gray draft horse to thunder by. Recoiling, they merely stared at them.

A moment of stunned silence buzzed over the hillside. No movement could be detected but the terrible flight of the boy and his big horse along the hillside, mounting the ridge with great strides.

Lukar had the presence of mind to lunge at Gray Eye during this distraction, but Kill Bear quickly interposed himself between them. It was a mistake. Hotheads are predictable, and Lukar had anticipated the move. Having feinted to his left at Gray Eye, drawing Kill Bear's too-eager head to a low extension, he pulled up short and wheeled upon the other's exposed nape with a lightning thrust of his fangs. Kill Bear threw his head back and screamed as the bite of death sunk deep into his flesh and took hold of his life, wrenching it violently from him.

Looking up from his kill, Lukar was startled to see Gray Eye storming the ridge with a third of his pack. Three Wolves drew up next to the white one, his jowls wet with the blood of Wumok, and the two of them set themselves to meet the oncoming rush of Gray Eye's wolves.

There was a hellish clash as the two walls of snarling bone and muscle collided upon the open field. The appalling clamor rose from that place and pierced far into the neighboring wolds and valleys, the sound of battle then drifting off into the moors and far reaches of the highlands where it was pummeled by the fierce winds.

Gildas and Rupert, apparently abandoned as inconsequential to the wolves, cast astonished looks at the ridge crest in time to see Aeryck astride the big, gray draft horse, pitched forward with his cloak a-wing and his legs flapping, and a hillside of spirited black-and-gray shapes fast converging on his hapless position. Each man's heart sank in despair, and from each throat there flowed a plaintive cry to its Creator on behalf of the doomed boy and his horse.

Aeryck looked over his shoulder at the windswept crown of the ridge, and a moment later it fairly swarmed with the rushing black spectacle of wolves. He spurred Sullie with a desperate kick of her flanks.

Ahead lay open ground, white on white for miles of rolling emptiness, the boy's only hope of outdistancing the shorter-legged carnivores. He glanced off to the right and saw the forest below him, sprawled darkly over the broad reach of the valley bending through the hills.

A shudder went through him as he remembered how the wolves had jumped him there. *Got to keep clear of the trees*, he thought.

The snow was deeper in the forest, swept into heavy drifts by the dark, wet trunks and the wind. They were treacherous snowdrifts that concealed any number of dangers beneath their beautiful white powder— hidden rocks, logs, sudden trenches—any one of which could reach up from the white deception and hurl the boy to the ground. Death was in there, he knew, bidding him to come. *Got to keep clear of the trees*, his mind chanted. *Got to keep clear of the trees. Got to keep* . . .

Meanwhile Lukar and his wolves fought valiantly against a greater foe. It was a grisly exhibition. For a battle wherein tooth and claw are employed—the snarling guttural yelps, the flashing, stabbing, ripping fangs and the attendant death screams—created such a mind-numbing furor that it beggared imagination. The fighting was as fierce and vehement as it was horrible and unnatural, and in every quarter acts of valor and cowardice, reticence and impulse—like those of men in the examinations of battle—were legion. And the carnage was soon great upon the once gleaming white field.

Lukar, realizing that there was no hope for his inferior forces against the superior foe, howled over the din of battle, then took off with about thirty wolves. Three Wolves and the rest of his pack fought on bravely against redoubtable odds, knowing full well their end; also knowing, however, that their valiant stand would provide Lukar with an avenue of escape.

Sullie was weakening. Aeryck could feel it in her stride. There rumored along her wet and foam-flecked sides the first epithets of death. No longer could he feel the massive long thrust of her muscles hammering against bone and rock. No longer could he hear the rhythmic, snorting bellows that fired a powerful engine, a wondrous invention that impelled her great bulk through the snow. Now he felt the tenuous strike of her hooves against the earth, a faltering here and there of her gait, her

163

wind coming in shallow gasps, in earnest reaches. Were it not for the strength of her courageous heart and love for the boy, she would have long since quit the struggle.

"God, have mercy," Aeryck prayed desperately. "Have mercy . . . have mercy . . . have mercy . . ." And though it pained him to do so, he dug his heels into Sullie's smoldering flanks, and immediately a hidden fire leaped into her legs.

But the wolves pursued them like tireless devils. They were gaining now, drawing closer and closer. And closing to within striking distance, they drew alongside Sullie's left flank, forcing her to veer southward into the clawing arms of the forest, into the deeper snow and the drifts awaiting them to the right. Aeryck knew then that his time had come.

There was a flush of birds as the forest first rushed them, then snatched them into its bowery embrace. The big gray slowed now and then to avoid the sundry obstacles presented, lurched here and there over and around the hidden treacheries, and the lighter, more nimble wolves gained advantage in their pursuit.

A wild blur of colors and fantastic shapes flashed by Aeryck's peripheral vision. He suddenly felt as though he were riding atop a rolling cloud in supreme solitude, so dreamlike was the effect of the rushing-by trees and the keening wind screaming through the canopy of frozen limbs.

Adding to the effect were the adrenaline surges careering through his veins that seemed to slow time to a crawl, and the muffled thundering of hooves and pads that drummed him senseless made time irrelevant. And then there was the wild hiss of branches all about him, some snatching at his cloak and hair with their bony fingers, some stabbing and swiping at him, tearing mercilessly at his flesh. He ducked and lurched to avoid the limbs, but time and again they found him. There was an intelligence in the trees, it seemed, a concerted mind and will to swat him to the wolves.

And the wolves were rushing alongside them now, drawing nearer and nearer with their snapping jaws, the deadly jaws lined with gleaming teeth and lolling with purple tongues. And above the slavering snouts were the hateful yellow eyes that seemed almost surreal in their thrusting leaps. And the whole of the rush was like an illusion, a fantasy of wolves bounding along quiet, floating, timeless arcs, looking up at him—and the boy glancing down at the yellow eyes, while ducking a limb swipe . . . his mind in a kind of dreamy peace amid the all-encompassing terror . . . and the wolves drawing nearer and nearer . . . their teeth clicking . . . snapping . . . eyes burning . . . then everything quieting to only the hissing of wind through the trees . . . and the thrusting, the thrusting, and . . .

164

Then they were upon them. Sullie screamed as a big wolf sank its yellow fangs deep into her hind leg. Immediately her great, heavy buttocks dipped and her hind leg cocked and struck out against the wolf with a sharp crack of her hoof, and the wolf reeled away. And then there was another wolf, and another.

Aeryck began to furiously work both flanks with his sword like one hacking a snarl of weeds, aiming at snapping heads, at anything that moved. Howls pierced the intertwining canopy as he occasionally made contact with bone and tissue. Still the wolves came rushing, their barks creating a solid web of noise that closed in around the boy's mind.

As he reined Sullie away from a jutting snag, four wolves leaped from the blinds of tree trunks upon the big gray and pulled her down, and the boy was hurled from the saddle. He hit the ground with a jolt and came rolling up with sword in hand, his eyes glaring wide in terror at the rushing black shapes through the trees.

A wolf lunged at him but was met with the full length of his sword. Retrieving his blade, he set himself squarely in time to face another in mid-leap. He felt the violent shudder go through his arms as his blade struck deep, then, whirling about, he fixed his gaze on another wolf as it came charging through a tangle of shrubs. He lowered his shoulders, waited for it, then came up slicing a sharp, crimson streak through the air, felt the punch, and the wolf crumpled headlong into the snow.

Then the boy turned and faced another wolf, and then another, his sword a single extension of his mind, hacking and thrusting, adroitly finding the vital places as he worked toward a higher elevation.

But there were too many of them. They kept coming. Crowding into the wooded aisles, they came a relentless approach. And he began to feel in his tiring arms the sentence of death.

He saw in a frantic glimpse Sullie struggling to her feet with wolves clinging to every part of her body. Her nostrils were flaring with unpent anger and fear. Shaking the attackers free of her with a desperate shudder, she hurled herself at those pressing the flagging boy, raining death upon the unwary wolves from behind with iron hooves. Enraged, the brutes turned upon the mare as one beast, giving the boy a brief respite and a terrible vision, for in a twinkling she was down again.

"No!" Aeryck cried, as he ran toward the mare.

An imperious call to battle sounded in his breast, and the boy, his thoughts affixed on the stricken form of Sullie before him, fought like a wildcat to get to her. He struck savagely at some vague wall of yellow eyes encompassing him. A kind of madness burned upon his ruddy brow, one kindled by fervent zeal and a dauntless reproach of death. The sword of Caelryck fell time and again with hammerlike blows, time and again meting out deadly wounds to those that chanced its edge. But the boy was withheld from the big gray by the wolves' sheer numbers, and he was forced back.

Quickly he scrambled onto a large flat rock that rose about two feet off the ground before a sharp acclivity of trees, and, felling a lunging wolf with a backhand swipe of his blade, he positioned himself for his final stand. His jaw was set with a determined grimness, his limbs cocked and waiting for the next trigger release of his brain. He stood atop the rock gasping, his back arched, chest heaving, with silvery blasts of air streaming from his torn mouth. His face was a contortion of dark lines.

Shifting his weight from foot to foot, he wagged the tip of his sword in their faces. "Come on then, come on," he snarled tauntingly. "You want more of this? Here it is then!"

The wolves came slowly now, deliberately, circling the rock to flank him, with the confidence of knowing that they had won their prize.

There was no need for a rush now. They had him. The whelp stood before them, helpless but for that long, shiny claw in his hand. But no matter, they had many claws. And so they drew nearer. And nearer. The cat upon the mouse.

Gray Eye preceded the others, his arrogant eyes narrowing on the boy with a malignancy kindled by some infernal source. His animal brain reduced the human to a helpless prey—a whelp is all, little more than a pathetic deer. A growl rattled wickedly in his throat. Then the large red wolf drew to within ten feet of the rock and gathered himself to leap.

Aeryck set his feet squarely.

Suddenly the ground trembled around the boy, and at once a great shadow fell over him from behind, startling him. Thinking the wolves had flanked him, he reeled, and immediately the forest resounded with a deafening roar, the concussion of which nearly bowled him over.

His eyes widened with horror, for it seemed a massive black wall was crashing through the trees and bearing down on him—a wall with burning eyes and snapping jowls, and angry snarls jerking in its throat.

Aeryck hit the rock immediately before the massive shape leaped over him, roaring, drawing with it a rush of wind, and, turning, he watched incredulously as the monster plunged headlong into the advancing press of wolves. Startled, the brutes fell back several feet and gaped spellbound at the giant bear.

"Hauwka!" the boy cried, as he scrambled to his feet.

Gray Eye leaped out of the bear's path, startled that the great creature was still alive.

But Hauwka was very much alive. And with the advantage of surprise in his favor he tore an indiscriminate wedge into the midst of the wolves, effecting great ruin among them. He was berserk with rage, a relentless killing behemoth that came wheeling about and charging into the wolves' crumbling flanks on either side of the wedge with devastating fury.

Many of the wolves fled, overwhelmed as they were by the sudden terror, their numbers disintegrating into a panicked rout. The woods were rife with the screams of dying wolves that lay in the terrible wake of the giant bear. Of the wolves too terrified to flee, many were crushed beneath Hauwka's gargantuan weight; others were killed or maimed by his powerful blows or by the lightning rakes of two-inch claws that ripped mercilessly through their flesh.

It was as though a mighty oak tree had taken fiery breath, sprouted legs, then gone on a rampage, felling puny saplings. His terrible roaring, like peals of thunder, stunned the senses of those in the vicinity.

The wolves scattered a short distance with their tails tucked neatly between their legs, some pausing tentatively to cast astonished looks over their shoulders, others yelping like frightened pups into the trees. It was a vivid demonstration of a most peculiar marvel of nature, namely, that one might put to flight a thousand, and this because each of the thousand believes himself to bear the singular scrutiny and wrath of the one. Passion will win the day.

But Gray Eye, infused with his own passion, was quick to recover his faculties and ran snarling through his scattering forces, threatening a greater violence upon them, regrouping the floundering ranks, grabbing the napes of his terrified lessers with his jowls, and jerking them back into the fight. He knew, as did Hauwka, that his superior numbers were more than even the giant bear could deter for very long, if they would but fight. And so he was quick to turn the rout.

But as Gray Eye and his company made ready their counterattack, the trees on their blind side disgorged another fury of wolves, and immediately Lukar and his small force were among them, killing at once those too stunned to comprehend the moment. And in the confusion that quickly boiled, many of Gray Eye's wolves turned on one another, thinking each other the enemy, and inflicted a great sum of casualties on their own kind.

Taking advantage of the diversion, Hauwka turned back to the boy and swatted two wolves from his path, breaking the spine of one, the neck of the other.

"Where have you been?" Aeryck cried elatedly as the bear drew alongside him.

The bear growled at him in retort.

Aeryck quickly clambered onto Hauwka's massive back, and immediately the great bear took off through the trees like a shot, distancing himself from the uproar of the battle.

"How did you find—" the boy started to say, but he broke off when he remembered the big gray. Shooting a desperate look over his shoulder, he cried, "Sullie!"

But her lifeless form was obscured by a confusion of battling wolves.

At once there were trees rushing past the boy's eyes in a blinding procession as the slope fell away from them with astonishing speed. And soon there was nothing left of the battle sounds but the wind rifling through the bowery and the roar of it over his ears. His eyes watered from the cold and the speed, and the ground was a thundering, rolling treachery beneath him. Aeryck feared he might be thrown off the bear's massive back, and he clung to it desperately with two thick handfuls of bearhide.

Then as they broke from the woods, the bear immediately took a northeasterly heading into the low ranks of hills before them, hoping to put as much distance between them and Gray Eye as Lukar could buy. However it was but a breath of time before Aeryck could hear the furious howls of wolves in the distance, breaking through the quiet, sometimes drawing nearer, sometimes falling away, it seemed, for the echoes now rebounding off the hills, now carried by the vagaries of the wind, played tricks on his ears.

Aeryck's mind was awhirl with the preceding events, and he hadn't had time to collect his thoughts. As the bear bounded across the earth with great strides, he clung to his broad back, and the rush of winter wind against his face was as exhilarating in its effect as it was terrifying in its cause.

Strangely, the boy had a difficult time holding onto the bear, for he found himself skewing to the right and was continually having to readjust his seat. It was not as he remembered it, he thought abstractedly, perhaps making a mental comparison with Sullie's smooth, easygoing gait.

Then as the boy began to muster his wits, his instincts informed him with a dawning awareness that something was dreadfully wrong. But what? Feeling a prickling along his spine, he looked around and scanned the hills forward and aft for mischief, but there was only the muted sound of the wolves ducking in and out of the wind. Nothing that he could see. But something was wrong. And then he felt it. The rhythm was wrong. The gait. Something was wrong with the . . .

"Hauwka, you're limping!" he exclaimed, looking down at the bear's front right leg. "You've been hurt!"

Then he noticed that the limp wasn't the only pronounced difference in his friend since the last time he saw him. One of his ears was torn and flapped about on his head in dreadful need of stitching. There was no blood though, so it hadn't happened just now but some time ago—months ago perhaps.

Then he felt a network of long, hardened ridges beneath the thick fur, crisscrossing the length and breadth of his great girth. He knew these at once to be scars, the salient reminders—like little grave mounds—of buried trauma. His face went blank for a moment as his mind assimilated the unsettling bits of information. And then his eyes started open.

"You've been in a terrible fight, haven't you, Hauwka?" he said thoughtfully, smoothing his hand over the scars.

The great bear glanced back at him with his small, black, watery eyes.

"You need rest, big fella." Aeryck smiled at him. "Food too, no doubt."

The bear looked away with a snort and continued with what had to be a punishing pace.

They had long since exited the woods, and the sound of the wolves had diminished. Hauwka sought to cover his tracks—a difficult task in the traitorous snow—traveling along frozen streams and ponds, keeping downwind as much as possible, and using the full arsenal of his instincts to elude Gray Eye's wolves.

They arrived at one of several fords, and the bear followed the river north for several miles off their course. However such a detour would not fool the wolves for long. He knew instinctively that their only hope of survival lay in speed of travel and cunning—two things sorely taxed because of his unhealed wounds and deprivation of sleep.

In time the bear began to falter, each time catching himself in time to quickly regain his pace. But Aeryck could see the stress of his wounds tolling away his strength. It worried him.

The boy cast a grim look over his shoulder and studied their back trail. He could see nothing but their tracks winding into the infinite white distance, clearly betraying their course. A prayer escaped his lips that it might snow. Snow would sweep away their trail and give them a suitable shield under which to escape. Hauwka would be able to slow down, maybe even hole up somewhere for a while to rest.

Then he looked beyond the rolling white hills to the place, many miles away now, where Sullie lay quiet in the snow. An image of the terrible scene suddenly flared in his mind, ambushing his thoughts, an image of snarling wolf faces as they pulled her down, tearing at her fiercely, and the look of terror in Sullie's eyes as she fought valiantly to save her life—to save his life. The sound of her cries suddenly overwhelmed him.

The boy spun around and forced the image from his mind, a shiver going through him. But as he gazed at the back of Hauwka's dark brown head, trying to collect his senses, another scene took its place.

169

In this scene he saw the face of a boy peering across a shadowy tavern at him, smiling at him with his bright blue eyes twinkling in a yellow aureole of light. The face continued to gaze at him, smiling kindly, even as the dark of the room was gradually eclipsed by a brilliant white. And the white became a field of snow with only the smile and the eyes remaining of the face, and the eyes dimmed in the whiteness of it, becoming dark and bloodless and hideous looking, with the smile twisting into the shape of an unuttered moan.

What he heard, though, was only the sound of a continual hissing. Like a laugh.

The image was more than Aeryck could endure, and he felt something go inside him, like a dam bursting. He buried his face in his hands and wept. "No . . . no . . . no . . . I didn't mean it! I didn't mean it. Can't you see I didn't mean it?"

The bear looked back at him, his eyes dark and glistening, and moaned empathetically.

After a long while the boy looked up. His eyes were red and torn with grief, and his cheeks glistened in the cold sunlight. A distraught expression darkened his features as he pondered the past few days. His thoughts performed soliloquies upon the stage of his ruddy visage, such that the basest patron of the arts might easily comprehend the dramatic sweeps of pathos, the pride and humility, the anger and angst, the little shadows of revenge and hatred that moved in and about the lines and folds of his face. When at last the stage was clear, the boy cast his eyes plaintively to the heavens.

"Why, Father?" he groaned. "Why must others die because of me?"

But the heavens were mute, the voice of God silent in his travail, as though He were bronzing the skies against his prayers, and the silence was a hammer in his face. Aeryck lowered his eyes to the horizon. He saw that the sky was lowering and dark in the east, coming on with a meanness, and the wind whistled its shrill winter notes over the broken terrain.

The boy shook his head and sighed.

Over the next few hours he lapsed into a morose faithlessness, his sullen mind taking in the harsh contrasts of the terrain with dispassionate perusal. And everywhere the white and the cold and the unnatural blue of sky, and the jagged rocks jutting through the snow, were like a mirror to his soul, polished in brass and showing a cruel and untoward expanse.

The storm front was coming on strong now, drawing a great curtain of darkness over the winterscape, blueing the whites and soft magenta hues with a cruel hardness. Winds from the north began to howl over the low hills, stinging the boy's nose and cheeks, hurting his ears, and he hunkered down into his cloak for warmth, his mind benumbed with the grimness of the day's events. Powdery snow snakes wriggled about in the crosscurrents before dissipating into the billowy drifts, and the boy watched them with heavy, solemn eyes that seemed dead in their sockets.

Hauwka was faltering more frequently now, even stumbling a few times, adding weight to the boy's concerns. They were not making near the time that they had earlier. In fact, they were hardly moving faster than a walk. He had tried twice to climb off the bear's back to give him a respite, but each time was withheld by a fierce growl, as a sow might growl at one of her wayward cubs. He stayed, worrying, wondering what drove the heart of this great bear, fearful that he too would forfeit his life because of him. The boy groaned in his spirit and fell sullen again.

Then as they approached the crest of a small knoll, the bear paused and looked back on their trail and sniffed the air. A low growl rumbled about in his breast.

Startling out of his dark mood, Aeryck looked over his shoulder and saw in the distance, about a mile away, black specks moving tirelessly over the rise of a low hill, moving resolutely toward their prey. Hauwka wheeled and redoubled his efforts.

And a groan of pain escaped his mouth.

PART TWO
CHRIST'S MASS

OF OLD TOADS AND
PICTISH CHIEFTAINS

The Pictish village of Loch na Huric lay beneath a comforter of snow, and the once thunderous roar of the River Annan, encompassing its environs, was hushed beneath a rustling trickle of ice. And except for the odd muffled bark of a dog, that was the only sound that murmured dimly along the steep blue hills of the river valley.

Festoons of silvery mist, spun from some mystic wheel, hung low over the winter dawn and draped here and about sharp purple crags and dark trees and folds in the land. The air was cold and glittery as though shot through a diamond. The scene, if chanced upon by some traveler, would conjure a sublime thought, a resonant hymn of worship. It might evoke from his throat an involuntary "Ah!"

Inside the chieftain's estate house (more a quaint country cottage, consisting of two bedrooms, a kitchen area, a great room with a generous stone hearth, and a loft overlooking it), Tillie buzzed hither and thither like a hummingbird, whistling and singing a tune that had no discernible melody, just random notes flung together into a kind of chaotic assault of the Muse.

She was performing an ancient rite, one indigenous to her gender and the bane of husbands, namely, the "rite of sweeps," which foreshadows the arrival of guests, particularly guests of the feminine stripe, and the melodyless tune was the anthem of the rite.

For the unenlightened, the rite consists of straightening furniture (any number of times), rearranging decorations and fixtures (likewise), dusting, scrubbing, sweeping, and an incessant whirlwind of other activities in which no man is safe.

Brynwald knew this from an earlier initiation, and he wisely maintained a masculine front of opposition: that is to say, moving into whatever room where his wife wasn't and appearing to be absorbed with some manly task or other. At the present he was standing off to one side of the smoldering hearth, a big, well-muscled hulk of a man, struggling with a little twist in his belt, and mumbling to himself. Upon his taut visage there churned a turbulent squall, as though he was troubled by a matter. And indeed he was.

Word had reached him before sunup that the Britons had just left the main road at the Roman ruins of Birrens and would be arriving sometime within the hour. As he regarded the matter, reenacting the history of fighting between their two peoples—particularly the great battle that he fought against Allyndaar and his longbowmen along Hadrian's Wall twenty years past—his eyes were framed with a certain apprehension as they gazed steadily out from beneath his leathery brow, focusing on nothing in particular across the room.

"Is that the hearth I smell, Bryn?" Tillie called out from the guest bedroom.

Brynwald knew better than to answer her directly, and so he feigned deafness. Anything else would have opened him up to any number of possible assaults on his tenuous retreat. For some reason, understood only by the Predeterminate Council of God, woman was created to help man, a help meet for him as it were, but by some cruel twist of fate, or mutation of gene, or quirk of societal evolution (some attribute this phenomenon to the Fall of Adam), man was destined to become a helpmeet for woman.

"Did you not hear me then, Bryn?"

"What's that, Tillie? Did you say something?"

"*Och*, but you're deaf sometimes," Tillie thundered, as she entered the great room a little breathless from ministration of the aforesaid rite. Then without breaking stride, she swept past the chieftain and adjusted his belt from behind with a dexterous flick of her wrists. "There," she said, then grabbed the poker and began to stoke the fire.

"Here, let me do that," Brynwald offered, stricken by a sudden glower of conscience.

"Hoot! And have you turn our hame into a smokehouse?" Tillie protested. "Not likely." And with the strength of history on her side, she prevailed. "Though you might bring in another load or two of firewood, if it wouldnay be too much trouble."

"Troth, woman! I just got you a load not ten minutes past," Brynwald countered in a pathetic voice. "See—there're yet two or three logs to burn there."

Tillie's eyes flashed, and she snatched up the two or three logs and tossed them onto the fire. "And now we have nane," she said. "Now be a dear, Brynnie. I dinna want to be concerning myself with the hearth once the guests arrive. And you ken they'll be here in a trice!"

Brynwald grunted as he slipped his ceremonial ax into the frog at his waist. Then, donning a bright blue woolen cloak, he dutifully went outside into the winter cold to collect more wood from one of their outbuildings.

The village was beginning to stir from the night's cozy slumber. Here and there cold blue shadows crept forth from their purpled hill haunts to the east, marking their subtle progress in long, inarticulate parallels across the snow. Here and there fists of black smoke silently punched through snow-crowned chimneys as fires were kindled and roared furiously below. Soon the brisk morning air would be rife with woodsmoke, a welcome scent to the traveler, no doubt weary and in want of a hot meal to break fast.

Glancing across the village, which fell away gently from the promontory of his steading, Brynwald noticed two or three men trudging wearily through the snow carrying armloads of wood into their homes. Another was disposing of a brazier of soot. Yet another was hefting two pails of milk. Each man was undoubtedly cast forth into the cold by his helpmate, and each wore the same resigned look of men whose wives were zealous in their observances of the rite. From one cottage a dog rushed forth into the snow, yelping before the broom of his mistress. The chieftain clucked his tongue and smiled.

Meanwhile, amid a renewed flurry of devotion, Tillie thought to pause before a mirror in the master bedroom and check her appearance. The pause begat another pause, which begat a certain look in her eyes that betrayed a pent anxiety. Her eyes were charged with an electric-blue intensity as they appraised the image gazing back at her, taunting her mercilessly, jeering at the memory of a girl with the once lithe feminine curves and sweeps that had conquered Brynwald's heart.

As Tillie regarded the burnished phantom in the mirror, whose figure was now best described as short, round, and full, and whose flower of youth was clearly showing the assault of middle age, a scowl crossed her brow. Quickly, as though to conjure some departed shade of beauty, she waved her hands over her hair in a kind of sleight of hand, and villainous strands of red and gray magically fell into place. Even so, she looked resignedly at herself and sighed. "'Tis nay good. 'Tis nay good at all."

At once her shoulders rolled forward into an exasperated slump. Then, setting aside her broom and scuttle, she clutched her face with her right hand and folded into herself, a kind of pitiful heap. She, in such mournful attitude of head and posture, began to softly weep, her shoulders heaving and shuddering a little as she did.

At that moment Brynwald kicked open the door and entered the cottage behind a shrill draft of wind and a terrific armload of firewood.

177

"What's this then?" he said, seeing Tillie framed by the bedroom doorway, obviously in tears. He dumped the wood next to the hearth, then strode over to her side. "What're you frothin' aboot, woman?"

"Nothing," Tillie replied, as she quickly gathered herself together.

"Nothing, is it?"

"*Och,* you wouldnay understand," she said, again reaching for the broom. "You being a man and all."

Brynwald, being a man and all, quickly surveyed the rooms in both directions. "The house looks fine to me—clean as an eel," he remarked. "Any cleaner and Allyndaar and his wife will think we dinna live here!"

"The house is fine! It's—" She broke off and, collapsing into his great, powerful arms, began to weep again.

Brynwald was stunned, and he looked down at her with a bewildered frown, his hands uncertain what to do.

"Oh, Bryn. I'm such an old toad," she sobbed. "Such an ugly old toad."

"Here, here now, girl," Brynwald said, somewhat relieved, and he began to pat her shoulders comfortingly. "What's this that's come over you? 'Tis nay like my smiling lassie to be puttin' up such a blow." He stroked her wet cheeks. "Put away your tears now, here?" he resumed. "I dinna like to see you cry."

Tillie sobbed a while longer, and Brynwald held her close to him.

"I'm told that the wife of Allyndaar is a beautiful lady," she finally said into his shoulder. "Of Latin descent, she is, and nay doubt well-educated and living in a right muckle house."

"So that's it, is it?" her husband replied. He lay his big hands on her shoulders, held her tenderly out before him, and from his noble height gazed down into her smallness. "Aye, and perhaps you're right aboot that. A right fine lady nay doubt, with servants running aboot her, a-primpin' her hair and toes and giving her a grand shine." He smiled, wiping a tear off her round, wet cheek. "But speakin' for myself, I've an eye for old toads with bonnie blue eyes, who live in wee mud hooses by the river."

She looked up into his eyes, her own glistening with tears. "Do you love me then, Bryn? Do you still?"

"Do I love you?" Brynwald threw his head back and guffawed. "Do I love you? By the oaks, woman! Like the biggest, boldest old bull-toad in the pond, I do! Come now and give us a croak. *Bwrawk, brwaak!*" And he began to tickle her and make silly toad faces, bugging out his eyes.

"Hoot now, Brynnie! Stop it!" she said, as she began to giggle.

"There's my bonnie toad now," Brynwald boomed, and he tickled her some more.

"*Och,* stop it now! Whist, Brynwald. I'll not stand for it." She scowled, feigning disapproval.

"*Bwaaark! Brroppop!* Here comes the old bull toad hopping doon the lane, a-lookin' for his wee lassie toad!" he bellowed. "*Bwaark!*"

"You dinna even sound like a toad." Tillie squealed with laughter.

"Is that so? How's this then? *Beeorp! Brreedeep! Brrribbitt!*"

"Now you sound like an old frog!"

"An old frog, is it? I'll show you an old frog! Come here, lass!"

And so it went as Brynwald chased his round, squealing wife about the cottage, here and there hopping up onto a chair or table and making grand leaps into the air, bellowing and booming and acting every bit the toad, or frog, or amphibious Pictish chieftain that he was.

Across the broad tract of land that spilled forth from the narrow river pass that cut through the southern hills surrounding Loch na Huric, a rider came galloping through the snow toward the village like an unleashed banshee, whooping and waving his arms wildly and shouting. "Halloo! Halloo! They're coming! They're coming! The Britons have arrived!"

Immediately the quiet, snow-burdened cottages of the village disgorged a great throng of people into the streets.

"Halloo! Halloo! The Britons are coming!" the rider heralded, as he rode through the village.

And the Picts, seeing in the distance the long line of horses and wagons and colorful cloaks like banners, snapping happily in the chill breeze, raised their voices in jubilant furor.

Children ran heroically beyond the crowd to welcome these the guests of their first Christ's Mass feast, waving holly boughs and branches of mistletoe (certain carryovers from their druidic heritage, symbolizing divine favor and protection from the winter elements) wildly in the air.

In the distance, the yet tiny file of Britons could be seen waving return salutes, and here and there the breaking light of dawn glinted off their metal accoutrements of battle.

179

21
A WELCOME
OF ENEMIES

I t was a most curious phenomenon. The nearer the Britons drew upon their horses and wagons to the village precincts, with their colorful cloaks snapping proudly in the breeze, the more the wind seemed driven from the jubilant furor of the crowd. And soon as the Britons reined their horses to a halt before the gates, there was not heard a sound but the wind brushing through the pines and the occasional snorting of horses that seemed to punctuate and call attention to the silence.

The vanguard of squealing children had long since tested the limits of their daring. From there they were driven back a step at a time to the invisible bulwarks encircling their parents' legs, their eyes blinking in wonder, their little fists still clutched tightly around boughs of holly and mistletoe.

For several moments the two peoples eyed one another as they stood in opposing groups—the Pictish villagers from the ground eyeing the long line of Britons warily, and the long line of Britons from their saddles eyeing the Pictish villagers warily. There was expressed between them a singular look of astonishment, of fear perhaps, a look of wonder such as children might have when appraising a new boy in their midst, one who has been preceded with a certain notorious reputation. No one was quite sure what to do next, since neither group had had the benefit of such experience to inform its etiquette.

And so the silence that had descended upon them drew itself into a supreme awkwardness. In time, however, the wary, astonished, appraising eyes began to unlink from their opposing fascinations and began to collect upon each of their respective chieftains.

Brynwald, sensing the moment overripe, grunted magnificently, then took a step forward from his warriors and raised his hand in salute. "Hail and well met, Britons!" he boomed, with a voice that seemed akin to the first Voice.

Allyndaar, wearing his emerald green cloak, raised his hand responsively and replied in equal voice, "Hail and well met, Brynwald and people of Loch na Huric."

Immediately he dismounted Daktahr, strode over to the Pictish chieftain, and extended his arms. Brynwald took hold of them with a terrific slap upon each, and the two leaders stared into each other's eyes.

There was a tense moment between them as each chieftain, men once sworn enemies, seemed to be calculating the sum of the other's mettle. Brynwald clearly had the advantage of size over the Briton, standing a half head taller, and of such stature that was rivaled only by a few; but there was a keenness in Allyndaar's eyes that was so piercing, like steel, it seemed to look through whatever they fell upon.

Brynwald found it difficult to hold his gaze.

"'Tis a fine, grand moment we neither might have kenned, Allyndaar, but by the grace of God and only by His grace do we live to see it," the large Pict said for all to hear. "We welcome you now into our bosoms as friends, to sup beneath our roofs, to take warmth before our hearths, and to coddle a fair love that we have in the wounds of the Savior. Let there be nay more war between our peoples, Allyndaar—nay, but an everlasting peace."

Allyndaar smiled warmly at him. "To my own shame I never would have thought this day possible," he replied. "We now, with such full hearts, with such inexpressible joy in the great mercies of Christ, gladly put behind us the sword that once rent our peoples and accept your peace and hospice to its fullest bounty. We come to you now, no longer as enemies, but as friends and more, Brynwald, as brothers."

At this point both Picts and Britons alike released a pent and fervent shout, and the hills thundered about them. Helena, looking on from her carpentum, smiled and took hold of Aurelius's hand, patting it gently. And from so full a gracecote that was framed within the monk's breast, a prayer of thanksgiving winged heavenward on its homing course. And upon their faces it seemed there shone a ray of shekinah.

Dagmere, riding beside them, however, was stirred by another matter altogether. And as her eyes busily searched the faceless crowd for the one familiar face, her heart was pounding with the anticipation of discovery. Her first look had been a quick sweep of the crowd surreptitiously, so as not to be too conspicuous. Finding nothing, her second look had been a more deliberate glance. But now after the third sweep and then a fourth, and after finding nothing of her eye's quest, her head began to wag quite noticeably. "Mama, I don't see Aeryck," she said, voicing concern.

"Are you sure, Dagmere?"

"Where could he be? Why isn't he here to meet us?" Dagmere asked, with a little panic edging into her voice. "Mama, you don't suppose something might have happened to him, do you?"

"I'm sure he'll be along presently. Don't worry," her mother replied comfortingly. However she was somewhat distracted by the proceedings, for Allyndaar was now receiving introductions of Brynwald's warriors and various men of standing.

Still scanning the crowd, Dagmere started as she suddenly felt someone draw alongside her left flank, and, turning to look, she half expected, half hoped, to find Aeryck smiling at her.

But it was Fiona. And though she was certainly smiling, there was little humor about her face.

"You do look like a silly goose craning your neck so," Fiona remarked, cocking her head to one side with a superior air. "I expect you'll put it out of joint." And then she giggled with her airless twittering voice, a sound so strident that it could easily sour a regiment of goodwill.

"Perhaps you'd care for another taste of snow," Dagmere countered, threatening the girl with her crop.

Fiona threw her head back haughtily. "You may have your way with horses, little girl," she sneered. "I will have mine with men." Then she giggled a long string of sour notes and reined her horse to a less hazardous place in the column.

Dagmere stared at her, fuming.

Terryll was staring at Gwyneth (as he was wont to do of late), and Gwyneth, unaware of her audience, was gazing steadfastly into the crimson luster of the ruby that hung about her neck, caressing it thoughtfully between her fingers. Then, at last feeling Terryll's eyes upon her, she looked over at him and beamed radiantly.

Terryll's cheeks flushed remarkably as he beheld her dazzling green eyes sparkling within their delicious settings, and the thick tresses of fiery, red hair that splashed playfully about her face. For a moment the boy could do nothing but gaze at her with his mouth hanging slightly ajar and the construction of a thought disintegrating pathetically on his lips.

"It feels wonderful to be here again, Terryll, don't you think?" she asked, rescuing him from his stupor.

"Huh . . . er . . . yes," Terryll replied, collecting himself.

Gwyneth turned and looked over the village. "I never thought I'd be coming here again of my own will." She sighed. "I only wish we could have talked father into coming."

"Perhaps in time he will," Terryll said. "He has a stubborn heart, but God can change a stubborn heart, can't He?"

182

Gwyneth smiled at him. "Yes, He can." And she reached over and patted his hand. "But you are here, my love, and my happiness is complete."

Terryll glowed. Then there came over the boy a shift in his demeanor. His chest swelled noticeably, and his expression took on a rather lofty glaze. "Even so I must leave you for a moment, Gwinnie, and join my father," he said, a little too full of himself. "It is proper that I should be next to him—being the chieftain's son and all."

Gwyneth released him with a vigorous nod. "Oh, yes, but of course. You must," she replied with a facetious edge in her voice. "It is your rightful place, being the chieftain's son and all." And as the boy began to swing from his saddle, she quipped, "Mind you don't bump your head now; the sun is just overhead."

"Huh?" Terryll queried, not perceiving her tease.

Then the young hunter dismounted Tempest and walked proudly over to Brynwald and extended his arms with a grand flourish of his cloak, knowing that his love's eyes were fast upon him. "Hail and well met, Brynwald," he said, heartily and a mite overplayed. "It is good to see you and Tillie again."

Upon seeing Terryll threading his way through the horses and the snow, Tillie smiled broadly. The line of her lips pushed her cheeks up into two round, red heaps upon her face, and tears spurted from her eyes.

"Oh, Brynwald!" Then she rushed forward and took hold of the boy before he had reached the chieftain and gave him such a great long hug that it squeezed the last swaggering ranks of pageantry from his limbs.

Terryll was so taken aback at the sudden display that he blushed profusely. His eyes worked the snickering crowd both fore and aft with a helpless submission.

When at last Tillie let go of him, Helena and Dagmere were at the boy's side. Tillie's eyes started a little at the sight of the beautiful and stately figure of Helena standing before her. She moved back a step, but Helena caught hold of her hand and clasped it warmly in hers.

"I feel as though I already know you both," Helena said graciously, and she drew Tillie close to embrace her. Then her eyes moved from Tillie's to Brynwald's and back again. "Especially you, Tillie. Terryll has told us so many kind things about you—most of which I'm sure he grossly understated—that I just had to come and meet this wondrous wife of Brynwald's."

A blush of color rushed into Tillie's face, and she giggled embarrassedly. Then retrieving her hand, she held it in her other, regarding it as though it had been suddenly accorded some high value.

Feeling it the proper time, Dagmere edged up next to her mother. She cleared her throat and gave her a subtle nudge.

"Oh. And I would like to present our daughter, Dagmere," Helena said, taking the hint.

At which point Dagmere stepped forward and smiled.

"*Och!* So this is Dagmere!" Tillie enthused heartily. "Brynnie, take a look at this girl! Is she not a bonnie lass then? Hoot!" she exclaimed, as she looked the girl over, as a woman would. "Hoot! 'Tis nay wonder Aeryck has talked of little else since he come to stay wi' us! By the oaks! Troth, she's got the bloom of heather aboot her, dinna you think, Bryn?"

"Aye," Brynwald agreed, as he smiled and cast a fatherly wink at Allyndaar. "Aye."

"Aye, indeed!" Tillie smiled. "And I can see how your eyes take the light at the mention of Aeryck's name! Dinna you be concerned, lass—the lad should be to hame any time now," she said, taking a pinch of her cheek. "He's gone off on an errand for the chieftain. Supposed to be back two days ago, but the storm's withheld him, nay doubt. Aye, but he'll come jaunting along in a trice, him and his handsome smiling face, I'll warrant you!"

"Gone to Whithorn to greet some of Patrick's men," Brynwald explained in a ceremonious aside to Allyndaar, as men are wont to do under such circumstances. "My surrogate he is—a good lad too, you ken. Aye, a good lad."

"That he is! That he is!" Dunnald, Brynwald's stoutly built second in command, concurred. And there was added a round of ayes from several warriors who were gathered around the chieftains, most of whom were in awe of the legendary longbowman of Killwyn Eden and gazed steadily at him.

Allyndaar smiled and nodded as he regarded Brynwald thoughtfully. He had detected a measure of pride in the man's voice, much like that a father might have for a son.

Meanwhile Dagmere was about to burst with joy at Tillie's unsolicited revelation. *So Aeryck has talked of little else*, she mused, and her mind was a party of rapturous thoughts. Presently a wicked little idea intruded upon the celebration, and the girl subtly, ever so subtly, glanced behind her to see if perhaps, just perhaps, Fiona might have overheard Tillie's pronouncement.

She had.

Fiona was glowering at her darkly from beneath her hood as she sat ladylike and, oh, so prettily upon her sidesaddle, with her lower lip having begun to push out into a little rosy shelf.

Dagmere sent her a triumphant little smile and blessed the day.

In the hour that followed, introductions were made between the two peoples, and at once the strongholds of culture and tradition and enmities began to crumble before the triumphal shouts of the Picts. And the once-daunted children, again empowered with their rightful abandon, stormed the invisible fortifications that had withheld them and ran squealing in every direction, assailing the Britons with their bounty of holly and mistletoe.

Homes were quickly assigned to accommodate the guests by Dunnald, who decided—from some military perspective, it seemed—which homes would be best suited for whom. And he having executed his charge with military precision, the Britons were then led by their hosts to their respective homes and given hot meals, cozy lodging, and the warmest of highland hospitality.

Riding a few paces behind her family as Brynwald and Tillie led them along a little tree-shaded lane toward their cottage, Dagmere fairly glowed while she rehearsed Tillie's words over and over. There beat in her heart a lively little skip, like that of a pent child who has suddenly been loosed from the tyranny of a governess and allowed to play. And the sheeny undulations of snow were to her an airy field of clouds over which she soared exultantly in the beatific currents of love.

In her mind she entertained myriad trysts with the handsome son of Caelryck, sequestered assignations where she entertained the singular audience of his eyes, the touch of his lips upon her cheek, upon her ready lips. A shiver scurried along her limbs and escaped her mouth a giggle.

Life was good again.

However, as Fiona and her parents were guided to a home on the far end of the village, the girl with the raven hair and flashing green eyes paused momentarily upon her mount, and, turning to the hinder scene of her contempt, cast Dagmere a strange look. As she sat staring intently at her rival, her green eyes simmering coldly in their pretty little caldrons, every hue of complexion, every supple line and plane and contour of beauty now seemed wrung from her face.

It was as though some invisible hand had reached under her woolen hood and took hold of her malleable features with a violent promiscuity, then twisted them into something altogether dark and wicked and ugly. A low chortle danced about in her throat. It seemed she had picked up some thrown gauntlet. And if looks could kill . . .

22

TWAIN
BECOMING ONE

That afternoon, after the visitors had settled comfortably into their host homes, Dunnald, a few of his warriors, and some Britons were gathered in the orchard adjacent to the chieftain's cottage. Allyndaar had just presented to Brynwald a longbow that he had made for the occasion, and the Pictish chieftain was testing its pull.

"Made of yew, is it?" he asked.

"Yes." The British bowyer smiled and added with a certain appreciation, "The yew is God's gift to the bowman."

"God's gift, you say?"

Dunnald and his warriors looked at one another curiously. Their own bowyers would not have dared defile such a tree to make a bow. Instead, they made their bows out of ash and lemon woods. For in their culture the yew tree was considered sacred, one revered by the druids for its immortal properties (because of its lush, year-round dark green foliage and longevity). They used the trees in their rites for the dead and planted them in burial grounds as symbols of eternal life. Never would they have imagined its use for a weapon.

"It has a good pull," Brynwald said, drawing the bowstring to his chin. "Aye. It's got a springiness, still 'tis stout enough to give it power. Not like our short bows, eh, Dunnald?"

"Give it a try then, Brynwald," the stout warrior replied.

"Aye, show us how it's done!" the other men said, egging him on.

"No, no, no." Brynwald chuckled. "I'll just have a go with it later."

Dunnald stepped forward and said as an aside, "'Twould nay look good to not try the gift, Bryn. 'Twould be bad manners."

"Would it now?" Brynwald said, cocking an eye at him.

"Aye, and as you can see, we've set a target for you to shoot at. Give it a try, if you think you can hit it."

Brynwald grunted at him. Then he noted the bale of straw leaning against an apple tree, twenty-five yards away, with a small red cloth pinned to it. The mark. Grunting again, he turned to the British chieftain and said, "You've brought an arrow, have you, Allyn? Aye, that you have, I can see," he added, with a note of surrender in his voice.

Taking the arrow, Brynwald fit it to the bow and cast Dunnald a sour look. Clearly he was out of his element. He drew the bowstring to the point of his chin.

Allyndaar noted his form and arched an eyebrow.

Then Brynwald loosed the arrow and shot a foot wide of the red cloth.

His men groaned.

"What happened then?" Brynwald muttered, presuming there to be something wrong with the bow.

"Perhaps if you were to anchor your draw thumb against the corner of your mouth," Allyndaar offered delicately. "It lines the shaft better with the mark and steadies the aim."

Brynwald mumbled something to himself as Allyndaar proffered another arrow. Then, drawing the nock back to the corner of his mouth, he asked, "Like this then?"

Allyndaar studied his form. "That's it," he said, then again added delicately, "and this time, don't pluck the string . . . release it. Feel the mark, don't aim at it."

"Feel it, eh?" Brynwald, muttering to himself ("And how do you feel the mark then?"), took careful aim and loosed the arrow. It caromed off the edge of the bale into the snow.

His men groaned again.

Brynwald shot them a crimson scowl. *"Och!* I dinna think I can hit anything with these things," he growled. Then, taking hold of his ax, he hurled it at the mark and hit it dead-center. Turning to Allyndaar with a self-satisfied grin, he added, "Put an ax in my hand, though—now there's a weapon I can split skulls with."

Allyndaar smiled at him wryly. "Unless, perhaps, the mark were a hundred yards farther," he jested.

Dunnald and his men laughed.

Brynwald snorted, however, failing to see the humor in it.

Then one of the younger warriors asked Allyndaar, "Iffen it's not too bold of me to ask of you, would you be givin' us a demonstration then?"

"Aye. Aye," the others agreed. They had heard many tales of the legendary bowman, and they stood watching him now with rapt, schoolboy fascination.

Allyndaar looked at Brynwald, indicating his longbow. "May I?"

"Och, yes," Brynwald boomed, then added sarcastically, "but would you not be preferring your mark a hundred yards farther then?"

Allyndaar smiled at him as he took the bow. "So be it." And two of Brynwald's men paced off the distance with the bale.

Allyndaar fit an arrow to the bow. Then, taking sight of the target, he loosed the arrow. The men followed its trajectory as the missile whistled through the air and hit the mark dead-on.

The Pictish warriors elbowed one another as they oohed and ahed, punctuating them with head nods and winks.

Now it was Brynwald's turn to smile wryly, "'Twould be grand if your enemy were so kind as to stand in front of you with a red circle painted on his chest."

That drew a little tension over the air, but Allyndaar took the ribbing good-naturedly. "Indeed it would," he said, then looking around he found a broken branch in the snow, about two feet in length and two inches thick.

"Young fellow," he said, tossing it to Duncan, one of Dunnald's young warriors, "when I give you the go, would you mind giving that a toss? High, mind you."

"Aye." And hefting the limb's weight the young warrior waited for Allyndaar's signal.

Allyndaar selected two arrows, fitted one to his bow, and the other he gripped in his left hand.

Dunnald's men looked at one another bewilderedly.

"Are you ready?"

"Aye."

"Give it a wing!"

Duncan coiled back and threw the branch high into the air. Then, in what seemed a blink of time, Allyndaar's arrow was rifling toward its mark, hitting the branch, kicking it higher into the air, and, before it fell to the ground, his second arrow striking it.

There was a collective gasp of astonishment.

Duncan quickly fetched the branch and showed it around to Brynwald's men, who gaped dumbfounded at the two arrows neatly sticking in it. Never before had they witnessed such marksmanship. Then, as each of them looked up at Allyndaar, the legendary longbowman suddenly grew in stature.

Brynwald nodded, eyeing the British chieftain with rekindled respect. "Och, I can see now why we once thought you were the deffil on the wind, Allyn. 'Tis a boon that he fights with us now, eh, Dunnald?"

"Aye, that 'tis."

And the others agreed in unison.

Tillie glanced nervously at her hands, folded around a cup of cider in her lap. Then, careful to avoid Helena's eyes, she darted a look at the hearth. She had just put a log on a bed of glowing peat and stoked it, so repeating that business wouldn't do. Perhaps . . . no, that wouldn't do, either, so she looked down at her hands again. Her mind was in a scramble. What to do? What to say?

The conversation, once the social amenities had been observed, had dropped off and fallen into one of those uncomfortable interludes, the kind that suggests people are trying too hard to look as though they're not trying too hard. Every second of silence seemed to stretch a tension over the room, until it was tight as a drum. Sighs beat against the silence, thumped the drum as it were, relieving the tension for a second as well as sounding a greater silence. There was a lot of smiling and friendly raising of eyebrows going back and forth.

Tillie glanced furtively at Helena, whose eyes were quietly moving about the room, noting its fixtures for the tenth time. She made a sweeping appraisal of the British woman. Helena was even more beautiful than she had imagined, Tillie thought: her beautiful Latin features, the way she carried herself, so poised and refined, how she held her cup just so as she daintily sipped her cider, yet there was a winsomeness about her that was endearing. She liked her. She wanted to be liked by her.

Their eyes met briefly and smiled, then they each took a sip of cider like mirror images and looked away in opposite directions. Tillie stifled a small groan. And as she studied the little leaps of flame in the hearth, the logs shifting under their weight, suddenly she too felt her insides crumbling. Panic edged into her thoughts.

She looked over at Dagmere who was seated nearby in a bay window niche, staring somewhat despondently outside, then cleared her throat. But the sound of it startled her, and she flushed. Recovering, she looked at Helena and her eyes twinkled with a single thought. "We might get snow, dinna you think?"

Helena perked. "Pardon? Oh!" Then she glanced briefly out the window. "Looks like it."

"We certainly get a lot of it in the winter," Tillie said. Her thoughts whipped her, and she glowed a bright red. Panic set in now with a whirl of images.

Helena must have noted the anxiety on her brow. "The apple cider is delicious," she offered, struggling to put the woman at ease.

Tillie giggled embarrassedly. "Hoot! 'Tis nothing . . ." She brightened. "*Och*—silly me! Would you like some more then?"

"Why, yes, thank you."

Tillie sprang to her feet and took her mug, then hurried over to the hearth and swung out the pot on the little brass hob.

"How do you make it?" Helena asked. "It has a nice flavor to it. I like it."

189

Smiling, Tillie ladled the cider into the cup, then pushed the hob back into the hearth. "Just apples and a bit of ginger root sprinkled in, then leave it be. The fermentation does the rest. Mustn't let it go too lang, or it'll snap at you!" She giggled as she handed the cup to Helena.

Helena took a sip, felt the warmth of the liquid slide down through her middle and spread out evenly to her extremeties. "It's quite delicious," she said, her mind struggling to keep the conversation flowing. "It does have a bit of a bite to it, though."

"Aye. I've seen Brynnie so bitten by the apple that he dinna care what bit him." She let out a roar of laughter, then abruptly covered her mouth. *"Och!* Listen to me now!"

Helena giggled at her and, taking another sip of cider, said, "I like it when you smile, Tillie. It suits you so."

Tillie flushed. "Hoot! Like a fool, you mean!" But she cherished the remark, and turning to Dagmere she said, "And would you like some more then, lassie?"

But Dagmere only sighed and leaned wistfully against the wall.

Helena and Tillie exchanged looks, crooking their eyebrows with hidden knowledge.

There was a knock on the door.

Springing from her chair, Tillie said, "Now who can that be?" She cast Helena a knowing wink.

She opened the door, and there were two teenage girls smiling sheepishly at her—one a tall, loose-limbed girl with blonde hair and long features, brown eyes, and teeth that stuck out a little too far from her face, and the other shorter, plumpish, with bright red hair and a sprinkling of freckles on her red cheeks. Her blue eyes twinkled apprehensively, then looking into the cottage past Tillie, she said, "We come by, thinkin' maybe the lass from Britain might like a turn aboot the village."

"Aye," the taller one said to Tillie. "We come like you asked us to."

The shorter one gave her an elbow in the side. "Shh! You dinna want to be spoutin' like that."

"Well, come in, come in," Tillie gushed. "It's too cold to be standin' out in the elements. Come in!"

"Thank you kindly," the plump one said as the girls scraped their feet of snow and stepped into the cottage.

Tillie closed the door behind them.

Helena came to the door and smiled warmly at the girls. "Hello. What have we here?"

The girls gazed at her shyly. They were apparently startled at her beauty and seemed to wilt. The taller one's jaw went slack.

"They've come to visit with Dagmere," Tillie offered.

The girls nodded and continued to stare and gape unabashedly.

Helena smiled and called across the room, "Dagmere, you have company."

Dagmere appeared from out of the window bay a moment later and smiled politely at the visitors.

The girls shifted their eyes from Helena and now stared at Dagmere awkwardly, tensing, seeming to have forgotten their purpose. Their eyes made surreptitious appraisals of her hair, her clothes, and her pretty face. She was an exact copy of the mother. A foreign thing was before them, and it astonished them. There was an awkward silence that rushed in and heckled.

The taller girl stepped forward at the other's prodding. "Er . . . would you like to come with us? We thought . . . maybe you'd like to come—" she stammered but quickly ran out of steam.

"Tell her who we are then, you ninny," the shorter one chided. "Have you no upbringing?"

"Huh? Oh, yes! Oona—I'm Oona," she said, collecting her wits, and she smiled broadly so that her overbite protruded conspicuously. "And this is—"

"Meara!" the plump girl interposed fiercely.

Dagmere nodded a smile to each of them, then introduced herself.

"We noted your horses when you come in—" Meara said.

"Ooie, such bonnie ones too!" Oona added.

Meara frowned at her. "We thought you wouldnay mind letting us have a look at them with you."

"We just love horses!" Oona enthused, then giggled. "We like boys too, of course, but horses dinna give us trouble."

The plump girl rolled her eyes, and Dagmere smiled.

"We could take a walk to the stables," Meara said. "That is, lessen you're too busy."

This seemed to stir Dagmere out of her melancholy. "No, no, I'm not too busy. It would be fun," she said, then looked at Helena. "Mama?"

"I think it would be wonderful for you to get out and enjoy yourself, Dagmere. Don't worry. If Aeryck comes in, we'll let him know where you are."

"Troth, lass!" Tillie added. "There'll be nay keeping him away from you!"

The two girls giggled. "Aye, that's the truth, 'tis!" Meara said. "We've heard of no one else since he come to Loch na Huric."

Dagmere beamed. "Let me just get my cloak, and I'll be right with you."

Helena stood in the doorway for a few moments, smiling as she watched the three girls treading away toward the village. They were laughing already.

Tillie looked into Helena's cup after she closed the door. "Och, but you're empty! Would you care for another then?"

"I'd love some," Helena said. "It's really quite wonderful! You must show me how you make it."

Though the sky hung low with black clouds, the temperature had risen enough so that several clutches of people were out and about taking in the bracing air. Children squealed as they played in the snow, and dogs barked and leaped about. There was an excitement in the air. It vibrated in the trees and glowed on people's faces, sprang from their lips in joyous salutations. For the feast of Christ's Mass would be here in two days—the first ever in Loch na Huric—and the people looked forward to it with the anticipation of brides.

Many of the homes were decorated with festoons of holly boughs and mistletoe sprigs in preparation for it. Candles were placed in windows and lighted, more out of the Celtic tradition of celebrating the birth of the unconquered sun than the birth of Christ. But the tradition seemed to fit in well with their new belief, that Jesus Christ, the Light of the world, came to forever conquer the powers of darkness, and so the candles remained.

As the girls walked past the hall in the center of town, Dagmere paused at a window and looked in, for she had heard a familiar voice. A knot of men was gathered inside around Brother Lucius, and they were asking him questions about the faith. Tolc was there, the onetime priest of Dagda, listening intently to the Roman monk describe man's salvific need for the Incarnation—how the Baby of Bethlehem had come specifically to die for the sin of the world. His eyes glistened with tears.

Dagmere caught Aurelius's eye, and he winked at her. Smiling, she turned away, and the girls headed across the village toward the stables.

Seeking a quiet place, Terryll and Gwyneth climbed the blunted hillock in the middle of the village. The hills were dark with cold behind them, and the sky was black with snow, but there was a brightness in the air, a glowing something that was indefinable. Reaching the summit, they made their way through the ring of fifteen-foot monoliths that dominated the skyline to the sacrificial altar in the center. Terryll brushed the snow away from its surface and sat against it, and Gwyneth leaned against him, curling snugly in his cloak.

Terryll looked over her at the village, at the little groups of people moving about, and smiled as he spotted the small figures of Dagmere and two girls threading through a little orchard. He watched them for a while, then looked ahead of them to see where they were going and smiled when he saw the stables. He looked beyond the village and let his eyes roam freely about the dark winter-blue hills. His eyes narrowed as he found three deer traversing the steep slope, and he followed them for several minutes before they reached the crest and disappeared over it.

"What's wrong, Terryll?" Gwyneth asked, looking up at him. "You seem distracted."

"Huh? Oh, nothing."

"Is it your bear again?"

Terryll looked at her and smiled. "How many times do I have to tell you that he's not my bear? Not like a pet or anything. But yes, I was thinking about him." He marveled at how often they were doing that now, reading one another's thoughts. It was almost eerie.

"Do you miss being out in the hills with him, hunting?" she asked.

Terryll stared wistfully at the distant slopes, at the dark clouds gathering there, threatening. The three deer appeared again farther along the crest. A little breeze picked up, and Terryll breathed it in, and his eyes sparkled with a wildness.

"Yes, I do."

Gwyneth sighed and pulled him close to her, laying her head on his breast. Her eyes lazily traced the runic lettering that was chiseled around the edge of the altar, noted the brass rings at each of the corners, used to bind the victims. "Isn't it strange that only two months ago Corrie was lying here about to be killed by that awful high priest. It seems like a lifetime ago."

Terryll chuckled.

"What's so funny?"

Terryll shook his head, thinking. "Aeryck. I can't forget how silly he looked sneaking up the hill wearing those priest's robes." His eyes lifted heavenward.

"It was a brave thing to do."

"Yes, stupid and brave."

"You miss him, don't you?"

"More than you know." Terryll said. "He's like a brother to me." He glanced over the village and noticed another group of people heading toward the stable. "He's made a home for himself here. A good home. You can see it in Brynwald and Tillie's eyes when they talk about him. Not just them, but everyone else here in the village." He sighed, and a big white cloud streamed into the air, then dissipated quickly on the breeze. "I don't suppose he'll be wanting to come back to Killwyn Eden in the spring."

Gwyneth said nothing for a moment. She was content listening to the booming of his voice through his chest. It was a comforting voice, making her feel warm and secure. Then, looking up into his dark blue eyes, she said, "I love you, Terryll. I will come to live with you in the spring."

Roused out of his thoughts, Terryll smiled at her. "I love you too, Gwinnie." He pulled her close to him, and they kissed. It was a lovely kiss.

Moments later Terryll pulled away with a determined look on his face.

Gwyneth gazed expectantly into his eyes.

"If he's not here by tomorrow, I'm going to go look for him," he said, with the notorious poor timing of his sex.

Gwyneth lay her head against his breast and, letting out a pitiable sigh, frowned.

"This is Daktahr," Dagmere said, patting his cheek. "It's all right—you can pet him. He's friendly."

Oona reached her hand into the stall and stroked the horse's sleek, hard-muscled neck. The dapple-gray swung his head up and down and whickered softly. "There's a boy, there's a boy," Oona said soothingly. Glancing quickly at Dagmere, she said, "I've never seen such a beautiful horse. What kind is he?"

"He's an Arabian—from Egypt."

Oona scrunched her nose. "Egypt? Is that a town in Britain then?"

Meara rolled her eyes. "No, it's in the south of Gaul, you ninny," she said, with a superior air.

Dagmere's eyes widened.

"Oh." The tall girl blushed embarrassedly. "Well, they do have lovely horses there just the same."

Changing the subject, Dagmere said, "Several of our mares are in foal by Daktahr. Come spring, we hope to have lots of little Arab colts leaping about."

"Ooie, would I like to see one of them!" Oona squealed.

"You shall," Dagmere promised.

Across the stable a horse snorted contemptuously. Dagmere turned as Tempest thrust his head over the stall door and shook his mane.

"Have we been ignoring you, Tempest?" Dagmere cooed as she went over to him. She scooped a handful of oats out of a swollen burlap sack and offered them to the spirited black stallion. He shoveled them greedily out of her hand. "There you go. Does that make you feel better?"

The other girls collected around the stall. Meara sat on a wooden crate and rested, pondering a matter, while Oona patted Tempest's neck. There was a sweet, musky smell of horses in the stables, of sweat and soaped tack and manure mixed with straw.

"I hear the people run aboot in sheets there," Meara said, adjusting her seat.

Oona frowned down at her. "Who's running aboot in sheets?"

"Egyptians," Meara said matter-of-factly. "When the Irish traders come through here last summer, I heard one of them say so. Said it was because they worshiped frogs and such."

"Frogs?"

"It's true."

Oona arched her brows in amazement. "Imagine that. Whatever for?"

"Because the ferrils tell them to, that's why."

"Ferrils?"

Meara cast a pitiful look at Dagmere. Then, scowling at Oona, she explained, "They're like kings, silly! Only worse. The ferrils make their subjects give all their gold and jewels to the frogs, so they can live forever under huge pointed rocks."

"The frogs?"

"No, the ferrils!"

Oona thought about that for a moment. "No wonder them poor Egyptians have to run aboot in sheets." Glancing over at Daktahr she said, "It's a wonder they have sense enough to breed such lovely horses."

Dagmere looked away politely. A scrawny orange cat was in a corner with a mouse pinned beneath its paws, torturing it. She was about to rescue the hapless creature when a sudden draft blew down the corridor. The girls turned to see who had opened the stable doors and saw a huddle of silhouettes in the bay, the light shining bright behind and through them.

"Well, if it isn't the little horse girl playing with all the pretty horses!" a voice called out. "Get tired of playing with the bow and arrow, have you?" An airless twittering followed that spooked several of the horses.

Dagmere groaned as Fiona and a string of pie-eyed local boys in tow entered the stables.

Not waiting for a reply, Fiona wiggled over to one of the stalls. "And this is my horse," she said, indicating her speckled gray gelding to the boys.

They glanced briefly at the horse, then turned their eyes studiously to the raven-haired beauty with the flashing green eyes.

"He comes from the finest breeding stock in all of Britain."

"Is that why your father had him cut?" Dagmere asked sweetly. "To preserve the line?"

Fiona bristled. Then she walked over to Dagmere and the two girls, and the boys followed her like spaniels. A couple of them, seeming to notice Dagmere for the first time, brightened considerably with senseless expressions.

"Just ignore her," Dagmere said to Oona and Meara.

"You can ignore me now, little horsey girl, but when you-know-who arrives, you won't be so smug."

"Who's you-know-who?" Oona wanted to know.

"Go on and tell them, Dagmere," Fiona snarled. "Tell them how he kissed me not two months ago." She ran her tongue deliciously over her lips. "Mmm, it was wonderful!"

The spaniels looked at one another, bewildered.

Color jumped into Dagmere's face as she clenched her fists. "Why don't you just be still, Fiona?"

"Why don't I—" Fiona threw her hand dramatically to her mouth. "For telling everyone here the truth, you want me to shut up?"

"Who's you-know-who?" Oona leaned over and asked one of the spaniels.

The spaniel shrugged his shoulders.

Dagmere glowered at her. "Well, if you don't shut up, I'm going to put something in your disgusting little mouth." She glanced about the stable floor.

Fiona winced. "It's no wonder Aeryck prefers me. Why, you're nothing but a dirty little girl who plays with horse droppings! Come, boys!" She turned hurriedly and started away, and the spaniels followed obediently.

Dagmere stared at her retreating form.

As Fiona reached the door she turned, and, indicating Oona and Meara with a turn of her nose, she sneered, "I see you've little enough to worry about in the way of competition, Dagmere. Why, even a wilted daisy would look good in a patch of weeds." She giggled wickedly and sauntered out of the stable.

"That does it!" Dagmere flew to the doors, and a moment later there was a wild scream.

Oona and Meara looked wide-eyed at each other, then ran after her. When they exited the stables, Dagmere and Fiona were rolling around in the snow, pulling each other's hair, and scratching and slapping.

"Here! Here! Come now, girls!" a man yelled.

As Dunnald raced over to the fight, the spaniels looked up and quickly scattered.

When Allyndaar and Brynwald entered the cottage, Helena and Tillie were squealing with laughter. Helena's face was flushed. Tillie's was beet red.

Tillie looked up at the men. "Hoot, Brynnie! Cume on in then— have some cider! You too, Allyn!" She threw a sudden hand to her mouth. "Ooie! I hope that were no' too forward of me, callin' your husband Allyn!"

"No, no," Helena chortled. "Call him anything you like. Watch me." She waved a hand at her husband. "Yoo-hoo . . . Allyn, sweetie! Do come in and have some cider, won't you?" She winked at Tillie then hiccuped. "Oh, dear," she said, covering her mouth, then she blew an intemperate strand of hair out of her eyes.

The men looked dubiously at one another.

Then both women jumped up quickly and looked into the pot.

"Aw!" Tillie groaned. "I don't think there's any left."

"We've been bitten by all the apples," Helena added sadly, trailing it with another hiccup.

And then the women looked at each other, first sorrowfully, then, stifling a snicker, they burst out laughing. It was the mouth-open, head-back kind of howl that sounded like mules braying. Then, catching themselves, they threw their hands to their faces and snorted. Both of their eyes shot open at the other. Helena hiccuped again and chased it with a burp. This got them going even more, and they began to laugh uncontrollably, slapping their knees, with their eyes squirting water.

The men gazed dumbfounded at their wives, then exchanged even more dubious looks.

Brynwald shrugged his shoulders. "I dinna ken what to say."

"I've never seen her this way before," Allyndaar said in quiet amazement.

"It must be the higher altitude," Brynwald offered. "Aye. Iffen you're no' used to it, you need to take it in slowly."

Allyndaar said, "Yes, that must be it."

Then the two chieftains turned quietly around and went back outside into the snow.

197

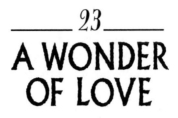

23

A WONDER OF LOVE

That night Dagmere lay in her bed, thinking what a fine mess she'd made of their first day in Loch na Huric. It had surprised her earlier when, entering the cottage, she related the sorry event to her parents, and her mother, looking unusually pale and peaked, moaned, "I am ruined, Allyn. Ruined! How could this have happened?" Then she asked him to help her into bed.

Dagmere thought her reaction severe and watched contritely as her father helped Helena across the room, thinking the shock must have been too great for her cultured constitution to endure.

The shock must have been too great for Tillie also, she mused horror-stricken, for a moment later the plump woman collapsed in a heap off to one side of the hearth and lay there gurgling with the queerest look on her face.

Brynwald had then carried her into their bedroom, with Tillie babbling something about there being stew in the pot and to watch out for biting apples. Supper had gone unheeded, and Dagmere, feeling ashamed and sick to her stomach, retired to the garret upstairs and troubled the throne of God with her broken catechism.

The house quickly fell to a quiet repose, and the noises of the night crept in stealthily behind: the crackling of the waning fire in the hearth and the sounds of snoring, intermingled with the distant murmur of the river gurgling through ice and stones.

Dagmere rolled over onto her side and blinked into the darkness, her mind a whirl of activity. In time her penitent thoughts yielded to those of an implacable burden, to the millstone hung about her heart that pulled her into a disconsolate gloom. Aeryck.

She wondered whether he cared for her as much as she did for him, wondered if what she felt burning deep in her breast was love or merely the cruel infatuation of youth. Either way, she hated this thing

198

that had gotten hold of her, that wracked her mind and heart with pangs of sorrow. So quickly had she forgotten Tillie's many warm and comforting words of his devotion. A single word of Fiona's had forced them out into the cold. A shiver of misery went through her.

She searched the darkness for his eyes, found them, then searched them for the telltale signs of love that her mother assured her would be there if love were in bloom. But she saw nothing in them, felt nothing of the bloom, and then his eyes spirited away into the night. She let out a sigh and closed her own, hoping for the comforting wash of sleep. But sleep would not come, she knew. Only tears.

She heard the door open below, and the muffled voices of Terryll and Gwyneth as they stole into the cottage, as lovers do when they are sure the world will not comprehend their love, and then the rustle of outer garments coming off and being hung onto the doorway pegs.

Someone jabbed the fire carefully with a poker, then placed a log onto it. The fire crackled and popped, then settled into a comforting roar. And then there was more whispering—love whispers, she knew instinctively—followed by a long silence during which she imagined them to be kissing. More whispers trailed the interlude, laced with giggles, and moments later there was the soft brush of Gwyneth's feet ascending the wooden stairs to the garret.

Dagmere listened as Gwyneth undressed in the dark, listened to the clothes rustling, falling to the floor, the girl picking them up and folding them away in her corner, listened as she dressed quietly in her nightclothes, an airy muse attending her surreptitious movements. Dagmere imagined the melody, and her own heart ached in counterpoint.

And then there was the quiet pad of Gwyneth's bare feet over the floor, a stifled groan as she stubbed her toe against the bedpost, and the ruffling of wool blankets as she climbed into bed and settled. There was a winsome sigh, and then Dagmere waited for the heavy sounds of sleep to follow, but they didn't come. For several minutes she waited, blinking into the darkness. And then she heard another rustling of blankets.

The garret, being a kind of loft, had a shuttered window that opened upon the great room below. Gwyneth had stolen away from her bed and situated herself on a small stool beside the window, which she opened just enough to see through. Dagmere followed her with her eyes.

The fireglow, ascending to the window with renewed vigor, cast flickering bars of shadow and light over her face, revealing the soft lines and contours of her beauty and the tender smile of love that played between the bars. The ruby hanging about her neck stole light from the fire and twinkled.

199

"Is it wonderful to be in love, Gwinnie?" Dagmere whispered across the room.

Gwyneth stifled a gasp and turned. "Oh! Did I wake you? I'm sorry, I—"

"No. No, you didn't wake me," Dagmere assured her. "I couldn't sleep."

Gwyneth was relieved. "Neither could I. I thought I would just sit here for a while, and . . . well, you know . . ."

Dagmere smiled. "Is it wonderful to be in love, Gwinnie?" she repeated.

"In love?" Gwyneth looked down at Terryll's reclining form upon a pallet next to the hearth. The boy moaned and rolled over onto his side and shrugged the blankets over his shoulders. Then he grew still, and the firelight traced his handsome features, shimmered warmly over the long, black shiny hair that spread on the pillow. Gwyneth's eyes glowed with adoration. "Oh, yes. Yes, it is," she said convincingly.

Dagmere raised up onto her elbow. "How did you know? I mean, when you knew that he first loved you?"

Gwyneth reflected on her question for a moment, and then a thought brought a smile to her lips. "When he handed me the ptarmigan."

"The ptarmigan?"

"Yes, that was it. On our trip home from Loch na Huric, after our rescue, Terryll killed two ptarmigans with his bow. That evening when we made camp, he made a little fire and cooked them—they were delicious!" She paused, as she looked back on the scene in her mind, savoring it. "I could see the love in his hands."

"His hands?" Dagmere sounded perplexed. "Not his eyes?"

"His eyes?" Gwyneth giggled. "Oh, no, I was afraid to look into his eyes. I was afraid that if I did he would know how I felt about him. I couldn't have that. Isn't that silly?" She clicked her tongue against the back of her teeth. "So like a coward I watched his hands as he prepared the meal. He has such beautiful, masculine hands—strong hands, you know—I couldn't take my eyes off them. Then as he handed me the ptarmigan, I saw his fingers trembling, and I knew." She looked back at the boy. "Yes, I knew then that he was in love with me."

Dagmere was quiet for a while. "Gwinnie?"

"Yes?"

"Do you think girls who like horses or girls who happen to be good at archery are unattractive to boys?"

Gwyneth shot her a queer look. "Where did you hear that nonsense? No, don't tell me. I know where you heard it—from that black-haired girl, right?"

200

Dagmere did not respond.

"Can't you see that she's just jealous of you?"

Dagmere's eyes started. "Jealous? of me?"

"Sure! Who wouldn't be? I'm just glad that Terryll is your brother, so I don't have to compete with you. Dagmere, you're intelligent, personable . . . and you're probably the prettiest girl I've ever seen!"

"That's kind of you to say, Gwinnie. But—"

"It's true."

"Do you think that Fiona is pretty?"

"That green-eyed witch?" Gwyneth shuddered. "She gives me the gooseflesh, that girl does. I can't see what any boy might see in her."

"You mean, besides her beautiful face and gorgeous figure?"

"Yes, besides those." Gwyneth chuckled. "By the way, Terryll and I were looking down from the hill and saw the fight. We never laughed so hard."

"I wish I could die," Dagmere said, lying back on her pillow. She stared at the ceiling and sighed. "I'm afraid I've really made a mess of things, Gwinnie. I know Mama and Tillie were beside themselves, it upset them so."

"Are you sure?" Gwyneth grunted. "Well, you know how people can get when they're trying to keep up appearances."

"If I just didn't have such a temper . . ."

Gwyneth stole one last look at Terryll, closed the shutters, then quietly padded over to her bed. "Enough of that talk. By the morrow everyone will have quite forgotten about it," she said, climbing into her covers.

"Not everyone," Dagmere muttered.

"Well, Terryll said she had it coming." Gwyneth looked up at the ceiling. "Ah! It should be a wonderful day, don't you think, Dag?—the celebration, and all."

"Yes, wonderful."

Gwyneth glanced over at Dagmere, the wan light catching the whites of her eyes and glistening in the darkness. "He'll be here, Dag, don't you worry. He'll come riding in on the morrow with his Uncle Finn and the men from Eire, and everything will be good again, you'll see."

"I do hope you're right."

"I am. Now, let's get some sleep. Good night."

"Good night, Gwinnie."

Gwyneth rolled over, and minutes later there was a soft murmuring of delicious sleep coming from her bed.

Dagmere blinked into the darkness, wondering about many things.

24

TERROR IN
THE BLACK

Aeryck blinked into the darkness, wondering if he were going to be alive in five minutes. He looked over his shoulder, and he could just make out several of the faster wolves gaining on them.

Hauwka was running along a low, treeless ridge now—his gait noticeably more halting and slower—and the boy was clinging to his fur with one hand. With the other he was ready with his sword. Prayers escaped his mouth rhythmically, but he had little confidence in prayers of late, for he had prayed earlier for snow that it might cover their tracks and scent, and almost immediately the dark storm clouds had opened up to a beautiful blue sky.

It had been nip and tuck all day long—the wolves gaining, and Hauwka losing them through some cunning of his; the wolves gaining again, and again the bear losing them. However it seemed likely that the wolves were going to overrun them now at last, and then it would be over.

Ahead was a large grove of scrub oaks and thickets, spread out along a stream and showing black against the night sky at the end of it, and the bear angled toward the trees, following the dictates of his kind. There was no outrunning the wolves in the open ground anymore. Perhaps in the thicket he could slow them down, force them to separate, take them on in smaller numbers, get into the trees.

It seemed a good idea to Aeryck at the moment, guessing the bear's strategy. But had he known anything about the nature of bears he would have had cause to despair. For bears heading for the trees usually means one thing: their cunning, or speed, or luck has been all used up and they are preparing themselves for a desperate last stand.

The bear cleared the first rank of bushes, nearly pitching the boy, who was busy looking over his shoulder, and then a second rank, landing in a broad clearing, the moon lighting it with a brilliant silver pallor. They found themselves suddenly in the midst of several large, black shapes that looked to be huge boulders—boulders that unexpectedly came to life, with the heads turning on the newcomers and the beady eyes mean and intense.

The bear wheeled to his left, his nostrils flaring angrily as he blew out several furious snorts, but there were others of the creatures, trotting out of the thicket with their little eyes glinting menacingly, stopping abruptly to stare.

Suddenly Aeryck felt a terrific jolt through Hauwka's right front leg and was thrown forward onto the bear's thick neck. "What?" he yelled, scrambling desperately, pulling himself back with a handful of fur.

Growling, Hauwka spun to face his attacker and took a swipe at it, but the creature whirled out of his reach and stood squared off and braced solid, eyeing the bear intensely and sniffing his scent. Others of the things were up and coming at him with quick, choppy gaits, several—maybe thirty—large, compact shapes with long, flat-ended snouts and tusks flashing dully in the moon light.

"Wild boars!" Aeryck gasped.

They had stumbled into a large herd of tuskers—big, thick, three-to-four-hundred-pounders that were rooting about in the scrub oaks for food. Boars are naturally testy animals, but when surprised at feeding time by the likes of a giant bear with a human rider, their disposition is likely to turn surly in short order. It did.

One of the larger boars charged Hauwka. It came at him fast, with the little legs scissoring over the ground, and, as the head dipped in low with the tusks, Hauwka spun around and batted it with his paw (Aeryck feeling the jolt in his teeth), bowling the pig over into the snow several feet away.

The boar rolled up onto its feet and shuddered off the blow, then squaring off, legs straight, the muscled flanks taut and gleaming, the coarse hairs showing in the light, he glared at the bear with intense, little mean eyes, appraising him curiously. Then he blew out an angry snort. The blow would have killed a wolf or a man, but the pig made ready to charge again, appearing to be little more than dazed. Others of the boars pawed the ground with their tiny hooves and raised a ruckus with their snorting.

Typically the boar will charge fast and, closing, will lower its snout and throw its taut bulk into its enemy to knock it off balance. Then, hooking a lip of flesh with the lower tusks, it will lift the animal with its powerful head and slash from side to side, fast, like a knife fighter, using the upper tusks now with the lower, to open huge gashes along the flanks of the beast, spilling its bowels. There was no retreat instinct bred into the brain of the wild pig, only attack, attack fiercely until either its enemy is dead or the pig itself is dead.

Aeryck had had nightmares about the creatures ever since he saw the head of the monster boar hanging in the great hall at Killwyn Eden. He'd hoped he'd never have to encounter one of them in the wild. And certainly not under these conditions. That a wild boar could tear a man to shreds with its tusks in a matter of seconds was no fancy of the imagination, and Aeryck was forcing the grisly images from his mind.

The whole herd of boars stampeded then as if they'd been insulted, and they came at the bear snorting and squealing, and Aeryck brought his sword down across the thick, coarse-haired nape of a smaller boar, and the pig screamed and corkscrewed into the ground, squealing awfully, the bear trampling it as he wheeled away from a broadside of deadly tusks, letting out an earsplitting roar. The pigs jerked to a stop, turned snorting as they made a new appraisal of the bear. Their flat noses twitching, they prepared for another charge.

Suddenly the air was rife with the chilling snarls of wolves in the thicket. In the confusion Aeryck had forgotten them, and he reeled in time to see the forward pack leaping into the clearing from several quarters, beheld with some satisfaction the startled looks in their eyes as they saw the boars. Many of the pigs trotted away from the bear, now sensing a greater threat to their feeding grounds, and, collecting in bunches, each animal stood stolid and red-eyed and snorted at the latest nuisances. For just a moment there was dead silence over the clearing as the animals looked at one another, pig ears flicking angrily, tails curling, wolf ears pinned back with the big canines showing under the snouts, and then there was a rush of pigs into the wolves.

Immediately a boil of confusion ensued, as the din of snarls and snorts and squeals quickly rose over the clearing. The pigs came in fast, their heads low, tusks clashing with the big canines as they pummeled the wolves with terrific body blows, then hooking, lifting, and slashing with the quick knife-fighter tactics.

The wolves, scrambling into smaller attacking groups, ganged on the smaller pigs, nipping at their hocks to cripple them, to get them down that they might sink their fangs into the thick hides. But they were having little success. The pigs were quick, turning on the open flanks of the wolves with their lethal tusks or ducking into the thickets, reappearing with charges to their blind sides. The overall effect produced a mind-numbing cacophony, and the wolves were having a time of it.

"C'mon, Hauwka! Let's go!" Aeryck yelled, seizing the moment to escape. And Hauwka let out a thunderous roar and felled a wolf that was backing away from a large tusker. The pig trampled it, made quick

204

work of it with its four-inch tusks, then turned on the bear with a snort. But Hauwka was already into the trees and heading for open ground.

When Aeryck looked back on the scene, the pigs had the first rush of wolves scattering into the thickets, but lifting his eyes beyond these he could see through the trees the bulk of the pack running black against the moon-washed snow, coming as a relentless killing machine.

He knew the wild boars might slow them down, but they certainly wouldn't stop them. The wolves would come. They would circumvent the nuisance. It is the nature of the predator.

And so the bear limped away as best he could, a cruel gash opened along his already crippled right shoulder, leaving a blood spoor that the weakest nose in the pack could follow.

25

COMINGS
AND GOINGS

Dagmere was awakened by some great noise. A roaring, it seemed, like a fast-moving watercourse. A thought floated sleepily through her mind: the river. That was it, of course.

Opening her eyes sluggishly (having dozed off only two hours earlier), she blinked at the rough-hewn planks of the ceiling, thinking she was still asleep. Practically speaking she still was, and she rolled over onto her other side to prove it. And then she heard the noise again—the river—but now it didn't sound like a river at all. It sounded like something different, like people yelling perhaps. *Let them yell,* she mused, dozing off to a delicious dream tryst.

"Dagmere! Are you going to sleep the day away?" Gwyneth yelled up the garret stairs. "Come quickly! There are riders coming!"

"Hm?" Dagmere purred dreamily.

"Tillie says it's probably Aeryck!"

Dagmere sighed, "That's nice. Ask him what's kept him so—" Suddenly one eye shot open. *"Aeryck!"*

The girl kicked off her blankets with a squeal and hit the floor running, her body dashing around the loft frantically looking for something to wear, while her mind was desperately trying to catch up to it.

The sky was gray and overcast, and the snow was lightly falling over the village with large fluffy flakes. Just inside the gates of the village the monks Gildas and Rupert were somberly relaying to the assembled crowd everything they knew concerning the boy, his last words to them, their last sight of him fleeing over a hill with scores of rabid wolves on his tail.

Oswald, the chieftain of Glenlochar, and the others of his men who had escorted the two monks on the final leg of their journey, nodded grimly at Brynwald as though to confirm their words. There was an unspoken understanding between the men.

Tillie threw her hands to her face and began to cry as she grasped it.

Brynwald took her into his arms and held her, patting her shoulder tenderly. "There, there," he tried to console her, reeling from the news himself. "The kipper will be all right. By the oaks, woman, the Laird'll look after him."

The other women fell in quick succession, both Helena and Dagmere crumpling into Allyndaar's arms and weeping bitterly, Gwyneth into Terryll's. Brynwald and Allyndaar exchanged grim looks, then gazed out over the dark, snow-grayed hills to the west, as though some hidden recourse were to be found there.

A pall of gloom descended quickly over the village as the news was relayed from person to person. Men looked at one another quietly and then down at their feet, shaking their heads, their lips compressed in thought as they calculated the odds. Some of them gazed out on the hills as well. The women wiped their eyes as they listened to their men for words of hope, and hearing none they clutched their faces. Children looked up at their parents, feeling sad about something but not understanding why. There was a pervading sense of helplessness in the air, the dread of irretrievable loss falling. A collective bitter sigh was exhaled.

Terryll stepped away from Gwyneth and said, "I'm going after him, Papa. I cannot believe that he is dead."

"I'll go with you, lad," a voice boomed. It was Bolstroem, the giant blacksmith.

"Aye," Dunnald said, stepping toward the boy. "I'll not believe he's dead till I see it with my own eyes."

There was a sudden murmuring of assent alighting here and there amid the villagers, sparked to life by the new course of action. Men nodded their heads at one another, grunting their approval as men do when there is a noble goal to achieve. And the women stood wondering anxiously as they do when their men suddenly start acting like men. This new shift in the mood released the children from their indiscernible burdens, and they scattered squealing into the falling snow, sticking out their tongues to catch the big new flakes.

"I'm going too!" Dagmere said, stepping away from her father.

"No, Dagmere," he said, catching her arm. "I want you to stay here with your mother."

"But, Papa—"

"You will stay here with your mother!"

She had seen that look before in his eyes, the piercing blue steel of his gaze that could cut through any pretense or affront, and she lowered her eyes before it.

Allyndaar went over to Brynwald and the others to make plans.

Helena put her arms around the girl and held her close. "We will pray for him, Dagmere," she said, looking apprehensively at the back of her husband. "Prayer is more powerful than any army of ten thousand."

"Yes, but I can shoot better with the bow than I can pray, Mama. Better than any of those men, I shouldn't wonder."

"All the more reason to stay here and practice."

"But he might need me!"

"Would you have me go against your father's wishes?"

"No," the girl said resignedly. Suddenly Dagmere looked imploringly into her mother's eyes, tears spurting from her own. "Mama, it's Aeryck. What if he's . . . what if he's really dead?" she cried, as though the thought had just struck her.

Helena said nothing. She just looked sadly at her daughter, then pulled her close again and began to pray quietly.

Dagmere wept miserably.

Fiona turned away from the group with a bewildered look on her face. She was wondering how all of this was going to affect her life. She walked back to her house and had herself a good cry.

Fifty men were quickly assembled to hunt for the boy, their horses packed and ready with two days' provisions. Brynwald organized them into two groups.

Oswald and the twenty men who had come with him were to look for Aeryck along the trail to Glenlochar and then beyond to where Rupert and Gildas last saw him alive. They were to pick up his trail and follow it as best they could, providing the snow had not covered it completely.

Brynwald, Allyndaar, and the rest of the party were to look for the boy more to the north, working westward along a parallel course to Oswald's, converging at a place known to both chieftains—a farm between the headwaters of the Rivers Clyde and Tweed. If either group found him, they were to send a rider to the place of rendezvous and let the other group know. Hopefully with Godspeed they would find him, but every man knew in his heart it would be like looking for the proverbial needle in a haystack.

Her eyes red and her face streaked with tears, Dagmere watched as the men rode away from the village, their shapes quickly turning gray and then dark and somber in the slanting snow. A silent prayer struggled weakly from her lips. "Have mercy, God. Please have mercy on my Aeryck."

And sniffling she turned and walked sadly back to the house with the other women.

26
LIKE THE HARE

Aeryck and Hauwka had been resting now for two hours—two precious hours sacrificed—and he hoped the much needed respite would not have cost them their lives.

He gazed out from the mouth of a black cave over the bleak and untoward snowscape that was heavy with dark clouds, angry, oppressive clouds that were slung low over the horizon of pitch, holding in them the threat of snow but as yet yielding only intermittent flurries. But the wind was up, blowing increasingly fierce now like banshees shrieking shrilly, and his ears were trained to it. A blizzard was on the way by the sound of it, or a monster of a storm at least. During the lulls he could hear the stealthy night scurryings of voles and mice over the snow, their little gnawings in the shadows, or the thumping of hares, warning of owls and foxes. But he heard no wolves. Thank God, no wolves.

The cave, a shelf of rock over a little hollow of beaten-down earth, loomed over a wide and rocky swale of land, bereft of trees and sloping away like a large fan, low ridges radiating away from the mouth on either side. Here and there naked shrubs protruded through the snow, their bony fingers rattling in the wind. And when the clouds permitted, the moon would spill through and light everything for miles around in the ghostly night hues of winter.

Earlier in the morning, the wolves had once again closed to within a mile of them, having been delayed some by the wild boars. And at once espying them in the distance, the brutes sent up hellish cries that resounded off the low hills and cloud ceiling, giving Aeryck the terrifying sensation that they were all around them, converging on them like several packs of demon wraiths.

His eyes were anxiously deployed over the low hills and sweeps before him and on either side. He fully expected a sudden rush from any quarter. But there was nothing: no sign of wolves, no sign of life whatsoever, nothing but the vast and broken emptiness of the moorlands, covered with a clean blanket of snow.

However, glancing over his shoulder, he saw the hills behind them were crawling with swarms of tiny black specks. The earth was moving, it appeared, boiling over with a black ooze, and it seemed likely that it would overrun them any moment.

And then the snow began to fall, drawing a white veil between them, covering their tracks and burying their scent, affording them a glimmer of hope. And when they entered another wood, Hauwka instinctively changed his course, swung wide and doubled back, hobbling terribly now as he padded tentatively along icy streams whenever possible, using every trick of cunning to bury their scent, then headed on a gradual northeasterly trail toward Loch na Huric.

Aeryck could hear the wolf howls dipping in and out of the wind, strong at first, then growing weaker in the distance with every mile. And then there was nothing. Only the wind. He sighed a prayer of thanksgiving. It was a weak prayer, one of tenuous faith, for the boy knew that the wolves were creatures of instinct also and would not be fooled long. They too would double back, would pick up their scent again, or guess it. They would come.

They were wolves.

Presently the boy sat bone tired, cold, and hunkered down in his cloak, his knees pulled up under the wrap with his joints aching in rebellion to the day's toil and bitterness. And his stomach was stabbing him with hunger pangs, like a thousand little needles pricking, and because of it he was feeling all-over miserable and sorry for himself.

Apparitions of roasted mutton legs and steaming plates of broiled whitefish and boiled cabbage rose before him and taunted him with their senseless vapors. Then he remembered his last meal when he broke fast at the tavern of Pea Gants yesterday morning: two bowls of hot porridge, a wedge of cheese, and half a loaf of warm, freshly baked bread, washed down with mugs of piping-hot apple cider—everything served straight off the stove and quick and with unbounded supply, and by the hands of the fiery tavern maid Silvie, who wouldn't take no for an answer.

It seemed a lifetime ago. Food was a remembered thing, taken for granted, a prospect of the past. But he was hungry now. He scooped up a little handful of snow and sucked on it, hoping the water trickling into his stomach would feign a meal and ease its constriction. It didn't. It only added shivers to his miseries.

But his mind was keen and bright, his contrary circumstances honing it to a fine edge. Thoughts of the morning played over his vision in sharp relief. Events after the meal, before the wolves, paraded before him, when his only concern had been that his Uncle Finn had failed to show. He remembered his sullen behavior toward the two monks all too clearly, his curt responses to their inquiries, his deliberate aloofness to

210

their fellowship, and his conscience was pricked with pangs of guilt. Both body and soul smarted now to the lack of nourishment.

What a fool, he thought, shaking his head contritely. *What a childish fool I have been. Oh, to hear their voices now, the song of human tongues warbling in the ear, the warm touch of their hands. I do hope they made it to Glenlochar all right,* he mused. *If they did, then Oswald will see them safely to Loch na Huric to celebrate Christ's Mass.* He took a little comfort in that, then thought of all the delicious food that was to be prepared for the occasion. The boy let out a sigh and looked grimly over at Hauwka a yard away, a great mound of fur breathing heavily now, struggling through a fitful, troubled sleep.

That the bear was in desperate throes was evident in his labored breath and attendant moans, his right shoulder trembling terribly with spasms of pain. His leg was a mat of dried blood from where the boar's tusk had opened it with a cruel gash. The detour, though certainly saving their lives, had added time and distance to their journey, two things that Hauwka's tortured body could ill afford.

Suddenly the moon spilled brightly through a dark aperture in the clouds, illumining the great loneliness of the terrain and marking the dips and swells with shadow and light. Drawn by the light, his eyes traced the black rim of distant hills to the east and reached beyond them with a glimmer of hope to the warming hearth and heath nestled cozily in the little river valley of the Annan.

Loch na Huric. The company of Britons had no doubt arrived there by now and with them the beautiful daughter of Allyndaar. She was but a phantom in his mind now, an ethereal wisp that flitted teasingly in the peripheral vision of his mind's eye. But the thought of her was strong in him, a resonant clangor that thundered like the hammer of Thor. But, alas! Would she ever look at him again after the unfortunate scene with Fiona? The fateful kiss? He thought not.

A white hare darted into view, sat upright, back bowed and rigid, ears perking to the wind, its shadow shooting out dark and crisp from its feet. Aeryck started from his wistful reverie and instinctively grabbed the hilt of his sword before he realized the utter foolishness of it. And then he watched helplessly as the hare bounded away into the black embrace of the night. In that moment he regretted his lack of the hunting skills that Terryll possessed, realized now the presumption he had had of life without the knowledge of bow and arrow.

The dark aperture began to close over the moon, narrowing its glistening field to a tiny spot of light on the snow, and then it leaped off the earth into a net of darkness. Immediately a shrill wind whistled over the snow, curled about in the cave, ferreting out the exposed patches of Aeryck's skin, and bit him with bitter cold.

Aeryck turtled into his cloak, pulled it up over his ears, and thought of food again, thought of the full satchel of provisions that were lost with Sullie. And the loss of her welled up in him again, her easy-going temperament, the look in her big brown eyes as she glanced back at him, and he sighed. Feelings of remorse and guilt and anger and hunger and all-over miserableness overwhelmed him, and he wanted to cry.

He looked to the heavens for consolation, but his heart was weighed down by a sudden heaviness, as though the dark, impenetrable ceiling clouded over his soul, downcasting him with chilling thoughts that fell lightly over the terrain of his soul like snow.

Is God there? Is He? *Yes, He is there, and He is angry with me. Isn't He? Why do I feel so? I didn't before I knew Him. How can I ease the terrible scrutiny of His countenance?*

And doubts scurried about just inside the shadows of his soul like the little night creatures, for so they were. And, like the warm-blooded variety, he could hear their gnawings but couldn't see them, couldn't get hold of them. They were always just beyond his reach. He felt as though no matter how hard he tried to overcome his doubts—to lay the ax, as it were, at the bitter roots that were entwining around his heart and choking the life out of him—the more entangled he became.

Brother Thomas's words came to mind. "Hate is a deffil of a thing. It'll take from a man his youth—eat it through like a canker till there's nothing left of his soul but the black hate itself. 'Tis an insatiable appetite that works within you, Aeryck . . . but the Laird by His grace will work His sweet mercy in you, if you dinnay withhold Him."

Oh, for such mercy, leaped the thought. *But how? How is it that I may withhold Him, when I know not where He is?*

The boy covered his face in shame. For it seemed to him that his fledgling faith was, like his sword, a useless thing—the grasp of God ever eluding him like the white hare. And then a gentle whisper stirred in his breast, like a moist breeze over a dry ground:

> "Come now, Immaculate fount of God,
> O wretched man draw near;
> Take hold the Lamb on Calvary's sod,
> Be cleansed and no more fear."

The whisper, stronger now in timbre, reached up through his tongue as his spirit rose in song, repeating the stanza with renewed vigor. He was moved to look heavenward again, to seek the elusive One beyond the canopy of gloom. And as his eyes searched the dark and terrible heavens that lowered over the eternal rim, no longer did they seem an implacable barrier to his prayers. Indeed, they seemed to invite his inquiry.

"Holy! Holy! Holy!
Omnipotent King of Kings;
The heavens declare Thy glory,
And angels rush to sing."

A glimmer of faith took wick on his soul, and immediately the little cave was filled with a sweet Presence, enveloping the downcast boy, filling him to overflowing with rapturous song. It seemed the cords of death that were entwined about his heart relaxed their grip and withered, their malignant black roots shriveling back into the infernal soil. He felt a oneness with God as he never had before, too much for him to comprehend. Tears welled into the boy's eyes, brimmed, then trickled joyfully down his cheeks as he communed with his God.

And then exhaustion took its toll. Full of hope, he nestled into the thick fur of the bear to rest a little while, to close his eyes over the day, and so to shut it forever in the past. Laying his head against the bear's flank, he listened to the great heart pounding slow and steady, the blood chugging heavily through the spent frame and limbs, listened to the wheeze of breath toiling in and out of the lungs. And, as he closed his eyes, the day's troubles came at him in quick snatches, ambushing him, rushing him from every quarter, and he slept fitfully.

Suddenly the fur on Hauwka's coat bristled, and the great animal, in a singular move, shuddered to his feet with a low growl steaming through his teeth.

Aeryck was awake with a start, his eyes wide and his chest pounding with the knowledge of imminent danger.

Three hares bounded across the clearing, darting along zigzag courses, their eyes bugged in terror.

The wolves came over the low rise that dipped into the swale, then passed before the little cave, a long line of black silhouettes, like specters floating silently over the earth with their yellow eyes sweeping for prey.

Aeryck blinked incredulously at the spectacle of death padding a mere twenty yards in front of him, the wind strong in his face, burning his eyes. He counted more then one hundred wolves, noted the large red one in the lead. He could hear the grunts rattling in their throats, even smell them—smelled the hatred on them.

One brute glanced in his direction and stared into the black mouth of the cave. The boy's heart leaped into his throat, and his hand moved furtively to his hilt. He gathered himself for the rush that would come any second should the wind shift and they be discovered.

But the wolf looked away, its curiosity satisfied, and the floating silhouettes disappeared over the other rise.

The boy exhaled quietly, and he felt a rush of blood suddenly pounding against his chest and temples. His hand was trembling on the hilt.

Immediately Hauwka started out of the cave and stopped, looked in the direction the wolves had gone, and raised his snout to the air. Then he lowered it to the snow and sniffed the scent. Looking up, he snorted and glanced back at the boy with a look that made his intentions clear.

So Aeryck quickly scaled the great back, and the bear hobbled away into the night, heading opposite the wolves on their very trail. And then it began to snow again, lightly at first, then a steady downpour.

As he looked back on the receding cave, the little scoop of earth, the thought entered Aeryck's mind that God had been holding him there in the hollow of His hand. A little prayer of thanksgiving winged brightly away. It was a good, strong prayer this time.

And the snow fell. The wolves' trail before them was soon obliterated, and so they struck a new one, heading in an easterly direction and climbing, always moving up a steady grade it seemed. There were dips, of course, little valleys frozen over and billowing with drifts of snow, but overall there was a general upward sweep in the terrain.

The boy had no idea where they were and peered into the dark snowfall for any landmarks or man-made structures that he might recognize. He didn't see any. He didn't recognize the grade either, but he knew that sooner or later they would have to run into the River Nith, which flowed north-south through the Southern Uplands. From there he would know how to get to Loch na Huric.

They moved haltingly over hill and dale, keeping to the high ground wherever possible. But still the going was treacherous. Every so often the ground would suddenly fall away into a crevice beneath a deceptive snowdrift, and with no way to see the fissure in the dark, the bear would fall into it and tax the reserves of his strength climbing out.

Hauwka began to halt many times and look back on their trail, raising his snout to the wind. However Aeryck knew that it wasn't to smell for wolves any longer, but to rest. The boy could see in his coallike eyes, once wet and glistening bright with vigor, the telling dull sheen of exhaustion.

At one point he slid off the bear's back, and this time Hauwka sounded no objection. He simply hobbled away with his massive head hung low on the great neck, his right shoulder shuddering terribly under the wicked, dark scab. And Aeryck followed him wearily, feeling the cold now that he was away from Hauwka's warm fur. The boy knew that, unless they found shelter and nourishment soon, the bear would perish, that he too would perish. And so they kept moving.

When they came to the old Roman road, Hauwka froze.

"What is it, boy?" Aeryck whispered, his eyes glaring into the night. And then he saw it—light, a tiny yellow halo flickering through the swirls of falling snow. The boy's face lit up excitedly. "A farm!"

But a low growl rattled in the bear's throat.

"What's wrong?"

Moments later they came, the horsemen did, a line of fifty Pictish warriors plodding along the road toward them.

Aeryck crouched instinctively into the shadows of some shrubbery, not knowing if they were friendly or not. The bear remained rock rigid, resembling a rather large bush covered in snow.

The Picts did not see them, for it was dark and snowing and visibility was poor, and their cloak hoods were pulled over their heads against the weather, and, not wanting to fall over into the ditch on either side of the road, they kept their eyes intent only on the horse's tail in front.

There was an air of black surliness grumbling along the line, and one of the men called out, *"Och,* what's the hurry? We could lodge in yon cottage for the night and get a fresh start on the morrow."

"Aye. Aye." Several of the men grunted their consent.

The man at the head of the column turned and answered gruffly, "By the oaks! Perhaps you'll have me telling Sarteham then that a pack of old crones have signed on with him."

That voice! Aeryck thought, starting. *I know that voice!*

And when the man at the head of the column turned about, a blush of light caught the features under the hood, and for an instant the sneer twisting cruelly over the face was lit with a wan pallor before the shadows reclaimed it. Aeryck felt the blood rushing from his head.

It was Spang.

Immediately a flame of anger leaped into the boy's limbs, roared throughout the length and breadth of his body until he was consumed by white-hot hatred. Again the call sounded in his breast, the resonant clarion to execute swift judgment on this killer of boy monks. And as the man drew nearer, not twenty feet away from him now, drawing closer and none the wiser, his course of action became lucidly clear. All he needed to do was simply step forward out of the shadows, and, with a lightning flick of silver, Spang, his bitter enemy, would be dead before he or anyone else would know what had struck him.

His dark, glowering eyes fastened on the approaching black shape of the man he had sworn on oath to kill, to kill swiftly, coolly, and without mercy. He deserved none. Fifteen feet . . . thirteen feet . . . drawing nearer.

His mind reasoned with him: the coincidence of meeting Spang out here, at night, in the middle of a snowstorm, was nothing of chance. It was by divine providence—*God has given your enemy into your hands. He has provided you a shield of darkness and snow behind which to escape. Do it now, Aeryck! Execute the judgment! Eleven feet . . . nine feet . . .*

The boy took a deliberate step forward, his hand reaching for his sword, seizing it, sliding it stealthily from its scabbard, with a single burning thought hammering in his brain. *Now! Now! Kill him now! Execute the sentence!* Seven feet . . .

And as Spang passed five feet before him, a throaty chortle popping in his throat, the man continued northward along the old Roman road. He did not see the dark killing shape recede back into the shadows, nor did he hear the sword of Caelryck sliding silently into its sheath, neither the cursing of his name that fell dead to the ground. He heard only the crimson oaths of his men, the grumbling of cold and bitter mercenaries bound under a wicked scheme, and he was pleased with himself. Yes, he had gathered a fair group of cutthroats to Sarteham's side, and he was mighty pleased with himself.

As Aeryck watched the column of Picts ride away into the darkness heading north, the doubts of his soul scurried from their shadow haunts and began to gnaw at him again. And as he turned and followed after the bear toward the glimmer of yellow light, he heard another voice. It spoke to him in a hoarse, fiendish whisper.

You see, Worm? You have not changed. You are still full of hate. Have done with this Christian foolishness. Have done with it, Worm.

27
OLD POOT

It was a queer sound that pecked away at Aeryck's subconscious mind, beginning at the end of a long, dark tunnel in his mindscape where there was a tiny point of light. And then he moved closer to the sound as he was drawn through the tunnel, and the point of light grew larger, and the sounds became louder and more distinct. However they were as yet indiscernible, and the dreams attending the sound and the light were wild and hallucinative, full of long-tusked boars and yellow-eyed wolves.

Aeryck blinked away sleep as the gray light of dawn slanted through the many openings in the thatched roof, one of which fell over his eyes with a bright spot of warming glory. It was cold and bright, there was a dampness in the air, and his breath hung over him in little clouds. He was happy for his warm, woolen cloak that he pulled over himself. When his eyes adjusted to the light he noticed that a chicken was staring down at his face, cocking its head to one side to see him with its little yellow eye, and it was clucking and pecking at the straws tangled in his hair.

At first the boy didn't know what it was, for it was perched on something behind him, so the chicken appeared to be standing on its head. Aeryck stared at it for a moment, collecting his bearings, realizing that he wasn't dreaming, then looked away to acquaint himself with his surroundings.

That he was in a barn he knew from last night when he and Hauwka stole into it. It was long and narrow, made of wattle and daub that needed new mudding, with a low, pitched roof that needed thatching and accounted for the many little spots of light over the dirt floor. And puddles were here and there where the snow melted through, trickled along the cross-spars, and dripped.

There were three weathered stalls on one side of the barn with gates tilting on worn leather hinges. A cow bawling to be milked was in one; a huge, dirty white draft horse was in the middle one, its big head hanging listlessly over the gate and snorting at the boy; and the third was empty, except for the chickens roosting in it.

There was the fetid smell of old urine and manure pervading the place, as though the stalls hadn't been tended to in months. Hanging on the other wall were the harness and traces, the leather neglected and cracked, the plow beneath them, and some pitching forks and rakes with some tines missing, and a wooden bucket for the milk. And up in the corners were hornets' nests of dried mud, long since abandoned, and below them in the corners little mice scurried about in some broken ale casks discarded there. Two or three plump cats watched them greedily.

Aeryck felt the eye on him again and, turning, saw the upside-down chicken sidestepping behind him now, clucking softly, its head low and jerking tentatively this way and that to get a better look at him. And then the boy saw that his head lay against a wooden crib that was stacked high with hay to a loft overhead.

Two dozen or more chickens, red-and-white ones and some with liver speckles, roosted on various perches around the barn. He could hear some in the loft, scratching around and kicking bits of hay into the air. A few more were in the third stall next to the draft horse (one was in an old grain sack propped in the corner where the mice were) and other nooks and crannies where they sought to sequester their eggs. Others were milling about, pecking in the light spots for grist.

The boy wondered what manner of caretaker presided here, or if there even was a caretaker, for the barn seemed abandoned to a happy neglect. His eyes shifted stealthily to the chicken again. A basal urge sounded in his belly and quick as a flash he snatched its neck.

"Food!"

The chicken let out a choked squawk and flapped its wings furiously, which excited the others. The draft horse whickered loudly, and the cow bawled, and for a moment there was a tremendous row.

Suddenly a big square of light opened into the barn, cut by the silhouette of a man, the gray light glowing dully around him and through his hair.

"Here, here . . . what's going—hey! And what is he doing in the barn?" a voice growled. "A thief, is he?"

Aeryck climbed to his feet from the thick bed of straw and squinted into the light. "I used to be," he said, eyeing the dark shape warily.

"Used to be, huh? What's that in his hands then, you wonder? That dinna look like no 'used to be.' Looks like one of your chickens."

The man stepped into the barn with a stealthy bounce in his gait, and the shadows stripped away from him, allowing Aeryck to see his features at last in the even light. He reeled at the sight.

He was a smallish, fiftyish, wiry-built man with a wizened face, reddened by the elements, and his long brows were pinched into a fiery scowl beetling over the eyes, which swept the place with a wild expression. His hair was a riot of coarse gray, sticking out every which way from beneath an old leather skullcap, and the scraggy gray beard was a redundancy. Over an ill-fitting woolen shirt he wore a jerkin of stitched-together pieces of leather. And his woolen trousers, which seemed more an assortment of mismatched patches over stripes, were tucked into heavy mud boots that were clogged and spattered with the same and bent up at the toes. He seemed a mirror image of his environs.

"I'll pay for what we eat," Aeryck said, wondering what feather of mischief had befallen him.

"Pay?" The man's eyes swelled with interest and focused on the boy now, a light twinkling in them. "Aye, that you will, mannie—and dearly too," he snarled. "That's his best egg-layer you got in your— We?" he interrupted himself.

The man reached over and took up one of the pitchforks and eyed the confines of the barn suspiciously, squinting this way and that. Indeed his face seemed made of rubber for the way the skin stretched and shrank over his thoughts.

Suddenly a large stack of straw in the corner behind Aeryck began to rustle. The man's eyes brightened, then narrowed, the right eye lost in the squint, and as he grinned knowingly there was revealed in his front teeth a large gap.

He went over to the stack, stepping cautiously and leading with the fork, shoulders stooped forward, knees crooked out and elbows up. "Ah, hidin' over here, is he?" he chortled, arching an elastic brow. "Come on then, lad, out with you! There's nay hidin' from old Poot!"

Poot? Aeryck sounded the name in his mind as he watched him with some bewilderment. His right hand was never far from his hilt. For indeed the man seemed a blurred reflection of both cunning and lunacy, and he wasn't sure which of them was in control of the pitchfork.

Poot was about to jab it into the mound of straw when a loud moan sounded from within it, startling him erect.

A moment later Hauwka rose out of the stack, covered with bits of straw that showered off his great height. Then, limping forward, he moaned again.

The man followed the bear up with his eyes, his mouth agape. Then, letting out a little shriek, he stumbled backward over the milking pail and landed in the midst of his chickens. There was a terrible squabble as the denizens of the barn squawked and whickered and bawled and meowed, and feathers and dust swirled into the air, and mice skittered into their holes.

Poot jumped to his feet and aimed his fork at the bear. He was blinking incredulously, and his jaw fell slack in wonder.

Hauwka gazed at the man for a moment, then, ignoring him, began to gingerly lick the wound on his shoulder.

"Och! What manner of beast is it? Or has the mountain sprouted legs then?"

"He's a bear."

"Aweel!" Poot exclaimed, eyeing the bear with amazement. His appraisal worked furiously over his face. "Such a beast you've never seen!"

The bear's eyes were on the fork now, and a low growl rumbled deep in his chest, the big canine teeth just showing below the snout curl.

Poot's eyes flew open in horror.

"He won't harm you so long as you don't point that thing at him," Aeryck said.

Poot tossed the fork into a corner as though it had caught fire. "There you have it," he said, gazing at a spot somewhere to the right of Aeryck's ear. "So he's stripped you to mercy, has he? And what've you got to say for yourself? By the oaks! What can he say?" The man suddenly giggled, then his eyes shifted to some other point over the boy's head. "Now if you're going to rob him, mannie, get on with it. He has chores need tending."

"I told you I'm not a thief," Aeryck said, beginning to feel a little flustered. "We only wish a decent meal, for which I will pay you fairly."

The man squinted. *"Och!* And so he's been flappin', Poot, but have you seen any gold? Nay!"

"And he won't . . . er . . . you won't either," Aeryck said, looking around him to see if there actually might be someone else in the barn. Then reaching into his cloak pocket, he pulled out a small silver coin and proffered it to the man. "But this should more than pay for what we eat."

The man's eyes widened at the gleam of the coin, and he snatched it from the boy's hand with an adder's speed. He examined both sides of it greedily, slowly turning it in one of the shafts of light. He was scratching his head through the skullcap, grinning, the gap in his teeth showing impishly.

"Roman, eh? Dinna see many of these anymore, do you now?" he chortled, casting a conspiratorial glance at the big, white draft horse. "Troth, nay! Hoot!" he whistled. "A scuttle of oats for you!"

The horse snorted happily, and the man squirreled the coin down his boot and gave it a stamp. "Well then, mannie, take your chickens and be oft with you now. Like he's said, old Poot has chores!"

"Do you mind if we eat first?"

"Do you min—" The man's expression flew wide, then collapsed into an indignant scowl. "Ooie! He's thinkin' old Poot is running an inn on the heather!" Shooing the boy with his hands, he added, "Oft with you now, gang—oft!"

Aeryck stared at the man thoroughly bewildered, but he didn't budge. Narrowing his eyes, he said, "I'll not leave until we've eaten what we've paid handsomely for."

Poot's face burned through a spectrum of reds until Aeryck thought he might burst. "He's an insolent scalawag, airn't he?" He scowled. Then throwing his hands in the air and stomping in a circle, he cried, "Well, he says to you nay! Nay! Nay! A thousand times nay!"

"And I prefer my meals cooked," Aeryck said, finishing his thought. "And the bear—well, he just likes his meals dead, and a little peace to enjoy them." He drew open his cloak and gently lay his hand on the pommel of his sword.

"Troth, so it's murder for old Poot, is it?" And his glowering eyes went from the boy to the sword hilt to the bear's teeth, quickly back to the sword, and then the man did a wee hop as the gleam of silver curling over the hilt caught his gaze.

"Och!" he said, falling into a kind of trance. His eyes, dull and transfixed by the piercing luster of its beauty, the exquisite lines and filigree around the hilt and haft, mirrored the surrender of his soul to the wonder and want of shining metal. "Such a bonnie . . . such a bonnie thing . . ." he gasped.

Then his hand, of its own will it seemed, stretched toward the gleaming hilt, the fingers trembling just a moment before there was a little jump in the hand, a spark of cognizance breaking the spell, and the hand snapped back into the other. "That s'ard," he said, reeling from the trance. And wringing his fingers, he looked at Aeryck as though he had seen a ghost. "Och! You've taken silver from a dead man, haven't you, Poot?"

"What are you saying?"

"That s'ard," Poot repeated, trembling. And his eyes darted to the hilt, then quickly away from it, looking beyond the boy now to some invisible horizon. "I've heard tell of a sword, one hammered in the forge of Goibhniu, that has fallen into the hands of a mortal creature—the child of gods, it is said. Troth, and by the oaks! You be the mannie what plucked the hand oft Sarteham's limb!"

A darkness swept over the boy's brow at the mention of his name. "I will take his head if ever our blades cross again."

"Aye . . . aye, that you will." The man stared at the boy—rather at his head, at his feet, never the eyes, now darting to the sword, then to the hands, still not convinced he wasn't looking at a spirit. His face

221

twitched with wonder, and the eyes ballooned. "Word on the wing is that the child is dead, Poot, felled by one of Sarteham's men, a cruel and merciless brute as ever were spawned in hate."

"Spang."

"Aye, aye, that's the cur. Spang."

"As you can see, I'm quite alive."

"Troth! That he is, Poot, that he is. Or so he says." The man grinned, looking off the boy's ear again. "Though you wouldnay give a dram for his life if it were whistled aboot, would you?"

"And I wouldn't give a cob for the bird that whistled the tune."

The man chuckled nervously through a cough, nodding his head wildly. Then he threw a wink at the cow. The cow bawled with understanding. "Nay more, nay more! You've chores to mend," Poot cried, as he sprang to the first stall of a sudden, snatched up his bucket and stool, and began to milk the old girl. Then as he got into a tempestuous rhythm, he struck up a hearty tune as though he were the only one in the place.

> "There was an old biddy,
>   frum the banks o' Loch Linnhe,
> Who took her new milk pail to bed;
> But when she awaken,
>   the pail had been taken,
> And she screamed, 'High-dee-ho,'
>   and fell dead."

Crazy as a loon, Aeryck thought, as he observed the man. He'd heard tales of old hermits that lived alone in the hills or in caves, or that wandered about in the peat bogs, their brains baked or boiled in the sun and elements so that their senses had stewed away, and he wondered if Poot was a hermit.

He'd never heard of hermits tending stock or chores, but then again he knew little enough of hermits. People considered them harmless old fools, he knew, and as such were invisible to society and perhaps privy to a number of clandestine businesses, much as lizards on the walls of a king's palace know well his affairs of state.

And then a thought entered his mind. "You wouldn't know why Spang and fifty others of his dreg-lickers were riding past your farm last night, would you?" he asked, as he angled over to the stall.

"Nay, nay!" Poot cried, without breaking his wild cadence. "'Tis nane of Poot's mind the industries of creatures, let alone the two-legged kind that take their fill of murder."

222

"Then you wouldn't know where they might have been heading?"

"Hoot and by troth, if he's not askin' you to slit your throat now, Poot," he said, trembling noticeably. And then he stepped up the tempo of his milking, and the cow cast him a curious glance. "But you dinna ken where, and you dinna care neither, and you're happy with both, if it please her!" he sang, and then let out a hoot and slapped his knee.

Aeryck shook his head in amazement. "I just want to know if there's a village or a—"

"Murder! Murder!" the man shrieked of a sudden. "And murder's the bairn of the same. There's nothing but murder to come of that uncertain light in his eye, Poot, and the wisdom of a fool cannay lie! Nay, you'll give his birds a good broiling and throw in a mug of hot brew to show the haleful hospice of old Poot, if he'll only leave you to your chores and creatures and solitary ways and speak nay more of the blackness that's lurkin' near his heart!"

The man leaped up from his stool and, snatching the chicken from Aeryck's hand, started out of the barn with a spry step. Then he drew up suddenly by the door and looked back at the boy. "Well, are you comin' or aren't you? Old Poot cannay tend to your bellies in the barn, now can he?"

The boy looked at him queerly until he disappeared around the door. "He's an odd one, isn't he, big fella?" he said as Hauwka padded over to him. "But he seems harmless enough . . . harmless like a fox in a hen house maybe."

Hauwka let out a moan.

"Come on," Aeryck said, starting for the door. "We'll be on our way soon."

Outside the barn he was at once struck with the view. The farm was situated on the heights of a mountainous region, the sky clear and bluing, and he could see for miles in every direction. A thick fog below them extended away to every horizon, as though the clouds, having spent themselves of snow during the night, had fallen to the earth and were now tucked in and around the lower hills like the cotton batting of an immense white comforter.

This accounts for the grade we kept climbing, the boy thought, startled by the altitude. And the sun was coming out of the cotton in the east and sending its warming fingers over the spread, and the view was glorious. He took a deep breath. The air was clear and bracing, and it hurt to take it in too fast, and the winter winds blew shrilly over the heights and bit the tip of his nose and ears. Then he noted the old Roman road winding up out of the fog from the south and passing in front of the farm about a hundred yards below—where he had espied Spang and his mercenaries the night before—and followed it north until it fell into the fog and disappeared.

"That storm must have really thrown us off our course," the boy thought aloud. "None of this looks familiar."

Glancing around the steading, he noted that the house was little more than a shed, a wee cottage made of wattle and daub. Its roof was thatched under the snow and bowed in the middle like a saddle, and vines climbed its walls and stone chimney, and a thin tongue of blue smoke was curling from its lip.

The yard was strewn with dozens of chickens that pecked about in the snow, and there were some pigs rooting near the house and some hairy goats in a wattle pen off to the side. Bramble and vines, stripped of leaves, grew about the place at will. Great tangles of them spilled out from behind the house and down to the road, marking its course into the fog.

Presently the man sprang from the tiny cottage carrying a mug of hot broth and a headless chicken, plucked of its feathers. A sow and two shoats followed him out, eyeing the chicken. However, at once seeing the bear, they high-tailed it back into the cottage, squealing, followed by some chickens and a scrawny dog.

"Such a beast!" Poot said, as he set the chicken down before Hauwka. "Such an unco beast of the earth you've never seen, Poot!"

The bear took the chicken in his mouth and padded over to the barn to eat it in peace.

Poot handed the mug to the boy and said, "There's one on the spit that should satisfy your belly, mannie. So let it not be said aboot old Poot that he isnay kind to strangers."

"Thank you," Aeryck said, taking a sip of broth. It was a hot chicken broth and tasted good all the way down. "Where are we anyway? I've been looking for the River Nith, but we haven't come across it."

"The River Nith? Ooie, but he's a sight oft his trail, isn't he?" Poot chortled, shooting an impish wink at the bear. "To the west, you'd say, a fair journey of four hours!"

Aeryck nearly choked on his broth. "To the west? But that's impossible! I've just come from the west, and I didn't see the river."

"And a fool would argue the nose on his face," Poot said. "He's a queer one, isn't he, Poot? And his speech—well, he's not from these parts, you'll wager."

"I'm from Britain."

"And are there many fools in Britain?" Poot asked innocentlike, with the note curling up at the end. Then, with a wry grin, he skipped into the house to tend the meal, singing another refrain from his song:

> "The fool and his money,
>   like a bee and his honey,
> Are too quickly parted 'tis said;
> Then along come a wise man,
>   from the shores o' Loch Lomond,
> And the fool went and lopped off his head."

Aeryck rolled his eyes and, sipping his broth, turned his head away. He looked out over the fog comforter to the west and wondered how they might have gotten to this place. Perhaps in the storm they had crossed the river without knowing it—over some kind of land bridge or ford. He remembered that many valleys they had passed over were frozen and covered with snow. Perhaps one of them was the Nith. There was no other explanation.

A growl rumbling in his throat, Hauwka raised up onto his haunches and sniffed the air.

"What is it, boy?" Aeryck asked, reaching for his sword.

"Riders," Poot cried, squinting from the doorway. "Lots of 'em."

Aeryck drew his blade and peered down the road. Out of the thick fog they came, a column of thirty horsemen, their gray shapes rising out of the mists like shades. He glanced about for a place to run, knowing there was none.

Poot galloped up to him and, waving a hand, whistled shrilly. "Ah, if it's not the chieftain of Loch na Huric!" he cried.

Aeryck strained his eyes into the fog. "Brynwald?"

"Aye, the same."

"You mean it's *Brynwald!*?"

"Hoot, but he is a slow one, isn't he, Poot? But, ah, he cannay help it if he's a bairn of Britain."

"Ho, Poot, you old fox, you!" Brynwald hallooed. "And who is that young scalawag dragging his chin on the ground before you?"

"Aeryck! Is that you?" Terryll cried out from behind him. "Hah, it is! And there's Hauwka!!"

"God be praised!" Allyndaar boomed.

Recognizing his friends, Aeryck let out a yell and ran down to the road, and a great cheer went up from the column.

The company waited until Oswald and his men, having swung up from a point south and west of Glenlochar, had rendezvoused with Brynwald at Poot's farm as they had determined the day before—everyone being well-fed and refreshed now—and were making ready to head back to Loch na Huric to celebrate Christ's Mass. "Dinna you worry nane aboot the beast," Poot said, clapping Aeryck on his shoulder. "Old

225

Poot'll take care of him, of that you can be sure! He'll be right as rain come the spring!"

Earlier Hauwka had caused quite a stir with the Picts, who had never seen such an animal, but they were reassured by the Britons that he was really quite a friendly bear. At least he was most of the time.

And when it was time for the column to depart, the bear had licked both of the boys, then, limping noticeably, padded slowly back into the barn where he settled into the warm, straw-filled corner to finish his winter's hibernation and heal from his many wounds.

It was a bittersweet moment for the boys (Terryll not having seen the bear in months), but they both knew it was for the best. It wasn't right nor was it natural for bears to be out and about in the dead of winter.

Then, mounting their horses, the column headed to Loch na Huric, a good day's journey to the southeast.

Aeryck, riding one of the pack horses and before dipping into the murky haze of the fog, looked back to wave at Poot. But the man was nowhere in sight. He heard him singing, though. He could see the chickens for a time and the pigs and goats as well, graying with every step of his horse, and then the happy, if neglected and disheveled, little farm was gone.

And riding now in the company of his friends—with Terryll beaming brightly at his side, and with his mind astir with thoughts of Hauwka and Sullie, of the wolves and the wild boars, and of the white wolf that had saved his life and wondering what had become of him, and of the lonely, cold, and bitter days on the trail, with the face of dead young Stephen before him and the sneer of Spang behind—the boy marveled at the grace of God that had brought him safely to this place. He let out a sigh and, sighing, turned his thoughts to Dagmere and was cheered.

28

HOMECOMING

When Dagmere found Aeryck's face in the column of riders coming through the gates of the village—his tentative smile finding her over the crowd—the sun was just touching the western rim of hills. And there was a fire lit in the dark clouds over them, a long crimson band glowing red and brightly for just a moment before all of it would go dark and loose the stars over the river valley, and the air was bright and clean, and the people gathered at the gates were cheering happily and smiling and embracing their loved ones, for it was the eve of Christ's Mass and everyone was home safe and sound at last, and it was all too much for the girl to take in at once, and she burst into tears.

She wept tears of joy, and when she looked up from her hands, there were Aeryck's eyes moving through the crowd haltingly toward her, and then they were gone, for a crowd was gathered around him and wishing him well, pressing his hands and hugging him and keeping him from her. And Tillie was there hugging him, and Helena too, and his eyes moved warmly through the crowd as he thanked people for their kind words.

But always they would come back to Dagmere, tagging her eyes with uncertainty at first, then working the crowd closer and closer to her and coming back to her eyes again. Always coming back, and each time with a little less uncertainty, until they were both smiling, and the smiles were genuine and without guile, and then he was standing before her.

"Hello, Dagmere."

"Hello, Aeryck. I am pleased that you are all right."

"Me too." And then color rushed to his face.

"It has been a long time," she said, giggling and rescuing him.

"Yes, yes, it has. What . . . two months, do you think?"

"At least. Maybe longer."

"Yes. How have you been?"

"Fine, thank you."

"That's good."

"And you?"

"And you? Oh! Fine, fine! I'm just fine." Aeryck chuckled embarrassedly.

"That's good."

"Yes."

There was a little awkward pause as the conversation ran out of breath, and the din of the bustling crowd around them rushed in. Meara and Oona walked by giggling, their eyes darting sideways. Then someone slapped Aeryck on the back in passing. "Welcome back!" the man said.

"Thank you!" Aeryck returned, waving at him. And catching a glimpse of Allyndaar through the crowd he caught a second wind. "Are you still practicing your archery?" he asked Dagmere.

"No, not so much anymore. I've been spending more time with Mama in the kitchen."

"You have?" he said with a mild surprise.

"Yes. I've even been thinking of taking up embroidery."

"That's too bad."

"Too bad?"

"Yes, you are such a good marksman. It seems a shame, is all—you loving it so."

"Well, I haven't given it up completely. I'm just not practicing as much as before—with the embroidery and cooking and all."

"Oh, that's good."

"Good?"

"Er . . . yes, good that you haven't given it up."

"Oh."

They both cleared their throats and glanced away briefly, as another awkward pause swept between them.

And then a young man appeared out of the throng and took Aeryck by his hand and shook it. "Welcome back, Aeryck! 'Tis good to see your smiling face!"

"Oh, hello, Duncan," Aeryck said, turning to the bright-faced youth. "Thank you. Yes, it's good to be back."

"When I heard the report of the wolves . . . well . . ."

"Yes, but I'm all right now."

There was another pause during which Duncan looked at the two, and the two looked at Duncan, and the silence that bullied into their midst was more than social etiquette could abide.

Then Duncan smiled at Dagmere. "Well, I see that you're busy here, so we will talk later, all right?" And as he walked away he looked back and smiled at her again.

"Yes, yes, we will talk later," Aeryck said, waving at him too and at some others who caught his attention.

Dagmere saw Terryll and Gwyneth walking away from the crowd, arm in arm, and she sighed. "I heard about your horse," she said, reclaiming Aeryck's eyes. "I'm very sorry. Sullie—that was her name?"

"Yes. She was a good horse." Aeryck looked at the ground and shoveled the snow with his boot. "A good horse."

"I'm sure the wolves were just horrible."

"Yes, they were."

"I can't imagine."

She was looking into his face closely for the magic signs but not finding anything that was conclusive. His eyes moved shyly away from her scrutiny. "Perhaps after supper we can talk more," he said. "About the wolves, I mean."

"We don't have to. We can talk about other things—happier things —like what you've been doing here for the past two months."

Aeryck smiled, then blurted out, "I would rather talk about you."

Dagmere took a deep breath, and her eyes lit up with a new lease of excitement. The rains of grace fell gently about her and brought a happy glow to her cheeks. "It should be a wonderful service tonight, don't you think?" She smiled.

"Service?"

"Christ's Mass," she said, and her eyes moved inquiringly to his hands.

"Oh, yes, yes, it shall be." He put them behind his back, not knowing why she was staring at them. "I've been looking forward to it."

"I have too."

Aeryck cleared his throat and looked away to the hills.

Dagmere knew that the conversation was about to shift to a different level. She knew that the preliminaries, however necessary and proper, had served their purpose and would bow graciously to the new thing, a refined and wonderful thing that had been aging quietly in the cellar of each heart for two months now, collecting dust. Being a female, she knew this intuitively.

Being a male, Aeryck knew only that his heart had suddenly begun to pound. He cleared his throat. "Dagmere?"

"Yes?"

He looked intently at her. "Uh . . . there's been something I've been wanting to ask you."

"Yes?" she asked, looking expectantly into his eyes, waiting for the wine to be brought forth.

And as he looked into her eyes, her big, beautiful, cobalt blue eyes with the tiny flecks of violet around the edges, and the large black pupils glistening in the center, and the thick black lashes sweeping away into her soft temples, a lump formed in his throat. And gazing at her long and thick tresses of auburn hair that stole a spectrum of reds and golds from the deepening sun, the lump swelled into a sudden terror. For it was the face of his dreams that was before him now, incarnate at last, the face he had rescued a thousand times from the hands of terrific evils along the shores of the Peloponnesus, the face that in his dreams had rewarded him with sweet kisses, the sweet and lingering kisses that filled his heart with a yearning that was all-consuming and terrible. And the face was now before him not two feet away, gazing up at him with the tiny sprinkle of freckles over the delicate nose and the full red lips below. It was an awesome vision.

Then he swallowed hard and asked, "Uh . . . how are your horses?"

She blinked at him incredulously. "My horses?"

"Yes . . . er . . . your horses," he stammered. "You haven't given them up too, have you?"

"My horses are fine."

"Aeryck, my love!"

"Huh?"

Aeryck turned as a woman shape winged out of the crowd like a dark bird and, interposing herself between Dagmere and him, threw her arms around his neck and kissed him passionately on his mouth. Aeryck, too stunned to move, stood staring bug-eyed into the emerald green that was flashing mercilessly between the eye-slits and the thick raven hair framing them, wondering what was happening to him. Indeed, his mind was a whirl of disintegrating confusion.

And Dagmere stood watching the spectacle dumbfounded, her feet frozen to the earth in horror, as Fiona took Aeryck by his arm and whisked him away.

"Come, my love, I have missed you so," the raven-haired beauty purred. "There is much we have to discuss."

Aeryck was looking over his shoulder at Dagmere with a stupid look on his face, as Fiona and he disappeared into the crowd.

Everything went suddenly quiet in Dagmere's brain.

The crimson band over the dark rim of hills darkened to a bright purple, then flared with a final appeal of light to the day, and then it was gone. And when Aeryck did not immediately return, Dagmere whirled in her tracks and, with the rage of her gender thundering in her breast, stormed back to the house, vowing never to set eyes on him again—a vow that she was able to keep for at least three hours.

The women bustled about the kitchen in a kind of beelike frenzy, dancing back and forth, in and out, around one another, with a graceful, mind-numbing choreography: peeling potatoes, plucking birds, stuffing birds, basting them, along with boiling vegetables, baking bread, roasting mutton over the hearth, and myriad other preparations that were necessary to pull off a memorable first-time Christ's Mass supper.

The men, on the other hand, assumed their duties before the hearth, occasionally jabbing the fire with the poker, and every so often adding a log or two to keep it roaring nicely. It was an important duty, and the men held to their end of it faithfully, requiring the girls to make only a few trips with trayfuls of hot apple cider to keep their spirits up, which they maintained admirably.

Then as a quiet, airy, philosophical glow settled over the great room, Aeryck began to relate his tale, describing in detail everything from the day he left for Whithorn until the morning before, when he was found by the search party. He kept the business of the wolf attacks brief, so as not to disturb the women (whose excursions from the kitchen into the room had taken a marked upswing during his account).

However he went into great detail over the business concerning Spang and his doings. Beginning with his encounter with the brute in the tavern of Pea Gants, Aeryck relayed every scrap of information he had gathered along the way: Sylvie's news obtained from Fek, Spang's murder of Stephen at the bluffs o'Dundragon, and finally the fifty or so horsemen he had seen with him heading north two nights earlier. It all pointed to one thing: Sarteham was building some kind of mercenary army to exact vengeance on Brynwald.

As the men reflected upon this, a somber mood descended over the airy glow, smothering it, and the hearth went untended.

"I should've taken his head when I had the beggar at my mercy," Brynwald growled, as anger colored his brow. "Aye, 'twere foolhardy of me."

Aeryck started at this. "Do you think I should've killed Spang when I had the chance?" he asked Brynwald.

Terryll looked quickly at his friend, surprised at the question.

"It is not for me to say what another man is to do, kipper," Brynwald replied. "But I will say that that man is surely marked for judgment. Aye, a sure and swift judgment."

"As we all were, but for God's grace," Allyndaar interposed gently. "No, Aeryck, mercy is the better course."

"Mercy? I wonder," Brynwald said, running his thick fingers through his hair. "And is there nay voice for justice?"

"Yes, what of justice?" Aeryck wanted to know.

Terryll looked at him again, studied him now in a new light. Aside from an added growth of stature to his height and build, a change had come over his friend. His eyes were quick to cloud over with a brooding darkness, lacking the youthful vigor and felicity he had known. He was troubled by it.

"Yes . . . and what of justice?" Allyndaar mused aloud. He looked into the fire that was glowing now a deep red around the black coals. "Justice is like one wing of a bird, but mercy is like the other. They are both needed for it to fly. I think if we are to err, it is better to err on the side of mercy."

"And which wing would you flap against your enemy's broad-ax, Allyn?" Brynwald grinned sardonically. "Would you not lift your sword in battle to kill?"

"In battle, yes. But if there were a way to prevent the battle, that would be better, wouldn't it?"

"*Och,* such talk! If I had taken Sarteham's head when I had the opportunity, then we wouldnay be concerned with battle now, would we?"

Allyndaar thought about that for a moment. "Perhaps, but God was glorified in your mercy, Brynwald," he said, "and pleased with it, I'm sure. I still say mercy is better."

"Troth, Allyn, this is hard. By the oaks, it is hard."

"Yes, it is. But no harder than the cross the Savior bore, is it?"

Brynwald thought it through, then quietly said, "Aye . . . aye."

Helena turned the mutton over the fire, and, waiting for a lull, wanted to know why Spang would kill a young monk.

Aeryck merely shrugged his shoulders. He looked away from her, and Terryll caught a glint of something in his eyes he had never seen before; it seemed a foreign thing was burning darkly in them.

"It's a shame," Helena said, shaking her head solemnly. "Such a shame."

"Yes, it is," Allyndaar said.

"Aye," Brynwald agreed.

"Did you know him, Aeryck?" Helena asked.

But Aeryck had pulled out his sword and was honing the blade with a whetstone and did not respond.

"Aeryck?"

"Huh?"

"I wondered if you knew the young monk?"

"No." And the way he said it ended the discussion.

Then Aeryck's eyes crept into the kitchen to Dagmere. She was wearing a light blue dress that was gathered at the waist, and she looked lovely in it. However she might have been wearing a burlap sack, and she would have looked just as lovely in it, he thought. He shook his head sullenly, then looked down at his sword, gazing thoughtfully at his father's work.

His was one of three swords fashioned by Caelryck, each a tribute to a Person of the Holy Trinity. Engraved along his blade were tongues of fire commemorating the gift of the Holy Spirit at Pentecost. And as the warm glow from the hearth flickered over its surface, the tongues sprang to life it seemed and leaped along the blade, giving it the appearance of a blazing shaft. He marveled at his father's craftsmanship, the exquisite lines and filigree tracing the hilt and haft, the bear wreath and chi-rho upon the pommel—his family crest—wonderfully engraved, every perfect detail a salient tribute to his father's pure and joyful devotion to his God.

As he gazed thoughtfully upon them, an ache swelled in Aeryck's breast at his memory and etched a sad reverie over his face. He laid down the whetstone, then polished the sword slowly with an oil cloth, bringing it to a fiery luster, then returned it to its scabbard. And then, looking into the hearth, he turned his thoughts to his Uncle Finn and to his mother's kinfolk, who lived beyond the sea—his kinfolk—and he was suddenly overwhelmed with a terrible aching loneliness.

When the women brought in the food, everyone gathered around the table. Aeryck sat at one end next to Brynwald, with Terryll and Gwyneth on his right. Dagmere sat at the other next to her father, her vow of eye-silence inviolate. Tillie sat between Helena, who was at Dagmere's right elbow, and her husband.

Then Brynwald stood up and asked the blessing. He began with gratitude for the occasion of Christ's Mass, the advent of Immanuel, covering the bulk of his theological understanding in as many words as decorum would permit. Then he moved on to the new friendships enjoyed with Allyndaar and his family and with the other British families in the village. He ended with a prayer of thanksgiving for the safe arrival of the Irish monks, sent from Patrick to establish a new church in Loch na Huric, and Aeryck's safe return home.

A moment of holy silence settled upon them with the benediction, pregnant with joyful thoughts of the Nativity. Amens went around the table, dipping in a couple of places, and when he sat down, Aeryck noticed a stream of tears rolling down his cheeks.

"Aye," Tillie said, her face also wet. "The Laird is good to us, isn't he? Such blessings."

Everyone but two agreed.

And then the business of eating got underway, with the ebb and flow of conversation surging and slipping festively around the table. Tillie beamed, and Brynwald boomed, and the fire crackled merrily in the hearth. The wine of mirth and goodwill was passed around the table, and all was good on the earth.

At one point Helena became aware of a significant gap in the flow, and she glanced over at Aeryck, who was eating quietly, and then at her daughter, who wasn't eating at all. It seemed there was a dark cloud hanging over each of their heads.

"Dagmere? Isn't it wonderful Aeryck's come home safely?"

"Oh, yes, wonderful," Dagmere said, not looking up from her plate. "Splendid, really." There was an edge of sarcasm in her voice.

Helena wasn't sure of the tone and tried again. "I'm sure you two did a lot of catching up. I saw you talking—"

"Catching up?" Dagmere interrupted, suddenly animated. "Oh, yes, there was much I had forgotten about him. We did have a delightful conversation, though. However I can't remember how it ended." She scrunched her nose and gazed ironically at the ceiling. "It seems to me we were talking about what a fine marksman I was—yes, that was it. And then there was something to do with horses. After that it gets fuzzy, or nondescript, or something or other." She looked coldly over at Aeryck, breaking her vow. "How *did* our conversation end, Aeryck? You must tell me some time. I'm sure it was wonderful."

Aeryck was looking down at his plate and brooding fiercely. An interlude of silence ensued during which everyone's eyes glanced back and forth across the table. It was the kind of silence that could choke a mule.

Helena was shocked. "Is there something wrong, Dagmere?"

"Wrong? Why would anything be wrong? On the contrary, I'm having a splendid time. Simply splendid." She took a deep breath and blew it out. "You see? I have now been relieved of a terrible misconception." She sighed, then chuckling, added, "It's funny how you can think one thing for so long, and then you find out it wasn't really what you thought at all. And then when you realize it is something else, there is a relief—yes, a relief that you don't have to waste energy on the first thing anymore."

"*Och,*" Brynwald grunted.

Terryll and Gwyneth cleared their throats and lowered their heads to their meal, like animals drinking warily at a watering hole.

Tillie forced a smile and wondered if anyone wanted more cider.

Helena declined.

Allyndaar grunted knowingly at Brynwald, and the circle was completed.

"Well, this is silly," Helena said, glaring at her daughter. "You apologize to everyone at once."

234

Dagmere stared at her plate, with her lips compressed into a grim slit of resistence. Suddenly her eyes brimmed with tears.

"Dagmere!"

However the girl pushed away from the table and ran upstairs to her bed.

Helena sat stunned as she looked at the empty flight of stairs. Then apologizing profusely to everyone present, she stood up and followed after her.

Aeryck got up and put on his cloak.

"Where are you going?" Terryll asked him.

"Out," he said curtly, then went outside.

"I'll go and talk to him," Terryll said, pushing away from the table. "This is crazy."

Those who remained seated looked at one another with various looks of astonishment, and the silence that followed found threads of the previous silence and wove them into something that was quite suffocating.

"*Och*," Brynwald boomed at last. "Has the world come to an end then?" He grunted, then added, "Pass the potatoes, will you, Allyn?"

Then Tillie jumped up from the table and smiled. "Would anyone like more cider?"

29

CHRIST'S MASS

W ait up, Aeryck!"
   Aeryck did not wait up. He continued on his course without breaking step. In fact, he quickened his pace. Down the snowy lane away from the chieftain's cottage he went on at a fair clip, as the tall black elms reached their spidery fingers over the path and the wind whistled strange melodies overhead, melodies unheard by the boy.

The moon winked through the dark scudding clouds, throwing shifting shadows and light over his path that defined the contours of the steading with shimmering blues and purples. Somewhere in the distance a wolf bayed, a long, sustained, haunting moan with a sinister echolalia ringing out. This too went unheard.

"What's gotten into you?" Terryll said, panting up alongside.

"Nothing."

And Aeryck continued through the trees undeterred, lengthening his stride.

Terryll matched him stride for stride. There was a muffled squeak of snow beneath their feet, and their breath trailed behind them hotly.

"Hey, hold on a minute," Terryll cried. "Where are you off to in such a hurry?"

No response.

"I can beat you in a race, you know," Terryll said.

"Then, why don't you?"

"Come on, Aeryck!" Terryll begged, catching his arm to stop him, but Aeryck yanked it free and continued on.

Undaunted, Terryll ran ahead and blocked his path.

Aeryck started to veer, but Terryll held out his arms and withheld him.

Aeryck stared at him for a moment, slightly winded. "Are you going to get out of my way, or do I have to knock you down?"

"You have to knock me down."

Aeryck rolled his eyes, then shook his head resignedly. "What do you want?"

"I want to know what happened to the friend I left behind here two months ago."

"Here I am, right here!" Aeryck growled, gesturing to himself. "If you don't like what you see, why don't you and everyone else in your perfect family just leave me alone!"

He brushed past Terryll and walked a few feet away and stopped. His head sank penitently to his chest, then immediately he turned around. "I'm sorry, Terryll, I didn't mean that. I'm just upset, you know. A lot has happened to me over the past two weeks. I just need some time alone to think it through. All right?"

"Sure."

"I didn't mean that about your family."

"You said that."

"We still friends?"

"We're still friends," Terryll said, then added wryly, "although I don't know why."

"It's my irresistible charm and good looks," Aeryck said, forcing a smile.

"That must be it. Now why don't you tell me what's troubling you. Is it Dagmere?"

Aeryck heaved a big sigh as he glanced back at the cottage.

Picking up the pause, Terryll asked, "What happened between you two? Earlier I saw you talking and smiling sickeningly at each other like you were the only two people on earth. Any blind person could see how much you care for each other."

"Is that right? Well, tell that to your sister. People that care for one another ought to at least trust each other. Your sister's got about as much trust in me as a rabbit has in a fox."

"What happened? You have an argument?" Terryll's expression changed suddenly. "It wasn't that business with her freckles again, was it?"

"No."

"What then?"

"What difference does it make?"

"Is it Fiona?"

Aeryck glared at him. "You can believe what you want." He looked plaintively at the sky. The moon was just peeking through some clouds, and then it was gone, as though the light were playing a game of hide-and-seek with him. He shook his head, tired of the game. "I wish everybody would just stay out of my life."

Terryll eyed him curiously. "There's something else, isn't there—troubling you, I mean?"

Aeryck blew out a cloud of smoke. "That's just it . . . I don't know what's troubling me. I just know that no matter what I do, it always seems to turn into one big disaster. I'm tired of it, Terryll. Tired of it. Things die around me . . . people die around me." He grimaced and started away. "You best watch yourself."

"What are you talking about?"

There was no answer.

"All right, but just hold on for a second, will you?"

Aeryck stopped.

Terryll reached into his cloak pocket and pulled out a small cloth-wrapped parcel. "Listen, I was going to give you this later, but since I don't know where you'll be later—well, here."

"What is it?"

"A gift. From that girl you saved at the altar. You know the one—"

"Corrie?"

"Yes, Corrie. She told me to give you this when I saw you." He handed Aeryck the little package.

Aeryck looked at it for a moment in his hand, not sure what to make of it. Then he untied the twine and opened the folds of cloth, and there was a wooden carving of a cross with a lamb against it. As the clouds swept away from the moon, the light played over it.

"It's the carving I told you to give her," he said bewildered.

"No, it isn't. She lost that one in the cave where we fought the Tuatha Baalg. She said she made this one for you as a way of saying thank you for what you did for her. You see, Aeryck, not everything you touch is destroyed. Corrie's doing quite nicely, actually. Without you, she'd be dead."

Aeryck thought about it for a moment as he studied the little carving of wood. "That seems like a thousand years ago, doesn't it?"

"Yes, it does."

Lines of tenderness around Aeryck's eyes pushed away the darkness from his brow.

"Now why don't you come on back to the house? I'm sure we can work this thing out between you and Dagmere. It's just a little lover's spat."

Aeryck looked up from the carving. "No," he said, and the tenderness was gone, the darkness was back, and he started away.

Terryll followed. "Come on, Aeryck, it's Christ's Mass. This is a time to be celebrating with your friends, not to be out walking in the snow, catching your death in the cold."

"I don't plan on staying out in the cold, so you can quit your mothering."

"Where are you going?"

"Somewhere."

"Where?"

"Just somewhere. Now leave it at that, will you?"

"I could follow you." Terryll chuckled. "You're easy to track, you know."

Aeryck stopped. "Are you going to leave me alone?"

"Not until you tell me what's eating at you."

"Right now, *you* are! Why don't you go and celebrate Christ's Mass with your family, Terryll, and just leave me be. Please, Terryll, just for tonight, all right?"

"You're not going to the service?"

"No." He looked down at the carving, then put it away in his cloak. "No, I'm not going." And then he walked away, leaving Terryll wondering what had become of the friend he had known two months ago.

As Aeryck approached the center of the village, he noted that in every home candles were glowing wonderfully, and upon their doors were hung wreaths of holly—the bygone entreaties to the angry Celtic gods of winter, now the apt symbols of Christ's eternal light and the crown of thorns worn upon His head. Many believed that the holly bush once had white berries, but they were forever changed to crimson by the blood of Christ's brow.

He heard laughter from time to time as the wind stirred, and Aeryck, familiar now with the families in each of the cottages, envisioned their faces gathered before roaring hearths and celebrating the advent of Christ.

As he passed Dunnald's small cottage on the left, he saw a warm glow of yellow light flickering through the shutters. There was a sudden outburst of laughter inside, followed by Dunnald's voice roaring amid the squeals of children. Aeryck knew from eating several meals there that it was a happy family of seven that took life, like the jocund head of the home, with zest and abandon. He smiled wistfully and went on, loneliness working heavily upon him now.

And as he passed the hall—the moon beaming bright on its white plaster walls—the door was flung open, and he could see the two Irish monks inside preparing for the midnight service, unrolling parchments, and lighting large candles, and Brother Lucius and Tolc were there helping them.

Aeryck paused, thinking he might talk to the once Roman centurion, but some women went inside with armloads of decorations and closed the door behind them, laughing. He shrugged woefully, then headed across the village in the direction of the stables.

Just before midnight the little warm cottages clumped about the village disgorged a throng of people into the frigid night air. From every direction they came in small knots of woolen bundles, some laughing, some hailing others as their paths met, some hurrying with heads down, all converging on the hall in the center of the village, which effused a bright and inviting warm light. The air was charged with joyful expectancy, as though something altogether new and glorious were about to transpire. Indeed, there was.

Allyndaar and his family stepped out of their glowing cottage into the cold of the Scottish winter. Helena shivered, whispered something about a trip to visit her relatives in the south of Gaul as soon as they returned home, then huddled under Allyndaar's arm. Gwyneth, likewise, snuggled next to Terryll, and the group trudged slowly down through the trees with the snow crunching beneath their feet, the winter air reaching icy fingers into exposed places and burning with its frigid touch.

As she trailed them, Dagmere's eyes darted to and fro from beneath the hood of her woolen cloak, appraising each of the dark shapes darting through the light spills in the distance. Her expression was grave and penitent, as none of the shapes was the one she dearly wished to behold.

Still inside their cottage, Brynwald was fumbling with the brooch to his cloak. "*Och*, but these big clubs of mine!"

"Here, let me help you," Tillie offered. And when he wouldn't move his fingers, she slapped them lightly and pushed them out of the way.

"By the oaks, woman!"

Tillie made a quick adjustment. "There!" And stepping back, she said, "You look grand, Bryn, just grand!"

"Is that so? Grand, you say?" The chieftain angled his head to get a look, but of course it was impossible to see under his chin without a mirror. So he grunted and fiddled with the brooch blindly, then finally took her word for it.

Hiding a smirk, Tillie threw on her cloak, and the two of them left the cottage, closing the door behind them.

"Where do you think he's got off to, Bryn?" Tillie asked, glancing anxiously over the steading.

"Quit your fretting, woman."

"I've never seen two people more in love, yet playing the deffil finding it out for themselves."

240

"Troth!" the chieftain grunted. "The ways of a young mannie with a lass are a mystery to behold. It says as much in the Proverbs," he added, proud to have remembered an appropriate Scripture for the moment.

Tillie nuzzled under his arm, proud of her man, and the two of them caught up with the others.

The northernmost hill overlooking the village of Loch na Huric was lined with trees and rose several hundred nearly sheer feet from the river, providing an insurmountable buttress against assault from that direction. However at the same time it was a terrific vantage point from which to observe the village precincts in all directions.

The moon, showing again over the clouds, silhouetted an uneven line of horsemen just inside the treeline, fifty warriors strong, each of whom was watching the Picts and Britons filing into the timbered hall below, each listening intently as Christian hymns began to rise reverently upon the winter breezes perhaps a quarter mile away.

That they were not listening to the words of peace and goodwill toward men was apparent in the way that each warrior fingered the haft or hilt of his weapon. How long they had been there was a matter of conjecture—long enough to have counted the Britons, it was certain.

A large man with a flat, misshapen nose and thick, leathery features leaned forward in his saddle to address an even larger man. "See? It is as I reported to you," Taelbork said. "Eighty Britons or better, come to celebrate the Christ's Mass with Brynwald."

The larger man grunted. *Eighty Britons,* he thought as he searched the crowd for the familiar shape of his enemy. Why? They were not a war party, obviously, though many of them were clearly warriors.

What was Brynwald doing? Had he formed some kind of alliance with the Britons? That seemed evident. But why? Brynwald hated the Britons. He had fought against them, raided their villages, dragged away their sons and daughters to be sacrificed on the altar to the sun god, lost many men to them in that terrible battle along the Wall twenty years ago. Why?

The fingers of his left hand began to scratch the scarred end of what was left of his sword arm. Not because it itched—no, that nuisance had ended over a month ago as the wound had healed. But he did so now out of force of habit. It was a long, ugly welt of hard skin, the scar was, that jagged wickedly across the end of his forearm like a little purple ridge, where the keen edge of the young Briton's sword had so neatly removed his hand from his arm just above the wrist.

The stitching of the wound had not been so neat. It had been done hurriedly that night by the old healer woman Myrna after she had cauterized the bleeders with a white-hot poker, turning the skin black. But no matter. The ugliness of the scar served as a grisly reminder of the hatred that burned in his heart for the chieftain of Loch na Huric and of the vengeance that he would soon exact.

Brynwald had changed, the large Pict reasoned, allowing his thoughts to drift into new territory. Ireland had changed him. This new religion of the Roman Britons had changed him. That was it, wasn't it? Brynwald had become a Christian. He had rejected the ways of his own people, of his fathers, and had embraced the ways of these accursed weak people, the once lapdogs of the Roman Empire.

That he was forming an alliance with them now was all too clear. Soon there would be many more Britons pouring north of the Wall with their culture, their religion, fighting men with their weapons. That could be trouble, the man reasoned. He could not allow it. No. He would have to destroy Brynwald and every vestige of Christianity north of the Wall now, lest the ancient ways vanish forever.

A sound caught his attention. His eyes jerked to it. There was Dunnald, he noted. The wind carried his distinctive laugh over the river and on up to the heights. *The fool,* the man thought, his face screwing into a cruel sneer. *Laugh while you can. You will not be laughing for long.*

"There he is, Sarteham," Taelbork rasped over the wind, "just entering the hall."

The large Pict's eyes shifted to the entrance, and, finding the familiar shape of Brynwald, tiny though it was, his eyes narrowed hatefully.

The moon spilled brightly through several slits in the walls, lighting the stables with slanting bars of light. One shone partly on a bale of straw, leaving the other part to the shadows. Sitting in the lighted area with his back to one of the stalls, Aeryck gazed dully at the little wooden carving in his hands, thinking of the girl who had made it.

He remembered the terrified look on her face as she lay upon the sacrificial altar awaiting the high priest's knife; and later the mousy darts of her eyes as she and the other rescued girls headed back to Bowness with Terryll and Gwyneth. He remembered praying that she might be made well in her mind, that she might be restored to a happy wholeness.

At the time, being new to the business of praying, he remembered thinking that his prayers were like little boats set adrift into the starry sea with burdens in them and with the hope that none would capsize before reaching the throne of God because of his lack of faith. And now, looking at the carving, it seemed as though one of the little boats had returned, no longer bearing a burden but a precious gift, a prayer answered, a life on the mend, a "yes" sailing back at him amid his stormy doubts. Would that every little boat returned with a yes. He let out a sigh. Yes, it seemed like a thousand years ago.

He looked up as the sound of singing began to filter in through the wall slits after the moon. For a time there was a great bustle of activity breaking into his solitude—little knots of people hurrying by, shogging through the snow, the horses whickering in concert.

At one point a man stuck his head in the stable door and called out, "You in here, Dobe?"

Aeryck started and said that he wasn't, to which the man grunted and closed the door. Dobe was a ten-year-old boy.

Moments later he heard someone else crying out for "Fen," another ten year old known to be an accomplice of Dobe's. And then there was an interlude of silence, followed by a burst of singing, and when that died down the only sounds he heard were the wind whistling over the thatch and an occasional snort of a horse complaining to the others about the cold. In such solitude Aeryck pondered many things. And with each one he sent out a little boat.

"So here you are," a girl's voice called out.

Aeryck turned as a woman shape, wrapped in a hooded cloak and blacker than the night, slipped through the door and closed it behind her. Then the black woman shape glided stealthily toward him, the folds of her cloak lightly winging over the draft of her approach, and, drawing up before him, she removed the hood and allowed a slanting shaft of light to extol her features.

"Fiona."

"You sound disappointed."

He was. "I came in here to be alone."

"The service has started, you know."

"Then why aren't you there?"

"I was. But when I didn't see you, I asked Duncan if he knew where you were, and he said he thought he saw you heading to the stables a while ago. I just slipped away to see." She giggled. "He was right."

"So you found me."

Fiona regarded him as though from a perch, her raven hair gleaming in a thin finger of light. "What's that you're holding? Ooh, let me see."

Aeryck put the carving into his pocket. "It's nothing."

"Is it a present?"

"Yes."

Fiona frowned in the shadows. "From Dagmere?"

"No. Do your parents know that you've slipped away from the service?"

"I'm not a little girl, you know. I'm nearly seventeen. I'm a woman now. I can go where I please." She winged away, not too far away, to prove it. And as she hovered in and out of the spindly fingers of light, glancing at the dark silhouettes of horses angling their heads inquisitively over their stalls, the moonlight caught a hawkish gleam curling over the green eyes that were affixed on the lone boy, and Aeryck was forced to look away from them.

"Don't you like me, Aeryck?" she asked, circling back.

"What kind of a question is that?"

"It's just a question."

He grunted. "I like you, I suppose."

"You suppose?"

"I like a lot of people."

"You don't think of me as someone special?"

"Special?"

"May I sit down?" And not waiting for his reply, she alighted next to him, and doing so her cool fingers brushed lightly over his hand.

Aeryck retrieved his hand into his lap.

"Silly boy." She giggled, and then pulling out a brush she began to preen herself.

Aeryck was surprised, for he had never seen a girl brushing her hair before, let alone doing it in public—if the shadowy stables, full of horses, could be considered public. Such things were simply not done. Were they? But then again, what did he know about girls and hair and the propriety of their brushing it in public? And so he stared, a little stupidly, at the sheen jumping around in her glimmering black locks, at the tiny crackling sparks of electricity which truly amazed him.

"I'm not going to hurt you, you know," she said. "Do I frighten you?"

"What are you talking about?" Aeryck jumped to his feet and glared at her from behind a buttress of boyish pride and resolve. "Look, Fiona, I told you earlier I'm not interested in you like this. We can be friends, all right? Just friends."

Fiona seemed hurt by his remark, and she looked sadly at her hands.

Aeryck eyed her warily. This was different. "What's wrong?"

But she didn't respond. And as she edged partly into the light, the boy could see a tear brim in one eye, then travel a lonely path of sorrow down her cheek.

"What? Are you crying? You're crying, aren't you? Why do girls have to cry all the time?" Four stupid questions in a row.

But she didn't answer any of them. Instead she looked away down the stables at the dark head shapes of horses.

244

Taking a step toward her, Aeryck said, "Look, I'm sorry if I hurt your feelings. There, does that make you feel better?" Another stupid question.

She looked up at him now. "It's all right, Aeryck. I'll be fine. I just hoped . . . " She looked away and stifled a sniffle.

This was really different. And suddenly he beheld her in a new light. She looked small, hurt, like a fledgling fallen from its nest, not at all like the bird of prey that had circled over him in his dreams, worrying his constitution to no end.

He sat beside her and lay his hand awkwardly on her shoulder to comfort her. "Look, Fiona, please stop your crying, won't you? Can't we just be friends and talk?"

Her shoulders rolled a little, flinched away at his touch, and she dabbed her eyes with a thin handkerchief that had materialized from somewhere.

Aeryck shook his head dolefully. "Why does life have to be so complicated?" The prayer sailed away with a groan, not to the throne of God but to the rafters, to the horses, to anyone in the universe with a sympathetic ear.

She looked up at him suddenly. "Is it complicated, Aeryck? Is life really complicated for you?"

And as he gazed into her lustrous green eyes, suddenly everything seemed so remarkably simple. The world with its cares and woes fell away in a single draft of wind: Spang, Brother Stephan, his Uncle Finn, Sullie . . . Dagmere—yes, even Dagmere. Nothing seemed to matter at all now except the solace of Fiona's lovely face and the invitation of her glistening, full lips.

And immediately the little boat was dashed upon the rocks.

When she leaned forward he didn't withdraw, and when she kissed him, he kissed her back. A few moments later he pulled away with a jolt, his eyes glaring with a terrible awareness.

But she caught him with her eyes. "Aren't I pleasing to you, Aeryck?"

"No . . . er . . ."

She giggled. Of course she was. "Ever since I first saw you, you were the only boy I ever wanted. Yes, I've seen it in your eyes too. I can see it now."

A thick lump swelled in his throat. "This is wrong."

"Wrong?" And as the clouds edged subtly over the moon, draping a chilling veil of darkness over the stable, she asked innocently, "Who says it is wrong?"

Inside the hall there was standing room only. All but the head table and chairs had been removed earlier in order to accommodate the large throng of worshipers. Even so, many were forced to huddle outside the door and windows, where several bonfires were going now to keep them warm. The Picts didn't seem to mind. Being a hearty lot, they actually preferred the outside over the stuffy press of the hall and, quickly learning the hymns, sang out with zealous enthusiasm.

Then as the final strains of the music drifted over the congregation of Picts and Britons, Brother Gildas opened the Scriptures to the gospel of Luke and began to read the account of Christ's birth. His big voice carried well outside and far beyond the bundled clutches of people into the gathering stillness of the night.

"'And it came to pass in those days, that there went out a decree from Caesar Augustus, that all the world should be taxed . . .'"

The Britons had heard the story many times, but somehow in this foreign place, in the presence of these once barbaric people, these once enemies of their land, many of whose arms and necks and places not exposed were indelibly tattooed with the images of the gods, goddesses, and symbols of their former religion, the words took on a whole new meaning.

Immanuel! God is with us! All of us!

Indeed it was mind numbing to ponder, knowing that the blood of Christ had washed away every stain and vestige of their old ways from their souls, making them whiter than snow, making them children and citizens of an eternal kingdom, one without deference to race, creed, gender, or former depth of depravity.

Yes, indeed, Immanuel had come, clothed in the helpless skin of a little baby, the eternal Lamb of God who takes away the sin of the world, nursing at the breast of a young virgin in a dirty stable!

It was too much for Helena to comprehend, and she began to weep. Allyndaar pulled her close. His own eyes welled from the great mystery. And glancing at Brynwald, he noticed that the big Pictish chieftain was shedding not a few tears as well.

However Dagmere's mind was not on the service; it was numbed with a different matter. Because of it she was not even aware that young Duncan had wended his way through the congregation and was now standing beside her, smiling. His eyes were making secret appraisals of her beauty.

"This is wrong," Aeryck said again, the resolve in his voice weakening.

"No, it's not, it's natural," she countered, taking his hand, pulling him closer. "Hasn't God made us so to enjoy one another?"

Aeryck's mind was in a whir of distortions, unable to string a reasonable thought together.

There *was* a thought flapping over his mind, however, a dark leathery thing, but his mind kept swatting at it, trying to keep it from landing. Every so often it would touch, chilling where it touched, and his mind would look at the thing for a moment and not want to swat it because it was a pleasant coldness. But his mind would swipe at it after the moment had passed, and the thought would flap up and continue its hovering, looking for a place to alight.

This went on for several moments as the boy looked at the girl, at her eyes pulling him. And it was sometime during this quiet, desperate exchange that a terror seized the boy's heart, and he pulled his hand away and fled from the stables, leaving Fiona alone in the shadows with the horses.

A frustrated scowl swept darkly over her brow as she covered herself with her cloak.

Sarteham scanned the village grounds, noting here and there small clumps of men patroling in a desultory manner along the encircling berm, most of whom seemed more interested in the goings-on in the hall than any outside threats.

Sarteham snickered.

"They have grown weak," Taelbork said, reading his thoughts. "The sentries move about like old women."

"Aye," Clynne, a smaller man, added. "We could rush in under the cover of night—half of us from the valley side north'ard, the other half through the river gorge."

It seemed like a good plan. And several of the men grunted their approval, itching to reclaim their lost homes and honor that were taken from them the day, two months before, when Brynwald and his men returned from Ireland and forced a third of their village to march northward into exile—men, women, and children who would not bow to this new and cursed religion.

The humiliation of that day burned hot in their breasts. It wasn't long after they had settled in the northern village of Old Glenlouden that their women began to chide them as cowards, to goad them into taking up their swords and to act like Pictish men, to avenge their honor, their homeland, and their gods.

Clynne chortled. *"Och,* by the time they'd kenned what was happening, old Bryn would be begging for mercy. By the oaks, he would."

"Aye," several of the men grunted.

"Perhaps."

Perhaps not, Sarteham didn't say. He was not a coward, but he knew well that Brynwald was a fierce warrior, that his men were fierce warriors. Neither of which were to be faced in battle without the odds of numbers and surprise on his side. He had surprise now, certainly. Brynwald would never expect a raid on such a night in the dead of winter. He might rush the village and kill many, but without greater numbers behind him, many of his own would be killed, and he couldn't have that.

No, Sarteham was not about to suffer a second defeat by the man. He would wait until a more opportune time, wait until spring, when his forces would have grown to such numbers that there would be no doubting the outcome.

A thin, baneful smile curled across his lips as he scratched the end of his stump. Vengeance would be his. Yes. Loch na Huric would be his. Yes. Nevermore would there be heard such blasphemous singing from the seat of the Pictish gods. They would smile on him. Yes, Sarteham was learning patience, and because of it he was becoming a dangerous man. A very dangerous man.

"Come," he snarled, reining his horse to the north, "let us return to Old Glenlouden and see if our friend Spang has returned."

Some of the men grumbled, but none voiced his objections. They had seen how quickly the large Pict had transferred his skills with the sword from his right hand to his left. And so they followed him off the ridge, the clangor of their battle accoutrements muffled by the wind and the steady gurgling of the river.

Aeryck stood huddled over one of the bonfires next to a window, rubbing warmth into his hands as he struggled to listen to Brother Gildas teaching just inside. He could hear the monk's voice with pristine clarity; however the scene he had left behind in the stables fought his concentration. It worried his mind.

He felt dirty inside somehow, tainted and cold, as though his soul had been penetrated by an evil that was spreading to every part of his being, pulling darkness through him, slithering like a phantom snake, and all the while hissing, *So you see, Worm, that you are not a Christian after all, are you? No. You are nothing but a vile sinner, a worthless beggar boy who would be better off falling on his sword.* A shudder trembled through Aeryck's body, and he clung to the light spilling from the window as though it had mystical properties in it. His face was florid in the glow of the bonfire, and he lay his hands over it for warmth.

And then a raft of thoughts flew about his mind, unbidden and unwelcome thoughts, swooping in fast, diving at him, thoughts of Spang and Brother Stephan and Sullie and . . . and Fiona. And attending them came an anger that flushed from some shady nook in his soul, from some hidden back-alley place in his soul where the prurient thoughts lurked in tireless imaginings, multiplying like little bats in the dark. *Give it up, Worm. Give it up. You are mine, you see.*

Aeryck lowered his head and stared into his soul. He stepped closer to the fire and felt the heat against his toes and shins.

"'For unto us a child is born, unto us a son is given,'" the voice of Brother Gildas boomed into the night. "'And the government shall be upon his shoulder: and his name shall be called Wonderful, Counsellor, The mighty God, The everlasting Father, the Prince of Peace.'"

Aeryck looked up and beheld the faces of those around him, their eyes flickering in the glow of the bonfires, a sweet awareness descending upon their brows as they listened to Brother Gildas's words. He saw the transformation in their eyes, from wonder . . . to awe . . . to joy . . . saw tears rolling down many of their cheeks, glistening in the fire, some on women, some on children, some on men—big ruddy men, warrior men—the great Light shining out of darkness, shooting out through their eyes as many welcomed the Babe into their hearts.

"'What shall we say to these things?'" Brother Gildas continued, drawing his message to a close from the epistle to the Romans. "'If God be for us, who can be against us? He that spared not his own Son, but delivered him up for us all, how shall he not with him also freely give us all things? Who shall lay any thing to the charge of God's elect? . . . Who is he that condemneth? . . . Who shall separate us from the love of Christ? . . . Nay, in all these things we are more than conquerors through him that loved us.'"

Aeryck started at these words. He had never heard them before, and they struck his heart like piercing firebrands. He felt the warmth move up from his hands along the surface of his arms and spread out. It was a little frightening at first, but it felt good as his mind began to clear of the other thoughts.

"'For I am persuaded, that neither death, nor life, nor angels, nor principalities, nor powers, nor things present, nor things to come, nor height, nor depth, nor any other creature, shall be able to separate us from the love of God, which is in Christ Jesus our Lord.'"

At this point tears were streaming from the boy's eyes, for he could see it now. Why hadn't he seen it before? He had, but he had forgotten. Things had gotten in the way, had clouded his mind. But he saw it again now, so clearly that he thought he could just reach out and touch it, and he marveled at it.

Now the light burned in his breast, spreading out evenly through his being, rooting out the little, dark breeders—the leathery wings flapping off at the approach of light. It hurt and indeed was a little frightening, but then it was so good and pure and right that he wondered how he could have forgotten. He got only tears in reply, and the host of stars slung low over the hills seemed to understand.

Brother Gildas led out with another hymn. And then the boy, feeling a warmth bubbling in him, was singing with the others around the bonfires. Their faces were wet too, and those that didn't know the words of the hymn hummed along, cutting in and out of the melody with their own, taking the words and giving them flesh, birthing them in their souls. And all in all it was a lovely hymn.

Inside, as the congregation lingered in the sweet spirit of the service, some beginning to leave now, nodding and smiling and wishing in low reverent tones a blessed Christ's Mass as they passed by others who were holding onto the glow, young Duncan smiled sweetly at Dagmere.

Feeling his eyes upon her, she looked up, a little startled at his proximity, and smiled back, more out of politeness than anything else. And stepping back a step she beheld something strange in his eyes.

"May I walk you home?" he asked, his eyes caressing her features.

"Walk me home?"

"With your parents, of course," the youth was quick to explain, chuckling. He was smiling at her still.

And looking up at him, at his eyes (they were brown, she noticed for the first time), Dagmere was struck by how handsome Duncan was.

"Walk me home?" she repeated, hearing his question now for the first time. She felt her ears go warm, and then her cheeks.

"Yes," Duncan said, and then he took her hand and held it gently in his.

She looked down at it, perplexed. At first she wondered why he had taken it. She looked back into his eyes as though for an explanation.

"I would like to walk you home." He smiled. "You see—"

"She's going home with me!" a voice interrupted.

Both Duncan and Dagmere glanced behind them, and across the hall, standing in the doorway, was Aeryck. He came toward them through the dispersing crowd, brushing off several friendly approaches, never once taking his eyes off Dagmere.

She looked at him, looked back at Duncan, then, remembering her hand, she pulled it away and held it in her other one to protect it. Then, watching Aeryck's approach, she allowed both to fall loosely folded in front of her.

He halted before them, his eyes darting briefly to Duncan with a certain look, and he said again, "She's going home with me."

There was something imperious in his voice that struck a primal chord in her. She slipped her hand into Duncan's again and said, "That won't be necessary, Aeryck. Duncan has offered to take me home."

"That's fine, but you're coming with me," Aeryck said, taking her other hand. And without listening to her numerous protests, he escorted her outside, gently but with firm resolve, leaving Duncan watching them with a stupid look on his face. Then he led her around to one side of the hall, just outside the light of a bonfire that seemed deserted of people. He glanced around quickly to make sure. It was.

Then, clearing his throat, he said, "I love you, Dagmere." And looking into her eyes, into her big blue eyes that were gazing up at him in wonder, eyes that were sparkling bright and beautiful in the waning glow of the bonfire, he added, "Do you hear me, Dagmere? I love you. I have always loved you. I've loved you ever since the first day I set eyes on you—that day when I felt your cool fingers touch my brow to see if I'd come out of the fever. You healed me of that fever, Dagmere, but you gave me another, and I don't ever want it to go away." And with that he leaned over and kissed her.

Dagmere was too shocked to realize what was happening, and she missed the first one. But when he kissed her again, she felt something tightly balled up inside of her begin to unwind. And unwinding and growing more and more comfortable with the moment she had longed for, Dagmere stretched her arms around the boy's neck. Stepping up onto her toes, she drew herself closer to him and kissed him back.

It was a lovely kiss.

Walking by in the distance, coming from the direction of the stables, Fiona glanced over at them. She stopped abruptly and scowled. Her fists clenched into balls of hatred.

Then noticing Duncan coming out the door of the hall, the youth wearing a dazed look on his face, she brightened. Flouncing over to him, waving and batting her eyelashes, she cried, "Duncan! Yoo-hoo! Oh, Duncan!"

Aeryck and Dagmere walked toward the cottage, holding each other. Neither was in any hurry to get there, and so they paused here and there to take in the sights and smells.

It was a beautiful night. The moon was bright, and they could see little huddles of people hurrying back to the warmth of their hearths. They saw Terryll and Gwyneth and waved at them as they passed by on their way home. Terryll was grinning wryly and mentioned something innocuous to Gwyneth about the ways of birds and bees.

Aeryck grunted. And as he and Dagmere approached the steading, they paused in the orchard to watch the moon and the way it lit up the hills and spangled the river that gurgled in the distance.

"It's lovely, isn't it?" Dagmere asked, as though seeing it for the first time.

"Yes, it is." He drew her closer to him, and they looked out upon the scene for several moments, letting their hearts do the speaking for a while. When he looked down at her, she was already looking into his eyes, and the two of them kissed again.

The sound of a familiar throat clearing interrupted the moment and startled them apart.

"Mama! Papa! I was . . . er . . . we were . . . uh . . ."

Feeling a surge of chivalry, Aeryck stepped forward to protect his damsel in distress. However, looking into the eyes of Allyndaar and Helena, he struggled with an explanation and managed only a sheepish chuckle.

"You come in soon, Dagmere," Helena said, putting on her best parental face. Somehow it didn't quite fit at the moment, and she cast it off with a smile. "You too, Aeryck. It's much too cold a night to be outdoors."

"We will, Mama," Dagmere said, relieved.

Aeryck nodded and kind of saluted with a roll of his fingers, trying to act nonchalant.

Brynwald gave him the eye as he and Tillie passed, but Aeryck caught a trace of a smile. Tillie stifled a giggle, then fifty feet later Brynwald grunted something at Allyndaar, and they laughed uproariously.

Aeryck looked at Dagmere and shrugged. He was about to kiss her again when a wolf's howl pulled his eyes back to the hills. It was long and baneful, and the sound of it clawed up his spine with a long rake of shivers. He heard that one.

"What is it, Aeryck?"

"The wolf," he said under his breath, peering up at the hills for any sign of movement. There wasn't any.

A second howl soon followed, from the opposite slope it seemed, and farther away. A few moments later there was a third, farther away still, and then a fourth that was barely audible. And then there was only silence and the hissing of the wind through the trees.

They had found him.

30

A LITTLE TRYST

Miles away, in a little cottage nestled in an ancient copse of yews, Norduk listened intently as the last faint echoes of the wolf's howl surrendered to the hush of the wind. A smile curled over his face in the shadows beneath the wolfskin shroud.

"It is good news, my lord Norduk—what the wolves say to you?" the woman asked.

"Yes, yes, it is good news," he said, thinking about it.

"I am pleased. I am pleased also that you have come to me, like the little druid said you would." She scolded him with her eyes. "I was growing worried that my lord was growing tired of me." She pouted as she wrapped the embroidered silk shawl around her shoulders. The blue in it matched her eyes. He had gotten it from a Gaulish trader who said it came all the way from China.

"There was no need for you to worry, my love," Norduk said, amused that she liked his gift. He had asked the druid to select something for him to give her, since he knew little of the tastes of women. "Some bauble that might amuse her," he had said before he left. *I shall have to reward him,* he thought—*perhaps a new glass eye.*

He glanced around him at the quaint furnishings, uncomfortable with them. They were too stuffy and confining—too feminine—not at all like the open, breezy chambers of his hill fort. His eyes were restless, taking everything in, wary like some animal sniffing at a trap.

"We are safe here?"

"Yes," she said, looking up with her blue eyes blinking brightly at him now. "This is my summer cottage. No one will disturb us here. I have given orders."

"And your husband? Will he not wonder why you are away and miss you?"

The woman laughed. "I told him that I needed time and solitude to contemplate the birth of my child—that women needed such times away from their husbands. He understood. He will not disturb us." She chuckled as she gazed into the fire that was burning in the hearth. "You see, the fool loves me."

Norduk did not say anything. His head oscillated slowly atop his neck as he took in her beauty that was lighted wonderfully by the fire, the long golden tresses folding over the blue shawl and down to the small of her back. He loved her too. Loved her like nothing else on the earth. He was frightened of the power that she held over him. With the flip of her fingernail she could reduce him to a blithering sycophant, if she so desired. But she was a beneficent despot, and he was pleased to serve her. For now.

Rowena was six months pregnant; still her beauty was unmarred. In fact, she was more beautiful, he thought. Her face glowed with the inner life of womanhood, the deep mysteries of her gender shining out through her eyes.

"You are beautiful," he said. There was a slight tremor in his voice.

"My lord should not have to see me so fat and ugly." She turned her back to him.

"You are beautiful," he repeated as he walked over to her. He walked lightly on his feet like a cat, his boots making little sound beneath his tread, and reached his arms around her. She clutched his hands, and he would not allow her to remove them. She relaxed and looked intently into the fire. Their shadows flickered strangely against one wall, the wolf's head dominant in profile.

"Your hair," he rasped, drinking deeeply of the heady aroma. "It is delicious."

She smiled. "It will not be long, my lord, until I will be rid of this foul thing." Her smile disintegrated into a sneer. "It disgusts me. I hate it. Were it not needed to sacrifice at Stonehenge I would have destroyed it months ago."

"Yes, but we need it, don't we?"

Rowena grew pensive. She knew that the death of the child upon the altar at Stonehenge would restore the druidic ways, infuse her with the lost power of the ancients. She knew that the gods had chosen Norduk to be their surrogate upon the earth, that through him they would establish a new and glorious kingdom and that she would rule at his side. It was a little thing that she was asked to do—to bear this indignity for a mere nine months. It would be over soon.

"Yes, we need it," she said, as she turned and looked up at him. "For you to win a kingdom, and I to gain a throne."

His eyes flared just perceptibly. "Yes. Indeed."

"And will my sovereign always wear such a thing in his king-dom?" she asked.

"What thing?"

"This," she said, indicating the wolfskin shroud. "It has a dis-tasteful odor—not at all fitting for a king." She stripped it from his head and tossed it to the floor. "There."

Norduk looked down at the cowl and then back at Rowena, and she saw the anger burning in his eyes, their color changing to a dull, deadly yellow. He tried to hide the anger, but it was there like a living thing on his brow, and she saw it. She saw him flinch and the knuckles on his hands go white.

Suddenly she beheld a very frightening man, if indeed he was a man. His face was taut, and he seemed to shudder like some wild thing coiling to leap.

She quickly bent to pick up the cowl. But the baby kicked just then, and, putting a hand against her stomach, she groaned.

Then the anger flew out of Norduk's eyes, the yellow going out of them too. He picked up the cowl himself and laid it gingerly over a settee.

She came over to him and put her arms around his waist and looked up into his eyes. They were cooling, she saw, turning a grayish blue. The change from blue to yellow to blue again had thrilled her, and she smoothed the hair that had gotten mussed and smiled.

"Come, my love," she cooed. "Let us not quarrel."

_____ 31 _____
THE END OF
THE BEGINNING

The days following Christ's Mass were the best in his life, Aeryck thought. There was no doubt of it. It seemed a long and somewhat bittersweet chapter in his life had finally come to a close and a new one was opening, the first few pages of which were full of promise and hope and the high ideals attendant to the fertile minds of youth.

It was as though a tiny seedling, after so long a period of gestation in the dark womb of the earth, had finally, worming its way tenaciously, burst through the cold and stony surface to face the sun, broad-leafed and pliant in its bright and warming rays. Aeryck was in love, in love as he dreamed love to be. Songs bubbled in his breast and came bursting forth with the earth in concert. With the weather turning pleasant and warming, he and Dagmere took long walks over the steading in the crisp mornings, through the orchards, and along the river and down into the snowy hollows of elm and maple dingles bared of leaves. And going along in a desultory manner, they took in the sights and sounds of nature, looking at the prints of little animal feet in the snow, crisscrossing each other, or glancing at the birds in their winter shelters, or listening to the river warbling over the rocks, or strolling through the village arm-in-arm as they talked about many things—the future mostly—as young lovers do.

And they took many deep breaths, and, breathing out their dreams, they were not at all aware of the sidelong looks that attended their way, the smiles, the thoughtful clucking of tongues of older people remembering.

It was a lovely time the two of them shared.

But every chapter must have an end, and this one was no exception. The Britons were leaving in two weeks, Aeryck knew, and he hoped to cram as much into them with Dagmere as he possibly could, holding onto each moment in hopes of drawing it out, filling it up with themselves, with their love swelling over and slowing down the inexorable march of time.

But the days sped by with uncanny indifference, "swifter than a weaver's shuttle," as Job once complained. The world wasn't about to slow up its turning and wait for them. And they both felt the great movements of the earth, the turning . . . turning . . . turning . . .

One night, as Dagmere and Gwyneth shared the window overlooking the great room where the two boys slept next to the hearth, the fire lighting their sprawled, recumbent forms warmly, the girls shared their secrets, secrets that boys wouldn't dare dream of sharing, not at any time, or place, or for any amount of money.

"When he kisses you, does it make you feel all warm and tingly inside?" one of the girls asked; it matters not which.

"Oh, yes," the other whispered, thinking about it. "And you?"

There was a gentle sigh of breath. "Oh, yes, yes, like nothing I ever imagined."

"Oh, good." There was a pause for reflection. "I was troubled."

"Troubled?"

"That such feelings were not . . . you know . . . normal."

"Normal? I don't know if they're normal. I don't care, either. I just know that they are wonderful."

Another sigh. "Yes, that's it, isn't it?"

"Mmm."

The two of them giggled, then gazed down through the slats in the window, with the light and the shadows flickering over their faces.

After some time, Gwyneth asked, "Do you think he loves you, Dagmere?"

"Oh, yes," Dagmere said matter-of-factly. There was no doubt of it in her mind.

"And when did you first know?" she asked, remembering their earlier conversation.

Dagmere thought about it for a moment and smiled. She hadn't seen it in his eyes, though it was certainly there had she looked closer. And she hadn't seen it in his hands. "It was when he told Duncan that he was taking me home after the service that I knew." She smiled, bringing the scene out of a treasured place in her heart. "I could hear it in his voice."

"His voice?"

"Yes. There was a certain tone in it . . . a tone completely devoid of uncertainty. I knew then."

"Ah!" Gwyneth said.

And the two of them looked down again at the sleeping forms, thinking about them, treasuring their thoughts, then sharing them long into the night.

On the evening before the Britons were to leave, Aeryck and Dagmere, strolling again along the river and heading into the hollow of stripped-clean maples, were weighted with the awareness of the slipping-by moments that were irretrievable. Their heads bowed sadly before this as they walked slowly, hand in hand. The path was worn clear of snow and showing the sodden dead grass all flat and matted at their feet.

"So you will not come with us on the morrow?" she asked him.

Aeryck did not answer. He looked away through the white aisles of the trees on his right.

"Aeryck?"

He looked down at his feet kicking out over the brown grass path that led through the trees, the toes of his boots wet and cold. "No, I cannot come with you."

"Why not? I don't understand."

"I don't understand either. Not fully. It's not that I don't want to come—of course I do. I can't bear the thought of being away from you for a minute."

"Then why don't you come?"

Coming out of the maples now, Aeryck looked up at the hills beyond the river, all blue and purple in shadow, with the pines dark and pointy against them as they jagged up the acclivity. The sky was quickly gathering the day's toils and memories and lighting a fire with them, and they burned quickly upon a glorious pyre with such an effulgence of reds and oranges and yellows pushing away at the coming blues of night that he had to stop and watch for a moment. Such a beautiful sunset. It too was the end of something.

"Aeryck?"

"Huh?"

"Did you hear me?"

"Yes."

"Then why won't you come?"

He thought about it. He could think of nothing he would rather do than go back to Killwyn Eden with his love. Then why not go? What was holding him back? There were three answers.

The first lay somewhere in the hills, just beyond the safe confines of the village. The wolves.

Though there had been no sign of them, he knew that they were lurking in the umbrage of the pines, watching him, waiting for him to make a mistake, waiting for him to expose himself in the open. He could feel them. He knew that wherever he was there was danger, and he was growing tired of it, tired of things dying around him. He knew that, if he left the village precincts with her, they would come for him, perhaps hurt her and others of her family as well. No, he would not endanger them. Or her, especially not her. He would die first.

258

The second answer had to do with the two monks from Ireland. To date he had been unable to spend any time with them at all learning about his family. Their time had been spent with preparations for Christ's Mass, with teaching new converts and admonishing the not-so-new ones, as well as drawing up plans to build a church. His time, of course, had been absorbed with Dagmere. But now that the Britons were leaving, things would quiet down. He would be able to hear more about his Uncle Finn and the rest of the MacLlewald clan, he hoped, something he very much needed to do.

The third was a bit more intangible. It had to do with his spiritual sense of things, an entirely new sense of things that had been building in him since the night of Christ's Mass. Wolves or no wolves, family or no family, he felt a compulsion to remain in Loch na Huric for a time, at least through the winter. But for whatever reason or purpose, he had no idea. He knew that if he were to leave right now he would be transgressing some innate command. Whether it was self-imposed or by divine decree, he had no discernment on this. But it was there. It was as though there were a great invisible hand withholding him, and he knew that he couldn't slip around it, or go over it or under it. The thought of doing so darkened in him an already heightened sense of dread.

He took a deep breath and briefly related the latter two answers, leaving the wolves out of it and ending with, "So you see, Dag, I just can't come. Not now. You must understand."

She looked at him crossly. "Why? Why does this keep happening to us—always leaving one another? If we truly love each other, why would God want to keep us apart? It doesn't make sense."

Aeryck shook his head in agreement.

"And why must you keep after the ghosts of your past? Aren't we your family now? Aren't I? You ask me to understand, Aeryck. Well, I don't. I don't understand—none of it!" She had said it harshly. She seemed to know that and turned away.

Aeryck looked at her back for a moment, compressing his lips together into a grim smile. Then he took her by her shoulders and gently turned her around. She would not look at him. She was looking down, but he could see the tears on her cheeks.

He lifted her chin between his forefinger and thumb, and her big blue eyes blinked away to the corners, averting his gaze. "You have to trust me, Dagmere," he said tenderly. "I love you. You have to trust me. We'll be together soon, I know. In the spring, I promise. That's not too far away, is it?" Yes, it was too far away. It was a lifetime away.

She looked at him now, her eyes brimming over. "I'm sorry, Aeryck . . . the things I said. I'm being very selfish. It's just that I do love you so." Then she buried her head in his chest and wept.

He drew her close and patted the rolling shoulders as he looked back to the hills growing dark against the blood red sky, where the wolves were watching him, he was sure. He let out a big sigh. Suddenly he was very tired. Very tired indeed. He kissed the top of her head.

And as they held each other it began to snow, softly at first, a thin lace of white slowly covering the dead, brown path at their feet. Then the flakes grew larger and larger, the cold wind bringing them in from over the hills, and they turned and headed back through the maple trees and on to the cottage.

By the first light of dawn they had all eaten breakfast, hitched their teams, saddled the horses, and were gathered in the center of town making ready to depart. A general sadness pervading the morning air seemed a reflection of the dismal, gray overcast. An awkwardness stirred in their midst. Friendships between Pictish hosts and British guests had been born and nurtured, and now they were bidding farewell. There were hugs and tears and promises of soon returns and invitations extended to visit Killwyn Eden, Brough, and Bowes.

Brynwald and Allyndaar, having become fast and bosom allies, clasped hands and bade each other farewell, reaffirming their oaths of troth to each other and to one another's people in time of need. The latter had been made the night before in the hall before men of both tribes and ratified with any number of drafts of ale.

Feeling an awkward reticence in the moment, Tillie stepped forward and handed Helena a woolen shawl she had knitted. "For your journey," she said, smiling shyly. "It's not very fancy—not like the ones you might knit yourself, but it should keep the chill off."

Helena looked down at the shawl and smoothed a hand over it. "It's beautiful, Tillie," she said, truly humbled by this Pictish woman. "I shall treasure it always."

Tillie blushed.

Helena immediately wrapped it around her shoulders and modeled it for her. And when their eyes met, no longer able to stay their emotions, they embraced one another with tears. "I shall miss you so very much, Tillie! I do hope you and Bryn will come and visit us soon."

"Hoot," Tillie said, wiping her eyes.

"*Och!*" Brynwald said, looking on. And the big man wiped away a tear that had gotten loose on his cheek.

"We'd best be going," Allyndaar said, sounding a little choked up himself. He took hold of Helena's arm and led her to their carpentum and helped her up next to Aurelius.

Helena looked intently at the chieftain and his wife. "I meant what

I said. You must come and visit us soon and let us return your wonderful hospitality."

"By the oaks, lassie!" Brynwald boomed up at her. "And why would you be wantin' a couple of old toads like us flopping aboot your lovely hame?"

"It would be an honor," Helena insisted. "Truly an honor. I won't take no for an answer."

Biting her lip, Tillie put her hand to her mouth. She was tired of wiping her eyes, so she just let the tears run freely down her round face.

Brynwald put his arm around her and held her close.

Terryll and Gwyneth walked their horses from the stables, Aeryck and Dagmere walking alongside. Aeryck was leading her horse.

Tempest was whickering fiercely and throwing his head about impatiently, not at all liking this business of being last out of the stables.

Terryll chuckled as he patted the black stallion's thick, muscular neck. "Easy, boy, easy!"

Steam rose off the stallion's flanks as they came out into the cold air, out his flared nostrils as he blew out snorts.

However Dagmere's and Gwyneth's mares were quite docile, preferring their nice warm stalls of straw to this nonsense.

Terryll looked and saw that people were about to mount their horses in the distance. Turning to Aeryck, he said, "I'll be looking forward to seeing you in a couple of months, Aeryck."

"Or sooner," Aeryck said hopefully. Two months sounded like such an awfully long time.

"You're sure about this?"

Aeryck gave him a look.

Terryll smiled wryly at Gwyneth. "He's sure about it." Terryll extended his hand, and Aeryck took it. "Take care of yourself, my friend."

"You too," Aeryck said.

They shook hands, then both Terryll and Gwyneth mounted. Tempest arched his neck proudly and pulled against the reins, clopping forward with high prancing steps, unhappy with how slow things were getting off.

"Let's go, Gwinnie," Terryll said.

"Good-bye, Aeryck," Gwyneth said, waving at him. Then the two of them cantered away.

Aeryck walked Dagmere to the carpentum, holding her hand. "I will see you in the spring, Dagmere. I promise." They looked at each other for a long moment. It was time, they knew.

Mindful of her parents nearby, she gave him a quick peck on the cheek and started to turn away. However he caught her and held her tight. "I promise," he repeated, whispering into her hair. "I love you."

She looked at him, and the tears were starting to come. "I told myself I wasn't going to do this," she said, smiling and wiping her eyes. "Now here I go getting all blubbery."

"I like it when you're blubbery."

She frowned and shook her head. "Oh, why do I put up with you?"

He grinned sheepishly. "Because you love me?"

"Yes, because I love you." She hugged him again. "Because I love you so very, very much."

Aeryck tied her horse to the carpentum, then helped her up onto the seat next to her mother and Brother Lucius. She would ride there for a while. She looked down at Aeryck, who was giving her a rakish smile.

"Till the spring then."

She smiled back. "I'll be waiting."

A few yards away Fiona made a great show of saying good-bye to Duncan, waiting to do so until Dagmere was within hearing distance. She gave him a huge kiss, said something innocuous, smote the air with her airless twittering, then insisted that he give her a leg up onto her horse—sidesaddle of course.

The boy gave her a weak, parting wave, then, as he turned away, a great surge of relief seemed to go over his face.

After the benedictions of farewell were duly bestowed from one side to the other, and from the other side back again, the Britons mounted their horses, climbed aboard their wagons and carpenti. Then the column trudged away through the fresh lay of snow toward the river pass that led through the hills.

Brynwald, Tillie, and Aeryck stood waving until the last of them were long out of sight.

Aeryck lowered his hand haltingly.

"You're certain aboot this, are you, kipper?" Brynwald asked, clapping him on the shoulder.

Aeryck shrugged, still looking ahead at the river pass. "No, I'm not."

"She's a bonnie lass, that girl," Brynwald said, smiling at the boy. "Smart as they come too. Why, iffen I were twenty years younger—"

"And what would you be doing if you were twenty years younger?" Tillie interposed with a gleam in her eye.

Brynwald grunted. "Why . . . why, I'd not be letting her get away from me, that's what I'd be doing, woman."

"Is that so?"

Aeryck looked up at Brynwald and grinned. "Are you trying to get rid of me?"

262

"*Och*, no, kipper!" the chieftain boomed. "We—"

"We just want to make sure you're not stayin' here because you feel sorry for old Bryn and me, son," Tillie interjected. She took Aeryck's hand and patted it warmly.

"That's not it at all," Aeryck said.

"Are you sure?"

"Of that, yes."

"Good." Tillie put one arm through Aeryck's, the other through Brynwald's, then led them back toward the cottage. "Well, men, what do you say we have a nice roast mutton for supper tonight?"

"That's the best news I've heard all day," Aeryck said. It was his favorite.

"With the little boiled potatoes and leeks?" Brynwald asked, indicating their size with his forefinger and thumb.

"Aye, the very same."

Brynwald grunted. "*Och*, I dinna ken if I'll be able to fit into my clothes after all this celebrating." He slapped his girth as he said this.

"No one says you have to eat any of it." Tillie smirked.

"You just try and stop me, girl."

They all laughed.

Then Aeryck looked back over his shoulder once more and prayed for spring.

PART THREE
THE RITES OF SPRING

32

THE BEGINNING
OF THE END

High up in the virile, glacier-carved mountains, stark in their rugged profile against the skies, the river came spurting forth from its subterranean fount through beds of snow and ice. The air was scarcer here at the headwaters, as was the vegetation. Only a few species of lichen and scrub pine could manage the cold and scant, chalky topsoil. Then as the river fell from the heights, it picked up speed over the stony parapets in cascades of white water, through the rushes, the current slapping up under the thin translucent shelves, breaking away little chunks of ice, floating them away downstream past steep meadows of blooming heather and tall pines and yews and great hawthorns; the snow warming, melting, and trickling into the river, swelling winter-hardened beds into raging freshets, spilling over the banks here and there and watering the land.

It came leveling, slowing down through the long, serpentine esses of the foothills, rustling over the stones in the shallows past stands of sycamores and maples and birches, their leaves unfurling bright and green and shimmering nervously in the cool off-river breezes, breezes rife with cool moisture and carrying the sweet, thick smell of ferns and bracken and bouying the flights of robins and goldfinches and diverse others, their beaks chock-full of worms and grist.

The river was golden brown from the smooth, flat stones in these shallow places, where the light shone through to the bottom and warmed the pebbly beds, showing the eelgrass undulating slowly in the currents and the little fry darting and hiding in it. Large brook trout angled into the placid pools made by windfalls and large boulders to catch the sweeping-by hatches of insects, snatching up at them with their smooth, speckled sides flashing in the sun, the eternal pulse of the spawn clicking on in their brains, burning in them and driving them up the river.

Then, as the river smoothed out around the broad, fertile bends of the plains, graceful and feminine in their contours, it grew quiet along muddy banks thick with sedge and cattails. Here the course was deeper

267

and running dark and strong and fast, flowing past green hills, impregnating them with rich, silt-laden nutrients, past the grasses gently waving in the warm breezes and the great swollen clumps of berry bushes crowding the banks, everything in velvet, waking from winter's long and indolent repose and bursting now with myriad wildflowers and scents and songs of birds on wing and bees droning along their secret paths to collect succulent treasures. Everywhere was heard the sound of squirrels chattering in the leafy theaters, arguing matters peculiar to their kind. And not far away the rutting clatter of young bucks was heard in the thickets, and in the distance there was heard the long, wailing cry of a woman in travail.

It was spring.

"Don't push, don't push! Hold it!" the midwife said.

"I can't. I've got to push," the woman cried. "It wants to come. It's coming!"

"No, it's not. Don't push! That's it. Don't push! Don't push!"

"It's coming!"

"Not just yet, girl."

The woman cursed the midwife.

The midwife paid her no mind. She just watched the woman's face grow taut.

Then the woman screamed.

The pain, climbing fast now, reaching its peak, digging in with its big talons, all over burning as it spread out, the weight of it pressing, pressing heavy against her stomach, tearing at her from inside, then slowly over the peak now, the talons easing out, lifting, the pain subsiding, easing out long over the great plain of her body and hovering over her.

The woman panted, breathing away the pain in waves, her fists unclenching, her eyes rolling open, fixing dully on the face of the midwife. She hated that face, the old crone, hated the touch of her old crone's hand on her brow with the cool rag, hated everything about this moment, this place—this everything.

Her tongue dabbed at the corners of her mouth. "Give me a drink."

"It's not good for you. Here—suck on this." The midwife proffered a towel soaked in water.

The woman slapped her hand away. "I don't want that! I want a drink of water!"

Undaunted, the midwife dabbed her lips with the moist towel.

The woman took it with her teeth, turning it greedily in her mouth and sucking out all the water.

"That's a girl," the midwife said, taking the towel from her. "Get me another basin of water," she commanded a wide-eyed girl in attendance.

The girl obeyed and left the room with the basin.

Turning back to the woman, she said, "You're doing fine. Just fine."

"No, I'm not." The woman groaned and cursed again. "Here it comes."

The talons, descending, pricking sharply, moving up and out over the great swell of her stomach.

"I feel that this is a genuine suit for peace," Vortigern said.

The graying, middle-aged man was pacing anxiously, as though trying to collect his thoughts, trying to keep them in some kind of order with all of these distractions. There were dark circles under his eyes, and his shoulders rolled forward as though unable to hold the weight of his arms, and the lines of his face were drawn in long, vertical creases. The gray in his hair and beard shone in the light coming through the small arched windows, showing the pinkish blotches over his pallid skin.

The room was crowded with men who were looking at him, waiting patiently in little knots, murmuring among themselves during the pauses. They had been summoned on a most important matter that had been unceremoniously interrupted. They would wait. He was the king, after all, though he looked more like a cadaver.

The sound of his wife's scream pierced the great chamber room. The king started and looked down the long hall in the direction of the bedroom. He frowned. When would this business end? he wondered. Surely it could not continue another minute; it had been going on for so long now. The men read his face, then looked at one another, shrugging their eyebrows. A low murmuring sifted through them.

Vortigern watched as a girl sped through the room with an empty basin, passing another girl going the other way with an armload of towels, one of which fell to the floor. The girl paused to look at it but left it there, hurrying away.

Sighing, the king turned abruptly to the men. "Yes, I feel that this is a genuine suit for peace," he repeated. "I have met several times with Hengist's envoys to talk over the details. They are tired of this war. We are tired of this war. I have decided that we will meet with him at Stonehenge on the eve of the feast of Eostre to celebrate the peace between us. There shall be a banquet. A great banquet to celebrate peace for all time!"

The men murmured happily.

"I have given each of you proclamations to take to the tribal chieftains. I have already sent envoys to the Brigantes, Parisi, and Coritani in the north. You men shall spread out over the southlands and tell the chieftains that I wish them present at the feast."

There was another scream. Vortigern took a step toward the sound, then stopped and pulled anxiously on his beard.

"That one's nearly got it," the midwife said. The baby's head was crowning. "Let's push on the next one, shall we?"

Rowena nodded absently and flung her arms to her sides, exhausted. Tears trickled from her eyes. Long dark scrolls of hair lay matted against her flushed cheeks and down over her shoulders. She looked as though someone had beaten her.

"Water," she groaned.

One of the girls dipped a towel in the water and handed it to her.

She took it without protest, sucked weakly, then rolled her head languidly from side to side, gazing at the midwife with lines of panic etched around her eyes.

"Give me those towels now," the midwife said to one of the girls. "And you—set that basin over there—quickly now! The baby won't wait because of your sloth. That's it." She set the clean towels in place, then turned to Rowena. "Now then——are you ready?"

Rowena looked at her desperately.

The two girls were looking on, their eyes blinking with an admixture of wonder and horror as Rowena's body arched and went rigid under the piercing talons.

"Here we go," the midwife said, moving in close.

The scream trailed off into a lengthy pause, everyone caught in it, listening, wondering fearfully, and then the pause was followed by the lusty cry of a baby.

The men turned as one man.

Vortigern arched upright. "That's it! Good show," he said, clapping his hands together. "Good show! Good show!"

"It's a boy!" The midwife beamed, holding the infant suspended before Rowena.

Rowena, laughing, crying, laughing again, angled her head to see the midwife cleaning the infant. The two girl attendants glowed happily.

The baby, a pasty purple from stem to stern, wailed a good healthy cry, his little wrinkled body rigid and quivering and his little black eyes blinking at the light.

Working quickly, the midwife deftly cut the umbilical. Then she wrapped him in a linen blanket. "Be a dear and hold the baby, while I take care of the rest of this," she said perfunctorily. She added, "And see you don't drop him now. He's your future king."

The girl gingerly held the child, and the other girl leaned in smiling to see his face. The baby quieted for moment, his black eyes rolling back and forth of their own accord as he searched the dark blurs over him.

Rowena tensed as the talons came again, but the fight had clearly gone out of the thing. And then it was gone.

"There! That takes care of it," the midwife said.

"Let me hold the baby," Rowena said, catching her breath.

"Of course, of course!" The midwife wiped her hands, then took the child and lay him against Rowena's breast. She smiled maternally. "He's a right ruddy lad, isn't he?" she gushed, smoothing her fingers over the baby's brow. "Got a touch of the king in his eyes, I'd say."

Rowena said nothing. She allowed only a weak smile. Then she touched the baby's tiny ball of a fist with her finger, and he took hold of it.

"That he has." The midwife grinned. "Stout little fellow, I can see too. Knows his own, he does."

"Yes, doesn't he." Rowena pulled the baby away and handed him back to the woman. "Here. Perhaps the king would like to see his son now.

The baby screamed.

"There, there." The midwife cooed, giving the infant her knuckle. He sucked on it and quieted. "There's a good boy." The woman looked sternly at the girls, who were gaping at the child in awe. "You two—get cleaning up this mess, and don't be dallying."

Then the midwife left the room.

The heavyset, elderly woman strode into the great chamber before the eyes of every man and handed the baby over to the king. "Here you are, my lord." She smiled proudly. "Your son."

Vortigern gazed down at the tiny pink face, searching the little pinched features. His eyes glanced briefly at the woman, then quickly fell back to the child. "A son?"

"Yes, my lord—your son!"

"My son," he said quietly.

The midwife beamed, looking on as the king's countenance went through a transformation. She saw years of the toil and stress of war, a war that had claimed the life of his only son, Vortimer, quickly shed from his face. The muscles in his shoulders and arms quickened, his back jolted

271

with forgotten vigor. The dull look in his eyes flickered, then roared to life.

Suddenly Vortigern threw his head back and laughed uproariously, startling the midwife. "I have gotten another son!" he shouted. "A son! Do you hear that, men? A son!" The king laughed deliriously.

The baby wailed.

Then Vortigern held the baby up before the men and proclaimed proudly, "Behold the next king of Britain!"

And the men let out a thunderous cheer.

Rowena, listening to the cheers rolling down the hall, watched impassively as the two attendant girls hurried about her chamber, cleaning the birthing debris.

The cheers continued unabated for several minutes, until finally they trailed off and there was only the sound of the baby crying. She heard her husband's voice booming but couldn't make out what he was saying. It didn't matter. She could guess it. And then as the girls hurried out of the room, each turning and bowing once before they left, a dark, malefic light shaded over the woman's brow.

Rowena narrowed her eyes and smiled.

33

THE ENVOYS

Dogs were barking in the distance as though they were onto something. Bolstroem looked up from his work as two riders advanced slowly toward him over a low knoll. They were coming on the road leading from the south, which wound, climbing gently, over fields that were defined by long, straight hedgerows. Big, mature hawthorns lined the road on either side and threw shade patterns over it.

The riders passed from the shade into the light, riding down the knoll into a shallow hollow, the dust rising and settling under the horses' hooves, and then they were into the shade again. The white walls of tiny farmhouses flickered through the trees, and before them were white sheep and red cattle grazing. And the dogs came running alongside the riders, barking.

As the horsemen drew near, it became apparent by the weary look of their pack animals that they had been traveling a long distance. The horses paid no mind to the dogs. Their heads were low and rocking, and their feet shoveled through the dust. However, smelling the water in the trough, they perked their heads.

"Hail!" one of the riders hallooed, seeing the big silhouette of the blacksmith.

"Hail and well met!" Bolstroem returned, laying his hammer and tongs against the anvil. He went over and stood in the bay doors and waited for the men to dismount. His big hands, black from soot, rested heavily on his hips. He looked away to the east. The sun was up now and drumming over the fields, lighting great grottos of white and yellow wildflowers. The dogs took off and headed back along the road when they saw everything was all right.

The first man swung down off his horse and tied it at the hitching rail next to the trough, then started toward the smithy. He was a tall man, with a wispy blond beard. Then the other fellow dismounted and caught up with him. He was shorter and balding but made up for it with the length of his black beard.

Bolstroem watched them walk toward him and knew by the way they were walking they were not local men.

When the two came nearer, they slowed as it became evident how large a man they were approaching. Likely as not neither had ever seen a man who was well over six feet tall, broad as an oak, and had eyes that burned like two fiery coals. They glanced at one another dubiously.

"We are on the king's business," the taller man said with a certain tone in his voice. He looked small now against the giant Bolstroem.

Bolstroem leaned forward and cupped his ear with a big hand. "The who? Speak up, man." He grinned. "I can't hear you over the furnace."

The man cleared his throat and repeated, "The king! We are here on the king's business." The tone was still there.

"The king, you say? Is that right? And what king would you be referring to now?"

The taller man was taken aback. "Why . . . er . . . King Vortigern, of course." There was less of the tone now.

Bolstroem arched back and roared. "And what pickle barrel has the old rascal gotten himself into this time?" he bellowed heartily. "Perhaps he has let the Hun in now to look after the Saxons and Jutes. You know—the ones he let in to look after the Picts and Scots! Heaven save us!"

He leaned close, his eyes shifting conspiratorially back and forth between their faces. "Do you think, perhaps—I wonder if he might consider letting the Britons in to look after him?" He threw his head back again and laughed uproariously.

The men looked at one another, a little perplexed. Then the taller one stepped forward and cleared his throat. "We have a message for the chieftain," he said with the tone back in it. "You are not Allyndaar, are you?"

"Me? Allyndaar? I dare say I am not!" The blacksmith was still chortling.

"Then we would be obliged if you would kindly point the way to his home. We have urgent business with the chieftain of the Brigantes, from the—"

"From the king, I know," Bolstroem said, his blue eyes twinkling fiercely in the climbing light. "I'll do better than that—I'll take you to him. I've got to see what this urgent business from our good King Vortigern is all about. Perhaps a rat has gotten into his larder." Grinning at them, he slipped off his leather apron and tossed it over the anvil, then started away.

The men looked at one another again.

"Step lively, lads!" Bolstroem cried.

And the two men stepped lively.

The villa estate, though smaller in scale perhaps than the villas of Gaul, was the pride of the Brigantes. People came riding in from miles around, stopped, and said, "See, there it is! There is where the chieftain and his family live. Isn't it a lovely place?" And it was a lovely place.

Designed and built in the last century by a nobleman from Châlons, turned captain of a Roman cohort and assigned to the distant outpost of Killwyn Eden in northern Britain, the estate was set upon a broad, rolling promontory with a commanding view of the village. The River Eden snaked through the middle of it, and the dark green mountains loomed beyond.

There was a manicured approach of trees and hedges leading one's eyes to the domicile of white plaster and red tile, drawing the viewer along trellised avenues and arbored lawns and over steps of carved flag-stones ascending through them. The steps opened at last into an array of marbled courtyards, landscaped with fountains and pools, tables and benches, each of which was accented by colorful Italian tiles and mosaics.

Meals could be served alfresco in the cool spring mornings and evenings, with the diners encompassed by gardens and floral grottos and ornamental trees, the sights and scents titillating the senses. Indeed it was a lovely place, the whole of it sitting upon the gleaming points of the terrain like a brilliant jewel, looking lovely and rubescent now with the red morning sun shining on it.

Allyndaar was busy smoothing out the lines of a six-foot longbow, working a fine wood rasp over its length, when he looked out his second-story workshop window and saw Bolstroem approaching. And behind him were two men, strangers at first glance, both pulling up on their horses and staring moon-eyed at his house, staring as if they'd never seen a house before. The chieftain opened the wood vise, pulled out the stave of yew, and set it in the adjacent wall rack.

"What's this about?" he wondered aloud, closing the door behind him.

"A banquet of peace?" Allyndaar said, reading the proclamation.

He and Bolstroem and the envoys from Vortigern were standing in the shade of a big hawthorn that was spreading out over the gate leading in to their villa.

"Yes," the taller man offered for the benefit of Helena, who was just walking down the long flight of stairs from the villa. "Hengist is suing for peace between our peoples."

Helena leaned closer, looking around her husband's shoulder. "Is it true, Allyn? Did I hear correctly?" she said, angling her head to read for herself. "The Saxons wish peace?"

The two envoys were watching her.

"It appears so," the chieftain said, reading it again. "It seems Vortigern would like all of the chieftains in Britain to travel to Stonehenge by the feast of Eostre to ratify the agreement."

"Why, that's just three weeks away."

"Yes."

Helena brightened. "Just think of it, Allyn—peace."

Her husband did not say anything; he merely read the proclamation a third time.

Helena scrunched her nose. "But Stonehenge? What an odd place for a banquet," she mused. "Why not Londinium?"

The shorter envoy said, "They wish it in a place far away from the war." He smiled happily at her, smoothing down his long black beard with a delicate hand. "It is to be a love feast. It is the king's idea." He said this showing all his teeth.

Bolstroem grunted. He was looming over Allyndaar from behind, looking down at the long sheet of parchment that he was reading.

"Will you be able to go, Allyn?" Helena asked.

Allyndaar looked over at Dagmere working Daktahr in the adjacent meadow. The fields were green and sloping away from the villa and stables, leveling out and reaching to the hedgerows that stood out dark along the estate borders. Dagmere looked fine riding the Arab, he thought, watching her take him over a jump. He glanced at the several mares in the field grazing in the purple and white clover; each of them in foal, with their swollen bellies weighing down their backs. He hoped they would soon deliver a fine new breed of faster, more beautiful horses. The next few weeks would tell.

He looked back at the two envoys who were gazing at him now and had begun to fidget waiting for him to respond. "No," he said. "I'm afraid I will not be able to attend your love feast."

"Not be able to attend?" the taller envoy asked, clearly not expecting this answer.

"Perhaps if it were at a later time," the chieftain said.

"I'm afraid that won't be possible. Really, you cannot attend?"

"What matters could be more important than obeying the proclamation of the king?" the shorter man wondered aloud.

A flash of anger jumped into Allyndaar's face. He did not like the tone in their voices. "I've matters here that will require my presence," he said, constraining himself. "I need not give further defense. Perhaps if there had been more warning I would have been able to make other arrangements."

A tension drew taut over them.

Then Bolstroem laughed, a big, belly-sourced laugh. The tension lifted into the air and dissipated quickly through the hawthorn leaves. Then he went over to the messengers and placed his enormous hands on each of their shoulders.

"Listen, my good lads," he bellowed, "I'll come straight out with it. We northerners have little regard for your rascal king, and I suggest you speak his name in these parts with a little less impudence." He dug his big fingers into their shoulders to impress the point.

Wincing under his viselike grip, the two envoys grinned up at him, then looked helplessly at the chieftain.

Allyndaar waved Bolstroem off with a nod, and the giant loosened his hold.

The two envoys looked at one another, rubbing their shoulders, seemingly wondering what to do next. Their meeting hadn't gone very well at all.

Then the taller one brightened and delicately stepped forward. "Perhaps you could send a surrogate," he suggested genially. "The king . . . er . . . Vortigern has impressed the utmost urgency that each of the tribes be represented at the banquet—to show solidarity, you understand? After all, we are all Britons, aren't we? The Saxons would think us divided and the weaker if we did not make a good show of it."

"A good spectacle, you mean," Allyndaar sneered. But he thought about it. A surrogate. But who?

"Hail!" a voice cried out.

Everyone turned and looked.

Through the big hawthorns lining the road Allyndaar could see the palisaded berm encircling the village and Terryll coming through the west gates, carrying something draped over his shoulders. He crossed the field between the berm and the road, and then came through the trees, everyone still watching and Terryll smiling at them. And as he entered through the villa gates he set his longbow against the stone wall, then hiked the deer off his shoulders and laid it on the ground.

The two riders looked at him briefly, then glanced down at the dead deer.

The boy asked what was happening, and his father explained it briefly to him, and Terryll said, "I could go in your place, Papa. I will be your surrogate."

"I need you to help me with the foaling."

"Dagmere can help you with the foaling, Papa. She's better at that sort of thing anyway. You've said so many times."

277

Allyndaar pulled on his chin and grunted, looking at him. Terryll was grinning as he always did when he knew he had a good case going.

"I could go with him, Allyn," Bolstroem offered. "I would like to see for myself this great love feast that Vortigern has cooked up for these Saxon devils. Perhaps I might even pull the old weasel aside and give him a good talking to." He said this last thing winking at the two envoys.

They grinned sheepishly, perhaps hoping he wouldn't put his big hands on their shoulders again.

"What do you say, Papa?" Terryll implored, moving along in the sweep of things. "I would be able to meet with the chieftains of the south-lands and perhaps renew our trade with them. You've said so yourself, if it were not for the war, how you wished we could do so."

"I did, did I? I said that too?" Allyndaar grunted, still eyeing the boy. Somewhere in this exchange there had been a shift in his countenance.

Terryll looked at his mother now, the next stronghold.

Helena looked from her husband to Terryll, to the two riders, and glancing at Bolstroem she looked back at her husband. Her face fell in resignation. "Is there any point in me objecting to this?"

Allyndaar said, "He's seventeen now, Helena. He's old enough. This will be a fine opportunity for him. And he'll meet the king." He glanced over at the two men, as though to confirm with them that the king would indeed be attending the banquet.

The men were looking at Helena though. Sensing the chieftain's eyes, the taller man flustered, saying, "The king? Oh . . . of course, the king . . . yes, he will be there! Yes, indeed!"

The shorter envoy nodded vigorously. "It will be a most officious occasion—a spendid moment in our history! Simply splendid!" He smiled, showing his teeth again, as he smoothed down his beard.

"Then it is settled."

Helena smiled. "Wonderful!" Then turning to the envoys, she asked, "Would you men care for some food and beverage to refresh you on your journey?"

The envoys smiled.

"Aye!" Bolstroem boomed, slapping the men on their backs. "And after you've supped, perhaps you might join us for a round of ale in the hall. What do you say, Allyn?"

"I've got chores, Bol, I'm pained to say." The chieftain grinned. "However, you could take our two friends over to the hall yourself and show them a hearty Brigantes welcome."

"Now there's a dandy idea!" Bolstroem agreed. Then looking at the men, he said, "I see the road has stripped the color off your cheeks. Not to worry! Nothing that a few tankards of ale apiece won't fix aright."

He took hold of their cheeks and gave them a good pinch. "There, I see the idea has already brought the color back into ye!" He laughed. And draping his enormous arms around their necks, the big blacksmith swept the two envoys away down the road before they could utter a protest.

The blacksmith towered over the two men, his voice trailing away but booming out now and again with laughter. "Say, we could talk more about our good King Vortigern—just the three of us. I hear he's taken a pretty young Saxon wife, since the passing of his first. Is it true? He's a rascal, you know. Aye, a right rascal of a fellow." He laughed, chucking the two men closer to him with his big hands. "Some say he's let the sun set on his pate a mite too long. It's a shame—having a fool for a king, I mean."

Allyndaar was chuckling to himself as he watched the three men growing smaller on the road. And when he finally looked over at Helena, she had her hands on her hips and was scowling at him.

Clearing his throat, he said, "Come on, son, I think it's time we dressed that deer of yours."

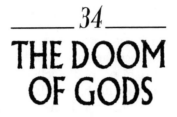

34

THE DOOM
OF GODS

Olaf was troubled by a matter that had been weighing on him for several weeks. And now, walking toward the Wolf's chambers, he wondered what kind of reception he would receive from the underlord. He was strangely unnerved by the thought of it.

Over the winter the underlord had grown noticeably detached, irritable, even snapping at him for no apparent reason. Some kind of a rift had come between them. Something was gnawing at his mind, Olaf was sure, something dark, intangible, something he could not quite discern. He had seen it in glimpses. But what?

Again he suspected the treachery of Ruddbane, suspected the burly, red-bearded warrior of poisoning the underlord's mind against him. Ruddbane was an ambitious man, as mean and cunning as a snake, and Olaf knew that sooner or later he would have to cross blades with him.

And then only the week before he had gone to Norduk's chambers to discuss details of the imminent campaign and there discovered the man sitting alone in a lightless ambience, the torch gone out, apparently given over to something that could only be described as a singularly dark and oppressive depravity.

Olaf's "Hail!" had gone unacknowledged. The underlord had not even looked at him. Instead he sat hunched, twisted into an anguished posture, as he stared out from beneath his wolfskin shroud into the umbrage of the room with unblinking, unseeing eyes. Occasionally he had groaned an utterance, of pain it seemed, shrugging his shoulders as though he were trying to shuck off invisible fetters of fire.

So oppressive was the air in the chamber, so smothering was the presence of evil, that the Norseman labored to move in it and indeed could scarce take it into his lungs. Whether Norduk was feeding the oppression or being consumed by it, Olaf could not tell.

He had left the Wolf's chambers gasping for breath. And immediately he heard a cry coming from behind the door. It was a tortured, inhuman cry, like that of a wounded animal. Then as Olaf hurried away through the dank, charnel halls of the hill fort contemplating the matter, he felt someone on his heels, felt a hot draft of wind, like a breath, on the back of his neck. Stopping cold in his tracks, he wheeled about and peered down the passage, but there was no one. And then a chilling terror rushed over his big frame. His legs began to tremble, and he had to steady himself against the wall.

It was then that he began to suspect a horrible truth.

That night Olaf climbed the hill overlooking Badonsward and sat upon a large flat stone beneath a certain ash tree with great overspreading boughs in full leaf. The tree reminded him of Ygdrassil, the fabled Tree of Life that grew upon the mount of Asgard, home of the gods, and bequeathed knowledge and wisdom to any who would listen.

Olaf came to this place often at night or in the early morning, when he needed time and a quiet place to think, and that night he needed to think about many things.

He sat there beneath the spreading boughs, with his chin cradled in the palm of his left hand in a contemplative attitude, giving audience to his thoughts and gazing upon the many campfires of the Angles, Jutes, and Saxons that burned bright against the warming, spring sky. His eyes, normally burning with an imposing fierceness, were locked in a kind of inquisitive trance, like that of a child's caught by some new distraction or horror, with the lights flickering faintly over them.

Druell, his Jutish kinsman, knew where to find him. The Viking was a creature of habit; his kinsman had often warned him about this. The Jute had climbed the hill, saw Olaf framed sharply by the overspreading ash, big and dark against the leaching lights of the campfires, and started toward him. As he approached the big Norseman's shape, Olaf reeled to his feet, clasping his battle-ax with a look of savagery twisting over his features.

"It is only me, Olaf," Druell said, stepping back and showing him the palms of his hands.

Olaf glared at him for a moment, the battle-ax quivering in his hand, ready to strike, then he cursed. "Fool!" he growled. "You are fortunate I did not split your skull." Cursing again, he sat upon the stone, and a brooding silence settled beneath the ash.

Druell stood for a few moments, looking over the plain of glowing fires. "It is a beautiful sight, isn't it?"

The big Norseman did not respond.

Druell looked up as a black shape winged overhead. Owls were out hunting for the mice that were scampering through the underbrush.

"The men are clawing for a good fight," he said. "They take wagers as to who will cleave the most heads, once they are in battle." He chuckled. "They are good men, these men of Horsa's—the best I have seen. Real fighters. Not even Attila could withstand such an army."

The big Norseman did not respond.

"What troubles you, Olaf?"

"*You* are troubling me."

Druell chuckled again, deflecting the remark. "I saw you leave the hill fort earlier," he said, the grin shrinking on his face. "Is it the war? It's the war, isn't it? I have known you too long for you to hide anything from me."

The Norseman remained sullenly quiet. He was gazing upon the fires below and the tiny shapes of men moving black and florid against them. The fierceness had gone out of his eyes, and the other thing was edging back into them. They were staring eyes, remote and lifeless.

"Do you remember our first raid together, Olaf?" Druell asked. "We were just boys—nine, ten years old maybe. Do you remember how we stole away in your father's fishing boat to prove we were fit to be Viking warriors?"

He was looking far away now, his eyes sweeping the black horizon beyond the fire-bleached fields of the army and into the shades of the past. He shook his head at the ascending reminiscence.

"Do you remember how, after we landed on the mainland, we fell upon the nearest village and stole those two goats and the cow? Some plunder it was, we thought. A king's ransom. And when we got back to the shore there were those two girls. Remember them? How they had followed us away from the village and wanted the animals back. That one girl—she was something, wasn't she?" The Jute scuffed his boot over the dirt and laughed. "I never told you before, Olaf, but I was glad when we couldn't figure out how to get those goats and cow into the boat without sinking it, and gave them back to the girls. I didn't want to have to fight that one—the big one, you remember her? She could have taken us both, easy. Ha, ha! So much for our first raid—one of our own villages too. Some Vikings. Thor must have smiled."

Druell finished his story and walked up to Olaf's side. He looked down at the campfires. "We have fought many battles together since then, haven't we, Olaf? We have taken much plunder. Yes, we have won much glory for ourselves since that night."

"Yes we have," the Norseman said, stirring out of his thoughts. His eyes twinkled to life. He looked briefly at the stout Jutish warrior, noticed how his thick shoulders sloped away from his neck on a line that was broken only by his elbows, then continued on to end at his thick hands, one hanging loosely at his side, the other clasped loosely about the haft of his battle-ax. Druell was looking at him intensely. As a brother might look.

282

"Is it the war?" he asked again.

Turning away, Olaf looked over at the hill fort. He could see torches lighting several of the windows from inside, lighting them to resemble glowing yellow eyes that peered out from the black face in the shadows. And then as he dared to look over and see the single eye flickering dimly in Norduk's chambers, the thoughts came and pressed against him. He could feel the oppression whistling out to him from that little window and roosting in the low branches of the tree.

"No, it is not the war," he said quietly, stifling a shudder that had jumped him.

"What is it then?" Druell asked. "That troubles you, I mean?"

The big Norseman did not answer.

"Olaf?"

"Leave me be, Druell."

"No."

"I do not wish to talk about it. Leave me be."

"You are my kinsman."

There was a long pause.

"Olaf?"

Olaf grunted. He shrugged his big shoulders. "I was thinking of Ragnarök."

"Ragnarök?" Druell had not expected this answer.

"Yes."

"This is what troubles you? The doom of gods?"

Olaf did not respond.

Druell looked away to the north. There was nothing there but a buttress of trees showing black against the night sky. "Do you think this war will be like Ragnarök?" he asked, looking back.

Olaf took a deep breath and blew it out hard. He ran the flat of his hand over the stone beneath him, felt the cool, sure hardness of it, the permanence of the thing. "I will tell you something I have never told a living soul," he said. "Not even Ingrid."

Druell leaned forward and waited patiently.

The Norseman's thoughts struggled to come forth. "I have long considered Norduk—the Wolf—to be the gods' surrogate upon the earth," Olaf began, his fierce blue eyes examining his dark fingers over the stone. "I believed him to be the one through whom Odin would extend his kingdom into this land. Because of it, I have overlooked the idiosyncrasies of the underlord." He grunted. "A surrogate of the gods is likely to be peculiar."

"Yes, yes, he is," Druell allowed.

"But lately . . ."

Olaf never finished his thought. His eyes, dimming of the fierceness, were drawn back to the hill fort as the light went out now in the Wolf's chambers. And then his mind drifted into the absolute blackness of that window.

Life to Olaf had been a Spartan adherence to a single creed, a warrior's creed. He was a Viking. Nothing less, nothing more—everything black and white. No grays. And with that creed he embraced the sum of its dictates: he would die a glorious death on the field of battle.

Since his earliest recollections, that had been his life's calling and duty. As a boy he would lie awake at night dreaming how it might happen—his death. The dream would always begin with his fighting and prevailing against insurmountable odds. And then amid the deafening clangor of battle there would come the sudden spear thrust through his heart, or the cleft of a battle-ax or sword, or the piercing hail of arrows that would lay him proudly upon the field of honor, spent of blood and wind.

And then the Valkyries would come, the beautiful battle maidens from Asgard, riding upon their luminous cloud steeds with fiery spears and shields flashing in the sun, their bodies clad in brilliant silver breastplates and helmets, with long golden hair flowing resplendent behind them. Searching the field of slain, they would choose those who had died as heroes, and in his dreams they would, upon finding his rent body amid scores of enemy slain, stand back and marvel.

Never had they seen such a hero. Then Brynhild, the youngest and by far the most beautiful of the sisters, would bend over and kiss his cheek softly, brush away the bloodied hair from his tragic brow with her porcelain white fingers, then proudly bear him back upon his shield to the Hall of the Slain, to Valhalla, where Odin and the other gods and slain heroes would give him a thunderous victor's welcome.

The dream sustained him through his childhood, growing each year with greater and greater feats of courage and prowess, as his imagination matured, until he was second to none among warriors of the earth. Indeed his exploits had grown to rival the mighty Thor's himself.

But as the years passed and his mind developed cunning and skill, and his body developed the frame and muscle and reflexes of young manhood, the dream took on flesh and became a living thing. He became a warrior, a devoted servant of the gods, of gods who smiled upon the acts of bravery and scorned the shrinking of cowards. And when it came time for him to be tested, he spilled his first blood in battle, took his first life, razed and plundered his first village, took his first woman.

Mercilessly.

In time there was none in all Jutland who could match the skill and fierceness of Olaf in battle, on land or on sea, against many or a few. He won glory for himself and his people, became a feared man, and his fame spread up and down the coasts of the mainland. It wasn't long before other men sought his blade, men such as Hengist and Horsa, and men like Norduk—powerful men of renown who had visions of grandeur and glory.

The dreams of his youth had served him well.

Lifting his eyes to the starry host, Olaf turned his thoughts to Odin, to Frigg his wife, seeking their wisdom and understanding on the matter that troubled him. He listened intently from beneath the canopy of the great ash tree, but they were silent.

He turned his thoughts to Thor, his favorite god, and Miölnir, the hammer made for him by the dwarfs of Svartheim. He thought of the other gods who lived in Asgard and the heroes who regaled them daily with their proud feats, demonstrating them in battle with one another. He longed for that day, as the Christian longs to be welcomed into the arms of the Savior on the day of his death. His fingers lightly touched the haft of his battle-ax as a smile edged wistfully into the corners of his mouth. They were pleasant thoughts.

Then somewhere in a faraway niche of his mind he felt a relief, like a boat slipping silently away from its cleat and disappearing into the floating mists of the night, and he knew that Druell had left him. His eyes widened imperceptibly at this knowledge, then narrowed with another.

A cool wind moaned in the overspreading boughs as the night settled into its quiet repose. The fires pulling the dark shades of coals over themselves retired to their glowing beds, with the dark and huddled shapes of men curling about them.

And then the other thoughts came—the intangible, spectral things that came at him in shades of gray, slithering into the battlefield of his soul like serpents worming their way under a hedge and spreading out, thoughts of other gods in the Norse pantheon, of gods who were evil and deceptive, gods who were jealous of his thoughts, of his sword, and those black-and-white places in his mind grew suddenly wary.

The chief of these was Loki, the trickster, the weaver of pranks, the demon god who first brought evil into the world, then multiplied it threefold by siring a terrible progeny. Of these there was Hel, the half-maiden half-corpse goddess who, because of her penchant for withering life, was hurled into the lowest bowels of Niflheim, where she ruled over the nine regions of the dead. And there was Jörmundgand, the Midgard serpent, whose destructive evil encircled the world with terror. And finally there was Fenris, the giant wolf, who was by far the most terrifying of the three. Because of Fenris's mighty power and wickedness the gods bound him to a rock with a six-stranded fetter named Gleipnir until the end of the world: in the Norse mind, Ragnarök.

The doom of gods.

At that time, according to Norse mythology, Fenris will break free of his fetters and, along with a host of giants and demons, war against Odin and the other gods and heroes in Valhalla to bring about the end of the present age. It will be a horrible day, a day when the earth will be consumed by a great conflagration and sink into the oceans, the sun and moon will be darkened, swallowed by wolves, and the stars will fall from the sky.

Baldur, the righteous son of Odin, will be slain by a mistletoe dart, and Odin himself will be swallowed by Fenris. It would be a terrible time, a time of weeping and gnashing of teeth, when all would seem lost for the gods and heroes of Asgard.

But then Vidar would come, another of Odin's sons, and avenge his father's death by stabbing the giant wolf in the heart with his sword. Thus would usher in the birth of a new and golden age. A new earth would rise from the seas, and a new sun and moon would shine from the heavens. It would be a world upon which no evil would dwell, no wolf would skulk or giant thunder. It would be a world where only glorious peace would reign for all time.

Olaf believed this fiercely. Every good and proud Viking did. Leaving the Wolf's chambers that day it struck him that perhaps he had made a terrible mistake, that Norduk was not the surrogate of Odin at all, that perhaps he was the surrogate of some dark and sinister spawn of Loki that had seduced him with its cunning.

For indeed it seemed to him that he had witnessed some evil thing in Norduk trying to break free of its fetters, like Fenris breaking free of Gleipnir. The thought of such a thing, the possibility that he might have been unwittingly serving the purposes of darkness, was almost more than the Norseman could bear. Truly he would rather fall on his sword than to bring reproach upon the beloved name of Odin.

Sweeping the heavens with his eyes, he took a deep breath and blew it out a long and troubled sigh. Oh, that he might meet his enemy face to face, flesh to flesh, blade against blade, face ten thousand or more of them if need be on the Plain of Vigard and have done with it. It was the only way for a true Viking to die. To live!

And then he remembered his dreams.

As Olaf made his way along the wide plank and beam-ceilinged corridors of the hill fort, he heard loud voices echoing down one of the halls. He stopped, listened warily, then as he turned into the passage it seemed the voices were laughing; laughter was coming from the under-lord's chamber.

He paused outside the large oaken doors and listened with a burning intensity. His eyes were dark and quick. He could hear Horsa and Norduk inside, both barking like old friends meeting after years apart. *Strange,* he thought.

Olaf waited until there was an interlude of silence. Then, filling his chest with resolve, he put his hand on the latch and entered the room with an animal wariness.

Horsa and Norduk turned as he strode to the center of the chamber and there smote his breast, bowing smartly to each of the men. Looking up he saw both grinning at him, as though they were in on some clever matter together. Olaf's eyes crept over to Norduk's, and peering into them he saw that the thing in the room that had troubled him a week earlier was gone.

"Come in, Commander." Horsa beamed. "Come in! *Wie geht es Ihnen?*"

Olaf looked at the overlord. *"Gut, Uberherr, danke,"* he replied tentatively. *"Und Ihnen?"*

"Gut! Gut! The underlord and I were just having a bit of celebration. News has reached us that phase one of our campaign is moving along splendidly. Just splendidly. The fools are flocking over the countryside, skipping happily to Stonehenge like sheep to the slaughter." The German slapped his hands together exultantly and let out a sharp laugh. He could scarce contain his rapture.

Olaf glanced over at Norduk. The Wolf was looking at Horsa, grinning at him. Not the grin of a week ago but of the other Norduk, the cunning general whom Olaf had admired as a young warrior, the general he had fought beside in many battles, to whom he had pledged his dying allegiance. He breathed deeply and blew out the air forcibly. The atmosphere in the chamber was clean, as though swept clear of any spectral debris. There was an invigorating tartness pervading. The other thing, whether real or imagined, was gone.

"Come, Olaf, let us review the next phase of our campaign." Horsa beckoned, waving him over to the table in the center of the room with a big arm. He threw his hands onto his thick girth and laughed. "Afterward we will drink to our most assured victory."

The Norseman smiled. Horsa had called him by name rather than by his rank. That pleased him, for it was a blessing of approval, a welcoming into an inner circle, into a greater sphere of power. He felt a surge of pride in his breast. The evening showed remarkable promise.

There was a map rolled on the table, and the Norseman went over to it with Horsa and the underlord, the sound of their boots striking smartly over the flagstones, and the chinking of swords and chains and mail, and the air smelling of leather and men.

Horsa smoothed his rough warrior's hands over the map and secured the corners of it with small stones, then set a lamp to one side so that its yellow light was cast over it. Then the three of them poured over the details of the campaign for what seemed the hundredth time, details that were now second nature to the Viking commander. But it did not matter; they were all men of Teutonic stock, a breed of men who were known to be sticklers for detail.

The briefing was short, Horsa dominating with his loud, barking voice. He alternately slapped Norduk and Olaf on the back after he had made a clever point of strategy or tactic that the other two knew was coming.

Killwyn Eden—that was the place. It had to be taken at any cost. Take that village and the north would fall, Britain would be won.

Olaf glanced over at Norduk and grinned. It was going to be a good war. He felt the thrill of it going through his body, streaming hot through his veins and burning out through his eyes, two beams of fierce crimson light.

Then Norduk stepped away as the briefing wound down, spoke to someone outside the door, and minutes later a girl came in with three flagons of ale, and the men drank them down heartily. They roared with laughter, looking over the map.

The girl waited, smiling up at them, then carried away the empty flagons and minutes later brought in another trayful.

The men drank them down heartily as well, each man going around now and drinking to the gods or to the success of their campaign or to their sons or wives or mistresses, and when they had come around to the gods again, the girl took the empty flagons and gave them each another, then left the room.

Good times were remembered, sins were forgotten. The thundering swell of manhood burst in each breast. Horsa took Olaf by his shoulders, slapped them, felt the thick, taut cords of muscle snapping under the skin.

"Ha! Ha! The man is a god!" he bellowed, slapping the big arms now. "A god, I tell you!" He grinned at Norduk. "The gods have come to earth and to lead our armies into glorious victory! Ha! Ha!" Then he drained his flagon. "More ale! More ale!" he cried. "Where is that wench! *Mädchen! Mädchen! Kommen sie hier, bitte! Schnell! Schnell!*"

Olaf drained his flagon and felt his head going tight, his lips going numb, but he didn't care. He laughed mockingly. It was going to be a good war, he knew, with much glory, and Odin would be proud.

"Where is that wench?" Horsa cried, then chortling winked an aside to Olaf.

It was going to be a good night, Olaf knew, as it should be. The dark thing was gone, and Norduk was over by the window, nodding his head and smiling, the moon shining in on him as he sipped his ale, and Olaf knew he was all right as before and phase one had gone well and phase two was about to get underway.

He drained his flagon, then threw his head back and roared.

And the old dreams soared in his breast.

The door opened quietly into the underlord's chamber. It was dark inside, save for the ambient light of stars filtering dully in through the window and forming a soft, trapezoidal pool of light upon the flagstones. Some time had passed since the briefing, though there was still a lingering smell of bitter ale and leather in the air.

A red-bearded man stepped into the room, cleared his throat nervously, then closed the door silently behind him and walked noiselessly to the center of the room and stood in the pool of wan light. He looked into the shadows before him and waited for his eyes to adjust. He could see nothing but a vague outline of a wolf's head and occasionally a glimmer of ocher light curling beneath it. He heard a faint guttural hissing, like an animal chortling, if that were possible, and then a sudden urge came over the man to turn around and flee.

"You must kill him," a voice rasped.

The bearded man started at the voice, then narrowed his eyes. "As you wish, my liege."

"You must kill him so it looks like an enemy killed him," the voice grated with a lilting meter.

"That will not be difficult."

"It must look like an enemy killed him in battle."

"It will be done, my liege."

"You will be rewarded greatly if you obey my commands."

"Serving you is reward enough, my liege."

Neither believed this, but it was appropriate. There was a pause. Again the sound of hissing, like an animal chuckling. The man with the red beard considered the yellow eyes blinking slowly in the darkness. He could not tell if they were looking at him or at something else. He found it difficult to look at the eyes. He found himself looking instead at the eyes in the wolfskin shroud, but the others—the yellow ones—would draw him back. They would not give him rest.

"Good," the Wolf rasped.

"And what of the Norseman?" Ruddbane asked.

"I have lost him. He has gone over to Horsa. But let us not speak of him now."

The Wolf moved forward surreptitiously, allowing what light there was in the chamber to illumine his features momentarily. Ruddbane's upper body recoiled an equal distance, goaded by something in his sub-consciousness, then advanced again as the Wolf sat back in his chair. This happened several times during the course of conversation, like the ebb and flow of the tide, back and forth—the yellow eyes advancing stealthily then retreating, then advancing. And retreating, the eyes blinked strangely in the darkness, and the man with the red beard did not want to look at them. He felt strangely naked before them, felt them probing his insides with leering scrutiny. He felt shame before the eyes.

"Horsa must die in battle," the Wolf intoned in the lilting voice. "It must look like an enemy has done it."

"Yes, yes, of course, my liege," Ruddbane said, clearing his throat. He did not like that the Wolf kept repeating himself. It made him feel patronized, like a child not trusted with a simple instruction. "He will die," he assured the underlord again. "An arrow will find his heart during the pitch of battle. The men will think him a hero. They will sing songs to him," he added sardonically. "He will be like a god to them."

"You are confident he will die then?"

"Yes, I am confident that he will die." The bearded man smiled as he said this, feeling the release of some red thing in his chest. He saw the event on a blaze in his mind: first Horsa, and then the Norseman, and the red thing winging free over the fire.

"Good, good, it is loose now," the lilting voice said. "That's it. You can see it now, can't you? Yes, you must kill Horsa, and it must look like an enemy has done it."

Ruddbane was looking into the eyes now, recoiling, advancing. "As you wish, my liege."

"Horsa will die, and then you may have the other."

"Yes, and then the other."

"You must kill Horsa first."

"I will, my liege."

"Kill him."

"Yes, kill him."

"Kill."

"Yes."

The eyes did not trouble Ruddbane now, for he did not think of them any longer. He was no longer ashamed of his nakedness. Something had changed in him. The red thing was gone, and he thought of nothing now as the yellow eyes came floating at him out of the shadows, came to within an inch of his face then orbited stealthily around his head, while a voice somewhere over him and around him spoke through him in the lilting voice.

Ruddbane, his eyes dull and fixed, stared ahead into the shadows at nothing. And then the yellow eyes were before him, coming out of him it seemed and hovering in the black void of space that was his mind.

There was a soft ring of metal and a glint of light off the blade as it came at the man's throat, slipped deftly under the beard, the edge brushing lightly over his Adam's apple. Then the Wolf, peering into the man's eyes, took hold of the beard and cut away a hank of it. He placed the hair in the man's cloak pocket, put his knife away, and stepped back.

Ruddbane stared ahead into the shadows at nothing.

The Wolf smiled.

It was then that the druid came out of his dark niche and toddled chimpishly across the room, his little flat feet slapping at the stones.

Norduk watched him as he came into the pool of faint light and stood next to Ruddbane, staring up at the impassive face. The little man was chuckling.

"Very well, very well."

Norduk grunted. "The man is a dolt. It was easy. There was nothing in his mind but murder."

"He will wonder how his beard ended up in his pocket though, won't he? That will fill his mind for a while." The druid chuckled at the thought. He stood up on his toes and waved his hand over Ruddbane's face.

The warrior did not flinch, the eyes did not blink.

Boadix stood back with his hands on his hips, staring at the man. "Remarkable," he said.

"Child's play," Norduk snarled, watching him. He turned and went over to the window and, placing his hands on the sill, gazed out upon the moon. "There is nothing in this," he said dourly.

"It is almost time—another week," the druid said. "You will have an army of such nothingness."

Norduk looked at him. "You are certain?"

"You doubt the will of the gods?"

The underlord gazed languidly out the window and stared over the cool sheen of the moon on the hills.

The druid studied him for several moments. "It is your dream again, isn't it?" he pressed. "The one with the fiery sword descending from the heavens and pointing at your breast?"

The underlord did not answer.

The druid smirked with a superior air. "I have told you before the dream's meaning. You are the chosen one—the sword bearer through whom Cernunnos will establish his kingdom upon this land."

"The dream is real," Norduk said, more to himself. "It comes to me in the daylight now—there is no escaping it. It haunts me like a fiend. I feel the anguish of the thing in my soul, the flames leaping about me until I am all but engulfed by them. And then it comes—the fiery sword. I can feel the point piercing through my breast until—" His head yawed painfully before the image, then, shuddering, he broke off from his thoughts.

"You are being purged," the druid said. "The Horned One is purging your soul to make ready for his coming."

Norduk grunted. A fierceness came back into his eyes. Then straightening from the sill, he looked over at Ruddbane and noticed that his head had begun to lower. From the window he made a little gesture with his hand, and the man's head rose and set itself upon its thick neck, looking straight ahead.

"You are ready to depart?" the Wolf asked, turning to the druid.

"Yes."

"And everything is in order with Rowena?"

"Yes. She has had a son."

"I know."

"You see? The gods did not lie to me."

"So you have told me many times."

The druid chuckled, looking up at Ruddbane's cropped beard. His eyes twinkled suddenly, then he took the man's knife from its sheath and put it in his hand.

Norduk watched him for a moment, then looked out the window. "You are sure that it is not necessary for me to attend the sacrifice at Stonehenge?"

The druid chuckled smugly. "Cernunnos knows where you are. It is not likely he will get lost."

"I must be here with the army. The gods know this."

The druid's brow arched dramatically. "Yes, of course," he sneered. "Of course the gods know this. Everything will be all right if you do your part."

"I will do my part."

"Then when I see you next, you will be king of Britain. I will be the high priest of Cernunnos." Boadix let out a little shriek of glee. "It will be a glorious time, won't it?"

The Wolf looked at him darkly, and then his lips curled subtly off his teeth into an inscrutable smile. "Yes, won't it, though."

The druid left the room, and the Wolf returned to his chair, thinking over the matter for hours, thinking of Rowena and the throne he would share with her, thinking of the other thing as well. They were pleasant thoughts, darkly pleasant. That is, until the first lights of dawn broke over the hills in the east and thrust a narrow blade of gray into the chamber.

Norduk's head bobbed upright with a jolt as a small tremor rippled over his body. His eyes registered fear—more than fear, for he knew what was coming. Another tremor struck him, confirming it, followed by another a moment later, and then another, each building on the other in intensity and frequency like the ascending travail of birth.

The Wolf flinched, twisting his head away from his neck as he fought against the thing he knew was coming, the pain ever building and building, making way for it to come, and he fighting it, as though struggling furiously against the swelling banks of a torrent. A groan ascended to his throat, his jaw yanking open to loose it into the air. And then there was nothing.

A pause.

It happened like this sometimes, quitting suddenly. But he didn't trust the respite.

The man blinked out of the darkness, his body still tensed against the memory of the tremors. The pause lengthened into a minute, and then two, then three. Exhaling slowly, he felt the cords of his arms slacken and go loose as though drained of their fluids. He waited, not trusting it, feeling contempt for it. Then his eyes shifted warily to the window where the gray blade of light was taking on a burnished gleam. A look of terror suddenly shot into his eyes, and he arched for it again. He saw it now, coming. The fit struck him. He cursed as his body began to shudder under the violent paroxysms. The dream came to him, the one of the fiery sword descending from the heavens and touching off a blaze at each of the four corners of the earth. It burned in his mind, the dream did, and he could not quench it, and quickly it raged out of control into a terrible conflagration that was all-consuming, coming at him until it was licking at his heels and reaching up through his limbs with its fiery tongues.

Norduk shrugged his shoulders, first one and then the other, groaning painfully, shucking away the anguish of the dream like an animal caught in a burning snare. And opening his eyes he saw the sword turning in his mind, and, pointing its flaming tip at his breast, it came with a single quick thrust, piercing through his soul like a fiery bolt.

Clasping his face, he augered violently out of the oaken chair and fell to the ground, writhing.

And Ruddbane stood, knife in hand, staring into the shadows at nothing.

293

35

A RUMOR
TO THE WISE

A capricious puff of wind billowed Terryll's emerald green cloak over the rump of the black stallion and flung it to one side where it hung limp and heavy with rain. Tempest picked up his head with a jolt, and with nostrils flaring struck ahead after the wind as though to catch it.

"Easy, boy, easy." Terryll laughed, reining the horse back into something that resembled a walk. "We'll get there in plenty of time. Easy, boy!"

The black whickered fiercely, snorted as he tossed his mane, then clipped forward into a prancing gait. His small, fast feet flicked sharply back and clattered defiantly against the worn, wet stones in a most complicated rhythm. Bolstroem's big, white draft horse looked over at Tempest and was confounded by his intricate gait; however, he had no mind to imitate it and rolled his head away back into a plodding *clip, clop, ka-clop, clop* cadence.

It suited Bolstroem just fine, for it was an easy gait for riding and pleasant for dozing.

Terryll looked up at the gray shield of sky with his piercing blue eyes. He saw that the rain clouds were breaking apart, narrow chinks opening in the armor and allowing long silver shafts of the sun, knifing through from the east, to stab the hills with its morning arsenal. Golden regiments of light descended and drove steadily against entrenched shadows, cascading down in silvery ripples over the fattened hills of dark, velvety grass that were slick with moisture.

The horses eyed the grass hungrily and raised their nostrils to the wind when it came tempting. Steam rose off their flanks and the road like ghostly sentinels quitting the earth. The air was newly washed and scented with the tartness of pine and the musky wet earth blowing off the dark hills. And at the same time it was sweet with the heady bouquet of wild-flowers, which were spreading their petals to the slanting sun and to the bees that hunted them.

It was overwhelming to the boy, and he stood in his stirrups, shook the rain from his hair, and took a deep breath of the thick vernal air.

"What a beautiful morning!" he cried, settling back into his saddle. His black shoulder-length hair shone with the greedy luster of youth as a finger of the sun struck it.

"Morning is my favorite time of the day, isn't it yours, Bol? Everything is so fresh and clean . . . the sun just coming up . . . the birds so full of song and cheer . . . woodland creatures scurrying about without a care in the world. Ah! And here we are, just like them—out on the open road, free from villages and chores and—"

"'He that blesses his friend with a loud voice, rising early in the morning, it shall be received as a curse,'" Bolstroem interrupted with a voice of sullen thunder.

"Huh?"

The big blacksmith cast the boy an ironic sneer. "A wise man that Solomon, don't you think?"

Terryll caught the gist of the remark and smiled. "What's the matter, Bol? Get a pine cone under your blanket last night? Come on, Bol, cheer up!" And not to be outwitted, he added, "Don't you know that 'a merry heart doeth good like a medicine'?"

The blacksmith's thick black eyebrows pinched over his broad nose.

Terryll turned away, smirking. "Ah, yes, a wise man that Solomon."

Bolstroem let out a snort, then tried to settle back into his dream.

But Terryll's enthusiasm was unflappable. He took a deep gulp of air, then burst out with another paean to the day's dawning miracle. "Can you believe it?—it's been a whole year already since Hauwka and I hunted in these parts. I'd almost forgotten how lovely it was! Isn't it lovely here, Bol?"

"Yes, isn't it though?" Bolstroem yawned sarcastically, giving up the dream ghost. He looked sleepily about the sodden countryside, then threw his massive arms skyward into a powerful stretch. "How much farther to Aquae Sulis?"

Terryll grinned. "Oh, I don't know. By this time on the morrow we should reach Corinium," he said, calculating the familiar reference points of the terrain. "And if everything goes well, by sundown the following day we should be eating a hot bowl of boar stew and fresh bread in one of the taverns of Aquae Sulis."

Bolstroem's eyes brightened at the thought.

Terryll crooked an impish brow at him and added, "Assuming, that is, that we don't get waylaid by robbers or eaten by wolves along the way."

Bolstroem grunted as he shifted his weight in his saddle. Robbers and wolves were the least of his concerns; they might even be a pleasant diversion after two weeks on the open road. "Two more days, huh?" he growled, pulling the wet trousers away from his legs. "And of course that means two more nights of sleeping out under the stars, doesn't it?—what stars we've seen since we set out on this fool's run."

The giant thrust out his chin and began fluffing beneath his thick black beard to air it of rain. "I tell you, lad, this traipsing about the countryside is for the birds—on a horse no wider than a blade, I might add."

Terryll looked incredulously at the huge draft horse that he was riding, standing at least seventeen hands at the withers and weighing easily eighteen hundred pounds. "A blade? Why, that plow-puller of yours is wider than a cask of ale!" He laughed. "You could pitch a tent on that broad rump of his! Two tents maybe!"

The plow-puller snorted indignantly.

Bolstroem snorted in concert and paid the boy no further mind. Now that he was resigned to another miserable day on the road he ran his big fingers through his hair, combing the black, wet snarl of ringlets into place.

Terryll snickered, watching from the corner of his eye. He knew that even though the gruff blacksmith spent most of his time sweating over a roaring furnace, or hammering an anvil, or fitting shoes at the back end of a horse, he was nonetheless a man who took keen pride in his appearance.

Dressed in his finest attire for the occasion, Bolstroem wore a pair of dark blue trousers made of thin tartan wool, light leather moccasins to keep his feet cool, and a bright blue cloak that was fastened at the neck with a brooch he'd hammered out of silver. He wore no tunic (wearing such a thing would be considered uncouth for a true Celt in spring or summer), and the thick mat of black curls that covered his barrel chest glistened proudly against the morning light. Indeed, but for his titan size he looked the very picture of a Celtic nobleman.

The British Celts were known for their bright, colorful apparel and finery, and Terryll was no exception. Wearing his father's torque (a neck collar of twisted gold and silver strands with an engraved boar's head at either end) and his favorite cloak of emerald green, the boy looked every bit the son of a British chieftain. A pair of low leather boots covered his feet, and over his sinewy frame he wore a loose-fitting, white linen tunic (his mother's Latin influence) and trousers of fine woolen tweed, with broad, red-and-yellow stripes running vertically along the legs. The two of them sat their horses well, as every self-respecting Celt did, and never was there a handsomer pair riding south to meet the king.

A red deer crashed out of the thicket ahead and skittered onto the wet road, startling horses and riders. The buck paused for a moment, looking warily at the two travelers, a sprig of blackberry bush dangling from its new antlers, then leaped, bounding away on its furious mission.

Terryll laughed as he watched its tail flag high into the trees on the other side of the road. "This is a good land for hunting!" he cried to his companion. "That's the fifth one this hour!" He strung his longbow and tested its pull. "Perhaps we might get some hunting in today. What do you say, Bol?"

"Not on your life," the blacksmith growled. "We'll not spend a minute longer on this road than we have to."

"Why, Bol, I never knew you to be such a dandy-legs." Terryll grinned.

"You mind your tongue, pup, or I'll show you the back of my hand," the blacksmith snarled. "Dandy-legs indeed. Hmph! The day I can't outride any three of you runny-nosed young bucks will be the day they're turning me under for the worms."

Terryll laughed. "Then you don't regret coming along after all?"

The giant shot him a fierce grin. "Lad, I wouldn't have missed this trip for the world. Just to see the look on the face of that scalawag king of ours when I walk up to him and tell him what a fool he's been. Ah, now that's a merriment that'll do my heart good!" He threw his head back and laughed heartily.

Terryll joined him, then trailed it with a familiar refrain.

> "When Love is fair, and fares thee well,
> The lonely soul takes wing;
> The turtle doves, though twain of breast,
> With single heart shall sing."

Bolstroem smiled to himself as he listened to the boy sing. Ah, young love! He gave his beard a few more airing fluffs, then wet his fingers and combed his thick eyebrows into place.

The song trailed away into a melancholy silence, and the two of them rode for a while, neither speaking, each taking in the lulls and flourishes of the country with appraising eyes, each entertained with his own thoughts.

Terryll saw no more deer for a time, or if he did his mind wasn't aware of it, for his mind was occupied with thoughts of his beautiful Gwyneth. He let go a sadness in his breast with a sigh. It was a good sadness though, the kind that autumn brings with its shorter days and falling leaves.

Bolstroem, on the other hand, was given to another matter.

They were a day's ride out of Venonae, where they had turned southwest onto the Fosse Way, the Roman road connecting through to Aquae Sulis, and were now well into the big forested hills of the Cotswolds, dripping wet and glistening with tiny prisms of silver from a warm spring rain. Little rivulets streamed from the hills, becoming larger confluences that filled the deep trenches along the road with a muddy run-off.

To the southwest the hills were rolling and green with trees clumping about, and the sun flashed over the puddled road that wound through the middle of them.

And to the east a long bank of fog obscured the horizon where the dark clouds were marshaling their ranks for a new campaign. Thunder boomed in the distance as it got underway. A huge bright rainbow sprang protectively over the countryside against the black reserves of clouds and thunder, shouting to them a warning of the Noahic Covenant, reminding them to go lightly over the earth.

Terryll could see a river snaking toward them in the distance—the Avon, he knew, having hunted along it with Hauwka the year before. Clumps of trees and shrubs pursued it greedily, and it was silvery and bright where the sun struck it.

A mile ahead a long curving hill sprawled indolently over the terrain like a big cat, thrusting a surly pack of shoulder into the road, and the young hunter remembered that beyond it they would meet the river and cross over on an old stone bridge. His eyes moved in restless darts over the terrain, looking for game or for any movement that might betray the position of a friend or enemy. And when they came to the Avon, crossing over the stone bridge, Terryll looked down into the river, muddied by the rain, and saw the water swells moving about where big trout were feeding just below the surface.

Bolstroem broke the silence. "Is it true what they say about the place, lad—that there is a spring in Aquae Sulis which bubbles up from the belly of the earth as hot as the River Styx itself?"

"A hot spring? Yes, so I've heard," Terryll replied, still watching the trout. "Why?"

Bolstroem had a dreamy look in his eyes. "Tell me more of it, lad—about the hot springs."

Terryll arched a brow at the man. "It's supposed to be full of minerals and medicinal properties. I hear the Romans have built baths around it too, though I don't know why. I've never been there, if that's what you're wondering."

"Ah, bless the Romans!" Bolstroem laughed. "I ask you, lad, do you know what I'm going to do after we get there and've had a good hot meal?"

Terryll shook his head.

"Why, I'm going to find those hot springs and have me a good soak! Minerals or no, I'll be a new man—right as rain, as they say!"

"The hot meal sounds good to me, but I'll leave you to those hot springs." Terryll smiled. "That sounds too much like taking a bath to me, and I've already had mine this month."

Bolstroem squinted an eye and made an exaggerated scrunch of one nostril. "Then I'm thinkin' you must be getting to the long end of the month, lad." He grinned wryly. "It wouldn't hurt you none to soak a bit of the road off you before we start sidling up to the likes of Vortigern. Why, that old popinjay might get a good strong whiff of you and faint dead away. We wouldn't want that to happen, now would we? Not at the banquet! What would the other chieftains think? They may get the wrong idea of our clan. They might even get to thinking we're no better than the Saxons."

"You go sidle up next to 'old popinjay' yourself if you want. I'm not taking another bath until I have to." Terryll frowned and looked away, settling the matter.

"Then you won't be minding if we ride upwind of you, will you, lad? I've a strong constitution—what with me working with stock and all—but the plow-puller here is getting a bit long in the tooth and has been complaining something fierce." Bolstroem goaded his horse forward, concealing a snicker.

Terryll grunted indignantly. Then, allowing Bolstroem to pass by, he surreptitiously sniffed at himself, crooked an eyebrow, and wondered what the fuss was all about.

Later that day, in the gloaming of the evening, Terryll looked up as a skein of ducks arrowed north against a bloodened palette of sky, seeking the clear mountain lakes in the north. The once golden regiments were drawn up quickly now into a grand crimson pageantry, passing in review as the sun marched to an ancient band behind the western rim of the Cotswolds.

The hills in the west drew upon the ranks of the fleeting spectrum, deepening every moment with purples and dark blues and sharpening their edges against the relentless advance of night. Those in the east were lighted still in the burnished hues of twilight, where the umbral struggle continued, but every minute sighing away their vigor in quiet exhales. The young hunter took them into his breast and held them.

"Corinium is probably another three miles off," he said in a tone of one reverencing the day's passing. "Should be a clear night though. No clouds."

Bolstroem glanced up from the road that wound a narrow blush of color over the countryside as it reflected the fading light, and eyed the horizons. "Aye. But they'll come sneaking, you can count on it."

"No point in wasting good money on an inn when a soft bed of pine needles will do just as well."

"Not tonight, laddie, not tonight," the big blacksmith contested. "You sleep on the pine needles if you've a mind. But as for me, I'll be finding the nearest inn and demanding the softest featherbed."

Terryll smiled and looked away. He let out the exhales he'd collected and patted the neck of Tempest. The horse whickered happily and raised his head against his toil. A boil of bats came charging clumsily overhead, laughing hysterically with their high-pitched voices, knowing full well that they were defying the laws of gravity with their comedic design.

Two hundred yards away a small herd of deer moved stealthily out of hiding into a large meadow to graze upon the cool, dark points of grass. The does looked up as Tempest whinnied and gathered nervously around the buck. Every so often a remnant of light would find their eyes and glow, betraying them.

Behind them the boy noted two low, dark mounds of earth that he knew to be long barrows, burial mounds of ancient Britons—the children of druids. They were gateways to the underworld, it was thought by some, the habitation of spirits, rife with lore and myth and places to be avoided. However, to the stout souls of grave robbers, they were troves containing gold and silver, jewels and armor, and other personal effects of the aristocratic dead.

Terryll was in neither of these camps, but he felt the hair edging anxiously up the back of his neck. He sensed that they had suddenly crossed into the domain of some dark lord of the air that came rushing out to challenge them. Watching the barrows, he felt his fingers go tight on his longbow.

"Strange place this, eh, lad?" Bolstroem said in a whisper, breaking into the eerie silence that had fallen upon them. "Aye, a strange devil of a place."

"You feel it too, huh?"

"Aye, lad. Evil lives here, or once did."

The horses exchanged whinnies and snorts. They sensed it too. The plow-puller quickened his gait to keep up with the black, his ears flicking warily back and forth. Wickedness was about. Surely some mischief had gotten loose in the air.

The riders rode on steadily for another mile, each sweeping the land for some dark thought of his to take form out of the darkening folds of the earth, or to appear from behind one of the trees, or to leap off one of the large boulders that loomed suddenly by the road.

But there was nothing they could see, only feelings. It was only some ill wind, perhaps, that was stirring over their fatigue-worn nerves, or perhaps it was the unfamiliarity of the terrain or the vague settling in of the night. Yes, that was it. The mind knows that evil things skulk in the night and that, without the witness of the eyes to contest it, it has a free run of itself.

The moon, a big waxing gibbous, loomed up from the east and cast a pale sallowness over the hills—a ghostly luminance—and the stars burned fiercely in their resolute courses. Occasionally one would break free its restraints and hurl wildly across the sky, a white streak of blazing hilarity and die upon the hills.

Terryll glanced over at the dark silhouette of Bolstroem. The man's head was bent forward with a menacing scowl, his eyes searching and daring, reflecting the moon's pallor, and the boy took comfort in the man. If ever there was a warrior to stand alongside in a fight, it was the giant blacksmith from Killwyn Eden.

As the riders rounded a bend in the road a cool breeze smote their faces, and Terryll pulled up on his reins. "Wait!"

Bolstroem drew up hard and grabbed the hilt of his sword. "What is it, lad?"

"Listen! Did you hear it?"

"Hear what?"

"Voices. Listen, there it is again!"

Cupping his ear, Bolstroem scowled into the night. "I must be going deef. I can't hear a thing but my heart thumping."

"Trust me," Terryll said, then reined Tempest to his left. "Come on, let's get off this road."

They leaped the ditch alongside the track and cut across a wide, open field toward a black palisade of trees at the base of a low hill, trotting their horses. The horses' hooves drummed quietly over the deep spring grass. The riders kept their eyes fixed on the trees, listening to the silences between the footfalls. Entering the trees, they climbed the hill and paused at the crest behind a screen of shrubbery.

Terryll was the first to see it. "Over there!"

"Aye, lad, I may be going deef, but my eyes are still as sharp as a widow's. And I can smell them too."

Over the dark tops of yews and pines, spread out for miles below them like a thick black carpet, they could see a soft glow of light spilling through the canopy into the sky. And upon the prevailing breeze there was the definitive smell of cooking smoke.

"It's a camp."

"Let's go, lad. I want to see what manner of fool builds a fire so large that every living thing for miles around can see him. Whatever he is, he must either be a mighty brave soul or one who has lost his senses—"

"Or a large party of men who don't care who sees them," Terryll added.

"Aye," Bolstroem mused, pulling on his beard. "What say we ride another couple hundred yards, then tie up the horses? We'll go the rest of the way on foot."

Terryll's eyes gleamed with interest. "Sounds good to me," he agreed. Anything to belay his eerie feelings.

Then they reined their horses down the hill.

Terryll and Bolstroem came sneaking through the dark columns of trees, from trunk to trunk, the soft floor of pine needles cushioning their feet silently. The voices and smoke guided them at first, and then, as they drew nearer, the firelight suddenly flickered through the thousand apertures of the black-backed leaves, opening with every step until they were at the perimeter and peeking through at the camp.

Six of them were sitting around a large fire, their faces lurid and rapt as they looked into the flames at the meat turning, and a few more milled about behind them in the lesser light, busy with chores. None of them was watching the trees for enemies.

Bolstroem winked knowingly at the boy. They had each been right—not only was this a fair-sized party of men, but they were fools as well.

"Gaulish traders, by the looks of them," Bolstroem whispered. Scanning their camp he saw several large tarpaulin-covered wagons at the far end and the teams beyond in the shadows. Then he looked back at the lamb turning on the spit. He watched as the fat juices dripped off the golden skin into the fire, the fire spitting, and his mouth began to water.

"Perhaps they've heard of the banquet at Stonehenge," Terryll suggested. "It would be quite a boon to their business, with all the chieftains in one place."

"Aye."

Terryll watched the men keenly and listened to their conversation, which centered primarily on the business of the camp: "One more turn should do it. . . . That's it. . . . Give those beans another stir, won't you? Don't want them sticking to the pot. . . . What a week this has been. . . . How are the horses? . . . They're fine. . . . Come and have some supper, won't you?" And so on, all in the fast tongue of Gauls, most of which he understood, having traded with Gauls before.

A man came out from one of the wagons holding a strange-looking cat on a leash. The cat was growling and looking over the camp as it pulled the man along.

Terryll stared incredulously at the thing. It was the size of a large dog, though its body was longer and it had a small round head. It was tawny in color, and there were little black spots covering it from head to toe. He'd heard tales of strange animals brought over from the East and from Egypt and points south, but he had never heard of anything like this before.

The man who was pulling on the cat's leash was having a difficult time of it now, and the cat was growling at him, showing its teeth, and its black-tipped tail was flicking furiously. One of the others by the fire threw a hunk of raw meat at it, and the cat trapped it with its paws and settled upon it hungrily. The men laughed. The one leading the big cat tied it to a fallen limb and joined the others, and the conversation centered on the cat for a while.

"They seem harmless enough," Terryll suggested, still eyeing the cat. "There's no further point in us dallying here."

But Bolstroem was still eyeing the lamb, his big hand working over his face and lips. He was about to throw discretion to the wind and step into the light when one of the Gauls said, "It's going to ruin our trade, this new thing."

"We'll survive somehow," a second man reasoned. "Wars or no wars, we've always managed."

"Wait!" Bolstroem whispered to the boy, who had started to back away. "Here's something!"

Terryll crept back, and the two of them inclined their heads to listen.

"There's no trading with them, I tell you," the third man said. He had a round face with tiny black eyes that moved constantly, and his belly was fat with profit. "Not with this lot. Look what happened to our trade in Londinium. *Phsst!* Gone! No more!"

"What of this treaty?"

"Don't believe it. It's a ruse," the fat Gaul declared. "These Saxons are clever, I tell you."

Terryll and Bolstroem listened intently.

The first man said, "It's getting so that wherever we establish a trade, there's a war on the wing."

"Or one roosting. I tell you, I'm going back to Gaul."

"Yes, maybe you can trade with Attila once he arrives." There was a bit of laughter.

"I'll take Huns over Saxons any day." The fat Gaul scowled. He bent over and picked another piece of meat out of a bowl and tossed it to the big cat, and the cat pounced on it. "There's no trading with them, I tell you. They never want to bend from their ridiculous offers."

"You keep trying to sell them perfumes and silks," the first man chuckled. "What do Saxons know about such things? They never bathe. Maybe you should try selling them pigs."

"Or cheetahs!" the one turning the spit put in, as he brushed some of the falling juices over the lamb.

"That cat will fetch a good price, I tell you!" the fat Gaul protested, glancing quickly at the animal.

A man snickered. "Yes, providing you can sell him before he eats away all your profits."

The men laughed again.

"You can make jests, but I tell you this island is finished," said the fat Gaul, his little black eyes darting from face to face. "First it was Londinium, and now there's this business in the north. Where else can we go?"

"There's always Eire."

"And get your ship scuttled by pirates? No, thank you."

Terryll and Bolstroem were looking at one another. *What business in the north?*

"That does it," Bolstroem growled.

"I'll cover you," Terryll said, drawing back on his bow.

The men standing were the first to see him. They froze dumbfounded and stared as the giant stepped out of the shadows into their camp, his blue eyes austere and riveting and his palm resting on the pommel of his sword.

One man dropped a stack of wooden plates, another called upon his god, and then in quick succession each of the others around the fire looked up at the man and gaped stupidly.

"Hail," Bolstroem boomed, gazing fiercely at each of their faces. His voice was like a clap of thunder, and the men around the fire stood up and backed away, blinking incredulously, no doubt wondering what manner of being had descended upon them. Bolstroem, standing closer to seven feet than to six, towered over the nervous little knot of Gauls.

An anxious murmuring rose from their midst as they closed in together.

"What? Have you lost your tongues then?" Bolstroem demanded. "They were wagging plenty a minute ago. Come on then, who is your man?"

The Gauls looked at one another, and the first man, a thin, balding fellow who wore a funny little cap and had a thick mustache that fell over his lip and puffed out when he spoke, raised his hand timidly.

"Hail and well met," he squeaked. "We welcome you into our humble camp."

304

Bolstroem grunted. "I daresay this camp is a wee bit short on humility, my good fellow," he sneered, looking them over.

The thin Gaul grinned sheepishly, then saw Bolstroem's eyes creeping to the lamb. "You are hungry, perhaps? Of course you are hungry! Please, my friend, it is clear that you have long been on the road—share our food. We have plenty, as you can see."

Bolstroem's gaze softened. "Aye, that I am, that I am. And I thank you kindly!"

One of the men carved off a joint and hurried over to the big blacksmith and handed it to him as one might stretch his arm to a ravenous bear.

The blacksmith took a big sniff then sank his teeth into it.

The thin Gaul's eyes narrowed shrewdly as he watched the man content himself with the meat, secretly scanning his fine cut of clothes for the betraying bulge of a purse or perhaps the tell-tale glimmer of jewelry. As he eyed the silver brooch at his neck, a thin, oily smile curled beneath his mustache.

"Mmm! Thish ish good!" Bolstroem bellowed. Then remembering his business, he started to speak but quickly found that he could not ask his questions and chew his food at the same time. So, licking his fingers, he waved the joint at the boy.

Terryll stepped warily into the light behind him, his bow held at the ready.

The Gaul's eyes lost their cunning as he looked from the giant to the boy and then at the bow in his hands. The others murmured behind him.

"We are peaceful men, my friends," the thin Gaul said warily, looking from Terryll's bow and then beyond into the shadows of the trees for any more of them.

"Then tell us of this business in the north," Terryll demanded, taking over as the spokesman. "Tell us of this matter that will ruin your trade there, and we will be on our way."

The Gauls looked at one another innocently. "What business in the north?"

"Do not play games with us." Terryll glowered. "We have been listening to you for some time."

Bolstroem nodded and shook the joint at them. "Thashh right!"

The thin Gaul took off his cap, twisted it with his hands, and smiled slyly. "We have no quarrel with any man," he said, eyeing the tip of the arrow. "We are peaceful traders." He indicated the others with his cap. "It is not our way to become involved in political differences between the peoples of a land."

"That way we can trade with all of them freely," the fat Gaul said happily, and grinning revealed a shiny gold tooth in front.

The thin Gaul censured him with a scowl.

Terryll narrowed his eyes. "Tell us what you know, or you will be involved more than you like."

The thin Gaul chuckled, holding up a conciliatory hand. "My friends, my friends, we are traders, that is all—nothing more, nothing less—just simple, peaceful traders from Gaul."

The others agreed, nodding their heads. Traders one and all.

"Who are withholding vital information," Terryll said.

Bolstroem arched a brow at the boy. "Shpies!"

"No, no, no, my friends! We are not spies. Not at all, not at all!" The thin Gaul laughed, and the others shook their heads in unison. "We are men of business. We deal in commodities, you see—in trade goods. That is all. You understand?"

The Gauls looked at one another, smiling in agreement. *Yes, that is all. Heh, heh, heh.*

The first man chuckled, placing his cap back on his head. "It is true that sometimes when we travel from town to town we hear things— you know, useless gossip like what man has taken a wife here, that has left a husband there, who was sleeping with the first man's wife over here again." He winked as he said this, drawing a finger through the air to illustrate the circle. "Sordid little affairs mostly."

Then, grinning shrewdly, he cinched up his waistband and added, "But if it happens—*if*, mind you—that every now and then we hear something of value—or vital, as you say—then what we have learned becomes . . . how shall I say it?—" He broke off, thinking, tapping a pulse on his nose, and then brightening, said, "Becomes like a commodity. That's it! A trade goods we might exchange for something else—say a bit of gold, or jewelry, or . . . silver." His eyes darted quickly to Bolstroem's brooch. "It is simple business, really, that is all. Do you understand?"

"Clearly." The boy raised the tip of his arrow and leveled it at the man's chest.

The man's eyes shot open. "My friends, my friends," he burst out with a chuckle, his mustache pumping as from a bellows. "On second thought it would be a poor business practice if we did not first give you a little something to show our good faith and intentions, would it not?"

The Gauls nodded their heads furiously.

"Of course! Of course! And perhaps you would allow us to trade in your fine village some day. As a way of exchange, you understand. Uh . . . and where did you say you were from?"

"We didn't," Terryll said flatly. "Now tell us what you know concerning this business in the north. And be quick about it. My fingers are getting tired holding this arrow."

The Gaul jumped to it. Clearing his throat, he spoke in a hushed tone, as though the very trees were listening. "It might interest you to know that there is a build-up of men in Badonsward."

"An army would be a more apt term for it," the fat Gaul interposed with a toothy grin.

The thin Gaul shot him a scowl.

Terryll frowned. "This is not news. The Saxons have long kept a contingent of men there."

"Is that so?" the thin Gaul resumed. "And does this contingent include five thousand of Horsa's men from Londinium?"

Terryll and Bolstroem looked at one another dumbfounded.

The Gaul snickered. "I thought not."

Bolstroem tossed the joint into the fire, where it crackled and spit up a flurry of sparks. "You have seen this army?" he demanded.

"No, but like I said, we are traders. We hear things."

"Go on," Terryll said.

"Some would pay handsomely for such information."

"You will pay handsomely if you don't get to it," Terryll snarled, hefting his bow.

The Gaul smiled wanly. "Yes, of course. You have such persuasive bargaining skills." *Like the rest of the barbarians on this island,* he didn't say. "There is not much more really—only rumors, mind you— but what we've heard is that this contingent of men is about to move north to secure the trade routes there."

Bolstroem wrinkled his brow. "Trade routes?"

"Yes—monopolize the trade routes, monopolize the world—it is a simple but effective law of business, or conquest . . ." *You great hairy dolt!* The thin Gaul smiled condescendingly up at him. "And now you have the whole of it."

"When is this supposed to happen?" Terryll asked.

The Gaul shook his head tiredly.

Terryll looked at the blacksmith, and suddenly a great many puzzle pieces fell into place: the reason that the Saxons had made so many bold ventures into the north over the summer and winter; the bits and pieces of information he had purloined from their camp when they had held him captive, indicating a possible link between Horsa and a movement of men to Badonsward; the two envoys from Vortigern with a supposed peace agreement that seemed too good to be true. And now this news, tying it together. Everything fit and pointed to one thing.

Terryll looked at the Gaul. "And you don't know which direction the army will move against the north?"

"I have told you, my friend. I have told you everything I know. Now won't you put down your arrow and have supper with us? We will discuss a trade venture with your village, as men of business. It is a big village where you are from?"

"There is no time," Terryll said. He pulled a small copper coin out of his purse and tossed it to the man, then darted into the thicket.

The thin Gaul looked nonplussed at the little coin in his palm, then rolled his eyes.

Bolstroem tore another joint off the lamb and saluted the Gauls with a grin. "For the lad."

The Gauls stood watching the trees for several moments after Bolstroem had disappeared into them. A great hush settled into the camp but for the crackling of the fire.

"I tell you we are finished on this island," the fat Gaul said, breaking the silence.

Then the big cat growled hungrily from its leash.

Tempest whickered and stamped a foot as Terryll untied his reins. "We must warn the chieftains of the trap, Bol."

"I will warn them. You must fly back to Killwyn Eden and tell your father."

"But—"

"Do not argue with me, lad. You're faster. You must go."

Terryll looked at Bolstroem, looked south into the blackness where he knew the road lay, then back at the man. He was right, of course. He smiled grimly. "It looks like your hot bath in Aquae Sulis is going to have to wait."

"Aye, that it will."

"Do you know how to get there? To Stonehenge, I mean?"

"Bear southeast once I reach Aquae Sulis, then twenty-five miles. I'll find it. Now do not tarry, lad. We must fly!"

Bolstroem reined the big draft horse away, then immediately wheeled him about again, as though struck by a thought. He looked at Terryll, the cool pallor of the moon flashing upon his broad face, capturing his grave expression. Then his fierce blue eyes twinkled brightly into a smile.

"Here," he bellowed, tossing the joint of lamb to the boy. "I'd almost forgotten your supper! Ha!" Then he rode away into the black wall of the night, waving a salute. "Godspeed to you, Terryll. Godspeed!"

"And to you, my friend," Terryll cried after him.

He listened as the heavy footfalls drummed away through the trees into an eerie silence. A cool wind stirred through the tree boughs, bringing with it a sadness that settled over the boy. He sat for a moment looking into the darkness, trying to remember the big face. But strangely he couldn't. He got his size, a big black shape in his mind, the huge arms swinging the hammer and the ringing report of the anvil, got the smell of burning coke and the roar of the furnace and the thrusting, barrel chest full of gleaming hair, and the sound of his booming voice and flashes of his teeth. But the face was gone. The moon had snatched it.

Hiking his longbow, Terryll reined Tempest to the north, and suddenly he felt a warm breath of wind on the back of his neck and a chill go down his spine. He pulled up and looked around him. There was nothing.

But there *was* something, he knew, something sinister, destructive. He felt it still, felt the vibrations buzzing in the air, shimmying up from the ground and through the stallion's legs and touching him, the destroyer reaching for him. He could almost hear the thing whistling and hissing around his ears, hawking over his head. He knew then that it had not been his imagination earlier, some by-product of a long and weary journey. Not this time. He knew now that he had entered the domain of some dark specter, some imp or fiend or band of devils, and that where he stood was an evil place, a place where the crosscurrent of some malevolence coursed through the air.

The stallion stamped away at it and shook his mane furiously.

"Come on, Tempest," the boy cried, looking over his shoulder as he patted the thick, muscular neck. "Let's see what your legs can do!"

And the black jumped away through the trees with a snort.

A GATHERING
OF DARKNESS

There was a fine pale corona around the moon, a ringed portent of rain to follow or of a coming storm. It was a sign of hope to farmers, whose haunted eyes had grown dark with worry over their parched fields, but it was a warning to mariners.

The little carpentum crawled like a large black tortoise to the edge of the trees and stopped. Lying before it the land was bathed in a bleaching wash of moonlight and rolled gently away for miles in every direction over a broad champaign like a vast and iridescent sea.

The moon, rising full in the east, shone over the undulating sea of low, flat hills and into the seating area of the small carpentum and lighted the covert faces of a man and a woman. The man held the reins. The woman was cradling a small dark bundle in her arms. The driver, a diminutive, bulbous-headed man with long floating hair and beard that shone like delicate spun glass in the moonlight, clambered up onto his seat, and his single living eye searched the horizon to the south. In the distance several fires were blazing, and he could just see the tiny shapes of men and tents black against them, like tiny ants.

"We are safe?" the woman asked.

"We are safe."

"Let us go then."

The driver climbed off the seat with a hop, took up the reins, and clucked his tongue. The little wagon lurched forward as the team of hairy ponies strained into their traces.

They rode for several miles, rising and dipping over the great sea plain, following the spangled course of the River Avon as it wound northward into the horizon. The wheels groaned plaintively over hidden stones and crevices, and the wooden frame shuddered and creaked over the torquing twists of ground like a little ship pitching on the dashing billows.

A funereal hush whined over the plain, rising solemnly from the earth like a diaphanous sheet of mist, and each was mindful of it, looking through it to the stars. The little man and the woman felt the slow turning of the earth beneath them, the precise gyres and movements of planets and moons and stars advancing one tick in the enormous cosmic clock, and their mortal skins trembled with fear and excitement. It was a holy night. And it was almost time.

They spoke only to observe a shift in the land or a turn in the river, and then only in laconic whispers. They continued for another mile or so in silence, and when at last they climbed over a phosphorescent swell of earth, the moon bright in their faces, they could see it looming stark and black on the horizon, anchored stolidly to the earth as it had been for centuries.

Stonehenge.

The druid pulled up on the reins from the suddenness of it, and the woman stifled a shriek of astonishment with her hand. A shudder jolted through her limbs. It struck her mind that a huddle of giants had gathered in a large circle around something they were about to eat. She half expected them to turn and demand of them an explanation for their intrusion. Then the bundle in her arms, startled from sleep by its mother's sudden movement, began to squirm and whimper.

Rowena chucked him with her arms to quiet him. "Hush, now, hush!" she whispered, rocking the infant gently. And when the baby began to cry she opened her dress and guided him to her breast.

Looking up she beheld the great circle of triloliths, reaching up—a seamless black extension of the earth, it seemed—breaking through the horizon as though in defiance of the heavens. Immediately she fell into a little trance. For there was a power in the thing, a force that was imminent and consuming, drawing energy like a lightning rod gathering the chaotic impulses of the air and channeling them into itself.

Rowena tried, but she could not look away. Her throat swelled with emotion: first with wonder, then with awe, and then with reptilian terror. An urge came over her to turn and flee, but she could not, for the power of the henge held her in place, bound her and drew her forward with invisible fetters, sucking her into its voracious vortex.

Even the ponies were mindful of the force reaching down into their primal fears, tapping them, and they stamped their tiny hooves restively. The druid snapped the reins, but they would not move. They fought against their traces, thrusting their long manes and snorting out their protestations into the cool spring night. Then the whip cracking over their ears snapped a stronger fear into them, and they jumped ahead, their eyes wide and white and filled with terror at the sight of the huge black stones dominating the skyline.

Veils of moisture gathered over the moon, cloaking its brilliance, giving it the color of a sun-bleached skull, with the dark hollows of its eyes gazing unblinking upon the living twirl of earth. The summit over-looking the hill fort of Badonsward was bathed in a diffusion of pale light. It gave the landscape the pallor of something dead. And then a silence crept over the earth, pervading the thickening air with imperceptible fingers, a living thing it seemed that stalked the noisemakers of the night and put them to flight, causing an aberration in the nocturnal rhythms.

Even the men encamped beyond the hill fort felt it, felt a mali-ciousness in the air that came pricking behind their ears with its cold, hollow touches, and they huddled around their fires and spoke to one another in throaty whispers. They attributed it to battle nerves. For it was the eve of the long march northward, a campaign of war where—many or few—some of them would die. And they believed the eerie si-lence was the chariot of the death specter, wending its way through their midst and marking the heads of those it would take.

But they were mistaken, for this silence had nothing to do with the destruction of transient flesh. It had everything to do with the destruction of their immortal souls.

Peering over a mountainous rim, the moon caught the silhouette of the Wolf leaving the hill fort, then lost him in the shadows of several large rowans, picked him up again in a small clearing giving orders to one of the sentries patroling the grounds. The sentry smote his chest, and the Wolf left him, strode to the base of the hill, and began to climb it. And reaching the summit he paused, looked down upon the settling quiet of the army, looked over his shoulder, then disappeared into a grove of oaks.

The carpentum drew up outside the encircling berm of the henge, and Boadix and Rowena stared at it for a moment. The druid's face was impassive, a stoic reflection of the consummate clock-watcher. The crystal orb filling his dead eye socket glinted dully in the half light.

However the woman's expression was rapt with tension, her eyes wide and glistening with a growing apprehension. Her tightly drawn lips were a demonstration of a fierce struggle.

The druid set the brake, tied the check reins, then climbed down over the large wheel, using the spokes as rungs, and Rowena followed him, the infant sated and asleep in her arms, with bubbles of milk grow-ing over his lips.

They approached the northeast corner of the berm, where a black monolith called the "Heel stone" stood sixteen feet above the earth like a giant sentinel at the gateway of the henge. It had been shaped of a thirty-five-ton sarsen and set in place by a Neolithic race of pre-Britons, a full century before God called Abram out of Ur of the Chaldees.

The druid placed the flat of his hand upon the moonstruck face of the stone and immediately felt the electrical vibrations pulsing through it and into his body like a ground. Some mystical circuit was completed, and the druid pulled his hand away with a startled giggle.

He paused, listening. It seemed to him there was a faint whine pulsing into the air. It was as though the stone were a huge tuning fork, sounding the pitch of some gargantuan engine grinding away at the center of the earth. He stretched a tentative hand and touched it again, held his palm flat against the stone, felt the current coursing through his body and speeding ever downward through the soles of his feet into the earth. His face glowed with a new power. Then he looked up the broad blade of stone thrusting into the heavens, saw Canis Major—the Dog Star—a silver coronet shining off the point, coming on line in a perfect tick of the clock.

"It is time," he said reverently.

"Yes, it is time," Rowena replied, sensing the moment rising in her spirit. There was a shift in her countenance, a resoluteness prevailing over the struggle and gathering in the anxious thoughts.

The druid looked up into her eyes, searching them. "You are certain of this?"

"Yes."

"It must be a willing sacrifice."

Rowena's eyes narrowed coldly. "It is, little man. Now let us be done with it."

A smile curled on the druid's face. "Give me the child then," he demanded.

Rowena handed the bundle down to him. "What would you have me do?"

"You will assist me."

"It does not matter that I am a woman?"

"There is no one else."

And the two began a slow procession down the long avenue of the sun, pacing solemnly toward the altar at the far end of the henge.

The druid's mind was a contemplation of the heavens, the stars gathered into their constellations, the whirling of planets and suns and the moons turning the seasons, raising and lowering the great oceans of the universe, everything connected, enmeshed, everything in the universal timepiece ticking along with perfect synchronization.

His thoughts raced ahead three months to the morning of the summer solstice. He knew that the sun and moon would then rise and set directly opposite the other along the axis of the avenue, with the sun's first slanting rays shooting its length and striking the altar with its blood red light. In this knowledge he felt the power of the sun on his back even now as the hour of midnight approached.

His mind praised the wisdom of his forebears, praised the gods' selection of him as the sole inheritor of that wisdom. His little chest swelled and could not contain the great burden of wisdom that grew in his bosom. He felt the ache of it pushing against his ribs. He knew that the lines of his life had drawn him to this place and time, that he was given breath for this moment, and, pacing along the avenue of the sun—the birth canal of some greater destiny—he sensed the quiet blessing of the stars upon his life.

Staring at the altar he felt the rhythms of the henge beating out the pulse in his breast, and as he fell in step with the dreadful cadence, he began to chant in the ancient tongue of the Celts.

"O most wise and venerable Cernunnos . . . lord of animalkind and keeper of the gates to the Underworld . . . thou who hast revealed the wisdom of the ages to vessels of earthen flesh . . . we draw humbly near to the devastations of your throne—I, as your high priest upon the earth, and the woman, as your devoted handmaiden and the betrothed of Norduk, thy chosen son. We have come with singular hearts and minds bearing this most holy offering."

The Wolf came out of the trees into a broad clearing of land and paused. He listened warily as an animal might before crossing over to a water hole or to graze in a meadow. There were no sounds, for they had been spirited away. But there was something in the air; he could sense it, like the galvanizing of ions before a lightning storm.

The man looked across the clearing, bright in the ascending moon, and saw the faint rings in the grass, nine of them—three sets of three concentric rings of three, each set within the larger set—worn through the grass by repeated ritual. He saw the old gnarled oaks beyond them growing in a tight huddle around the clearing, and the moon lighting the leaves and shining garishly upon their limbs that reached protectively over the rings. Satisfied that all was as it should be, he trod stealthily out into the clearing and set his foot within the depression of the outer ring.

Then he waited.

There was a stirring in the air, not of wind but of the other thing, and Norduk looked over his shoulder when he felt it coming through the trees and drawing the hair out on his neck. A glimmer of fear flared in his eyes, then settled after he felt the first shock of it.

It was as though a great stone had been thrown into the center of an immense and placid sea and the first of the ripples had come splashing against the banks, sounding out the distant echo of a drum. The Wolf knew that it was time and that he must now fulfill his part of the rite. He felt an exultation in his spirit—the culmination of a dream—bubbling up through his body.

And then he felt the shock of the second ripple, and then of the third, and fourth—the pulse of the henge *tapping, tapping, tapping* out the ancient rhythms, the cadence growing stronger in his breast with every beat of his heart. And falling into step with it, he began to trace the circumference of the outer circle.

Each of his carefully laid steps marked the tick of the dial, a timed and measured calibration that pleased the arcane eccentricities of the gods. He chanted in concert with the druid, in the soft-palated tongue of the ancient Britons, the monotone intonation pealing off his tongue like a dull clapper incessantly striking . . . *clap* . . . *clap* . . . *clap* . . .

Completing the outer circle, he turned and stepped inward without breaking cadence or chant, and staring ahead his eyes began to glaze over with an occultic sheen. The references of moon and stars and the circle of trees and other earthly objects began to fall away from his vision. His focus narrowed, straining away all traces of light but a single, distant point in his mind, a pinpoint of crimson light at the end of a long tunnel that grew before him with every footfall.

The druid continued his procession along the avenue, the chant resonating in the bell of his throat . . *gong* . . . *gong* . . . *gong* . . . ringing out a doxology to Cernunnos, the horned god of the ancient Britons. His single eye was fixed upon the altar, which was drawing nearer with every step.

Over the henge the air was charged in a frenetic whorl of forces, of lesser and greater malignancies, that came flapping in from their various haunts of rocks and pools, of twisted minds and the raging-eyed husks of tortured souls. They rose from the earth like tendrils of burning sulfur, the pulse of the henge drawing them, sucking them away from their seats of power and mischief. And joining others in their reprobate flights, they formed small peccant bands that grew into larger swarms of wickedness and droned over the earth in long undulating lashes, intertwining and writhing with other swarms like mating snakes. The snakes became one and begat a legion, and the legion grew into a great and terrible dragon. And the dragon begat others of its kind, and they came arcing in from every corner of the land to form a seething maelstrom of darkness around the circle of the moon, now swirling and growing, the forces circling and building into a huge thunderhead of powers and principalities and authorities, and the lightning rod of the henge sparking the incessant pulse and galvanizing them by the furious chant and working them into a demonic frenzy.

Miles away in the Monastery of St. John's, Brother Lucius Aurelius sat up in his cot with a start. His spirit was aware of a terrible breach in the heavenlies, and his mind struggled to comprehend it.

There was a light rapping on his door, and Brother Lupe stuck his head into the dark room.

"Brother Lucius?"

"Yes?"

"You are awake?"

"Yes."

"We must pray."

The brothers Gildas and Rupert—even the aged Patrick, miles across the Irish Sea—startled awake, praying.

Helena opened her eyes and blinked into the darkness, allowing the dim light in the room to define the outline of her husband's back. Her heart was racing before an indiscernible fear. A shiver of horror raced along her spine.

"Allyn," she whispered. "Are you awake?"

"Yes."

"Hold me, Allyn."

The druid and Rowena exited the avenue of the sun, and, treading over a broad skirt of moonlit ground, passed through the outer ring of the henge and entered the inner horseshoe-array of triloliths and bluestones, raised into place during the time of the Exodus.

Ahead the altar stone stood in the apogee of the bluestones, a large slab carved of bluestone itself, that was stained indelibly in the ancient bloodwash of its victims. The druid's eye was trained upon the altar with a fierce stare, his lips trembling with a feverish chant.

Norduk turned inward and began to pace the outer ring in the third set of rings. In his mind the long black tunnel was falling behind him now, and as he drew nearer to the pinpoint of crimson light, he saw that it was fast becoming a shape.

The thunderhead of devils ascended wildly, spiraling into the air like a frenzied boil of locusts, and the pulse from the henge struck the anvil of the thunderhead with a continual hammering, sending terrible shock waves across the heavens. Rumblings, indiscernible to the human ear, sounded out the clarion peals of a coming glory. Flashes of sulfuric light flickered excitedly beyond the spectrum of the human retina. Some terrible and awesome event was about to occur upon the earth, and the stars bore witness to it in silent vigil.

The druid drew up sharply before the altar and immediately went about his preparations for the sacrifice in a perfunctory manner. There was a supreme economy of movement. The limbs of the druid belonged

316

to those of a little machine. His mind and his fingers were not connected; they were moving in two distant planes, and there was a vast sea between them. Somewhere in his brain the chant drummed steadily from an ancient synapse, the throbbing, pounding, hammering monotony echoing lifelessly over a surreal mindscape.

At last he pulled out the glass orb from its fleshy crypt and held it aloft to the heavens. He rolled it between his fingers, allowing the light of the Dog Star and the moon to shine through it to the altar, a single terrifying beam of light. There was a surge of power, a little glow of heat that burned through to his subconsciousness.

As Norduk completed the third ring in the third set of rings, the last syllable of his chanting leaped off his tongue in a perfect clip. He stopped, looking forward, and the pinpoint of crimson light defined the image of the altar and the hazy shapes before it.

It was time.

He spread his arms—palms out—to his side, raised his face to the moon, and cried, "Thy will be done, master. Come, I bid thy terrible presence welcome."

Rowena felt an electric turbulence in the air, she felt the space around her head crackling with energy, revealing to her a hidden knowledge of the world. She glanced up at the glazed-over moon. Her eyes were vacant, and the moon filled them and pulled the tides of her soul, drawing her out of herself, it seemed, and over the banks of her mortal flesh.

A profound weightlessness rose in her breast like an enormous bubble of light. She felt herself ascending into the heavens and, setting upon the circle of the earth, she gazed upon the henge from the dark hollows of her eyes. Somewhere, as though from an infinite distance, she heard the incessant drone of the druid.

Time marched inexorably toward some salient point in the heavens, and once arriving there it seemed to stop. Or at least it slowed down to a crawl so that it gave the illusion of stopping. With vivid clarity she saw the little, stumpy fingers of the druid's hands working madly, even caught the tiny moons of his nails rising from their beds.

And then the chanting stopped. Its echo trailed away into a dreadful silence that came crashing back into the void of the pulse.

Then she saw the blade of bronze rising with an infinite slowness, tracing a burnished arc over the black of the stones. And as the blade reached its zenith, the moon struck it with a sudden flash of light, followed by a roaring clap of thunder that sounded like a million madding voices charging in battle, and immediately a bolt of power jagged invisibly across the heavens, and she was rushing before it.

Norduk reeled from the shock of the bolt. It struck him square in the back, and as he fell spinning to the ground his eyes described a glaring terror of realization. An inscrutable knowledge was revealed to him in the bolt, and he screamed the sum of its horror.

The moon shone pale upon the dark figure sprawled face down in the center of the rings, twisted in an attitude of death. A breathless hush descended upon it like a shroud. There was a subtle stirring in the bowery of the oaks, an impish breeze that slipped noiselessly through the trees and stole over the clearing, curling for a moment over the still form before whisking away, laughing it seemed.

Suddenly the body groaned, and the inert fingers twitched to life. The Wolf rolled his head to one side, and the yellow eyes blinked inquisitively at the sharp blades of grass. It seemed he was waking from a deep slumber and was coming to a new awareness of the world.

He grunted amusedly.

Then at last climbing to his feet and twisting into an arch, he flexed the taut muscles of his back and limbs and looked around the clearing as though seeing it for the first time. He stretched his hands before his face and studied them, both front and back, beholding in them a foreign thing, a curious and living thing. He felt the power of life coursing down through the veins in his arms and pulsing in the fingertips, and he clenched his fists over the pleasure of it. A throaty chortle rattled through his teeth.

There had been no pain this time, no agonizing paroxysms wracking his body, no torture of soul. But why should there have been? The opposition to his coming had been removed; the channel had been opened.

Norduk was no longer a problem.

The fool.

Now looking up at the moon, at the Dog Star running swiftly over the southern hills, Cernunnos knew that it was done, that the time of his renewed reign over the land had at last come.

The Wolf threw his head back into a violent lupine arch and let out a baneful cry of exultation. And a myriad delirious voices carried the echoes far into the night.

318

37

THE SWIFT
MARCH OF TERROR

Bolstroem made it to Aquae Sulis without mishap and from there turned southeast off the road toward Stonehenge as he knew to do. Twenty-five miles, he thought. An easy trot and he would be there in a few hours.

However the skies were lowering with storm, and his not being a woodsman there was no way for him to stay true to his course without benefit of the sun. One false turn led to another, each leading him farther astray, and a few hours later it dawned on him that he had no idea where he was. He put the big draft horse into a lope to make up for lost time, but this tactic only served to advance him closer to where he didn't want to go and at a faster pace.

Panic began to grow upon the man the moment he realized he might not arrive in time to warn his fellow Britons of the trap. The sum of their imperiled lives ignited a zeal upon his brow.

He began to charge the hills that obscured his vision as though assaulting strongholds. And attaining some lofty vantage from which to survey the terrain, he demanded of each new horizon a point of reference or landfall, some intuitive impulse or feeling or clue that would set him aright.

But all that he could see for miles and miles, from hilltop to hilltop, were unending folds of countryside, everything cast in the dismal ranks of grayness, vast and mocking under the sullen skies.

Hurling imprecations at the earth, at the sky, at the lathering draft horse, he would dead-reckon a new bearing and storm off the hill to attack other positions with greater abandon and fury. He was driven by a kind of madness. And in such a way the blacksmith found himself entangled in a labyrinth of endless possible routes, every one right and every one wrong. Hopelessly lost he was and mindful of what a poor mariner he would have made.

The eve of the equinox came and went with a strangeness crackling through the air, working some dark ministration upon his mind. Vagrant winds blew overhead and through the trees and shrubbery, moaning like disembodied souls. It seemed to him there were invisible flights of birds diving at his head.

But the fury of his duty burned in his eyes and drove him straight on into the night. And the night directed his path with a savage mischievousness. Shadows collected into the forms of boulders and shrubs and hurled themselves before him, forcing sudden turns one way or the other. Trees sprang from the earth and held out indicating limbs.

That way, go that way! And Bolstroem would rein his horse that way.

No, this way, go this way! And Bolstroem would wheel his horse this way.

Impenetrable thickets and sheer bluffs forced him back upon his path and along fathomless routes. It seemed the elements of the night worked in concert to see that he remain irreparably lost. Bolstroem had begun to unleash a string of expletives at the subterfuge of creation, when there was a sudden flash of light in his brain.

The blacksmith blinked curiously up at the gray light of dawn, saw the big tree limb overhead, hanging low and dark against the sky, and concluded that he had been knocked senseless by the thing during the night.

When he remembered his duty, his eyes recovered their fierceness. He sat up quickly, and a bolt of pain shot to his head. Groaning, he felt the place where the pain had collected on his forehead and discovered there a rather large lump.

He climbed to his feet and reconnoitered his immediate surroundings, smarting under the sting of the blow. He saw the plow-puller grazing peacefully nearby, with the reins dragging freely in the long wet grass and the saddle listing to one side. The horse looked up from his breakfast and whickered contentedly.

Bolstroem grunted. "I hope there's some jerky left in your saddle bags." He groaned again as he staggered over to the horse.

The sun rising gave him vague directions, and for several hours he rode in a quiet pessimism, not knowing if Stonehenge were before him or behind him or off to the side. He knew only that he was traveling in a general southerly direction and that sooner or later he would ride over a cliff into the channel. His eyes glared furiously from their tight sockets as he scoured the distant ranks of hills for any sign of the henge or a village that might know of its whereabouts.

By midday the sun was a vast dimness that spread out evenly behind an impenetrable gray vault of sky, concealing every point of the compass. The thought struck him that he might be riding in circles. This revelation came to him on a bolt of terror, and the blacksmith, pointing his horse at a spot on the horizon, resumed his maniacal charges.

Several times during the day he espied farmers in the fields and accosted them with a look of rage in his eyes, demanding of them directions. Each time he was set right on his course, sometimes to the east, sometimes to the west, only to lose it after a mile or two to the clandestine sun or to the zeal upon his brow.

The farmers were only too eager to oblige, for the sight of the giant, wild-eyed and caked with dried mud, was a terror to behold.

One poor fellow looked up from his plow when he felt the earth rumbling, thinking the world was coming to an end, and when he saw a giant thundering toward him astride a monstrous horse, he was convinced of it and ran screaming into his house.

The blacksmith went in after him and dragged him outside, kicking and screaming and clinging to a round woman with bulging eyes, his wife no doubt. And when a gaggle of small children appeared magically from various haunts, they immediately fell upon the giant's knees with savage ignorance.

After convincing the poor fool that he wasn't going to decapitate him or eat his children, he managed to extract from him three or four different directions to the henge, each of which was accompanied by an emphatic nodding of heads and a flailing of fingers pointing this way and that, and the blacksmith thundered away.

The day burned through the length of its wick and lay smoldering upon the distant hills in the west, still without any sign of the henge. Hope sank with the sun, and despair rose with the diffused glory of the moon. A melancholy fog settled over Bolstroem's head.

His mind envisioned the gathering throng of chieftains now, the expectant looks of hope and peace in their eyes turning to horror as the treachery coiled itself and struck. His eyes brimmed with tears of failure.

He reined his horse to a stop and gazed disconsolately to the south. A southerly breeze stirred and died, then lifted, and he thought he heard faint cries of laughter upon it. Turning in his saddle, he looked to the northeast. He wiped his eyes to be certain, looked again, and there it was: a ruddy glow of lights crowning the horizon behind him and flickering against the low ceiling of clouds.

Bonfires.

Several of them.

Bolstroem's eyes burned with the fierceness of discovery, and he spurred his flagging horse into a run.

From the precipice overlooking the hill fort of Badonsward,

Terryll watched grimly as the valley below him disgorged a tremendous army. He felt his blood going cold as he beheld it marching by in an interminable procession.

There were three parts to the army. First there were the horsemen at the head, and then there were several companies of foot soldiers in the center, and these were followed by a wagon train that wrapped around a hill and disappeared, reappearing a half mile farther down the road, then trailing away out of sight.

The sun hurled a glittering of firebrands over the sky, and they fell striking the horsemens' helmets and battle accoutrements, igniting them with crimson light. The points of their spears blazed like deadly tongues of fire. The iron-rimmed wagon wheels caught fire and burned like little suns whirling in space. The column was a living, burnished anger that consumed the road and breathed out fiery threats.

Terryll gaped down at the thing crawling along, watched the war machine grinding forward and advancing toward his kinsmen in the north. The young hunter was far enough away that he could see the whole of it moving along the northbound road, and it struck him with awe. Never had he ever imagined such a machine of war.

He was reminded of the first view he had had of the Pictish raiding party back in the fall, heading north to Loch na Huric under the command of that usurper Sarteham. That small army resembled to him a terrible serpent—a monstrous leviathan. But the image shriveled in the light of this new thing and became nothing more in his mind than a little wriggling snake.

Suddenly Terryll felt light-headed and warm, felt himself drifting away from his mental axis like a comet falling out of orbit and careering off into some bright and dangerous mist. An anguish of soul burned against his breast, for this new thing was a dreadful inspiration. It was coming to kill his people, he knew, to devour them. War was coming.

The boy took hold of his senses. He began to count with mounting horror the shapes of the horsemen—there were a thousand or more of them, he reckoned, but he could not be certain at this distance. There were so many horsemen. So he moved his ledger to the foot soldiers, but he couldn't hold their count either. They were beyond his mental tally, and he gave it up with a cry for God's mercy.

Terryll rode ahead of the army and found some trees on a low bluff with a closer view of the road. He had to see this thing up close, to smell it, as it were, to stalk it, to look into the menacing eyes of the war beast and dare its fangs. He was, after all, a hunter.

He waited, well-concealed in a copse of young alders and beeches, feeling the pulse thick in his neck.

Goldfinches and flycatchers darted in the trees, singing happily, and there was a fine wet scent in the air, cooling as the day drew to a close. Shadows thickened between the leaves, and the birds settled into them for the night. Then the shadows crept out from the bluff and pushed imperceptibly across the road like a spill of darkness. There was a heavy silence pervading, the kind that presages a storm. Terryll heard the rustling of birds around him.

And then he heard them coming—faint at first, like the muffled boomings of the surf, dipping in and out of the wind, and then the breakers rolling louder and stronger along the ceiling of clouds and finally crashing down over his head.

Terryll felt his heart racing violently, and his eyes narrowed warily on the crescent of road bending around the hill to the south. And when he saw the first flashing of light on their helmets and shields, the standards snapping bright and proud in the wind, it took his breath away. He was awed anew at the sight of the army.

The horsemen came four abreast, each man arrayed and fit for battle and displaying proudly his black shield with the crimson wolf's head arched fiercely against it. The clatter of so many horses—their hooves like flint against the hard smooth stones of the Roman road—and the drumming of the footmen and the wagons behind, laden with provisions for the insatiable belly of the army, made a roaring sound like that of a mountain runoff or a continual clapping of thunder.

It seemed a thunderhead of men was drawing over the countryside, flickering with lightning, with the horses' hooves hammering and the big, iron-rimmed wagon wheels grating over the stones, and there was nothing that could stop the coming of the front. Terryll felt the earth tremble through the stallion's legs. It seemed the world would collapse under the weight of the army.

Narrowing his gaze from the whole of the thing to its particulars, Terryll noticed the three men riding at the head of the column, just ahead of the standard-bearers. He recognized the nearest rider at once. With his long, blond mane unfurled to the wind, heralding his own private colors, and the white wings of his helmet soaring high and proud over the undulating column of lesser men, the man projected an unmistakable presence in the saddle. It was the Norseman.

Terryll marveled at him for a moment. His back was as straight as a mast, and his chest was bowed and trimmed before the wind of the army, and the muscles of his big arms gleamed in the twilight like smooth varnished spars. He was the pride of the horsemen, Terryll saw, for he caught their eyes upon him, saw the power of his bearing working fiercely through their ranks, impelling them forward. They rode as men returning victorious from a glorious campaign, carrying their heads high and shot through with the bravado attendant to superior numbers and the certitude of the Norseman's immortality.

He presumed the man in the center to be Horsa. Who else could it be but the Saxon overlord, prancing like some vain peacock at the fore of an endless demonstration of war? The man was wearing the finely tooled armor of a nobleman, glimmering like polished gold in the waning light, and the rich trappings of colorful raiment (no doubt imported from the East) as well as those other trappings of cloak and plume and spangled adornments that so fully commended the pomp of his station and bore his head upon so lofty a pedestal as his neck. Terryll had only a passing interest in the man.

However his eyes were strangely drawn to the man on the far side of him, to the one riding on a black charger and wearing a black jerkin over his mail with a wolf's head emblazoned upon it. And assigning his face to the shadows was what appeared to be a wolfskin cowl covering his head.

Terryll glared at the man for some time.

The Wolf!

A whirlwind of thoughts wheeled through his head: of the man's prowess in war, of his cruel subjugation of the land and its people, of the countless British men who had bravely given their lives opposing him. An image flickered through his mind of Aeryck's father, Caelryck, and the little knot of men who died with him at the Battle of Glenryth, and an urge came over the young hunter to send an arrow through the man's brisket.

But no sooner did he dismiss the thought than the Wolf turned and looked directly at him, giving the boy a start.

At first Terryll shrugged it away, for he knew that he was well concealed in the trees. Surely the man had turned his head only to observe some point in the terrain.

But still the Wolf was looking at him. Terryll could see the two yellow lights burning beneath the cowl, glowering at him, it seemed.

And then another thought occurred to him, one that sent shivers down his neck: perhaps the man had heard his thoughts. Terryll felt the blood draining from his head and collecting in his throat, and he hunkered down into his shoulders, drawing a veil of leaves and birds and shadows over his head.

And then the Wolf looked away, riding by below him now and away to the north.

Breathing easier, Terryll looked ahead on the road. He knew that once the army reached Biddlecairn it would either take the road leading to Ermine Street, the broad Roman road that wound north along the eastern part of the island, or it would strike directly north through the Pennines. The latter was a less traveled road, a more difficult one, perhaps, considering the mountainous region it ran through. However it was a more direct route. And should the Saxons decide to take it, it would lead them straight through Killwyn Eden and then on into the heart of the Eden Valley.

Terryll shuddered at the thought. He knew there would be no time for his father to organize any kind of resistance against such an army. They wouldn't stand a chance. War was coming, and he had to know which route it would take. And so the young hunter reined the stallion off the hill away from the passing-by troops and headed for Biddlecairn to wait and see.

The field where the festival was held was bright in the light of the moon and stars. Several long tables were set up end to end in a large circle, bonfires were going around them, and servant girls were hurrying around the tables clearing away the settings.

The pigs had been eaten, and the wine and ale were flowing over the happy glut, and the Saxons and Jutes and the British chieftains were flushed with the spirit of celebration. Empty flagons were quickly re-filled, such that there was never an empty vessel. Laughter boomed around the circle and rose upon the shimmering updrafts of the fires. The feast had gotten off to a ripping start. Hengist was having a roaring good time, it seemed to Vortigern, who was studying the man from across the circle. He might even decide to like this German fellow. Yes, and why shouldn't he? Hengist was, after all, his father-in-law, wasn't he? Yes, of course he was, and it was a fine celebration to make reparations, the king mused, as he took another draft of wine. It was a fine Gaulish wine with a heady bouquet too.

His face was a reverie of thoughts. The end of war had finally come! There was peace at last! After ten long years of bitter fighting, his army had prevailed. The Saxons had sued for peace. He clapped his flag-on down on the table as though punctuating the thought, and a servant girl stepped forward and quickly filled it to the brim.

Yes, I shall like this fellow, Vortigern decided, laughing to himself, and, drinking heartily, he glowed with the pride of his accomplishments.

The king glanced off into the distance. Stonehenge was a black speck on the silvery horizon, like a beacon of sorts. He raised his flagon in a mock toast.

What a grand idea it was to celebrate the truce here, he reflected, thinking back to the night when Rowena had made the suggestion. She said it would be a wonderful "love feast" honoring the goddess Eostre, and that the birth of their child would be a symbol of the new order that would descend upon the land. She was so insistent on the idea, so passionate. It had come to her like an oracle.

The king's eyes twinkled as he remembered the fire in her eyes. It was unfortunate that their son had taken ill at the last moment, so that she could not attend the celebration.

"It is only a little thing, really," she said. "Just a cough. Nothing to worry about."

And so he hadn't. He missed her though. Missed his son. Missed showing off his beautiful young wife and child to the other chieftains, some of whom were old friends that he hadn't seen since the beginning of the war. It was a shame. Truly.

The king sighed reflectively over the waves of his thoughts. He took another sip of wine, and the girl stepped forward with the pitcher. He smiled up at her and patted her hand, and she bowed demurely, stepping back and watching his cup.

Then the sound of a flagon hammering the table brought him back from his reverie. It was time for the speeches. The air cleared reverently, allowing the Muse of benediction to descend upon the gathering like a dove.

Vortigern looked around at the expectant faces of the British chieftains. Their eyes were fixed upon his, and he smiled paternally at each of them. But then they were like his children, weren't they? Come home to him after so long and gathering around his table. He felt as though he could look them in the eye now that everything was right again. Everyone's face was glowing in the light of this new thing in the air. The end of war! The beginning of peace!

The king knew there was some beatific speech hovering over their midst, fluttering its wings brightly, and, taking another drink, he felt a splendid speech of his own warming up through him to greet it. A splendid speech indeed.

Hengist, a taller, leaner man than his brother, raised his flagon and drew everyone's attention. He began by toasting Vortigern, and three cheers went up around the circle for the king.

Vortigern nodded modestly and waved a deprecating hand. He felt the speech in him aging splendidly in his breast now. He could taste it frothing on his tongue.

And then Hengist toasted the British chieftains—their "new brothers," as he called them, who had come from such great distances to attend this auspicious occasion.

Another cheer went up around the tables.

One of the Britons made some jest about the long ride. There was a gush of laughter, and Vortigern threw back his drink and roared. It was a wonderful jest, and he felt glad that one of his children had made it. He slapped the back of the Saxon on either side of him like a proud father.

Hengist had suggested that the seating should be Briton, Saxon, Briton, Saxon, and so on around the circle, so that there would be a fine spirit of brotherhood between the two peoples.

Vortigern thought it a fine idea. Yes, it was a fine idea, and a splendid celebration, and a splendid speech so far, he thought, listening to the overlord continue his eulogy. It was too bad that Rowena and their son were not present to hear it. There was such promise of peace and goodwill. Yes, it was a fine celebration. Splendid! Just splendid! He would mention how fine and splendid everything was in his speech.

A tremendous cheer went up as Hengist finished his address. And as it was settling, the overlord winked at one of his men.

Bolstroem heard the burst of ovation and spurred his horse over the last low hill, and reaching the summit he beheld the festival spread below him. There were scores of men sitting around a large circle of tables, dark against the bonfires, so that he couldn't tell Briton from Saxon.

A dreadful revelation rose in his breast.

"Forgive me, God, for failing You," he cried heavenward. "For failing my people. Have mercy on our souls." And with that he drew his sword, dug his heels into his mount's flanks, and the big, white draft horse leaped down the hill with a blast of his nostrils.

"Britons! Britons!" the blacksmith bellowed. "It is a trap! It is a trap, I tell you!"

The men, Saxon and Briton alike, turned at his voice, and for a moment every man seemed stunned at the vision of the giant roaring toward their camp.

Then Hengist, seizing his wits, cried, "Angles, Jutes, Saxons! Use your swords!"

And at once every one of his men drew his blade and stabbed his British neighbor through the heart.

Vortigern laughed in astonishment as the Saxons on either side of him seized his arms, for he thought the men were having a good lark, staging some mock demonstration on his behalf. He smiled happily through the fog in his brain. The scene was a happy blur, floating just beyond his reach. He felt a love for the world glowing warmly in him. The speech was coming now, bubbling on his lips.

And then his eyes focused upon his countrymen—his children— draped over the tables, their eyes gazing dully at him, their lives pouring out and mingling with the spilled wine, and the laughter gone out of the Saxon faces. Something in a distant part of his brain clicked dully. And

327

then the horror of the treachery fought through the fog and rushed into his eyes, and the only speech he managed to utter was a helpless "But . . ."

Bolstroem let out a battle cry as the plow-puller crashed into the midst of the camp, spilling tables and sending men flying. Those who were too slow were trampled, and the giant blacksmith reached over and finished them off with his sword. For a moment there was a riot of confusion. Men yelled, scrambling for cover as Bolstroem charged about with his broadsword swiping at flashes of limbs and faces.

And then he reined the horse to a halt in the midst of the tables. The horse blew out a snort of terror and stamped his big feet. And for a moment everything went quiet.

As Bolstroem looked around at his fallen kinsmen, fury smoldered in his breast. He looked over at Vortigern. The king was gazing stupidly at him, supported by two Saxons, with wine dribbling down his beard and onto his clothes.

And then he looked at Hengist, and his eyes flared with fierce anger.

In a glimmer of crimson light he saw the last of his duty burning upon the pyre of his heart, a thick column of smoke—his life—wafting to the heavens. He threw his head back and let out an exultant cry, then, spurring his horse, he lunged forward and an arrow caught him in his side.

He pulled up sharply, was wheeling around to face his assailant when another arrow sank deep into his chest and shuddered still. He reeled from the blow, twisting in his saddle, and a third arrow struck his thigh.

Then the Saxons let out a devilish scream and rushed the giant for the kill.

Bolstroem scythed along the flanks of his horse with a last desperate surge of strength, felling several warriors. However their numbers were too great, and the second attacking wave pulled him from his horse and ran him through with pikes.

Terryll reined Tempest to a halt and looked back over his shoulder. It was as though something had gone out of him, and he looked to see where it had flown. But there was only the night, and the singing of crickets, and the melancholy soughing of wind over the hills.

"Come on, boy," he said, patting the stallion's neck. "Let's go." And he quickly rode on ahead toward Biddlecairn to warn them, looking back every so often to monitor some feeling of dread.

Arriving in Biddlecairn Terryll rode to the center of town. "Citizens of Biddlecairn! To arms! To arms!" he cried, riding up and down the moonlit street. "The Saxons are marching on your village!" But the only response he heard was from several barking dogs. He flew off his horse and began pounding on the nearest door.

A minute later an old man called from inside, "Who's there?"

"I am the son of Allyndaar, the chieftain of Killwyn Eden. You must defend yourselves! There's an army coming!"

"Who?"

Terryll glared at the door and began pounding again. "Open up! There's an army of Saxons marching on the village! You must defend yourselves or flee!"

"Do you know what hour it is?" the old man shrieked.

"I don't care! There's an army coming to destroy you, I tell you!"

"And I say you're a lunatic," the old man shouted fearfully. "Now go away and leave me be!"

Across the street a man drew open the shutters of his second-story bedroom and leaned out the window. "What's that?" He grinned. "An army of Saxons, did you say?"

Terryll ran over to him. "Yes, yes, you must warn your townspeople. War is coming!"

The man laughed. "A war, you say? Perhaps you should find your bed and sleep it off."

Terryll was growing frustrated. "Don't you see? I'm trying tell you there is an army of at least five thousand Saxon warriors coming up the road! If you don't—"

"Five thousand, is it?"

"At least!" the boy cried. "Perhaps more. I couldn't count them all, there were so many!"

The man turned into the bedroom at the sound of a woman's voice. "Go back to sleep, woman," he said. "It's just some drunken fool out here saying there's some kind of army he's seen in his drink."

Terryll shot him an exasperated look. "There *is* an army marching on your village, I tell you!" he shouted.

Lights blinked on in several windows as candles and lamps were lighted. Doors began to open, and men still wearing their nightclothes stumbled groggily onto the street and moved cautiously toward the dark stranger. Soon a little knot of onlookers was gathered around him, sizing him up.

Terryll repeated his warning, implored them to listen to him. He went briefly into an explanation of the army's size, the number and weaponry of its horsemen, its foot soldiers, the number of supply wagons, but the men only eyed him suspiciously, doubtless thinking him a madman. They were looking warily at his longbow.

"What's going on out here?" another man demanded, exiting his front door. "What's the meaning of this furor so late at night?"

The onlookers parted way for him. He was a portly man and balding and had the look of authority about him.

"And what's this then?" he bellowed, setting eyes on Terryll. "Has someone caught a thief?"

"Are you the chieftain of this town?" Terryll asked, relieved that he might get somewhere now.

The portly man chortled. "And a saucy thief at that!"

"I'm no thief," Terryll snarled. "If you're the chieftain here, I beg you to listen to me."

The portly man chuckled with a superior air. "Our chieftain's away at Stonehenge with the king—invited there personally by him, I might add. Why, at this very minute they're celebrating a peace treaty with Hengist. Having a grand time of it too, I'll wager," he added, throwing a wink at one of the men.

A tittering went around the onlookers.

Then the portly man arched a skeptical brow at the boy. "Surprised you haven't heard of it, lad."

"That's what I'm trying to tell you," Terryll cried. "There *is* no peace treaty. It was a trap! A Saxon ruse to throw us off! Horsa's army is marching toward your village this very minute! I've seen it not three hours ago!"

"Say, who are you anyway?" a burly man demanded, holding a light up to Terryll's face.

"That's not important. I'm trying to warn your people that—"

"Says he's a chieftain," the old man from behind the first door said, peering out now and snapping a crooked finger at him. "I knew he was a lunatic. Been howling at the moon, I expect."

The portly man eyed the boy narrowly. "A chieftain, are you?"

"No, my father's a chieftain! He too was invited to Hengist's 'peace festival,' but I'm telling you it was a lie!"

Several of the men snickered and elbowed one another. It was a lie, all right.

"I say he's a troublemaker," the burly man said gruffly.

"He's drunk," another put in, to which several others agreed.

Terryll glowered at them in frustration. "Is there no one in this fool of a village who will listen to reason?" he shouted.

Suddenly the group turned ugly.

"Somebody take hold of this rabble-rouser!" a man growled. "Perhaps a night in the gaol will cool his temper!"

"Aye! Clap the drunken fool in irons!"

The burly fellow laid hold of Terryll's sleeve.

Terryll tore his arm away with a scowl and dashed fleet-footed to his horse. He mounted Tempest with a fluid sweep of his legs.

330

"I have warned you people!" he cried, reining the stallion about. "Your blood be upon your own heads! And may God have mercy on your souls!" He stared at them for a moment, shook his head, then rode out of the village with an angry clattering of hooves.

Once he had ridden into the hills, his heart full of rage and pity, Terryll found a stand of trees that offered a clear view of the village below, nestled securely in the crook of the two intersecting northbound roads.

He waited, praying that the townspeople were right, praying that he was indeed some kind of madman, or drunk, or fool, who was given to flights of fancy. He watched grimly as one by one the lights winked out in the village, and the citizens settled back into their beds. In time even the dogs quit their protests and screwed down into their hollows in the dirt. Then the village let out a tired sigh and became a black sleeping hulk sprawled happily under the soft hazy moonlight.

Two hours later Terryll was sitting with one leg crooked across the saddle and his longbow cradled loosely over his lap, listening to the jeering taunts of a million insects. His piercing blue eyes sparkled with intensity as they searched the dark and sullen humors of the terrain, jumping at every shadowy nuance and tracing filigrees of travail on the moonlit bent of road falling away over the rounded shoulders of earth like a shimmering train of silk.

He waited, standing a desperate vigil. A profound loneliness shook out of the stars and sprinkled over his head. His head began to bow under the enormous weight of it, and his eyes began to falter under the sleepless strain. And then a thought oscillated through his mind—his eyes rising to it—that the army might have made camp for the night.

A steady pulse of insects whined mockingly into the air. Tempest busied himself contentedly in the cool grass, and, except for an occasional lazy shake of his mane, horse and rider appeared to be some inanimate projection of the earth. An interlude of silence passed before something came fluttering toward them on a sibilant breath of air.

Immediately Tempest's head was up and his ears perking. An inquiry whickered low and heavily in his thick throat, blowing out through his flaring nostrils.

And then Terryll heard it, faintly now, heard the war beast beating proudly against its chest in the distance. *Thwump! . . . thwump! . . . thwump!*

The sound of the thing came advancing steadily up the road like the relentless reach of the tide. *Boom! . . . boom! . . . boom!* Its legions of hooves, pounding a dreadful drill on the road, grew louder and louder each minute, and its battle ware clattered angrily over the sky and sounded off the hills like distant peals of thunder.

A few lights flickered on below as the townspeople began to stir from their slumber. Some threw open their shutters and looked out at the sky to see what manner of storm was approaching.

But the sky was clear, and the moon was lowering on the hills and spreading a silvery gauze over the landscape and over the dark heaving shape of the war beast when at last it appeared, huffing out of the darkness. Light glinted dully off the points of its back, defining its appalling shape. Long shadows stretched out from the legs of the beast and kept time with it like a column of ghosts.

Terryll watched with astonishment as a dark appendage stripped away from the beast while the rest of the thing continued northeast toward Ermine Street; watched as the appendage disintegrated into what seemed a thousand black spiders that went skittering into the heart of the village.

Moments later the boy heard the sounds of war descending: men yelling, women screaming, the clatter of hooves from different quarters, everything fast becoming a disorienting clangor. And then there were the first leaps of fire flashing against buildings and trees and incredulous faces and lighting the horror of the scene as the flame tongues stretched, licking up at the sky. It seemed a blister of hell had burst open upon the world, revealing a wicked sore, the stench of it rising to the heavens with a great offense.

Terryll saw the villagers amid the growing conflagration, no bigger than tiny black insects, scattering in frantic little groups, and then the larger black spiders moving toward them with incredible speed and overtaking them, going around and herding them, it seemed, and Terryll watching with horror as the insects fell silent before them on the streets.

"God have mercy," he cried, clasping his face.

He looked away and observed the broad and glimmering flanks of the ongoing column thumping along the northeast route, the wagons not even in sight yet. He waited until he was sure of their course. Then reining Tempest away toward the Pennines, he cast a final grim look at the village—the first of the British villages having fallen without resistance—watched the black plumes of smoke curl over the rooftops and cocoon the fluttering moths of flame. A sustained lugubrious wail rose from the dying village of Biddlecairn, as its immortal soul writhed agonizingly out of the husk.

Terryll shook his head sadly and looked away, goading the black stallion out of the trees.

Tempest reeled suddenly, screaming as something struck hard against his hindquarters, and a swift dark shape missed Terryll's thigh by inches. A thought flashed into the boy's mind, as the horse's buttocks shuddered under him, that the black had stumbled into a hole. But he didn't believe it for a second.

Turning quickly in his saddle—the horizon sweeping by in slow-motion—he heard a throaty rattle bearing down on him, then caught a movement out of the corner of his eye. He saw a wolf, cutting hard and low and coming in on a tight curve now, head lowered and teeth bared, with its yellow eyes burning and fixed.

Finishing his turn with the longbow rising into line, Terryll caught a second wolf sweeping into his view as he dug his heels into the horse's flanks. Tempest shot forward away from the trees as the boy, his eyes set on the wolf's bulk, loosed an arrow.

The wolf screamed as the broadhead sank deep into its shoulder and pitched forward into a crumpling roll. The second wolf leaped at the very moment on a long ascending arc, aiming its fangs at the boy's leg. However it had misjudged the horse's speed and, coming down, snatched only a mouthful of tail.

Watching the horse and rider disappearing over the low hill and down and away into the night, the wolf threw its head back and bayed furiously at the moon. The voice shot over the boy's head and reached far ahead into the distance, and moments later the voice rolled back in fierce echoes.

Terryll hoped and prayed that they were echoes.

PART FOUR
SIGNS AND WONDERS

38

THE HASTY COUNCIL

Dagmere drew an arrow along the smooth flank of her yew bow. One hundred yards away was her mark: a red circle, one foot in diameter, painted on a burlap cloth tacked to a bale of straw. She lowered the point over the mark—a glaring red eye taunting her—and, touching its rounding zenith, she steadied her aim and loosed the arrow.

The shaft whistled over a flat trajectory and smacked the target directly, completing a loose grouping of six feathered shafts two inches north and one east of dead-center.

Dagmere frowned.

"You're pulling up as you release," her father said, passing behind her on his way to the stables. He was carrying a bag of carrots and set them down as he peered at the target. "See how your arrows have strayed from the mark."

Dagmere groaned. "I know. But it just keeps swimming around in little circles out there. I can't stay on it."

Allyndaar grinned wryly at her. "It's because you've got your mind somewhere else."

She looked at him abruptly, saw the knowing gleam in his eyes, then turned away and gazed upon the northern hills. "It's spring now, Papa." She sighed wistfully. "He said he'd be coming in the spring."

"He'll come," Allyndaar said, then added with a smirk, "but not if you keep watching the road instead of your mark. Now go collect your arrows and try it again."

"But I'm tired, Papa. I don't feel like practicing anymore today." Dagmere looked hopefully at her father's piercing stare. "Why don't we go and watch the new foals together? It will take my mind off Aeryck."

Allyndaar studied his daughter for a moment, allowing the humor to clear from his brow, and suddenly, as the morning sun blushed over her face and hair and twinkled upon the sapphires of her eyes, he saw her in a new and marvelous light. And it startled him, for it was a frightening revelation.

337

The person standing before him, he saw, was no longer his little girl—his once bouncing, cooing, effluent bundle of giggles, kisses, and secrets-telling little girl. She was transforming before his eyes into another being now, something altogether other, becoming a woman by all appearances. Strange that he had not noticed it before.

In that suddenness of dawning light he realized that he was no longer the center of her universe, the single pull of her happy, insouciant orbits. He realized now that there was someone else eclipsing his hallowed dominion of sixteen years. It pained him deeply, for he knew that soon he must let her go. He felt a little wind go out of him, a little breath of life sailing forever away.

"Come here," he said, taking her shoulders and pulling her close to him. He held her for a moment, cherishing the closeness, shepherding the little flock of memories with a bittersweet crook of a smile.

Dagmere felt a little flush of emotion from her father's sudden embrace. Folded into his big arms with her cheek pressed against his chest, she listened to his heart beating, smelled the wood and horse and the other distinctive Allyndaar smells upon him that for so long framed a secure, robust image of her father. These were intact, inviolate, but she sensed that some shift had occurred in the earth.

She raised her eyes. "What's wrong, Papa? Are you all right?"

"I'm fine, Dag." He smiled, holding her out at arm's length and admiring this new and wondrous creature. "Why?"

Dagmere searched her father's face, her eyes tentative and inquiring. "You're certain?"

"I'm just fine."

She chuckled skeptically. "Shall we go and look at the foals together then?"

"Yes," he said, then arched a brow at her. "But first, go and collect your arrows before someone sees them. It may be a fine group for a Saxon infidel but not for the daughter of a British chieftain."

There he was again. She smiled and looked adoringly into his eyes. "Oh, Papa." Then, stepping up onto her toes, she kissed his cheek and flounced away.

And watching her, Allyndaar beheld admiringly his skipping little girl of five.

Dagmere felt a rush of exhilaration just watching them prancing over the field, hammering their little dish-shaped heads and tossing their bristly roaches, celebrating life with abandon. Feeling the strong instincts of the herd driving in them, some of the colts went running after one another in furious dashes, vaulting about upon long shards of chiseled bone and throwing their hindquarters into the air with frolicking kicks.

Colors of black and chestnut, roan and white and dapple-gray splashed over the green canvas of the field with daring and passionate strokes. Others, still glistening in the wet sheen of new life, stood splay-legged as they suckled their mother's teats, pulling away now and then to answer some whinnying cry.

Dagmere watched with mounting glee how they wobbled about upon uncertain compasses, testing their bearings, stumbling now and then as they struggled to negotiate the spinning globe beneath them. She could repress her love of the horse no longer and, tossing her auburn mane behind, let out a squeal of laughter.

"Aren't they wonderful, Papa?"

Allyndaar, his hands extended upon the stone wall enclosure, allowed a proud smile as he gazed out over the firstfruits of his careful breeding. Through his stallion Daktahr he had sought to strip back into the flagging gene pool of his British stock the first true and untainted bloodlines of the Arabian horse—the First Cause of equine breeds. His eyes burned with the fever of success, and he slapped his palms against the stone.

"Of a truth, lass!" he boomed. "Of a truth, they are marvelous little beasts, aren't they?"

A small bay colt with white socks and a white blaze down his forehead trotted up, put his little nose over the wall, and nuzzled Dagmere's arm.

"Why, there you are, little fellow," she cried in a lilting voice. "Do you want me to give you a nice, juicy treat?" She produced a carrot and held it playfully over the colt's searching lips. "Sure you do." Then she fed it into his biting front teeth until there was only the palm of her hand brushing his whiskers and the sound of his molars crunching loudly.

Daktahr thrust his head through his stall and whickered fiercely, tossing his head and mane and demanding the freedom to romp with his children.

Allyndaar looked over at him and laughed. "Best let him out, Dagmere, or he's liable to wreak thunder and mayhem."

She giggled. However, as she turned her head, something caught her eyes down the road. Her brows knit into a puzzled expression. "Papa? Isn't that—"

"Terryll!" Allyndaar exclaimed, seeing him immediately. "What's he doing back so soon?"

A perplexed shade squirreled over his brow as he started slowly toward the road to meet his son, his mind assessing several possibilities. Then as the possibilities coalesced into a single thought he broke into a run.

The midday sun streamed hotly through the windows of the great hall—hot and wet with precipitation in the air and claustrophobic with the press—and the streamers falling through cast long oblongs of golden light over the floorboards and backs and shoulders of the men who stood in huddled astonishment.

A silence clapped after Terryll's initial briefing, then thinned away, ringing in everyone's ears like the sound after the report of an anvil. And something else came in, something heavy, something heavy and thick and choking like a woolen muffler wrapping thickly around everyone's head and neck.

"Y-you say an army of f-five *thousand?*" a man stuttered.

"Or more," Terryll replied grimly, glancing at his father next to him. "I couldn't count them all though, there were so many. A thousand or more of them were horsemen."

Every man was looking ahead at some place in his mind as the gravity of the news worked through its initial waves of shock. Myriad implications turned on frenetic wheels, spinning a fabric of garish images out of the threads of information. Every so often a face would look up at Terryll from the corporate trance of astonishment as if to say, "Surely this is a jest, isn't it?" then fall back into the sullen pool. There were no units in this, just pieces of a whole, one mind buzzing through it.

"Perhaps they won't come this far north," someone from the back of the hall suggested, breaking the silence, to which a few hopeful heads rose.

Terryll explained again the wagon train of supplies to the unbroken wall of perplexed faces, explained the northerly route they had taken, reminding them of the bits and pieces of information they had collected over the past several months. Then he went into a detailed description of the pogrom of Biddlecairn, his mind recalling vividly for them the tiny black shapes fleeing in ones and twos and in little groups through the burning streets, recounted the swift clattering rushes of the larger black shapes and their cold merciless savagery. He paused, remembering the cries, remembering the pitiful cries for mercy, and the silence rang thinning away.

"This is war then," a man said matter-of-factly. He said it with such stoicism that he might have been commenting on an unfortunate turn in the weather.

A few eyes sparkled to life as the grim reality of the news began to pierce through the unblinking wall, and a bubbling of thoughts began to pour forth through the holes.

"Could it be?"

"Surely it can't be true."

"What of the peace treaty with Hengist?"

"War?"

"There must be some explanation. Some sound reason."

Standing toward the front of the assembly, a short wizen-faced man with shining black eyes, named Clewes, glared fiercely into the square of light at his feet, glared at the tiny dust devils twirling mischievously through it. His mouth was compressed into a grim scar.

"You're certain, Terryll?" a lanky man asked. "You're certain they mean war?"

"What shall we do?" another asked.

Suddenly a guttural effervescence burst, deep-chested, from Clewes's throat, and he threw his hands over his face and wept. "We were to have peace!" he cried. "Peace! But now—woe! Woes upon woes!" And he trailed away in a sobbing upheaval.

Stunned at the outburst, every man turned and looked askance at him, embarrassed.

Terryll glanced at the man, then looked down at the floor and studied the cracks in the planks.

The man standing next to Clewes laid a hand upon his heaving shoulders to console him.

But the latter yanked away violently and reeled, facing the assembly, red-eyed and desperate, like a cornered criminal. His eyes burned with a dreadful prescience as he glared at the startled surge of faces.

"Don't you see?" he cried, the flames mounting in his eyes. "Don't you see that we are all dead men? Dead men, I tell you! Every last one of us. You ask what can we do—" he chortled fiercely at the one who had made the inquiry "—we can dig our graves. That is what we can do!"

Then he raised his eyes prophetlike to the rafters, as though beholding some dark vision of horror there. "Devastations of devastations," he pronounced gravely. "Nothing can stop the advance of the Destroyer. He will come like a great dragon, breathing fire over the land, consuming everything in its path, gorging himself on the sweet flesh and blood of men. He will come raping our wives and daughters before our eyes. Devastation is our lot, for there is no hope." He barked a laugh of contempt. "No, the Destroyer feeds on the vain hopes of puny souls!"

Something appalling crackled over the men's heads as they beheld the deep grooves bunching and twisting over Clewes's face. Each man stared in gaping disbelief at the malignant gleam burning through his wet, little black eyes. Fear rifled through their ranks, startling mental and emotional faculties, chilling them with terror.

"It is over! It is over!" the wizen-faced man cried. "It is over but for the Destroyer and the devastations that he will bring upon the land! Woes upon woes!" Then, as though to prevent further view of the thing that tormented his mind, he clasped his hands over his head and wept bitterly again, begging for mercy, his chest heaving like a bellows over the deep choking anguish.

The men gaped at him with wide, frightened sheeps' eyes.

Then Clewes came to himself abruptly with a jolt of his head, and the fire in his eyes cooled in the settling bobble as they lowered upon the taut faces of the men. He blinked queerly at them, as though not comprehending at first. Then his eyes began to glow in the approach of some disquieting light. And then the eyes glared out at the assembly from the sum of his shame.

Wiping his face, he hitched up his trousers, nodded curtly to Allyndaar, grunted something to him and to an indiscriminate pan of faces, then strode quick-footed out of the hall. Several women approached him outside to ascertain details of the briefing but drew up sharply when they saw his eyes.

His wife followed him home apprehensively. Upon his arrival Clewes proceeded to feed his livestock, milk his goats, turn his horses out to pasture, then, setting the barn on fire, hanged himself from the loft.

Meanwhile a boil of frantic discussion bubbled into the awful void opened by the man's departure. It happened at once, as though on cue, the stunned shock of horror drawing out into a thin wire, tauter and tauter, until nothing was left in it to draw out. And then it snapped. The once whole thing in the room disintegrated into a shattering of pieces, the fearful shards of personality stabbing wildly at the vagaries of this new and threatening wind.

Allyndaar raised his hand to settle the crowd. "Men! Men! Enough of this," he cried over the din. "Enough! We will get nowhere in this tumult."

Slowly, layer upon layer, veils of anxious quiet settled over the thing Clewes left behind until there was restored order and every eye was turned expectantly to the chieftain.

"That's better," he said, looking out at the drawn faces. "We've business at hand."

"What shall we do then, Allyn?" a voice cried out. "What can we do against so many of them?"

A murmuring simmered, bubbling quickly through the crowd.

"We must keep our heads, for one thing," the chieftain retorted, and the murmuring quieted.

"Aye, that's it," a man grunted.

"I think we should wait until we hear news from Bolstroem," another man suggested. "If indeed the Saxons have set a trap, then he will tell us."

This seemed reasonable and was met with nods and grunts of affirmation.

342

But Allyndaar shook his head. "No, my friends. I daresay there isn't a man in this room who doubts the word of my son. If there is, let us hear him now." He waited for a moment, searching their faces. "Now listen to me, men. I doubt seriously that any news Bolstroem might bring will change the fact that there is a large Saxon army marching north this very moment—one that has already destroyed a village of helpless people. If we wait and do nothing we will lose valuable time, time that we cannot afford to spare. No, we must act. We must face this threat against us now with every resource available to us."

"And what resources are those, Allyn?" a voice called out. "We have no army."

"Yes!" someone agreed. "We can scarce put five hundred men in the field, let alone five thousand!"

"Or *more!* Terryll said there were maybe more!"

Allyndaar nodded. "Then that is all the more reason we must act upon this information now. If we do not prepare ourselves for a fight, then we'd best take Clewes's advice and start digging graves."

A moment of silence intervened as every man remembered the face of Clewes. A chill fingered through their midst.

"I still say we should wait for Bolstroem," a man said.

"No. We should do as Allyn suggested," another countered.

And a heated debate ensued, some holding fast to waiting, others in agreement with Allyndaar. It seemed the individual shards of personality had galvanized into two fronts of sharp disagreement.

"I can't believe my ears," a stout man bellowed from one camp, pushing his way to the front of the assembly. "I thought I was in the company of Britons—nay, not Britons only but men of Killwyn Eden no less! And here I find out that someone has let the women in here." He threw a big hand into the air, waving off his last comment. "What am I saying? That's not really fair to the women, is it? On second thought, I say we should *let* them in here—aye—and then we might see some fighting spirit."

"What's that? Are you calling us cowards?" a burly man snarled from the other group, now bullying his way forward. "Is that what you're doing? Are you calling us cowards? By thunder, I'll not tolerate being called a coward!"

The two of them squared off. The first man's face and neck burned a bright crimson, the second man's eyes turned blood red.

"I'm saying we should let the women in here, that's what I'm saying," the first man growled, stabbing the air between them with his finger. "You make what you want of it."

"So you're calling us cowards then, is that it?" the second man cried. "I just want to know one thing—are you calling us cowards? Just say it!"

This went back and forth a few more rounds, the men fuming like two young pugilists on a playground, each thrusting his chin and shoulders with short, truculent jabs and threatening the other with his fists. It was sure to go to blows.

"That's enough!" Allyndaar roared, stepping between them. "There'll be plenty of fighting going round soon enough without us turning on each other."

The two men eyed one another menacingly, spat out closing remarks, then edged snarling back into the anonymity of the crowd.

A husky man with a fair crop of whiskers and a balding pate stepped forward. He was a respected man in the village and a friend of Allyndaar's.

"Allyn," he said, "we're behind you to a man, you know it. Each of us would give his life protecting his home and family, rather than let some Saxon devil put his filthy claws on them." Grunts of approval sounded from both camps. "You see, there's nary a coward in the lot of us, but facin' an army of five thousand—" he blew out a whistle "—it will be the deuce to pay, you can count on it."

"If we stand against them alone, we will surely die," Allyndaar said. "But what of the men of Brough, or of Bowes? Will they not come to our aid, and we to theirs? And what of the men of Whitley Castle?"

"They would rather drink sheep dip than help us," a voice called out.

Several men laughed.

Allyndaar joined them, for he needed a good laugh. "Then we must convince them otherwise," he said, letting the humor trail away. "Sheep dip or no, we must stand together in this thing—every village in the Brigantes, every man for his neighbor. And then, by God's grace, we will put up a fair show."

"Aye!" sounded from the crowd.

"Men, this is our homeland," he continued, building now into a driving cadence. "The Saxons do not know these hills like we do. For who among you doesn't know every stream and lake, every nook and crevice, every tree in every forest in every vale and wold? Terryll says there are at least a thousand horsemen coming. But what Saxon is there who can ride like even the poorest horseman in our tribe? He says they are well-armed with bow and spear and mace. But what are these compared to the range of our longbows?

"Men of Killwyn Eden, we will use what we have to our advantage. We will strike swift and true where they least expect it, then disappear like the wind into the hills. The Saxons will think the very earth has

344

risen against them. They will think they are fighting spirits and cringe in terror before the fighting men of the Brigantes!"

Several more "that's its" were added to the "ayes."

Then Terryll brightened with an idea. "What of Brynwald, Father? Surely Brynwald will come to our aid as well."

Several of the men looked at him incredulously.

"You would ask the Picts to come and fight with us?" one sneered. "Why, what would stop them from taking a share of their own?"

Terryll glared at the man. "I would trust Brynwald with my life. And he would give his own to save it."

Several voices rose in concert, having visited him at Christ's Mass, and the man was silenced.

"Now there's a turnabout for you," a voice cried out. "Vortigern brings in the Saxons to fight the Picts, and we bring in the Picts to fight the Saxons!"

The hall erupted into laughter. It was a good hearty laughter, chasing some pent flight of devils into the air. The laughter built on itself, swelling into a sustained and boisterous roar like a blast of cleansing wind, a strong mannish wind that worked thunderously through the flagging hearts of the men of Killwyn Eden, billowing their luffing sails and striking a fire in their bellies.

The men rose together on a surge of human spirit. Their eyes burned, and their jaws hardened with a singleness of purpose, a kindled zeal, and everyone pitched forward to the business of protecting his home and loved ones, and to blazes with the prophecy of Clewes.

Allyndaar began to select leaders according to their skills, and soon a chain of command was established. Having done this, he dismissed the rest of the men from the hall to ready their weapons and steadings. Then he put forth a rough plan of attack before the leaders.

Each man was given an area of responsibility, be it defense of the walls, or care of the women and children, or to lead groups of men on horseback or foot offensively against the Saxons. It would be left to the leaders to select men according to their abilities; any crossover disputes between them would be settled by Allyndaar. The plan was added to by others of the men, then modified by Allyndaar, refined several times through corporate discussion, and when everyone was of one mind, the matter was sealed. Envoys then were selected to ride to each of the neighboring villages in the tribe and bring them into the plan. A tight, well-rehearsed choreography between them would be essential for any hope of victory.

Allyndaar stepped out of the hall with Terryll after the last of the men went home to his supper. The clouds were dark and gathering low over the hills, and he immediately smelled rain in the air. He felt the change in the wind too.

He closed his eyes momentarily and filled his lungs to cleanse them of the briefing, to wash out some of the heaviness of his office. Opening them again, he could see Helena and Dagmere approaching along the road, silhouetted in the dappled shadows of the overarching trees.

Terryll was looking down at the ground in a brooding quiet.

"What is it, son?" Allyndaar asked, laying his hand on the boy's shoulder. "It's Bolstroem, isn't it?"

Terryll looked up at him with a start.

Allyndaar looked away with sad and heavy eyes. "I have been thinking of him too, son."

"He wouldn't let me go with him, Papa. If he had only let me go with him then—"

"Perhaps then you couldn't have come home to warn us. No, Terryll, don't look back on it. Never look back."

"Well, Allyn?" Helena asked, drawing up to them. Her face was a grave mask.

Allyndaar smiled at her and took her hands in his. "I will leave for Brough and Bowes at first light. Terryll will leave for Loch na Huric."

Dagmere perked.

"Alone," Allyndaar said, reading her mind.

"But, Papa!"

"You must stay here with your mother and help with preparations." And the matter was settled.

The family walked together under the blinking moonlight, discussing the details of the council, the men's part in it, the women's part in it, and the various tactics to be employed. Allyndaar put his arm around his wife and drew her close to his side.

"What will become of us, Allyn?" she asked. "Of our people, I mean."

"I don't know," he said. "I know that we are in God's hands though—and that nothing will happen to us that He doesn't allow in order to accomplish His good purpose."

Helena pondered the truth of this for several moments as they walked along, smelling the flowers and the wild scents rushing off the hills in the shifted wind. She took Dagmere's hand and squeezed it. "Yes," she sighed. She looked up at the tiny stars twinkling through holes in the closing dark clouds. "Yes, we must take comfort in this. We must hold onto this hope."

At length the fields and orchards of the estate opened before them. Everyone looked up, coming out from the overhanging trees and seeing it

346

at once—the white plastered walls of the villa that was their home, broad and gleaming in the moonlight, sprawling gracefully over a dark and silvery promontory of rolling sward. And suddenly everyone feeling something different about it.

Suddenly, because of the coming war, it seemed remote to them, no longer warm and welcoming. Like a living thing that palled at their approach, it appeared to draw away off the rise with its wings lifting brightly.

Everyone stopped, feeling a melancholy ache boring into them and letting in a kind of death. And then the colts came whinnying out over the fields to greet them, the whole new herd of them, prancing and bucking and dashing it all back to earth, thrusting their perfect, little dish-shaped faces over the stone wall, each one beaming in the gift of life.

Allyndaar looked over at them and smiled. Then starting forward to their house—their home—he let out a sigh, and the wind swept by and took it.

And the Saxon juggernaut struck Danum with the sword, then set it on fire, and the Britons fled screaming in terror.

---39---

THREE STARTLING VISITORS

A eryck had it in mind to camp at the ruins just north of Netherby. Night was coming on, and it would be safer there, he thought. Much safer. Yes, that is what he would do. Then in the morning he would ride out before dawn and hopefully reach the Wall and Britain a few hours later.

Britain. The thought of it sent a glad shiver up his spine. At last, after five months away, he was going back to his homeland, to the land of gentler clime and slopes; to the home of his birth and life and the girl he loved. That thought sent a little shiver too. But he couldn't hold onto it, not with the other thing pressing in the pit of his stomach.

He had been nurturing a fine dream over the past two days, envisioning Dagmere in his arms, looking up at him with those beautiful blue eyes, her full lips pursed with tingling eagerness, then kissing her until the dream swelled in his breast and burst under its own weight. When that happened he would quickly try to get the pieces back right away, arranging them into the image of her face.

But he couldn't, he knew, and he'd have to think about something else for a while, then sneak up on the dream from a different angle. But if he came at it too soon the pieces still wouldn't be right, and he'd lose that time and have to come at it again later.

However that business on the road a mile back had put a scattering end to it, and he was thinking about that now and the thick-walled ruins of the Roman garrison.

He had thought that business was over, since he hadn't seen or heard any of them for more than two weeks now—not since the equinox, when there had been that uproar in the hills and everyone in the village coming out of their homes and wondering what it was. It was a sound like nothing they'd ever heard before, "like Legion getting loose into the herd of swine," someone said, "then them turning on each other." Only these weren't swine. They were wolves.

Some in the village thought it a sign of something dreadful because of the equinox and went quickly indoors. Others thought it was just some territorial dispute aggravated by the severe cold of winter.

But Aeryck knew that the wolves were killing each other because of him. *It's mind numbing,* he'd think, gazing up into the dark screen of hills; terrifying, for it made no earthly sense. Not one bit of it.

Throughout the winter he had seen them on the hills, small and black against the gray skies, sitting sullen and motionless on their haunches. They were all around him it seemed, their heads lowered and looking down at him like statues of stone, with pinpoints of yellow light gleaming from their hollow eyes, boring untiringly into his mind, waiting for him to ease up his guard, to leave the village perhaps so that they might tear him to pieces. At night he heard them calling to one another, heard their voices going back and forth across the valley, its length and breadth, stitching a net of mischief over the sky, then occasionally dropping under the wind and penetrating through the walls of the cottage into his chest so that he thought he would go mad listening to them.

He would have too but for the other thoughts, those aching ones ripping the heart out of his chest that only got worse with the approach of spring—those of Dagmere.

For weeks he had been weighing the ache in his heart against the other—his love for Dagmere pitted against his maddening fear of the wolves—with the scales tipping back and forth, the ache winning over the madness sometimes, then the madness winning over the ache. He knew that, if he were to leave, the wolves would be on him in a snatch and make short, savage work of him. He had seen it described in a spate of nightmares: the flashing white canines buzzing in his face, snarling demonically—Legion loosed in the pack—with the yellow, boring eyes sweeping by in terrific rushes. And then, with everything slowing down to a terrifying dream-crawl, he would feel the hot, malodorous breath puffing against his neck and the sudden set of fangs at his throat. Then he would jolt upright in his bed, gasping for breath. And the scales would tip.

And then there was that awful-sounding night of the equinox, bringing everything to a head and bursting on the hills with a hellish fury, and now—for more than two weeks—not a peep. It was as though the wolves had been spirited away with the winter. There hadn't been a glimpse of them, only the skies blackening for days with the birds circling and descending, screeching exultantly over their feast, then ascending and the skies going clear.

Spring had come chattering with resolve, and Aeryck felt a release to go—the inner compulsion that had withheld him loosing its grip—and for two days now not a glimpse of a single wolf. Not until that business a mile back on the road.

A dozen or more of them he counted, flashing through the trees in dreamlike slow motion, their yellow eyes floating eerily through the haze. And now he was thinking of wolves instead of Dagmere, with the terror of them growing in his mind.

He was thinking of how he was out in the open, with only a sword to protect himself, and riding a horse that had to be the oldest, slowest, and certainly the ugliest rack of bones he had ever seen. It certainly wouldn't do in a test of speed, not unless it was heading back to the barn. He wished now he had taken that other horse that Brynwald had suggested, the red one with the blue eye that looked as if he could run—run? He looked as if he could fly!—but that was precisely why he hadn't taken him, that and the way that blue eye kept looking him over.

His eyes were taut and busy on the stark hills to his right. They flattened away into the broken barrenness of the peat bogs, a seismic upheaval of indiscriminate violence, softly shrouded in lowering veils of evening mist. Then his gaze swept anxiously over to the rolling barrenness on his left—the whole of it resembling the bleak grayness of a surreal dreamscape. And when he rode out of a dip and around a bend in the road, he saw a wolf on a little rise to his right, and he pulled up sharply on the reins.

His hand snapped over his sword, and a violent shudder staggered through his limbs and gurgled out his throat. He stared for a moment at the animal, gaping incredulously, his mind dully comprehending the image.

Then a wave of relief spread through the boy, slow, then building, then smoothing out over the terror, as he gazed in wonder at the wolf. For he had presumed him dead, killed that time before Christ's Mass.

It was the white one, alive.

The wolf was sitting and looking away into the distance as though he didn't know the boy was coming. But when Aeryck spurred his horse forward, he turned and gazed at him with those inscrutable yellow eyes of his, blinking placidly, knowingly, and Aeryck perceived that he was only waiting for him to arrive.

They stared at one another for several moments as the boy drew slowly by. Then as the white wolf looked away to gaze back on the hills, Aeryck caught something in his movement, something that was a little startling. He looked again, drawing closer, and saw it clearly now—saw the tired, gaunt lines of the wolf's face, saw the ribs showing sickly through the once glistening white fur, fur that was now a pale ashen color.

There were scars showing a wicked purple over the length of the wolf's body. A wedge of light cut through the left ear, and Aeryck realized that there was only the husk of him left—a broken and bruised shell of his former self—hammered down in recent battle.

350

Aeryck reined his horse again and stared at the wolf for a long while. Tears began to well in his eyes. Brother Stephen's dead face flashed upon a bolt through his mind. Sullie's death scream pierced the quiet of his soul with a disquieting thunder, and he felt a sudden desire to go over and put his arms around the wolf's neck and ask him why. Why would he spend the last ounce of his strength protecting him? Dying for him, as others had? *Why?* he wanted to shout.

It was then that the other wolves came, perhaps fifteen of them, some torn and ragged, others limping from sundry wounds. The white one led them away toward the dark green stretch of forest that was drawn over the hills about a half mile up the road. Aeryck felt the warm tears spread over his cheeks as he watched them lope brokenly away in a single haggard line. He glanced down at his hands, at the hilt of his sword glinting dully, and pondered many things.

The garrison had been deserted for more than a century. It had once served as a halfway post between the military stations at Netherby and Birrens. Now it lay in a rubble of ruin, the roof fallen in over most of it. Rafters protruded haphazardly from its broken back like the spreading ribs of a skeleton. Vines clung to its crumbling walls, crept over and down into the several rooms and barracks and spread out—the earth breaking down and reclaiming its stolen materials.

Most of what the Romans left behind had been picked clean by people and animals alike. However, here and there under a fallen beam or pile of rocks, a bit of leather strap, or brass brad, or tin utensil remained for the less discriminating scavenger to yet uncover.

Aeryck carefully built a large fire with windfalls and tinder on the charred remains of previous fires, all that endured of the transient civilizations of fellow travelers that crept in after the Romans. Then he struck the tinder with flint.

Flames quickly leaped from the layered ruins, greedy for life, licked up along the dry twigs and branches, then lashed out into the air, sparking and bucking and casting a lurid glow onto the leaves and the trees. They were old trees, heavy shouldered and thick limbed, bearded with hoary moss, and they crowded the ruins inquisitively.

Shades crawled out of the fire and danced airily against the thick walls of stone, laughing it seemed, as a new civilization was born and immediately began to consume itself. Then the night pushed against the fire and the fire against the night in a desperate, pitched battle that flickered eerily over the camp.

The boy went over to his horse, tied securely to a tree in a dark swale of grass, and retrieved his bedroll and saddle bags. He spread his bedding over the grass-grown flagstones of the garrison, felt their hardness under the blankets, grimaced at the thought of a night's sleep on them, thought about the soft bed of pine needles over by the horse. Then, remembering the wolves, he grimaced again and dug around in the bags for his supper rations: a joint of mutton that needed roasting, a small red potato, and a skin of cider. A feast fit for a king.

Aeryck made a spit of broken limbs, stripping off the excess twigs and leaves, then carefully whittling the ends with his knife, as Terryll had once shown him to do, until they were pointed. He held them up and smiled. He drove the first one into a gap in the flags, but the second one snapped under his weight. He held it up and eyed it, grumbled, tossed it into the fire, then quickly made another, leaving the twigs and leaves. He wedged it in tight, skewered the mutton, and set it in place over the crooks.

Then, satisfied that his camp was in order, the boy sat with his back in a corner, watching the flames crackle under the meat as the cooking aroma filled the air, hearing the night song of crickets and frogs and something that hummed a feverish monotone in the background. He gazed into the leaps of fire, listening to it snap for a while. Then in the dazing aftermath of preparations he began to imagine what manner of life there must have been within these walls more than a century ago, with the Spartan furnishings, with the Roman regimen and discipline.

He envisioned the shades of legionaries rising upon the shimmering fire waves, the ghosts of a forgotten past whispering to him through the stone and mortar, the overhanging trees and stars bearing witness to their tales. He thought he heard the laughter of huddled men over a rousing game of dice, the sound of their studded sandals clicking over the floor, and the rattle of battle accoutrements being honed and polished. He imagined them writing letters, each man with a context—a wife, a family, a sweetheart perhaps—reading their letters time and again, and all the while working through the throbbing, aching loneliness attendant to soldiers away from home. Like him.

Aeryck let out a sigh, then pulled out his little leather copy of the *Iliad*. Looking up once at the meat, he smiled, then let his mind drift, sailing over the pages. And in no time the dream was up like a wind off the crests and building, and Dagmere was angling her head the way she did so prettily to receive his tender kiss. And the next one . . . and the next . . .

After a time he wore out the dream from overrehearsing it. The bright pieces hurled across the jet of night like stars. Then he remembered the meat.

But when he looked up, a shudder of cold terror shook his body as he found himself staring into the eyes of a man shape, sitting on its haunches across the fire, with a twisted grin flickering on its fire-bleached face, the eyes gleaming like two coals of fire. Aeryck was so startled that he reeled to his feet, his sword ringing as it cleared scabbard, before he recognized who it was.

"Terryll!"

Terryll grinned ironically at him through the flames. "You looked so happy reading your little book that I didn't want to disturb you."

Aeryck coughed, choking out his fear in sputters. "Well, you disturbed me about half to death!" he snarled.

"Since when is there a Dagmere of Troy?" Terryll asked, abruptly changing the subject.

"What?"

"Your book. Interesting reading that. 'Dagmere, O Dagmere of Troy, let me kiss your sweet ruby lips!'" Terryll sprang to his feet and swept an imaginary girl into his arms and, bending over her, made passionate kissing noises into the air.

Aeryck burned red and shook his sword at him. "You were listening!"

"Still carrying around that useless slab of metal, I see," Terryll said, dropping the girl and clucking his tongue.

"You won't think it so useless when I prick your gizzard with it," Aeryck threatened. He was making his angry face, the one with the furrowed brow, the one with the jutting chin and the veins popping out of his neck, trying to hold onto the fierceness of it but knowing he couldn't because of the infernal bubbling inside of him.

Terryll knew it too and made a face, crossing his eyes and blowing up his cheeks.

It was too much for Aeryck to endure, and he burst into laughter. Then the two of them leaped at one another and embraced, each slapping the other's back. Terryll felt the taut bulk under Aeryck's tunic, the thick muscles rippling powerfully. "Put on some weight, I see," he said, looking him over admiringly. "Tillie must be feeding you well."

"She does." Aeryck shrugged. And then it dawned on him. "Hey! What are you doing here? I was on my way to see you."

Terryll's head lowered suddenly, and Aeryck saw the humor wing off his face.

"What is it?" he asked. "What'd I say?" Suddenly he was gravely serious. "Nothing's happened to *Dagmere*, has it?"

"No, she's fine."

"Your *parents*? What? What's happened? Tell me!"

Terryll eyed the mutton. "Mind if I share some of your supper?"

"No. But first you have to tell me what's going on."

"By then it'll be burned."

Aeryck followed his eyes to the mutton, then jumped to it, blowing on it and brushing off the smoking bits of char.

353

Terryll snickered. "It's a good thing Tillie's been feeding you. You'd be nothing but skin and bones on your own."

Aeryck glowered at him. "You want any of this, or don't you?"

"Me?" Terryll laughed. "Why, roast whatever-that-was is my favorite!"

So the boys sat down and ate supper, during which Terryll related everything concerning the Saxons: the proclamation of Vortigern, the trip to Stonehenge with Bolstroem, the information learned from the Gaulish traders, the razing of Biddlecairn, and finally the hasty war council in the great hall.

Terryll let the news settle in for a moment, allowing the shock to clear, then asked, "Do you think he'll come?"

But Aeryck was staring into the flames, which had grown small and red during the story, lost in a whirl of despairing thoughts.

"Aeryck?"

Still he did not reply.

"Are you all right, Aeryck?"

"Huh? Yes . . . er . . . no," Aeryck said thickly, his mind forcing the words out of his mouth. "No, I'm not all right. This is horrible. I can't imagine . . ." And he let his thoughts trail away.

Terryll just nodded his head and threw a chip of wood into the fire, watched the flames snatch at it greedily, then tossed a larger one in after it. The sparks flew, bursting up onto the draft of heat.

Aeryck looked up from the fire, his eyes suddenly tired and sick looking. "And Bolstroem?"

Terryll shook his head. "We haven't heard." There was a pause. "Aeryck, do you think Brynwald will come?"

"Brynwald?

"Without his help, we can't hope to defeat the Saxons."

Aeryck's eyes snapped to life. "Yes, of course Brynwald will come. He meant it what he said to Allyndaar."

"Good. How many men do you think he can muster?"

"I don't know. Five, six hundred, maybe. Maybe more if we go to the men of Glenlochar. Oswald's a good man."

"That will help. Yes, that will help," Terryll said, more to himself. His mind worked the numbers into his father's battle choreography. A weight seemed to lift off his shoulders. "It is the providence of God, me finding you here, Aeryck," he said in earnest. "There are others in Britain that I must warn. If you take this message back to Brynwald, it will save me three or four days."

"Yes, of course." Aeryck looked intently into his eyes. "You must see to it that Dagmere and your mother are safe in the hills."

354

"Don't worry. The women and children are being looked after. Whatever comes of this, no harm will befall them."

Aeryck glared at him. "You must see to it."

"You have my word on it. We'd best get some sleep now," Terryll suggested, looking suddenly weary. "Won't do anybody any good if we fall off our horses and break our necks, will it?" He took Aeryck's shoulder with a slap and gave it a good shake. "Yes, Brynwald and Tillie must be starving, keeping you fed." He grinned.

A smile struggled on Aeryck's face. "It's good to see you too, Terryll. I just wish—"

"I know." Suddenly Terryll's face went hard with anger. "It feels like the world's coming to an end, doesn't it? Like the Apocalypse." Then he disappeared into the trees to collect his bedroll off his horse.

Meanwhile Aeryck sat down with his back in the corner again, gazing thoughtfully at the sword across his lap. He studied the family crest his father had engraved on the hilt—the "bear wreath," as the boy had called it for so many years. He marveled at the tongues of fire tracing the length of the blade.

The intricate workmanship never ceased to amaze him. And then he saw his father's face gleaming in the blade, suddenly smiling warmly at him with the same grim smile he remembered him smiling the last time he saw him as a young boy.

Aeryck stared into the image, startled at the revelation, then shook his head when he realized that he was looking down at his own reflection. His fingers lightly touched his cheek, as though to confirm it. Then his thoughts turned to his father's death, recalling how he and a tiny knot of men had died bravely defending the village of Glenryth against the Saxon general known as the Wolf, the one riding north this very moment before an army of five thousand men. Killers all.

He smoothed his fingers along the tongues of fire on the sword, as a dark reverie shifted over his countenance. The tongues of fire seemed animated in the flickering glow of the campfire. His fingers grew warm at the touch, and he lifted them from the blade. Thoughts called unto thoughts.

Then he pulled out the bronze medallion from around his neck, the one with the matching bear wreath engraved on it and, twirling it absently between his fingers, thought how history seemed to be repeating itself, thought how he might, after eleven long years, finally avenge his father's death. The providence of God? Perhaps, he mused darkly. Perhaps not.

A shadow passed over his face.

"You all right?" Terryll asked, having returned as silently as he had gone.

Aeryck looked up. "Hmm?"

Terryll smiled. "Here, this is for you." He tossed Aeryck a thin leather valise. "Dagmere asked me to give it to you." Then he laughed. "She sure put up a good fight with Papa, not letting her come with me."

Aeryck looked down at the valise dumbfounded. Then he quickly glanced up at Terryll, who was giving him that knowing smirk of his.

"Seems like I'm always delivering things to you from your female admirers." Terryll snickered.

Aeryck looked at the valise and opened it. There was a letter inside. He took it out and stared expectantly at the handwriting for a moment before he began to read. He gave it up and moved closer to the fire, holding it up to the low, red flames.

Terryll shook his head and smiled, then, spreading out his blanket, curled up and within seconds was fast asleep.

Aeryck read the salutation several times, and each time finishing it he had to go back and start over because his mind kept spinning off the last word into a world of bright fantasy. "My dearest Love . . . My dearest Love . . . My dearest Love . . ."

And the wind was up in his soul and building to a gale.

When at last the night had prevailed, pushing the fire down into the tomb of blasted stones—the life of another civilization again smoldering in ruins—Aeryck lay huddled next to it, shivering with cold, or fear, or love. For even though his bedroll was spread out a mere three feet behind him, it had been forgotten at some point during the night's passage along the bright shores of the Peloponnesus, and remained unused. And the boy clutched the letter against his bosom for warmth.

Terryll's eyes opened with a start, and he rolled out of his sleep with a single fluid movement, coming up onto his knees with his longbow drawn and pointing into the dark gray mists of the pre-dawn. He waited, tensed, his mind blinking away the remnant of sleep, as he stared warily between the black boles of trees showing through the swirling mists.

Something was out there. He heard the dull wet snap of a twig. A cold thick wetness pervaded the air, muffling sound. There was a heady pungency of dripping vegetation fogging his brain.

There it was again! The muted crush of earth. The stealthy approach. And another one! And then he saw a movement, and then a shape appearing, vague and watery at first, dark and monstrous and growing, lumbering through the trees toward the garrison, about fifty yards away. And seeing it fully now the tenseness shivered out of his limbs, and he lowered his bow.

"Hauwka!"

The looming hulk let out a familiar moan, and Terryll, hopping a broken wall, ran and threw his arms around the bear's massive hairy neck. "Hauwka, my friend!" he cried, drinking in the bruin's damp scent. "How are you, big fella? You don't know how I've missed you! This is jolly!"

Hauwka let out a happy bawl, still plodding forward.

"I see you've put some fat on you since the last time I saw you," he said, kneading the thick skin under the fur. "That's good, that's good."

The two of them continued toward the garrison in the brightening grayness of dawn, the long spears of grass wet on their feet and slapping round their ankles. Aeryck's horse whickered when he caught wind of the bear. And somewhere in the distance Tempest answered him, his snorts sounding dully through the dense fog.

Entering the garrison, the bear padded over to Aeryck, who was sound asleep, and sniffed behind his ear.

Aeryck stirred and groaned, then went still, lazily smacking his lips.

Hauwka snorted. Then putting his snout next to the boy's face, he dragged his warm wet tongue over his cheek.

Aeryck chuckled in his sleep and mumbled, "Oh, Dagmere. My dearest love, Dagmere," then trailed off with a happy decrescendo of giggles.

"I think he's dead," Terryll thought aloud, gazing down at the stupid grin on Aeryck's face. "Struck down by Cupid's airy dart." He nudged him in the foot with his toe. "Time to wake up, my love!"

Aeryck's legs drew up to his chest, giving him the appearance of an overgrown baby.

Terryll gave him a sharper kick on the sole of his boot. "Come on, sweet lips. Up! Up with you now. Up!" And he kicked him again.

Aeryck groaned, opening one red eye that focused blearily on a big black snout with two wet eyes set over it, gazing at him. Hauwka licked his face again.

Aeryck screamed, scrambling backward. He hit the wall behind him with a jolt that seemed to clear his vision.

Terryll threw his head back and laughed. "You looked like one of those crabs you see on the coast!"

Ignoring him, Aeryck gaped fuzzily at the huge bruin, giving his brain a moment to clear. Then a big smile spread over his face. "Hauwka!" he cried, suddenly overwhelmed with emotion. "Is it really you? Yes— yes it is!" And leaping to his feet he flung himself at the bear, laughing.

The boys ate a hasty meal while Hauwka busied himself in a tangle of blackberry bushes, then struck camp and mounted their horses and

357

headed through the moss-covered trees to the road. The bear caught up to them and padded along behind, his massive head low and forward and swinging to the heavy rhythm of his gait. Once arriving at the road, the boys reined their horses in opposite directions and halted, looking at one another with uncompromising glances.

"Look for us in a week or so," Aeryck said.

Terryll stared at him hopefully. "You're sure?"

"We'll come, I promise," Aeryck said, then added fiercely, "The gates of hell won't keep me away."

"I believe you." Terryll nodded. "A week then."

Hauwka looked back and forth between the boys. His muzzle was stained with blackberry juice.

"You'd best go now." Terryll smiled, waving the bear to Aeryck. "It's safer up here." He looked quickly at Aeryck. "Never thought I'd hear myself say that."

The boys chuckled weakly.

Hauwka let out a moan.

Then with a parting salute and a wink, Terryll spurred Tempest down the road with a clattering of hooves.

Aeryck and Hauwka watched until they disappeared over a small rise, then the boy clucked his horse northward. "Come on, big fella," he said, looking down at the bear padding beside him. "It sure is good to see you. Still got that limp, I see. Are you all right?"

The bear bawled happily, gazing up at the boy with a look of keen animal intelligence sparkling through his eyes.

Aeryck marveled at him. "You truly are a wonder, Hauwka." He smiled affectionately. "You truly are."

Then Hauwka looked away at something off to his left.

Aeryck followed his eyes, and there, sitting on a low rise about three hundred feet away, was the white wolf slowly scanning the country-side. He could just see him through the dissipating mists. No other wolves were in sight. Aeryck paused, shaking his head in amazement.

"Let's go!" he clucked, goading the horse's flanks.

The horse needed no encouragement. He got wind of where he was going and took off as though his tail were on fire, nearly throwing the boy. "Whoa! Whoa!" he cried, first surprised, then angry. "Easy now! Easy! Whoa, I say, you worthless horse!"

And so it went. Hauwka kept up as best he could.

And the Saxon juggernaut struck Eburacum with the sword, then set it on fire, and the Britons fled screaming in terror.

40
THE GATES
OF HELL

Aeryck awoke with a startled gasp, his mind reeling with the terror that he had arrived too late. The last lingering image twisting through his mind was that of a burning village—the black curdling plumes of what was once Killwyn Eden ascending to the heavens, and the wicked black flights of ten thousand carrion-eaters descending upon some vague carnage. And of Dagmere, her face a mask of horror, being carried away by some devil who bore an uncanny resemblance to Spang.

The horror of the dream impelled him to his feet with a sense of urgency. His pulse sounded a reveille to action. His mind was bright and focused on the singular task of his day, and he sprang to it with an economy of movement. Time was his enemy. He would beat time.

Hurriedly he ate a meal of jerky and bread, washed down with several gulps of cider, then broke camp before dawn. While tying his bags to his saddle, he made a speedy calculation of the distance remaining to Loch na Huric. He reckoned that if he made as good time today as he did yesterday, he ought to be there sometime before sunset.

He quickly saddled his horse, cinching him tight, then untied the tether from his neck. And as he began to fit the bit in its teeth, the horse bolted, leaving the boy holding the bridle and a handful of mane.

Aeryck stood dumbstruck for three full seconds, watching his horse hightailing it back to the barn, stirrups and saddlebags full of provisions flapping wildly, before he fully grasped the situation. Then wave after wave of cold, hollow chills swept over his frame.

And then a curse flew out of his mouth.

"Stupid horse," he added to it, as he ran to the road. He shook his fist at the receding black speck. "Stupid, stupid horse!" But the sound of the hooves clattering away had a reckless hint of mockery in it.

Aeryck glanced plaintively at the graying light in the east. He could see the clouds now, black as soot. He could see the red flames glowing through them as though they were being stoked by an immense furnace. It seemed as though the day was coming with a terrible vengeance.

Then a renewed terror struck his mind, one that elicited a groan of despair. The dream hadn't been a nightmare after all. It had been a prophecy.

"God, why? Why?" he cried.

He looked down at the bridle, twisting through his hands, a chafing reminder of his plight. Then, compressing his lips into an angry slit, he flung it to the ground and kicked it. That wasn't enough. He went over and picked up the bridle, then flung it into the underbrush, letting go a violent scream.

Suddenly he felt a nudge on his back and, turning, saw the bear looking at him with those black, coal-like eyes of his twinkling brightly and something wet and purple dripping from his muzzle.

Immediately Aeryck's brow cleared of the maledictions like a flush of birds. He managed a weak smile. "Hello, big fella." He sighed. "I see you've had your breakfast."

The bear bawled cheerfully, then lowered his shoulder for the boy to climb onto his broad back.

"No, Hauwka—your shoulder," Aeryck said. Turning up the road, he stepped into a brisk jog. A minute later he was sprawled out on the trail, staring at a bug crawling out of crack between the stones.

The great bear loomed over him from behind, his wet eyes twinkling fiercely in the shadows of his face. He let out an imperious snort.

"All right, all right," the boy said, looking up at the bear's face. "Just for a little while." Then he climbed onto the bear's massive back, and Hauwka loped away.

A bright quartering wind was up, and they made fair time before it. The bear padded steadily along with his easy, rolling gait, sometimes loping, sometimes walking, always with the heavy mass of his head rocking from side to side, marking the forward tempo.

Hope stirred in Aeryck's heart. He believed he might make it to Loch na Huric before sunset after all.

Hours passed and with them the miles. Then the toil of the road began to show in Hauwka's stride. It began as a twinge at first, then a little shudder. Then the bear began to favor his right front leg more and more. Every so often a violent shudder would tremble along his right flank, as the bear shook away the mounting pain.

Thrice Aeryck tried to dismount, as he had tried that night the blizzard blew them off course, and thrice the bear swung his big head around and growled. Then he would leap ahead into a lope. The little hope foundered in Aeryck's breast.

More hours passed.

The clouds hung low in a smothering oppression of cold metallic planes, entombing the sun and its warmth and whatever hope he had for a swift day's journey.

The miles skulked by in a procession of boulders and gnarled shrubs over a series of broken tables of land shrouded in haze. The landscape was uniformed in grays and drab greens, reflecting the boy's sullen mood, with here and there tints of purple and pink lighting the blooming crowns of heather. A pervading melancholy clung to his spirit as his thoughts and gaze narrowed to the irregular rhythm of the bear's gait.

Hauwka mounted steadily out of the bleak desolation of the moors.

Low bosomy hills, spangled with rustling streams and small ponds, lined and ringed with cattails and sedge, rose gently out of the lowland girth. Then a coarse fabric of land stretched away in an expansive skirt, with a series of folds and pleats that swept for miles in every direction. Broad squares and rectangular shapes of planted fields crisscrossed to form tartan patterns in the soil.

Adornments of trees and shrubs laced the scalloped horizon, lined the borders of farms, and fluttered delicately against the imposing sky—a gray smear against which skeins of ducks and geese arrowed toward the mountain reaches of the Grampians, far away in the north.

Grazing sheep dotted the rolling landscape, white against the looming darkness of the hills. Their muted bleating and bell sounds were a comfort to Aeryck. Occasionally he would see a herder in the distance. Heartened at the sight of another human being, he would wave.

The shepherds would turn and gaze in wonder at the youth riding by on a monstrous bear.

The wind shifted. There was a steady breeze blowing from the northeast now, whistling under the overcast sky and carrying with it the sweet tart scent of cherry blossoms and wildflowers, carrying as well the tang of something untamed and stimulating, something imposing and forbidding that sprang from every virile pore in the soil; something alive and breeding life that was altogether indigenous to the land of Picts and Scots.

But Aeryck was not thinking of the lively highland scents or of the wild sights gliding past his peripheral vision. He was thinking of Hauwka's faltering gait. He was thinking of the Saxon army marching north toward Killwyn Eden, marching toward his Dagmere and everything he held dear in the world.

And he was thinking of how, once again, the ground beneath his feet was being torn out from under him and the sky rending into dangerous shards. He was thinking of death.

Presently the world came to an abrupt halt. Aeryck felt his head jolt upon its axis, then felt the earth begin to fall swiftly away from his view. He had the queerest sensation that he was flying—or falling as though he had stepped off some precipice in a dream. And then he realized that he *was* falling. For Hauwka had begun to rise inexplicably onto his hind legs, and Aeryck wasn't quite prepared for it.

"What—" The boy flung his arms around the bear's thick neck and hanging, feet dangling and suspended over the earth, wrapped his legs frantically around the bear's girth and clung to him piggyback. "What're you doing, Hauwka?" he cried.

A low menacing growl rattled deep in the bear's throat as he sniffed the air, the hackles up in a glistening roach along his thrusting nape, with the massive head bent low and forward and shuddering with animal ferocity. He blew out a contemptuous snort.

The hair went up on the back of Aeryck's neck, and his eyes darted anxiously back and forth over the terrain. He was thinking of only one thing now. "What is it, Hauwka? Is it—"

But the bear leaped forward, clearing the ditch alongside the road with a terrific bound, hurling Aeryck airborne for a single heart-stopping moment. Then he struck out across an open meadow in a dead run, heading northeast and cutting an oblique course away from the road.

Aeryck held onto the bear's mane for his life. "Hey!" he shrieked. "Where are you going! Stop!" He could scarce catch his breath for the rush of wind in his face. His body tingled from head to toe, forcing an involuntary shout from his throat.

He managed a glance over his shoulder and gaped in astonishment at the narrow strip of road getting smaller and smaller on the hinder rim of the earth. It fast became a thread of bright light that faded into the world between the former horizons. Panic seized him. A thought crossed his mind to leap, but the hurling sweep of earth at his feet convinced him otherwise.

"Hauwka, stop! What's gotten into you! Stop!"

But the bear paid him no heed. Instead he plotted an unwavering course toward several ranks of low hills directly ahead, with garlands of trees and shrubs draped around their bases. Dark ominous-looking trees. Dark wicked-looking shrubs. Where some impending disaster loomed, he was certain.

Aeryck's eyes were riveted on the jagged slash of dark green, rising like the blade of a terrible saw. He had no idea what was lurking there— what it was in the trees or hills that had aroused the feral instincts in the bear—though his imagination was quick to supply him with several horrible suggestions. His temples hammered against the sudden surge of adrenaline through his veins.

Reaching the treeline, the bear slowed to a stealthy gait as he began to climb a lofty mount of ground. A bulwark of trees obscured the summit, forbidding ascent. Gray patches of light quivered through the flickering bowery, casting vague ghost patterns over the rise.

Occasionally the bear would pause to sniff the air, his nape bristling in shudders of animal wariness, then start forward, prowling with the delicacy of a cat. There was a continual low growl chuckling in his throat, as though some primal savagery were being vented. His head moved back and forth, sweeping over the slope pantherlike.

Aeryck felt the bear's hide trembling beneath the thick fur, felt the tremors climbing up the flanks, through his own legs and spine, and chattering in his mouth. Creeping through the umbral density of the foliage, he was certain the trees and bushes were stretching out their leafy fingers to conceal hidden yellow eyes and deadly white fangs. He couldn't comprehend the thought of dismounting the bear now. Instead his thoughts raced to prepare for what he might see ahead over the lowering summit.

His eyes scrawled recitations of terror against the dark trunks, which he half expected to step aside at any moment and reveal something hideous and deadly. His hand was clasped firmly about his sword, his knuckles describing five jagged peaks of white, each rising precipitously from its taut leathery base.

Everything was quiet, deathly quiet, but for the silent crush of earth beneath Hauwka's footfalls. The quiet rushed in to claim the intervals between them.

Aeryck heard the thick chugging drum of his heart. Heard a buzzing ring in his ears, sounding as though from a great distance. Something rifled through the air and struck his neck. Reeling, the boy swiped at it with his hand, felt a papery crush between his palm and skin. Immediately a stinging bite of pain radiated from the point of impact. Opening his fingers he saw a crumpled wasp stabbing vainly at the air with its tiny stinger. A curse spat over his lips. He crushed its head and flicked it away, then nursed the wound on his neck.

Hauwka reached the summit and paused warily.

The hill—the forward slope of which cut away to form a wall of bluffs—overlooked a long and narrow valley that stretched off into the distance on a southerly trajectory. The bear's instincts tingled with cunning alertness. The air buzzed with the knowledge of certain danger.

The winds were capricious, racing up the valley, flying up the bluffs, and squirreling around in the trees, then racing back down the valley. The bear lifted his snout to the wind, caught some scent with a startling flare of his nostrils, then turning his head froze like a hound on the point. He stood shuddering in cold fury.

Aeryck, momentarily distracted by the burning welt on his neck, followed Hauwka's point. And when he saw, he immediately forgot about the wasp sting, and his face blanched. He blinked dazedly for a moment while his brain reeled violently. For what he saw dwarfed his imagination, crumpled the former images into a wad of refuse and tossed it to the wind.

"Oh, God, no," he gasped. "No. Not now! Not now."

It began as a grunt. There was contempt in it, but there was satisfaction in it as well. The grunt evolved into a throaty chortle, both contempt and satisfaction still present, each building on the other. Then, looking back at the long column behind him, Sarteham threw back his head and roared, and when he had finished there was only arrogance hissing through his clenched teeth.

Riding alongside, Spang beamed proudly. "They're a fine bunch, I'd say," he gloated, hoping for a nod of approval. "Aye! The deffil's own."

But Sarteham only grunted and looked away at the bluffs ahead. His eyes, vigilant and sharp, searched the trees lining the ridge on the left side of the valley for movement. There was none. Though it seemed a fine place for an ambush, he thought.

Spang bristled sourly, observing the large Pict out of the corner of his eye. *There's no pleasing him,* he thought. He had spent the past four months scouring the countryside, raising an army for Sarteham to command. And what did he get for it? Cold-shouldered contempt. His eyes narrowed hatefully on the side of the large Pict's head.

When Sarteham suddenly glanced back at him, Spang was slow in recovering his murderous stare and was caught unprepared. A full second passed before his brain processed the information, and when it did he flushed a bright crimson and jerked his head away, too obviously, throwing his startled glance at nothing on the horizon with a little shudder of his head.

Sarteham snickered coldly in triumph.

Spang melted back into the column, still looking at nothing on the horizon. Something inside him withered and crawled into a dark corner. And from that moment on he was mindful never to let his eyes sweep through the same plane that was dominated by the back of Sarteham's head. Instead, when looking from one side of the valley to the other, he was careful to observe some formation in the clouds or the flight of a passing bird while making the transition.

Occasionally he would turn in his saddle and review the men with a surly grunt, as if to reclaim some remnant of authority. His chin would jut forward just so, with the thick lower lip pursed proudly, and then, with a condescending nod, he would arch one of his brows so violently it seemed as though it might leap off his sloping skull. It was a menacing expression that he would wrangle his features into—a configuration of facial lines and planes that he had no doubt contrived in his youth, then honed to its present meanness. It was a brutish, simian meanness.

However the men were not impressed. They were thinking only of the great plunder they would take. Each wore a killer's mask. Their heads were bent forward with insatiable violent eyes that scoured the countryside, burning hotter and hotter in their lust for blood sate the nearer they drew to Loch na Huric.

Several hundred men were in the column, about half of whom were mounted. They were well-armed with battle-axes and broadswords and pole-axes, each man hefting his weapon with practiced facility. Some of them favored stout bows. But as a rule the Picts preferred to kill their enemies up close, so that they could look into their eyes while their lives were being torn from them.

It couldn't be said that they were warriors, not in the noblest sense of the word. Most were either thieves or murderers who had crawled out from some rock or back-alley haunt at the beck and call of Spang. Hired killers who, like Spang, would slit a throat for a farthing—any throat, man, woman, or child's—and derive sadistic pleasure from it.

But because it was Brynwald's throat they were after, every one of them would gladly have done it for nothing. For Brynwald had made many enemies on his rise to power, and each of them had a private vendetta to settle with the man.

Most of them were bare-chested, with limbs painted or tattooed with all manner of hideous designs and faces. Some had shaved their heads for battle, leaving only a topknot, then painted their faces and upper torsos solid red or blue, so as to instill fear in the hearts of their opponents. It did. For each of them looked more ghoul than man. Perhaps they were. They were certainly a fierce-looking lot. Or, as Spang had said, "the deffil's own."

Aeryck stared in disbelief as the column of Picts made its way toward his position. This was no mere raiding party; this was a small army fit for battle. He glowered at them, half hoping, half praying that the earth would open up before them and swallow their blasphemy as it had to Dathan and Abiram and their households.

But they came, a swaggering black affront to the earth, to the race of men, and to the God who made them.

Quickly the boy made another mental calculation. At the rate the Picts were traveling, and with the sequestered route they would have to take in order to avoid detection, they would arrive in Loch na Huric sometime the following afternoon—at night most likely.

His eyes glared wildly, traveling a desperate circuit from the column of Picts to the south, where Killwyn Eden lay, to the north, where

Loch na Huric lay, then back to the column of Picts. Sarteham and Spang were in that column, he knew, though the distance was too great to make out their forms. He cringed.

Then he felt something give way in his chest. It was as though the superstructure that was his life's work suddenly collapsed in a terrible heap, all about the tender quick of his soul. He was undone. There was nothing left in him but hollow bankruptcy. He was at a total loss as to what he should do. What hope there was remaining in him withered into a tiny pile of dust and was caught away by the capricious wind. He lowered his head and began to cry. "O God, have mercy . . . have mercy . . . have mercy . . ."

And then there was a sudden shift in the wind.

Suddenly the horses in the cavalcade began to whicker and stamp their hooves and violently toss their manes. Their eyes glared. Several began to buck and kick, snorting furiously and scattering the wary foot soldiers in their vicinity. One rider was thrown as his horse reared, and broke his neck on the unforgiving Roman road. The man on foot nearest the horse greedily took its reins.

"What is it, Sarteham?" Spang cried, goading his mount forward with sharp kicks.

Sarteham jerked his horse's head around, forcing it to obey his will by the brute strength of his left arm. He glared at the bluffs ahead, caught a glint of light off a blade.

"There! In those trees! I want him dead!" he bellowed, thrusting the stump of his right arm in his direction. Turning to Spang he shouted, "Take four bowmen and see to it!"

Spang strained his eyes but could not see the hidden threat.

"Now!" Sarteham growled. Then he whipped Spang's horse with his reins.

Aeryck watched with renewed horror as five riders broke away from the column and headed toward a glen that cut through the bluffs ahead of his position.

Hauwka growled menacingly, then blew out a snort.

"Come, Hauwka," Aeryck rasped. "We must go!"

The bear wheeled about and raced down the hill, cutting a diagonal slash through the trees. The speeding ground hurled itself at them—a wedge of dark on their right, a spear of light on their left, where the overcast sun cut in, and a swirl of colors whizzing by overhead.

Aeryck kept low for fear of the treacherous limbs that tore at his clothes and skin. He blinked away the tears from his eyes, made by the stinging wind against his face. It roared past his ears. A legion of chills flapped about in his throat, beating back his breath. It seemed his heart had ceased to beat. The boy fully expected to find himself a corpse at the foot of the slope.

Reaching the baseline of the trees, the bear headed across the meadow on a northwesterly course toward the road, toward the village of Loch na Huric still hours away.

The dark points of trees fell steadily behind them. Ahead was nothing but open rolling terrain for miles, wind-blasted and treeless but for a few clumps of scrub oak and outcroppings of boulders. Falling away to the right was the mouth of the glen cutting through the hills to the long narrow valley. Aeryck glanced into the opening as they passed by, in time to see five horsemen turning into it at the far end—five wicked-looking silhouettes bent on his violent death.

A single spear of light penetrated the overcast sky and struck the face of the lead horseman.

Aeryck blinked once. Twice. Then suddenly the roaring in his ears ceased. And then all movement ceased. Everything—the sweep of the earth at his feet, the falling-away crawl of the trees, even the five horsemen galloping toward him. Everything that was time and space, sight and sound, touch and smell was caught in that slanting bolt of light, compressing the whole of the world into a singular image of hate, burning it white-hot into his brain. Even at the distance there was no mistaking who it was.

"Spang!"

The brutish Pict caught sight of the boy, laughed drunkenly, then drove his heels mercilessly into his horse's flanks.

And the Saxon juggernaut struck Catterick with the sword, then set it on fire, and the Britons fled screaming in terror.

_41_
BURDENS
OF THE SOUL

A lone rider sat motionless upon a promontory overlooking the river valley of the Tees. He had been there for hours, brooding over the terrain below him as a great bird might peer over the tract of his realm from a lofty crag. The sky, blue and clear but for the white fluffs of clouds fleeting by in a continual procession, served as an ever-moving backdrop against which the stolid immutability of that dark and singular shape of nobility stood in sharp contrast.

Two horsemen approached from the east, climbed the finger of land spreading from the promontory to the river, and approached the lone rider. They waited quietly for him to acknowledge their presence. He did not.

Instead his eyes were trained upon the features of the valley with quiet scrutiny. Like a surveyor planning a city, the man noticed how the valley formed a dogleg bend as it followed the course of the river; noted how the thrusting headland pinched the valley at the bend, giving it the shape of an elongated hourglass.

He observed the trees stretching for miles in either direction over the rise of the valley walls, clumping here and there in the draws. He noted the various outcroppings of boulders along the nearer banks and the thickets of berry bushes, with stands of birch and willow digging their roots into the wet fertile soil. And then there was the flat plain of the valley floor itself, and the way the road wound over it, through the narrow pinch of land and on to Bowes, Brough, and Killwyn Eden beyond.

It was a good place for a battle.

Only the eyes moved, the steel blue bores of light that saw something in the valley below that was not there—was there only by the force of his intellect, his imagination, his will shaping some scene in his mind, moving the integrals into position as one might move the pieces of a chess game long before a single piece is ever lifted.

The man contemplated these time and again, playing out some strategy of attack in his mind, of retreat, rethinking it, playing another, pushing this piece here and that piece there. Attack. Retreat. Considering each possibility, each gambit, the sacrifices each would require, the possible vertical, horizontal, and diagonal thrusts that would lead to the end game. To the win. Again he considered them—the gambit . . . the play . . . the sacrifice. The gambit . . . the play . . . the sacrifice.

It always came back to the sacrifice.

And then he would try another strategy, the eagle eyes glowing with intensity.

One of the horses whickered impatiently, and the man, almost as an afterthought, looked over at the two scouts.

"Yes?" He coughed, as though waking suddenly from a deep slumber.

"They've taken Catterick, Allyn," the first scout said. "Set it to the torch."

The chieftain's eyes started, and he looked away as though the eastern horizon were too painful for him to bear. But he could not escape it. A terrible image of devastation rose over the rim of his mind, and he was reminded of the prophecy of Clewes. He saw the village burning—the curling fingers of smoke reaching to the heavens with their offerings of destruction; heard the cries of the Britons—the men, the women, the children—saw their souls dangling from the dissipating black fingertips.

He had met the chieftain there once, met his wife and four sons, but he could not think of them now. It was too great a burden.

"They've turned west, Allyn," the second scout added, searching the chieftain's eyes, "and are heading toward Greta Bridge."

"We warned the people there. Some of the men will stay and fight. The rest will flee into the hills with the women and children."

"They will probably strike Bowes next, Allyn," the first scout said at last, glancing away to the east, "just like you said they would." Then he looked over at the chieftain. "Should we warn the people to leave?"

Allyndaar considered each of their faces. They were both so young, he observed, no older than Terryll. It was as though he had just seen them for the first time. "Yes, of course . . . the women and children. Move them into the hills." Then he looked away and studied the terrain.

The two men watched him, looked at one another, fidgeted uncomfortably, then settled, letting go their reins and allowing their horses to graze. They fell silent for a time, as they too gazed at the valley below. However they saw only the trees and rocks and the road winding along, saw how the valley was pinched where the promontory jutted into it, and a fast-moving river. They saw nothing of a battle but the one they had just left behind.

"It's true what Terryll said, Allyn," the second scout said, looking to the east from whence he had come. "There's more than five thousand of the beggars. The horsemen riding in front, followed by the footmen." He blew out a sigh. "Never have I imagined such an army. As many as the stars."

The chieftain glanced at him. "And the wagons?"

"The wagons?"

"Yes."

"They are to the rear."

"How far? What distance between the wagons and the foot soldiers?"

"Perhaps a half mile."

"Yes, about a half mile," the other scout agreed.

Allyndaar looked away and pondered the great chessboard below, added the new pieces, reconsidered the gambit . . . the play . . . the . . . Suddenly the chieftain looked at the two scouts. "Assemble the men of Bowes and Brough. I will join you in a few minutes."

"As you wish, Allyn!"

Then the scouts collected their reins and galloped away, leaving the chieftain of Killwyn Eden brooding over the game, his strong back and shoulders bent under the weight of the sky. He could scarce lift his eyes to the heavens.

"O merciful God, what would You have me to do?" he whispered. "I am but a man. Who am I that I should lead such men—nay, such boys—into battle? Give me your wisdom, O Father of lights. Give me Your wisdom that I might do what is right."

He felt something go out of him, but the weight remained, heavier now. Then he reined Daktahr down the hill, thinking of the gambit . . . the play . . .

He could not think of the other.

Hauwka knew instinctively that he could not outrun the horses. They were gaining on him. There was a desperate shift in his brain. Soon he would have to turn and fight.

Then his keen eyes saw a shallow depression ahead through the afternoon haze—a gully made by the runoff from the hills—saw how it angled to the right toward the ridgeline—saw the trees! His instincts blazed with a command. Coming upon the gully, he disappeared over the brim; then, hidden from view of the horsemen, he headed for the trees, splashing through a trickle of water.

Minutes later the five horsemen rode into the ravine. The horses leaped the stream and climbed out onto the flat plain on the other side

370

and into the haze. They continued blindly for several hundred yards on the same bearing, before realizing at last that they had lost sight of the bear.

Spang reined his horse to a trot and scanned the horizon, wondering whether or not he were chasing a ghost. Then, peering through a translucent veil of moisture that clung low to the earth, he caught sight of the animal, a dark speck now, entering the trees along the ridge.

He cursed. And whipping his horse as though it were somehow to blame, he renewed the fury of pursuit.

Hauwka climbed halfway up the slope, then traversed steadily along its northerly course, snorting under the strain of the toil and the barking pain in his shoulder.

Aeryck looked back, his eyes quick and glaring, and through a gossamer mist that seemed snagged in the trees he could just make out the tiny shapes of the horsemen entering the incline of the ridge a quarter mile behind them.

Hauwka had gained them a little distance. But he was limping terribly, and the boy knew that the gap would be quickly reclaimed by his pursuers.

Hauwka appeared to know too. He descended into a draw, thick with scrub oak and pine along its sides and narrow floor. Then quickly descending to the foot of the incline, the bear loped through the trees to the base of the forward slope of the draw. Coming to a small clearing in the shrubbery, he pulled up sharply and unceremoniously pitched the boy from his back.

Aeryck landed with a startled jolt. "What'd you do that for?" he cried angrily.

Hauwka answered him with a menacing growl, startling him further.

Aeryck gaped, bewildered. There was a fierceness in Hauwka's eyes that he had never witnessed before. He scrambled to his feet and, eyeing the bear strangely, moved toward him.

"What's the matter, big fella?" he asked, stretching out his hand to stroke the bear's face. He did so haltingly, not knowing what had come over his hairy friend. "It's me. I'm not going to hurt you. That's it . . ."

Hauwka snapped at his hand, then charged him, snarling ferociously.

Aeryck staggered backward, dumbstruck. And then a thought jumped into his mind. *The bear's shoulder. That must be it.*

He remembered that wounded animals often behaved erratically, sometimes turning on their owners or keepers with uncharacteristic viciousness. It was as though the pain of the wound burned away every good-natured thought in their brains, leaving only a smoldering madness.

371

If that were true of domesticated animals, how much more so with wild ones—wild animals as big as small trees, with very large fangs and very sharp claws.

Suddenly the boy was frightened of the bear. He backed away cautiously.

And then the sound of horses crashing through the trees in the distance cut through his mind with an even greater fright.

The bear looked in their direction for a moment. Then, turning his attention to Aeryck, he growled and charged him again, forcing the boy back into the thick shrubs.

It was in that moment that Aeryck understood the bear's intent, and his heart burst with emotion. "No, Hauwka," he cried. "I won't let you do it!"

He started toward the bear, but Hauwka cuffed him alongside his head, not too hard but hard enough to send him sprawling to the ground in a daze.

Hauwka lowered his head and sniffed him, let out a mournful cry, then turned and rushed up the slope, heading northeast.

Aeryck groaned. He opened his eyes and blinked dazedly at the sky. It was spinning. He sat up and let his head clear. The ground, swirling at first, then slowing, came into focus with the twigs and grass and small white stones narrowing into single images, crisp and glittering, and astounding him with a sudden feeling of remoteness. He touched the ground to assure himself that it was there.

Then he felt the horsemen coming, felt the thunder of hooves rumbling, building terrifically beneath him, and thought the earth might give way. He tensed when he saw their speeding shapes flickering down through the trees, leveling out over the floor.

Then he heard the horses breathing hard, heard the shock of spent wind punching through their nostrils and the crescendo of their flashing hooves. The men were grunting and coughing, their violent eyes gleaming through the foliage.

The boy dived behind a bush, looked up in time to see them pass by through the trees with flashes of black and brown and gray; saw their weapons glinting through the hazy light, yards away now, then climbing the other slope, the five of them; saw Spang in the lead kicking his horse brutally, then cresting the ridge and going over.

And then there was silence, and the feeling of remoteness returning.

Aeryck climbed to his feet in the silence and looked up the ridge. There was a ringing in his right ear from where the bear had cuffed him, and he nursed the place with his fingertips. It was warm to the touch.

He shook his head thinking about the bear—that marvelous bear —then he remembered Dagmere and Killwyn Eden, remembered the column of Picts advancing upon Loch na Huric, and he started running toward the mouth of the draw. When he came to the edge of the trees, a bit of shade spilling before him, he was stunned to see a rider blocking his path. Aeryck recognized him at once.

It was Spang.

The man grinned when he saw the boy, then reined his horse toward him, advancing slowly. "Thought I saw something move through here," he said, chortling wickedly. "Came back to see. Sent the others on after the beast."

Drawing closer, the man snickered through his teeth. "By the oaks! It ain't nothing but a shoat. Heh, heh, heh. Well, mannie, have you lost your way—"

The man choked on his last word as his face went sheet white.

"What's the matter, Spang?" the boy said coolly. "You look as though you've just seen a ghost."

"Y-y-you. N-no, no it can't be," the Pict stammered. "But I—"

"Thought you killed me?"

He stared at the boy—at the ghost—a word hanging lost on his tongue as a winter scene immediately resurrected in his mind. There upon the bluffs o' Dundragon he saw himself perched in a cleft of rocks, waiting in ambush.

He saw the boy, wearing the brown cloak, riding through the trees toward the broken back of the dragon; saw the pretty smile on his face when the boy looked up at him and his men rising from the rocks; saw the look of wonder in his eyes as the arrow struck deep in his chest.

He saw the boy cast his gaze heavenward, heard his strangely exultant cry, before crumpling over into the snow—he presumed dead. Yes, dead. No one could have survived that arrow.

And then the wolves were upon them, and the scene dissolved in a swirl of white.

"Aye, mannie," Spang reflected. "You've made a fool of me twice then. The first time in the tavern of Pea Gants . . . the second at the dragon, when I thought my arrow had taken care of you. But I can see plain that it didn't. All these past months you've been fooling old Spang, and he dinna take to that."

Spang ran his thumb over the haft of his battle-ax, peering into the boy's face. "You've got the luck of a deffil, shoat."

"And yours has just run out," the boy snarled, drawing his sword.

Spang laughed throatily, then grunted as his eyes narrowed on the boy. "Perhaps, mannie. Perhaps not." He spat viciously. "I ken 'twere a lucky flick of your sword what pricked my shoulder. Aye, that I'll warrant you. But this time there will be nay Pea Gants to interfere. It's just between you and me." He laughed. "And there'll be nay wolves to keep me from taking your head this time."

"Do you intend to talk me to death?" Aeryck retorted.

Spang's expression went cold. Then he dug his heels sharply into his horse's flanks and charged the boy.

Aeryck leaped out of the way, diving just below the deadly wedge of Spang's blade. Hitting the ground, he rolled up onto his feet and readied himself for another charge.

Spang wheeled his horse around and rushed him again, a sneer scrawled over his face.

Aeryck waited, holding his sword with both hands, the tip forward and tracing a tight circle of silver light in the air. He bounced lightly from foot to foot, keeping his weight low and on the balls of his feet as Aurelius had taught him.

Balance! Balance! Balance! The monk's voice echoed in his mind.

The boy's focus was honed to two pinpoint glows of light burning in Spang's face. He waited until the horse was nearly on top of him, using its bulk as a shield, then rolling away in a spin . . . ducking . . . feeling the sharp cleft of wind over his head . . . then pushing away off his feet . . . leaping . . . feeling his body flattening, thrusting like a blade . . . driving his sword into the back of Spang's thigh.

The Pict let out a scream as he reeled out of the saddle, screwing backward into the ground with a bone-jarring crunch. He writhed, clutching his thigh. His face contorted. Then his eyes, jerking open with a start of horror, darted fiercely around him, looking for the boy. And finding him looming off to one side, he locked onto his face—his eyes.

A curse spat through Spang's clenched teeth. Then as he began to edge up onto his right elbow with little hops, he winced. His left arm, broken, hung useless at his side. Again he cursed. He managed to sit upright with a supreme effort, and doing so he gaped incredulously at the blood streaming from the wound in his thigh.

Aeryck approached the man warily, as one might approach a wounded animal or a coiled snake, with the tip of his sword pointed at his throat. Glaring down at Spang, he too resurrected that scene upon the bluffs. He too saw the look on Brother Stephen's face—that sweet, gentle face, and the smile, the sad smile without a hint of guile in it, and those dead eyes gazing up at him.

Grimacing, the boy painfully buried the shades of that scene, everything but the hate and the anger. He felt the sum of them surge in

374

his breast, swell into his throat, then stream out through his eyes a murderous fire.

"Go ahead, mannie, kill me," Spang spat, squinting up at him. "I can see the want of it in your eyes. Aye, those deffil eyes of yours, and your deffil luck. Go ahead and kill me!" He laughed contemptuously. "Aye, kill me, and I'll beat you yet!"

"Shut up! Just shut up!" Aeryck snarled, glaring down at the foul wretch who deserved nothing but death, who deserved a thousand deaths for his crimes. He took a half step forward, trembling with rage. His sword blade quivered as his fingers flexed over the handle.

That's right, Worm, he deserves to die, he heard a voice whispering in his soul. *Go ahead and kill him. Have your vengeance. You will be at peace then. Go ahead, Worm, kill him. Kill him!*

The boy raised his sword obediently. And then he heard another voice, from a place deeper in his soul. *Hate is a deffil of a thing, lad—a terrible master, if you 'low it. It'll take from a man his youth—eat it through like a canker till there's nothing left of his soul but the black hate itself.*

The tip of Aeryck's sword bobbled, then lowered and hung suspended before him, rage quivering over its length. His eyes alternately burned, then cooled, as a fierce battle tore his soul wide open. He felt himself buffeted back and forth between infinite points in the heavenlies with the speed of thought as the two voices strove against the other.

Spang's face became a blur before him, then a vague splotch of white at the end of a long dark tunnel. Featureless. Then lost to his mind.

But Spang was watching him, was eyeing him with fierce animal cunning. His eyes shifted furtively, looking for his battle-ax—the wounded animal seeking to stretch out its wretched existence another wretched minute. He caught sight of the thing three feet away in the grass, off to his right.

He looked up at the boy, who seemed caught in a trance. He narrowed his eyes shrewdly, then glanced back at the weapon. Three feet away. An arm's length. His good arm's length. He inched his hand toward the ax, his eyes fixed on the stupid stare of the boy. Then clutching the haft, he swung it.

But the violent action was more than his broken arm would allow, and he crumpled to the ground under the pain. The battle-ax fell harmlessly at the boy's feet.

And Aeryck jolted to his senses. He looked down at the ax, looked back at Spang, then bent over and picked up the weapon. "You won't be needing this anymore."

Spang was of no mind to object. His features were clenched into a scowl of pain. Then, screwing open an eye, he glared at the boy, glared at the tip of his sword, all the while striving with his features to conjure some brutish caricature of himself that was designed to intimidate. But he looked nothing more than a pathetic imbecile.

Aeryck stared at him coldly, his hand flexing on the haft of his sword. And then he realized that the hate that once burdened his mind was nothing more than a hollow shell, a dark passageway through which some ranting brute had been given access into the terrain of his soul, free to storm about at will, to bully him, to stalk him, ambush him, to eat away at the very marrow of his being. But now it was gone, collapsed in on itself with a terrific weight and consumed by a fiery judgment, until there was nothing more of the thing but a tiny glimmer of pity.

The boy stared at the man and felt a black thing taking flight from his soul, leaving nothing behind but a sorry anecdote. He took a deep breath.

Spang glowered at him, forcing a grin of defiance.

Aeryck shook his head. "You lose." He looked up and saw the Pict's horse grazing in the cool grass beneath the trees, then walked over to it and took up the loose reins.

Spang followed him with his eyes, studying him curiously. "Where do you think you're going? That's my horse!"

Aeryck mounted the animal without a retort.

"You're weak, mannie," Spang spat viciously. "Just like Brynwald is weak. You and your weak Christian god. You should have killed Sarteham and me when you had the chance." He waited. Still no response. "Many more will die because of your weakness. Women and children. Aye, think of it, lad—the children too." He laughed wickedly. "But then I guess you ken aboot that, don't you? Aboot the fair-faced ones taking your arrows, I mean."

Aeryck rode past him without looking down. He goaded the horse gently into a trot.

Spang laughed. "You're a fool, mannie! A fool, d'you hear? Dinna think you can sing to Brynwald. My men are all aboot these hills looking for your bonnie face!" He hiked up onto his elbow, winced in pain, then called out, "Dinna think you've seen the last of me, boy! *Och*, no! Nay matter where you go, old Spang'll be looking over your shoulder. Aye! I'll come ridin' into the gates of hell after you, if need be!"

Spang chortled, pleased with his revilements.

Then he grunted in his misery. He twisted, struggling to lift himself into a sitting position, grimaced. He clasped the wound in his thigh again and looked around for any sign of his men. A bewildered look spread over his face. They should have caught up to that beast and killed it by now. Should be on their way back.

He chortled at some base thought. Then, frowning, he muttered something incoherent. His brain could not determine whether to be happy he was alive or angry that the boy got away. He glanced up and saw the youth in the distance—a gray shape now—galloping away, heading north-west into the haze.

"The *fool*," he growled.

A movement in the trees off to his left caught his attention. Look-ing up he saw a white streak through the underbrush. He brightened. "That you, Clynne? Ha, ha. That you, Ruppie?" Then he saw the eyes, the yellow eyes looking down at him through the apertures in the foliage —several pairs of them—coming toward him, snarling with bared fangs.

Terrified, Spang climbed to his feet, and, cradling his broken arm, began to hobble away, whimpering.

Aeryck turned when he heard the scream.

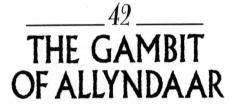

42
THE GAMBIT
OF ALLYNDAAR

Olaf did not like the way the valley narrowed ahead. Neither did he like the sudden rise of hills on either side of the road nor the way the river came up close on the left. He did not like the trees, or the rocks, but especially those hills, lush with heather and shrubbery, on the other side of the river. It would be an ideal place for an ambush. He halted the cavalcade of horsemen, throwing a big arm in the air, then ordered several scouts ahead to reconnoiter.

The scouts left at a gallop, and when they returned the news was favorable, each saying that the Britons had fled, that there was only a handful of men left in the village of Bowes to defend it.

The Viking frowned. A handful of men. This campaign had not gone as he had anticipated or as he had hoped. He looked back on his men. He saw it in their faces too—a perfunctory listlessness that had dulled the fierceness in their eyes. It had been too easy. The Britons were a beaten people, and there was no glory in defeating a beaten people.

Olaf signaled his men forward, and the column lurched ahead with a loud grunt. The bunched-up companies of horsemen and foot soldiers quickly stretched out along the road into their marching intervals, with the men looking down at the road and back into their minds as they tried to remember the faces of their wives and sweethearts; or looking ahead to the evening camp, thinking of the ale and wine and the gambling that would break the monotony.

But the Norseman was gazing warily at the hills on the far side of the river and thinking that he didn't like them.

The men of Bowes watched from their places of concealment as the horsemen entered the narrow pass, proudly bearing their shields of black and red and their standards hanging limp in the thick air. The Britons were hidden behind rocks and trees, hidden in the thick bracken on the hills and in the thickets along the river, and were invisible to the passing leviathan. Each man held his longbow at the ready. Each eye was trained on a mark—a spot about a foot above the crimson wolf's head on a shield—waiting for the signal to attack.

The horsemen rode through the pass, and immediately the river fell away, allowing broad green swards to open on either flank and with the hills falling back to a respectable distance.

Olaf breathed easier in the open and looked back upon the monstrous army. He could see the end of the cavalry now, and beyond, stretching away through the pass and around the dogleg bend in the valley, were Horsa and the Wolf and an army the likes of which he had imagined time and again from the earliest days of his childhood.

A surge of pride boomed in his chest. The gods had fashioned him for this moment. They had given him a body fit for battle, one perfect in frame and symmetry, with the muscles and sinews taut and honed to serve a singular purpose—to kill one's enemies on the field of battle. Then they had breathed into his mortal sheath a burning zeal for war, had forged in him a skill and cunning to execute it, had placed him at the head of a great demonstration of war as their chosen son.

The Norseman felt an energy vibrating over the surface of his skin, as though his body could not contain the glory of his being. A shudder of delight rippled through his limbs and burned through his eyes. He felt the great wind of power on his back. *Ah, such glory!*

He took a deep breath and blew it out a laughing triumph, exulting in the knowledge that the gods had favored him above all others. He laid his palm against the solid haft of his sword and thought of Odin.

Now for an army to pit himself against, an army of fighting men against whom he might test his strength and cunning. Now for a worthy adversary that might bequeath to him much glory and prove to the gods that they had chosen wisely.

Olaf looked ahead and thought of the villages of Bowes and Brough, wondering what manner of men he would find there. Would they be rabbits like the others—those pitiful wretches whose screams for mercy only elicited in him chilling contempt? Or would he find there men who would fight and die well?

Then his mind reached beyond these to the village of Killwyn Eden, to the British chieftain named Allyndaar, the legendary bowman of whom he had heard such tales of valor. His brow was ablaze with a terrible reverie, and he smiled in it.

Secret eyes watched keenly as the foot warriors followed the horsemen into the pass, sounding like continuous rolling thunder, and waited until a third of them had marched through it.

Hidden well below the line of the ridge, an archer was crouched in waiting. When he saw the warrior on the summit turn toward him and lower his arm, he loosed an arrow with a red streamer tied to it. The arrow landed several hundred feet away, toward the rear of the Saxon army.

A second archer saw it fall and ran to it. He took careful aim and loosed the arrow, sending it rifling several hundred more feet, below the line of the ridge.

And likewise did several other bowmen retrieve the arrow and loose it to the next link in the chain, over trees, across meadows and streams, always out of sight of the Saxon army marching toward Bowes in the opposite direction.

When the last archer retrieved the arrow, he saw that the streamer was red and not white, and he smiled. Then he hurriedly climbed a small knoll, took note of the line of wagons clattering along the road, saw the contingent of horsemen assigned to guard them, smiled again, then signaled to a man atop the hill on the farther side of the river.

The man across the river returned his signal and disappeared from sight.

For a few moments there was heard only the incessant drone of iron wheels clattering over the stone road, mingled with the sound of the River Tees rushing alongside. Birds flirted playfully in the trees along the banks, and butterflies winked about on the heavy currents of spring air, playing tag.

Heads of riders and teamsters nodded sleepily to the languid symphonies of the late afternoon and would jolt occasionally to an upbeat in the tempo.

Many of the horsemen thought it a curious turn in the wind that made the unusual sound, the sharp quarter note that broke the lazy rhythm of the music. Those who looked up and saw the streaks of light and dark falling toward them knew too late what had caused it. Several managed to gasp.

Immediately an outcry arose along the wagon train as British arrows found their marks, piercing the hides of man and beast. Men and horses screamed as the dead and wounded fell to the ground. The wagons shuddered to a halt as horses were felled and writhed in their traces.

The horsemen wheeled their mounts, furiously looking for their assailants—anything—a shape, a face, a quiver of betraying movement. But there was nothing, nothing that they could see. There was only the whistling scream of another shower of arrows, then the sickening sounds of the broadheads thudding into their midst and finding the killing places. More men fell. Horses screamed, rearing in terror, pitching their riders to the ground, then trampling them. Those pulling the wagons careered off the road into the ditches, overturning them.

Still volley after volley of arrows fell to their marks. The men shouted to one another with astonished expressions. Riders charged this way and that, without aim or purpose other than to flee the deadly fusillades.

Several horsemen charged the river in a desperate tactical strike at anything, seeing nothing but the rocks and shrubs along the bank and then the sudden spray of feathered shafts that rifled toward them. Other horsemen charged the opposite wall of the valley, equally desperate, but were felled by a hail of deadly missiles that had appeared suddenly from the sky.

Terror gripped the hearts of the Saxons, who, not seeing their enemy, believed that the earth had risen against them and that the sky had fallen upon them, both of them like enormous cymbals striking the other in a clangorous crescendo.

Then panic danced among the wagons, piping a little discordant tune and inciting chaos. Though none of the men were cowards, each man's will for courage was violently torn from his breast by the snarling beast of war, and the concerted will of the whole quickly degenerated into a boiling cacophony.

Suddenly a great shout arose, stunning the horsemen. Even the foot soldiers in the main body a half mile ahead heard it and turned.

And then the rocks and shrubs and trees and banks disgorged a throng of Britons, startling the Saxon horsemen further. They sought to flee, but everywhere they turned they were met by a charging wall. Clumps of furious fighting dotted along the wagon train, as the men of Bowes fell upon the confused rearguard with sword, battle-ax, and well-aimed arrow, showing no mercy to these rapers of their homeland. Torches were set to the wagons, and soon scores of smoke columns were rising like black snakes against the sky.

News of this buzzed along the forward column of Saxons.

When Olaf wheeled his horse about and saw the smoke rising in the distance, he spat out a curse. With the pass clogged with foot soldiers, he knew there was no way for his cavalry to get through to the rear without trampling his own men. And he realized in that moment that the supply train was lost. Something else whined in his brain as well, just out of his sight.

Then one of his men cried out. "Olaf! Across the river!"

The Norseman followed his point and beheld the hills coming to life with scores of British archers. His eyes glared open with a terrible thought. There it was, shouting now—he had led his men into a trap! Again he cursed.

He charged his horse over the field as he assessed their predicament, several thoughts rifling through his mind on a single blaze of fury. He knew that, with the river between them, there was no way for his men to mount a counteroffensive. He knew that they would be cut down like so many dogs by the longer range of the British longbows. He knew also that they could not retreat, neither could they swing to the right or left, but that they could only advance to the west.

"To Bowes, men!" he cried, spurring his mount forward. "Lest we all perish in this place!"

And then the sky became suddenly dark with British arrows.

Three hours later the Saxons had cleared the pass, leaving behind hundreds of slain warriors and the charred remains of two hundred supply wagons.

The Saxon juggernaut, though limping somewhat, took Bowes (if marching into the village unopposed could be rightly called "taking it"). They did not set it to the torch, for they needed the village to lick their wounds. Neither did they strike it with the sword, for the men of Bowes who had remained earlier as part of Allyndaar's ruse had cleared out once the battle in the pass commenced, taking with them whatever foodstuffs or supplies that might be considered useful to their enemy.

The little hall of Bowes was filled with captains and lieutenants who, in the leaden aftermath of battle, were awaiting the arrival of the overlord. Olaf was there, as was the Wolf, who stood across the room from him, looking out a window. The room was enshrouded with a dark encumbrance. Men looked up from the floor and cast secretive eyes at one another. They looked back at the floor. They moved and breathed in a collective guilt. There was a need for a collective atonement. Their low murmuring was evidence of this.

The young captain who had been in command of the rearguard stood off to one side of the somber gathering, waiting anxiously to brief Horsa on the attack on the wagons. His thoughts were drawn into a singular line of defense. It was not his fault. He was innocent of wrongdoing.

When Horsa stormed into the hall, he paused just inside the door and made a quick sweep of the officers. The room clapped to silence. Then locking onto the young captain, the overlord strode over to him.

The captain stiffened.

Horsa peered fiercely into his eyes. "Why did you run?" he demanded.

The captain held his stare. "They were everywhere, Overlord," he said evenly. "When I saw that the wagons were lost—that there was nothing more to—"

"You are a coward," the overlord interrupted coldly. "I will not suffer a coward" And having said this, he drew the captain's sword from its scabbard and ran him through.

The young captain blinked at him in disbelief, then crumpled to the floor and was left to die.

There was a sudden release of guilt in the air.

"It could have been avoided," Horsa glowered, brandishing the sword at his officers. "It will not happen again!" Then, flinging the blade to the floor with a clatter, he launched into a tirade, upbraiding each of the men, calling them out by name, sparing no one.

Norduk watched him, his ocher eyes narrowing bitterly as he chafed under the overlord's insults. A thought went through his mind to walk over to the man and seize his throat, to have done with the fool and the charade of his power. That was Norduk's thought. It was a mannish thought, a smoldering flame of sentient light that yet glimmered on the tortured wick of his humanity.

But the other thing raging in him would not permit it, the tyrant that controlled his mind, his body, and his soul. No, Cernunnos would not allow Norduk to assert his way. Instead he would allow Horsa to have his day in the sun, to go on strutting petulantly behind a facade of power until there was no further need for him.

The Wolf chuckled throatily, amused with the overlord's little tirade. It was such a pleasant diversion.

But Olaf kept silent. He made no protestations. He had already redressed himself far more severely than the overlord ever could.

The overlord's voice became a drone as the Norseman's mind moved back into itself, recalling each event of the day, observing with amazement the scattered pieces over the board. He too saw the battle as a game, however now as a player in defeat demanding a mental rematch to see where he had gone wrong.

But he knew where that had happened, didn't he? He knew it going into the narrow pass. It had been obvious to him then; he had seen it coming, and yet he hadn't seen it. Why not? He had underestimated his adversary, that was why. He had been outthought, outstrategized, outmanuevered, and because of it had witnessed a flawless execution of battle tactics against himself. It left him feeling as though his heart had been ripped out of his chest, with a terrible hollowness rushing into its place. He wouldn't let that happen again. No. A wise man will learn from his mistakes, but a fool will continue in them without profit.

And so he pored over the field of play in his mind. He saw the river, the narrow pass, the hills on either side bending like the joint of a gargantuan arm. He saw the screen of shrubs and trees and outcroppings of boulders, from which hidden archers could strike. Yes, it was a good place for an ambush.

He retraced each of the moves: first his move, then his opponent's, then his again, then his opponent's, back and forth, cause and effect, the quick forward thrusts and retreats . . . the gambit . . . the play . . . the end game. With every move he sought to catch a glimpse into the mind facing him, the way it thought through a strategy given the circumstances—how it might think and strategize again given new circumstances, given a new field of battle.

He turned the board around in his mind in order to view the game from his opponent's perspective, to study the game from his skin, as it were, to see it through his eyes—the eyes that he could feel upon him even now, studying his own side of the board, scrutinizing his moves from the vantage point of the victor, mocking his failure.

The Norseman shook his head bitterly. No, he would not let that happen again.

Olaf looked up from his thoughts at the overlord. The man was still droning fiercely, would drone on for another hour perhaps. He had repeated his diatribe three times already and showed no sign of letting up.

Then he noted the look on the Wolf's face, and he felt a little shiver go through his limbs like a heralding cry of warning. For something about the face was unnerving, sinister, something human yet inhuman, compelling his eyes yet repulsing him. Olaf remembered the last time he had met with the man alone in his chamber—remembered the smothering presence of evil in which he could scarce move or breathe.

While he was yet considering the matter, the Wolf looked over at him with a quick snap of his head, as though he had read his thoughts. The Wolf stared at him for a moment with a wondrous incandescence burning beneath the wolfskin shroud, holding Olaf's gaze in a snare of growing horror.

And then he smiled, the Wolf did. And the smile completed the horror of the eyes, for it was nothing but a thin humorless slit in his face, benign of expression, with the lips turned up ever so slightly at the corners. The smile had all the warmth of a stone radiating from it, all the sincerity of a dead man's grin, and together with the eyes and the shroud, and something altogether inscrutable, it composed the face of a monster.

Olaf again felt a rush of suffocating terror clutch his throat, and he gasped. His mind reeling, he returned a salute with a curt nod of his head, then quickly tore his eyes from the man and gazed out the window, taking in several large drafts of air.

Later the Norseman strode alone through the encampment to clear his mind of the briefing, to cleanse his soul of that monster face. Everywhere he looked he saw the faces of men gazing inwardly at their souls, every man sifting through the ashes of defeat for some kind of expiation.

This was good, he thought. It was necessary. He knew that from the ashes there would arise a blaze of anger, a corporate cry for vengeance that would rekindle the fierceness in the men's eyes. The Norseman chortled to himself. He wondered if the Britons were aware that they had inadvertently done him a great service.

As he walked along the perimeter of the village, something in the distance caught his attention, and turning to it he noticed that it was a rider sitting on the top of a distant ridge—a solitary black shape cut against the burning hues of the sunset like a sentinel keeping watch. Even at the distance Olaf could sense twin bores of light drilling into his mind, studying him, trying to intimidate him, daring him to make his next move.

Olaf grunted. A British scout perhaps? No. There was a certain bearing that the horseman projected, the way he sat with stoic appraisal against the sky, as though he commanded everything in his sight. No, he was not a scout, Olaf was certain. He was someone greater—much greater. He smiled.

Druell walked up to Olaf and stood beside him for a while, gazing at the lone horseman. "He has been there like that for over an hour now, Olaf," he said, breaking the silence. "Should I send riders after him?"

The Norseman chortled. "No. They would only be chasing after the wind," he replied, "a wind that would likely send a downpour of deadly bolts upon them."

A low animal cough rattled deep in Olaf's chest. He knew, beyond any doubt now, that he had at last found a worthy adversary, one whose defeat would earn him the glory he so rightly deserved. He was pleased. And a thin, arrogant grin spread beneath his ropelike mustache.

He would not underestimate him again.

It was a spectacle the likes of which Allyndaar had never seen in all his years. The village was teeming with warriors—Angles, Saxons, and Jutes—making preparations for the evening camp, and the men hovered around the cooking fires, clattering their tinware and grumbling in time-worn tradition as the great armored beast demanded sustenance for its day's toil.

The village could not contain the beast—only the head of it. The rest of the thing—the broad, scaly mass of its back and tail—spilled beyond the gates, glinting in the waning daylight. It stretched as far as the chieftain could see up the river valley, with bonfires blazing and tents for the commanders and captains going up in the broad fields on either side of the road, then disappearing around some hills in the distance.

Allyndaar shook his head in amazement. Such an army! He knew in that terrible sweep of his eyes that the day had gone better than he could ever have hoped. He knew that God had given them a great victory, for not one of his men was lost, and only a few were wounded. The gambit had worked. Flawlessly. The leviathan could bleed.

However, as the chieftain gazed down upon the village of Bowes, he knew that the beast would not be so easily tricked again.

His eyes shifted to the broad river valley of Brough, ten miles to the west. Surrounding the village were miles of rolling farmland, dotted here and there with forest, with the river swinging a mile to the south. Such an ambush would be impossible there, given the openness of its approach.

He would have to conceive another plan. He had to wound the beast again before it advanced upon Killwyn Eden. As he began to give it thought he heard a rider approaching him from behind. Turning, he smiled.

"Terryll!"

The boy waved a salute. "Hail, Papa!" he cried. He drew alongside his father and gazed down at the Saxon encampment. "Is it true, Papa—what the men said about the battle today?"

Allyndaar looked back toward the valley where the fighting had taken place. His face was calm, without pride. "God was with us," he said quietly.

Terryll beamed. "We can beat them, Papa! I know we can!"

Allyndaar smiled at his son. "You met with Brynwald?"

"Not exactly," Terryll said.

Allyndaar winced. "Not exactly?"

Terryll explained how he had met Aeryck on the road and given him the message. "He said that Brynwald could send maybe five or six hundred men—maybe more, if they can get Oswald's help."

Allyndaar's face turned suddenly grave.

"What's wrong, Papa?"

"You're telling me that we really don't know if Brynwald will come?"

"Aeryck said he would."

Allyndaar glared at him. "Aeryck is not Brynwald! I told you to go to Brynwald—to hear it from his own mouth."

Terryll appeared stunned. "I-I just thought that—"

"How can I plan a defense without knowing for certain?" Allyndaar snapped. "I've got to know what my strengths are." There was an interlude of furious silence. "Terryll—why?"

The boy groaned. "I just thought that if I could warn the people at Caer Luhl and Bowness that—"

386

"You mean you thought that you might just stop by for a quick visit with Gwyneth!"

Terryll stared at him, hurt. Then he looked away.

Allyndaar saw the look and shook his head remorsefully. He waited a moment, then took a deep breath and blew out a draft of anger and tension. "I didn't mean that, Terryll," he said, changing his tone. "I know that you meant well. But don't you see it, son? If the Saxons take Killwyn Eden, the rest of the villages will fall without contest. I needed the assurance that Brynwald would come."

Terryll sank into a sullen mood and gazed thoughtlessly into the distance. "Maybe I should just ride back up there and ask him."

Allyndaar ignored the remark. Instead he looked back at the Saxon encampment and studied it for a long while, considering his next move, considering several next moves. Finally he asked, "When did Aeryck say Brynwald would come?"

Stirring from his heavy thoughts, Terryll seemed to do a quick calculation in his head. "Four—maybe five days. No, four days at the most."

Allyndaar took a deep breath. "Four days . . . four days. Let us pray that you are right."

Terryll brightened. "They'll come, Papa," he said earnestly. "Brynwald said he'd come whenever we needed him. You remember."

"I know, son. I know." Allyndaar looked at him and smiled grimly. "Now come with me, and I'll tell you what I want you and the men of Bowes and Brough to do. We'll see if we can't set a fitting snare for this beast."

Terryll brightened. "We can beat them, Papa. I know we can."

Allyndaar nodded his head thoughtfully. "With God's help, son."

The chieftain cast a final glance back at the village, now almost dark with the sun going down in the west. Then he looked north toward the land of Picts and Scots. An anxiousness edged into his features.

"Four days." It was like a prayer. He thought about it for a moment, calculating the distance, then said to himself, *Brynwald should be on the road by now. O God, I pray that he is on the road.*

Then the two of them rode off the hill.

43
A STORMING
OF THE GATES

Long dark clouds passed slowly over the moon like a procession of barges, traveling silently up the meandering valley of the Annon with their airy freight. Every cloud barge drew a momentary curtain of darkness over the silvery terrain. And each having passed, the moon would shine luminous over the village of Loch na Huric, almost as bright as day, and flicker over the surface of the river like a million tiny stars. Some darker clouds, moving in quickly from the east, looked as if they had rain in them.

It was just past midnight. Still a few lights were burning, showing like tiny yellow squares on a sea of black. A dog barked somewhere; it was not the bark of warning but of some primal loneliness, and he kept at it for a long while. It was an annoying sound to the listening ear, like a continual grating. Then everything went quiet, and there was only the sound of the river rustling along its banks and a light breeze stirring through the trees.

Sarteham gazed down upon the hamlet from one of the steep hills overlooking it. His eyes shifted warily to the village hall, ferreting out any sign of movement, then shifted to the stables, and then to a few of the homes. He saw nothing. The village was peaceful, in quiet repose for the evening, except where the lights shone with their little halos of saffron gold.

Then his eyes locked onto the hillock and noted that the ring of monoliths had been recently torn down. He could just make out their black shapes fallen away from the ring like the staves of a barrel spread out on the ground. He grunted. The altar was still there, he noted, standing bleached and desecrated in the moonlight. A curse escaped his lips.

His eyes shifted when he heard a rider approaching.

The horseman drew up next to him and also looked over the village. "Looks quiet to me," he rasped.

Sarteham ignored the remark.

"The men are through the pass now and waiting along the river," the horseman added, after a few moments more of considering the village.

"Sentries?"

"Just one. By the south gate. He's asleep."

The man grunted. "Brynwald has grown weak."

Sarteham did not respond. Instead he watched intently as a rectangle of light opened on one of the houses and the silhouette of a man passed through it, carrying a bundle in his arms—refuse likely.

Moments later the silhouette passed back through the light. The rectangle closed behind him, the tiny square of light blinked off, and the house was dark. One by one the other remaining squares of light in the village blinked off, and then everything was dark under the passing-by clouds, and there was only the rush of the river.

Sarteham turned to the rider. "When you hear the shout, it will be your signal to storm the village. You ken what to do."

The rider's teeth gleamed in the faint light. "Aye."

Sarteham saw his look. "Brynwald is mine."

"Aye."

The rider reined his horse down the ridge, angling back toward the river pass on the south end of the village, where more than two hundred footmen were spread out, hidden in the bulrushes, clutching their weapons anxiously.

Sarteham rode along the ridge, heading the opposite direction to where the other half of his force was waiting for him at the north end of the valley. His eyes swept the broad river basin below him and imagined the rush of his horsemen. He felt a shiver of excitement go through him. He glanced over his shoulder at the receding black rise of the village. *Finally*, he thought, chortling. *It is time.*

A light drizzle began to fall as the black clouds swept in from the east, though the moon was still clear of them and shining over the hills. The large Pict lifted his eyes to the sky, and the wet felt good on his face.

The horsemen were gathered by the mouth of the valley, a long dark formation against the wet shine of the hills. A low murmur buzzed through the ranks, then trailed away into a brooding silence. The horses' heads hung low and still.

Someone cursed. "I didn't sign on for no rain."

A few sullen moments passed.

"We ride through blizzards, then sit around and freeze in the rain. I didn't reckon on this at all."

"Keep it to yourself," the horseman next to him said.

And then a few more sullen moments passed.

There was a grunt. "I surely hate this waiting. What are we waiting for?"

"For Sarteham to get here, fool," the second horseman said.

"*Och,* and who are you calling a fool then?"

"Shut up, you two," a third man said. It was Clynne, one of Spang's men.

"What's wrong with him?" the first man whispered.

"He's still sore from that thing with the bear," the second man said, lower.

"Bear? What bear? I heard it was wolves."

"You heard it wrong. Spang was the wolves . . . Clynne and the others was the bear."

"Troth! And I hear it was a good day for wolves," the first man said, sniggering, forgetting the rain.

"I hear it was a bad day for Spang," the second man added, joining him.

"No loss. Serves him right, chasing after bears."

"It looked like someone though."

"What looked like someone?"

"Riding the bear."

"You're daft in the bean," the first man said with a sneer. "What kind of outfit did I hitch up with anyway?"

"I told you two to shut up," Clynne snarled.

There was an interlude of silence during which the drizzle thickened into a steady rain, quickly soaking the troop of riders. Some of the horses began to snort and shudder off the water. Most remained sullen and quiet.

The men turned when they saw a dark shape angling toward them.

Seeing who it was, Clynne drew his battle-ax. "It is time."

"Good."

"I dinna like this rain though," the first man said. "It clouds my thinking." He laughed at his little joke.

The second man looked at him. "You are truly a fool."

Aeryck lay flat against the earthen berm that encircled the village. The rain had gathered into little muddy rivulets and trickled down the slope and soaked him through to the skin. The smell of the wet earth rose into his face, and the wetness of everything, and the cold, and the thought of what lay ahead chilled him to the bone and made him feel miserable.

Then the clouds passed by, and the moon shone bright again, illuminating the valley and the fields beyond the berm, and there was a sudden rush of cold air. The boy shivered, thinking about everything and trying not to think. Then he felt something go cold and hollow inside him.

Brynwald crouched beside him. He was thinking about what lay ahead also, but there was no fear in him. The anger in him had burned it away. He chided himself over and over for not having killed Sarteham when he had the opportunity months before. He looked up the valley and caught a glint of light off something in the distance. And then he saw the black mass of horsemen advancing silently around the hills, with the bright moon outlining one side of them.

"This is it, lads," he whispered. And the news buzzed from man to man.

A few minutes later everyone along the berm could feel the ground shudder, and soon afterward they could hear the horses and the chafing leather and the muffled tinkling of battle gear. Everyone took hold of his weapon and narrowed his thoughts.

When Brynwald recognized Sarteham's shape riding at the head, he grunted. "You were right, kipper," he whispered to the boy. "'Tis the deffil himself, come for a vengeance."

Aeryck peered over the berm, saw the undulating wall of shapes spread out and coming down the valley, and felt his stomach turn in the great hollowness that was his chest.

He looked over his shoulder and saw several of Brynwald's men mounted and hidden in the groves of oaks. They were like parts of the trees, and because of the shadows he couldn't distinguish one from the other. But he could feel their presence, feel the intensity of their eyes burning out of the darkness. There were other warriors with Dunnald, he knew, hidden behind houses and barns, lying flat along the south berm that faced out toward the river pass across the village.

"Will Oswald get here in time, do you think?" he whispered. *"Och.* Dinna you fret nane aboot Oswald," Brynwald said. "We'll give Sarteham's men a fair welcome." He chuckled. "'Twill be a muckle show, eh, kipper?"

Aeryck wasn't feeling so grand about it. He was thinking of the horror of it. He was thinking of something else as well.

Brynwald glanced over at him and read his mind. "You're thinkin' aboot your troth again, I'll wager."

"Huh? Uh . . . yes," Aeryck said, startled out of his thoughts. "We should've been on the road by now."

Brynwald winked at the boy. "Troth, kipper, one scrape at a time." He grinned. "As soon as we take care of this rabble, we'll be on our way to the help of your bonny lass."

Aeryck looked at him and smiled. Inwardly, however, he wished that he had the same confidence. He peered back over the berm, and the horsemen were nearer now, still advancing stealthily. His stomach did another turn, and he felt a fluttering queasiness pressing out against his rib cage and robbing his lungs of air.

Gazing ahead at the black swell of the village, Sarteham spurred his horse into a gallop. Then the other horsemen put their mounts into a gallop and spread out into their battle intervals, their eyes suddenly fierce with violence and rage. The horses thundered over the wet valley floor, and their eyes glistened in the moonlight.

When they got to within two hundred yards of the berm, Sarteham goaded his horse into a run with a sharp kick and let out a bloodcurdling war cry. The others joined him, picking up the shout and sustaining it, sounding like a horde of devils ascending out of the pit. The horses were caught up in the fury of the charge, and it became a race.

The others of Sarteham's men, crouched among the bulrushes, heard the cry and rose with a howl. They stormed across the moon-washed field brandishing their weapons, all of them wild-eyed and raising a terrible uproar.

The sentry by the gate, having fulfilled his part in Brynwald's facade, ran into the village where Dunnald and the others were waiting, gathered now for the imminent clash of battle. Each man held fast, anxiously clutching his bow or battle-ax, waiting until the last moment to rush.

Brynwald waited until the horses narrowed to enter the gates, then he stood and cried, "By the Laird Christ, give it to them, lads!"

The man on his right jumped to his feet and blew a ram's horn, and immediately the archers hidden on the hill and along the berm stood and loosed a volley of arrows at the charging horsemen. Several riders fell as arrows streaked into their midst from every quarter. Others wore various expressions of perplexity, not comprehending at first that they were riding into a trap.

When Sarteham saw that Brynwald was set for him, it seemed to unhinge a madness in him. He let out another cry and thundered through the gates, laughing fiendishly, as though riding with a troop through the gates of hell.

Brynwald's warriors rushed the horsemen with a shout and fell upon them with a terrific clash of metal that pealed up and down the length of the valley. It was as though the heavens were being rent in two, so deafening was the clap of violence. Those of his mounted warriors waiting in the groves stormed out of the trees and drove a wedge though Sarteham's forces, dividing them and driving the lead contingent of horsemen (including Sarteham) to another part of the field.

Immediately an outcry of rage ascended over the battlefield as the two opposing forces converged, then disintegrated into sundry pockets of fighting—Pict against Pict, savagery upon savagery.

The battle immediately took on the ambience of a dream. Everything moved in a surreal progression of shadowy contours and shapes and snatches of lighted faces, speeding by at once in blurred rushes and crawling with incredible lethargy. Edges of silver flashed in the moonlight, and the clangor of battle was deafening—the clash of metal, the rending of bone and flesh, men screaming, horses screaming.

It seemed the battle was a living thing that made a continual roaring. It had an insatiable appetite for men. Warriors glared at one another in profound disbelief, as the horror of death went about the throng, snatching throats.

Aeryck stood in a small clearing, bouncing lightly back and forth on the balls of his feet, gripping his sword with both hands, and looking anxiously about him for an enemy to fight. Strangely, there were none. It seemed the storm of battle was moving out from him like an ever-widening wall, leaving him in an eye of incredible calm.

He saw Brynwald off to one side, felling a man with his battle-ax, and was awed by the fierceness of his countenance. A bolt of pride tore through his mind.

And then he heard a clash behind him, piercing the eye of calm, heard the angry peal of battle tearing high over the village, and he knew that Dunnald and the others were into it now. He didn't have time to give them a thought, however, for a riderless horse careering through the press nearly bowled him over.

Diving out of its way, he rolled to his feet and came face to face with a warrior who, pitching out of the whirling-by wall, swiped at him with a broadsword. Aeryck jumped back, feeling the cleft air go by his throat, then readied himself for another assault.

Immediately the man thrust his blade at the boy's chest. Aeryck parried, rang clear of the blade, then stepped to one side and set himself to counterattack. His mind was clear now of all thoughts and emotions—all but those concerning the preservation of his life. A buzz of intensity blazed down the blade of his being, honing his every instinct to a pristine edge. And the animal roar of battle thinned away to a distant part of his brain. Every detail of movement on the man's face, his hands, even the necklace of cheap beads around his neck, was caught and stood out in stark relief. Aeryck saw fear leap into the man's eyes now that he had missed with his sword twice. The story was always in the eyes. One of Spang's choice men, he thought. Probably some thief or murderer who preyed on helpless victims in dark alleys, ambushing them from behind, then crowing about his bravery in the taverns. He could see this in his eyes as well. He also saw, by the way the man stood and by the way he held his sword, that he was a clumsy swordsman.

Then he saw the man's eyes narrow as though he had made up his mind on a matter. The Pict yelled something at him. The voice sounded thin, distorted, disembodied, as though the voice and the man were crossing one another at the same moment and joined briefly to form a curse. Then the man drew his sword back as though he were going to chop wood, and Aeryck dispatched him deftly with a quick thrust.

And the once wall of calm closed about him with a violent clasp, and he was in the thick of battle now, going around in it like a leaf caught in a gale. There were blades going by his face, clicking with dreamlike remoteness. And there were faces of men rising before him—their features contorted in nightmarish extremes of hate and violence—then the men falling away as though they were never there.

The roar of battle alternately rushed in close and receded into the background, pressing in, then sucking away, ascending, descending, near and far. And he felt the report of his blade hammering rhythmically, ringing off the anvils of flashing metal, though his sword seemed weightless to him—nothing more than a shard of light that moved before him of its own will, creating some devastation that the boy was loathe to observe.

Somewhere in the torrent and the roaring he saw the face of Dagmere floating by, smiling up at him with her big blue eyes, then kissing him, again kissing him, and waving good-bye and kissing him again. And he saw the Roman monk Aurelius drilling before him in his brown birrus —*to the right . . . forward . . . to the left . . . backward*—saw the silver sparks winging off the blades, and the faces of Brother Stephen and Spang looking up at him, and Hauwka looking down—the bear growling and warning him to flee.

Sensing imminent peril, the boy whirled about and, ducking, brought his sword up in time to catch the devastating blade of a large broadsword. Reeling from the blow, Aeryck found himself staring into the eyes of a fierce-looking fellow, one whose bare torso and arms and shaved head were painted red. There was a fleeting moment of eyes locking onto the other, the battle shuddering to a halt as each of them recognized that the Fates had selected them for private contest.

The Pictish warrior barked a laugh of contempt. Then he glared at the boy with taunting eyes, the whites showing luminous through the red paint and boring two savage holes through him. A long topknot sprang from the back of his gleaming pate and curled down his broad back, bouncing with his truculence. That this man was one who had lived through many battles was immediately evident by the fresh blood on his sword and the three heads dangling from his belt.

"*Och*, but you've a bonny face, mannie," the Pict sneered through clenched teeth. "Has Brynwald run out of warriors then, that he must fight with lassies?"

Aeryck swayed back and forth, keeping his weight low and evenly distributed on the balls of his feet. He forced himself not to look at anything but the man's eyes. However even they were a distraction—those two holes of wicked light.

Seeing the look on the boy's face, the Pict chortled wickedly. "Your head will look a bonny sight hangin' from my belt, dinna you think?"

"Come and take it then."

The warrior snarled savagely, then rushed him, and their blades met with a tremendous clash of sparks. Aeryck felt the shudder go up through his arms and into his teeth, and he knew without a doubt that he had his hands full.

Meanwhile Sarteham finally fought clear of Brynwald's horsemen and galloped to an opening in the trees, away from the immediacy of fighting, from whence he could survey the battlefield.

Peering over the heaving swell of men, he espied the chieftain near the gates, battling two warriors. Immediately his eyes burned with consuming rage and tore his features into a violent grin. Quickly he secured the reins in the crook of his right arm, wrapping them around the stump, then spurred the horse through the press.

Aeryck, sidestepping a blade thrust, caught sight of the large Pict mounting over the battle toward Brynwald. He turned briefly toward the chieftain and tried to call out a warning but in such distraction was struck to the ground by a punishing blow from his opponent's sword. The fall knocked the wind out of him, and looking up he saw the Pictish warrior looming closer with a murderous snarl.

The Pict swung his blade at the boy's head with a lightning strike.

Aeryck rammed his sword against it, barely catching it over his face, and felt the stunning impact go down through him into the earth.

Enraged, the Pict raised his sword to strike again.

But the boy, seizing the opportunity, slipped his toe behind the man's calf and drove the heel of his other boot as hard as he could into his leg. He felt the knee go, heard the scream, then, rolling to one side, thrust his blade upward.

The man doubled over and looked at the boy for a moment, staring incredulously, then dropped his sword and crumpled to the ground.

Scrambling to his feet, Aeryck looked frantically about and saw

Sarteham bearing down on Brynwald, brandishing his ax. He guessed his intent at once.

The boy took off over the littered ground, hurdling fallen men, jostling others, stumbling, spinning, fighting his way toward the chieftain, who was battling a man and unaware of his peril. With a sweep of his eyes Aeryck saw Sarteham hurl the ax, saw the twirling blade snatch a flash of light, saw Brynwald's back in the path, and knew there was no time.

"Brynwald!" he cried, leaping off the belly of a fallen horse. He hit the chieftain solidly and, in the falling sweep of motion, heard the ax whirl close, then strike with a hollow cleft of bone. The two of them fetched the ground with a bone-jarring shudder.

"By the oaks, kipper!" Brynwald swore, swiping the boy off him as though he were a rodent.

Both sprang to their feet. Brynwald jerked his head back and forth, then saw the man he had been fighting, splayed out on the ground with an ax buried in his chest. His eyes went wide. "How—"

"Sarteham!" the boy cried, pointing at the oncoming horseman.

"Aye," Brynwald snarled, following his point. "It is indeed."

Sarteham let out a hellish cry of laughter. Then he pulled up his horse with a brutal yank of the reins and, throwing them to one side, immediately drew his sword.

But as he swung his leg off the saddle, a streak of light was already rifling over the battle. It struck him high in his rib cage, just under the shoulder blade. Sarteham's body twisted fantastically as he grabbed at the arrow, a gasp of astonishment caught on his lips. Then he fell hard to the ground.

Immediately he climbed onto his elbows and looked up at Brynwald standing only a few feet before him. Rage and frustration worked over his features, as his mind assessed the transgression to his body. "No!" he cried. "No!"

He would not allow vengeance to escape him, not when it was so close to his grasp. All that was left of his fury and hate and frustration burned in his eyes, and the large Pict, clawing through the mud, pulled himself closer and closer toward his hated enemy. He felt death taking hold of him with its long talons, but he would deny death. He would have his vengeance.

"*Och*, but if it isn't the old serpent crawling on its belly," Brynwald taunted. "A fitting image, wouldn't you say, kipper?"

Aeryck just looked at the arrow jutting from the man's back, saw that it had penetrated deep.

Then Sarteham recognized Aeryck standing next to the chieftain, and his eyes widened in amazement. "*You!* I thought—"

"You thought Spang killed me months ago," Aeryck said without emotion. "But as you can see I'm very much alive." He grunted. "But then I don't suppose Spang was able to tell you, was he? Not with the wolves and all."

Sarteham gaped at him, bewildered, until several things came into focus. "You were there today . . . on the bluffs." He winced. "Aye, it was you, Briton, riding the bear. It was you." His eyes burned in a fever of rage.

Aeryck stared at him coldly. He said nothing. He felt nothing.

Brynwald laughed. *"Och,* Sarteham. 'Tis the second time now the kipper has fouled you. You're not having much of a go at this, are you?"

Sarteham shifted his eyes to the chieftain. Then, drawing upon the last of his strength and hate, he threw out his arm and grabbed Brynwald's boot with a viselike grip. He dug his fingers into the boot. "No! I won't allow it! Not until . . . no . . . ."

Then the fingers loosened. He glared at the chieftain with pained defiance. But he knew he was through. "I'll be waiting for you at the gates of the Underworld, Brynwald," he snarled. "We'll finish it there. By troth, I swear it!"

"'Tis not likely, Sarteham," Brynwald said, stepping free of his fingers. "Not likely at all."

Sarteham spat a curse, and then, with a final violent lurch, his body went still.

Aeryck stared at him, shaking his head in amazement. It seemed impossible to him that this large Pict lying sprawled in the mud—the fingers of his left hand still outstretched and curled in their final reach for vengeance—could have caused so much destruction and grief.

The thought struck his mind that now the man was nothing more than a mere husk, a shell, like one of those mollusks he had seen washed up on the beach with its insides eaten away. He seemed so small now. So pathetically irrelevant.

The boy was startled out of his thoughts when he heard the drumming of hooves. And whirling about, sword swinging to the ready, he saw an army of horsemen coming toward them, riding furiously and black against the falling moon.

44
GAMBIT
OF THE FOX

Allyndaar had hoped to draw the Saxons into a series of skirmishes that would wear down their resources and buy the Britons some time. He had not expected them to bypass Brough though. It seemed too good a plum to leave unpicked. But they did. And now, with one massive circumventing sweep of the board, all his strategic planning to defend the village and hurt the enemy was suddenly rendered inconsequential.

"What will we do now?" Terryll asked. He was alone with his father on the mount overlooking Brough. The two of them were on horseback, looking down at the road winding through the hills into the distance. "They will reach Killwyn Eden in two days. Maybe less."

The chieftain gazed at the sprawling length of the army bending steadily away to the northwest. Then he looked over to the east. The first gold rays of the sun were bursting over the cloudless rim of hills, shooting fingers of color into the sky, the fingers advancing tirelessly over the broad lay of the earth. "We will have to slow them down somehow."

"Slow them down?"

The chieftain did not answer, but Terryll could see the mind working quickly behind the piercing blue eyes.

"You're sure they're heading to Killwyn Eden?" the boy asked. He glanced away from his father to the thick black cord of men snaking away in the distance. "They went around Brough, didn't they?"

Still the chieftain did not answer. He was silent for a long while in a brooding darkness, his eyes and mind clearly moving in different planes. Then his eyes began to glow in the light of some unveiled knowledge. "I should have anticipated it," he chided himself under his breath. "I see it now. We could have been waiting for them in the forest of Teesbrough. I should have seen it."

"But how could you—"

"They have no supplies, Terryll," his father interrupted, the two planes sharply focusing on a single point of light. "Don't you see they cannot afford a delay now? What is Brough to them? Killwyn Eden is the mark. They have to strike quickly—throw everything they've got at us."

Allyndaar let out a sigh, looking back over the game in his mind, rethinking the moves. Yes, he saw it now. The light of understanding settled over his brow, and his head bent slightly to the weight of it. "Our little victory may prove to be a costly mistake . . . a very costly mistake."

Terryll was perplexed. He wanted to reach over and lift his father's head and remind him that they had beaten them once already—that they could beat them again. But the light on his father's brow was unapproachable.

Then the chieftain stiffened. "If they take Killwyn Eden, all will be lost." Allyndaar looked quickly at his son, his mind suddenly made up on a matter. There was a fierceness in his eyes that bored through the boy's brain.

"I want you to take the men of Bowes with you and harass the advance," he said earnestly. "Don't engage them in battle though, son. Just hit and run . . . work on their nerves . . . get their minds off their objective. Do you understand?"

"What will you do, Papa?"

"Do you understand?" the chieftain snapped.

"Yes, Papa, I understand," Terryll said. "We will not engage the enemy—just whittle away at their flanks."

"That's it. You must delay them, son. A day . . . a half day . . . even an hour would help."

"We'll do our best, Papa. The men of Bowes are fine archers."

"Yes . . . yes . . ." Allyndaar agreed, but his thoughts were somewhere else. The eyes cooled, then withdrew to find some place in the terrain over the boy's shoulder. "That might do it."

Terryll saw something strange burning in his father's eyes. "What might do it, Papa?"

But his father didn't hear him.

"Papa?"

"Yes . . . we can strike them at the fords," Allyndaar said, resolve growing in his voice. "The river will be high. They will have to cross there."

Terryll was unable to believe his ears. "You can't hold off the entire army, Papa. There are too many of them."

"We can slow them down," Allyndaar said, cutting off his son's objections. Not hearing them. "Watch the flanks, son—this Saxon commander is a fox. He'll be sure to have patrols out."

Terryll saw the resoluteness in his father's eyes. There was a recklessness pulling at the corners, and he knew that there was no point in arguing with him. Suddenly he was full of contempt. "A fox?" he sneered. "I've snared many a fox."

Allyndaar looked intently at his son. "A fox that runs with a wolf?" Then the warmth returned, and, turning to leave, he said, "God-speed, Terryll."

"And to you, Papa." Terryll stretched out his hand suddenly. "Papa . . ."

Allyndaar reined the Arab and looked back at the boy. "Yes?"

Terryll just looked at him. Then his hand withered into a parting salute. "I'll see you at home."

"Until then." Allyndaar grinned. Then, waving, he spurred the gray Arabian down the hill.

Terryll watched him leave, wondering if it were possible that the world could get any darker. "Come on, Tempest." He sighed, reining the black stallion's head. "We'll see if we can't get us another fox."

Tempest whickered fiercely and leaped forward.

Terryll and the men of Bowes shadowed the army like a pack of wolves, eyeing the herd of Saxon warriors with hungry eyes, looking for weaknesses along the broad exposed belly of the herd, looking for stragglers. Throughout the day they rushed their flanks with lightning hit-and-run raids, nipped at their heels, riding suddenly out of a screen of trees or draw, striking quickly with their longbows, drawing blood, then disappearing back into the trees and into the hills as though they were never there.

The column began to constrict and bunch together like cattle, eyes darting back and forth as they scanned the ridge lines for the predators.

Olaf widened his flanking patrols, sending them after the Britons when they appeared. He did not want to do it, knowing that his men were unfamiliar with the countryside, but the orders had come from Horsa.

Quick to seize any small edge, Terryll turned his knowledge of the terrain and his woodsman's skills to advantage. Skillfully he and a small contingent drew the enemy horsemen into box draws, into forests, or along streams, where the bulk of his men were waiting in ambush, waiting to loose volleys of arrows at the unsuspecting Saxons. One hundred horsemen were killed in this way, without a single dead Briton to show for it.

Many of the Saxons began to think that they were spirits of the land, that the myths they'd heard were indeed true. It worked on their nerves. The patrols stopped. Horsa's orders.

Bolstered with their successes, Terryll and his men rode alongside in the distance, disappearing in and out of the folds in the terrain, allowing the foot warriors to get a good look at them, taunting them, again rushing in suddenly, striking, and dashing away, every time daring the cavalry to pursue. They would not.

Terryll kept this up all day, taking a fair toll of men and horses. And seeing the frustration on the faces of the Saxon riders, he smiled because he knew he was making a little difference—like a flea troubling the hide of a great beast. Nothing more than a nuisance, but a nuisance nevertheless. However the beast was undaunted and continued its adamantine pace, advancing with the sun, never slowing down, not even to assist those wounded by the peppering assaults.

That night Terryll separated his men into two groups: one large (a hundred archers or so) and the other only a handful. The smaller group were men he knew to be especially skilled hunters—good game stalkers. His plan was to lead these men into the camp of the Saxon cavalry at the head of the column, cut the tethers holding their horses, and stampede them. Then the larger group, hearing the uproar, were to shoot their arrows into the Saxons while they slept, hitting them from all sides. Terryll hoped to create such confusion that it would take the army a good day or two to wrangle all its horses and to reorganize itself.

It was a bold plan. But then again, Terryll was a hunter, and he loved bold plans.

He and his men tethered their horses in a stand of alders situated on a gentle rise of land and waited. A broad field sloped gently away from them, a field pleasant for picnicking, clear and bright and shimmering in the moonlight, and then the jagged black line of the forest rose like a rake of teeth.

The horsemen were camped somewhere beyond by the river—they had seen their fires against the sky. Terryll and his men waited until the yellow firelight spilled down into the trees like the sand in an hourglass, leaving the sky dark with a residual glitter of stars. They waited until the moon was low over the hills, until there were long shadows creeping over the earth to cover their approach. They waited until everything was dark and still, waited until the spirits of the night drew a quiet comforter over the terrain, leaving only the muffled sound of the river that threaded through it in the distance.

Then they moved stealthily out of the stand of alders and crossed the field, moving like shadows over the ground, and disappearing one by one into the umbrage of the trees. No sentries were roving about, none that they could see.

Strange, Terryll thought. *There should be sentries.* And then he remembered the arrogance of these men, remembered how lax they were when he had come upon them that time in their winter camp. He wished now he had sent an arrow into the Norseman's breast when he had had the opportunity.

The Britons picked their way through the trees and shrubs and came to a broad meadow—the hunters in their element now, the air whispering its secrets to them. Then every one of them froze as though they had suddenly come upon game. Indeed they had.

The young hunter peered through a blind of shrubs and scanned the camp, his eyes wary and covering the ground quickly. A slight wind was blowing in their favor. The camp spread out before them across a field that was lined with a thick forest of pines and yews.

The trees were black against the dark sky, and he could see the shapes of sleeping men, lying in groups around the glowing remains of their campfires. He saw a few men walking idly about—the sentries, he thought—gathering occasionally in small huddles to converse, to laugh, then separating. They moved as though they hadn't a care in the world. Terryll frowned.

Off to one side the horses grazed in the long grass. Everything was quiet, except for an occasional snort from a contented horse and the low roar of the river. There was a continual dripping coming from somewhere in the distance, and every so often the looping song of a night bird.

But something was wrong. They all felt it, the hunters did. The wind withdrew to a dreadful hush.

"Where are the rest of the horses?" a man whispered to Terryll. "There should be twice as many."

The boy looked around. "Horses?" He hadn't noticed. Yes, the horses. "I don't know. There must be another field of them."

"Something odd about those men," someone else said, sweeping over the area with his hand. "The ones sleeping."

Terryll looked again at the black shapes strewn over the field. His eyes narrowed. "Yes . . . unless . . ." He saw it then, and he felt the hair go up on his neck. "Let's get out of here."

"What?"

"Let's get out of here. Now!"

Terryll heard a noise, then reeled as an arrow whistled past his nose and caught his fellow in the chest. Terryll saw him fall away and disappear into the shadows as though the earth had opened up and swallowed him.

Then several more arrows rifled into their midst, sounding like angry hornets. There were impact noises all around the boy, sudden gasps and cries, and he knew that if he remained where he was he would be dead in seconds.

He turned his head in the breadth of a wink and saw several vague man shapes rising out of the shadows like a troop of ogres, gathering light and form as they came surging forward in a violent rush. He felt the heat leaving his face, then the blood coming back and squishing through the

402

veins at his temples. Other man shapes were rising behind the first rank, and beyond these was the sound of horses galloping toward the battle scene.

Wasting no time for mental debate, Terryll took off through the trees in a dead run, away from the man shapes, heading in the general direction of their horses. The black outline of trees and bushes fell swiftly behind him as he ran for all his worth.

Somewhere off to his left he heard the sound of running horses and the clatter of metal, closer now. He caught flashes of their shapes, gaining on his position—perhaps a dozen or more of them galloping in the clearing beyond the edge of the trees. The moon glinted silvery on shards of armor and weapons and burned savagely upon the corneas of their eyes.

He cast a quick glance over his shoulder and saw five of his men on his heels. The moon flickered through the black lace of the bowery over their grim faces and gathered a collective expression of wonder. He had no idea what had happened to the rest of his men—whether they had fallen or had fled in other directions. He prayed the latter. There had been no time for planning, so sudden was the cleft of death. It was every man for himself.

"Have mercy, God," he cried. "Have mercy." And he felt sudden shame for having failed them.

The lead horseman, loping along a parallel course in the field, turned and, glancing into the trees, saw the Britons. He called to his men with an exultant cry and cut into the trees, crashing through the bushes after them.

Horses whickered in the charge, and the ground shook with a terrible convulsion, and the Britons redirected their steps. Immediately arrows buzzed all around their heads, the maddened hornets striking trees, glancing off the trunks, and piercing the ground at their feet.

Terryll zigzagged through the trees, looking for aisles of gray light, and, finding them, darted into them, hurdling windfalls and boulders, and occasionally catching his toe and stumbling, then running out of the falls by the sheer force of his will and youth's agility. All the while he was thinking of the Saxons, thundering, gaining, loosing their killer darts, and thinking of Tempest ahead and getting to him, and how he had failed his men.

He felt the blunt points of the earth going by under his feet. It was like running on stones spanning a rushing river. He picked his steps in the dark, with the speed and the fear and with the ground in a general uprising. Low branches struck him in the face. Thickets clawed at his clothes and tore his skin. Rocks rose out of the forest bed in defiance, dashing themselves against his feet. It seemed the earth that once favored the Britons had turned against him.

Several black silhouettes with drawn bows rose suddenly before them. There was an immediate exchange of arrows, followed by the sounds of broadheads impacting flesh in both camps and man shapes careering out of sight.

Terryll heard the man behind him go down, felt the jolt of the earth as he hit, and glancing back was struck in the face by a limb. He heard the crack of the branch and felt it pull away, then he felt something strike his side, felt the sudden rip of pain, and knew that one of the hornets had found him.

He looked down for the telling black shaft jutting from his body but there wasn't one. Then he felt a warm wetness trickling down his left side, and he felt his tunic slapping against it as he ran and the skin cooling along his flank as the air was caught inside. He put the wound out of his mind and thought only of reaching the horses.

He knew they were across the field in the stand of alders but couldn't see them. A thought jolted his mind that he might have overshot the stand, but running toward the edge of the forest he saw the trees on the rise of the field. Thank God! The meadow was less bright now, but still he could see the black outlines of the horses idling about in the grass.

Terryll glanced behind him before exiting the forest. He saw only three of his men now. One turned and loosed an arrow at the galloping horsemen, slowing down now among the trees, and he saw a rider fall. The man resumed his flight, then lurched forward suddenly and screwed to the ground with an arrow in his back.

Terryll broke out of the forest and was struck by a rush of horror. Cresting the rise before him was another group of horsemen—fifty or more—quickly bearing down on his position. His heart sank. Then he gritted his teeth and sprinted for the stand of alders.

He heard the shuddering twang of bowstrings, saw the black bolts slanting past the moon into the trees behind him, and then, to his amazement, striking the Saxon horsemen who were pressing on his heels. Animals reared, and men fell from their mounts.

Terryll let out a hoot, for he knew that the second troop of horsemen was the larger force of his men returning.

"Is that you, Terryll?" one of them cried out.

"Yes," Terryll shouted. Then, reaching the horses, he grabbed his reins and flew up onto the back of Tempest.

Immediately he felt the bite of pain, reminding him of his wound, and he glanced down at his side. To his horror he could see a dark, wet swath in the moonlight, shining wickedly, and he felt the weight of his tunic pulling thickly along his flank. He felt gingerly for the wound and, locating it, winced in pain. However he was relieved that the arrow had not cut too deeply into him. A flesh wound, he hoped. He pressed his fingers against it to stop the bleeding. Again he winced.

"Quickly, lad. The devils are right on our heels!"

The two men who had been fleeing with Terryll reached the trees and quickly mounted. Then the three of them charged out of the cover and joined the rest of his force, now galloping across the field away from the Saxon camp.

Terryll glanced over his men and noted that his force was considerably diminished.

"They surprised us," a man said, drawing alongside the boy.

"Aye," another added. "They were waiting for us."

"Is this all that are left of you?" Terryll cried.

"Some got away into the hills," the first man answered. "But too many are left behind."

A thick mist hovered over the ground, giving everything a dismal cast. There were no colors, only gradations of gray and a wet brightness off to one side in the east, pushing through with the dawn. Strange-looking figures rose darkly in the mist, and the thick dark boughs of trees in full leaf draped heavily over them. There was the smooth full sound of a river, moving high and swiftly along the banks, bending the sharp spears of sedge grass and bulrushes. Other sounds were flattened into the ground.

Allyndaar and the men from Brough were hidden among the shapes across the ford and along the northwestern bank of the river. The ford was really a narrow stone bridge, built by the Romans, and the men peered into the obfuscation beyond it.

They heard them coming first, heard the muffled tinkling of battle gear drawing nearer and nearer, the dull clinking of the killing tools clapping against iron and mail; heard the horses clattering mutedly over the road, and then a sound that could only be described as a low humming noise, a savage pulsing that sounded in regular intervals like the seething breath of a rising monster.

Allyndaar watched as the advancing beast rose out of the mists, watched as it began to take the shape of the Saxon army—the sound giving definition to the shape. First it resembled nothing more than a light gray smear stretching away into the fog. Then the horsemen began to take form—the man shapes and horse shapes growing darker every moment and defining themselves out of the smear. Beyond them were the foot warriors, the great bulk of the war beast that was still an indiscriminate serpentine mass as it curled back into the gray wash.

Arriving at the turnoff, the beast shuddered to a halt and paused momentarily. It was thinking, Allyndaar knew. It was looking, hunting, cunningly tracking the scent of Britons. Then, catching the scent, it turned toward the ford and angled toward them with a menacing snort.

An apprehension of imminent battle shuddered through the men of Brough as they beheld the coming behemoth.

Riding at the head of the column, Allyndaar could just make out, was the silhouette of a large man wearing a winged helmet, the head thrown back proudly off the bow of his chest and his charger prancing with like conceit. It seemed to the chieftain that he resembled some general appraising his conquered domain with the arrogance of a king, subjugating everything in the sweep of his glance by some fiat of his will. Allyndaar knew at once that it was the man he had been waiting to kill.

He tested the pull of his bowstring, felt the brush of the arrow shaft over the meat of his extended hand. There was nothing so sure, so secure, as the heft of his yew bow, its singular lithe curve breaking the plane of earth and sky. He smiled, then looked down the line of his men on either side of him. Every one of them was looking at him now, longbows at the ready, waiting for him to give the signal.

He looked back across the river. The head of the beast was just coming into range. He could barely make out the dark hollows of its eyes—hundreds of them. He nodded to his longbowmen. Without a sound the archers rose deliberately from the bulrushes and found their marks.

Then suddenly the ground began to tremble beneath their feet. It was a strange phenomenon.

Allyndaar struggled to connect the shuddering of the ground with the steady advance of the army, but they wouldn't connect. Then he realized what it was. He wheeled about with a prickling of horror along his neck and saw several hundred horsemen pouring over the broad knoll to their rear.

"How'd they get around us?" one of his men cried.

The chieftain did not respond. He knew full well what had happened. The Saxons had sent an advance contingent of riders to the fords, while he and his men were building an irrelevant defense of Brough. He cursed his foolishness. A terrific roar yanked Allyndaar's eyes back across the river. The main army of horsemen was charging now, howling fiendishly, adding its violence to the earth. The Britons were caught in the middle, with death on either side. A scowl burned across Allyndaar's brow as he looked for the winged helmet. *I'll take you at least,* he thought. But the Norseman was lost somewhere in the surging wall of horses and men.

Selecting another mark, he quickly stripped a man shape away from the anonymity of the wall, fixed his eye on it, then loosed his arrow and saw the flat trajectory of the missile going out from him and the impact.

The men of Brough loosed a desperate flight of arrows, and several dozen Saxons pitched off their mounts.

"To your horses, men!" Allyndaar cried, running as he fit another arrow to his bow.

The Britons quickly mounted and whirled to face the hinder force of Saxons, the lesser of the two evils. They loosed a hail of arrows into their midst. Horses and riders fell. Then Allyndaar let out a battle cry and, charging, drove a wedge into the wall of horsemen, and there was a sudden violent concussion of horses and metal.

By midday Terryll and the men of Bowes had finally eluded their pursuers, riding far to the northeast, then doubling back. They crossed the river at the second ford north of Teesbrough, intending to locate Allyndaar and the men of Brough and join forces with them. Almost immediately they spotted three riders loping toward them—Britons, they could tell by the way they rode. One was doubled over with his head pressed against the horse's mane.

"Hail!" Terryll called out apprehensively. His expression turned to alarm once he recognized them as men of Brough. Each was bleeding and spent, it appeared, from some recent battle. The one who was doubled over had an arrow jutting from his chest and didn't look long for this world. Terryll glared at the other two. "What news do you bring?"

"It was a trap," the first man said.

"Aye, they tore into us good," the second man added. "Wasn't nothing could be done."

"What of my father?" Terryll demanded.

The wounded man looked up at him. His eyes were wild. "I saw him fall, Terryll. I don't know what's come of him. But I saw him go down."

Terryll's head reeled as though he had taken a lash.

The boy turned quickly and gazed in the direction of the fords of Teesbrough, as though to confirm the man's words there. His thoughts began churning into a whir. A horror went round in his chest, like a funnel sucking everything out, leaving him cold and numb and empty.

"I tried to warn him," the boy said dazedly to the horizon. "He wouldn't listen." His eyes swept despairingly over the gray sky. "Papa . . ." He let it trail.

His men stared at him, then looked sadly at one another. "I don't know, lad," the first man said, seeing the look on the boy's face. "It mightn't of been your father. It weren't nothing but confusion there. Men hollering . . . falling every which way . . . Saxons and Britons alike. Who's to say who was falling and who was riding?"

"Aye. They were all over us," the severely wounded man added. "Who's to say?" He choked. Then he fell off his horse and lay in the grass, gasping, the arrow heaving with his breath. "We slowed 'em down though. Aye, we gave them a good fight of it." The man smiled, then rolled his eyes heavenward as the arrow lowered to a point and grew still.

Something clicked in the air.

One of Terryll's men drew alongside him. "It's time to be thinking of your mother and sister now, Terryll. If your father's alive, he can fend for himself, don't you think? If he's dead—well, like I said, it's time to be thinking of your womenfolk."

Terryll stared at him hard, then looked away in the direction of Killwyn Eden. His eyes burned with hot tears.

45
THE PRELUDE

Helena sat on the veranda of the villa, staring out at the hills in the west as the sun slanted slowly toward them. Her fingers worked anxiously along the hem of her shawl. Her face was impassive. The moorings connecting the heart to the face had gotten loose, it seemed.

Dagmere sat nearby on a marble bench, looking down at something on the flagstones. A tiny pool of tears seeped into a crack. One launched off her cheek and splattered against the stone. Every so often she would look up bleary-eyed at Terryll, who was standing before them, as though he had made some dreadful mistake. Then, seeing his face, she would lower her head and add to the pool.

A moment later she looked sharply at her brother. Her expression had changed. "I want to stay, Terryll."

Terryll shook his head. "No, Dag, we've already been through this. I want you to go with Mama. She needs you. Besides, I don't want to have to be worrying about you here."

"But what if Papa—" She caught her words, glancing suddenly at her mother. Helena had begun to sway slightly.

Terryll frowned. "You're going with Mama, and that's final," he said, sounding like his father. He looked up as the carpentum clattered to a stop in front of their gates. Brother Lucius Aurelius was driving the team.

"It's time to go now, Mama," Terryll said, bending to his mother.

Helena looked at her son. Though her face was still void of animation, her eyes were moist, and Terryll saw the cry of anguish in them. She seemed suddenly older to him, suddenly frail. As she stood to her feet she wavered, and Terryll steadied her with his hand. It was in that moment that the boy realized that his mother was a mortal being. Something mortal showed itself in him as well. He walked with her down the flight of stairs, steadying her with one arm and carrying a small satchel of her belongings with the other. Then they passed through the villa gates, and he helped her up into the wagon.

Terryll looked into the monk's eyes, handing the satchel to him. Each knew what the other was thinking.

Aurelius said, "There have been stragglers coming in all day from the fords, Terryll. Only the one man you talked to said your father had fallen." He took hold of Helena's hand and patted it.

She smiled appreciatively for the news, but the eyes did not change.

Terryll glanced away, thinking, then looked back into the monk's eyes. "Why, Brother Lucius? Why would God allow such a thing?"

"I do not know, Terryll," the monk said. "I have been asking God this question for many weeks now. Why is there pain in the world? Why is there sorrow? Why must the wicked prosper on the backs of the innocent?" Looking away at the reddening sky, he let out a heavy sigh. "It is to strengthen us in some way perhaps—our faith." He smiled. "Perhaps it is only to give us strong backs."

Helena's eyes lowered, and she studied her hands in her lap, one held protectively in the other. The fingers were trembling, so she smoothed them over her dress, then took hold of the shawl again and began to work her thoughts over the hem.

"Right now my faith is weak," Terryll said, glancing at his mother, seeing the mortal thing growing in her. "It seems as though God has turned His face from us."

"No, Terryll," the monk chided gently, "He would never turn His face from His children. We just don't always know what He is doing, that's all. Never lose hope in this, Terryll. Nothing can separate us from the love of God . . . neither life nor death . . . nor any fiery trial that comes our way. It is what Saint Paul said to the—"

"Romans. I know," Terryll said, then he changed the subject. "You must go now, Brother Lucius. The women and children should be safe in Old Penrith. I will send word to you when it is safe . . . when it is safe to return."

"I will pray that it is soon," the monk said. "May God be with you, Terryll."

Terryll almost said, "And with you too," but caught himself. He just nodded his head and smiled grimly. "I will send for you when we have sent these savages fleeing," he said instead. Then he looked up at the house for Dagmere, but she was gone. "Now where did she go?" he muttered to himself.

Then he saw her riding out of the stables, carrying her longbow. She galloped over to the field gate and let herself through to the road.

Terryll looked at his mother. "I must go now, Mama. Brother Lucius will take good care of you and the others."

Helena looked at her son. Something was struggling in her eyes, a

410

pent thing tearing at the corners of her mouth. A course of tears began to stream over her cheeks, then she clutched her face and wept.

Terryll looked at the ground.

Brother Lucius clucked his tongue, and the horses lurched ahead, kicking up little clouds of dust in the road. Terryll watched the carpentum roll away, pitching and shuddering, then dipping into the avenue of trees and up onto the rise of the road where Dagmere joined them.

Terryll looked heavenward. "Why, God? Why?" he cried. But he heard only the wind soughing through the heavy leaves of the hawthorns. And the sky began to deepen with color.

A steep earthen berm, surmounted with a palisade of thick timbers, encircled the village. There were two gates, both made of heavy iron-banded oak, leading into the city from the north and south, and a stone road running through the village connecting them.

The hamlet was set upon an escarpment of chalky ground (gently rising to the north and west walls, with a steep incline along the south and east) and commanded a sweeping view of the countryside in every direction. To the west were hills rising sharply—big mounds of granite that formed the northernmost reach of the Pennine Chain—then falling away gently into the broad valley of the Eden, flattening out, wind-blasted and treeless, flowing north and away to the Solway Firth. To the east were low hills and ridges, stacked one against the other with forested dells and dingles bunching along the base works, and more of the same to the south.

The men of Killwyn Eden gazed numbly over the irregular crenellations of timber as the exodus of wagons and horses rolled northwest out of the village on the road to Old Penrith. They waved as their loved ones looked back from the receding column, waving with enthusiasm, then waving just to wave, waving to squeeze every last feeling out of the moment—each man capturing the last images of his loved ones' faces and smiling to hide the pain. The column grew small, then tiny on the horizon, then dipped altogether out of view behind the hills.

And then a great void rushed into the village, the soul having gone out of it with a moan. Every man felt the burning in his heart, held onto that for a while, viewing the captured images in his mind, and once these began to fade—his face changing, hardening, putting away its smile against the advance of the other thing—he turned his thoughts to the business of war. Almost to a man everyone looked down at his sword or battle-ax or hefted the length of his bow as his mind made the transition.

Earlier the men had turned the Roman engines of war—the catapults and the larger ballistae—to the northeast, from whence the army must come through the hills. Each was fitted with new rope and tested—

their ranges carefully noted and the stones collected. Then stockpiles of boulders and small rocks were gathered beside each one.

The thick oaken gates opened in the berm and allowed Terryll and the men of Bowes and those stragglers of Brough who were rested and fit for battle to exit on horseback, their quivers stuffed with arrows. Then the gates closed solidly behind them.

Terryll turned in his saddle and was struck by the austerity of the walls. His home had suddenly become a fortress. It had always been, he supposed, but he felt it now. He waved at the men along the wall. Their faces were red and glowing in the sunset, and they raised their weapons into it.

"Godspeed, Terryll!" one of the men cried out.

"Aye, Godspeed to you, lad!" another added.

Suddenly a shout went up from the walls.

Terryll smiled, feeling a surge of strength. "Godspeed to you too!" he shouted back.

Immediately the line of British horsemen separated into two groups, Terryll leading one into the thick forests to the east and a man named Conlan leading the other group west into the trees along the hills.

And the men along the walls waited. And they waited as the darkness of night descended over the countryside and gathered into the vulnerable places of each man's soul.

They never did see the Saxons arrive. But they knew they had come, for the heavens were suddenly ablaze with their bonfires in the distance, and the moon was awash in crimson light. The Britons watched the skies in amazement. Those who knew the Scriptures were reminded of the prophecy of Joel that went, "I will show wonders in the heavens and in the earth: blood, and fire, and pillars of smoke. The sun shall be turned into darkness, and the moon into blood, before the great and terrible day of the Lord come."

And every man along the wall made his peace with God, believing in his heart that that day had certainly come. Every so often they could hear peals of laughter on the shifting winds, wicked, throaty laughter, and they knew them to be devils.

By daybreak the early mists peeled away to reveal a thin black line stretched across the horizon from one end of the valley to the other. There was a collective gasp of astonishment, followed by an anxious murmuring. The men quickly spread several barrows of dirt before the gates, then poured buckets of water over them, until the approach was a muddy slick. Then they began watering the slopes of the berm and the oaken door until they glistened in the dawning light.

And then there was the sound. The men of Killwyn Eden had never heard anything like it. It was like the consecutive claps of a thousand thunderbolts, lasting for several minutes.

Instinctively the men lifted their eyes to the sky. Clouds were floating by—big fleecy ones heading south—but they were not the kind of clouds that made noise. And then everything went suddenly quiet, and the clouds continued on their way.

A small group of riders rode out a little distance from the Saxon army and paused on a low rise of ground.

"What a glorious field!" Olaf cried, assessing the broad sward before them, glittering with a million tiny jewels in the breaking light. "By Odin, it is a field to die on!"

But Horsa was staring at the rise of the village, the steep berm and palisades encompassing it. He grunted. "And die you might, Commander," he said with less exuberance than the Norseman. "It is a formidable village by the look of things. And we do not know if they have siege engines."

He turned to the Wolf alongside him and with a disdainful look said, "Pity you were not able to reconnoiter the area better, Underlord."

Olaf glanced at the Wolf, saw an ocher light kindle beneath the wolfskin shroud.

"Perhaps my lord Horsa would prefer attacking another village," the Wolf countered with a touch of irony. "There are several that are unwalled just north of us."

"Walls come down," Olaf interposed, feeling caught between the two men. He hated this business of politics. War would be honorable and clean but for the politics.

The overlord turned away from the Wolf in disgust. He was tired of the man. He had become insolent, challenging his authority at every opportunity, it seemed—not openly, not in words or actions, but Horsa could feel it just under the surface. He could see it in the eyes, see an intangible something, something sinister, wickedlike, simmering. Something dangerous. Changing, every day changing more and more. Like a dog turning wild. The overlord let out a grunt. He would deal with the Wolf later—and dismissed him from his mind.

After several minutes of looking over the field, and the village, and the trees lining the approach, he said, "Commander, I will lead the first assault with the army."

The Norseman turned sharply to him.

Horsa read his objection and quickly added, "The cavalry will serve little purpose until we have breached the gates, Commander. I want your men to ride along either flank, protecting our advance from the trees

413

over there . . . and there," he said, indicating the trees with sharp sweeps of his hand. "We will attack the north gates and swing round to the western walls. It appears more expedient from that approach, wouldn't you say, Commander?"

The Norseman nodded, not at all pleased with a supporting role.

"Yes, that is what we shall do." Horsa grinned at the Norseman. "Once my men have smashed through the gates, Commander, then you are to come riding through the breach like your lives were dependent on it. Understood?"

Olaf looked intently at the overlord. "I live to obey your will, my lord Horsa."

"Good." Then, looking ahead at the field, Horsa said, "Underlord, you will follow with the second wave of men, swinging round and attacking the western berm. There should be little resistance there after we've settled accounts with their main defense, but see to it that you don't dally."

The Wolf bowed slightly and smiled. "As you wish, Overlord." Then he turned to the man just behind him and nodded subtly.

Ruddbane smiled in reply.

Horsa took a deep breath, suddenly suffused with good humor. He glanced at the Norseman and laughed. "Do not fret, my proud Viking. There will be glory enough for all of us by day's end. By Thor, we shall have a day of it!"

Olaf struck his chest, grinning now as he felt the glory of war descending upon him. Then he led his horsemen forward. Immediately they broke off into two flanking columns, Olaf taking the left and Druell the right.

Horsa raised his arm and then lowered it.

The footmen behind him, moving forward in bunches, began to beat their swords against their shields again, drumming themselves into a battle frenzy. And then they began chanting to the god of war, first low and with measured cadence, then building in tempo and volume. "Thor . . . Thor . . . Thor . . . Thor . . ."

The noise was deafening, and the hills surrounding the village resounded with an unrelenting clapping of thunder.

When the Saxon juggernaut had approached to within three hundred yards of the village, the Norseman let out an exultant cry, lifting his battle-ax to the heavens. Then he spurred his horse forward into a lope. The footmen began to run, thinning out into their battle intervals, clapping their shields and shouting as they charged. The entire field was a movement of men.

"Here they come," one of the Britons along the wall shouted. "Steady now, lads!"

414

46
THE BATTLE OF KILLWYN EDEN

Terryll and his men watched intently as they came up the valley. The horsemen were riding about two hundred yards out from the trees, double file, looking over the rim of their shields into the forest, seeing nothing, then looking ahead at the walls going round the village berm.

And then there was the roar of the army as it came sweeping across the valley floor like a flood, rushing, crashing, as the men ran quickstridedly, shoulder-to-shoulder, brandishing their weapons and hammering them against their shields. Some were holding grappling hooks and ropes; others carried ladders, running awkwardly with them, and at the fore of the advance was a group of men charging with the battering ram— a long heavy spar of fir, the branches trimmed for handles.

"Easy, easy," Terryll said, looking from the running men, to the enemy horsemen, to the walls, and back to the running men, the first of them coming alongside now.

More horsemen trotted past their position, peering over their shields —the early sun got over the trees and glanced off their helmets—and seeing nothing they also turned their attention to the men along the walls.

There were several sudden shocks, sounding like felled trees crashing with solid *ka-whunking* sounds, and then whipping, whirring noises following immediately.

Terryll looked up and saw the sky suddenly darken with projectiles, looking like a flush of ducks winging fast against the sky, then falling, wings folded, and crashing into the rushing men. Men augered to the ground with fantastic twirls as the boulders impacted their bodies, crushing bone and flesh and splintering their wooden shields. Other footmen swung out wide in either direction away from the downward approach of another flight of boulders and in doing so swept into range of the British longbowmen waiting just inside the trees.

"Now!" Terryll cried.

The men of Bowes darted forward on their mounts and loosed a barrage of arrows into the outward sweep of warriors. At the same instant Conlan and his men rushed the right flank across the valley, pouring arrows into those men. Suddenly the dead and dying were strewn about the field, and the timbre of battle modulated to a dramatic pitch.

By the time Olaf realized what had happened, Terryll's archers had refit their longbows with arrows and, loosing them, were expertly finding their second and third marks.

Enraged, the Norseman wheeled his charger about and galloped toward them with his cavalry.

"That's it! Follow us, you devils!" Terryll cried, spurring Tempest. "Let's get out of here!" And the men of Bowes turned heel and bolted.

Outnumbered four to one, the Britons fled south, making a broad, doubling-back sweep through the hills and vales. Knowing the terrain, they headed east, then south, through forests, galloping over wolds, down into stream beds, splashing along, then mounting over the banks, then bending away to the west and back into another forest.

Not knowing the terrain, Olaf and his horsemen drummed after them blindly and closed to within a hundred yards.

The terrain opened into a broad meadow surrounded by a labyrinth of tree-bald hills—one hillock looking like the other. Leading them through the maze, Terryll glanced back, saw the Saxons gaining, grinned, then swung back around to the north, completing a broad circuitous loop.

Olaf stayed with them and closed to within fifty yards.

Meanwhile, the Saxons attacked the berm like an army of fighter ants. However, clambering up the slopes, the warriors lost their footing on the wetted grass and, falling, bunched up along the base and became easy marks for the British archers. Still they came with a single mind—ants swarming a lump of sugar—climbing over fallen men, trampling them, using them to gain footholds up the deadly incline.

Grappling ropes were tossed and, hooked over the crenellations, were cut at once by the Britons with their axes. More hooks were thrown.

The Britons worked feverishly along the walls, hacking ropes, loosing arrows, hurling javelins, hurling anything to repel the relentless advance of the Saxon juggernaut.

The warriors with the battering ram charged shouting toward the north gates—running heavily, ten men to a side and their shields held overhead against the continual hail of arrows. However, once reaching the mud slick, many of them slipped and fell, tripping others, and the ram nose-dived, thick-ended, into the stones of the road and bucked out of their hands.

Scrambling to their feet, the warriors lifted the ram but were quickly felled by the British marksmen above them.

Horsa, sitting astride his horse just out of range of the long-bowmen, was furious. "Bring up the archers!" he shouted. "Give those men covering fire!"

Two lines of bowmen quickly formed just back from the gates and directed their fire at the Britons. Volleys of arrows whistled away. Britons were falling along the wall now with Saxons falling in the field as the men of Killwyn Eden returned their fire.

Several men rushed in to replace those slain before the gates. Dragging their bodies out of the way—using them, in effect, to sweep away the mud from the approach—the Saxons took hold of the ram and, finding their footing, charged anew against the gates, coming at them with short, choppy rushes, then backing away, thrusting again, time and again, like a pendulum, pounding with a drumming cadence that sent shock waves oscillating through the walls.

When a man was struck down by a British arrow, another would jump in to take his place, and so on, man after man after man, like a machine. There was no end to Saxon replacements. There was no end to the hammering of the gates.

The Britons angled the catapults and ballistae toward the flanks and hurled payloads of rocks and boulders over the walls into the rushing men, one after the other—the felling-of-tree sounds, *ka-whunk*, whipping, whirring sounds—punishing the war beast.

Still the beast came, roaring with rage.

Ladders were tilted against the palisade only to be poled off the walls by the Britons. More ladders were slanted against the palisade with men climbing now . . . with men shinnying up alongside, shooting at the men behind the crenellations . . . men being shot off the ladders, and more taking their place . . . men being shot behind the walls, leaving gaps here and there . . . more ladders tilting . . . the defense weakening, the offense mounting with a violent tenacity.

A grimness began to set into the faces of the Britons, for it was clear they could not win a battle of attrition.

Terryll and his men broke out of the trees, galloping pell-mell into an open field and crossing it toward the berm at the south end of the village. The escarpment rose steeply there and wrapped around, falling away just as steeply along the eastern wall, to make any assault of the palisade on these fronts impossible. He angled his horse toward the eastern base of the escarpment, descending sharply with the slope so that the berm loomed high over his left shoulder.

Olaf and two hundred of his men were right on their tails, still closing, descending now to follow the Britons along the base of the escarpment. Having been disoriented in the pursuit, the Norseman grinned when he saw that the fool Britons had led them back to the battle. It wasn't until arrows began falling from the sky that he realized the boy had led them into range of the longbowmen waiting for them along the eastern wall.

Olaf's horse reared as an arrow struck its left flank, and the Viking was thrown clear. He landed with a jolt, and his head glanced off the ground and broke one of the wings on his helmet, so that it flapped like a wounded bird.

Not wasting their advantage, the British archers continued to fire volley after volley of arrows into the confused riders, decimating their numbers.

Olaf jumped to his feet with a curse, grabbed the reins of a riderless horse and, swinging up into the saddle, galloped out of range of the archers with the broken wing on his helmet flopping miserably.

Terryll and his men looked over their shoulders and laughed. And laughing, they spurred their mounts up the eastern slope and around to the northern end of the village, still reveling in their little victory.

But once seeing the black mass of men battering against the palisade there, and the Britons' desperate defense of the walls, the humor quickly left their faces. They disappeared silently into the forest to rejoin Conlan and the others at the rendezvous, every one of their faces glaring with the spectacle they were leaving behind.

Dagmere opened her eyes with a start, her heart pounding furiously in her chest. She blinked at the ceiling, wondering for a moment where she was, and, remembering, her thoughts slowly came into focus. She saw it clearly now, lying there in a makeshift bed in the quiet of the morning, looking up at the ceiling and thinking through it. It had come to her like a revelation from on high. It terrified her. She took a deep breath to calm the fury in her heart. The sun slanted through the open window over the bed and spread an oblong of light over the smooth wooden floor. A light breeze from the west carried the wild tart scent of heather into the room. She could hear the cheerful song of finches and flycatchers just outside in the trees and every so often catch their tiny shapes darting past the window.

To be a bird, she thought. *To be a bird and be able to fly away at will.* What a lovely thought. Then she thought of Aeryck—another lovely thought. Yes, she would fly to him. But the other thing—the revelation—lighted darkly upon her reverie, and she let out a sigh.

418

She glanced briefly around the room, acquainting herself with their new surroundings. A table and three chairs commanded the center of the chamber, some fresh wildflowers stood in a ceramic vase on the table, a rack of coats was in the corner by the door, a wooden coal scuttle by the hearth, and kitchen utensils hanging neatly from the mantle. In short, the furnishings of simple country folk.

Arriving late the night before, she hadn't been able to see anything but vague shapes and the dazed eyes of those simple country folk upon hearing the dreadful news.

The girl looked over at her mother sleeping soundly next to her. She watched the back of her head for a few moments, as the sun lit her hair ablaze with a rich palette of reds and golds and browns. She watched the blanket rise and fall with her mother's breathing, listening to her soft sleeping sounds.

Helena had finally, after several hours of fitful tossing and turning, fallen off to sleep, mumbling at first, then weeping in some deep anguish of spirit, thrice calling out to Allyndaar, then growing still.

Dagmere compressed her lips and frowned. Then she slipped out of bed surreptitiously and stole across the room, dressed quickly, collected her longbow and quiver, and opened the door. She looked back at her mother, and whispered, "I'm sorry, Mama, but I've got to do this." Then she sneaked outside, closing the door silently behind her.

Minutes later she was galloping south along the road, heading back to Killwyn Eden.

Brother Lucius Aurelius and Brother Lupe were in the hills overlooking the village of Old Penrith, where they had spent the night in prayer.

Lupe, a heavyset swarthy man from the Iberian peninsula, had just nodded off and begun to snore. It had commenced with a gentle blowing noise—little cooings that were soft and babelike—then following came the windless whistles. As he got into the deep rhythms of sleep, he began to rasp, then wheeze, then, after lacing several short blasts into the mix, he settled into something of a continuous drone, sounding much like a lion stricken with adenoid problems.

Brother Lucius reached over and jostled him. "Wake up, Brother Lupe. Wake up." He smiled. "I cannot concentrate with all thy roaring."

Brother Lupe bolted upright with a loud snort, wiped the drool off his chin with the back of his thick hand, looking embarrassed for his crime.

"'The spirit is willing,'" Brother Lucius quoted, "but the flesh would prefer a soft down bed, wouldn't it?"

Brother Lupe lowered his eyes penitentially.

Then Aurelius's face turned suddenly grave, and as he began to speak an intensity grew in his voice and burned out through his eyes.

"We must not lose heart, my brother. We must pray. Fiercely we must pray. Pray that God will have mercy on His little flock—that they will not scatter at the hands of these wolves. Pray that they will no longer be divided in their faith but come together as one, as the Godhead is one. Pray, Brother Lupe, that this darkness overwhelming the land will not extinguish the holy lamp of Christ. Pray, Brother Lupe. Pray fervently!"

Brother Lupe nodded vigorously, then both monks—their forms tiny against the shining grandeur of creation—reverently lowered their heads and stormed the throne of God.

Terryll and the men of Bowes were to meet the other half of their troop at the ancient dolmen situated in a grove of oaks about five miles northeast of Killwyn Eden. Every few minutes he looked over his shoulder, then, seeing nothing, looked ahead, his eyes warily working the terrain. So far there had been no sign of the Norseman and the survivors of his cavalry, so he eased their pace to a gentle lope to spare the horses.

They had long since left the forest, and the countryside was gathered before them now into a series of low hills, mounding away in a brilliant spectrum of greens—the wet soil-rich green of a British countryside in spring. There were myriad wildflowers covering entire hillsides, scenting the air, and with the sun now and then breaking through a scattering of clouds and spreading a golden incandescence over the green, the vistas were spectacular. But the Britons were of no mind to admire them.

They wound up the steep grade of a ridge, the horses tired and chugging, traversing back and forth. Then, cresting the summit, with the horizon lowering and spreading out to reveal that spectacular green-on-green vista, they saw the grove of oaks in the distance.

"There they are, Terryll!" one of the men cried.

They could see the troop clearly through the trees, cool in the shade as they were gathered around the dolmen, and the horses grazing down the lee of the slope in the long grasses. They could see the men looking up, not their faces, just the shape of their heads coming up and holding as Terryll and his men rode toward them. A few came forward into the sun.

"Hail!" Terryll shouted, waving an arm.

"Hail and well met," a man returned, waving his arm in a universal salute. "That you, Terryll?"

"Yes, it is—" And suddenly his eyes went wide. "Papa?"

Then the boy was flying off his horse and running, the father and son running toward the other, and, meeting, they embraced happily.

"Papa, Papa! I thought you were—"

"I'm all right, son," Allyndaar said. "Just a little sore in the head." Allyndaar held his son out at arm's length and gazed upon him.

There were streams of tears washing over the boy's cheeks. Then he noticed Terryll's tunic. "What's this? You're wounded?"

Terryll glanced down at the dark, red stain on his side. "A scratch. It's nothing." The boy looked at his father, noticing the bandage wrapped around his head. "What happened to you? We heard that you had fallen."

Allyndaar laughed. "I fell all right! That Saxon liked to take my head off." He laughed again, glancing back at the trees. "But it will take more than some glancing blow from a battle-ax to keep me down. Isn't that right, men?"

Laughter came from the trees.

Terryll followed his look and noticed several of the men of Brough there, perhaps as many as twenty, besides Conlan and his men. He looked back at his father. "Mama thinks you might've been killed, Papa."

Allyndaar looked suddenly at the boy.

"She's not taking it very well," Terryll continued. "Dag's not taking it very well either."

"They are safe?"

"Yes, Aurelius took them to Old Penrith." Terryll's expression changed. "Papa, there are too many of them. They just keep coming."

The chieftain gazed off in the direction of Killwyn Eden.

Thick dark clouds were rolling in from the west now, closing in over the fleecy blue of the sky.

"God have mercy," he said quietly, his face looking worn and drawn. Wrinkle lines radiated from his eyes like spokes in a wheel. Then turning abruptly, he commanded, "Mount your horses, men. We must go and fight. We must fight until we can fight no more."

The men mounted and were quickly on their way south to Killwyn Eden.

Terryll drew up next to his father at the head of the column—Tempest straining to take the lead from Daktahr—and said, "It is good to see you well, Papa."

"It is good to see you well too, son."

They rode a little way, then Terryll asked, "Can we beat them, Papa?"

Allyndaar smiled grimly. "The battle is the Lord's, son. It is for Him to decide."

Toom . . . Toom . . . Toom . . .

The battering ram continued to pummel the gates with unrelenting monotony.

"A few more whacks ought to do it!" one of the Saxons shouted. "Lay your backs into it, men!"

Toom . . . Toom . . . Toom . . .

And the heavy oaken gates shuddered with each punishing blow.

Horsa's face mirrored the ebb and flow of battle—alternately beaming happily or burning in furious rage as he stormed back and forth across the battlefield on his white charger.

"That's it! Keep hammering at it, men," he shouted. "It'll give way any minute." He directed others with broad sweeps of his hands. "There! Over there, you fools!" he cried. "There's a gap opened up on the wall . . . get the ladders up there! Up there, and over there! Step to it, men!"

Several more ladders slanted against the palisade, with warriors ascending, then falling, then others pulling them out of the way and ascending, then battling with the Britons along the parapets.

"That's it! That's it!" Horsa bellowed.

But one of the archers along the wall cried out, "Take heart, men of Killwyn Eden! We are Britons all! Let us fight as Britons! Die as Britons if Christ wills it!"

And the Britons loosed more arrows into the crush of men, driving them back.

However the war beast gathered itself into a crouch, then sprang at them with a roar, pummeling the gates with unpent rage.

Toom . . . Toom . . . Toom . . .

And suddenly a loud crack rent the clangor of battle. There was a brief moment of silence as the shock of it rang high in the air, drawing out into a thin mantle of gloom over the Britons. Every eye turned to the gates. The Saxons, seeing the thick planks begin to give way, were the first to respond and redoubled their efforts.

Toom . . . Toom . . . Toom . . .

And the gates staggered on their hinges like a battered pugilist.

The Britons scrambled before a surge of panic, concentrating more of their fire on the Saxons at the gates. Those manning the siege engines rolled one of the ballistae to the entrance and tipped it over against the gates, hoping to forestall the inevitable. Then they picked up their swords and clambered up the walls to fight alongside the longbowmen. One by one the war machines fell silent in this way, as the drama moved to the desperate defense of the palisade.

Saxons were getting over the walls now—the flood rising, brinking on the lip, holding, then going over in trickles here and there, men finding the gaps and swinging their arms and legs over, then dropping into the compound. Their faces were clenched in various attitudes of violence, some grunting savagely, others laughing with blood lust, others snarling and shouting obscenities, every one of them swollen with the surety of the kill.

Still the men of Killwyn Eden fought valiantly to keep from being overwhelmed. Little knots of warriors rushed back and forth, filling in the gaps—too many gaps now, more gaps than men to fill them—battling hand-to-hand with their enemies coming over the walls, their blades rising, falling, thrusting, flashing, the men pressing forward, snarling with animal ferocity, then falling back, groaning, now waxing in strength, now flagging, as they struggled desperately to shore up the crumbling defense.

The gates continued to shudder before the punishing blows of the battering ram.

Toom . . . Toom . . . Toom . . .

There was another crack, and then another. A shout went up. And then again as the thick timbers began to tear away from the iron hinges and the wood splintered into thick shards, knifing away and allowing daylight to shine through the gaps. The glaring faces of men could be seen through the gaps, grinning menacingly as they drove the ram steadily against the bashed-in places—the juggernaut pounding . . . pounding . . . pounding . . .

And the roar of battle was impossible to comprehend.

Allyndaar and the troop of archers galloped through the forest at a punishing pace. Flecks of foam lathered the horses' flanks, where the saddles and reins slapped hard against them. Their heads hammering the air, their nostrils flared and blasting furious snorts, the horses drummed fleet-footedly over the earth.

Now the Britons could hear the roar of battle, ascending like a moan over the earth. As they raced over a treeless hill everyone could see the crown of the village rising in the distance and the boil of men encompassing it.

And then they heard a great shout. It shot over their heads like an airy sheet of glass; then striking the distant hills, it caromed off and returned a shattering of echoes. The riders, reining sharply, looked at one another dumbstruck.

"Are those our men?" one wondered out loud.

No one answered, but everyone knew what had happened.

"The gates!" Allyndaar cried, digging his heels into Daktahr's flanks.

As the Britons sped away, every man felt as though his soul had been rent in two.

The skies over Killwyn Eden were a dark oppression, lowering and slung over the village like a ceiling of slate. Lightning flickered in the hills, followed by the bully rumblings of thunder. A chilling wind shrieked down the Eden valley like so many banshees, causing leaves to shimmer nervously in the silvery glow of the pre-storm.

And the Saxon warriors began to pour through the breach with heartless abandon.

The dispirited Britons inside fought desperately to hold back the deluge, but one by one the men fell, leaving greater gaps along the wall. And the war beast rushed into them with machinelike efficiency.

"That's it! We've got them now!" Horsa boomed, unable to contain himself. He clapped his hands with a shout. "We've done it, Hengist! We've done it at last, by Woden!"

He looked over his shoulder to see how the second wave was advancing, and immediately his eyes burned angrily. The Wolf was advancing too slow, he thought. Indeed it appeared as though he was deliberately holding back. Jerking his horse about, he shouted, "Advance, you fool! Advance, or so help me I'll strip you of command!"

If the Wolf heard him, he made no indication, neither did he adjust the speed of his approach. He simply gazed at the overlord with cold yellow eyes and a thin maleficent twist of the lips that begged a smile.

Horsa shook his head with disgust. And then he lurched forward with a cough, feeling the sudden jolt of an arrow through his back. He blinked perplexedly for a moment, thinking there had been some horrible mistake. Then his eyes jerked wide with the realization that death was upon him. He whirled in his saddle, clutching his throat, and found Ruddbane hidden in the umbrage of the treeline, grinning, saw the cold devilish treason in the man's eyes as he came trotting out of the shadows. A curse formed upon the overlord's lips, then aborted into a groan as he pitched headlong to the earth.

The Wolf rode forward, glanced down at the crumpled body of the overlord, and grunted dispassionately. Then he raised his hand and signaled the advance of the second wave.

His warriors ran forward, brandishing their weapons and shouting the battle cry, greedy to get into the killing.

Ruddbane drew alongside the Wolf and gazed down at the dead body of Horsa. "You are now in command, my liege," he said proudly.

"Now?" The Wolf chortled throatily. "My friend, I have been in command for some time."

Looking into the Wolf's yellow eyes—inhuman eyes that glowed with supernatural intensity—Ruddbane felt a shiver go through him. He made some feeble attempt at a laugh to cover it, but the laugh got caught in his throat. The Wolf looked away. "Go now and do what you must."

"As you wish, my liege," the red-bearded warrior said, striking his chest. Then he galloped away, feeling a sudden release of evil in his brain.

Allyndaar and his troop of archers drew up at the edge of the forest, and immediately their hearts sank. Across the field they could see a black mass of Saxon warriors pouring through the breach and going over the walls. And occasionally they could see British defenders mounting here and there over the surge, their faces blanched in a desperate vigilance.

Brilliant shards of lightning jagged flickeringly across the angry skies, followed at once by a deafening clap of thunder. Dark streaks of rain slanted over the hills, and the thunder rolled back with a menacing afterword. A few raindrops began to find their way through the forest canopy, spattering heavily against leaves and the backs of men. Horses shuddered stoically. Then the shower stiffened abruptly and made a continual hissing sound in the leaves, as though the forest itself were jeering at them.

A profound gloom settled over the men of Bowes and Brough.

"All is lost!" one of the riders despaired.

"What shall we do, Papa?"

Allyndaar turned heavily to his son. "I want you to ride to Old Penrith and tell Aurelius that the village has fallen."

"No, Father, I won't leave you again."

"Take your mother and sister to Bowness," the chieftain continued, ignoring his son's protests. "They will be safe there."

"But—"

"Do as I tell you, son. Go quickly now."

Terryll looked at his father, stricken with horror. His father had spoken with such a calm deliberateness, such stoic surrender, that it seemed as though his spirit had already flown from his body—that the laying down of his husk would only be a formality. However the imperious look in his eyes compelled him to obey.

The boy bade farewell and, turning away, glanced into the men's eyes, then quickly averted his own to the ground. He felt shame spidering all over him. He spurred Tempest into a trot, wanting to get away quickly, his head tucked into his shoulders like a criminal's. Then, stealing into the dismal sanctuary of the forest, he felt as though some invisible hand had reached into his chest and was squeezing his heart. Tears flowed and mingled with the drops of rain. Terryll reined Tempest, looked back through a drizzling corridor in the trees, and could just make out the dark gray shape of his father as he was giving final instructions to the men. They all looked like ghosts. And then everything became a blurry wash.

"O God," he wept bitterly, "O God, have mercy."

Then he reined the black slowly away.

A gentle wind coming from the north sifted through the rain-soaked bowery that flickered by overhead, then stiffened its intent. The rain eased of a sudden, then trickled away, sheeting off the leaves into large drops. There was a musky smell of wet earth and wood and leaves pervading the forest and the wet breeze blowing through it. Thick mists cottoned around the dark boles of trees.

Tempest, plodding slowly along, raised his nose, scenting the wind shift, then blew out a snort.

Terryll jerked his head at the same moment. His eyes shot wide as he pulled up on the reins. He craned his head, listening, frowning, then leaped off the horse and pressed his ear to the drenched ground.

He looked up suddenly. *"Papa!"*

Then he flew back into the saddle and took off like a shot.

"And then we'll work along the left flank there until we reach the gates," Allyndaar said, finishing his hasty briefing. "Once there—well, you know what to do."

The men glanced away from the battlefield and looked grimly at one another. Gazing at the long line of horsemen stretching out on either side of him, their young faces flinty for the grim task ahead, Allyndaar felt a sudden swell of pride in his bosom. "It has been an honor to have fought alongside each of you," he said fondly. "May we sing songs of how God has wrought a great deliverance through you in the years to come. May our children remember this day proudly. Godspeed to you now."

Every man nodded, taking heart. Without a word, each secured his reins beneath his thigh, keeping a slack in them, then pulled two or three arrows from his quiver and clasped them in his bow hand for faster delivery. Then every eye fixed on the chieftain.

"Are you ready?" he said.

"We are ready to die with you, Allyn," one answered, arching his back proudly.

"Aye, Allyn," another put in, "we'll give them a fair show of it."

There was a round of ayes.

Glancing heavenward, Allyndaar raised his hand and held it suspended for one terrible moment.

A thundering of hooves broke the dreadful pause.

"Wait, Papa! Wait!" Terryll cried, crashing through the forest.

Allyndaar and the Britons turned, pulling up on their reins.

Suddenly the horses began to whicker and toss their wet manes, sensing something in the air. The men struggled angrily to control them.

Then the ground began to tremble beneath their feet. And then the trembling became a steady rumbling, building every second without letup. There was a flash of lightning, brightening the hills with a deathly luminance, and then the cymbal crash of thunder. And when it rang off behind the hills, the rumbling continued, building to something.

The men glanced northward when they heard the sound. It was faint at first, like a single sustained note whining in the distance, then building louder and more vigorous every second.

"What is this?" one of the men cried.

The Britons looked at one another in astonishment, many feeling chills going over them as if something either terribly frightful or wonderful were happening. The air was charged with an awful expectancy. The horses blew loud snorts and stamped their feet at the ground, pawing it anxiously.

The sound coming out of the north was more robust now and lower in pitch, sounding no longer like a single note but like a multitude of voices—voices increasing in amplitude and coming out over the rolling thunder of the earth like the rushing of many waters.

Many of the men still fighting—Britons and Saxons alike—turned fully in their places to see what it was, forgetting momentarily the business of war. And just for a moment the din of bloodletting surrendered to a reverent hush.

The Wolf turned, and immediately his head jolted as though struck by a blow. His eyes widened into an impenitent glare. He knew exactly what it was.

The sound, booming now, came rolling beneath the thick black clouds. It caromed off the iron-cast ceiling and fell over the battlefield, with every moment passing lending articulation to the voices.

Fear began to grip the hearts of man and beast. Warriors gaped at the cloud ceiling, for indeed it sounded as though some heavenly host were descending. Nothing in their history could prepare them for what their eyes and ears were about to witness.

"What is it, Papa?" Terryll cried, gazing up at the overcast sky. "It—it almost sounds like singing."

Allyndaar looked wondrously at the horizon. "It is, son," he said. "It is singing."

"It sounds like angels."

"I do not doubt there are angels present, Terryll." The chieftain smiled. "But those are clearly the voices of men."

"You mean—"

And then the black snarl of clouds burst open with a sudden effulgence. Golden bars of light shot through the holes and struck the field of battle as though heaven itself were breaking through to the earth. The chorus of singing men swelled to fortissimo strength, and the ground trembled before them.

The Saxons continued to look up wonderingly, fearfully, thinking the British gods were descending upon them to exact some vengeance.

Men began to tremble. Hearts fluttered and failed. A few warriors dropped their weapons.

The dark pack of storm clouds slunk away behind the hills, rumbling petulantly.

And then the sun burst upon the northern rim of the earth with splashes of radiant gold, revealing a translucent wall of riders advancing suddenly out of the misty horizon. They appeared as though out of thin air, and the rising waves of heat gave the illusion that they were galloping above the glistening earth like an army of mythic heroes, shining brightly, with their swords and armor flashing in the sun as they sang.

> "Alleluia! Alleluia!
> Salvation and glory and honor and power
> unto the Lord our God,
> who reigns forever and ever!
>
> "Alleluia! Alleluia!
> For the Lord God omnipotent reigns.
> Let us be glad and rejoice
> and give honor to Him!"

Again they sang the chorus, and again and again, louder and louder, building to a terrible crescendo. An army from the north was coming, an army of Picts and Scots singing the alleluia chorus.

And as they drew near to the battlefield, Terryll could just see Aeryck in the lead, brandishing his sword in the sun, and there was Brynwald beside him wielding his battle-ax, and righteous Dunnald with the men of Loch na Huric, and Oswald with all of his warriors, every one of them shouting, "Alleluia! Alleluia!" And it seemed the heavens and the earth were singing in concert. "God be praised!" Allyndaar shouted over the roaring.

Then he and his troop of riders galloped from the trees, adding their voices to the holy anthem, and together with Brynwald's army they drove a wedge through the center of the Saxon offense, trailing a wake of devastation.

Brynwald and Aeryck led an assault against the right flank, charging fiercely into them, driving them toward the hills. And Oswald and Dunnald charged against the left, the Saxons melting before them and scattering toward the trees.

The Britons inside the compound let out a shout, then rushed into those men they were battling with rekindled fury. The Saxons dashed about ineffectually, inside and outside the camp, as though suddenly stricken with some madness. Confusion rifled through their ranks. Warriors gaped at one another with profound horror.

The rout began with one man throwing his sword down and running. Seeing him go, another man, witnessing in the act a mirror of his own terror, threw down his weapons and ran, and then another bolted—the fear working through their midst like cracks of ice radiating from some point of impact, then networking out over the surface. And then they began to flee in twos and threes, the fear touching, connecting them, impelling them outward, and then small groups of them turned heel and ran, and then larger groups turned and fled, and the juggernaut disintegrated. The battlefield was a rout of running men, no two going off together.

"Strike them doon!" Brynwald cried, his eyes blazing with holy fire, "lest they live to trouble us again!" And the Picts fell upon the Saxons with a terrible wrath.

"For the glory of the Laird Christ!" Oswald thundered, raising his blade to the heavens. And the Scotti cut through them without mercy.

Enraged with the turn of events, Olaf galloped about the field trying to rally the fleeing men. "Turn and fight, you cowards!" he shouted, charging into their paths.

But the men swerved and, running past, only glanced up at him—the fear of the herd glaring in their eyes—not missing a beat in their stride. And when the Norseman saw that victory was slipping through his fingers, he began to hack away at them with his battle-ax, venting his fury like a madman.

Even Druell ran. He rushed up to Olaf, his face craven, crying, "We are doomed, Olaf. Doomed! Flee for your life!"

Olaf took a swipe at him with his ax, but the Jute bolted away at a full gallop.

Olaf hurled his ax at the nearest man, then drew his sword. Suddenly his horse reeled, screaming, its eyes white in terror, and fell over backward onto him, pinning his left leg beneath its hindquarters. A battle-ax angled up from behind its skull.

The Norseman tugged at his leg, trying to extricate it from under the dead weight of the horse, then he screamed as he felt a knife of excruciating pain tear over his body. Propped up on his elbows, his head thrown back, he cursed at the sky when he realized that his leg was broken.

He waited a moment, allowing the pain to seep out of him, then tried to budge the horse. Another jolt of pain threw him back to the ground. Again he waited. Unclenching his eyes, he blinked at the sky and cursed. He could do nothing but lie there, caught in some ignominious malaise, stripped of honor, of pride, saddled with the intermittent drummings of feet and flashes of legs rushing by adding insult to injury.

A shadow passed over him. Looking up, Olaf beheld the backlighted silhouette of a horseman looming over him. He could not tell if he were Saxon or Briton.

The rider eyed the Viking's helmet and began to chortle. "Seems you've had your wings clipped and fallen into a bad way."

Olaf narrowed his eyes, searching the dark folds of his face. "Ruddbane," he snarled. He shot a glance at the battle-ax.

Ruddbane chortled. "That's right, Commander, you're onto me now."

Olaf looked around for his sword, but he had lost it in the fall. Then he thought of the ax. He swung his arm at the haft, wincing. But it was just out of his reach.

The red-bearded warrior, looking down at him, laughed. He was enjoying himself immensely. Then he swung off his horse and strode, heavy-legged, over to the Viking. "I'll just collect this," he said, retrieving his ax from the horse's neck.

Olaf glared at him, his mind working fast.

Ruddbane shook his head as he glanced around at the confused rabble. He clucked his tongue. "It doesn't look good for our noble campaign, does it, *Commander?*" he said contemptuously. "Pity, isn't it? Ahh, but no matter. I will have my little pleasure."

He snickered, savoring the thought. "I've waited a long time for this moment, Olaf. I've lived in your shadow, years now, biding my time, knowing that one day I would have you. And now I have you, don't I?"

The man stepped forward with the ax, and his eyes, gleaming wickedly, narrowed into a menacing scowl. "You once deprived me of my rightful kill, do you remember? The young Briton. I'll just collect my due."

"Unless you put down your weapon, Ruddbane," a voice cried out in broken German, "the only collecting you will do will be at the gates of hell!"

Ruddbane whirled to see a handsome young Briton—hair black and shining, with piercing blue eyes—sitting astride a black charger and pointing an arrow at his chest.

Ruddbane's eyes widened, then narrowed with comprehension. "Well, as I live and breathe . . . if it isn't . . ." The warrior threw his head back and laughed. "Ho, ho, Olaf. How is it that men doubt the providence of the gods? See how they've given me the both of you!"

Terryll drew back on his bow. "I said to put your weapon down, Ruddbane," he repeated. "Or would you prefer that I let a little air into your miserable hide?"

A crimson light flared in the warrior's eyes. "Not likely," he said coldly. Then he turned to the Norseman, laughing again, his eyes shifting serpentlike. "Did you hear that, Olaf? The lad thinks to prick me with his—" Quick as a flash he hurled his ax at the boy's torso and lunged to one side.

Terryll ducked and loosed his arrow at the same moment, immediately hearing the *whuh-whuh-whoosh* of the battle-ax over his head and seeing the arrow strike high in Ruddbane's chest.

Olaf glanced at Ruddbane, marveled at the skill of the shot, then looked up at the boy.

They stared at one another for a long moment.

"Wie heissen Sie?" the Norseman asked.

Terryll did not answer him.

Olaf hiked himself up on his elbow, winced, then chortled. "Seems you've bested me after all, young Briton." He spoke in the British tongue. "You are a fine warrior. And a proud one, I can see." He laughed. "I still say you would've made a good Viking."

Terryll frowned, thinking how much misery and death this man had caused his people. He thought of Bolstroem's big face beaming at him, heard the big echo of his laugh booming in his mind. He thought of the faces of those who had fallen bravely this day in battle; thought of the people of Biddlecairn and the horror of their cries for mercy. He drew the last arrow from his quiver and fit it to his bow, then leveled it at the man's chest.

Olaf's expression changed. He glanced at the tip of the arrow, then peered into the boy's eyes. He saw the hesitation in them.

"What are you waiting for?"

Terryll eased the pull of his bow, scowling angrily. "You showed me a kindness once, Norseman. Today the debt is paid."

Olaf grunted. "I do not want your pity, Briton," he snarled. "Or have you become a woman that you dishonor me so? I have fallen in battle; now kill me like a warrior. There is honor in it."

Terryll shook his head. "I'm not going to kill you, Norseman. I wouldn't give you the satisfaction."

Olaf glowered. "Give me Ruddbane's sword then, and I will finish his work if you haven't the stomach for it."

"Auf Wiedersehen," the boy said contemptuously, then reined Tempest away.

"A knife then, a stone—anything!"

Terryll let out a yell and spurred the black into a gallop.

Olaf watched him leave, his eyes glaring. Then, with a mounting frustration, he grasped around for his sword and, not finding it, was consumed by a violent rage. "Odin! Odin, hear me!" he shouted furiously. "Do not let me die like some animal. There is no glory in this."

But he heard only the sounds of a defeated army, of men fleeing wide-eyed into the trees, with the British cavalry now hotly pursuing. Then vainly he beat his fists against the horse, the very symbol of his defeat.

"Odin! Odin! Odin!"

Dagmere feared she was too late. Galloping around the final bend in the road, the village and the field of battle opening to her left, she scanned the scene quickly. Immediately horror rushed her, as the terrible spectacle and stench of battle smacked her in the face. Loud groans rose like departing spirits over the grim plot of earth.

Looking about hopelessly, she saw several groups of horsemen galloping to and fro, running down men, mopping up the remaining debris of battle; and men running here and there, wearing masks of primal terror as they scattered before the horsemen, sometimes turning to fight like cornered animals, then buckling to lance or ax. The field was strewn with several hundred men, some propped up on their elbows, others on their hands and knees, others deathly still.

"O God, this cannot be!" Dagmere cried, thinking the day lost.

It was then that she espied her brother racing after a flight of Saxons, looking like an avenging angel. "Terryll?" she said, blinking incredulously. Then she realized with a jolt of excitement that those horsemen were Britons. And then she saw her father by the gates, directing some men into the compound to aid the Britons still fighting there.

"Papa," she whispered. Then she cried happily, "Papa! Papa!"

She let out a happy shriek and spurred her horse onto the field, guiding the mare through the fallen men—Saxons mostly—mindful not to look down at their faces. However, drawing near the gates, she was alarmed to see an archer rising from the among the dead behind her father, fitting an arrow to his bow, and sighting on his back.

"Papa! Look out!" she cried, galloping and drawing back on her longbow.

Allyndaar whirled about and in one moment of time saw the white dash of an arrow wing past him to shudder harmlessly in the palisade, saw the archer pitch forward with an arrow quivering in his back, and beyond him saw some wild horse maiden, with a mane of auburn hair billowing in the wind, charging at him and screaming—a frantic-looking creature who bore an uncanny resemblance to his daughter.

"Papa!" the frantic-looking creature cried, waving her bow.

"Dagmere?"

432

The girl drew alongside her father and flung herself at him, nearly unseating him. "You're alive, Papa! You're really alive!"

The chieftain was incredulous. "Yes . . . yes, I'm alive," he said, still not believing his eyes. Then he frowned. "Dagmere, what are you doing here? This is no place for a young woman."

Dagmere looked at him fiercely. "This is no place for a man either, Papa."

"Dagmere!"

"I had to come, Papa. I felt a fire in my chest—like the voice of God burning in me. I had to come, Papa. I just had to." She smiled weakly at him. "Aren't you glad I did?"

Allyndaar glanced down at the slain Saxon. He grunted. "We'll discuss this later. Right now, let's get you to a safe place."

Dagmere's eyes darted anxiously about the field. "Have you seen Aeryck, Papa? Did he come like you hoped?"

"Yes, he came," the chieftain growled, his tone softening. "I saw him with Brynwald, over by the west gate—there!"

Dagmere followed his point to the broad gentle slope of ground that fell away from the western berm before it rose sharply into the hills. Immediately she saw Brynwald and a throng of Pictish warriors putting a disorderly mob of Saxons to flight, and in the midst of them, charging heroically, was Aeryck.

She beamed, watching happily as the boy whirled from his attack and swung back toward the village, leaving the Saxons high-tailing it south.

Brynwald charged up to Aeryck, his bronzed and tattooed body glistening in the sun. "Ha! The day belongs to the Laird Christ, kipper!" he boomed over the receding din. "See how the heathen scatter before His mighty arm! By the oaks, lad, 'tis a glorious victory!"

Aeryck turned to him and smiled grimly.

Then the chieftain thundered away, howling some Pictish war cry, leaving Aeryck suddenly alone in the midst of a grisly desolation. The boy looked around at the carnage, then let out a sigh. His arms ached, his shoulders ached, his entire body was spent from fighting. He was tired of the killing.

"Aeryck!" a girl's voice cried out.

The boy reeled and saw a girl galloping furiously toward him. "Dagmere!"

He let out a whoop and thundered in her direction.

Dagmere burst into tears of joy, and meeting on the brow of a low swell of earth, they both flew off their horses and embraced each other tearfully.

A span of minutes passed with Dagmere weeping into his shoulder and Aeryck pulling her head close and stroking her hair, stroking her cheeks, kissing her head, and drawing strength from her. Then looking into the other's eyes, they could scarce speak for the release of emotions.

"I thought I would never see you again, Dagmere," he said, his voice trembling.

"See me again?" Dagmere buried her head in his chest, squeezing him hard. "Oh, Aeryck, I've missed you so."

Allyndaar laughed as he rode up to them.

Aeryck pulled away abruptly. "Hail, sir," he said sheepishly.

The chieftain let his laugh trail. "Hail and well met," he returned. He smiled generously at him. "The Lord has brought a timely deliverance through you and Brynwald, Aeryck," he added sincerely. "The people of Killwyn Eden will be forever in your debt." He stretched his arm to the boy.

Aeryck looked at it, turning bright red, then clasped it firmly. "The debt is mine, sir."

Dagmere wiped her eyes. "I'll be safe here with Aeryck, don't you think, Papa?"

Allyndaar crooked an eyebrow at her, then grunted. "You stay right here, young lady," he said, feigning a stern voice.

Dagmere lowered her eyes appropriately, adding to the charade. "I will, Papa." She cast a playful smile at Aeryck.

Aeryck had no clue as to what was going on. He and Dagmere watched the chieftain gallop away toward the north gates, then looked at one another, both smiling shyly.

Aeryck drew her close again. Then seeing that look in her eyes, that big, pools-of-glistening-blue-with-lashes-fluttering look in her eyes and those full lips pursed and moist, he felt a sudden swelling in his throat. His heart thundered in his breast. His knees weakened. He thought he might pass out.

Dagmere smiled. Then, inclining her head, she rose up onto her toes, and Aeryck kissed her. The battle fell suddenly away into another universe, and everything was wonderful.

After several moments or hours (time was irrelevant), Aeryck, a bit dizzied by it all, pulled away when a movement caught his eye. He turned abruptly and saw a dark shape disappear into some trees a few hundred feet away.

"What is it, Aeryck?" Dagmere asked, following his eyes to a low, forested ridge.

"Huh? Oh, nothing, I guess. Just thought I saw something."

Dagmere frowned. "Look at me, silly," she teased.

He turned, and she lightly kissed the corners of his mouth.

Aeryck gazed into her eyes. "I love you, Dagmere."

"I love you too."

"Aeryck?"

"Yes?" He looked at her.

Dagmere was peering over his shoulder. She stared at something queerly.

"What is it?"

"I'm not sure. It looks like a wolf."

Aeryck looked quickly and saw it moving through the trees. The creature was dark in the umbrage of the forest. Still the lupine shape was unmistakable.

"Strange-looking wolf, though," she added. "Look how it moves . . . almost as though it were floating."

Aeryck peered at it curiously. Something was not right about this; it did seem as though the wolf were floating through the trees.

And then he saw a black horse rise into view from behind the ridgeline, coming up and over in dark silhouette, then halting in a sun-washed clearing in the trees. Aeryck frowned when he saw that the rider wore a wolfskin shroud and sported a black shield with a crimson wolf's head arched against it.

The horseman gazed sullenly upon the battlefield, his body bent in dark contemplation like some lord surveying the ruin of his estate. Then he turned, the horse stepping forward, and the horseman's eyes swept over the village, sweeping past the boy and girl, then jerking back to the boy. Even across the distance, the two yellow orbs smoldering angrily beneath the shroud transfixed Aeryck's eyes and bored into his mind.

It was a summons. *I have you, Worm. You cannot escape me now.*

Aeryck reeled, immediately feeling something cold and deathlike touch his soul, then crawl up the back of his neck. "It's him," he said, voicing some dark thought that was suddenly resurrected from his past.

"Who is he, Aeryck?" Dagmere asked fearfully. "Do you know him?"

"Yes, I know him," Aeryck said coldly, glaring at the horseman now. "He is the one they call the Wolf. The man—if he can be called a man—who was responsible for my father's death."

Dagmere was aghast. "Are you certain?"

"Stay here, Dagmere," Aeryck said, then ran over to his horse and mounted.

"Where are you going?" she cried, running after him.

Aeryck glanced down at the girl. "To settle a debt."

Dagmere looked up at the Wolf, saw the yellow eyes glinting darkly beneath the shroud. "No, Aeryck, you mustn't go! Just leave him be."

"I can't. Now please back away."

"No, I'm coming with you."

"You're staying here!" Aeryck snapped. Then, hefting his sword, he reined the horse away from her and galloped toward the low ridge.

Dagmere ran after him. *"Aeryck!"*

47
THE FENRIS WOLF

Aeryck charged up the ridge after the Wolf, feeling the sum of his angers and fears burning in his breast, feeling the torments of his mind and soul and body—and every lost thing of love and beauty torn from his tender life because of this man going up on a pyre of unquenchable indignation. His mind was fired with a single blazing thought. His arms, his legs, the sum of his flesh and bones were the keepers of the flame and drove him to the contest at the summit. He rushed to the edge of the clearing, pulled up on his reins and glanced around, fully expecting to see the Wolf where he had last seen him. But there was no sign of him. Aeryck had lost sight of him for a moment through the trees, but only for a moment. Where was he? He looked carefully now.

There was a strange quiet in the clearing. There were no birds chirping or flitting about in the bowery, no chattering of squirrels, no drone of insects. It was as though every beating breast and wing had been driven away by some shift in the air. Even the air had grown still as if it had died.

And then he felt the evil. There was a suddenness to it, as though a flight of ravens had just lighted in the trees, some dark presence roosting in the bowery, peering at him. A shiver crawled over him. He knew the Wolf was there. He could feel him amid the evil, brooding somewhere in the umbrage, watching. He could feel the eyes upon him, feel the malignant reach of those yellow eyes penetrating his mind.

Aeryck spurred the horse forward, walking cautiously around the perimeter of the clearing, feeling the eyes as he glanced warily into the trees. He looked down at the ground for tracks. There were none that he could see.

And then the quiet. There was nothing but the sound of his horse's footsteps resounding over the dead silence of the glade, and the pounding of his heart. The hairs on the back of his neck suddenly bristled with alarm. He jerked his head. He saw nothing. The Wolf, or the evil, or his mind was toying with him. And his fingers flexed anxiously over his sword.

Hauwka padded along the stream bed, limping terribly. Still he kept moving. Some imperious instinct sounded in his cavernous breast and drove him forward. He had been traveling south for many days now without letup, taking only brief respites for sleep and food and to ease the nagging pain in his shoulder.

Fleeing Sarteham's men and horses, he had circled wide to the north and east, leading them ever away from the boy. Then he had doubled back, trailed the horsemen for a few miles, and surprised them out of a blind of thick underbrush. He had fallen upon them with fierce anger, inflicted terrible wounds upon both man and beast until they fled with their tails in the air.

But the bear was not thinking of this now as he padded steadily along, his shoulder smarting terribly. He was thinking that he had to move south, wanting to stop and rest but racing against some clock that thundered in his brain. The village lay just ahead, perhaps a mile or so in the hills. He climbed out of the stream bed onto a grassy rock-strewn hill, and a growl rattled deep in his throat. He paused and raised his great bulk onto his hind legs—full-bodied, head thrust forward, lower lip hanging like a black cup—and sniffed the air. The standing hair bristled along his nape, and lowering himself he snorted.

Then the great bear lunged forward into a lope, shuddering off the pain.

Aeryck made a complete circle of the clearing, seeing nothing, hearing nothing, but feeling closer to—whatever it was. He began to doubt his eyes. He had seen the man though. Dagmere had seen him too. But where was he? And then he felt a strange prickling along his neck, like an electrical charge loosed over him. He yanked his head and saw nothing.

He pulled up angrily on the reins and looked around. Still nothing. Not a bird, not a creature, not the stirring of a leaf. He upbraided himself for his foolishness. The flame of his indignation flickered on its wick. Obviously the man had flown, gotten away into the trees while he could. The flame died in a grunt of contempt.

He reined his horse away from the trees, thinking of that last image of the man on the summit, looking at him with those eyes. He had expected the Wolf to be here.

Then something in him clicked, buzzed hot, and, whirling, he saw the downward flash of metal over his head. And in one split second of time he sprang, twisting backward out of the saddle, felt the sudden sharp cleft of air past his face, and heard the sickening shock as a blinding swipe of steel severed his horse's head.

438

Aeryck hit the ground and rolled to his feet, sword at the ready. He glanced quickly at his prostrate horse, not comprehending at first, then, seeing the head off to one side, was stunned by the terrible power of the blow that had severed it.

Then he felt a sudden rush of evil shrieking out of the trees and encompassing him with a frenetic chatter, the teeth of the things working fast and sounding like a whir of locusts. He could almost hear the leathery flap of wings beating about his face in a whorl of fiendish mischief, sucking the wind from his chest.

And then he looked up into the eyes of the Wolf, glaring at him from the height of his black charger. Immediately he felt some numbing darkness worming its way into his brain, reaching in through the eyes with icy talons, clawing down toward his soul. He felt the first glimmerings of cold terror pricking in him.

He averted his eyes from those of the Wolf to the black-and-crimson shield, not wanting to look back at the yellow eyes, frightened of the eyes but feeling himself drawn back to them. And looking into the shadows beneath the wolfskin shroud, he felt himself drawn out and over some dark and immeasurable void of space. And out of the void came the eyes, the two yellow orbs suddenly floating toward him.

He could do nothing, staring at the yellow orbs and feeling his life being clawed out of his shell and too paralyzed to do anything about it but surrender to the void. A prayer fought its way to his lips through the frenzied chatter in his brain, but was choked into a mental scream.

"Jesus!" he cried. "Holy Savior!"

Hauwka threaded his way up the back side of the slope, the grass wet and glistening in the sun after the rain. Then he was into the trees. The wood was sparse at first with tall pines and firs, then it closed toward the summit with old forest, black and bent with age. A rabbit started out of some brush as the bear passed by, paused partway down the slope, hiked up on its haunches, and sniffing bolted down the hill. Then some birds winged overhead toward the west, several flights of them moving fast with their wings tucked scissorlike, then beating away.

There was a shift in the wind coming over the summit through the trees, and the bear ran smack into it as if he'd suddenly come around a corner into a wall. He reeled to one side, growling warily, then lifting off his forepaws with a little hop and scenting—every part of him burning now with animal cunning—he blew out a snort and took off into the trees like a shot.

Aeryck's head bobbled to life with a jolt of adrenaline. Fear buzzed round his head and over his chest as his eyes fluttered into focus. When he saw that the Wolf had closed to within a few feet of him, he jumped back out of reflex and crouched, chest pounding, into his battle stance and jerked up his sword. He wasn't sure what had just happened or how the Wolf had gotten around the horse carcass, but his head was clearing now with the fear and his eyes working.

He shifted back and forth on the balls of his feet, his hands flexing on the sword handle, the tip up and extended toward the horseman, and his mind drummed a practiced catechism: *Balance! Balance! Balance!*

The Wolf reined his black steed, eyeing the boy as one might eye a bug and in no apparent hurry to squash it. Then he glanced at Aeryck's sword, noticing perhaps the tongues of fire engraved along the blade. He recoiled slightly.

Then bending forward he chuckled throatily. "I have been expecting you, Worm." He smiled. "You are surprised that I know who you are. There is much that I know about you."

Aeryck's eyes flirted with the shadows under the shroud, mindful not to connect with the yellow orbs, then darted away.

"Yes," the Wolf continued, snickering humorlessly, "when my wolves did not return I knew that you would come. And here you are."

His voice seemed to come out from him in waves—large, billowing swells of oily fluid—making the boy feel as though the ground were pitching beneath him. The voice had a bestial timbre, human but not all human, and, feeling it washing over him, set after set of smoothing oiliness, sent shivers careering over his limbs.

"I can see the fear in your eyes, Worm. There is no need for that. For what are you to me? You are nothing to me."

Aeryck's eyes edged closer to the shroud. He felt a bit nauseous from the rolling.

"Perhaps you think that I am going to kill you, just as I killed your father."

Aeryck looked at him quickly.

A thin baneful smile curled over the Wolf's mouth. "That's right," he said, fixing his gaze on the boy. "It was I who killed him." He clicked his tongue. "Would you like for me to describe how he begged for mercy on his hands and knees? It was pitiful."

Aeryck glared at the man. "You're a black liar," he heard himself shout, his voice sounding thin and outside of him.

The Wolf chortled. "Yes . . . yes . . . and you are a pathetic worm," he spoke in that billowing, oily, smoothing voice. "But you know that, don't you? Yes, of course . . . an insignificant sack of scum. A wretched worm."

"My name is Aeryck."

"A dweller of dung heaps."

440

"No."

"Yes . . . a nothing worm."

"No."

"You are nothing."

"No . . ."

". . . thing."

The eyes glowed like twin suns hurling across the jet of space.

As Aeryck felt invisible fetters crisscrossing over his mind, he struggled briefly against them but felt himself sinking back into the black nothingness of the void, the ropes of his will loosing and his mind powerless to grab hold of them. He felt himself slipping away from his moorings into the void and the blackness chilling his soul and enveloping him with a swell of impish chatter coming up and beating around his ears. He would resign to it, have done with it, surrender to the darkness, to sleep. He would welcome sleep. Just a little sleep.

He saw only a silvery shard of light racing over the twin suns like a comet. And he saw the tip of his sword rising in slow motion, of its own will it seemed, rising to intercept its course. Then there was a tremendous clash and an explosion of sparks winging every which way as the comet struck, and the jolt shuddering through his body felt as though worlds were being torn apart. And the earth was loosed under his feet.

He hit the ground hard, and somewhere in his brain he heard himself scream, *Roll! Roll!* And rolling he staggered drunkenly to his feet, the world reeling about him, and he threw up his sword in time to catch another stunning blow, one that hurled him again across the clearing like a thrown toy.

Landing with a jounce, his mind racing to catch up with his body, he saw the black shape of the Wolf in mid-leap, saw the two yellow tracers arcing toward him on a bolt of silver light. He twirled to his right an instant before the blade slammed into the earth where his head had been.

The Wolf landed, crouching in animal fury, then immediately sprang with a guttural snarl jerking in his throat and with a scything curl of his sword.

Finding his feet, Aeryck braced himself, brought his sword across his chest, and caught the Wolf's blade with a terrific clangor, steel on steel, the sparks winging off like tiny shooting stars.

And as he closed with the man, time quit for an instant, and in that instant he caught the engraving along the Wolf's blade, his mind instantly recording the least detail: a broken loaf of bread overlaid with silver and set on a bronze platter, and an ornate wine chalice overlaid with beaten gold, both enwreathed by a brazen plait of thorns; its motif carrying down the length of the blade on both sides, along the swordhilt and around the bear-wreath crest, around the pommel of the handle.

The Wolf glared fiercely into his eyes. "That's right, Worm," he hissed into the boy's face. "It is your father's sword. And I shall kill you with it."

The eyes were not human. They were not animal either. They were clearly something other, like two burning coals, and Aeryck dared not look into them. And the stench of his breath was noxious-smelling like burning sulfur, and he knew now that he was fighting some incarnate devil.

The Wolf snickered through his teeth. Then, freeing his left hand, he struck the boy with an effortless swat that sent him tottering across the clearing. Aeryck stumbled and, scrambling to his feet, had scarce enough time to regain his footing when the Wolf was upon him, hammering him with his sword, relentlessly driving him ever backward and off-balance.

Aeryck staggered before the devastating blows, time and again, always on the defensive, always catching the lightning blade just a split second before the edge caught his throat. His catechism of sword drills was a forgotten thing; he was in a desperate scramble just to remain on his feet.

Then he saw the Wolf's sword shoot forward, swinging around and up and describing a perfect orbit of light. He brought his own blade up to parry the imminent blow—too slow, he knew. He shuddered in that knowledge, then felt the sword, like a sledge-hammer, crashing against his body, lifting him off his feet and hurling him through the air. Then to his horror he felt his sword leaving his hands, saw it twirling out of reach one way as he twirled the other.

He fetched the earth hard and, landing, coughed the wind out of his lungs. He shot a desperate glance at his weapon lying eight feet away and knew it was over. Glancing up, gasping, he saw the Wolf coming on, the eyes burning hot, his sword high and lowering, and then saw a whistling whirl of light rifle deep into the man's flank.

The Wolf shuddered, reeling stagger-footed to a halt as he grabbed at his side. Something horrible crossed over his face.

Aeryck turned and saw Dagmere galloping into the clearing, calling his name as she reached for another arrow.

The Wolf let out an enraged snarl, glaring, looking like a stricken animal. Then, whirling about, he raised his sword over the boy.

Aeryck sprang for his sword. Grabbing the hilt with his fingertips, he swung the blade around and caught the Wolf, coming on in a demonic fury, just below his sternum. And crabbing away, he saw the Wolf's blade flash past his shoulder and stab into the dirt.

The Wolf staggered backward, knees bent and buckling, the yellow eyes wide in disbelief, then torn with rage. As he fell forward, bracing himself with one hand against the earth, then going over hard onto his side, his body began to shake violently, the rage in his eyes becoming terror.

Then he arched his back, and the demon twisted out of the mouth with a scream. The body breached mid-air, then collapsed on itself, and, shuddering, went still with an exhale of sulfur wheezing out into the air as though it had somewhere to go.

A sudden blast of wind shrieked over the clearing, then whisked away through the trees. And everything went quiet and smelling of spring.

Moments passed. Norduk opened his eyes and blinked dully at the shape moving slowly toward him, seeing the boy now looming over him with his sword pointing at his chest. His eyes traced the length of the blade, up and down.

"It is the sword," he said, rolling his head back to see it better. "The one in the dream." He coughed, then gazed up at the boy. "You are Arthgen, cub of the great bear, the one wielding the sword of fire."

Aeryck stared at him, not knowing what he was talking about.

Norduk grunted. "The little wretch got it wrong, after all." Then his eyes jerked open and fixed over his last terrible thought, and the yellow went out of them.

Aeryck stared down at the lifeless body of the underlord.

"What an awful man," Dagmere said, putting her arm through Aeryck's. A shudder went over her.

Aeryck looked at her and smiled. He had not heard her come up to him.

"Aeryck, you're bleeding."

Aeryck glanced at his shoulder, saw that it was only a flesh wound, then looked down at the grass. He saw the glint of metal and bent over and picked up the Wolf's sword—weight for weight and steel for steel, the perfect match of his own. He looked at it for several moments, studying the symbols of the cup and the bread and the plait of thorns, thinking of how his father had carried it to his death. And now he was holding it in his hands. Tears began to stream from his eyes.

Dagmere studied his face. "What's wrong, Aeryck?"

He smoothed his fingers over the crest. "It was my father's sword —the one he made to honor Christ. I thought it was long buried in the past."

Dagmere smiled at him. "Then it's kind of like a resurrection, isn't it?—you having it now."

Aeryck looked at her. "Yes . . . yes, it is." He laid the swords down tenderly in the grass, then put his arms around her. "Dagmere, you saved my life. I—"

"Let's not talk about it, Aeryck," she said, and she threw her arms around him. "Just hold me. Don't ever let me go."

He folded his big tired arms around her and drew her close with the weight of them. For several long moments neither spoke, though both of their hearts conversed at great length.

Aeryck looked up when he heard a crashing through the trees. "What is it?" Dagmere said, turning.

The great bear roared furiously as he loped into the clearing. And without pausing for ceremony he padded over to the dead underlord, his hackles still up and bristling, sniffed him, then blew out a snort of contempt.

"Hauwka!"

Aeryck ran tiredly over to him and threw his arms around the bear's massive neck. "Oh, Hauwka! Hauwka! You're alive!"

The bear looked at him with his wet, coal-like eyes glistening in the sun, then bawled happily and licked his face.

"Hey, big fella, cut it out!" The boy laughed. "C'mon now."

Dagmere let out a squeal of delight.

Somewhere in the distant south a little carpentum clattered over the fog-enshrouded moors toward the coast. Everything was gray and dreary, and suddenly the distant howl of a wolf broke the monotony of the wheels and the tiny hooves clipping along the road.

The little druid looked nervously about as he snapped the whip but could see only the vague and desolate grayness of the terrain, with objects suddenly appearing here and there out of it. The team of hairy ponies snorted, not liking the sting of the whip, not liking the little human either, but lurched forward when they heard the howl of a second wolf that sounded much nearer than the first one. The wagon clattered along, pitching and yawing over the broken ground, and the druid's single nervous eye busily worked the fog.

Then out of the gray came a streak of white, sudden and fast-moving, and, turning to it, Boadix let out a shriek and lost his glass eye over the side as the wolf leaped.

48
A TIME TO HEAL

The dead were buried. It was an ordeal that took several days of digging long trenches and laying out the British warriors with their weapons and shields, covering their faces with linen, then reverently mounding the earth over them. The Saxons were gathered and thrown into large pits with rocks dumped on top.

Afterward Brother Lucius held a funeral service for the British dead in the stone church at Killwyn Eden, concluding the rites with a hymn:

"Thou holy spark, which once did shine,
So bright and strong in darkest night;
With warrior's arm and hope divine,
Stood sure against the godless might.

"Though thou be torn from wick of clay,
By winds of woe or length of days;
Thou fleeting gleam—in Christ delight,
For thou dost burn with endless light."

There was much weeping, for scarcely was there a home among the villages of the Brigantes that was not touched by the terrible battle. The skies over the Eden valley darkened, and the rain falling cleansed the soil of blood and the stench of death, and a season of mourning draped solemnly over the land.

Days passed following the funeral service, and at last there was a break in the dark mantle of clouds. Bright blue shapes of sky moved slowly over the hills, pushing ever southward before the driving fleece of white.

Brynwald, Oswald, and the men of the north, rested now and anxious to return to their own land to mourn those who had fallen in battle against Sarteham, gathered at the north gates to bid farewell to the people of Killwyn Eden.

Allyndaar and his family stood in a little group before the other Britons, and, stepping forward, the chieftain took Brynwald by his arms and clasped them firmly.

"There are no words to convey the depth of our gratitude, Brynwald," he said looking into the large Pict's eyes. "Your kindness to our people will long be remembered and sung about in our halls."

"*Och*, 'twere nothing but a wee thing, Allyn." Brynwald grinned. "We men of the north need a good fight from time to time to keep us from getting too womanly. Isn't that right, men?"

There were a few ayes and amens and a ripple of laughter.

"We'd best be going, Bryn," Dunnald added, "lest we have a bigger fight on our hands when we get hame to our wives."

Everyone laughed.

"Troth! You've said it, lad!" Brynwald roared.

Helena stepped up holding a jar of preserves and a bundle containing a few ivory combs, a silver brooch, and a silk shawl. "Will you give this to Tillie, Brynwald?" she said, handing him the bundle. Then, smiling, she gave him the jar. "And this is for you. You said you liked them so."

Brynwald's eyes lit up. "Are these your blackberry preserves then?"

Helena crooked an eyebrow at him. "Do leave Tillie a taste, won't you?"

He crooked an eyebrow back at her. "Troth, lassie, that I'll nay promise you."

Dunnald laughed. "Aye, the bounty of his kindness dinnay reach down as far as his stomach."

The men guffawed, and Brynwald shot them a look.

Helena smiled and gave him a big hug.

Then Brynwald turned to Aeryck, who hadn't said a word so far. They just looked at one another for a few moments, as everyone watched and the mood suddenly changed.

"Well, kipper," he said, seemingly not knowing what to do with his hands. He put them behind his back. "I trust you'll nay be forgetting old Bryn and Tillie—the sweet smell of heather off the hills of our fair north." His voice cracked, and he cleared his throat to cover it. "By the oaks, son, it has been grand having you with us. You'll come visit us from time to time?"

Aeryck's eyes suddenly brimmed over, and he threw his arms around the big chieftain. "I love you, Brynwald."

Brynwald, taken aback, folded his arms around the boy's neck and hugged him. They held each other for several moments, and the chieftain's big shoulders began to heave.

Dunnald wiped his eyes and looked heavenward. "Praise be."

446

Helena and Allyndaar looked at one another.

Dagmere looked at the ground and wept.

Brynwald slapped Aeryck's back. *"Och,* kipper, you're a fine lad."
Then he broke away, tears streaming from his eyes—tears streaming
from everyone's eyes—and tousled the boy's hair. "A fine lad, indeed."
Then with a quick swipe of his eyes, he turned and swung up into his
saddle, looking like a giant against the sweeping blue sky.

Allyndaar said, "You let us know when to come up to help you
build your church, Bryn. We've plenty of strong backs."

"Aye, that I will, Allyn." Brynwald smiled. "That I will." Then
he reined his horse away with a salute and with a booming voice cried,
"May the Lord bless you and keep you, and may He make His holy face
to shine upon you!"

Allyndaar returned his salute. "And to you, brothers. Godspeed."

An offering of Godspeeds and farewells followed as the Britons
waved. Children chased the men as they headed north to the land of Picts
and Scots, then, quickly tiring of the pursuit, ran squealing every which
way and chasing each other up and down the berm as they reenacted the
battle.

Dagmere went over to Aeryck and slipped her arm through his
and laid her head against his shoulder.

He put his arm around her waist and watched the Picts growing
small against the emerald green of the hills, feeling a heavy sadness coming over him. They stayed there long after the other Britons had filtered
back into the village, long after the hills had closed around the tiny
riders.

During the days following Brynwald's departure, the pall of death
began to slowly lift from over the land. Rain fell intermittently, gently,
and cool breezes blew up and down the reach of the Eden as the land
exhaled the stench of killing and inhaled the warming spring. The sun
streamed radiantly over the broad valley stretching out and away from the
village, and the skies brightened over the Pennine chain. Birds were up
and at it again, and the air was thick with insects and moisture, and the
sun was everywhere drying up the rains.

Riders were sent throughout the land, heralding the victory and
announcing that there would be a great feast in the hall of Killwyn Eden.
People gathered in cheerful knots and talked about the news. Myriad industries resumed their turning. Tradesmen crisscrossed the countryside
selling goods and singing songs, dogs chased cats, children chased dogs,
and young lovers stole away to private retreats.

There was a happy sense of renewal in the air.

Terryll rode up to Bowness and a few days later arrived back home with Belfourt and Gwyneth. The portly chieftain was in fine spirits and, not waiting to settle into the villa, dragged Allyndaar off to the hall to prove it, bellowing boisterously over several mugs of ale. He was in fine spirits all right.

Terryll and Gwyneth spent their days walking in the fields hand in hand, marveling at one another, pausing frequently to kiss, looking at everything and nothing, then stooping now and then to pluck some tiny flower to strip it of its petals.

Hauwka frequented their strolls, lumbering along behind, every so often moaning plaintively, though the limp in his shoulder was less pronounced.

On the day before the great feast they were together in the cool shade of the orchard. Terryll's head lay in her lap, and she ran her long fingers through his hair, smiling down at him.

Hauwka padded over to them. Looking at them, his eyes shifted back and forth between their faces, then he let out a moan.

Terryll opened one eye, then closed it. "Don't you worry, Hauwka," he said, dreamily smacking his lips. "We'll go hunting soon."

The bear let out a disgruntled snort and ambled away to the other side of the orchard, scratched himself against a trunk, then went to sleep.

That night at supper Terryll, swollen with a matter, announced that he and Gwyneth were getting married.

Helena burst into tears, and Belfourt let out a thunderous "By Toutatis! What ho!"

Dagmere hugged Gwyneth and gushed, "I'm so happy for you, Gwinnie!" Then she looked brightly at her and squealed, "Just think, we'll be sisters!"

After supper Allyndaar and Belfourt took Terryll to the great hall—"To get a little pre-feast celebrating in," Belfourt said devoutly to Helena, to reassure her that he wouldn't corrupt the lad.

The moon hung like a porcelain dish over the rim of the Pennines and bathed the village in silver light. Hauwka rooted around the base of the trees for windfalls. There weren't any; he had polished them off earlier. A disgusted snort fluttered through his snout.

Then he looked up as Dagmere went by in the distance, seeing her silhouetted through the apple trees and walking over to Aeryck, who was in the field behind the orchard. The bear blinked at them for a moment, his eyes glistening in the light patterns shifting over him, then padded over to another tree.

Aeryck watched Dagmere approaching.

"Hello, Dag."

"Hello again." She smiled. "I've been looking for you."

"Here I am," he said, then glanced down at the sword in his hands.

"Looking at your father's sword?"

"Yes," Aeryck said, his eyes scrutinizing the bear wreath on the hilt.

She studied it in the moonlight. "It's lovely. Your father was a wonderful craftsman."

"Yes, he was," he said, then put the sword back into its scabbard and looked away at the hills.

Dagmere glanced at his profile briefly, then took hold of his arm and looked where he was looking. After a while she said, "Why didn't you go to the hall with Terryll?"

"The hall?"

"Yes, the hall. Papa and Bellie are celebrating with Terryll." She giggled, thinking about it. "Poor Terryll." She looked at Aeryck. "Didn't they ask you to come?"

"Yes. I'll be along."

She waited a few moments. "Isn't it wonderful Terryll and Gwyneth getting married?"

"What? Yes, yes, it is . . . wonderful."

Dagmere let go a sigh, letting her head fall against his shoulder. "What's troubling you, Aeryck? You've been somewhere else ever since Brynwald left."

Aeryck looked at her. "I'm right here."

"No, you're not. You're miles away. Do you want to go back to Scotland?"

He looked at the hills again.

She studied his face. "That's not it, is it?" Then her expression changed. "It's Ireland, isn't it? You want to go to Ireland."

He didn't answer.

Then she looked at the hills, letting her thoughts unhinge and move away from her. A silence came between them.

Aeryck looked at her. "I thought maybe the desire would go . . . coming down here . . . being with you. But seeing my father's sword . . . I don't know," he said, struggling for words. "Dagmere, if I don't go now, I'll never be any good to you. I'll always be wondering."

Dagmere's eyes shifted away.

"Now you're crying."

"No, I'm not."

Aeryck groaned, then looked plaintively to the heavens.

"Perhaps this is best, Aeryck," Dagmere said, turning away and folding her arms. "Go away and find yourself. Heaven knows how hard you've tried here."

Aeryck frowned at her, suddenly angry. "You just don't understand. How could you? You've got a family. You've always had a family. Well, I've got a family too, and I'd like to see them. Is it so wrong that I should want to see them? Is it?"

"You said one time that we were your family."

"It's not the same," he snapped. "Why is this so difficult for you?"

Dagmere looked at him sharply. "It isn't for you?"

They looked into the other's eyes for a long moment.

Dagmere felt something spinning away from her. Frightened, she wrapped her arms around him to stop the movement and burst into tears. "Oh, Aeryck, let's not quarrel. I just don't want to lose you."

Aeryck held her. "Lose me?" He sighed, then kissed the top of her head. "You're the best thing that's ever happened to me, Dagmere. If I ever lost you, I would shrivel up and blow away."

She looked up at him, her cheeks glistening with tears.

He held her face tenderly in his hands and gazed into her eyes. Then he kissed her on each cheek, and then he kissed her on her lips. They held each other for a long while, watching the hills, letting the still cool quietness of the night embrace them. It was such a lovely night.

A wolf howled in the distance against the full brightness of the moon. They both turned to it. It was a long and mournful cry that reached down into some sad place in her soul.

"Why do you think they do that, Aeryck? Howl like that against the moon."

"I don't know. Lonely I guess," he said. "Who knows why wolves do what they do?"

"He does sound lonely, doesn't he?"

Aeryck sighed. "Lonely as a night without stars." He looked back into her eyes—those big blue sapphires of glistening light—and he brightened. "Dagmere, will you marry me?"

Dagmere's head did a little jolt. "Marry you?"

"Yes, marry me," he said, moving along with it under full sail. "Will you, Dag? Will you marry me, so that we'll never have to be apart again? Will you?"

She stared at him, dumfounded.

He was bright with inspiration. "We could go to Ireland together, Dag. Just you and me—husband and wife! We could meet my family— my Uncle Finn—and they could meet you! Think of it, Dagmere."

Tears streamed from the girl's eyes. "Oh, yes, Aeryck," she squealed. "Yes, I'll marry you." She threw her arms around his neck and

450

squeezed, laughing. She pulled back, looked to make sure she had heard him correctly, and squeezed again. Then she looked excitedly at him. "We could have a double wedding! Wouldn't that be wonderful?"

"Yes, it would be."

Dagmere beamed with delight. "Oh, Aeryck, I love you so!"

They embraced, then sealed their covenant with a long and soulful kiss.

It was such a lovely kiss.

The wolf howled again. A cool spring breeze took it away into the distant ranks of hills, then brought it back an echo. It had a lonesome, mournful sound to it.

Hauwka looked over at the field and saw the boy and girl walking away in the moonlight, walking slowly as lovers do, arm in arm, pausing to kiss, pausing to pick up a blade of grass and strip it, then walking on toward the paddocks where the spring colts were skipping happily about, talking of love, of beauty, and dreaming of glorious days to come.

The bear blew out a snort and sat down in disgust, sitting on his right hip with one hind leg thrown under the other. Suddenly a shudder trembled along his right shoulder. He looked back at it, waited for it, then like a flash dug his teeth into his hide, clipping here and there and snorting through his fur. He paused, moaned. Then, climbing to his feet, he rubbed up against the nearest tree trunk and bore into it fiercely.

He had a powerful itch coming on.